EVERYMAN,
I WILL GO WITH THEE,
AND BE THY GUIDE,
IN THY MOST NEED
TO GO BY THY SIDE

RICHARD YATES

REVOLUTIONARY ROAD

THE EASTER PARADE

ELEVEN KINDS OF LONELINESS

WITH AN INTRODUCTION
BY RICHARD PRICE

EVERYMAN'S LIBRARY
Alfred A. Knopf New York London Toronto

THIS IS A BORZOI BOOK

PUBLISHED BY ALFRED A. KNOPF

First included in Everyman's Library, 2009

C O N T E N T S

INTRODUCTION

All she could muster was the weak, meek little phrase she had hated herself for using since childhood: "I see."
 – Emily Grimes, *The Easter Parade*

Richard Yates (1926–92), author of seven novels and three collections of short stories, was the poet laureate of the Age of Anxiety, a master purveyor of the crushed suburban life, of the great con known as the American Promise. He was a tender connoisseur of the verbal seedlings implanted, say, in a child's visit to a father's place of work; or in the bedroom, or the bar car; at the dining table, or the two-couple cocktail party: those genteel, mostly oblivious verbal cuts and pernicious grafts that will metastasize into a hushed, lifelong dying.

Yates country lies slightly to the south of Cheever, to the west of O'Hara, east of Carver, and north of Tobias Wolff and Richard Ford. Over the last century there have been many riders on that particular literary range but what sets Yates apart, the true marvel of his legacy, is the very writing itself. His deft and miraculously weightless prose was Shaker-simple, a levitation act of declarative sentences, near-neutral observations and unremarkable utterances, as if the author were as powerless as the reader in controlling the destinies of his characters – the slow-motion train wreck of the lives to come, the soul-killing self-realizations that will invariably be their lot. In part, the beauty and the genius of his voice lies in how its gently inexorable tone so eerily mirrors the muffled helplessness of the characters themselves.

April and Frank Wheeler in *Revolutionary Road*; all the bruised young men and women who inhabit the short stories of *Eleven Kinds of Loneliness*; the Grimes sisters and their hapless mother Pookie in *The Easter Parade*: in his no-exit, unblinking honesty, in his bone-deep sorrowful conviction that loneliness is our inescapable lot, Yates pities his characters but has no choice but to doom them.

In Yates country knowledge invariably ends in suffering, but none of his people are ever without hope – they dream and they want, they endure and they yearn.

In the beginning of things their eyes are as wide as dishes.

In the end, their longing will be the very knife that runs them through.

*

As crystalline as he was on the page, in the flesh Richard Yates was a magnificent wreck, a chaotic and wild-hearted presence, a tall but stooped smoke-cloud of a man, Kennedyesque in dress and manner, gaunt and bearded with hung eyes and a cigarette-slaughtered voice, the words barreling out of him in a low breathless rumble as ash flew into salads, into beer mugs, into the laps of others with every gesture, his demeanor invariably lurching between courtly-solicitous and edge-of-bitter cavalier.

*

I first met Yates in 1974 at the School of the Arts, Columbia University, in an MFA fiction workshop. For a few thousand dollars a semester, he entered the room every week wearing a nubby sports jacket and askew knit tie to critique and counsel a table of students sporting frayed bell-bottoms, Prince Valiant bangs and sarcastic hats. It had been thirteen years since *Revolutionary Road. Disturbing the Peace* was a year away.

We were in our early twenties, and most of us had neither read nor even heard of him. In class he called you by your last name, no title: a brusque, slightly boarding-schoolish and utterly seductive form of address. He regularly and passionately savaged those writers whom he perceived to be his more validated ("lucky," he called them) peers, but he treated a student's work, no matter how hapless, with shocking earnestness.

He was a nurturer of grudges; an incubator of slights.

His personal gods were Hemingway and Fitzgerald.

He was bitter.

He had every right to be bitter.

He was really bitter.

At twenty-four, I had just published my first novel *The Wanderers*, making me the literary hot dog of the month, and when he came to my name during the first class roll call he added "Oh, so *you're* our billion dollar bonus baby" in a voice that turned my spine to chalk.

And if anyone had been so obtuse or patronizing as to call him a "Writers' Writer"....

After class, he loved to talk in the West End bar while working his way through a pack of smokes.

"So, Price," he would semi-growl, his elbow beer-damp on the varnish, "they paying you a lotta dough? Are you raking it in? Make sure the bastards pay for it," hacking like a Model T while palming his chest for the next fresh twenty. "I wrote a good novel once, you probably never heard of it, well you were a kid, you're still a kid, no reason why you should," slowly stripping the seal. "Just make sure the bastards pay you through the nose."

*

In 1992, after having completed a brief teaching stint at the University of Alabama and hard up for cash, he was living alone in Tuscaloosa in order to take advantage of the local VA hospital for his rapidly deteriorating emphysema. Word of his situation had made it up north to a number of his former students and devotees who ponied up a ten-thousand-dollar honorarium and offered him a reading at the Donnell Library in midtown Manhattan.

Emphysemics really shouldn't fly.

He came off the plane on a gurney.

Later that night in the dining room of the Algonquin Hotel he made his entrance in a wheelchair with an oxygen tank strapped to its back, air buds swooping down from his ears to his nose. It was a very short dinner.

"Price, I need...I think you should take me back upstairs. My apologies to all." In his room he asked me to call for an ambulance, and while we waited, he struggled through a tale, half confession, half grievance, of how a casual offhand comment tossed his way by a successful former student at a cocktail party three years earlier still had him burning with humiliation and rage.

He gave me a message to deliver to this, this, *individual* in case he didn't make it through the night. It contained no profanity, no threat; just a wounded fiery promise to meet his obligations.

The medics came in to the room all business, speaking in the unnecessarily loud and brisk tone of frontliners in a slow motion combat zone. "So, Dick, it's Dick, right? You got emphysema, Dick? Yes?" strapping him in, "So how come you still smoke?"

"I don't smoke. I'm not crazy."

"Oh yeah?" – pulling a pack of unfiltered cigarettes out of Yates's chest pocket. "Then what are these?" Despite his pulmonary collapse, he turned crimson with embarrassment.

The following day the hospital wouldn't let him out to do his reading at the Donnell.

He refused to accept the honorarium.

Everyone pleaded that he just take the damn money and get well. After a bruisy moment of impasse he requested a tape recorder and a copy of *Revolutionary Road*.

That night, those who attended the reading sat facing an empty lectern flanked by two speakers and listened to a recording of a dying man whistle-gasp his way through the great first chapter of *Revolutionary Road*: April Wheeler's excruciating attack of stage fright during an amateur production of *The Petrified Forest*.

At the hospital two days later we walked in to see him sitting up in bed. If not exactly robust, he was in considerably better shape – and mood. Hospital rules; no booze, no cigs. And ya gotta eat.

Like ants working a jamjar, a stream of visitors stretched from the bed to the hallway. He looked happy as hell. Happier than I'd ever seen him.

Six months later he was gone.

*

INTRODUCTION

His personal gods were Hemingway and Fitzgerald. And now more than a decade after his death he's become something of a god himself.

Would that piss him off. . . .

*

"Yes, I'm tired," she said. *"And do you know a funny thing? I'm almost fifty years old and I've never understood anything in my whole life."*
– Emily Grimes, *The Easter Parade*

Richard Price

RICHARD PRICE is the author of eight novels, including *Lush Life*, *Freedomland*, and *Clockers*, which was nominated for a National Book Critics Circle Award. He lives in New York City.

SELECT BIBLIOGRAPHY

WORKS BY RICHARD YATES
Revolutionary Road, Little, Brown, 1961.
Eleven Kinds of Loneliness, Little, Brown, 1962.
A Special Providence, Knopf, 1969.
Disturbing the Peace, Delacorte Press/Seymour Lawrence, 1975.
The Easter Parade, Delacorte Press/Seymour Lawrence, 1976.
A Good School, Delacorte Press/Seymour Lawrence, 1978.
Liars in Love, Delacorte Press/Seymour Lawrence, 1981.
Young Hearts Crying, Delacorte Press/Seymour Lawrence, 1984.
Cold Spring Harbor, Delacorte Press/Seymour Lawrence, 1986.
The Collected Stories of Richard Yates, Picador, 2001.

BIOGRAPHY AND CRITICISM
BLAKE BAILEY, *A Tragic Honesty: The Life and Work of Richard Yates*, Picador, 2003.
BLAKE BAILEY, "Poor Dick: Looking for the Real Richard Yates," *Harvard Review 25*, Fall 2003.
SCOTT BRADFIELD, "Follow the Long and Revolutionary Road," *The Independent*, November 21, 1992, p. 31.
DAVID CASTRONOVO AND STEVEN GOLDLEAF, *Richard Yates*, Twayne Publishers, 1996.
GEOFFREY CLARK, "The Best I Can Wish You," *NORTHEAST CORRIDOR 1, No. 2*, 1994.
ANDRE DUBUS, "A Salute to Mr. Yates," *Black Warrior Review 15, No. 2*, Spring 1989.
STEVE FEATHERSTONE, "November 7, 1992," *Black Warrior Review 21, No. 1*, Fall/Winter 1994.
RICHARD FORD, Introduction to *Revolutionary Road*, Vintage, 2000.
NICK FRASIER, "Rebirth of a Dark Genius," *The Guardian*, February 17, 2008.
DEWITT HENRY AND GEOFFREY CLARK, "An Interview with Richard Yates," *Ploughshares 1, No. 3*, Winter 1972.
ROBERT LACY, "Remembering Richard Yates," *North Stone Review 12*, 1995.
MARTIN NAPERSTECK, "Drinking with Dick Yates," *North American Review*, May–August 2001.
STEWART O'NAN, "The Lost World of Richard Yates," *Boston Review*, October/November 1999.

RICHARD RUSSO, Introduction to *The Collected Stories of Richard Yates*, Holt, 2001.

ELIZABETH VENANT, "A Fresh Twist in the Road," *Los Angeles Times*, July 9, 1989, section 6, page 8.

KURT VONNEGUT, "Remarks at the Yates Memorial Service," *Harvard Review 25*, Fall 2003.

RICHARD YATES, "Correspondence, 1960–1," *Harvard Review 25*, Fall 2003.

RICHARD YATES, "Some Very Good Masters," *New York Times Book Review*, April 19, 1981, page 3.

CHRONOLOGY

DATE	AUTHOR'S LIFE	LITERARY CONTEXT
1926	Birth of Richard Walden Yates at Yonkers, New York (February 3), the second of two children, to Ruth (Dookie) and Vincent Yates.	1926 Hemingway: *The Sun Also Rises*. O'Neill: *The Great God Brown*.
1927		
1928		
1929	Divorce of Yates's parents. Family moves from place to place, eventually settling in Greenwich Village, where Dookie attempts to make a living as a sculptor.	1929 Faulkner: *The Sound and the Fury*. Hemingway: *A Farewell to Arms*. Hammet: *Red Harvest*.
1930		1930 Faulkner: *As I Lay Dying*. Hammett: *The Maltese Falcon*.
1932		Faulkner: *Light in August*.
1933	Moves with family to Scarsdale, a northern suburb of New York City.	1933 Hemingway: *Winner Take Nothing*. N. West: *Miss Lonelyhearts*.
1934		1934 Fitzgerald: *Tender is the Night*. H. Miller: *Tropic of Cancer*. Cain: *The Postman Always Rings Twice*.
1935		1935 Steinbeck: *Tortilla Flat*. Lewis: *It Can't Happen Here*.
1936		Faulkner: *Absalom, Absalom!*
1937	Moves to Scarborough-on-Hudson, Westchester County. Attends Scarborough Country Day School.	1937 Steinbeck: *Of Mice and Men*. Hemingway: *To Have and Have Not*.
1938		1938 Dos Passos: *USA*.
1939	Fleeing mounting debts, the family moves back to Greenwich Village; Yates attends Grace Church School.	1939 Steinbeck: *The Grapes of Wrath*. H. Miller: *Tropic of Capricorn*. Chandler: *The Big Sleep*.
1940		1940 Hemingway: *For Whom the Bell Tolls*. Chandler: *Farewell, My Lovely*.

1926 Germany admitted to League of Nations. General Strike in UK.

1927 Lindbergh's solo Atlantic flight. First "talkie" – *The Jazz Singer*.
1928 Hoover elected US president. First Five Year Plan in USSR.
1929 Wall Street Crash. Period of worldwide Depression begins.

1930 Mahatma Gandhi begins civil disobedience movement in India.

1932 Roosevelt elected US president. Nazis become largest party in German Reichstag.
1933 Roosevelt announces "New Deal." Prohibition repealed. Hitler becomes German chancellor.

1934 Stalin's great purge of the Communist Party begins.

1935 National Labor Relations Act gives workers in the USA the right to join unions.
1936 Outbreak of Spanish Civil War. Hitler and Mussolini form Rome–Berlin Axis. In the UK Edward VIII abdicates and is succeeded by George VI.
1937 Japanese invasion of China. First jet engine and nylon stockings.

1938 Germany annexes Austria; Munich crisis.
1939 Nazi–Soviet Pact; Hitler invades Poland. World War II begins. First commercial transatlantic flights.

1940 Churchill prime minister in UK. Fall of France; battle of Britain. Penicillin developed.

xvii

DATE	AUTHOR'S LIFE	LITERARY CONTEXT
1941	Begins boarding at Avon Old Farms, a prep school in Connecticut. Marriage of Yates's sister Ruth (Dec).	1941 Fitzgerald: *The Last Tycoon*.
1942	Begins editing and writing for the school magazine. Death of Yates's father.	1942 Chandler: *The High Window*.
1944	Enlists in the army.	1944 Williams: *The Glass Menagerie*.
1945	Travels to England, France and Belgium as part of the 75th Division. Contracts pneumonia while serving as a runner; active service in Germany.	
1946	Demobilized from the army; returns to New York. Begins writing for a trade journal. Takes evening courses in creative writing at Columbia University.	
1947	Works for the United Press on the financial news desk.	1947 Williams: *A Streetcar Named Desire*.
1948	Marries Sheila Bryant. Begins submitting stories to magazines, without success.	1948 Mailer: *The Naked and the Dead*.
1949	Hired by Remington Rand to write copy for the business machine company's monthly magazine.	1949 A. Miller: *Death of a Salesman*.
1950	Birth of first child, Sharon Elizabeth. Diagnosed with advanced tuberculosis.	1950 Highsmith: *Strangers on a Train*.
1951	Partially recovered, Yates moves with his wife and child to Paris (April). Moves to Juan-les-Pins, near Cannes (Oct).	1951 Salinger: *The Catcher in the Rye*. Styron: *Lie Down in Darkness*.
1952	Taken on by a literary agent, Monica McCall. Moves to London (Oct). Yates receives $250 for a short story, "Jody Rolled the Bones," from the *Atlantic Monthly*.	1952 Hemingway: *The Old Man and the Sea*. M. McCarthy: *The Groves of Academe*. A. Miller: *The Crucible*.
1953	Sheila returns to the US to care for her brother. Sells "Lament for a Tenor" and "A Glutton for Punishment" to *Cosmopolitan*. Returns to the US. Works as a	1953 Bellow: *The Adventures of Augie March*. Salinger: *Nine Stories*.

CHRONOLOGY

1941 Japan attacks Pearl Harbor; USA enters war. Hitler invades the Soviet Union.

1942 North African campaign (to 1943). Battle of Midway. The world's first nuclear reactor constructed at Chicago University.

1944 Allied (D-Day) landings in Normandy.

1945 Roosevelt dies; Truman becomes president. Unconditional surrender of Germany. US drops atomic bombs on Hiroshima and Nagasaki. End of World War II. Wave of strikes in America (to 1946). Attlee forms Labour government in UK. United Nations founded.

1946–7 USSR extends influence in Eastern Europe. Beginning of Cold War.

1947 Independence of India and Pakistan.

1948 Jewish state of Israel comes into existence. Russian blockade of West Berlin. Assassination of Gandhi in India. Apartheid introduced in South Africa.

1949 Communists win Chinese Civil War. North Atlantic Treaty signed.

1950 Korean War begins.

1952 Eisenhower elected US president. Accession of Elizabeth II in UK. First contraceptive pills.

1953 Korean War ends. Eisenhower elected US president. Death of Stalin.

DATE	AUTHOR'S LIFE	LITERARY CONTEXT
1953 *cont.*	ghost writer for Remington Rand. Wins the Atlantic Monthly "First" Award.	
1954	Sells two short stories, "Nuptials" and "The Best of Everything" to *Charm* magazine.	
1955	Moves to Redding, Connecticut. Begins work on a novel, provisionally titled *The Getaway*.	1955 Nabokov: *Lolita*. Williams: *Cat on a Hot Tin Roof*. Highsmith: *The Talented Mr. Ripley*.
1956	Moves to Mahopac, Putnam County, New York.	1956 O'Neill: *Long Day's Journey into Night*.
1957	Birth of second daughter, Monica Jane.	1957 Kerouac: *On the Road*. Cheever: *The Wapshot Chronicle*. Nabokov: *Pnin*.
1958	*Esquire* accepts "B.A.R. Man." Four short stories, "Jody Rolled the Bones," "The Best of Everything," "Fun with a Stranger," and "A Really Good Jazz Piano'" included in *Short Story 1*, a Scribner volume showcasing talented new writers.	1958 Capote: *Breakfast at Tiffany's*.
1959	Separates from his wife. Moves back to New York and begins teaching a writing class.	1959 Burroughs: *Naked Lunch*. Bellow: *Henderson the Rain King*.
1960	Completes first novel, *Revolutionary Road*. Receives $2,500 as an advance from Little, Brown.	1960 Updike: *Rabbit, Run*.
1961	Publication of *Revolutionary Road* to mixed reviews. Suffers the first of many mental breakdowns.	1961 Heller: *Catch-22*. Salinger: *Franny and Zooey*.
1962	Edits *Stories for the Sixties*, an anthology of new writers. Travels to Hollywood to work on the screenplay of Styron's *Lie Down in Darkness*. *Eleven Kinds of Loneliness* (stories). Guggenheim Award. Begins a lifelong course of treatment for mental illness.	1962 Nabokov: *Pale Fire*. Albee: *Who's Afraid of Virginia Woolf?*
1963	National Institute of Arts and Letters Award. Works as a speechwriter for Robert F. Kennedy.	1963 Pynchon: *V.* Salinger: *Raise High the Roof Beam, Carpenters and Seymour: An Introduction*. Plath: *The Bell Jar*.

CHRONOLOGY

1954 Vietnam War begins.

1956 Soviets invade Hungary. Suez crisis. Transatlantic telephone service linking USA and UK.
1957 Civil Rights Commission established in USA to safeguard voting rights.

1958 Alaska becomes 49th state of the USA.

1959 Castro seizes power in Cuba.

1960 Kennedy elected US president.

1961 Erection of Berlin Wall. Yuri Gagarin becomes first man in space. Bay of Pigs invasion.

1962 Cuban missile crisis.

1963 Assassination of Kennedy. Johnson becomes US president.

DATE	AUTHOR'S LIFE	LITERARY CONTEXT
1964	United Artists pull out of the movie deal for *Lie Down in Darkness*. Begins teaching creative writing at the University of Iowa Writers' Workshop.	1964 Bellow: *Herzog.* Cheever: *The Wapshot Scandal.*
1965	Returns to Hollywood to work as a screenwriter.	1965 Mailer: *An American Dream.*
1966	"A Good and Gallant Woman" and "To Be a Hero," excerpts from second novel, published in *Saturday Evening Post*. Second screenplay turned down by Columbia.	1966 Pynchon: *The Crying of Lot 49.* Capote: *In Cold Blood.*
1967	Returns from Hollywood to teach at Iowa.	1967 Styron: *The Confessions of Nat Turner.*
1968	Marries Martha Speer, a graduate student at Iowa. Death of Yates's sister, Ruth, and his mother.	1968 Updike: *Couples.*
1969	Publication of *A Special Providence*; poor sales leave Yates in debt to Knopf for almost $13,000.	1969 P. Roth: *Portnoy's Complaint.* Vonnegut: *Slaughterhous-Five.* Oates: *Them.*
1970	Takes up a writer-in-residence post at Wichita State University.	1970 Updike: *Bech: A Book.* Didion: *Play It As It Lays.*
1971		1971 Updike: *Rabbit Redux.*
1972	Birth of daughter, Gina Catherine.	1972 DeLillo: *End Zone.*
1973		1973 Pynchon: *Gravity's Rainbow.*
1974	Break-up of second marriage; mental collapse.	1974 P. Roth: *My Life as a Man.*
1975	*Disturbing the Peace.*	
1976	Suffers lung damage and third-degree burns after setting his New York apartment on fire. *The Easter Parade* is nominated for National Book Critics' Circle Award. Moves to Boston.	1976 Carver: *Will You Please Be Quiet, Please?*
1977		1977 Morrison: *Song of Solomon.* Herr: *Dispatches.*
1978	*A Good School.*	
1979		1979 Updike: *The Coup.* C. McCarthy: *Suttree.* Styron: *Sophie's Choice.*

CHRONOLOGY

1964 Civil Rights Act prohibits discrimination in USA. Martin Luther King wins Nobel Peace Prize. Brezhnev becomes Communist Party General Secretary in USSR.

1965 Human rights activist Malcolm X assassinated. US military intervention in Dominican Republic.
1966 Mao launches Cultural Revolution in China.

1967 Arab–Israeli Six-Day War.

1968 Student unrest in USA and throughout Europe. Assassination of Martin Luther King. Soviet invasion of Czechoslovakia. Nixon elected US president.

1969 Americans land first man on the moon.

1970 Salvador Allende becomes president of Chile, the first Marxist head of state to be democratically elected.

1972 USSR and USA sign Strategic Arms Limitation Treaty (SALT).

1973 Yom Kippur War. Oil crisis. Allende deposed by military coup. Legalization of abortion in US.
1974 Nixon resigns in wake of Watergate scandal; Ford becomes US president.
1975 Vietnam War ends. G6 Group founded (becomes G7 1976, G8 1997).
1976 Death of Mao Tse-Tung. Carter elected US president.

1978 Camp David agreement between US, Egypt and Israel. P. W. Botha comes to power in South Africa.
1979 Carter and Brezhnev sign SALT-2 Arms Limitation Treaty. Soviets occupy Afghanistan. Iranian revolution; Iran hostage crisis.
Margaret Thatcher first woman prime minister in UK.

RICHARD YATES

DATE	AUTHOR'S LIFE	LITERARY CONTEXT
1980		
1981	*Liars in Love* (stories).	1981 Updike: *Rabbit Is Rich.* P. Roth: *Zuckerman Unbound.* Carver: *What We Talk About When We Talk About Love.*
1982	Teaches creative writing at Boston University.	1982 Updike: *Bech Is Back.* Munro: *The Moons of Jupiter.*
1983		
1984	Awarded an NEA Fellowship worth $25,000. *Young Hearts Crying.*	1984 Carver: *Cathedral.* Updike: *The Witches of Eastwick.*
1985	Publication of Yates's screenplay for Styron's *Lie Down in Darkness.* Moves to a small apartment above the Crossroads, an Irish pub in Boston.	1985 C. McCarthy: *Blood Meridian.* Atwood: *The Handmaid's Tale.* DeLillo: *White Noise.*
1986	*Cold Spring Harbor.*	1986 R. Ford: *The Sportswriter.* Munro: *The Progress of Love.*
1987		1987 Morrison: *Beloved.*
1988	Works for a former student, writing treatments for TV pilots in Los Angeles.	1988 Tyler: *Breathing Lessons.* Atwood: *Cat's Eye.*
1989	Teaches at University of Southern California.	1989 DeLillo: *Libra.*
1990	Despite increasing ill health, begins teaching at the University of Alabama.	1990 Updike: *Rabbit at Rest.*
1991		
1992	Dies from emphysema in Birmingham, Alabama.	1992 C. McCarthy: *All the Pretty Horses.* Smiley: *A Thousand Acres.* Oates: *Black Water.*

CHRONOLOGY

1980 Lech Walesa leads strikes in Gdansk, Poland. Reagan US president.
1981 President Sadat assassinated in Egypt. Mitterand elected president of
France. First cases of AIDS detected in USA.

1982 Falklands War.

1983 US troops invade Grenada.
1984 Famine in Ethiopia. Indira Gandhi assassinated.

1985 Gorbachev becomes General Secretary in USSR.

1986 Gorbachev–Reagan summit. US bombs Tripoli. State of Emergency in
South Africa. Chernobyl nuclear power accident.

1988 Gorbachev announces big troop reductions, suggesting end of Cold
War.

1989 Collapse of Communism in Eastern Europe. Fall of the Berlin Wall.
First democratic elections in USSR. Tiananmen Square massacre in China.
1990 End of Communist monopoly in USSR. Yeltsin elected first leader of
Russian Federation. Reunification of Germany. Nelson Mandela released
from jail after 27 years' imprisonment.
1991 Gulf War. Central government in USSR suspended. War begins in
former Yugoslavia. End of apartheid in South Africa.
1992 Riots in Los Angeles. Clinton elected US president.

REVOLUTIONARY ROAD

To Sheila

Alas! when passion is both meek and wild!
—JOHN KEATS

PART ONE

ONE

THE FINAL DYING sounds of their dress rehearsal left the Laurel Players with nothing to do but stand there, silent and helpless, blinking out over the footlights of an empty auditorium. They hardly dared to breathe as the short, solemn figure of their director emerged from the naked seats to join them on stage, as he pulled a stepladder raspingly from the wings and climbed halfway up its rungs to turn and tell them, with several clearings of his throat, that they were a damned talented group of people and a wonderful group of people to work with.

"It hasn't been an easy job," he said, his glasses glinting soberly around the stage. "We've had a lot of problems here, and quite frankly I'd more or less resigned myself not to expect too much. Well, listen. Maybe this sounds corny, but something happened up here tonight. Sitting out there tonight I suddenly knew, deep down, that you were all putting your hearts into your work for the first time." He let the fingers of one hand splay out across the pocket of his shirt to show what a simple, physical thing the heart was; then he made the same hand into a fist, which he shook slowly and wordlessly in a long dramatic pause, closing one eye and allowing his moist lower lip to curl out in a grimace of triumph and pride. "Do that again tomorrow night," he said, "and we'll have one hell of a show."

They could have wept with relief. Instead, trembling, they cheered and laughed and shook hands and kissed one another, and somebody went out for a case of beer and they all sang songs around the auditorium piano until the time came to agree, unanimously, that they'd better knock it off and get a good night's sleep.

"See you tomorrow!" they called, as happy as children, and riding home under the moon they found they could roll down the windows of their cars and let the air in, with its health-giving smells of loam and young flowers. It was the first time many of the Laurel Players had allowed themselves to acknowledge the coming of spring.

The year was 1955 and the place was a part of western Connecticut where three swollen villages had lately been merged by a wide and clamorous highway called Route Twelve. The Laurel Players were an amateur company, but a costly and very serious one, carefully recruited from among the younger adults of all three towns, and this was to be their maiden production. All winter, gathering in one another's living rooms for excited talks about Ibsen and Shaw and O'Neill, and then for the show of hands in which a common-sense majority chose *The Petrified Forest*, and then for preliminary casting, they had felt their dedication growing stronger every week. They might privately consider their director a funny little man (and he was, in a way: he seemed incapable of any but a very earnest manner of speaking, and would often conclude his remarks with a little shake of the head that caused his cheeks to wobble) but they liked and respected him, and they fully believed in most of the things he said. "Any play deserves the best that any actor has to give," he'd told them once, and another time: "Remember this. We're not just putting on a play here. We're establishing a community theater, and that's a pretty important thing to be doing."

The trouble was that from the very beginning they had been afraid they would end by making fools of themselves, and they had compounded that fear by being afraid to admit it. At first their rehearsals had been held on Saturdays—always, it seemed, on the kind of windless February or March afternoon when the sky is white, the trees are black, and the brown fields and hummocks of the earth lie naked and tender between curds of shriveled snow. The Players, coming out of their various kitchen doors and hesitating for a minute to button their coats or pull on their gloves, would see a landscape in which only a few very old, weathered houses seemed to belong; it made their own homes look as weightless and impermanent, as foolishly misplaced as a great many bright new toys that had been left outdoors overnight and rained on. Their automobiles didn't look right either—unnecessarily wide and gleaming in the colors of candy and ice cream, seeming to wince at each splatter of mud, they crawled apologetically down the broken roads that led from all directions to the deep, level slab of Route Twelve. Once there the cars seemed able to relax in an environment all their own, a long bright valley of colored plastic and plate glass and stainless steel— KING KONE, MOBILGAS, SHOPORAMA, EAT—but eventually they had to turn off, one by one, and make their way up the winding country road that led to the central high school; they had to pull up and stop in the quiet parking lot outside the high-school auditorium.

"Hi!" the Players would shyly call to one another.

"Hi! ..." "Hi! ..." And they'd go reluctantly inside.

Clumping their heavy galoshes around the stage, blotting at their noses with Kleenex and frowning at the unsteady print of their scripts, they would disarm each other at last with peals of forgiving laughter, and they would agree, over and over, that there was plenty of time to smooth the thing out. But there wasn't plenty of time, and they all knew it, and a doubling and redoubling of their rehearsal schedule seemed only to make matters worse. Long after the time had come for what the director called "really getting this thing off the ground; really making it happen," it remained a static, shapeless, inhumanly heavy weight; time and again they read the promise of failure in each other's eyes, in the apologetic nods and smiles of their parting and the spastic haste with which they broke for their cars and drove home to whatever older, less explicit promises of failure might lie in wait for them there.

And now tonight, with twenty-four hours to go, they had somehow managed to bring it off. Giddy in the unfamiliar feel of make-up and costumes on this first warm evening of the year, they had forgotten to be afraid: they had let the movement of the play come and carry them and break like a wave; and maybe it sounded corny (and what if it did?) but they had all put their hearts into their work. Could anyone ever ask for more than that?

The audience, arriving in a long clean serpent of cars the following night, were very serious too. Like the Players, they were mostly on the young side of middle age, and they were attractively dressed in what the New York clothing stores describe as Country Casuals. Anyone could see they were a better than average crowd, in terms of education and employment and good health, and it was clear too that they considered this a significant evening. They all knew, of course, and said so again and again as they filed inside and took their seats, that *The Petrified Forest* was hardly one of the world's great plays. But it was, after all, a fine theater piece with a basic point of view that was every bit as valid today as in the thirties ("Even more valid," one man kept telling his wife, who chewed her lips and nodded, seeing what he meant; "even more valid, when you think about it"). The main thing, though, was not the play itself but the company—the brave idea of it, the healthy, hopeful sound of it: the birth of a really good community theater right here, among themselves. This was what had drawn them, enough of them to fill more than half the auditorium, and it was what held them hushed and tense in readiness for pleasure as the house lights dimmed.

The curtain went up on a set whose rear wall was still shaking with the impact of a stagehand's last-minute escape, and the first few lines of dialogue were blurred by the scrape and bang of accidental offstage noises. These small disorders were signs of a mounting hysteria among the Laurel Players, but across the footlights they seemed only to add to a sense of impending excellence. They seemed to say, engagingly: Wait a minute; it hasn't really started yet. We're all a little nervous here, but please bear with us. And soon there was no further need for apologies, for the audience was watching the girl who played the heroine, Gabrielle.

Her name was April Wheeler, and she caused the whispered word "lovely" to roll out over the auditorium the first time she walked across the stage. A little later there were hopeful nudges and whispers of "She's *good*," and there were stately nods of pride among the several people who happened to know that she had attended one of the leading dramatic schools of New York less than ten years before. She was twenty-nine, a tall ash blonde with a patrician kind of beauty that no amount of amateur lighting could distort, and she seemed ideally cast in the role. It didn't even matter that bearing two children had left her a shade too heavy in the hips and thighs, for she moved with the shyly sensual grace of maidenhood; anyone happening to glance at Frank Wheeler, the round-faced, intelligent-looking young man who sat biting his fist in the last row of the audience, would have said he looked more like her suitor than her husband.

"Sometimes I can feel as if I were sparkling all over," she was saying, *"and I want to go out and do something that's absolutely crazy, and marvelous . . ."*

Backstage, huddled and listening, the other actors suddenly loved her. Or at least they were prepared to love her, even those who had resented her occasional lack of humility at rehearsals, for she was suddenly the only hope they had.

The leading man had come down with a kind of intestinal flu that morning. He had arrived at the theater in a high fever, insisting that he felt well enough to go on, but five minutes before curtain time he had begun to vomit in his dressing room, and there had been nothing for the director to do but send him home and take over the role himself. The thing happened so quickly that nobody had time to think of going out front to announce the substitution; a few of the minor actors didn't even know about it until they heard the director's voice out there in the lights, speaking the familiar words they'd expected to hear from the other man. He was doing his fervent best and delivering each line with a high semi-professional finish, but there was no denying that he looked all wrong in the part of Alan Squiers—squat and partly bald and all but unable to see without his glasses, which he'd refused to wear on stage. From the moment of his entrance he had caused the supporting actors to interrupt each other and forget where to stand, and now in the middle of his important first-act speech about his own futility—*"Yes, brains without purpose; noise without sound; shape without substance*—" one of his gesturing hands upset a glass of water that flooded the table. He tried to cover it with a giggle and a series of improvised lines—*"You see? That's how useless I am. Here, let me help you wipe it up*—" but the rest of the speech was ruined. The virus of calamity, dormant and threatening all these weeks, had erupted now and spread from the helplessly vomiting man until it infected everyone in the cast but April Wheeler.

"*Wouldn't you like to be loved by me?*" she was saying.

"*Yes, Gabrielle,*" said the director, gleaming with sweat. "*I should like to be loved by you.*"

"*You think I'm attractive?*"

Under the table the director's leg began to jiggle up and down on the spring of its flexed foot. "*There are better words than that for what you are.*"

"*Then why don't we at least make a start at it?*"

She was working alone, and visibly weakening with every line. Before the end of the first act the audience could tell as well as the Players that she'd lost her grip, and soon they were all embarrassed for her. She had begun to alternate between false theatrical gestures and a white-knuckled immobility; she was carrying her shoulders high and square, and despite her heavy make-up you could see the warmth of humiliation rising in her face and neck.

Then came the bouncing entrance of Shep Campbell, the burly young red-haired engineer who played the gangster, Duke Mantee. The whole company had worried about Shep from the beginning, but he and his wife Milly, who had helped with the props and the publicity, were such enthusiastic and friendly people that nobody'd had the heart to suggest replacing him. The result of this indulgence now, and of Campbell's own nervous guilt about it, was that he forgot one of his key lines, said others in a voice so quick and faint that it couldn't be heard beyond the sixth row, and handled himself less like an outlaw than an obliging grocery clerk, bobbing head, rolled-up sleeves and all.

At intermission the audience straggled out to smoke and wander in uncomfortable groups around the high-school corridor, examining the high-school bulletin board and wiping damp palms down their slim-cut trousers and their graceful cotton skirts. None of them wanted to go back and go through with the second and final act, but they all did.

And so did the Players, whose one thought now, as plain as the sweat on their faces, was to put the whole sorry business behind them as fast as possible. It seemed to go on for hours, a cruel and protracted endurance test in which April Wheeler's performance was as bad as the others, if not worse. At the climax, where the stage directions call for the poignance of the death scene to be *punctuated with shots from outside and bursts from* DUKE'S *Tommy gun*, Shep Campbell timed his bursts so sloppily, and the answering offstage gunfire was so much too loud, that all the lovers' words were lost in a deafening smoky shambles. When the curtain fell at last it was an act of mercy.

The applause, not loud, was conscientiously long enough to permit two curtain calls, one that caught all the Players in motion as they walked to the wings, turned back and collided with one another, and another that revealed the three principals in a brief tableau of human desolation: the director blinking myopically, Shep Campbell looking appropriately fierce for the first time all evening, April Wheeler paralyzed in a formal smile.

Then the house lights came up, and nobody in the auditorium knew how to look or what to say. The uncertain voice of Mrs. Helen Givings, the real-estate broker, could be heard repeating "*Very* nice," over and over again, but most of the people were silent and stiff, fingering packs of cigarettes as they rose and turned to the aisles. An efficient high-school boy, hired for the evening to help with the lights, vaulted up onto the stage with a squeak of his sneakers and began calling instructions to an unseen partner high in the flies. He stood posing self-consciously in the footlights, managing to keep most of his bright pimples in shadow while proudly turning his body to show that the tools of the electrician's trade—knife, pliers, coils of wire—were slung in a professional-looking holster of oiled leather and worn low on one tense buttock of his dungarees. Then the bank of lights clicked off, the boy made a pale exit and the curtain became a dull wall of green velvet, faded and streaked with dust. There was nothing to watch now but the massed faces of the audience as they pressed up the aisles and out the main doors. Anxious, round-eyed, two by two, they looked and moved as if a calm and orderly escape from this place had become the one great necessity of their lives; as if, in fact, they wouldn't be able to begin to live at all until they were out beyond the rumbling pink billows of exhaust and the crunching gravel of this parking lot, out where the black sky went up and up forever and there were hundreds of thousands of stars.

TWO

FRANKLIN H. WHEELER was among the few who bucked the current. He did so with apologetic slowness and with what he hoped was dignity, making his way in sidling steps down the aisle toward the stage door, saying "Excuse me . . . Excuse me," nodding and smiling to several faces he knew, carrying one hand in his pocket to conceal and dry the knuckles he had sucked and bitten throughout the play.

He was neat and solid, a few days less than thirty years old, with closely cut black hair and the kind of unemphatic good looks that an advertising photographer might use to portray the discerning consumer of well-made but inexpensive merchandise (Why Pay More?). But for all its lack of structural distinction, his face did have an unusual mobility: it was able to suggest wholly different personalities with each flickering change of expression. Smiling, he was a man who knew perfectly well that the failure of an amateur play was nothing much to worry about, a kindly, witty man who would have exactly the right words of comfort for his wife backstage; but in the intervals between his smiles, when he shouldered ahead through the crowd and you could see the faint chronic fever of bewilderment in his eyes, it seemed more that he himself was in need of comforting.

The trouble was that all afternoon in the city, stultified at what he liked to call "the dullest job you can possibly imagine," he had drawn strength from a mental projection of scenes to unfold tonight: himself rushing home to swing his children laughing in the air, to gulp a cocktail and chatter through an early dinner with his wife; himself driving her to the high school, with her thigh tense and warm under his reassuring hand ("If only I weren't so *nervous*, Frank!"); himself sitting spellbound in pride and then rising to join a thunderous ovation as the curtain fell;

14

himself glowing and disheveled, pushing his way through jubilant backstage crowds to claim her first tearful kiss ("Was it really
good, darling? Was it really good?"); and then the two of them,
stopping for a drink in the admiring company of Shep and Milly
Campbell, holding hands under the table while they talked it all
out. Nowhere in these plans had he foreseen the weight and
shock of reality; nothing had warned him that he might be overwhelmed by the swaying, shining vision of a girl he hadn't seen
in years, a girl whose every glance and gesture could make his
throat fill up with longing ("*Wouldn't you like to be loved by me?*"),
and that then before his very eyes she would dissolve and change
into the graceless, suffering creature whose existence he tried
every day of his life to deny but whom he knew as well and as
painfully as he knew himself, a gaunt constricted woman whose
red eyes flashed reproach, whose false smile in the curtain call
was as homely as his own sore feet, his own damp climbing
underwear and his own sour smell.

At the door he paused to withdraw and examine the pink-
blotched hand from his pocket, half expecting to find it torn to
a pulp of blood and gristle. Then, pulling his coat straight, he
went through the door and up the steps into a high dusty chamber filled with the raw glare and deep shadows cast by naked light
bulbs, where the Laurel Players, ablaze with cosmetics, stood
talking to their sallow visitors in nervous, widely spaced groups
of two and three around the floor. She wasn't there.

"No, I mean seriously," somebody was saying. "Could you
hear me, or not?" And somebody else said, "Well, hell, it was a
lot of fun anyway." The director, in a scanty cluster of his New
York friends, was pulling hungrily on a cigarette and shaking
his head. Shep Campbell, pebbled with sweat, still holding his
Tommy gun but clearly himself again, was standing near the curtain rope with his free arm around his small, rumpled wife, and
they were both demonstrating their decision to laugh the whole
thing off.

"*Frank?*" Milly Campbell had waved and risen on tiptoe to
shout his name through cupped hands, as if pretending that the
crowd were thicker and noisier than it really was. "Frank! We'll
see you and April later, okay? For a drink?"

"Fine!" he called back. "Couple of minutes!" And he winked and nodded as Shep raised his machine gun in a comic salute.

Around the corner he found one of the lesser gangsters talking with a plump girl who had caused a thirty-second rupture in the first act by missing her entrance cue, who had evidently been crying but now was hilariously pounding her temple and saying "God! I could've *killed* myself!" while the gangster, tremulously wiping grease paint from his mouth, said "No, but I mean it was a lot of fun anyway, you know what I mean? That's the main thing, in a thing like this."

"Excuse me," Frank Wheeler said, squeezing past them to the door of the dressing room that his wife shared with several other women. He knocked and waited, and when he thought he heard her say "Come in," he opened it tentatively and peeked inside.

She was alone, sitting very straight at a mirror and removing her make-up. Her eyes were still red and blinking, but she gave him a small replica of her curtain-call smile before turning back to the mirror. "Hi," she said. "You ready to leave?"

He closed the door and started toward her with the corners of his mouth stretched tight in a look that he hoped would be full of love and humor and compassion; what he planned to do was bend down and kiss her and say "Listen: you were wonderful." But an almost imperceptible recoil of her shoulders told him that she didn't want to be touched, which left him uncertain what to do with his hands, and that was when it occurred to him that "You were wonderful" might be exactly the wrong thing to say—condescending, or at the very least naive and sentimental, and much too serious.

"Well," he said instead. "I guess it wasn't exactly a triumph or anything, was it?" And he stuck a cigarette jauntily in his lips and lit it with a flourish of his clicking Zippo.

"I guess not," she said. "I'll be ready in a minute."

"No, that's okay, take your time."

He pocketed both hands and curled the tired toes inside his shoes, looking down at them. Would "You were wonderful" have been a better thing to say, after all? Almost anything, it now seemed, would have been a better thing to say than what he'd said. But he would have to think of better things to say later;

right now it was all he could do to stand here and think about the double bourbon he would have when they stopped on the way home with the Campbells. He looked at himself in the mirror, tightening his jaw and turning his head a little to one side to give it a leaner, more commanding look, the face he had given himself in mirrors since boyhood and which no photograph had ever quite achieved, until with a start he found that she was watching him. Her own eyes were there in the mirror, trained on his for an uncomfortable moment before she lowered them to stare at the middle button of his coat.

"Listen," she said. "Will you do me a favor? The thing is—" It seemed that all the slender strength of her back was needed to keep her voice from wavering. "The thing is, Milly and Shep wanted us to go out with them afterwards. Will you say we can't? Say it's because of the baby sitter, or something?"

He moved well away and stood stiff-legged and hump-shouldered, hands in his pockets, like a stage lawyer considering a fine point of ethics. "Well," he said, "the thing is, I already said we could. I mean I just saw them out there and I said we would."

"Oh. Then would you mind going out again and saying you were mistaken? That should be simple enough."

"Look," he said. "Don't start getting this way. The point is I thought it might be fun, is all. Besides, it's going to look kind of rude, isn't it? I mean isn't it?"

"You mean you won't." She closed her eyes. "All right, I will, then. Thanks a lot." Her face in the mirror, nude and shining with cold cream, looked forty years old and as haggard as if it were set to endure a physical pain.

"Wait a second," he told her. "Take it easy, will you please? I didn't say that. I just said they're going to think it's damn rude, that's all. And they are. I can't help that."

"All right. You go along with them, if you want to, and give me the car keys."

"Oh, Jesus, don't start this business about the car keys. Why do you always have to—"

"Look, Frank." Her eyes were still shut. "I'm not going out with those people. I don't happen to feel very well, and I—"

"Okay." He was backing away, holding out both stiff trembling hands like a man intently describing the length of a short fish. "Okay. Okay. I'm sorry. I'll tell them. I'll be right back. I'm sorry."

The floor rode under his feet like the deck of a moving ship as he made his way back to the wings, where a man was taking pictures with a miniature flash camera ("Hold it now—that's fine. That's fine") and the actor who played Gabrielle's father was telling the plump girl, who looked ready to cry again, that the only thing to do was write the whole thing off to experience.

"You folks about ready?" Shep Campbell demanded.

"Well," Frank said, "actually, I'm afraid we'll have to cut out. April promised this baby sitter we'd be home early, you see, and we really—"

Both their faces sagged in hurt and disappointment. Milly drew a section of her lower lip between her teeth and slowly released it. "Gee," she said. "I guess April feels awful about this whole thing, doesn't she? Poor kid."

"No, no, she's okay," he told them. "Really, it's not that. She's okay. It's just this business of the baby sitter, you see." It was the first lie of its kind in the two years of their friendship, and it caused them all three to look at the floor as they labored through a halting ritual of smiles and goodnights; but it couldn't be helped.

She was waiting for him in the dressing room, ready with a pleasant social face for any of the Laurel Players they might happen to meet on the way out, but they managed to avoid them all. She led him through a side door that opened onto fifty yards of empty, echoing high-school corridor and they walked without touching each other and without speaking, moving in and out of the oblongs of moonlight that lay on the marble floor.

The smell of school in the darkness, pencils and apples and library paste, brought a sweet nostalgic pain to his eyes and he was fourteen again, and it was the year he'd lived in Chester, Pennsylvania—no, in Englewood, New Jersey—and spent all his free time in a plan for riding the rails to the West Coast. He had traced several alternate routes on a railroad map, he had rehearsed many times the way he would handle himself (politely, but with fist fights if necessary) in the hobo jungles along the way, and he'd chosen all the items of his wardrobe from the window of an

Army and Navy store: Levi jacket and pants, an army-type khaki shirt with shoulder tabs, high-cut work shoes with steel caps at heel and toe. An old felt hat of his father's, which could be made to fit with a wad of newspaper folded into its sweatband, would lend the right note of honest poverty to the outfit, and he could take whatever else he needed in his Boy Scout knapsack, artfully reinforced with adhesive tape to conceal the Boy Scout emblem. The best thing about the plan was its absolute secrecy, until the day in the school corridor when he impulsively asked a fat boy named Krebs, who was the closest thing to a best friend he had that year, to go along with him. Krebs was dumfounded—"On a *freight* train, you mean?"—and soon he was laughing aloud. "Jeez, you kill me, Wheeler. How far do you think *you'd* get on a freight train? Where do you get these weird ideas, anyway? The movies or someplace? You want to know something, Wheeler? You want to know why everybody thinks you're a jerk? Because you're a jerk, that's why."

Walking now through the same smells and looking at the pale shape of April's profile as she walked beside him, he allowed his rising sense of poignance to encompass her as well, and the sadness of her own childhood. He wasn't often able to do this, for most of her memories were crisply told and hard to sentimentalize ("I always knew nobody cared about me and I always let everybody know I knew it"), but the school smell made him think of one particular time she had told about, a morning in Rye Country Day when a menstrual flow of unusual suddenness and volume had taken her by surprise in the middle of a class. "At first I just sat there," she'd told him. "That was the stupid thing; and then it was too late." And he thought of how she must have lurched from her desk and run from the room with a red stain the size of a maple leaf on the seat of her white linen skirt while thirty boys and girls looked up in dumb surprise, how she must have fled down the corridor in a nightmarish silence past the doors of other murmuring classrooms, spilling books and picking them up and running again, leaving a tidy, well-spaced trail of blood drops on the floor, how she had run to the first-aid room and been afraid to go inside, how instead she had run all the way down another corridor to a fire-exit door, where she pulled off her cardigan and tied it around her waist and hips; how then, hearing or imagining the approach of footsteps in her wake, she had pushed through to the sunny lawn outside and set off for home, walking not too quickly and with her head high, so that anyone happening to glance from any of a hundred windows would think her on some perfectly normal errand from school, wearing her sweater in a perfectly normal way.

Her face must have looked almost exactly the way it did now, as they opened this other fire-exit door and walked out across these other school grounds not many miles from Rye, and her way of walking must have been similar too.

He had hoped she would sit close to him in the car—he wanted to hold her shoulders while he drove—but she made herself very small and pressed against the passenger's door, turning away to watch the passing lights and shadows of the road. This caused his eyes to grow round and his mouth solemn as he steered and shifted gears, until finally, licking his lips, he thought of something to say.

"You know something? You were the only person in that whole play. No kidding, April. I mean it."

"All right," she said. "Thank you."

"It's just that we never should've let you get mixed up in the damned thing, is all." With his free hand he opened his collar, both to cool his neck and to find reassurance in the grown-up, sophisticated feel of the silk tie and Oxford shirt. "I'd just like to get my hands on that what's his name, that's all. That director."

"It wasn't his fault."

"Well, the whole pack of them, then. God knows they all stank. The whole point is we should've known better in the first place. I should've known better, is what it amounts to. You never would've joined the damn group if the Campbells and I hadn't talked you into it. Remember when we first heard about it? And you said they'd probably turn out to be a bunch of idiots? Well, I should've listened to you, that's all."

"All right. Could we sort of stop talking about it now?"

"Sure we will." He tried to pat her thigh but it was out of reach across the wide seat. "Sure we will. I just don't want you feeling bad about it, that's all."

With a confident, fluid grace he steered the car out of the bouncing side road and onto the hard clean straightaway of Route Twelve, feeling that his attitude was on solid ground at last. A refreshing wind rushed in to ruffle his short hair and cool his brains, and he began to see the fiasco of the Laurel Players in its true perspective. It simply wasn't worth feeling bad about. Intelligent, thinking people could take things like this in their stride, just as they took the larger absurdities of deadly dull jobs in the city and deadly dull homes in the suburbs. Economic circumstance might force you to live in this environment, but the important thing was to keep from being contaminated. The important thing, always, was to remember who you were.

And now, as it often did in the effort to remember who he was, his mind went back to the first few years after the war and to a crumbling block of Bethune Street, in that part of New York where the gentle western edge of the Village flakes off into silent waterfront warehouses, where the salt breeze of evening and the deep river horns of night enrich the air with a promise of voyages. In his very early twenties, wearing the proud mantles of "veteran" and "intellectual" as bravely as he wore his carefully aged tweed jacket and washed-out khakis, he had owned one of three keys to a one-room apartment on that street. The other two keys, and rights to "the use of the place" every second and third week, had belonged to two of his Columbia College classmates, each of whom paid a third of its twenty-seven-dollar rent. These other two, an ex-fighter pilot and an ex-marine, were older and more relaxed in their worldliness than Frank— they seemed able to draw on endless reserves of willing girls with whom to use the place—but it wasn't long before Frank, to his own shy amazement, began to catch up with them; that was a time of wondrously rapid catching-up in many ways, of dizzily mounting self-confidence. The solitary tracer of railroad maps had never hopped his freight, but it had begun to seem unlikely that any Krebs would ever call him a jerk again. The army had taken him at eighteen, had thrust him into the final spring offensive of the war in Germany and given him a confused but exhilarating tour of Europe for another year before it set him free, and life since then had carried him from strength to strength.

Loose strands of his character—the very traits that had kept him dreaming and lonely among schoolboys and later among soldiers—these seemed suddenly to have coalesced into a substantial and attractive whole. For the first time in his life he was admired, and the fact that girls could actually want to go to bed with him was only slightly more remarkable than his other concurrent discovery—that men, and intelligent men at that, could actually want to listen to him talk. His marks at school were seldom better than average, but there was nothing average about his performance in the beery, all-night talks that had begun to form around him—talks that would often end in a general murmur of agreement, accompanied by a significant tapping of temples, that old Wheeler really had it. All he would ever need, it was said, was the time and the freedom to find himself. Various ultimate careers were predicted for him, the consensus being that his work would lie somewhere "in the humanities" if not precisely in the arts—it would, at any rate, be something that called for a long and steadfast dedication—and that it would involve his early and permanent withdrawal to Europe, which he often described as the only part of the world worth living in. And Frank himself, walking the streets at daybreak after some of those talks, or lying and thinking on Bethune Street on nights when he had the use of the place but had no girl to use it with, hardly ever entertained a doubt of his own exceptional merit. Weren't the biographies of all great men filled with this same kind of youthful groping, this same kind of rebellion against their fathers and their fathers' ways? He could even be grateful in a sense that he had no particular area of interest: in avoiding specific goals he had avoided specific limitations. For the time being the world, life itself, could be his chosen field.

But as college wore on he began to be haunted by numberless small depressions, and these tended to increase in the weeks after college was over, when the other two men had taken to using their keys less and less frequently and he was staying alone in the Bethune Street place, taking odd jobs to buy his food while he thought things out. It nagged him, in particular, that none of the girls he'd known so far had given him a sense of unalloyed triumph. One had been very pretty except for unpardonably thick ankles, and one had been intelligent, though possessed of an annoying tendency to mother him, but he had to admit that none had been first-rate. Nor was he ever in doubt of what he meant by a first-rate girl, though he'd never yet come close enough to one to touch her hand. There had been two or three of them in the various high schools he'd attended, disdainfully unaware of him in their concern with college boys from out of town; what few he'd seen in the army had most often been seen in flickering miniature, on strains of dance music, through the distant golden windows of an officers' club, and though he'd seen plenty of them since then, in New York, they had always been climbing in or out of taxicabs, followed by the grimly hovering presences of men who looked as if they'd never been boys at all.

Why not let well enough alone? As an intense, nicotine-stained, Jean-Paul Sartre sort of man, wasn't it simple logic to expect that he'd be limited to intense, nicotine-stained, Jean-Paul Sartre sorts of women? But this was the counsel of defeat, and one night, bolstered by four straight gulps of whiskey at a party in Morningside Heights, he followed the counsel of victory. "I guess I didn't get your name," he said to the exceptionally first-rate girl whose shining hair and splendid legs had drawn him halfway across a roomful of strangers. "Are you Pamela?"

"No," she said. "That's Pamela over there. I'm April. April Johnson."

Within five minutes he found he could make April Johnson laugh, that he could not only hold the steady attention of her wide gray eyes but could make their pupils dart up and down and around in little arcs while he talked to her, as if the very shape and texture of his face were matters of absorbing interest.

"What do you do?"

"I'm a longshoreman."

"No, I mean really."

"I mean really too." And he would have showed her his palms to prove it if he hadn't been afraid she could tell the difference between calluses and blisters. For the past week, under the guidance of a roughhewn college friend, he had been self-consciously "shaping up" on the docks each morning and swaying under the weight of fruit crates. "Starting Monday, though, I've got a better job. Night cashier in a cafeteria."

"Well but I don't mean things like that. I mean what are you really interested in?"

"Honey—" (and he was still young enough so that the audacity of saying "Honey" on such short acquaintance made him blush) "—Honey, if I had the answer to that one I bet I'd bore us both to death in half an hour."

Five minutes later, dancing, he found that the small of April Johnson's back rode as neatly in his hand as if it had been made for that purpose; and a week after that, almost to the day, she was lying miraculously nude beside him in the first blue light of day on Bethune Street, drawing her delicate forefinger down his face from brow to chin and whispering: "It's true, Frank. I mean it. You're the most interesting person I've ever met."

"Because it's just not worth it," he was saying now, allowing the blue-lit needle of the speedometer to tremble up through sixty for the final mile of highway. They were almost home. They would have a few drinks and maybe she would cry a little— it would do her good—and then they would laugh about it and shut themselves in the bedroom and take off their clothes, and in the moonlight her plump little breasts would nod and sway and point at him, and there wasn't any reason why it couldn't be like the old days.

"I mean it's bad enough having to *live* among all these damn little suburban types—and I'm including the Campbells in that, let's be honest—it's bad enough having to *live* among these people, without letting ourselves get hurt by every little half-assed—what'd you say?" He glanced briefly away from the road and was startled to see, by the light of the dashboard, that she was covering her face with both hands.

"I said *yes*. All *right*, Frank. Could you just please stop talking now, before you drive me crazy?"

He slowed down quickly and brought the car to a sandy halt on the shoulder of the road, cutting the engine and the lights. Then he slid across the seat and tried to take her in his arms.

"No, Frank, please don't do that. Just leave me alone, okay?"

"Baby, it's only that I want to—"

"Leave me alone. Leave me *alone!*"

He drew himself back to the wheel and put the lights on, but his hands refused to undertake the job of starting the car. Instead he sat there for a minute, listening to the beating of blood in his eardrums.

"It strikes me," he said at last, "that there's a considerable amount of bullshit going on here. I mean you seem to be doing a pretty good imitation of Madame Bovary here, and there's one or two points I'd like to clear up. Number one, it's not my fault the play was lousy. Number two, it's sure as hell not my fault you didn't turn out to be an actress, and the sooner you get over *that* little piece of soap opera the better off we're all going to be. Number three, I don't happen to fit the role of dumb, insensitive suburban husband; you've been trying to hang that one on me ever since we moved *out* here, and I'm damned if I'll wear it. Number four—"

She was out of the car and running away in the headlights, quick and graceful, a little too wide in the hips. For a second, as he clambered out and started after her, he thought she meant to kill herself—she was capable of damn near anything at times like this—but she stopped in the dark roadside weeds thirty yards ahead, beside a luminous sign that read no passing. He came up behind her and stood uncertainly, breathing hard, keeping his distance. She wasn't crying; she was only standing there, with her back to him.

"What the hell," he said. "What the hell's this all about? Come on back to the car."

"No. I will in a minute. Just let me stand here a minute, all right?"

His arms flapped and fell; then, as the sound and the lights of an approaching car came up behind them, he put one hand in his pocket and assumed a conversational slouch for the sake of appearances. The car overtook them, lighting up the sign and the tense shape of her back; then its taillights sped away and the drone of its tires flattened out to a buzz in the distance, and finally to silence. On their right, in a black marsh, the spring peepers were in full and desperate song. Straight ahead, two or three hundred yards away, the earth rose high above the moonlit telephone wires to form the mound of Revolutionary Hill, along whose summit winked the friendly picture windows of the Revolutionary Hill Estates. The Campbells lived in one of those houses; the Campbells might well be in one of the cars whose lights were coming up behind them right now.

"April?"

She didn't answer.

"Look," he said. "Couldn't we sit in the car and talk about it? Instead of running all over Route Twelve?"

"Haven't I made it clear," she said, "that I don't particularly want to talk about it?"

"*Okay,*" he said. "*Okay.* Jesus, April, I'm trying as hard as I can to be nice about this thing, but I—"

"How kind of you," she said. "How terribly, terribly kind of you."

"*Wait* a minute—" he pulled the hand from his pocket and stood straight, but then he put it back because other cars were coming. "Listen a minute." He tried to swallow but his throat was very dry. "I don't know what you're trying to prove here," he said, "and frankly I don't think you do either. But I do know one thing. I know damn well I don't deserve this."

"You're always so wonderfully definite, aren't you," she said, "on the subject of what you do and don't deserve." She swept past him and walked back to the car.

"Now, *wait* a minute!" He was stumbling after her in the weeds. Other cars were rushing past now, both ways, but he'd stopped caring. "*Wait* a minute, God damn it!"

She leaned the backs of her thighs against the fender and folded her arms in an elaborate display of resignation while he jabbed and shook a forefinger in her face.

"You listen to me. This is one time you're not going to get away with twisting everything I say. This just happens to be *one* damn time I *know* I'm not in the wrong. You know what you are when you're like this?"

"Oh God, if only you'd stayed home tonight."

"You know what you are when you're like this? You're sick. I really mean that."

"And do you know what you are?" Her eyes raked him up and down. "You're disgusting."

Then the fight went out of control. It quivered their arms and legs and wrenched their faces into shapes of hatred, it urged them harder and deeper into each other's weakest points, showing them cunning ways around each other's strongholds and quick chances to switch tactics, feint, and strike again. In the space of a gasp for breath it sent their memories racing back over the years for old weapons to rip the scabs off old wounds; it went on and on.

"Oh, you've never fooled me, Frank, never once. All your precious moral maxims and your 'love' and your mealy-mouthed little—do you think I've *forgotten* the time you hit me in the face because I said I wouldn't forgive you? Oh, I've always known I had to be your conscience and your guts—*and* your punching bag. Just because you've got me safely in a trap you think you—"

"*You* in a trap! *You* in a trap! *Jesus*, don't make me laugh!"

"Yes, me." She made a claw of her hand and clutched at her collarbone. "Me. Me. Me. Oh, you poor, self-deluded—*Look* at you! *Look* at you, and tell me how by any *stretch*"—she tossed her head, and the grin of her teeth glistened white in the moonlight—"by any *stretch* of the imagination you can call yourself a man!"

He swung out one trembling fist for a backhanded blow to her head and she cowered against the fender in an ugly crumple of fear; then instead of hitting her he danced away in a travesty of boxer's footwork and brought the fist down on the roof of the car with all his strength. He hit the car four times that way: *Bong! Bong! Bong! Bong!*—while she stood and watched. When he was finished, the shrill, liquid chant of the peepers was the only sound for miles.

"God damn you," he said quietly. "God damn you, April."

"All right. Could we please go home now?"

With parched, hard-breathing mouths, with wobbling heads and shaking limbs, they settled themselves in the car like very old and tired people. He started the engine and drove carefully away, down to the turn at the base of Revolutionary Hill and on up the winding blacktop grade of Revolutionary Road.

This was the way they had first come, two years ago, as cordially nodding passengers in the station wagon of Mrs. Helen Givings, the real-estate broker. She had been polite but guarded over the phone—so many city people were apt to come out and waste her time demanding impossible bargains—but from the moment they'd stepped off the train, as she would later tell her husband, she had recognized them as the kind of couple one did take a little trouble with, even in the low-price bracket. "They're *sweet*," she told her husband. "The girl is *ab*solutely ravishing, and I think the boy must do something very brilliant in town— he's very nice, rather reserved—and really, it *is* so refreshing to deal with people of that sort." Mrs. Givings had understood at once that they wanted something out of the ordinary—a small remodeled barn or carriage house, or an old guest cottage— something with a little charm—and she did hate having to tell them that those things simply weren't available any more. But she implored them not to lose heart; she did know of one little place they might like.

"Now of course it isn't a very desirable road down at this end," she explained, her glance switching birdlike between the road and their pleased, attentive faces as she made the turn off Route Twelve. "As you see, it's mostly these little cinder-blocky, pickup-trucky places—plumbers, carpenters, little local people of that sort. And then *eventually*"—she aimed the stiff pistol of her index finger straight through the windshield in fair warning, causing a number of metal bracelets to jingle and click against the steering wheel—"*eventually* it leads on up and around to a perfectly dreadful new development called Revolutionary Hill Estates—great hulking split levels, all in the most nauseous pastels and dreadfully expensive too, I can't think why. No, but the place I want to show you has absolutely no connection with that. One of our nice little local builders put it up right after the war, you see, before all the really awful building began. It's really rather a sweet little house and a sweet little setting. Simple, clean lines, good lawns, marvelous for children. It's right around this next curve, and you see the road *is* nicer along in here, isn't it? Now you'll see it—there. See the little white one? Sweet, isn't it? The perky way it sits there on its little slope?"

"Oh yes," April said as the house emerged through the spindly trunks of second-growth oak and slowly turned toward them, small and wooden, riding high on its naked concrete foundation, its outsized central window staring like a big black mirror. "Yes, I think it's sort of—nice, don't you, darling? Of course it does have the picture window; I guess there's no escaping that."

"I guess not," Frank said. "Still, I don't suppose one picture window is necessarily going to destroy our personalities."

"Oh, that's *marvelous*," Mrs. Givings cried, and her laughter enclosed them in a warm shelter of flattery as they rolled up the driveway and climbed out to have a look. She hovered near them, reassuring and protective, while they walked the naked floors of the house in whispering speculation. The place did have possibilities. Their sofa could go here and their big table there; their solid wall of books would take the curse off the picture window; a sparse, skillful arrangement of furniture would counteract the prim suburban look of this too-symmetrical living room. On the other hand, the very symmetry of the place was undeniably appealing—the fact that all its corners made right angles, that each of its floorboards lay straight and true, that its doors hung in perfect balance and closed without scraping in efficient clicks. Enjoying the light heft and feel of these door-knobs, they could fancy themselves at home here. Inspecting the flawless bathroom, they could sense the pleasure of steaming in its ample tub; they could see their children running barefoot down this hallway free of mildew and splinters and cockroaches and grit. It did have possibilities. The gathering disorder of their lives might still be sorted out and made to fit these rooms, among these trees; and what if it did take time? Who could be frightened in as wide and bright, as clean and quiet a house as this?

Now, as the house swam up close in the darkness with its cheerful blaze of kitchen and carport lights, they tensed their shoulders and set their jaws in attitudes of brute endurance. April went first, swaying blindly through the kitchen, pausing to steady herself against the great refrigerator, and Frank came blinking behind her. Then she touched a wall switch, and the living room exploded into clarity. In the first shock of light it seemed to be floating, all its contents adrift, and even after it held still it had a tentative look. The sofa was here and the big table there, but they might just as well have been reversed; there was the wall of books, obediently competing for dominance with the picture window, but it might as well have been a lending library. The other pieces of furniture had indeed removed the suggestion of primness, but they had failed to replace it with any other quality. Chairs, coffee table, floor lamp and desk, they stood like items arbitrarily grouped for auction. Only one corner of the room showed signs of pleasant human congress—carpet worn, cushions dented, ash trays full—and this was the alcove they had established with reluctance less than six months ago: the province of the television set ("Why not? Don't we really owe it to the kids? Besides, it's silly to go on being snobbish about television . . .").

Mrs. Lundquist, the baby sitter, had fallen asleep on the sofa and lay hidden beneath its back. Now she rose abruptly into view as she sat up squinting and trying to smile, her false teeth clacking and her hands fumbling at the pins of her loosened white hair.

"Mommy?" came a high wide-awake voice from the children's room down the hall. It was Jennifer, the six-year-old. "Mommy? Was it a good play?"

Frank took two wrong turns in driving Mrs. Lundquist home (Mrs. Lundquist, lurching against door and dashboard, tried to cover her fear by smiling fixedly in the darkness; she thought he was drunk), and all the way back, alone, he rode with one hand pressed to his mouth. He was doing his best to reconstruct the quarrel in his mind, but it was hopeless. He couldn't even tell whether he was angry or contrite, whether it was forgiveness he wanted or the power to forgive. His throat was still raw from shouting and his hand still throbbed from hitting the car—he remembered that part well enough—but his only other memory was of the high-shouldered way she had stood in the curtain call, with that false, vulnerable smile, and this made him weak with remorse. Of all the nights to have a fight! He had to hold the wheel tight in both hands because the road lights were blurring and swimming in his eyes.

The house was dark, and the sight of it as he drove up, a long milky shape in the greater darkness of trees and sky, made him think of death. He padded quickly through the kitchen and living room and went down the hall on careful tiptoe, past the children's room and into the bedroom, where he softly shut the door behind him.

"April, listen," he whispered. Stripping off his coat, he went to the dim bed and sat slumped on its edge in a classic pose of contrition. "Please listen. I won't touch you. I just want to say I'm—there isn't anything to say except I'm sorry."

This was going to be a bad one; it was going to be the kind that went on for days. But at least they were here, alone and quiet in their own room, instead of shouting on the highway; at least the thing had passed into its second phase now, the long quiet aftermath that always before, however implausibly, had led to reconciliation. She wouldn't run away from him now, nor was there any chance of his boiling into a rage again; they were both too tired. Early in his marriage these numb periods had seemed even worse than the humiliating noise that set them off: each time he would think, There can't be any dignified way out of it this time. But there always had been a way, dignified or not, discovered through the simple process of apologizing first and then waiting, trying not to think about it too much. By now the feel of this attitude was as familiar as an unbecoming, comfortable old coat. He could wear it with a certain voluptuous ease, for it allowed him a total suspension of will and pride.

"I don't know what happened back there," he said, "but whatever it was, believe me, I—April?" Then his reaching hand discovered that the bed was empty. The long shape he'd been talking to was a wad of thrown-back covers and a pillow; she had torn the bed apart.

"April?"

He ran frightened to the empty bathroom and down the hall.

"Please go away," her voice said. She was rolled up in a blanket on the living-room sofa, where Mrs. Lundquist had lain.

"Listen a minute. I won't touch you. I just want to say I'm sorry."

"That's wonderful. Now will you please leave me alone?"

THREE

A SHRILL METALLIC whine cut through the silence of his sleep. He tried to hide from it, huddling deeper into a cool darkness where the mists of an absorbing dream still floated, but it came tearing back again and again until his eyes popped open in the sunshine.

It was after eleven o'clock, Saturday morning. Both his nostrils were plugged as if with rubber cement, his head ached, and the first fly of the season was crawling up the inside of a clouded whiskey glass that stood on the floor beside a nearly empty bottle. Only after making these discoveries did he begin to remember the events of the night—how he'd sat here drinking until four in the morning, methodically scratching his scalp with both hands, convinced that sleep was out of the question. And only after remembering this did his mind come into focus on an explanation of the noise: it was his own rusty lawnmower, which needed oiling. Somebody was cutting the grass in the back yard, a thing he had promised to do last weekend.

He rolled heavily upright and groped for his bathrobe, moistening the wrinkled roof of his mouth. Then he went and squinted through the brilliant window. It was April herself, stolidly pushing and hauling the old machine, wearing a man's shirt and a pair of loose, flapping slacks, while both children romped behind her with handfuls of cut grass.

In the bathroom he used enough cold water and toothpaste and Kleenex to revive the working parts of his head; he restored its ability to gather oxygen and regained a certain muscular control over its features. But nothing could be done about his hands. Bloated and pale, they felt as if all their bones had been painlessly removed. A command to clench them into fists would have sent him whimpering to his knees. Looking at them, and particularly at the bitten-down nails that never in his life had had a chance to grow, he wanted to beat and bruise them against the edge of the sink. He thought then of his father's hands, and this reminded him that his dream just now, just before the lawnmower and the headache and the sun, had been of a dim and deeply tranquil time long ago. Both his parents had been there, and he'd heard his mother say, "Oh, don't wake him, Earl; let him sleep." He tried his best to remember more of it, and couldn't; but the tenderness of it brought him close to tears for a moment until it faded away.

They had both been dead for several years now, and it sometimes troubled him that he could remember neither of their faces very well. To his waking memory, without the aid of photographs, his father was a vague bald head with dense eyebrows and a mouth forever fixed in the shape either of disgruntlement or exasperation, his mother a pair of rimless spectacles, a hair net, and a timorous smear of lipstick. He remembered too, of both of them, that they'd always been tired. Middle-aged at the time of his birth and already tired then from having raised two other sons, they had grown steadily more and more tired as long as he'd known them, until finally, tired out, they had died with equal ease, in their sleep, within six months of each other. But there had never been anything tired about his father's hands, and no amount of time and forgetfulness had ever dimmed their image in his mind's eye.

"Open it!" That was one of his earliest memories: the challenge to loosen one big fist, and his frantic two-handed efforts, never succeeding, to uncoil a single finger from its massively quivering grip, while his father's laughter rang from the kitchen walls. But it wasn't only their strength he envied, it was their sureness and sensitivity—when they held a thing, you could see how it felt—and the aura of mastery they imparted to everything Earl Wheeler used: the creaking pigskin handle of his salesman's briefcase, the hafts of all his woodworking tools, the thrillingly dangerous stock and trigger of his shotgun. The briefcase had been of particular fascination to Frank at the age of five or six; it always stood in the shadows of the front hallway in the evenings, and sometimes after supper he would saunter manfully up to it and pretend it was his own. How fine and smooth, yet how impossibly thick its handle felt! It was heavy (Whew!) yet how lightly it would swing at his father's side in the morning! Later, at ten or twelve, he had become familiar with the carpentry tools as well, but none of his memories of them were pleasant. "No, boy, no!" his father would shout over the scream of the power saw. "You're ruining it! Can't you see you're ruining it? That's no way to handle a tool." The tool, whatever obstinate thing it was, chisel or gouge or brace-and-bit, would be snatched away from the failure of its dismally sweat-stained woodwork and held aloft to be minutely inspected for damage. Then there would be a lecture on the proper care and handling of tools, to be followed by a gracefully expert demonstration (during which the grains of wood clung like gold in the hair of his father's forearm) or more likely by a sigh of manly endurance pressed to the breaking point and the quiet words: "All right. You'd better go on upstairs." Things had always ended that way in the woodworking shop, and even today he could never breathe the yellow smell of sawdust without a sense of humiliation. The shotgun, luckily, had never come to a test. By the time he was old enough to go along on one of his father's increasingly rare hunting trips the chronic discord between them had long precluded any chance of it. It would never have occurred to the old man to suggest such a thing, and what's more—for this was the period of his freight-train dreams—it would never have occurred to Frank to desire the suggestion. Who wanted to sit in a puddle and kill a lot of ducks? Who, for that matter, wanted to be good with hobbyist's tools? And who wanted to be a dopey salesman in the first place, acting like a big deal with a briefcase full of boring catalogues, talking about machines all day to a bunch of dumb executives with cigars?

Yet even in those days and afterwards, even in the extremities of rebellion on Bethune Street, when his father had become a dreary, querulous old fool nodding to sleep over the *Reader's Digest*, then as now he continued to believe that something unique and splendid had lived in his father's hands. On Earl Wheeler's very deathbed, when he was shrunken and blind and cackling ("Who's that? Frank? Is that Frank?") the dry clasp of his hands had been as positive as ever, and when they lay loose and still on the hospital sheet at last they still looked stronger and better than his son's.

"Boy, I guess the headshrinkers could really have a ball with me," he liked to say, wryly, among friends. "I mean the whole deal of my relationship with my father alone'd be enough to fill a textbook, not to mention my mother. Jesus, what a little nest of neuroses we must've been." All the same, in moments of troubled solitude like this, he was glad he could muster some vestige of honest affection for his parents. He was grateful that however uneasy the rest of his life had turned out to be, it had once contained enough peace to give him pleasant dreams; and he often suspected, with more than a little righteousness, that this might be what kept him essentially more stable than his wife. Because if the headshrinkers could have a ball with him, God only knew what kind of a time they would have with April.

In all the scanty stories she told about them, her parents were as alien to his sympathetic understanding as anything in the novels of Evelyn Waugh. Had people like that ever really existed? He could picture them only as flickering caricatures of the twenties, the Playboy and the Flapper, mysteriously rich and careless and cruel, married by a ship's captain in mid-Atlantic and divorced within a year of the birth of their only child.

"I think my mother must've taken me straight from the hospital to Aunt Mary's," she'd told him. "At any rate I don't think I ever lived with anyone but Aunt Mary until I was five, and then there were a couple of other aunts, or friends of hers or something, before I went to Aunt Claire, in Rye." The rest of the story was that her father had shot himself in a Boston hotel room in 1938, and that her mother had died some years later after long incarceration in a West Coast alcoholic retreat.

"Jesus," Frank said on first hearing these facts, one irritably hot summer night in the Bethune Street place (though he wasn't quite sure at the time, as he hung and shook his head, whether what he felt was sorrow for the unhappiness of the story or envy because it was so much more dramatic a story than his own). "Well," he said. "I guess your aunt always really seemed like your mother, though, didn't she?"

But April shrugged, drawing her mouth a little to one side in a way that he'd lately decided he didn't like—her "tough" look. "Which aunt do you mean? I hardly remember Mary, or the others in between, and I always hated Claire."

"Oh, come on. How can you say you 'always hated' her? I mean maybe it seems that way now, looking back, but over the years she must've given you a certain feeling of—*you* know, love, and security and everything."

"She didn't, though. The only real fun I ever had was when one of my parents came for a visit. They were the ones I loved."

"But they hardly ever *came* for visits. I mean you couldn't have had much sense of their *being* your parents, in a deal like that; you didn't even know them. How could you love them?"

"I did, that's all." And she began picking up and putting away again, in her jewelry box, the souvenirs she had spread before him on the bed: snapshots of herself at various ages, on various lawns, standing with one or the other parent; a miniature painting of her mother's pretty head; a yellowed, leather-framed photograph showing both parents, tall and elegantly dressed beside a palm tree, with the inscription *Cannes, 1925*; her mother's wedding ring; an ancient brooch containing a lock of her maternal grandmother's hair; a tiny white plastic horse, the size of a watch charm, which had a net value of two or three cents and had been saved for years because "my father gave it to me."

"Oh, all right, sure," he conceded. "Maybe they did seem romantic and everything; they probably seemed very dazzling and glamorous and all that. The point is, I don't mean that. I mean love."

"So do I. I did love them." Her grave silence following this statement, as she fastened the clasp of the jewelry box, was so prolonged that he thought she had finished with the subject. He decided he was finished with it anyway, at least for the time being. It was too hot a night to have an argument. But it turned out that she was only thinking it over, preparing her next words with great care to make sure they would say exactly what she meant. When she began to speak at last she looked so much like the little girl in the photographs that he was ashamed of himself. "I loved their clothes," she said. "I loved the way they talked. I loved to hear them tell about their lives."

And there was nothing for him to do but take her in his arms, full of pity for the meagerness of her treasure and full of a reverent, silent promise, soon to be broken, that he would never again disparage it.

A small stain of drying milk and cereal on the table was all that remained of the children's breakfast; the rest of the kitchen gleamed to an industrial perfection of cleanliness. He planned, as soon as he'd had some coffee, to get dressed and go out and take the lawnmower away from her, by force if necessary, in order to restore as much balance to the morning as possible. But he was still in his bathrobe, unshaven and fumbling at the knobs of the electric stove, when Mrs. Givings's station wagon came crackling up the driveway. For a second he thought of hiding, but it was too late. She had already seen him through the screen door, and April, trudging along the far border of the back yard, had already escaped her with a wave across the wide expanse of grass and gone on mowing. He was caught. He had to open the door and stand there in an attitude of welcome. Why did this woman keep bothering them all the time?

"I can't stay a minute!" she cried, staggering toward him under the weight of a damp cardboard box full of earth and wobbling vegetation. "I just wanted to bring over this sedum for the rocky place at the foot of your drive. My, don't you look comfy."

He bent into an ungainly pose, trying to hold the door open with one trailing foot while he took the box from her arms. "Well," he said, smiling very close to her tense, powdery face. Mrs. Givings's cosmetics seemed always to have been applied in a frenzy of haste, of impatience to get the whole silly business over and done with, and she was constantly in motion, a trim, leather-skinned woman in her fifties whose eyes expressed a religious belief in the importance of keeping busy. Even when she stood still there was kinetic energy in the set of her shoulders and the hang of her loose, angrily buttoned-up clothes; when sitting was inevitable she always chose straight chairs and used them sparingly, and it was hard to imagine her ever lying down. Nor was it easy to picture her face asleep, free from the tension of its false smiles, its little bursts of social laughter and its talk.

"I really think this is just what's called for down there, don't you?" she was saying. "Have you worked with this type of sedum before? You'll find it's the most marvelous ground cover, even in this acid soil."

"Well," he said again. "That's fine. Thanks a lot, Mrs. Givings." Nearly two years ago she had asked them to call her Helen, a name his tongue seemed all but unable to pronounce. Usually he solved the problem by calling her nothing, covering the lack with friendly nods and smiles, and she had taken to calling him nothing either. Now, as her small eyes seemed to take in for the first time the fact that his wife was cutting the grass while he lounged around the kitchen in a bathrobe, they stood smiling at each other with uncommon brilliance. He let the screen clap shut behind him and adjusted his grip on the box, which wobbled in his arms and sent a fine stream of sand down his naked ankle.

"What should we—you know, do with it?" he asked her. "I mean, *you* know, to make it grow and everything."

"Well, nothing really. All it wants is just a tiny dollop of water the first few days, and then you'll find it absolutely thrives. It's rather like the European houseleek, you see, except of course that has the lovely pink flower and this has the yellow."

"Oh, yeah," he said. "House leak." She told him a good many other things about the plants, while he nodded and watched her and wished she would go away, listening to the whir and whine of the lawnmower. "Well," he said when her voice stopped. "That's swell, thanks a lot. Can I—offer you a cup of coffee?"

"Oh, no, thanks ever so much—" She skittered four or five feet away, retreating, as if he had offered her a soiled handkerchief to blow her nose in. Then, from the safety of her new position, she displayed all her long teeth in an elaborate smile. "Do tell April we loved the play last night—or wait, I'll tell her myself." She craned and squinted into the sun, judging the distance her voice would have to travel, and then she let it loose:

"*April! April!* I just wanted to *tell* you we *loved* the *play!*" Her strained, shouting face could have been the picture of a woman in agony.

After a second the sound of the lawnmower stopped and April's distant voice said, "What's that?"

"I say, we LOVED, the PLAY!"

And at last, on hearing April's faint "Oh—thanks, Helen," she was able to slacken her features. She turned back to Frank, who was still clumsily holding the box. "You really do have a very gifted wife. I can't tell you how much Howard and I enjoyed it."

"Good," he said. "Actually, I think the general consensus is that it wasn't too great. I mean I think most people seemed to feel that way."

"Oh, no, it was charming. I did think your nice friend up on the Hill was rather unfortunately cast—Mr. Crandall?—but otherwise—"

"Campbell, yes. Actually, I don't think he was any worse than some of the others; and of course he did have a difficult part." He always felt it necessary to defend the Campbells to Mrs. Givings, whose view seemed to be that anyone who lived in the Revolutionary Hill Estates deserved at best a tactful condescension.

"I suppose that's true. I was surprised not to see *Mrs.* Crandall in the group—or Campbell, is it? Still, I don't expect she'd have the time, with all those children."

"She worked backstage." He was trying to shift the box so that the sand would stop trickling, or trickle somewhere else. "She was quite active in the whole thing, as a matter of fact."

"Oh, good. I'm sure she would be; such a friendly, willing little soul. All right, then—" She began sidling toward her car. "I won't keep you." This was the moment for her saying "Oh, one other thing, while I think of it." She nearly always did that, and the other thing would turn out to be the thing she had really come for in the first place. Now she hesitated, visibly wondering whether to say it or not; then her face showed her decision not to, under the circumstances. Whatever it was would have to wait. "Fine, then. I simply love the stone path you've started down the front lawn."

"Oh," he said. "Thanks. I haven't hardly started it yet."

"Oh, I know," she assured him. "It *is* hard work." Then she trilled a gracious little two-note song of goodbye and twitched into her station wagon, which rolled slowly away.

"Mommy, look what Daddy's got," Jennifer was calling. "Mrs. Givings brought it."

And Michael, the four-year-old, said, "It's flowers. Is it flowers, or what?"

They were hurrying toward him over the cropped grass, while April slowly and heavily brought up the rear, pulling the lawn-mower behind her, blowing damp strands of hair away from her eyes with a stuck-out lower lip. Everything about her seemed determined to prove, with a new, flat-footed emphasis, that a sensible middle-class housewife was all she had ever wanted to be and that all she had ever wanted of love was a husband who would get out and cut the grass once in a while, instead of sleeping all day.

"It's leaking, Daddy," Jennifer said.

"I know it's leaking. Quiet a minute. Listen," he said to his wife, without quite looking at her. "Would you mind telling me what I'm supposed to do with this stuff?"

"How should I know? What is it?"

"I don't know what the hell it is. It's European house leak or something."

"European what?"

"Oh no, wait a second. It's *like* house leak, only it's pink instead of yellow. Yellow instead of pink. I thought you'd probably know all about it."

"Whatever made you think that?" She came up close to squint at the plants, fingering one of their fleshy stems. "What's it for? Didn't she say?"

His mind was a blank. "Wait a second. It's called beecham. Or wait—seecham. I'm pretty sure it's seecham." He licked his lips and changed his grip on the box. "It's marvelous in acid soil. Does that ring a bell?"

The children were switching their hopeful eyes from one parent to the other, and Jennifer was beginning to look worried.

April ran her fingers into her hip pockets. "Marvelous for what? You mean you didn't even ask her?"

The plants were quivering in his arms. "Look, could you kind of take it easy? I haven't had any coffee yet, and I—"

"Oh, this is swell. What am I supposed to do with this stuff? What am I supposed to *tell* the woman the next time I see her?"

"Tell her any God damn thing you like," he said. "Maybe you could tell her to mind her own God damn business for a change."

"Don't *shout*, Daddy." Jennifer was bouncing up and down in her grass-stained sneakers, flapping her hands and starting to cry.

"I'm *not* shouting," he told her, with all the indignation of the falsely accused. She held still then and put her thumb in her mouth, which seemed to make her eyes go out of focus, while Michael clutched at the fly of his pants and took two backward steps, solemn with embarrassment.

April sighed and raked back a lock of hair. "All right," she said. "Take it down to the cellar, then. The least we can do is get it out of sight. Then you'd better get dressed. It's time for lunch."

He carried the box down the cellar stairs, dropped it on the floor with a rustling thud and kicked it into a corner, sending a sharp pain through the tendon of his big toe.

He spent the afternoon in an old pair of army pants and a torn shirt, working on his stone path. The idea was to lay a long, curving walk from the front door to the road, to divert visitors from coming in through the kitchen. It had seemed simple enough last weekend, when he'd started it, but now as the ground sloped off more sharply he found that flat stones wouldn't work. He had to make steps, of stones nearly as thick as they were wide, stones that had to be dislodged from the steep woods behind the house and carried on tottering legs around to the front lawn. And he had to dig a pit for each step, in ground so rocky that it took ten minutes to get a foot below the surface. It was turning into mindless, unrewarding work, the kind of work that makes you clumsy with fatigue and petulant with lack of progress, and it looked as if it would take all summer.

Even so, once the first puffing and dizziness was over, he began to like the muscular pull and the sweat of it, and the smell of the earth. At least it was a man's work. At least, squatting to rest on the wooded slope, he could look down and see his house the way a house ought to look on a fine spring day, safe on its carpet of green, the frail white sanctuary of a man's love, a man's wife and children. Lowering his eyes with the solemnity of this thought, he could take pleasure in the sight of his own flexed thigh, lean and straining under the old O.D., and of the heavily veined forearm that lay across it and the dirty hand that hung there—not to be compared with his father's hand, maybe, but a serviceable, good-enough hand all the same—so that his temples ached in zeal and triumph as he heaved a rock up from the suck of its white-wormed socket and let it roll end over end down the shuddering leafmold, because he was a man. Following it down to the edge of the lawn, he squatted over it again, grunted, wrestled it up to his thighs and from there to his waist, cradling it in the tender flesh of his forearms; then he moved out, glassy-eyed and staggering on the soft grass, out around the white blur of the house and into the sun of the front lawn and all the way over to the path, where he dropped it and nearly fell in a heap on top of it.

"We're helping you, aren't we, Daddy?" Jennifer said. Both children had come to sit near him on the grass. The sun made perfect circles of yellow on their two blond heads and gave their T-shirts a dazzling whiteness.

"You sure are," he said.

"Yes, because you like to have us keep you company, don't you?"

"I sure do, baby. Don't get too close now, you'll kick dirt in the hole." And he fell to work with the long-handled shovel to deepen the hollow he had dug, enjoying the rhythmic rasp and grip of the blade against a loosening edge of buried rock.

"Daddy?" Michael inquired. "Why does the shovel make sparks?"

"Because it's hitting rock. When you hit rock with steel, you get a spark."

"Why don't you take the rock out?"

"That's what I'm trying to do. Don't get so close now, you might get hurt."

The piece of rock came free at last; he lifted it out and knelt to claw at the sliding tan pebbles of the pit until the depth and the shape of it looked right. Then he heaved and rolled the boulder into place and packed it tight, and another step was completed. A light swarm of gnats had come to hover around his head, tickling and barely visible as they hung and flicked past his eyes.

"Daddy?" Jennifer said. "How come Mommy slept on the sofa?"

"I don't know. Just happened to feel like it, I guess. You wait here, now, while I go and get another stone."

And the more he thought about it, as he plodded back up through the trees behind the house, the more he realized that this was the best answer he could have given, from the standpoint of simple honesty as well as tact. She just happened to feel like it. Wasn't that, after all, the only reason there was? Had she ever had a less selfish, more complicated reason for doing anything in her life?

"I love you when you're nice," she'd told him once, before they were married, and it had made him furious.

"Don't *say* that. Christ's sake, you don't 'love' people when they're 'nice.' Don't you see that's the same as saying 'What's in it for me?' Look." (They were standing on Sixth Avenue in the middle of the night, and he was holding her at arm's length, his hands placed firmly on either side of the warm rib cage inside her polo coat.) "Look. You either love me or you don't, and you're going to have to make up your mind."

Oh, she'd made up her mind, all right. It had been easy to decide in favor of love on Bethune Street, in favor of walking proud and naked on the grass rug of an apartment that caught the morning sun among its makeshift chairs, its French travel posters and its bookcase made of packing-crate slats—an apartment where half the fun of having an affair was that it was just like being married, and where later, after a trip to City Hall and back, after a ceremonial collecting of the other two keys from the other two men, half the fun of being married was that it was just like having an affair. She'd decided in favor of that, all right. And why not? Wasn't it the first love of any kind she'd ever known? Even on the level of practical advantage it must have held an undeniable appeal: it freed her from the gritty round of disappointment she would otherwise have faced as an only mildly talented, mildly enthusiastic graduate of dramatic school; it let her languish attractively through a part-time office job ("just until my husband finds the kind of work he really wants to do") while saving her best energies for animated discussions of books and pictures and the shortcomings of other people's personalities, for trying new ways of fixing her hair and new kinds of inexpensive clothes ("Do you really like the sandals, or are they too Villagey?") and for hours of unhurried dalliance deep in their double bed. But even in those days she'd held herself poised for immediate flight; she had always been ready to take off the minute she happened to feel like it ("Don't *talk* to me that way, Frank, or I'm *leaving*. I *mean* it") or the minute anything went wrong.

And one big thing went wrong right away. According to their plan, which called for an eventual family of four, her first pregnancy came seven years too soon. That was the trouble, and if he'd known her better then he might have guessed how she would take it and what she would happen to feel like doing about it. At the time, though, coming home from the doctor's office in a steaming crosstown bus, he was wholly in the dark. She refused to look at him as they rode; she carried her head high in a state of shock or disbelief or anger or blame—it could have been any or all or none of these things, for all he knew. Pressed close and sweating beside her with his jaw set numbly in a brave smile, trying to think of things to say, he knew only that everything was out of kilter. Whatever you felt on hearing the news of conception, even if it was chagrin instead of joy, wasn't it supposed to be something the two of you shared? Your wife wasn't supposed to turn away from you, was she? You weren't supposed to have to work and wheedle to win her back, with little jokes and hand-holdings, as if you were afraid she might evaporate at the very moment of this first authentic involvement of your lives—that couldn't be right. Then what the hell was the matter?

It wasn't until a week later that he came home to find her stalking the apartment with folded arms, her eyes remote and her face fixed in the special look that meant she had made up her mind about something and would stand for no nonsense.

"Frank, listen. Try not to start talking until I finish, and just listen." And in an oddly stifled voice, as if she'd rehearsed her speech several times without allowing for the fact that she'd have to breathe while delivering it, she told him of a girl in dramatic school who knew, from first-hand experience, an absolutely infallible way to induce a miscarriage. It was simplicity itself: you waited until just the right time, the end of the third month; then you took a sterilized rubber syringe and a little bit of sterilized water, and you very carefully . . .

Even as he filled his lungs for shouting he knew it wasn't the idea itself that repelled him—the idea itself, God knew, was more than a little attractive—it was that she had done all this on her own, in secret, had sought out the girl and obtained the facts and bought the rubber syringe and rehearsed the speech; that if she'd thought about him at all it was only as a possible hitch in the scheme, a source of tiresome objections that would have to be cleared up and disposed of if the thing were to be carried out with maximum efficiency. That was the intolerable part of it; that was what enriched his voice with a tremor of outrage:

"Christ's *sake*, don't be an idiot. You want to kill yourself? I don't even want to hear about it."

She sighed patiently. "All right, Frank. In that case there's certainly no need for you to hear about it. I only told you because I thought you might be willing to help me in this thing. Obviously, I should have known better."

"Listen. *Listen* to me. You do this—you do this and I swear to God I'll—"

"Oh, you'll what? You'll leave me? What's that supposed to be—a threat or a promise?"

And the fight went on all night. It caused them to hiss and grapple and knock over a chair, it spilled outside and downstairs and into the street ("Get *away* from me! Get *away* from me!"); it washed them trembling up against the high wire fence of a waterfront junkyard, until a waterfront drunk came to stare at them and make them waver home, and he could feel the panic and the shame of it even now, leaning here against this tree with these gnats tickling his neck. All that saved him, all that enabled him now to crouch and lift a new stone from its socket and follow its rumbling fall with the steady and dignified tread of self-respect, was that the next day he had won. The next day, weeping in his arms, she had allowed herself to be dissuaded.

"Oh, I know, I know," she had whispered against his shirt, "I know you're right. I'm sorry. I love you. We'll name it Frank and we'll send it to college and everything. I promise, promise."

And it seemed to him now that no single moment of his life had ever contained a better proof of manhood than that, if any proof were needed: holding that tamed, submissive girl and saying, "Oh, my lovely; oh, my lovely," while she promised she would bear his child. Lurching and swaying under the weight of the stone in the sun, dropping it at last and wiping his sore hands, he picked up the shovel and went to work again, while the children's voices fluted and chirped around him, as insidiously torturing as the gnats.

And I didn't even *want* a baby, he thought to the rhythm of his digging. Isn't that the damnedest thing? I didn't want a baby any more than *she* did. Wasn't it true, then, that everything in his life from that point on had been a succession of things he hadn't really wanted to do? Taking a hopelessly dull job to prove he could be as responsible as any other family man, moving to an overpriced, genteel apartment to prove his mature belief in the fundamentals of orderliness and good health, having another child to prove that the first one hadn't been a mistake, buying a house in the country because that was the next logical step and he had to prove himself capable of taking it. Proving, proving; and for no other reason than that he was married to a woman who had somehow managed to put him forever on the defensive, who loved him when he was nice, who lived according to what she happened to feel like doing and who might at any time—this was the hell of it—who might at any time of day or night just happen to feel like leaving him. It was as ludicrous and as simple as that.

"Are you hitting rock again, Daddy?"

"Not this time," he said. "This is a root. I think it's too deep to matter, though. If you'll just get out of the way now, I'll try and fit the stone in."

Kneeling, he rolled the boulder into place, but it wouldn't settle. It wobbled, and it sat three inches too high.

"That's too high, Daddy."

"I know it, baby." He laboriously pried the stone out again and began hacking at the root, trying to cut it, using the shovel like a clumsy ax. It was as tough as cartilage.

"Sweetie, I said don't come so *close*. You're kicking *dirt* in the hole."

"I'm *helping*, Daddy."

Jennifer looked hurt and surprised, and he thought she might be going to cry again. He tried to make his voice very low and gentle. "Look, everybody. Why don't you find something else to do? You've got the whole yard to play in. Come on, now. That's the idea. I'll call you if I need any help."

But in a minute they were back, sitting too close and talking quietly together. Dizzy with effort and blind with sweat, he was straddling the pit and holding the shovel vertically, like a pile driver, lifting it high and bringing it down with all his strength on the root. He had torn a ragged wound in it, laying open its moist white meat, but it wouldn't break, it wouldn't give, and it made the children laugh each time the shovel bounced and rang in his hands. The delicate noise of their laughter, the look of their tulip-soft skin and of their two sunny skulls, as fragile as eggshell, made a terrible contrast to the feel of biting steel and shuddering pulp, and it was his sense of this that made his eyes commit a distortion of truth. For a split second, in the act of bringing the shovel blade down, he thought he saw Michael's white sneaker slip into its path. Even as he swerved and threw the shovel away with a clang he knew it hadn't really happened— but it *could* have happened, that was the point—and his anger was so quick that the next thing he knew he had grabbed him by the belt and spun him around and hit him hard on the buttocks with the flat of his hand, twice, surprised at the stunning vigor of the blows and at the roar of his own voice: "Get *outa* here now! Get *outa* here!"

Leaping and twisting, clutching the seat of his pants with both hands, Michael found his need to cry so sudden and so deep that for several seconds after the first shocked squeal no sound could break from him. His eyes wrinkled shut, his mouth opened and was locked in that position while his lungs fought for breath; then out it came, a long high wail of pain and humiliation. Jennifer watched him, round-eyed, and in the next breath her own face began to twitch and crumple and she was crying too.

"I kept telling you and telling you," he explained to them,

waving his arms. "I *told* you there'd be trouble if you got too close. Didn't I? Didn't I? All right now, take off. Both of you."

They didn't need to be told. They were moving steadily away from him across the grass, crying, looking back at him with infinite reproachfulness. In another second he might have been running after them with apologies, he might have been crying too, if he hadn't forced himself to pick up the shovel and bang it at the root again; and as he worked he prepared an anxious, silent brief in his own defense. Well, damn it, I *did* keep telling them and telling them, he assured himself, and by now his mind had mercifully amended the facts. The kid put his foot right the hell in my *way*, for God's sake. If I hadn't swerved just in time he wouldn't *have* a foot, for God's sake. . . .

When he looked up again he saw that April had come out of the kitchen door and around the side of the house, and he saw that the children had run to her and hidden their faces in her trousers.

FOUR

THEN IT WAS Sunday, with the living room deep in the rustling torpor of Sunday newspapers, and no words had passed between Frank Wheeler and his wife for what seemed a year. She had gone alone to the second and final performance of *The Petrified Forest*, and afterwards had slept on the sofa again.

He was trying now to take his ease in an armchair, looking through the magazine section of the *Times*, while the children played quietly in the corner and April washed the dishes in the kitchen. He had thumbed through the magazine more than once, put it down and picked it up again, and he kept returning to a full-page, dramatically lighted fashion photograph whose caption began "A frankly flattering, definitely feminine dress to go happily wherever you go . . ." and whose subject was a tall, proud girl with deeper breasts and hips than he'd thought fashion models were supposed to have. At first he thought she looked not unlike a girl in his office named Maureen Grube; then he decided this one was much better looking and probably more intelligent. Still, there was a distinct resemblance; and as he studied this frankly flattering, definitely feminine girl his mind slid away in a fuddled erotic reverie. At the last office Christmas party, not nearly as drunk as he was pretending to be, he had backed Maureen Grube up against a filing cabinet and kissed her long and hard on the mouth.

Displeased with himself, he dropped the paper on the rug and lit a cigarette without noticing that another one, quite long, was smoldering in the ash tray beside him. Then, if only because the afternoon was bright and the children were quiet and the fight with April was now another day in the past, he went into the kitchen and took hold of both her elbows as she bent over a sinkful of suds.

"Listen," he whispered. "I don't care who's right or who's

wrong or what this whole damn thing is all about. Couldn't we just cut it out and start acting like human beings for a change?"

"Until the next time, you mean? Make everything all nice and comfy-cozy until the next time? I'm afraid not, thanks. I'm tired of playing that game."

"Don't you see how unfair you're being? What do you want from me?"

"Two things, at the moment. I want you to take your hands off me and I want you to keep your voice down."

"Will you tell me one thing? Will you tell me just what the hell you're trying to do?"

"Certainly. I'm trying to wash the dishes."

"Daddy?" Jennifer said when he went back to the living room. "What?"

"Would you please read us the funnies?"

The shyness of this request, and the sight of their trusting eyes, made him want to weep. "You bet I will," he said. "Let's sit down over here, all three of us, and we'll read the funnies."

He found it hard to keep his voice from thickening into a sentimental husk as he began to read aloud, with their two heads pressed close to his ribs on either side and their thin legs lying straight out on the sofa cushions, warm against his own. *They* knew what forgiveness was; *they* were willing to take him for better or worse; they loved him. Why couldn't April realize how simple and necessary it was to love? Why did she have to complicate everything?

The only trouble was that the funnies seemed to go on forever; the turning of each dense, muddled page of them brought the job no nearer to completion. Before long his voice had become a strained, hurrying monotone and his right knee had begun to jiggle in a little dance of irritation.

"Daddy, we skipped a funny."

"No we didn't, sweetie. That's just an advertisement. You don't want to read that."

"Yes I do."

"I do too."

"But it isn't a *funny*. It's just made to look like one. It's an advertisement for some kind of toothpaste."

"Read us it anyway."

He set his bite. All the nerves at the roots of his teeth seemed to have entwined with the nerves at the roots of his scalp in a tingling knot. "All right," he said. "See, in the first picture this lady wants to dance with this man but he won't ask her to, and here in the next picture she's crying and her friend says maybe the reason he won't dance with her is because her breath doesn't smell too nice, and then in the next picture she's talking to this dentist, and he says . . ."

He felt as if he were sinking helplessly into the cushions and the papers and the bodies of his children like a man in quicksand. When the funnies were finished at last he struggled to his feet, quietly gasping, and stood for several minutes in the middle of the carpet, making tight fists in his pockets to restrain himself from doing what suddenly seemed the only thing in the world he really and truly wanted to do: picking up a chair and throwing it through the picture window.

What the hell kind of a life was this? What in God's name was the point or the meaning or the purpose of a life like this?

When evening came, heavy with beer, he began to look forward to the fact that the Campbells were coming over. Ordinarily it might have depressed him ("Why don't we ever see anyone else? Do you realize they're practically the only friends we have?"), but tonight it held a certain promise. At least she would have to laugh and talk in their company; at least she would have to smile at him from time to time and call him "darling." Besides, it couldn't be denied that the Campbells did seem to bring out the best in both of them.

"Hi!" They called to one another.

"Hi! . . ." "Hi! . . ."

This one glad syllable, borne up through the gathering twilight and redoubling back from the Wheelers' kitchen door, was the traditional herald of an evening's entertainment. Then came the handshakings, the stately puckered kissings, the sighs of amiable exhaustion—"Ah-h-h"; "Whoo-o"—suggesting that miles of hot sand had been traveled for the finding of this oasis or that living breath itself had been held, painfully, against the promise of this release. In the living room, having sipped and grimaced at the first frosty brimming of their drinks, they pulled themselves together for a moment of mutual admiration; then they sank into various postures of controlled collapse.

Milly Campbell dropped her shoes and squirmed deep into the sofa cushions, her ankles snug beneath her buttocks and her uplifted face crinkling into a good sport's smile—not the prettiest girl in the world, maybe, but cute and quick and fun to have around.

Beside her, Frank slid down on the nape of his spine until his cocked leg was as high as his head. His eyes were already alert for conversational openings and his thin mouth already moving in the curly shape of wit, as if he were rolling a small, bitter lozenge on his tongue.

Shep, massive and dependable, a steadying influence on the group, set his meaty knees wide apart and worked his tie loose with muscular fingers to free his throat for gusts of laughter.

And finally, the last to settle, April arranged herself with careless elegance in the sling chair, her head thrown back on the canvas to blow sad, aristocratic spires of cigarette smoke at the ceiling. They were ready to begin.

At first it seemed, to everyone's surprise and relief, that the delicate topic of the Laurel Players could be rapidly disposed of. A brief exchange of words and a few deprecating, head-shaking chuckles seemed to take care of it. Milly insisted that the second performance had really been much better than the first—"I mean at least the audience did seem more—well, more appreciative, I thought. Didn't you, sweetie?" Shep said that he personally was glad to have the damn thing over with; and April, to whom all their anxious glances now turned, put them at ease with a smile.

"To coin a phrase," she said, "it was a lot of fun anyway. Wasn't it awful how many people were saying that last night? I must've heard those same words fifty times."

Within a minute the talk had turned to children and disease (the Campbells' eldest boy was underweight and Milly wondered if he might be suffering from an obscure blood ailment, until Shep said that whatever he was suffering from it sure hadn't weakened his throwing arm), and from there to an agreement that the elementary school was really doing a fine job, considering the reactionary board it was saddled with, and from there to the fact that prices had been unaccountably high in the supermarket. It was only then, during a dissertation by Milly on lamb chops, that an almost palpable discomfort settled over the room. They shifted in their seats, they filled awkward pauses with elaborate courtesies about the freshening of drinks, they avoided one another's eyes and did their best to avoid the alarming, indisputable knowledge that they had nothing to talk about. It was a new experience.

Two years or even a year ago it could never have happened, for then if nothing else there had always been a topic in the outrageous state of the nation. "How do you *like* this Oppenheimer business?" one of them would demand, and the others would fight for the floor with revolutionary zeal. The cancerous growth of Senator McCarthy had poisoned the United States, and with the pouring of second or third drinks they could begin to see themselves as members of an embattled, dwindling intellectual underground. Clippings from the *Observer* or the *Manchester Guardian* would be produced and read aloud, to slow and respectful nods; Frank might talk wistfully of Europe—"God, I wish we'd taken off and gone there when we had the chance"—and this might lead to a quick general lust for expatriation: "Let's *all* go!" (Once it went as far as a practical discussion of how much they'd need for boat fare and rent and schools, until Shep, after a sobering round of coffee, explained what he'd read about the difficulty of getting jobs in foreign countries.)

And even after politics had palled there had still been the elusive but endlessly absorbing subject of Conformity, or The Suburbs, or Madison Avenue, or American Society Today. "Oh Jesus," Shep might begin, "you know this character next door to us? Donaldson? The one that's always out fooling with his power mower and talking about the rat race and the soft sell? Well, listen: did I tell you what he said about his barbecue pit?" And there would follow an anecdote of extreme suburban smugness that left them weak with laughter.

"Oh, I don't believe it," April would insist. "Do they really talk that way?"

And Frank would develop the theme. "The point is it wouldn't be so bad if it weren't so typical. It isn't only the Donaldsons—it's the Cramers too, and the whaddyacallits, the Wingates, and a million others. It's all the idiots I ride with on the train every day. It's a disease. Nobody thinks or feels or cares any more; nobody gets excited or believes in anything except their own comfortable little God damn mediocrity."

Milly Campbell would writhe in pleasure. "Oh, that's so true. Isn't that true, darling?"

They would all agree, and the happy implication was that they alone, the four of them, were painfully alive in a drugged and dying culture. It was in the face of this defiance, and in tentative reply to this loneliness, that the idea of the Laurel Players had made its first appeal. Milly had brought the news: some people she'd met from the other side of the Hill were trying to organize a theater group. They planned to hire a New York director and to produce serious plays, if only they could arouse enough community interest. Oh, it probably wouldn't amount to much— Milly knew that—but she wondered, shyly, if it might not be fun. April had been disdainful at first: "Oh, God, I know these damn little artsy-craftsy things. There'll be a woman with blue hair and wooden beads who met Max Reinhardt once, and there'll be two or three slightly homosexual young men and seven girls with bad complexions." But then a tasteful advertisement began to appear in the local paper ("We are looking for actors . . ."); then the Wheelers met the people too, at an otherwise boring party, and had to admit that they were what April called "genuine." At Christmastime they met the director himself and agreed with Shep that he did seem like a man who knew what he was doing, and within a month they were all committed. Even Frank, while refusing to try out for a part ("I'd be lousy"), helped write some of the promotional material and got it multigraphed at his office, and it was Frank who talked most hopefully about the larger social and philosophical possibilities of the thing. If a really good, really serious community theater could be established here, wouldn't it be a step in the right direction? God knew they would probably never inspire the Donaldsons—and who cared?—but at least they might give the Donaldsons pause; they might show the Donaldsons a way of life beyond the commuting train and the Republican Party and the barbecue pit. Besides, what did they have to lose?

Whatever it was, they had lost it now. Blame for the failure of the Laurel Players could hardly be fobbed off on Conformity or The Suburbs or American Society Today. How could new jokes be told about their neighbors when these very neighbors had sat and sweated in their audience? Donaldsons, Cramers, Wingates and all, they had come to *The Petrified Forest* with a surprisingly generous openness of mind, and had been let down.

Milly was talking about gardening now, about the difficulty of raising a healthy lawn on Revolutionary Hill, and her eyes were taking on a glaze of panic. Her voice had been the only sound in the room for ten minutes or more, and it had been continuous. She seemed keenly aware of this, but aware too that if she allowed herself to stop the house would fill with a silence as thick as water, an impossibly deep, wide pool in which she would flounder and drown.

It was Frank who came to her rescue. "Oh, hey listen, Milly. I meant to ask you. Do you know what seecham is? Or beecham? A kind of plant?"

"Seecham," she repeated, pretending to think, while a blush of gratitude suffused her softening face. "Offhand I'm afraid I don't know, Frank. I can certainly look it *up* for you, though. We have this book at home."

"Doesn't really matter, I guess," he said. "It's just that Mrs. Givings came barrel-assing over here yesterday with a big box of this crazy—"

"Mrs. Givings!" Milly cried in a sudden ecstasy of remembrance and relief. "Oh my goodness, I haven't even *told* you people about that! I guess I haven't even told Shep yet, have I, sweetie? About their son? It's fantastic."

She was off again, but this was a wholly different kind of monologue: everyone was listening. The urgency of her voice and the eager way she leaned forward to tug her skirt down over her wrinkled knees had galvanized them all with the promise of a new theme, and Milly savored the capture of her audience, wanting to let the revelation come out as slowly as possible. First of all, did the Wheelers know the Givingses had a son?

Certainly they did; and Milly sat nodding wisely, allowing herself to be interrupted, while they reminded each other of the thin sailor whose photograph had grinned from the Givingses' mantelpiece the one time they had gone there for dinner; they remembered Mrs. Givings explaining that this was John, who had loathed the navy, had done marvelously well at M.I.T. and now was doing marvelously well as an instructor of mathematics at some Western university.

"Well," Milly said. "He isn't teaching any mathematics now, and he isn't out West either. You know where he is? You know where he's been for the past two months? He's over here in Greenacres. *You* know," she added, when they all looked blank. "The State hospital. The insane asylum."

They all began chattering at once, drawing close and tense together in the fog of cigarette smoke; it was almost like old times. Wasn't this the damnedest, weirdest, saddest thing? Was Milly absolutely certain of her facts?

Oh yes, oh yes, she was certain. "And what's more," she went on, "he didn't just *go* to Greenacres. He was taken in and put there, by the State Police."

A Mrs. Macready, who worked for the Givingses as a part-time cleaning woman, had told Milly the whole story only yesterday, at the shopping center, unable to believe she hadn't heard it long before. "She said she thought everybody'd heard it by now. Anyway, it seems he's been—you know, mentally disturbed for a long time. She said they practically went broke trying to pay for this private sanatorium out in California; he'd go in there for months at a time and then come out—that's when he'd teach, I guess—and then go back again. Then he seemed all right for a long time, until he suddenly quit his job out there and disappeared. Then he turned up here, without any warning, and came storming into the house and sort of held them captive there for about three days." She giggled uneasily at this, aware that a phrase like "held them captive" might sound too melodramatic to be true. "That's what Mrs. Macready called it anyway. I mean he probably didn't have a gun or a knife or anything, but he must've scared them half to death. Especially with Mr. Givings being so old and all, and his heart trouble. What he did was, he locked them in and cut the telephone wires and said he wasn't going to leave until they gave him what he'd come for, only he wouldn't say what it *was* he'd come for. One time he said it was his birth certificate, and they looked through all their old papers and stuff until they found it and gave it to him, and he tore it up. The rest of the time he just walked around talking and talking—raving, I guess—and breaking things. Furniture, pictures off the wall, dishes—everything. And in the middle of it all Mrs. Macready came over to go to work and he locked her in too—that's how she found out, you see—and I guess she was there for about ten hours before she got out through the garage. Then she called the State Troopers, and they came and took him to Greenacres."

"God," April said. "The State Troopers. How awful." And they all shook their heads in solemn agreement.

Shep was inclined to doubt the cleaning woman's veracity—"After all, the whole thing's just hearsay"—but the others talked him down. Hearsay or not, it had the unmistakable ring of truth to it.

April pointed out how significant it now seemed that Mrs. Givings had been dropping in so often lately for seemingly aimless little visits: "It's the funniest thing, I've always had the feeling she wanted something here, or wanted to tell us something and couldn't quite get the words out—haven't you felt that?" (Here she turned to her husband, but without quite meeting his eyes and without adding the "darling" or even the "Frank" that would have filled his heart with hope. He muttered that he guessed he had.) "God, isn't that sad," April said. "She's probably been dying to talk about it, or to find out how much we know, or something."

Milly, happily relaxing, wanted to explore the thing from the woman's angle. What *would* a mother feel on learning that her only child was mentally deranged? Shep hitched his chair up close to Frank, excluding the girls, bent on a plain, hard-headed discussion of the practical aspects. What was the deal? Could a man be forcibly committed to the nuthouse just like that? Didn't it sound fishy somehow, from a legal standpoint?

Frank began to see that if he allowed things to go on this way the excitement of the topic would soon be dispelled; without it, the evening might then degenerate into the dreariest kind of suburban time filler, the very kind of evening he had always imagined the Donaldsons and the Wingates and the Cramers having, in which women consulted with women about recipes and clothes, while men settled down with men to talk of jobs and cars. In a minute Shep might even say, "How's the job going, Frank?" in dead earnest, just as if Frank hadn't made it clear, time and again, that his job was the very least important part of his life, never to be mentioned except in irony. It was time to act.

He took a deep drink, leaned forward, and raised his voice enough to leave no doubt of his intention to address the group. Wasn't this, he asked, a beautifully typical story of these times and this place? A man could rant and smash and grapple with the State Police, and still the sprinklers whirled at dusk on every lawn and the television droned in every living room. A woman's only son came home insane, confronting her with God only knew what agonies of grief and guilt, and still she busied herself with the doings of the zoning board, with little chirrups of neighborly good cheer and cardboard boxes full of garden plants.

"I mean talk about decadence," he declared, "how decadent can a society get? Look at it this way. This country's probably the psychiatric, psychoanalytical capital of the world. Old Freud himself could never've dreamed up a more devoted bunch of disciples than the population of the United States—isn't that right? Our whole damn culture is geared to it; it's the new religion; it's everybody's intellectual and spiritual sugar-tit. And for all that, look what happens when a man really does blow his top. Call the Troopers, get him out of sight quick, hustle him off and lock him up before he wakes the neighbors. Christ's sake, when it comes to any kind of a showdown we're still in the Middle Ages. It's as if everybody'd made this tacit agreement to live in a state of total self-deception. The hell with reality! Let's have a whole bunch of cute little winding roads and cute little houses painted white and pink and baby blue; let's all be good consumers and have a lot of Togetherness and bring our children up in a bath of sentimentality—Daddy's a great man because he makes a living, Mummy's a great woman because she's stuck by Daddy all these years—and if old reality ever does pop out and say Boo we'll all get busy and pretend it never happened."

It was the kind of outburst that normally won their clamorous approval, or at the very least caused Milly to cry, "Oh that's so true!" But it seemed to have no effect. The three of them sat watching politely while he talked, and when he stopped they looked mildly relieved, like pupils at the end of a lecture.

There was nothing for him to do but get up and collect the glasses and retreat to the kitchen, where he petulantly wrenched and banged at the ice tray. The black kitchen window gave him a vivid reflection of his face, round and full of weakness, and he stared at it with loathing. That was when he remembered something—and the thought seemed to follow rather than precede the stricken look it caused on his mirrored face—something that shocked him and then filled him with a sense of ironic justice. The face in the glass, again seeming to anticipate rather than reflect his mood, had changed now from a look of dismay to a wise and bitter smile, and it nodded at him several times. Then he busied himself with the drinks, anxious to get back to the company. The thing he had remembered, whatever else it might mean, would be something to talk about.

"I just thought of something," he announced, and they all looked up. "Tomorrow's my birthday."

"Well!" The Campbells said in tired, congratulatory unison.

"I'll be thirty years old. Can you beat that?"

"Hell yes, I can beat it," said Shep, who was thirty-two, and Milly, who was thirty-four, began brushing cigarette ashes off her lap.

"No, but I mean it's funny to think you're not in your twenties any more," he said, re-establishing himself on the sofa. "It's kind of—*you* know, the end of an era or something. I don't know." He was getting drunk; he was drunk already. In another minute he'd be saying even sillier things than this, and repeating himself—he knew that, and the desperation of knowing it made him talk all the more.

"Birthdays," he was saying. "It's funny how they all run together when you look back. I do remember one of them damn well, though, and that was my twentieth." And he began to tell them how he had spent it, or part of it, pinned down by mortar and machine-gun fire in the last week of the war. One small, cold-sober part of his mind knew why he was doing this: it was because humorous talk of the army and the war had more than once turned out to be the final salvation of evenings with the Campbells. There was nothing Shep seemed to relish more, and though the girls might laugh in the wrong places and jokingly insist they would never fathom the interests and the loyalties of men, there was no denying that their listening faces would shine with a glow of romance. One of the most memorable nights of the whole friendship, in fact, had been built on a series of well-turned army stories and had found its climax in a roar of masculine song. Shep Campbell and Frank Wheeler, exultantly laughing and sweating and bathed in the sleepy admiration of their wives, had thumped their fists in marching cadence on the coffee table and bellowed out, at three in the morning:

> "Oh-h-h-h—
> Hidey, tidey, Christ Almighty
> Who the hell are we?
> Flim, flam, God damn
> We're the infantry . . ."

And so he told his anecdote, as carefully and well as he could, using all the tricks of wry self-disparagement that had come to form his style of military reminiscence over the years. It wasn't until he got to the part that went "—so I poked the guy next to me and said 'Hey, what day is this?' " that he began to feel uneasy, and by then it was too late. There was nothing to do but finish it: "And it turned out to be my birthday." He knew now that he'd told this same story to the Campbells before, using almost the same words; it must have been a year ago that he'd told it, in connection with his turning twenty-nine.

Both the Campbells made conscientious little clucks of amusement, and Shep discreetly inspected his watch. But the worst part—the worst part of the whole weekend, if not of his life to date—was the way April was looking at him. He had never seen such a stare of pitying boredom in her eyes.

It haunted him all night, while he slept alone; it was still there in the morning, when he swallowed his coffee and backed down the driveway in the crumpled old Ford he used for a station car. And riding to work, one of the youngest and healthiest passengers on the train, he sat with the look of a man condemned to a very slow, painless death. He felt middle-aged.

FIVE

THE ARCHITECTS OF the Knox Building had wasted no time in trying to make it look taller than its twenty stories, with the result that it looked shorter. They hadn't bothered trying to make it handsome, either, and so it was ugly: slab-sided and flat-topped, with a narrow pea-green cornice that jutted like the lip of a driven stake. It stood in an appropriately humdrum section of lower midtown, and from the very day of its grand opening, early in the century, it must clearly have been destined to settle deep into that smoke-hung clutter of numberless rectilinear shapes out of which, in aerial photographs, the mightier towers of New York emerge and rise.

But for all its plainness, the Knox Building did convey a quality of massive common sense. If it lacked grandeur, at least it had bulk; if there was nothing heroic about it, there was certainly nothing frivolous; it was a building that meant business.

"There it is, Frank," Earl Wheeler said to his son on a summer morning in 1935. "Straight ahead. That's the Home Office. Better take my hand here, this is a bad crossing . . ."

It was the only time Frank had ever been brought to New York by his father, and it had come as the climax to an exhilarating several weeks that always seemed, in retrospect, the only time his father could ever have been described as jovial. During that time the cryptic phrase "Oat Fields" had flown in happy profusion through his father's dinner-table talk, along with "New York" and "The Home Office," and had repeatedly caused his mother to say "Oh, that's wonderful, Earl," and "Oh, I'm so glad." Frank had eventually figured out that Oat Fields had nothing whatever to do with Quaker Oats but was in fact the odd name of a man—Mr. Oat Fields—a man remarkable not only in his size ("One of the biggest men in the Home Office") but in his intellectual astuteness. And he'd scarcely put this information

straight in his mind before being presented, by his mother, with
some startling news. Mr. Oat Fields, upon learning that Mr. Earl
Wheeler had a son of ten, had invited that son to accompany his
father on a visit to the Home Office. Father and son would then
be the guests of Mr. Fields at luncheon (it was the first time he'd
ever heard her use that word instead of lunch), following which
Mr. Fields would take them to a ball game at Yankee Stadium.
In the next few days the suspense had grown all but intolerable
until it threatened to spoil everything on the morning of the trip:
he very nearly threw up his breakfast from tension and trainsick-
ness on the way to town, and might have done it in the taxi too
if they hadn't gotten out to walk the last several blocks in the
fresh air; but with the clearing of his head as they walked it began
to seem that everything was going to be fine.

"There," his father said when they'd crossed the street. "Now,
here's the barbershop, that's where we're going for our haircuts
in a minute, and here's the subway—see how they've built the
subway entrance right into the building?—and look over here,
this is the display room. These windows run the entire length
of the building, from here on. Lot bigger than our dinky old
showroom out home, isn't it? And look—these are just a few of
the products we make. Here's your typewriters, of course, and
your adders and calculators and some of your different kinds of
filing systems, and that's one of the new bookkeeping machines
back there in the corner; and then look over here, in the next
window. These are your punched-card machines. That big one
is your tabulator, and the little one beside it is your sorter. When
you watch a demonstration of that baby, it's really a sight to see.
Fella takes a deck of punched cards, stacks 'em, puts 'em in there
and presses a button, and those old cards go flying through
there lickety-split."

But Frank's eyes kept wandering from the machines to his own
reflection in the plate glass. He thought he looked surprisingly
dignified in his new suit, with its coat and tie almost exactly like
his father's, and it pleased him to see this bright image of the two
of them, man and boy, with the endless swarm of people moving
past on the sidewalk behind them. After a minute he backed several steps away and looked straight up, until his collar cramped

the back of his neck, and Wow! He would admit he'd hoped for a skyscraper, but the last of his disappointment was vanishing now in this one long look. Up and up and up the tiers of windows rose, each smaller and more foreshortened than the one beneath, until their ever-narrowing sills and lintels seemed to merge. Imagine falling from the very top floor! Then he saw that the high, high cornice was moving slowly and steadily forward against the sky—the building was falling over on them!—but there was no time for panic before he saw his mistake: it was the sky that moved, white clouds floating back over the ledge of the roof, and at the instant his mind came into focus on this fact he felt a shiver of wonder down his spine at the enormous granite strength and stillness of the building. Wow!

"All set?" his father was saying. "Let's go to the barber's, then, and get fixed up, and then we'll go on inside. We're going to ride the elevator all the way up to the top."

But as things turned out, that preliminary moment on the sidewalk was the high point of the day. The barbershop proved to be nice enough, and so did the echoing marble-flagged lobby, which smelled of cigars and umbrellas and ladies' perfume, but from there on the pleasures of the day began to dwindle steadily. The elevator gave no sense of flight, for one thing, but only of confinement and nausea. Of the office itself, the top floor, he remembered only an acre of white lights and a very thin lady whose openwork blouse revealed an incredible number of straps that were apparently connected with her underwear, who called him Sonny and showed him how the water cooler worked ("Look, Sonny; watch the big bubble come up when I press the button—Blurp!—isn't that funny? Here, you try it"); and he would never forget the instantaneous revulsion he felt in the presence of Mr. Oat Fields, who if not the biggest was certainly the fattest man he had ever seen. Oat Fields's glasses mirrored staring images of the office lights, so that you couldn't see what his eyes were doing when he talked to you, and he talked in a very loud voice without seeming to hear your replies.

"Well, aren't *you* a big fella! What's your name? Huh? You like school? Well, that's fine. You like baseball? Huh?"

The worst part of him was his mouth, which was so wet that

a dozen shining strands of spittle clung and trembled between his moving lips; and it was this as much as anything that hampered Frank's enjoyment of the lunch, or luncheon, which took place in the restaurant of a great hotel. Oat Fields's mouth did not close while chewing and it left white streaks of food on the rim of his water glass. Once he softened the hard crust of a roll by holding it submerged in the gravy boat for some time before he lifted it to his reaching lips, allowing part of it to fall and leave a bright tan stain on his vest.

"You're absolutely right, Oat," Earl Wheeler kept saying throughout the meal, and "I certainly do agree with you on that," and the few times he glanced at Frank it was with startled eyes, as if surprised to find him sitting there. The ball game was a letdown too: nobody hit a home run, and in Frank's limited knowledge of the game a home run was all that mattered. For the last hour of it the sun slanted straight in his eyes, giving him a headache, and he had to go to the bathroom but didn't know how to broach the subject. Then came the grimy ordeal of subway connections to Penn Station, during which his father took him angrily to task for having failed to say "Thank you I had a very nice time" to Oat Fields. In the bleak light of the trainshed, as they stood waiting for the gates to open, he stared unnoticed at the physical exhaustion and moral defeat in his father's face, which looked loose and porous and very old. Then, lowering his eyes, he discovered that his father's trouser leg was slightly and rhythmically twitching with the anxious movement of his pocketed fingers on his genitals.

And that, ultimately, would become his most vivid single remembrance of the day; at the time, though, later that same night as he staggered and crouched barefoot in the tilting, oddly shrunken bathroom of his home, it was his memory's vision of Oat Fields's eating mouth that made the spasms of vomiting come again and again.

Not until years later was he able to piece the simple facts of the case together. Earl Wheeler, having clung to an assistant branch managership in Newark through any number of Depression layoffs and cutbacks, had somehow come to Home Office attention as a candidate for the job of right-hand man to Oat Fields (and not until later still did he guess the explanation of that name—the fact that in a world of mandatory diminutives, a corporation of jolly Bills and Jacks and Herbs and Teds in which an unabbreviable given name like Earl must always have been a minor handicap, "Oat" was the best that could be done for a man with the given name of Otis). But the promotion had fallen through; higher authority had decreed that Oat Fields could get along without a right-hand man, and Earl Wheeler must either have learned or guessed this outcome at some point during the luncheon or the ball game.

And whether or not he ever came to accept the disappointment, Frank knew that to the end of his life he never understood it. It must, for that matter, have been the first of many events that passed Earl Wheeler's understanding, for it came at the beginning of his decline. In the years after that he was transferred from one field assignment to another until his retirement soon after the war (and not long after Oat Fields's own retirement and death), by which time he had slipped from the assistant-manager level to that of an ordinary salesman in Harrisburg, Pennsylvania. And in those years too, with increasing bewilderment, he had failed to understand the weakening of his health, the rapid difficult aging of his wife, the indifference of his two older sons—and finally the shrill rebellion, the desertion and the moral collapse of his youngest.

A longshoreman! A cafeteria cashier! An ungrateful, spiteful, foul-mouthed weakling, boozing his way through Greenwich Village with God only knew what kind of companions; a punk kid with no more sense of decency than to drive his mother nearly out of her mind not writing for six, eight months and then mailing a letter with no return address and the postscript: "Got married last week—might bring her out sometime."

It was a lucky thing for Earl Wheeler, then, that he wasn't present in a cheap bar near the Columbia campus one noontime in 1948, when his son sat in conference with another slouching youth named Sam, a graduate student in philosophy who held a part-time job in the student placement office.

"So what's the problem, Frank? I thought you'd be back in Europe by now."

"Big joke. April's knocked up."

"Oh Jesus."

"No, but listen; there're all different kinds of ways of looking at a thing like this, Sam. Look at it this way. I need a job; okay. Is that any reason why the job I get has to louse me up? Look. All I want is to get enough dough coming in to keep us solvent for the next year or so, till I can figure things out; meanwhile I want to retain my own identity. Therefore the thing I'm most anxious to avoid is any kind of work that can be considered 'interesting' in its own right. I want something that can't possibly touch me. I want some big, swollen old corporation that's been bumbling along making money in its sleep for a hundred years, where they have to hire eight guys for every one job because none of them can be expected to care about whatever boring thing it is they're supposed to be doing. I want to go into that kind of place and say, Look. You can have my body and my nice college-boy smile for so many hours a day, in exchange for so many dollars, and beyond that we'll leave each other strictly alone. Get the picture?"

"I think so," said the philosophy student. "Come on back to the office." And there, adjusting his glasses and thumbing through a card index, Sam began to write out a list of companies that seemed to fit the picture: a great copper-and-brass manufacturer, a great public utility, a gigantic firm that made all kinds of paper bags . . .

But when Frank saw the awesome name of Knox Business Machines being added to the list he thought there must be some mistake. "Hey, no, wait a minute; I know that can't be right—" and he gave a brief oral summary of his father's career, which caused the philosophy student to enjoy a pleasant chuckle.

"I think you'll find things've changed a little since your old man's time, Frank," he said. "That was the Depression, don't forget. Besides, he was out in the field; you'd be in the home office. As a matter of fact this place is just what you're looking for. I happen to know they've got guys sitting around that building that never lift a finger except to pick up their checks. I'd certainly mention your father, though, when you go for the interview. Probably help things along."

But Frank, as he walked into the shadow of the Knox Building with the ghosts of that other visit crowding his head ("Better take my hand here, this is a bad crossing . . ."), decided it would be more fun not to mention his father in the interview at all. And he didn't, and he got a job that very day on the fifteenth floor, in something called the Sales Promotion Department.

"The sales what?" April inquired. " 'Promotion'? I don't get it. What does that mean you're supposed to do?"

"Who the hell knows? They explained it to me for half an hour and I still don't know, and I don't think they do either. No, but it's pretty funny, isn't it? Old Knox Business Machines. Wait'll I tell the old man. Wait'll he hears I didn't even use his name."

And so it started as a kind of joke. Others might fail to see the humor of it, but it filled Frank Wheeler with a secret, astringent delight as he discharged his lazy duties, walking around the office in a way that had lately become almost habitual with him, if not quite truly characteristic, since having been described by his wife as "terrifically sexy"—a slow, catlike stride, proudly muscular but expressing a sleepy disdain of tension or hurry. And the best part of the joke was what happened every afternoon at five. Buttoned-up and smiling among the Knox men, nodding good-night as the elevator set him free, he would take a crosstown bus and a downtown bus to Bethune Street, where he'd mount two flights of slope-treaded, creaking stairs, open a white door so overlayed with many generations of soiled and blistered paint that its surface felt like the flesh of a toadstool, and let himself into a wide clean room that smelled faintly of cigarettes and candlewax and tangerine peel and eau de cologne; and there a beautiful, disheveled girl would be waiting, a girl as totally unlike the wife of a Knox man as the apartment was unlike a Knox man's home. Instead of after-work cocktails they would make after-work love, sometimes on the bed and sometimes on the floor; sometimes it was ten o'clock before they roused themselves and strolled into the gentle evening streets for dinner, and by then the Knox Building could have been a thousand miles away.

By the end of the first year the joke had worn thin, and the inability of others to see the humor of it had become depressing. "Oh, you mean your *father* worked there," they would say when he tried to explain it, and their eyes, as often as not, would then begin to film over with the look that people reserve for earnest, obedient, unadventurous young men. Before long (and particularly after the second year, with both his parents dead) he had stopped trying to explain that part of it, and begun to dwell instead on other comic aspects of the job: the absurd discrepancy between his own ideals and those of Knox Business Machines; the gulf between the amount of energy he was supposed to give the company and the amount he actually gave. "I mean the great advantage of a place like Knox is that you can sort of turn off your mind every morning at nine and leave it off all day, and nobody knows the difference."

More recently still, and particularly since moving to the country, he had taken to avoiding the whole topic whenever possible by replying, to the question of what he did for a living, that he didn't do anything, really; that he had the dullest job you could possibly imagine.

On the Monday morning after the end of the Laurel Players, he walked into the Knox Building like an automaton. The show windows were featuring a new display, bright cardboard images of thin, fashionable young women who grinned and pointed their pencils at emblazoned lists of product benefits—SPEED, ACCURACY, CONTROL—and beyond them, across the deep-carpeted expanse of the display floor, a generous sampling of the products themselves stood poised for demonstration. Some of them, the simpler ones, were much like the machines that had kindled his father's enthusiasm twenty years before, though the angular black designs of those days had all been modified to fit the globular "sculptured forms" of their new casings, which were the color of oyster meat; but there were others equipped to deal with the facts of business at speeds more lickety-split than anything Earl Wheeler could have dreamed of. These, ready to purr and blink with electronic mystery, grew more and more imposing across the floor until they culminated in the big inscrutable components of the Knox "500" Electronic Computer, a machine which, according to the museum card displayed at its base, could "perform the lifetime work of a man with a desk calculator in thirty minutes."

But Frank moved past the display room without a glance, and his actions on entering the lobby were absent-mindedly expert: he obeyed the pointed finger of the elevator starter without quite being aware of it, nor did he notice which of the six elevator operators it was who sleepily made him welcome (he almost never did, unless it happened to be one of the two whose presence could be faintly oppressive: the very old man whose knees were so sprung that painful-looking bulges pressed against the backs of his trousers, or the enormous boy whom some glandular disorder had afflicted with the high hips of a woman and the downy head and beardless face of an infant). Pressed well back in the polite bondage of the car, he heard the sliding door clamp shut and the safety gate go rattling after it, and as the car began to rise he was surrounded by the dissonant conversations of his colleagues. He heard a deep, measured voice of the Great Plains, rich with distance and travel and the best accommodations ("... course, we did hit a little bumpy weather comin' inta Chicawgo ..."), sound out in counterpoint to the abrupt and sibilant accents of the city ("... so I siz 'Whaddya—kiddin'?' He siz 'No, listen, *I'm* not kiddin' ...") while a softer medley of eight or ten voices, male and female, repeated their hushed morning courtesies under the buzz of the overhead fan; then it was time to begin the nodding, side-stepping ritual of making way for the people who edged toward the front with murmurs of "Out, please ... Out, please" and to wait while the door slid open and shut, open and shut again. The eighth, the eleventh, the twelfth, the fourteenth ...

At first glance, all the upper floors of the Knox Building looked alike. Each was a big open room, ablaze with fluorescent ceiling lights, that had been divided into a maze of aisles and cubicles by shoulder-high partitions. The upper panels of these dividers, waist to shoulder, were made of thick unframed plate glass that was slightly corrugated to achieve a blue-white semitransparency; and the overall effect of this, to a man getting off the elevator and looking out across the room, was that of the wide indoor lake in which swimmers far and near were moving, some making steady headway, some treading water, others seen in the act of breaking to the surface or going under, and many submerged, their faces loosened into wavering pink blurs as they drowned at their desks. But the illusion was quickly dispelled on walking further into the office, for here the air was of an over-whelming dryness—it was, as Frank Wheeler often complained, "enough to dry your God damned eyeballs out."

For all his complaints, though, he was sometimes guiltily aware of taking a dim pleasure in the very discomfort of the office. When he said, as he'd been saying for years, that in a funny way he guessed he would miss old Knox when he quit, he meant of course that it was the people he would miss ("I mean hell, they're a pretty decent crowd; some of them, anyway") and yet in all honesty he could not have denied a homely affection for the place itself, the Fifteenth Floor. Over the years he had discovered slight sensory distinctions between it and all the others of the building; it was no more or less pleasant, but different for being "his" floor. It was his bright, dry, daily ordeal, his personal mea-sure of tedium. It had taught him new ways of spacing out the hours of the day—almost time to go down for coffee; almost time to go out for lunch; almost time to go home—and he had come to rely on the desolate wastes of time that lay between these pleasures as an invalid comes to rely on the certainty of recurring pain. It was a part of him.

"Morning, Frank," said Vince Lathrop.

"Morning, Frank," said Ed Small.

"Morning, Mr. Wheeler," said Grace Mancuso, who worked for Herb Underwood in Market Research.

His feet knew where to turn at the aisle marked sales promo-tion, and they knew how many steps would bring him past the first three cubicles and where he would have to turn again to enter the fourth; he could have done it in his sleep.

"Hello," said Maureen Grube, who served as floor reception-ist and worked in Mrs. Jorgensen's typing pool. She said it in a frankly flattering, definitely feminine way, and as she swayed aside to let him pass he wanted to put his arm around her and lead her away somewhere (the mail room? the freight elevator?) where he could sit down and take her on his lap and remove her royal blue sweater and fill his mouth with one and then the other of her breasts.

It wasn't the first time this idea had occurred to him; the difference was that this time it had no sooner occurred to him than he thought, Why not?

His feet had led him to the entrance of the cubicle whose plastic nameplate read:

J. R. ORDWAY

F. H. WHEELER

and he paused there, one hand hooked over the rim of the plate glass, to turn and look back at her. She was all the way down to the end of the aisle, now, her buttocks moving nicely in her flannel skirt, and he watched her until she disappeared beneath the waterline of partition tops to take her place at the reception desk.

Take it easy, he counseled himself. A thing like this would need a little planning. The first thing to do, he knew, was to go on inside and say good morning to Jack Ordway and take off his coat and sit down. He did that, instantly shutting out his view of everything beyond the cubicle walls, and as he settled himself sideways at his desk with his right foot automatically toeing open a lower drawer and using its edge as a foot rest (the pressure of his shoe over the years had worn a little saddle in the edge of that particular drawer), he allowed a slow wave of delight to break over him. Why not? Hadn't she given him every possible encouragement for months? Undulating past him in the aisle like that, bending close over his desk to hand him a folder, smiling in a special, oblique way that he'd never seen her use on anyone else? And that time at the Christmas party (he could still remember the taste of her mouth) hadn't she trembled in his arms, and hadn't she whispered, "You're sweet"?

Why not? Oh, not in the mail room or the freight elevator, but didn't she probably have an apartment somewhere, with a roommate, and wouldn't the roommate probably be out all day?

Jack Ordway was talking to him, requiring him against his will to look up and say "What's that?" An intrusion by almost anyone else wouldn't have mattered—he could have nodded and made the right replies while keeping most of his mind free for Maureen Grube—but Ordway was different.

"I said I'm going to need your help this morning, Franklin," he was saying. "This is an emergency. I'm dead serious, old scout." He was apparently studying a sheaf of typewritten papers on his desk, the picture of concentration; only someone who knew what to look for could have told that the hand which seemed to be shading his eyes was really holding his head up, and that his eyes were shut. In his early forties, slight and trim, with the graying hair and wittily handsome face of a romantic actor, he was the kind of borderline alcoholic whose salvation seems to lie in endless renewals of his ability to laugh the whole thing off, and he was the sentimental hero of the office. Everybody loved Jack Ordway. Today he was wearing his English suit—the suit he had ordered from a touring London tailor some years before, at the cost of half a month's salary, the suit whose cuff buttons really buttoned and whose high-backed trousers could only be worn with suspenders, or "braces," the suit that was never seen without a fresh linen handkerchief spilling from its breast pocket—but his long narrow feet, which lay splayed with childish awkwardness under the desk, betrayed a pitifully all-American look. They were encased in cheap orange-brown loafers, badly scuffed; and the reason for this clashing note was that the one thing Jack Ordway could not do in the grip of a really bad hangover was to tie a pair of shoelaces.

"For the next—" he was saying in a hoarse, unsteady voice, "for the next two or possibly three hours you're to warn me of Bandy's every approach; you're to protect me from Mrs. Jorgensen, and you may have to screen me from public view in case I begin to throw up. It's that bad."

The capsuled story of Jack Ordway's life had become a minor legend of the Fifteenth Floor: everyone knew of how he'd married a rich girl and lived on her inheritance until it vanished just before the war, how since then his business career had been spent entirely in the Knox Building, in one glass cubicle after another, and how it had been distinguished by an almost flawless lack of work. Even here in Sales Promotion, where nobody worked very hard except old Bandy, the manager, he had managed to retain his unique reputation. Except when a really bad hangover laid him low he was up and around and talking all day,

setting off little choruses of laughter wherever he went, sometimes even winning a tolerant chuckle from Bandy himself, driving Mrs. Jorgensen into fits of helpless giggles that made her
weep.

"First of all," he was saying now, "on Saturday these crazy
friends of Sally's flew in from the Coast all eager for the treat.
Could we show them the town? Oh, indeed we could. Old, old
buddies of hers and all that, and besides, they always bring
pocketfuls of loot. So. Started off with lunch at André's, and dear
God you've never seen such whopping great martinis in your
life. Oh, and none of this sissy business of one or two apiece,
either, buddy. I lost count. And then let's see. Oh, yes. Then
there was nothing to do but sit around and drink until cocktail
time. Then came cocktail time." He had abandoned his working
posture now, pushed the false papers aside and leaned delicately
back in the chair to hold his head with both hands; he was moving it from side to side in the rhythm of his narrative, laughing
and talking through his laughter, while Frank watched him with
a mixture of pity and distaste. Most of his hangover stories
seemed to begin with a flying-in of Sally's crazy friends from the
Coast, or from the Bahamas, or from Europe, with pocketfuls of
loot, and Sally herself was always featured at the center of the
fun—the former debutante, the chic, childless wife and irrepress-
ible playmate. That, at least, was the way his listeners on the Fifteenth Floor were expected to picture her; Frank had been able
to do so, and to picture their apartment as a kind of Noël Coward
stage setting, until the time he went home with Ordway for a
drink and found that Sally was massively soft and wrinkled, a
sodden, aging woman with lips forever painted in the petulant
cupid's bow of her youth. Her every whining intonation of
Jack's name that night, as she swayed bewildered through rooms
of rotting leather and dusty silver and glass, showed how deeply
she blamed him for allowing the world to collapse; once she had
turned up her eyes to the paint-flaked ceiling as if calling on
God to punish him—this weak, foolish little man for whom she'd
sacrificed her very life, who poisoned all her friendships with
his endless counting of pennies, who insisted on grubbing at his
dreary, dreary white-collar job and bringing dreary office people

home with him. And Jack, apologetically hovering and making little jokes, had called her "Mother."

". . . and as for how we got *back* from Idlewild," he was saying, "it's a thing I'll never know. My last completely clear recollection is of standing in the Idlewild lounge at three o'clock this morning and wondering if someone would please tell me how we'd gotten there in the first place. Or no, wait. After that there was something about a hamburger joint—or no, I think that was earlier . . ." When the story was over at last he removed his hands from his head, experimentally, and frowned and blinked several times. Then he announced that he was beginning to feel a little better.

"Good." Frank dropped his foot from the drawer and got settled at his desk. He had to think, and the best way to think was to go through the motions of working. This morning's batch of papers was waiting in his IN basket, on top of last Friday's, and so his first action was to turn the whole stack upside down on his desk and start from the bottom. As he did each day (or rather on the days when he bothered with the IN basket, for there were many days when he left it alone) he tried first to see how many papers he could get rid of without actually reading their contents. Some could be thrown away, others could be almost as rapidly disposed of by scrawling "What about this?" in their margins, with his initials, and sending them to Bandy, or by writing "Know anything on this?" and sending them to someone like Ed Small, next door; but the danger here was that the same papers might come back in a few days marked "Do" from Bandy and "No" from Small. A safer course was to mark a thing "File" for Mrs. Jorgensen and the girls, after the briefest possible glance had established that it wasn't of urgent importance; if it was, he might mark it "File & Follow 1 wk.," or he might put it aside and go on to the next one. The gradual accumulation of papers put aside in this way was what he turned to as soon as he was finished with, or tired of, the IN basket. Arranging them in an approximate order of importance, he would interleave them, in the same order, with those of the six- or eight-inch stack that always lay near the center of the desk, held down by a glazed ceramic paperweight that Jennifer had made for him in kindergarten. This was his current work pile. Many of the papers in it bore the insignia of Bandy's "Do" or Ed Small's "No," and some had been through the "File & Follow" cycle as many as three or four times; some, bearing notes like "Frank—might look into this," were the gifts of men who used him as he used Small. Occasionally he would remove a piece of current work and place it in the equally high secondary pile that lay on the far right-hand corner of the desk, under a leaden scale model of the Knox "500" Electronic Computer. This was the pile of things he couldn't bring himself to face just now, and the worst of them, sometimes whole bulging folders filled with scrawled-over typewritten sheets and loose, sliding paper clips, would eventually go into the stuffed bottom right-hand drawer of the desk. The papers in there were of the kind that Ordway called Real Goodies, and that drawer, opposite to the one that served as a foot rest, had come to occupy a small nagging place in Frank's conscience: he was as shy of opening it as if it held live snakes.

Why not? Wouldn't it be perfectly easy to walk up and ask her out to lunch? No, it wouldn't; that was the trouble. An unspoken rule of the Fifteenth Floor divided the men from the girls on all but business matters, except at Christmas parties. The girls made separate arrangements for lunch in the same inviolable way that they used a separate lavatory, and only a fool would openly defy the system. This would need a little planning.

He was still in the middle of the IN basket when a thin smiling face and a round solemn one appeared above the glass wall, looking in from the next cubicle. They were the faces of Vince Lathrop and Ed Small, and this meant it was time to go down for coffee.

"Gentlemen," said Vince Lathrop. "Shall we dance?"

Half an hour later they were back in the office, having heard at some length about Ed Small's difficulties with grass seed and lawn care in Roslyn, Long Island. The coffee had helped to strengthen Ordway, though it was clear now that what he really needed was a drink, and to prove how much better he felt he was pacing up and down the cubicle and going through his impersonation of Bandy, wobbling his head and repeatedly sucking at a side tooth with little kissing sounds.

"Well, but I wonder if we're really being effective, that's the thing (kiss). Because if we really want to be effective, then we're going to have to get in there and be more, be more (kiss), be more *effective* . . ."

Frank was trying for the second or third time to read the top paper on his current work pile, which seemed to be a letter from the branch manager in Toledo; but its paragraphs were as opaque as if it had been typed in a foreign language. He closed his eyes and rubbed them and tried again, and this time he made it.

The branch manager in Toledo, who in the Knox tradition referred to himself as "we," wished to know what action had been taken on his previous correspondence with regard to the many serious errors and misleading statements in SP-1109, a copy of which was attached. This proved to be a thick, coated-stock, four-color brochure entitled *Pinpoint Your Production Control with the Knox "500,"* and the sight of it brought back uneasy memories. It had been produced many months before by a nameless copywriter in an agency that had since lost its Knox account, and had been released to the field in tens of thousands of copies marked "Address all inquiries F. H. Wheeler, Home Office." Frank had known at the time that it was a mess—its densely printed pages defied simple logic, as well as readership, and its illustrations were only sporadically related to its text—but he'd let it go anyway, chiefly because Bandy had confronted him in the aisle one day with a kiss of the side tooth and said, "Haven't we released that brochure yet?"

Since then the inquiries addressed to F. H. Wheeler had come in slow, embarrassing streams from all parts of the United States, and he was dimly aware of something particularly urgent about those that had been coming from Toledo. The next paragraph reminded him.

As you will recall, it was our intention to order 5,000 additional copies of the brochure for distribution at the annual NAPE Convention (Nat'l. Assn. of Production Executives) here June 10–13. However, as stated in previous correspondence, the brochure is in our opinion so inferior that it does not fulfill its purpose in any way, shape, or manner.

> Therefore please advise immediately re our inquiry in
> previous correspondence, namely: what arrangements are
> being made to have a revised version of the brochure in our
> office not later than June 8 in the required number of copies?

He looked quickly at the upper left-hand corner and was
relieved to find that the letter had not carried a carbon to Bandy.
That was a piece of luck; but even so, this had all the earmarks
of a Real Goody. Even if there were still time to arrange for a
new brochure to be produced (and there probably wasn't), he
would have to clear the job through Bandy, and Bandy would
want to know why he hadn't been told about it two months
earlier.

He was in the act of laying the thing on his secondary pile
when the beginnings of a bright idea came through his confusion; and suddenly he was out of the cubicle and walking toward
the front of the office with his heart in his mouth.

She was at her desk in the reception area with nothing to do,
and when she looked up her eyes were so full of pleased expec-
tancy—of complicity, it almost seemed—that he nearly forgot
what it was he had to pretend he'd come for.

"Maureen," he said, moving up close and taking hold of the
back of her chair, "if you're not too busy here I wonder if you'd
help me find some stuff in the central file. You see this?" He laid
the brochure on her desk as if it were an intimate revelation, and
she leaned forward from the hips to examine it, so that her breasts
swung close to his pointing hand.

"Mm?"

"The thing is, it's got to be revised. That means I've got to dig
up all the material that went into it, right from scratch. Now, if
you'll look in the inactive file under SP-1109 you'll find copies
of all the stuff we sent to the agency; then if you check each of
those papers you'll find another code number referring you to
other files; that way we can trace the thing back to original
sources. Come on, I'll help you get started."

"All right."

As he moved up the aisle behind her hips he felt the promise
of triumph in his expanding chest, and soon they were alone

together in the labyrinth of the central file, enveloped in her perfume as they fingered nervously through a drawer of folders.

"Eleven-oh-what, did you say?"

"Eleven-oh-nine. Should be right there somewhere."

For the first time he allowed himself to scrutinize her face. It was round and wide-nosed and not really very pretty—he could afford to admit that now—and its too-heavy make-up was probably there to hide a bad complexion, just as the little black tails she had drawn at the corners of her eyes were there to make the eyes look larger and farther apart. Her carefully arranged hair was probably her greatest problem—it must have been a shapeless frizzled bush when she was a child, and must still give her trouble in the rain—but her mouth was wonderful: perfect teeth and plump, subtly shaped lips that had the texture of marzipan. He found that if he focused his eyes on her mouth so that the rest of her face was slightly blurred, and then drew back to include the whole length and shape of her in that hazy image, it was possible to believe he was looking at the most desirable woman in the world.

"Here," she said. "Now, you want all the folders relating to all these other code numbers. Is that it?"

"That's it. It may take a little time; I hope you weren't planning on an early lunch."

"No. I didn't have any special plans."

"Good. I'll stop back in a while and see how you're doing. Thanks a lot, Maureen."

"You're very welcome."

And he went back to his cubicle and sat down. It was a perfect arrangement. He could wait here until the rest of the floor had emptied out for lunch; then he would go back and get her. His only problem now was to think up an excuse for not going out to lunch in the usual way, with the usual crowd—an excuse, if possible, that would cover him for the rest of the afternoon.

"Eat?" a deep masculine voice inquired, and this time three heads hung above the partition. They were the heads of Lathrop, Small, and the man who had spoken, a gray mountain of a man with heavy eyebrows and a clenched pipe, whose bulk rose high enough above the glass to reveal that he wore a defiantly unbusinesslike checked shirt, hairy wool tie and pepper-and-salt jacket. This was Sid Roscoe, the literary and political sage of the Fifteenth Floor, a self-described "old newspaper guy" who contemptuously edited the employee house organ, *Knox Knews*. "Come on, you characters," he said heartily. "On your feet."

Jack Ordway obeyed him, pausing only to murmur "Ready, Franklin?" But Frank held back, inspecting his watch with the look of a man pressed for time.

"Guess I won't be able to make it today," he said. "Got some people to see uptown this afternoon; I'll probably stop for a bite up there."

"Oh, for God's sake, Wheeler," Ordway said, turning on him. There was a disproportionate amount of shock and disappointment in his face, a look of *But you've got to come with us*; and it took Frank a second to realize what the trouble was. Ordway needed him. With Frank along for moral support, it would be possible to steer the group to what Ordway called the Nice place, the dark German restaurant where a round of weak but adequate martinis came floating to your table almost as a matter of course; without him, under Roscoe's leadership, they would almost certainly go to the Awful place—a bright, mercilessly clean luncheonette called Waffle Heaven where you couldn't even get a glass of beer and where the cloying smells of melting butter and maple syrup were enough to make you retch into your tiny paper napkin. There would then be nothing for Jack Ordway to do but sit and hold himself together until they brought him back to the office and set him free to slip out again for the couple of quick ones he would need to survive the afternoon. *Please*, his comically round eyes implored as they led him away, *please* don't let this happen to me.

But Frank sat firm, thumbing the edges of his current work file. He waited until they were safely in the elevator, and then he continued to wait. Ten minutes went by, and twenty, and still the office seemed much too crowded; then at last he half rose from his chair and peeked out over the surface of the partition-tops in all directions.

Maureen's head moved alone above the waterline of the central file. There were a few other heads bunched near the elevators and a few others scattered in far corners, but there was no point in waiting any longer. The office would never be emptier than this. He buttoned his coat and stalked out of the cubicle.

"That's fine, Maureen," he said, bearing down on her and taking the batch of folders and papers from her hand. "I don't think we'll need any more than that."

"Well, but it's only about half the stuff, though. I mean didn't you want all of it?"

"Tell you what: let's not worry about it. How about some lunch?"

"All right. I'd love to."

He was all action as he hurried back to his desk to drop the papers and dodged into the men's room to wash up, but when he went to stand by the elevators, waiting for her to come out of the ladies' room, he was all worry. The small crowd around the elevators was beginning to include people coming *back* from lunch; if she didn't hurry up they might run into Ordway and the others. What the hell was she doing in there? Standing with her arms around three other girls in a paralysis of laughter at the very idea of going out with Mr. Wheeler?

Then suddenly she was walking toward him in a light coat, and the elevator door was sliding open and the operator's voice was saying "Down!"

He stood a little behind her and held himself in a rigid parade rest as they dropped through space. All the restaurants for blocks around would be loaded with Knox people; he would have to get her out of the neighborhood, and as they moved through the lobby he touched her elbow as hesitantly as if it were her breast. "Listen," he mumbled. "There aren't any decent places to eat around here. You mind taking a short trip?"

They were out on the sidewalk now, jostled by the crowd, and he stood smiling like an idiot for what seemed a full minute of indecision before the word "taxi" popped into his head; then all at once it made him feel so fine to see one slowing down under the command of his wagging arm, and so splendid to see her smile and bend and climb gracefully into its deep seat, that he didn't give a damn about what he saw from the corner of his eye at that moment: the unmistakable bulk of Sid Roscoe in the crowd, flanked by the familiar shapes of Lathrop and Small and Ordway, coming from the direction of the Awful place. It was impossible to tell whether they'd seen him or not, and he instantly decided that it didn't matter. He slammed the door and allowed himself one more glance through the window of the cab as it pulled away from the curb, and he wanted to laugh aloud at the sight of Jack Ordway's orange loafers flapping along through the forest of legs and feet.

SIX

"EVERYTHING'S SORT OF going out of focus," she said. "I mean I feel fine and everything, but I guess we'd better eat something."

They were in an expensive brick-walled restaurant on West Tenth Street, and Maureen had talked for half an hour in a breathless autobiographical rush, pausing only once to let him telephone Mrs. Jorgensen and arrange for one of the other girls to take the reception desk for the afternoon. ("The thing is," he had explained, "I had to borrow Maureen to help me locate some stuff here in Visual Aids, and it looks like we're going to be tied up here for the rest of the day." There was no department or subdepartment anywhere in the Knox Building called Visual Aids, but he was reasonably sure that Mrs. Jorgensen didn't know it, and that anyone she'd be likely to ask would not be certain either. He had handled the call so adroitly that he didn't realize how close he was to being drunk until he came within an inch of upsetting a tray of French pastries on his way back from the phone booth.) The rest of his time had been devoted to steady drinking and listening, with mixed emotions.

These were some of the things he'd learned: that she was twenty-two and came from a town far upstate, where her father owned a hardware store; that she hated her name ("I mean 'Maureen's' all right but 'Grube' sounds so awful with it; I guess that was one reason I was so crazy to get married"); that she'd been married at eighteen and had it annulled six months later—"It was completely ridiculous"—and had spent the following year or two "just moping around home and working at the gas company and feeling depressed" until it struck her that what she'd always really and truly wanted to do was to come to New York "and live."

All this was pleasing, and so was the way she had shyly slipped into calling him "Frank," and so was the news that she did indeed have an apartment with another girl—a "perfectly adorable" apartment right here in the Village—but after a while he found he had to keep reminding himself to be pleased. The trouble, he guessed, was mainly that she talked too much. It was also that so much of her talk rang false, that so many of its possibilities for charm were blocked and buried under the stylized ceremony of its cuteness. Soon he was able to guess that most if not all of her inanity could be blamed on her roommate, whose name was Norma and for whom she seemed to feel an unqualified admiration. The more she told him about this other girl, or "gal"—that she was older and twice divorced, that she worked for a big magazine and knew "all sorts of fabulous people"—the more annoyingly clear it became that she and Norma enjoyed classic roles of mentor and novice in an all-girl orthodoxy of fun. There were signs of this tutelage in Maureen's too-heavy make-up and too-careful hairdo, as well as in her every studied mannerism and prattling phrase—her overuse of words like "mad" and "fabulous" and "appalling," her wide-eyed recitals of facts concerning apartment maintenance, and her endless supply of anecdotes involving sweet little Italian grocers and sweet little Chinese laundrymen and gruff but lovable cops on the beat, all of whom, in the telling, became the stock supporting actors in a confectionery Hollywood romance of bachelor-girls in Manhattan.

Under the oppressive weight of this outpouring he had called for round after round of drinks, and now her meek announcement that everything was sort of out of focus filled him with guilt. All Norma's brittle animation had fled from Maureen's face; she looked as honest and as helpless as a child about to be sick on her party dress. He called the waiter and helped her to choose the most wholesome items on the menu with all the care of a conscientious father; and when she had settled down to eat, looking up now and then to assure him that she felt much better, it was his turn to talk.

He made the most of it. Sentences poured from him, paragraphs composed themselves and took wing, appropriate anecdotes sprang to his service and fell back to make way for the stately passage of epigrams.

Beginning with a quick, audacious dismantling of the Knox

Business Machines Corporation, which made her laugh, he moved out confidently onto broader fields of damnation until he had laid the punctured myth of Free Enterprise at her feet; then, just at the point where any further talk of economics might have threatened to bore her, he swept her away into cloudy realms of philosophy and brought her lightly back to earth with a wise-crack.

And how did she feel about the death of Dylan Thomas? And didn't she agree that this generation was the least vital and most terrified in modern times? He was at the top of his form. He was making use of material that had caused Milly Campbell to say "Oh that's so true, Frank!" and of older, richer stuff that had once helped to make him the most interesting person April Johnson had ever met. He even touched on his having been a longshoreman. Through it all, though, ran a bright and skillfully woven thread that was just for Maureen: a portrait of himself as decent but disillusioned young family man, sadly and bravely at war with his environment.

By the time the coffee came he could see that it was all taking effect. Her face had become an automatic register of quick responses to everything he said: he could make it leap into delighted laughter or frown and nod in solemn agreement or soften into romantic contemplation; if he'd wanted to he could very easily have made it weep. When she looked briefly away from him, down at her cup or off misty-eyed into the room, it was only for a kind of emotional catching of breath; once he could have sworn he saw her planning how she would tell Norma about him tonight ("*Oh*, the most fascinating man . . ."), and the way she seemed to melt when he helped her on with her coat, the way she swayed against him as they walked out of the place for a stroll in the sunshine, made it clear that the last shred of doubt could be safely abandoned. He had it made.

The only problem now was where to go. They were heading vaguely toward the trees of Washington Square; and the trouble with taking a walk in the park, aside from its waste of valuable time, was that this was the hour when the park would be full of women who had once been April's friends and neighbors. Anne Snyder and Susan Cross and God only knew how many others would be there, lifting their softening cheeks to the sun or wiping ice cream from the mouths of their children as they talked of nursery schools and outrageous rents and perfectly marvelous Japanese movies, waiting until it was time to gather up their toys and graham crackers and stroll home to fix their husbands' cocktails, and they'd spot him in a minute ("Well, of *course* it's Frank Wheeler, but who's that *with* him? Isn't that funny?"). But he had scarcely allowed this uneasiness to develop before Maureen came to a stop on the sidewalk.

"This is my place. Would you like to come up for a drink or something?"

Then he was following her hips up a dim carpeted stairway, and then a door had clicked shut behind him and he was standing in a room that smelled of vacuum cleaning and breakfast bacon and perfume, a high, silent room where everything lay richly bathed in yellow light from windows whose blinds of split bamboo had turned the sun into fine horizontal stripes of tan and gold. He stood feeling tall and strong as she ducked and curtsied around him in her stockinged feet, straightening ash trays and magazines—"I'm afraid the place is an awful mess; won't you sit down?"—and when she sank one knee into a studio couch to reach across it for the cord that opened one of the blinds, he moved up close behind her and put his hand on her waist. That was all it took. With a moist little whimpering groan she turned and pressed herself into his arms, offering up her mouth. Then they were on the couch and the only problem in the world was the bondage of their clothing. Twisting and gasping together, they worked urgently at knots and buttons and buckles and hooks until the last impediment slipped away; and then in the warmth and rhythm of her flesh he found an overwhelming sense of *this* is what I needed; *this* is what I needed; his self-absorption was so complete that he was only dimly aware of her whispering, "Oh, yes; yes; yes . . ."

When it was over, though, when they had fallen apart and rejoined each other in a lightly sweating tangle of arms and legs, he knew he had never been more grateful to anyone in his life. The only trouble was that he couldn't think of anything to say.

He tried to get a look at her face, to give himself a clue, but she had clasped her head against his chest so that all he could see was the black disorder of her hair; she was waiting for him to speak first. He rolled his head a little and found he was looking through a crooked opening of the window blind, which she had managed to raise a few inches before falling into his arms. He studied the weathered brick cornice of a house across the street, whose chimney pots and television aerials made intricate silhouettes against the vibrant blue of the sky. From somewhere high and far away came the faint crawling drone of a plane. He looked the other way, into the room where everything—Picasso prints, Book-of-the-Month Club selections, sling chair, mantelpiece bristling with snapshots—everything swam in the vivid yellow light; and his first consecutive thought was that his flung coat and shirt were lying over there, near the chair, and his shoes and pants and underwear were here, closer at hand. He could be up and dressed and out of this place in thirty seconds.

"Well," he said at last, "I guess this wasn't exactly what you had in mind when you went to work this morning, was it?"

The silence continued, so complete that he was aware for the first time of the ticking of an alarm clock in the next room. Then:

"No," she said. "It certainly wasn't." And she quickly sat up. She groped for the royal blue sweater and snatched it up to cover herself. Then, hesitating, she seemed to decide that modesty could hardly be said to matter any more, and let it drop; but in a flurry of embarrassment she picked it up again, evidently wondering if this wasn't exactly the kind of a time when modesty mattered most, and covered her breasts with it again and crossed her arms over it. Her hair was as unattractively wild now as it must have been in childhood; it seemed to have exploded upward from her skull into hundreds of little kinks. She touched it delicately with her fingertips in several places, not in any effort to smooth it but rather in the furtive, half-conscious way that he himself had sometimes touched his pimples at sixteen, just to make sure the horrible things were still there. Her face and neck were pale but a deep red blush had begun to mottle both her cheeks, as if she'd been slapped, and she looked so vulnerable that for a second or two he was certain he could read her thoughts. What would Norma say? Would Norma be appalled at her for having been so easy to get? No; surely Norma's feeling would be that in a really adult, really sophisticated affair it was hopelessly banal to think in such terms as being "easy" or "hard" to "get." Yes, but still, if it was as adult and sophisticated as all that, why couldn't she decide what to do with her sweater? Why was she having such an awful time thinking of what in the world she could possibly *say* to the man?

Finally she composed herself. She lifted her chin as if to toss back a smooth, heavy lock of hair and willed her face into a drawing-room comedy smile, looking him straight in the eyes for the first time.

"Do you have a cigarette, Frank?"

"Sure. Here." And at last, mercifully, the dialogue began to flow.

"What was the name of that department you invented?"

"Mm?"

"You know. The place you told her we'd be. Mrs. Jorgensen."

"Oh. Visual Aids. I didn't really invent it. There used to be something called that, down on I think the eighth floor. Don't worry, though, she'll never figure it out."

"It does sound wonderfully real. Visual Aids. Excuse me a sec, Frank." And she skittered across the apartment, crouching awkwardly as if that would make her less naked, into the room where the alarm clock ticked.

When she came out, wearing a floor-length dressing gown and with her hair almost completely restored to its former shape, she found him fully dressed and politely inspecting the snapshots on the mantelpiece, like a visitor who hasn't yet been asked to sit down. She showed him where the bathroom was, and when he came back she had straightened up the couch and was moving indecisively around the kitchenette.

"Can I get you a drink or anything?"

"No thanks, Maureen. Actually, I guess I'd better be cutting out. It's getting kind of late."

"Gee, that's right, it is. Have you missed your train?"

"That's all right. I'll get the next one."

"It's a shame you have to rush off." She seemed determined to be calm and dignified, and she carried it off with elegance until the moment of her opening the door for him, when her eyes strayed to the corner near the couch and discovered that something flimsy and white, a brassiere or a garter belt, had been overlooked in her straightening-up and still lay twisted on the carpet. She started, visibly fighting an impulse to run over and grab it and stuff it behind the cushions—or possibly tear it to shreds—and when she turned back to him her eyes were pitiably wide and bright.

It couldn't be avoided; he would have to put something into words. But the only honest thing he could say was that he'd never felt more grateful to anyone—to thank her—and he wondered if this mightn't have exactly the wrong effect, almost as if he were offering her money. Another idea occurred to him: he could be sad and tender; he could take her by the shoulders and say "Look, Maureen. There can't be any future in a thing like this." But then she might say "Oh, I know," and hide her face in his coat, and that would leave him nothing to say but "I don't want to think I've taken any kind of unfair advantage here; if I have, well, I'm—" and that was the trouble. He would have to say "I'm sorry," and the last thing he wanted to do—the very last thing in God's world he wanted to do was apologize. Did the swan apologize to Leda? Did an eagle apologize? Did a lion apologize? Hell, no.

What he did instead was to smile at her—a subtle, worldly, attractive smile—and hold his face in that position until she falteringly smiled back. Then he bent and kissed her lightly on the lips and said, "Listen: you were swell. Take care, now."

He was down the stairs and out on the street and walking; before he'd gone half a block he had broken into an exultant run, and he ran all the way to Fifth Avenue. Once he had to swerve to keep from stepping into a baby carriage, and a woman shouted "Can't you watch where you're going?" but he refused, no less than an eagle or a lion would have refused, to look back. He felt like a man.

Could a man ride home in the rear smoker, primly adjusting his pants at the knees to protect their crease and rattling his evening paper into a narrow panel to give his neighbor elbow room? Could a man sit meekly massaging his headache and allowing himself to be surrounded by the chatter of beaten, amiable husks of men who sat and swayed and played bridge in a stagnant smell of newsprint and tobacco and bad breath and overheated radiators?

Hell, no. The way for a man to ride was erect and out in the open, out in the loud iron passageway where the wind whipped his necktie, standing with his feet set wide apart on the shuddering, clangoring floorplates, taking deep pulls from a pinched cigarette until its burning end was a needle of fire and quivering paper ash and then snapping it straight as a bullet into the roaring speed of the roadbed, while the suburban towns wheeled slowly along the pink and gray dust of seven o'clock. And when he came to his own station, the way for a man to alight was to swing down the iron steps and leap before the train had stopped, to land running and slow down to an easy, athletic stride as he made for his parked automobile.

The curtains were drawn in the picture window. He saw that from the road before he'd reached the driveway; then, when he'd made the turn, he saw April come running from the kitchen door and stand waiting for him in the carport. She was wearing her black cocktail dress, ballet slippers, and a very small apron of crisp white gauze that he'd never seen before. And he'd barely had time to switch off the ignition before she wrenched open the car and took hold of his forearm with both hands, talking. Her hands were thinner and more nervous than Maureen Grube's; she was taller and older and used a completely different kind of perfume, and she spoke more rapidly in a higher-pitched voice.

"Frank, listen. Before you come in I've got to talk to you. It's terribly important."

"What?"

"Oh, so many things. First of all I missed you all day and I'm terribly sorry for everything and I love you. The rest can wait. Now come on inside."

If he'd had a year to devote to it and nothing else to do, he couldn't for the life of him have sorted out and weighed the emotions that filled him in the two or three seconds of his lumbering to the kitchen steps with April fastened to his arm.

It was like walking through a sandstorm; it was like walking on the ocean floor; it was like walking on air. And this was the funny part: for all the depth of his bafflement he couldn't help noticing that April's voice, different as it was, possessed a quality that made it oddly similar to Maureen Grube's voice telling of the fabulous people Norma knew, or saying "Visual Aids"—a quality of play-acting, of slightly false intensity, a way of seeming to speak less to him than to some romantic abstraction.

"Wait here, my darling," she was saying. "Just for a minute, till I call you," and she left him alone in the kitchen, where the hot brown smell of roasting beef brought tears to his eyes. She handed him an Old-Fashioned glass full of ice and whiskey and disappeared into the darkened living room from which, now, he could hear an ill-suppressed giggle of children and the scrape of a match.

"All right," she called. "Now."

They were at the table, and he looked into all three of their faces before he saw what it was that bathed them in a flickering yellow light. It was a cake with candles. Then came their slow, shrill singing:

"Hap-py birth-day to you . . ."

Jennifer's voice was the loudest and April's was the only one in tune when they took the high note—"Hap-py *birth*day, dear Dad-dy . . ." but Michael was doing the best he could, and his was the widest smile.

SEVEN

"FORGIVE YOU FOR *what*, April?" They were standing alone on the living room carpet, and she took a tentative step toward him.

"Oh, for everything," she said. "For everything. The way I was all weekend. The way I've been ever since I got mixed up in that awful play. Oh, I've got so much to tell you, and I've got the most wonderful *plan*, Frank. Listen."

But it wasn't easy to listen to anything over the outraged silence in his head. He felt like a monster. He had wolfed his dinner like a starving man and topped it off with seven cloying forkfuls of chocolate cake; he had repeatedly exclaimed, over the unwrapping of his birthday gifts, the very word he'd used to describe what Maureen Grube had been to him—"Swell ... Swell ..."—he had heard his children's bedtime prayers and tiptoed from their room; now he was allowing his wife to ask forgiveness, and at the same time, with a cold eye, he was discovering that she wasn't really very much to look at: she was too old and too tall and too intense.

He wanted to rush outdoors and make some dramatic atonement—smash his fist against a tree or run for miles, leaping stone walls, until he fell exhausted in a morass of mud and brambles. Instead he shut his eyes and reached out and drew her close against him, crushing her cocktail apron in a desperate embrace, letting all his torment dissolve in pressing and stroking the inward curve of her back while he urged his groaning, muttering mouth into her throat. "Oh, my lovely," he said. "Oh, my lovely girl."

"No, wait, listen. Do you know what I did all day? I missed you. And Frank, I've thought of the most wonderful—no, wait. I mean I love you and everything, but listen a minute. I—"

The only way to stop her talking and get her out of sight was to kiss her mouth; then the floor began to tilt at dangerous angles and they might have fallen into the coffee table if they hadn't

taken three tottering steps and gone over instead into the voluptuous safety of the sofa.

"Darling?" she whispered, fighting for breath. "I do love you
terribly, but don't you think we ought to—oh, no, don't stop.
Don't stop."

"Ought to what?"

"Ought to sort of try and get into the bedroom first. But not
if it makes you cross. We'll stay here if you like. I love you."

"No, you're right. We will." He forced himself up, dragging
her with him. "I better take a shower first, too."

"Oh, no, don't. Please don't take a shower. I won't let you."

"I've got to, April."

"Why?"

"Just because. I've got to." It took all his will to move one
heavy, swaying step at a time.

"I think you're terribly mean," she was saying, clinging to his
arm. "Terribly, terribly mean. Frank, did you like the presents?
Was the tie all right? I went to about fourteen different places
and none of them had any decent ties."

"It's a swell tie. It's the nicest tie I've ever had."

Under the stiff pelting of hot water, in which Maureen Grube
had become an adhesive second skin that only the most desperate
scrubbing would shed, he decided he would have to tell her. He
would soberly take hold of both her hands and say "Listen, April.
This afternoon I—"

He turned off all the hot water and turned up the cold, a thing
he hadn't done in years. The shock of it sent him dancing and
gasping but he made himself stay under it until he'd counted to
thirty, the way he used to do in the army, and he came out feeling
like a million dollars. Tell her? Why, of course he wasn't going
to tell her. What the hell would be the point of that?

"Oh, you look so clean," she said, whirling from the closet in
her best white nightgown. "You look so clean and peaceful.
Come sit beside me and let's talk a minute first, all right? Look
what I've got."

She had set a bottle of brandy and two glasses on the night
table, but it was a long time before he allowed her to pour it, or
to say anything else. When she did pull away from him, once, it

was only to remove the constriction of lace from her shoulders and let it fall away from her breasts, whose nipples were hardening and rising even before he covered them with his hands.

For the second time that day he discovered that the act of love could leave him speechless, and he hoped she would be willing to let the talking wait for tomorrow. He knew that whatever she had to say would be said with that odd, theatrical emphasis, and he didn't feel equipped to deal with it just now. All he wanted was to lie here smiling in the dark, confused and guilty and happy, and submit to the gathering weight of sleep.

"Darling?" Her voice sounded very far away. "Darling? You're not going to sleep, are you? Because I do have so much to say and we're letting the brandy go to waste and I haven't even had a chance to tell you about my plan."

After a minute he found it easy to stay awake, if only for the pleasure of sitting with her under the double cloak of a blanket, sipping brandy in the moonlight and hearing the rise and fall of her voice. Play-acting or not, her voice in moods of love had always been a pretty sound. At last, with some reluctance, he began to pay attention to what she was saying.

Her plan, the idea born of her sorrow and her missing him all day and her loving him, was an elaborate new program for going to Europe "for good" in the fall. Did he realize how much money they had? With their savings, with the proceeds from the sale of house and car and with what they could save between now and September, they'd have enough to live comfortably for six months. "And it won't take anything like six months before we're established and self-supporting again for as long as we like—that's the best part."

He cleared his throat. "Look, baby. In the first place, what kind of a job could I possibly—"

"No kind of a job. Oh, I know you could get a job anywhere in the world if you had to, but that's not the point. The point is you won't be getting any kind of a job, because I will. Don't laugh—listen a minute. Have you any idea how much they pay for secretarial work in all these government agencies overseas? NATO and the ECA and those places? And do you realize how low the cost of living is, compared to here?" She had it all figured out; she had read an article in a magazine. Her skills at typing and shorthand would bring them enough to live on and more— enough for a part-time servant to take care of the children while she worked. It was, she insisted, such a marvelously simple plan that she was amazed at having never thought of it before. But she had to keep interrupting herself, with mounting impatience, to tell him not to laugh.

This laughter of his was not quite genuine, nor was the way he kept squeezing her shoulder as if to dismiss the whole thing as an endearing whimsy. He was trying to conceal from her, if not from himself, that the plan had instantly frightened him.

"I'm serious about this, Frank," she said. "Do you think I'm kidding or something?"

"No, I know. I just have a couple of questions, is all. For one thing, what exactly am I supposed to be doing while you're out earning all this dough?"

She drew back and tried to examine his face in the dim light, as if she couldn't believe he had failed to understand. "Don't you see? Don't you see that's the whole idea? You'll be doing what you should've been allowed to do seven years ago. You'll be find- ing yourself. You'll be reading and studying and taking long walks and thinking. You'll have *time.* For the first time in your life you'll have time to find out what it is you want to do, and when you find it you'll have the time and the freedom to start doing it."

And that, he knew as he chuckled and shook his head, was what he'd been afraid she would say. He had a quick disquieting vision of her coming home from a day at the office—wearing a Parisian tailored suit, briskly pulling off her gloves—coming home and finding him hunched in an egg-stained bathrobe, on an unmade bed, picking his nose.

"Look," he began. He let his hand slide off her shoulder and work its way up under her arm to fondle the shape and light weight of her breast. "In the first place, all this is very sweet and very—"

"It's not 'sweet'!" She pronounced the word as if it were the quintessence of everything she despised, and she caught at his hand and threw it down as if it were despicable too. "For God's sake, Frank, I'm not being 'sweet.' I'm not making any big altruistic sacrifice—can't you see that?"

"Okay; okay; it's not sweet. Don't get sore. Whatever it is, though, I think you'll have to agree it isn't very realistic; that's all I meant."

"In order to agree with that," she said, "I'd have to have a very strange and very low opinion of reality. Because you see I happen to think *this* is unrealistic. I think it's unrealistic for a man with a fine mind to go on working like a dog year after year at a job he can't stand, coming home to a house he can't stand in a place he can't stand either, to a wife who's equally unable to stand the same things, living among a bunch of frightened little— my God, Frank, I don't have to tell you what's wrong with this environment—I'm practically *quoting* you. Just last night when the Campbells were here, remember what you said about the whole idea of suburbia being to keep reality at bay? You said everybody wanted to bring up their children in a bath of sentimentality. You said—"

"I know what I said. I didn't think you were listening, though. You looked sort of bored."

"I *was* bored. That's part of what I'm trying to say. I don't think I've ever been more bored and depressed and fed up in my life than I was last night. All that business about Helen Givings's son on top of everything else, and the way we all grabbed at it like dogs after meat; I remember looking at you and thinking 'God, if only he'd stop talking.' Because everything you said was based on this great premise of ours that we're somehow very special and superior to the whole thing, and I wanted to say 'But we're not! Look at us! We're just like the people you're talking about! We *are* the people you're talking about!' I sort of had—I don't know, contempt for you, because you couldn't see the terrific fallacy of the thing. And then this morning when you left, when you were backing the car around down at the turn, I saw you look back up at the house as if it was going to bite you. You looked so miserable I started to cry, and then I started feeling lonely as hell and I thought, Well, how *did* everything get so awful then? If it's not his fault, whose fault is it? How did we ever get *into* this strange little dream world of

the Donaldsons and the Cramers and the Wingates—oh yes, and
the Campbells, too, because another thing I figured out today
is that both those Campbells are a big, big, big, colossal waste of
time. And it suddenly began to dawn on me—honestly, Frank, it
was like a revelation or something—I was standing there in the
kitchen and it suddenly began to dawn on me that it's my fault.
It's always been my fault, and I can tell you when it began.
I can tell you the exact moment in time when it began. Don't
interrupt me."

But he knew better than to interrupt her now. She must have
spent the morning in an agony of thought, pacing up and down
the rooms of a dead-silent, dead-clean house and twisting her
fingers at her waist until they ached; she must have spent the
afternoon in a frenzy of action at the shopping center, lurching
her car imperiously through mazes of NO LEFT TURN signs and
angry traffic cops, racing in and out of stores to buy the birthday
gifts and the roast of beef and the cake and the cocktail apron.
Her whole day had been a heroic build-up for this moment of
self-abasement; now it was here, and she was damned if she'd
stand for any interference.

"It was way back on Bethune Street," she said. "It was when
I first got pregnant with Jennifer and told you I was going to—
you know abort it, abort her. I mean up until that moment you
didn't want a baby any more than I did—why *should* you have?—
but when I went out and bought that rubber syringe I put the
whole burden of the thing on you. It was like saying, All right,
then, if you want this baby it's going to be All Your Responsibility. You're going to have to turn yourself inside out to provide
for us. You'll have to give up any idea of being anything in the
world but a father. Oh, Frank, if only you'd given me what
I deserved—if only you'd called me a bitch and turned your back
on me, you could've called my bluff in a minute. I'd probably
never have gone through with the thing—I probably wouldn't
have had the courage, for one thing—but you didn't. You were
too good and young and scared; you played right along with it,
and that's how the whole thing started. That's how we both got
committed to this enormous delusion—because that's what it is,
an enormous, obscene delusion—this idea that people have to

resign from real life and 'settle down' when they have families. It's the great sentimental lie of the suburbs, and I've been making you subscribe to it all this time. I've been making you *live* by it! My God, I've even gone as far as to work up this completely corny, soap-opera picture of myself—and I guess this is what really brought it home to me—this picture of myself as the girl who could have been The Actress if she hadn't gotten married too young. And I mean you know perfectly well I was never any kind of an actress and never really wanted to be; you know I only went to the Academy to get away from home, and I know it too. I've always known it. And here for three months I've been walking around with this noble, bittersweet expression on my face—I mean how self-deluded can you get? Do you see how neurotic all this is? I wanted to have it both ways. It wasn't enough that I'd spoiled your life; I wanted to bring the whole monstrous thing full-circle and make it seem that you'd spoiled mine, so I could end up being the victim. Isn't that awful? But it's true! It's true!"

And at each "true!" she thumped a tight little fist on her naked knee. "Now do you see what you have to forgive me for? And why we have to get out of here and over to Europe as fast as we possibly can? It isn't a case of my being 'sweet' or generous or anything else. *I'm* not doing you any favors. All I'm giving you is what you've always been entitled to, and I'm only sorry it has to come so late."

"All right. Can I talk now?"

"Yes. You do understand, though, don't you? And could I have a little more of the brandy? Just a splash—that's fine. Thanks." When she'd sipped at it she threw back her hair, allowing the blanket to slide from her shoulders, and drew a little away from him in order to sit back against the wall, tucking her legs up beneath her. She looked wholly relaxed and confident, ready to listen, happy in the knowledge that she'd stated her case. The blue-white luminescence of her body was a powerful force; he knew he wouldn't be able to think straight if he looked at her, so he willed himself to look at the moonlit floor between his feet, and he took longer than necessary over the lighting of a cigarette, stalling for time. He would have to get his bearings. When she came home to the Paris apartment her spike-heeled pumps would click decisively on the tile floor and her hair would be pulled back into a neat bun; her face would be drawn with fatigue so that the little vertical line between her eyes would show, even when she smiled. On the other hand . . .

"In the first place," he said at last, "I think you're being much too hard on yourself. Nothing's ever that black and white. You didn't force me to take the job at Knox. Besides, look at it this way. You say you've always known you weren't really an actress, and therefore it's not too legitimate for you to go around feeling cheated. Well, let's face it: isn't it just possible the same thing applies to me? I mean who ever said I was supposed to be a big deal?"

"I don't know what you mean," she said calmly. "I think it might be rather tiresome if you *were* a big deal. But if you mean who ever said you were exceptional, if you mean who ever said you had a first-rate, original mind—well my God, Frank, the answer is everybody. When I first met you, you were—"

"Oh, hell, I was a little wise guy with a big mouth. I was showing off a lot of erudition I didn't have. I was—"

"You were not! How can you talk that way? Frank, has it gotten so bad that you've lost all your belief in yourself?"

Well, no; he had to admit it hadn't gotten quite that bad. Besides, he was afraid he could detect a note of honest doubt in her voice—a faint suggestion that it might be possible to persuade her he *had* been a little wise guy, after all—and this was distressing.

"Okay," he conceded. "Okay, let's say I was a promising kid. The point is there were plenty of promising kids at Columbia; that doesn't necessarily mean—"

"There weren't plenty like you," she said, sounding reassured. "I'll never forget what's-his-name, you know? The one you always admired so much? The one who'd been the fighter pilot and had all the girls? Bill Croft. I'll never forget the way he used to talk about you. He said to me once: 'If I had half that guy's brains I'd quit worrying.' And he meant it! Everybody knew there was nothing in the world you couldn't do or be if you only had a chance to find yourself. Anway, all that's beside the point.

You wouldn't have to be the least bit exceptional, and this would still be a thing that has to be done. Don't you see that?"

"Will you let me finish? In the first place . . ." But instead of allowing his voice to run on he felt a need to be quiet for a minute. He took a deep drink of brandy, letting it burn the roof of his mouth and send out waves of warmth across his shoulders and down his spine as he solemnly stared at the floor.

Had Bill Croft really said that?

"Everything you say might make a certain amount of sense," he began again, and one of the ways he could tell he was losing the argument was that his voice had taken on a resonance that made it every bit as theatrical as hers. It was the voice of a hero, a voice befitting the kind of person Bill Croft could admire. "Might make a certain amount of sense if I had some definite, measurable talent. If I were an artist, say, or a writer, or a—"

"Oh, Frank. Can you really think artists and writers are the only people entitled to lives of their own? Listen: I don't care if it takes you five years of doing nothing at all; I don't care if you decide after five years that what you really want is to be a brick-layer or a mechanic or a merchant seaman. Don't you see what I'm saying? It's got nothing to do with definite, measurable talents—it's your very *essence* that's being stifled here. It's what you *are* that's being denied and denied and denied in this kind of life."

"And what's that?" For the first time he allowed himself to look at her—not only to look but to put down his glass and take hold of her leg, and she covered and pressed his hand with both of her own.

"Oh, don't you know?" She brought his hand gently up her hip and around to the flat of her abdomen, where she pressed it close again. "Don't you know? You're the most valuable and wonderful thing in the world. You're a man."

And of all the capitulations in his life, this was the one that seemed most like a victory. Never before had elation welled more powerfully inside him; never had beauty grown more purely out of truth; never in taking his wife had he triumphed more completely over time and space. The past could dissolve at his will and so could the future; so could the walls of this house and the whole imprisoning wasteland beyond it, towns and trees. He had taken command of the universe because he was a man, and because the marvelous creature who opened and moved for him, tender and strong, was a woman.

At the first bright, hesitant calls of awakening birds, when the massed trees were turning from gray to olive green in a rising mist, she gently touched his lips with her fingertips.

"Darling? We really are going to do it, aren't we? I mean it hasn't just been a lot of talk or anything, has it?"

He was on his back, taking pleasure in the slow rise and fall of his own chest, which felt broad and deep and muscled enough to fill the modeling of a medieval breastplate. Was there anything he couldn't do? Was there any voyage he couldn't undertake and any prize in life he couldn't promise her?

"No," he said.

"Because I mean I'd like to get started on it right away. Tomorrow. Writing letters and whatnot, and seeing about the passports. And I think we ought to tell Niffer and Mike about it right away too, don't you? They'll need a little time to get used to it, and besides, I want them to know before anybody else. Don't you?"

"Yes."

"But I mean I don't want to tell them unless you're absolutely sure."

"I'm absolutely sure."

"That's wonderful. Oh darling, look at the time. And it's practically light outside. You'll be dead tired."

"No I won't. I can sleep on the train. I can sleep at the office. It's all right."

"All right. I love you."

And they fell asleep like children.

PART TWO

ONE

THERE NOW BEGAN a time of such joyous derangement, of such exultant carelessness, that Frank Wheeler could never afterwards remember how long it lasted. It could have been a week or two weeks or more before his life began to come back into focus, with its customary concern for the passage of time and its anxious need to measure and apportion it; and by then, looking back, he was unable to tell how long it had been otherwise. The only day that would always stand clear and sharp in his memory was the first one, the day after his birthday.

He did sleep on the train, riding with his head fallen back on the dusty plush and his *Times* sliding from his lap; and he stood for a long time over scalding cups of coffee in the echoing tan vault of Grand Central, allowing himself to be late for work. How small and neat and comically serious the other men looked, with their gray-flecked crew cuts and their button-down collars and their brisk little hurrying feet! There were endless desperate swarms of them, hurrying through the station and the streets, and an hour from now they would all be still. The waiting midtown office buildings would swallow them up and contain them, so that to stand in one tower looking out across the canyon to another would be to inspect a great silent insectarium displaying hundreds of tiny pink men in white shirts, forever shifting papers and frowning into telephones, acting out their passionate little dumb show under the supreme indifference of the rolling spring clouds.

In the meantime, Frank Wheeler's coffee was delicious, his paper napkin was excellently white and dry, and the grand-motherly woman who served him was so courteous and so clearly pleased with the rhythm of her own efficiency ("Yes, sir, thank *you* sir; will that be all, sir?") that he wanted to lean over and press a kiss into her wrinkled cheek. By the time he reached the office he had passed into that euphoria of half-refreshed exhaustion in which all sounds are muffled, all sights are blurred and every task is easy.

First things first: and the first thing he had to do, when the elevator door slid open at the Fifteenth Floor, was to walk up and deal like a man with Maureen Grube. She was alone at her reception desk, in a dark suit that she'd probably worn because it was the most severe, least provocative thing in her wardrobe, and when she saw him coming she looked badly flustered. But his smile was so expert—not the least bit furtive or the least bit vain, a perfectly open, friendly smile—that he could see the assurance come back into her face before he got to the desk. Had she been afraid he would think her a tramp? That he'd spend the day whispering and chuckling about her with the other men? If so, the smile told her she could relax. Had she been afraid, on the other hand, that he would try to make a big romantic thing out of it? That he'd embarrass the life out of her with messy little importunings in corners ("I've got to see you . . .")? The smile told her she could stop worrying about that, too; and these two possibilities, for the moment, were the only ones that seemed likely enough to bother with.

"Hi," he said kindly. "You have any trouble about yesterday? With Mrs. Jorgensen, I mean?"

"No. She didn't say anything." She seemed to be having some difficulty in meeting his eyes; she was looking mostly at the knot of his tie. Standing there and smiling down at her, with the constant hum and bustle of people milling just out of earshot in the dry lake beyond them, he could easily have been stopping to pass the time of day or to ask her about a typing job; there was nothing in his face or his stance to arouse the curiosity of onlookers. Yet at close range, from where she sat, he knew there could be no doubt of his intimate sincerity.

"Look, Maureen," he began. "If I thought there was anything to be gained by it, for either of us, I'd say let's go somewhere this afternoon and have a talk. And if you want to, if there's anything at all you want to tell me or ask me, that's what we'll do. Is there?"

"No. Except that I—well, no. There isn't really. You're right."

"It isn't a question of being 'right.' I don't want you to think I'm—well, never mind. But listen: the important thing in a thing like this is not to have any regrets. I don't; I hope you don't, and if you do I hope you'll tell me."

"No," she said. "I don't."

"I'm glad. And listen: You're swell, Maureen. If there's ever anything I can—you know, do for you or anything, I hope you'll let me know. I guess that sounds sort of crummy. All I mean is that I'd like us to be friends."

"All right," she said. "So would I."

And he walked away up the aisle of cubicles, moving slowly and confidently in a new, more mature version of the old "ter-rifically sexy walk" of Bethune Street. As simple as that! If he'd spent days planning and rehearsing it, filling page after page of scratch paper with revised and crossed-out sentences, he could never have come up with a more dignified, more satisfactory speech. And all on the spur of the moment! Was there anything in the world he couldn't do?

"Morning, Dad," he said to Jack Ordway.

"Franklin, my son. How good to see your shining morning face."

But first things first; and the next thing now was his IN basket. No; it was the batch of papers he'd dropped on the middle of his desk yesterday, the things Maureen had pulled from the central file, which brought up the whole disorderly problem of the branch manager in Toledo and the production control brochure. Was he going to let a thing like that harass him? Certainly not.

"Intra-company letter to Toledo," he said into the mouth-piece of his Dictaphone, leaning back in his swivel chair and working his foot into its wooden saddle on the drawer edge. "Attention B. F. Chalmers, branch manager. Subject: NAPE conference. Paragraph. With regard to recent and previous cor-respondence, this is to advise that the matter has been very satisfactorily taken in hand, period, paragraph."

He went that far without any idea of how the matter was going to be taken in hand, if at all; but as he sat fingering the mouth-piece he began to get ideas, and soon he was intoning one smooth sentence after another, pausing only to smile in satisfaction. The branch manager in Toledo was turning out to be as easy to handle as Maureen Grube.

F. H. Wheeler, or "we," wholly agreed that the existing brochure was unsuitable. Fortunately, the problem had now been solved in a way which "we" were confident would meet with the branch manager's approval. As the branch manager doubtless knew, the NAPE delegates would be given dozens of competitive promotion brochures, most of which were certain to end up in the wastebaskets of the convention floor. The problem, then, was to develop something different for Knox—something that would catch the delegate's eye, that he would want to put in his pocket and take back to his hotel room. Just such a piece was now in production, designed specifically for the NAPE conference: a brief, straightforward sales message entitled "Speaking of Production Control." As the branch manager would see, this document relied on no slick format, no fancy artwork or advertising jargon to tell its story. Crisply printed in large, easy-to-read type, in black and white, it had all the immediacy of plain talk. It would "give the NAPE delegate nothing more or less than what he wants, colon: the facts."

After putting a new belt in the Dictaphone machine, he leaned back again and said, "Copy for Veritype. Heading: Speaking of Production Control, dot, dot, dot. Paragraph. Production control is, comma, after all, comma, nothing more or less than the job of putting the right materials in the right place at the right time, comma, according to a varying schedule. Period, paragraph. This is simple arithmetic, period. Given all the variables, comma, a man can do it with a pencil and paper, period. But the Knox '500' Electronic Computer can do it—dash—literally—dash—thousands of times faster, period. That's why . . ."

"Coming down for coffee, Franklin?"

"I guess not, Jack. I better finish this thing."

And he did finish it, though it took him all morning. Fingering through the papers from the central file with his free hand, lifting a sentence here and a paragraph there, he continued to recite into the Dictaphone until he'd explained all the advantages of using a computer to coordinate the details of factory production. It sounded very authoritative when he played it back ("Once the bill of materials has been exploded," he heard his own voice saying, "the computer's next step is to scan the updated parts inventory"). No one could have told that he didn't quite know what he was talking about. When the typescript came back he would polish it up—maybe he'd have it checked over by one of the technical men, just to be safe—and then he'd have it Veri-typed and sent to Toledo in the required number of copies. For self-protection he would send one copy to Bandy, with a note saying "Hope this is okay—Toledo wanted something short & sweet for the NAPE thing," and with luck he'd be off the hook. In the meantime he could safely remove all the troublesome Toledo correspondence from the stack of things he couldn't bring him-self to face just now, and put it in his OUT basket marked "File," along with all the brochure material.

This made such a surprising reduction in the clutter of his desk that he was encouraged, after lunch, to tackle two or three other matters in the stack of things he couldn't face. One of them involved a ticklish letter explaining why "we" had allowed an obsolete model of adding-machine demonstrator to be shipped to the Chicago Business Fair, and he made it an airtight master-piece of evasion; another, a thick sheaf of letters that he'd been avoiding for weeks, turned out to be much simpler than he'd thought in that it all boiled down to a decision left squarely up to him. Should solid-gold tie clasps ($14.49) or solid-gold lapel buttons ($8.98) be offered as the prizes in a quota-breaking con-test among the tabulating-equipment salesmen of Minneapolis-St. Paul? Tie clasps! And into the OUT basket it went.

He was a demon of energy; and it wasn't until four o'clock, walking blearily to the water cooler ("Watch the big bubble come up—Blurp!—Isn't that funny?") that he realized why. It was because April had left a small pocket of guilt in his mind last night by saying that he'd "worked like a dog year after year." He had meant to point out that whatever it was he'd been doing here year after year, it could hardly be called working like a dog—but she hadn't given him a chance. And now, by trying to clear all the papers off his desk in one day, he guessed he was trying to make up for having misled her. But what kind of nonsense was that? How could it possibly matter what he'd been doing here year after year, or what she thought he'd been doing, or what he thought she thought he'd been doing? None of it mattered any more; couldn't he get that through his head? And as he stumbled back from the water cooler, wiping his cold mouth with a warm hand, he began to understand for the first time that in another few months he would leave this place forever. All of it—lights, glass partitions, chattering typewriters—the whole slow, dry agony of this place would be cut away from his life like a tumor from his brain; and good riddance.

His final act of that day in the office involved no work at all and very little energy, though it did take a certain amount of courage. He opened the big bottom drawer of his desk, carefully lifted out the whole stack of Real Goodies—it weighed as much as a couple of telephone books—and tipped it into the wastebasket.

For an indeterminate number of days after that, the office all but vanished from his consciousness. He went through the motions, shuffling his papers, having conferences with Bandy, having lunch with Ordway and the others, smiling with dignity whenever he passed Maureen Grube in the corridors and even stopping to chat with her now and then, to show that they were friends—but the fact was that the daytime had ceased to have any meaning except as a period of rest and preparation for the evening.

He never seemed to come fully awake until the moment he swung down from the train at sunset and climbed into his station car. Then came the stimulation of drinks with April, while the children lay silenced by television, and then the pleasure of dinner, which in conversational intensity was very like the dinners they'd had before they were married. But the day didn't really begin until later still, when the children were in bed with their door firmly shut for the night. Then they would take their places in the living room—April curled attractively on the sofa, usually, and Frank standing with his back to the bookcase, each with a cup of black Italian coffee and a cigarette—and give way to their love affair.

He would begin to pace slowly around and around the room as he talked, and she would follow him with her eyes, often with the tilt of her whole head and shoulders. From time to time when he felt he'd made a trenchant point he would wheel and stare at her in triumph; then it would be her turn to talk, while he walked and nodded, and when her turn was over their looks would meet exultantly again. Sometimes there was a glint of humor in these embraces of the eye: I know I'm showing off, they seemed to say, but so are you, and I love you.

And what did it matter? The very substance of their talk, after all, the message and the rhyme of it, whatever else they might be saying, was that they were going to be new and better people from now on. April, tucked up on the sofa with her skirt arranged in a graceful whirl from waist to ankle, her tall neck very white in the soft light and her face held in perfect composure, bore hardly any resemblance to the stiff, humiliated actress who had stood in the curtain call—and still less to the angrily sweating wife who had hauled the lawnmower, or to the jaded matron who had endured the evening of false friendship with the Campbells, or to the embarrassed, embarrassingly ardent woman who had welcomed him to his birthday party. Her voice was subtle and low, as low as in the first act of *The Petrified Forest*, and when she tipped back her head to laugh or leaned forward to reach out and tap the ash from her cigarette, she made it a maneuver of classic beauty. Anyone could picture her conquering Europe.

And Frank was modestly aware that something of the same kind of change was taking place in himself. He knew for one thing that he had developed a new way of talking, slower and more deliberate than usual, deeper in tone and more fluent: he almost never had recourse to the stammering, apologetic little bridges ("No, but I mean—I don't know—*you* know—") that normally laced his speech, nor did his head duck and weave in the familiar nervous effort to make himself clear. Catching sight of his walking reflection in the black picture window, he had to admit that his appearance was not yet as accomplished as hers— his face was too plump and his mouth too bland, his pants too well pressed and his shirt too fussily Madison Avenue—but sometimes late at night when his throat had gone sore and his eyes hot from talking, when he hunched his shoulders and set his jaw and pulled his necktie loose and let it hang like a rope, he

could glare at the window and see the brave beginnings of a
personage.

It was a strange time for the children, too. What exactly did
going to France in the fall mean? And why did their mother keep
insisting it was going to be fun, as if daring them to doubt it? For
that matter, why was she so funny about a lot of things? In the
afternoons she would hug them and ask them questions in a rush
of ebullience that suggested Christmas Eve, and then her eyes
would go out of focus during their replies, and a minute later
she'd be saying "Yes, darling, but don't talk *quite* so much, okay?
Give Mommy a break."

Nor did their father's homecoming do much to help: he might
throw them high in the air and give them airplane rides around
the house until they were dizzy, but only after having failed to
see them altogether during the disturbingly long time it took him
to greet their mother at the kitchen door. And the talking at
dinner! It was hopeless for either child to try and get a word in
edgewise. Michael found he could jiggle in his chair, repeat baby
words over and over in a shrill idiot's monotone or stuff his
mouth with mashed potato and hang his jaws open, all without
any adult reproof; Jennifer would sit very straight at the table
and refuse to look at him, feigning great interest in whatever her
parents were saying, though afterwards, waiting for bedtime, she
would sometimes go off quietly by herself and suck her thumb.

There was one consolation: they could go to sleep without
any fear of being waked in an hour by the abrupt, thumping,
hard-breathing, door-slamming sounds of a fight; all that, apparently, was a thing of the past. They could lie drowsing now
under the sound of kindly voices in the living room, a sound
whose intricately rhythmic rise and fall would slowly turn into
the shape of their dreams. And if they came awake later to turn
over and reach with their toes for new cool places in the sheets,
they knew the sound would still be there—one voice very deep
and the other soft and pretty, talking and talking, as substantial
and soothing as a blue range of mountains seen from far away.

"This whole country's *rotten* with sentimentality," Frank said
one night, turning ponderously from the window to walk the

carpet. "It's been spreading like a disease for years, for generations, until now everything you touch is flabby with it."

"Exactly," she said, enraptured with him.

"I mean isn't that really what's the matter, when you get right
down to it? I mean even more than the profit motive or the loss
of spiritual values or the fear of the bomb or any of those things?
Or maybe it's the result of those things; maybe it's what happens
when all those things start working at once without any real
cultural tradition to absorb them. Anyway, whatever it's the
result of, *it's* what's killing the United States. I mean isn't it? This
steady, insistent vulgarizing of every idea and every emotion into
some kind of pre-digested intellectual baby food; this optimistic,
smiling-through, easy-way-out sentimentality in everybody's
view of life?"

"Yes," she said. "Yes."

"And I mean is it any wonder all the men end up emasculated?
Because that *is* what happens; that *is* what's reflected in all this
bleating about 'adjustment' and 'security' and 'togetherness'—
and I mean Christ, you see it everywhere: all this television crap
where every joke is built on the premise that daddy's an idiot
and mother's always on to him; and these loathsome little signs
people put up in their front yards—you ever notice those signs up
on the Hill?"

"The 'The' signs, you mean; with the people's name in the
plural? Like 'The Donaldsons'?"

"Right!" He turned and smiled down at her in triumphant
congratulation for having seen exactly what he meant. "Never
'Donaldson' or 'John J. Donaldson' or whatever the hell his name
is. Always 'The Donaldsons.' You picture the whole cozy little
bunch of them sitting around all snug as bunnies in their pajamas,
for God's sake, toasting marshmallows. I guess the Campbells
haven't put up a sign like that yet, but give 'em time. The rate
they're going now, they will." He paused here for a deep-
throated laugh. "And my God, when you think how close *we*
came to settling into that kind of an existence."

"But we didn't," she told him. "That's the important thing."

Another time, quite late, he walked up close to the sofa and
sat down on the edge of the coffee table, facing her. "You know

what this is like, April? Talking like this? The whole idea of taking off to Europe this way?" He felt tense and keyed up; the very act of sitting on a coffee table seemed an original and wonderful thing to do. "It's like coming out of a Cellophane bag. It's like having been encased in some kind of Cellophane for years without knowing it, and suddenly breaking out. It's a little like the way I felt going up to the line the first time, in the war. I remember acting very grim and scared because that was the fashionable way to act, but I couldn't really put my heart in it. I mean I was scared, of course, but that's not the point. What I really felt didn't have anything to do with being scared or not scared. I just felt this terrific sense of life. I felt full of blood. Everything looked realer than real; the snow on the fields, the road, the trees, the terrific blue sky all marked up with vapor trails—everything. And all the helmets and overcoats and rifles, and the way the guys were walking; I sort of loved them, even the guys I didn't like. And I remember being very conscious of the way my own body worked, and the sound of the breathing in my nose. I remember we went through this shelled-out town, all broken walls and rubble, and I thought it was beautiful. Hell, I was probably just as dumb and scared as anybody else, but inside I'd never felt better. I kept thinking: this is really true. This is the truth."

"I felt that way once too," she said, and in the shyness of her lips he saw that something overpoweringly tender was coming next.

"When?" He was as bashful as a schoolboy, unable to look her full in the face.

"The first time you made love to me."

The coffee table tipped absurdly and banged straight again, rattling its cups, as he moved from its edge to the edge of the sofa and took her in his arms; and the evening was over.

It wasn't until a good many such evenings had passed—until the time, in fact, when he had again begun to think in terms of time passing—that the first faint discordances crept into their talk.

Once he interrupted her to say, "Listen, why do we keep talking about Paris? Don't they have government agencies pretty much all over Europe? Why not Rome? Or Venice, or some place like Greece, even? I mean let's keep an open mind; Paris isn't the only place."

"Of course it isn't." She was impatiently brushing a fleck of ash off her lap. "But it does seem the most logical place to start, doesn't it? With the advantage of your knowing the language and everything?"

If he'd looked at the window at that moment he would have seen the picture of a frightened liar. The language! Had he ever really led her to believe he could speak French?

"Well," he said, chuckling and walking away from her, "I wouldn't be too sure about that. I've probably forgotten most of what little I knew, and I mean I never did know the language in the sense of—you know, being able to speak it fluently or any-thing; just barely enough to get by."

"That's all we'll need. You'll pick it up again in no time. We both will. And besides, at least you've been there. You know how the city's laid out and what the various neighborhoods are like; that's important."

And he silently assured himself that this, after all, was sub-stantially true. He knew where most of the picture-postcard landmarks were, on the strength of his several three-day passes in the city long ago; he also knew how to go from any of those places to where the American PX and Red Cross Club had once been established, and how to go from those points to the Place Pigalle, and how to choose the better kind of prostitute there and what her room would probably smell like. He knew those things, and he knew too that the best part of Paris, the part where the people really knew how to live, began around St. Germain des Prés and extended southeast (or was it southwest?) as far as the Café Dome. But this latter knowledge was based more on his reading of *The Sun Also Rises* in high school than in his real-life venturings into the district, which had mostly been lonely and footsore. He had admired the ancient delicacy of the buildings and the way the street lamps made soft explosions of light green in the trees at night, and the way each long, bright café awning would prove to reveal a sea of intelligently walking faces as he passed; but the white wine gave him a headache and the talking

faces all seemed, on closer inspection, to belong either to intimi-
dating men with beards or to women whose eyes could sum him
up and dismiss him in less than a second. The place had filled him
with a sense of wisdom hovering just out of reach, of unspeakable
grace prepared and waiting just around the corner, but he'd
walked himself weak down its endless blue streets and all the
people who knew how to live had kept their tantalizing secret
to themselves, and time after time he had ended up drunk and
puking over the tailgate of the truck that bore him jolting back
into the army.

Je suis, he practiced to himself while April went on talking; *tu
es; nous sommes; vous êtes; ils sont.*

". . . better once we get settled," she was saying, "don't you
think? You're not listening."

"Sure I am. No, I'm sorry, I guess I wasn't." And he sat down
on the coffee table, smiling with what he hoped was a disarming
candor. "I was just thinking that none of this is going to be easy—
taking off to a foreign country with the kids and all. I mean,
we'll be running into a lot of problems we can't even begin to
anticipate from this end."

"Well, certainly we will," she said. "And certainly it's not
going to be easy. Do you know anything worth doing that is?"

"Of course not. You're right. I'm just kind of tired tonight,
I guess. Would you like a drink?"

"No thanks."

He went to the kitchen and got one for himself, which brightened him; and there were no further difficulties until the next
night, or the next, when she made a startling disclosure about
how she'd spent her day.

He had assumed that she too would be lazy and absent-minded
in the daytime; he had pictured her taking long baths and devot-
ing whole hours to the bedroom mirror, trying on different
dresses and new ways of fixing her hair—perhaps leaving the
mirror only to waltz lightly away on the strains of imaginary
violins, whirling in a dream through the sunlit house and returning to smile over her shoulder at her own flushed image, and
then having to hurry to get the beds made and the rooms in
order in time for his homecoming. But it turned out that on this

particular day she had driven to New York right after breakfast, had undergone an interview and filled out a lengthy job application with an overseas employment office, had gone from there to make the necessary arrangements for their passports, had obtained three travel brochures and the schedules of half a dozen steamship companies and airlines, had bought two new traveling bags, a French dictionary, a street guide to Paris, a copy of *Babar the Elephant* for the children and a book called *Brighter French* ("For Bright People Who Already Know Some"), and had sped home and relieved the baby sitter just in time to get the dinner started and mix a pitcherful of martinis.

"Aren't you tired?"

"Not really. It was sort of invigorating. Do you realize how long it's been since I spent a day in town? I was going to pop into the office at lunchtime and surprise you, but there wasn't time. What's the matter?"

"Nothing. It just sort of throws me, that's all; the amount of stuff you can get done in one day. Pretty impressive."

"You're annoyed," she said, "aren't you. Oh, and I don't blame you." She puckered her face into what looked distressingly like the understanding simper of the wife in a television comedy. "It must seem as if I'm sort of taking over, doesn't it— taking charge of everything."

"No," he protested, "no, listen, don't be silly; I'm not annoyed. It doesn't matter."

"It does matter, though. It's like when I mow the lawn, or something. I *knew* I should've left the passports and the travel agent for you to handle, but I was right there in the neighborhood and it seemed silly not to stop in. Oh, but I *am* sorry."

"Look, will you cut it out? I'm going to start *getting* annoyed in a minute, if you keep on at this. Will you please forget it?"

"All right."

"This probably won't be much use to us," he said, fingering through the pages of *Brighter French*. "I mean, I think it's a little advanced."

"Oh, that. Yes, I guess it's sort of a supercilious little book; I just grabbed it in a hurry. That's another thing I should've left

for you to do. You're always much better at things like that than
I am."

It was the night after that when she told him, looking remorse-
ful, that she had some bad news. "I mean not really bad, but
annoying. First of all Mrs. Givings called up today and issued this
very formal invitation to dinner tomorrow night, and naturally
I said no; I said we couldn't get a baby sitter. Then she started
trying to pin me down for a night next week and I kept begging
off, until I realized we *are* going to have to see her soon anyway,
about putting the house on the market, so I said why didn't they
come *here* for dinner."

"Oh Jesus."

"No, don't worry, they're not coming—you know how she
is. She kept babbling about not wanting to put us to any
trouble—Lord, what a pain that woman can be—and I kept
insisting we did want to see her anyway, on business, and this
went on for half an hour until I finally worked her around to
saying she'd come over alone tomorrow night. So it'll be after
dinner, strictly business, and with any kind of luck we'll never
have to see her again except to sell the house."

"Fine."

"Yes, but here's the trouble. I'd completely forgotten we were
supposed to be going to the Campbells' tomorrow night. So
I called Milly and tried using the same lie about the baby sitter,
and she seemed—I don't know, really upset. You know how
Milly is sometimes? It's like dealing with a child. And the first
thing I knew she had me saying yes, we'd come tonight instead.
So there goes the weekend—Campbells tonight, Givings tomorrow. I'm awfully sorry, Frank."

"Hell, that's all right. Is that all you meant by bad news?"

"You're sure you don't mind?"

He didn't mind at all. In fact, he realized as he washed up
and changed his shirt, he was looking forward with eagerness to
telling the Campbells of the plan. A thing like this never really
seemed real until you'd told somebody about it.

"Listen, though, April," he said, stuffing in his shirttail.
"When we're breaking it to Mrs. Givings, there isn't any reason

why we have to tell her what we're going to *do* in Europe, is there? I mean I think she thinks I'm enough of a creep as it is."

"Of course not." She looked surprised at the very idea of telling Mrs. Givings anything at all beyond the simple fact of their wish to sell the house. "What possible business is it of hers? There's no need to tell the Campbells either, for that matter."

"Oh no," he said quickly, "we have to tell them—" and he almost said, "They're our *friends*" before he caught himself. "I mean, *you* know; of course we don't have to. But why not?"

TWO

SHEPPARD SEARS CAMPBELL loved to shine his shoes. It was a love he had learned in the army (he was a veteran of three campaigns with a famous airborne division) and even now, though civilian cordovans were far less rewarding than the heavy jump boots of the old days, the acrid smell and crouching vigor of the job held rich associations of *esprit de corps*. He sang a kind of old time, big-band swing while he did it, alternating the husky lyrics with a squint-eyed, loose-lipped sound—Buddappa banh! Banh! Banh!"—to simulate the brass section, and now and then he would pause to take a swig from the can of beer that stood on the floor beside him. Then he would stretch his back, scratch the yellowed armpits of his T-shirt and permit himself a long and satisfying belch.

"What time the Wheelers coming, doll?" he asked his wife, who was studying herself, sensibly, in the mirror of her flounced dressing table.

"Eight-thirty, sweetie."

"Jesus," he said. "If I want to get a shower, I better haul ass." Squinting, he flexed the toes in his right shoe to test its gleam before he crouched again, snapped his rag, and went to work on the left one.

The stolid peasant's look that glazed his face as he worked was only an occasional expression with Shep Campbell nowadays—he saved it for his shoe-shining mood or his tire-changing mood—but it held the vestige of a force that had once laid claim to the whole of his heart. For years, boy and man, he had yearned above all to be insensitive and ill-bred, to hold his own among the sullen boys and men whose real or imagined jeers had haunted his childhood, to deny by an effort of will what for a long time had been the most shameful facts of his life: that he'd been raised in a succession of brownstone and penthouse apartments in the vicinity of Sutton Place, schooled by private tutors and allowed

to play with other children only under the smiling eye of his
English nanny or his French ma'm'selle, and that his wealthily
divorced mother had insisted, until he was eleven years old, on
dressing him every Sunday in "adorable" tartan kilts that came
from Bergdorf Goodman.

"She woulda made a God damn *lollypop* outa me!" he sometimes ranted even now, to the few friends with whom he could
bring himself to talk about his mother, but in calmer, wiser
moments he had long since found the compassion to forgive her.
Nobody's parents were perfect; and besides, whatever her intentions might have been, he knew she'd never really had a chance.
From earliest adolescence, from the time his child's physique
began to coarsen into the slope-shouldered build of a wrestler, if
not before, he had been lost forever to her fluttering grasp. Anything in the world that could even faintly be connected with
what his mother called "cultivated" or "nice" was anathema to
Shep Campbell in those formative years, and everything she
called "vulgar" was his heart's desire. At his small and expensive
prep school he found it easy to become the ill-dressed, hell-
raising lout of the student body, feared and admired and vaguely
pitied on the assumption that he was one of the charity boys;
after being expelled in his senior year he moved straight, to his
mother's horror, into the swarm of a Manhattan high school,
and into minor scrapes with the police, until the arrival of his
eighteenth birthday sent him whooping and hollering into the
paratroops, resolved to acquit himself not only with conspicuous
bravery but with that other attribute so highly prized by soldiers,
the quality of being a tough son of a bitch.

He made the grade on both counts, and the war seemed only
to deepen the urgency of his quest. Afterwards it seemed entirely
logical for him to shrug off all his mother's tearful arguments for
Princeton or Williams and go slouching away instead to a third-
rate institute of technology in the Middle West ("On the G.I.
Bill," he had always explained, as if any possibility of private
means would have made him effete). There, dozing through his
classes in a leather jacket or lurching at night in the spit-and-
sawdust company of other campus toughs, growling his beer-
bloated disdain for the very idea of liberal arts, he learned the

unquestionably masculine, unquestionably middle-class trade of mechanical engineering. It was there too that he found his wife, a small, soft, worshipful clerk in the bursar's office, and fathered the first of his sons; and it wasn't until several years later that the great reaction set in.

What happened then—he was later to call it "the time I sort of went crazy"—was that he woke up to find himself employed in a hydraulic machinery plant a hundred miles from Phoenix, Arizona, and living in one of four hundred close-set, identical houses in the desert, a sun-baked box of a house with four framed mountain scenes from the dime-store on its walls and five brown engineering manuals in the whole naked width of its book-shelves, a box that rang every night to the boom of television or the shrill noise of neighbors dropping in for Canasta.

Sheppard Sears Campbell had to admit he felt forlorn among these young men with blunt, prematurely settled faces, and these girls who shrieked in paralyzing laughter over bathroom jokes ("Harry, Harry, tell the one about the man got caught in the ladies' john!") or folded their lips in respectful silence while their husbands argued automobiles ("Now, you take the Chevy; far as I'm concerned you can have any Chevy ever built, bar none") and he rapidly began to see himself as an impostor and a fool. All at once it seemed that the high adventure of pretending to be something he was not had led him into a way of life he didn't want and couldn't stand, that in defying his mother he had turned his back on his birthright.

Bright visions came to haunt him of a world that could and should have been his, a world of intellect and sensibility that now lay forever mixed in his mind with "the East." In the East, he then believed, a man went to college not for vocational training but in disciplined search for wisdom and beauty, and nobody over the age of twelve believed that those words were for sissies. In the East, wearing rumpled tweeds and flannels, he could have strolled for hours among ancient elms and clock towers, talking with his friends, and his friends would have been the cream of their generation. The girls of the East were marvelously slim and graceful; they moved with the authority of places like Bennington and Holyoke; they spoke intelligently in low, subtle voices, and they never giggled. On sharp winter evenings you could meet them for cocktails at the Biltmore and take them to the theater, and afterwards, warmed with brandy, they would come with you for a drive to a snowbound New England inn, where they'd slip happily into bed with you under an eiderdown quilt. In the East, when college was over, you could put off going seriously to work until you'd spent a few years in a book-lined bachelor flat, with intervals of European travel, and when you found your true vocation at last it was through a process of informed and unhurried selection; just as when you married at last it was to solemnize the last and best of your many long, sophisticated affairs.

Brooding on these fantasies, it wasn't long before Shep Campbell gained a reputation as a snob at the hydraulics plant. He antagonized Milly, too, and frightened her, for he had become a moody listener to classical music and a sulking reader of literary quarterlies. He seldom talked to her, and when he did it was never in his old unique blend of New York street boy and Indiana farmer, a mixture she had always found "real cute," but in a new rhythm of brisk impatience that sounded alarmingly like an English accent. And then one Sunday night, after he'd been drinking all day and snapping at the children, she found herself cowering in tears with the baby at her breast while her husband called her an ignorant cunt and broke three bones of his fist against the wall.

A week later, still pale and shaken, she had helped him load clothes and blankets and kitchenware into the car and they'd set off on their dusty Eastward pilgrimage; and the six months in New York that followed, while he tried to decide whether to go on being an engineer—that period had been, Shep knew, the hardest time of Milly's life. The first rude surprise was that his mother's money was gone (there had never really been very much of it in the first place, and now there was barely enough to keep her decently in a residence hotel, a querulous, genteel old lady with a cat), and there were hundreds of other rude surprises in the overwhelming fact of New York itself, which turned out to be big and dirty and loud and cruel. Dribbling their savings away on cheap food and furnished rooms, never knowing where Shep was or what kind of a mood he'd be in when he came home, never knowing what to say when he talked disjointedly of graduate courses in music and philosophy, or when he wanted to lounge for hours in the dry fountain of Washington Square with a four-day growth of beard, she had more than once gone as far as to look up "psychiatrists" in the Classified New York Telephone Directory. But at last he had settled for the job with Allied Precision in Stamford, they had moved out to a rented house and then to the Revolutionary Hill Estates, and Milly's life had taken on a normal texture once again.

For Shep, too, the past few years had been a time of comparative peace. Or so it seemed, at any rate, in the glowing dusk of this fine spring evening. He was pleasantly full of roast lamb and beer, he was looking forward to a session of good talk with the Wheelers, and things could have been an awful lot worse. True enough, the job in Stamford and the Revolutionary Hill Estates and the Laurel Players were not exactly what he'd pictured in his Arizona visions of the East, but what the hell. If nothing else, the mellowing of these past few years had enabled him to look back without regret.

Because who could deny that his tough-guy phase, neurotic or not, had done him a lot of good? Hadn't it helped him on the way to a Silver Star and a field commission at twenty-one? Those things were real, they were a damned sight more than most men his age could claim (Field commission! The very forming of the words in his mind could still make warm tendrils of pride spread out in his throat and chest) and no psychiatrist would ever be able to take them away. Nor was he plagued any longer by the sense of having culturally missed out and fallen behind his generation. He could certainly feel himself to be the equal of a man like Frank Wheeler, for example, and Frank was a product of all the things that once had made him writhe in envy—the Eastern university, the liberal arts, the years of casual knocking around in Greenwich Village. What was so terrible, then, in having gone to State Tech?

Besides, if he hadn't gone to State Tech he would never have met Milly, and he didn't need any damn psychiatrist to tell him he would really be sick, really be in trouble, if he ever caught himself regretting that again. Maybe their backgrounds were different; maybe he'd married her for reasons that were hard to remember and maybe it wasn't the most romantic marriage in the world, but Milly was the girl for him. Two things about her had become a constant source of his sentimental amazement: that she had stuck right by him through all the panic in Arizona and New York—he vowed he would never forget it—and that she had taken so well to his new way of life.

The things she had learned! For a girl whose father was a semi-literate housepainter and whose brothers and sisters all said things like "It don't matter none," it couldn't have been easy. The more he thought about it, the more remarkable it was that she could dress very nearly as well as April Wheeler and talk very nearly as well on any subject you wanted to name; that she could live in an ugly, efficient suburban house like this and know why and how it had to be apologized for in terms of the job and the kids ("Otherwise of course we'd live in the city, or else further out, in the real country . . ."). And she had managed to give every room of it the spare, stripped-down, intellectual look that April Wheeler called "interesting." Well, almost every room. Feeling fond and tolerant as he rolled his shoe rag into a waxy cylinder, Shep Campbell had to admit that this particular room, this bedroom, was not a very sophisticated place. Its narrow walls, papered in a big floral design of pink and lavender, held careful bracket shelves that in turn held rows of little winking frail things made of glass; its windows served less as windows than as settings for puffed effusions of dimity curtains, and the matching dimity skirts of its bed and dressing table fell in overabundant pleats and billows to the carpet. It was a room that might have been dreamed by a little girl alone with her dolls and obsessed with the notion of making things nice for them among broken orange crates and scraps of cloth in a secret shady corner of the back yard, a little girl who would sweep the bald earth until it was as smooth as breadcrust and sweep it again if it started to crumble, a scurrying, whispering, damp-fingered little girl whose cheeks would quiver with each primping of gauze and tugging of soiled ribbon into place ("There . . . There . . .") and whose quick, frightened eyes, as she worked, would look very much like the eyes that now searched this mirror for signs of encroaching middle age.

"Sweetie?" she said.

"Mm?"

She turned around slowly on the quilted bench, tense with a troubling thought. "Well—I don't know, you'll just laugh, but listen. Do you think the Wheelers are getting sort of—stuck up, or something?"

"Oh, now, don't be silly," he told her, allowing his voice to grow heavy and rich with common sense. "What makes you want to think a thing like that?"

"I don't know. I can just tell. I mean I know she was upset about the play and everything, but it wasn't *our* fault, was it? And then when we were over there the last time, everything seemed so sort of—I don't know. Remember when I tried to describe the way your mother looked at me that time? Well, April was looking at me that exact same way that night. And now this whole business of forgetting our invitation—I don't know. It's funny, that's all."

He snapped the lid on his can of shoe polish and put it away with the rolled-up rag and the brushes. "Honey," he said, "you're just imagining all that. You're going to spoil the whole evening for yourself."

"I knew you'd say that." She got to her feet, looking aimless and pathetic in her pink slip.

"I'm only saying what's true. Come on, now; let's just take it easy and have a good time." He walked over and gave her a little hug; but his smile froze into an anxious grimace against her ear, because in bending close to her shoulder he had caught a faint whiff of something rancid.

"Oh, I guess you're right," she was saying. "I'm sorry. You go and have your shower, now, and I'll finish up in the kitchen."

"No big rush," he said. "They're always a little late. Why don't you have a shower too, if you want to?"

"No, I'm all ready, soon as I put on my dress."

In the shower, pensively soaping and scrubbing, Shep Campbell wondered what the hell it was that made her smell that way sometimes. It wasn't that she didn't take enough baths—he knew damn well she'd had one last night—and it didn't have anything to do with the time of the month; he had checked that out long ago. It seemed to be a thing brought on by nerves, like a skin rash or a bad stomach; he guessed it was just that she tended to perspire more in times of tension.

But he had to acknowledge, as he toweled himself in the steam, that it was more than just the smell of sweat. That alone, God knew, could be an exciting thing on a woman. And suddenly he was full of the time last summer when he'd held April Wheeler half drunk on the stifling, jam-packed dance floor of Vito's Log Cabin, when her soaked dress was stuck to her back and her temple slid greasily under his cheek as they swayed to the buzz and clip of a snare drum and the moan of a saxophone. Oh, she was sweating, all right, and the smell of her was as strong and clean as lemons; it was the smell of her as much as the tall rhythmic feel of her that had made his—that had made him want to—oh, Jesus. It had happened nearly a year ago, and the memory of it could still make his fingers tremble in the buttoning of his shirt.

The house seemed unnaturally still. Carrying his empty beer can, he went downstairs to see what Milly was doing, and he was halfway across the living room before he realized that he had four sons.

He almost tripped over them. They were lying on their bellies in a row, their eight-, seven-, five-, and four-year-old bodies identically dressed in blue knit pajamas, all propped on their elbows to stare at the flickering blue of the television screen. Their four snub-nosed blond faces, in profile, looked remarkably alike and remarkably like Milly's, and their jaws were all working in cadence on cuds of bubble gum, the pink wrappers of which lay strewn on the carpet.

"Hi, gang," he said, but none of them looked up. He walked carefully around them and out to the kitchen, frowning. Did other men ever feel distaste at the sight of their own children? Because it wasn't just that they'd taken him by surprise; there was nothing unusual in that. Quite often, in fact, he would happen on them suddenly and think, Who are these four guys? And it would take him a second or two to bring his mind into focus on the fact that they were his own. But damn it, if anyone ever asked him what he *felt* at those moments, he could have described it in all honesty as a deep twinge of pleasure—the same feeling he got when he checked them in their beds at night or when they galloped under his high-thrown softball on the lawn. This was different. This time he had to admit that he'd felt a distinct, mild revulsion.

Milly was there in the kitchen, spreading some kind of meat paste on crackers, licking her fingers as she worked.

" 'Scuse me, honey," he said, sidling around her. "I'll get right out of your way."

He got a cold, fresh can of beer from the refrigerator and took it out to the back lawn, where he sipped it soberly. From here, looking down over the shadowy tops of trees, he could just make out the edge of the Wheelers' roof; farther down, beyond it and to the right, under the telephone wires, the endless humming parade of cars on Route Twelve had just turned on its lights. He looked away into the shimmering distance of the highway for a long time, trying to figure it out.

If it wasn't revulsion he'd felt, what exactly was it? An over-fastidious, snobbish disapproval, maybe, because their sprawled staring and chewing had made them look sort of knuckle-headed and—well, middle-class? But what kind of nonsense was that? Would he rather see them sitting at a God damn miniature tea table, for Christ's sake? Wearing tartan kilts? No, it had to be more than that. Probably it was just that the sight of them had broken in on his thoughts of April Wheeler—and he did have thoughts about her! All kinds of thoughts! Wasn't it healthier to own up to a thing like that than to hide from it?—had broken in on his thoughts of April Wheeler and shocked him a little; that was all. And now that he'd faced up to it, he gave himself permission to quit looking up Route Twelve and to concentrate instead on the Wheelers' roof. In winter, when the trees were bare, you could see most of the house and part of its lawn from here, and at night you could see the light in the bedroom window. He began to wonder what April was doing right now. Combing her hair? Putting on her stockings? He hoped she would wear her dark blue dress.

"I love you, April," he whispered, just to see what it felt like. "I love you. I love you."

"Sweetie?" Milly was calling. "What're you *doing* out there?" She was standing in the bright kitchen doorway, squinting out into the gloaming, and behind her smiled the Wheelers.

"Oh!" he said, starting back across the lawn. "Hi! Didn't see you folks drive up." Then, feeling foolish, he paused to drink the last of his beer and found he had drunk the last of it some minutes before; the can was already warm in his hand.

It was an awkward evening from the start—so awkward, in fact, that for the whole first hour of it Shep had to avoid meeting Milly's eyes for fear his own expression would confirm her worry. He couldn't deny it: there *was* something damned peculiar going on here. The Wheelers weren't participating; they didn't relax and move around. Neither of them wandered talking out to the kitchen to help with the drinks; all they did was sit politely glued to the sofa, side by side. It would have taken a pistol shot to separate them.

April had indeed decided to wear her dark blue dress, and she'd never been lovelier, but there was an odd, distant look in her eyes—the look of a cordial spectator more than a guest, let alone a friend—and it was all you could do to get anything more than a "Yes" or an "Oh, really" out of her.

And Frank was the same, only ten times worse. It wasn't just that he wasn't talking (though that alone, for Frank, was about as far out of character as you could get) or that he made no effort to conceal the fact that he wasn't listening to anything Milly said; it was that he was acting like a God damned snob. His eyes kept straying around the room, examining each piece of furniture and each picture as if he'd never found himself in quite such an amusingly typical suburban living room as this before—as if, for Christ's sake, he hadn't spent the last two years spilling his ashes and slopping his booze all over every available surface *in* this room; as if he hadn't burned a hole in the upholstery of this very sofa last summer and passed out drunk and snoring on this very rug. Once, while Milly was talking, he leaned slightly forward and squinted past her like a man peering in between the bars of a darkened rat cage, and it took Shep a minute to figure out what he was doing: he was reading the book titles on the shelves across the room. And the worst part of it was, that Shep, for all his annoyance, had to fight an impulse to spring jovially to his feet and start apologizing ("Well, of course it's not much of a library, I mean I'd hate to have you judge our reading tastes on the basis of—actually, they're mostly just the kind of junk that accumulates over the years, most of our really good books have a way of . . ."). Instead, with his jaws shut tight, he collected all the glasses and went out to the kitchen. Jesus!

He gave both the Wheelers double shots in their next drinks, to help things along, and he held Milly's down to half a shot because if she went on putting it away like this, in the shape she was in, she'd be out cold in another hour.

And at last the Wheelers began to loosen up—though by the time their loosening-up was over, Shep wasn't at all sure but that he'd liked them better the other way.

It began with Frank clearing his throat and saying, "Actually, we've got some pretty important news. We're going—" and there he stopped and blushed and looked at April. "You tell it."

April smiled at her husband—not like a spectator or a guest or a friend, but in a way that made Shep's envious heart turn over—and then she turned back to address her audience. "We're going to Europe," she said. "To Paris. For good."

What? When? How? Why? The Campbells, husband and wife, exploded in a ferocious battery of questions as the Wheelers subsided into laughing, kindly answerers. Everybody was talking at once.

". . . Oh, about a week or two now," April was saying in reply to Milly's insistence on knowing how long all this had been going on. "It's hard to remember. We just suddenly decided to go, that's all."

"Well, but I mean what's the deal?" Shep was demanding of Frank for the second or third time. "I mean, you get a job over there, or what?"

"Well—no, not exactly." And all the talking stopped dead while he and April looked at each other again in their private, infuriating way. All right, Shep wanted to say; tell us or don't tell us. Who the hell cares?

Then the talking began again. Leaning forward, interrupting each other and squeezing each other's hands like a pair of kids, the Wheelers came out with the whole story. Shep did what he always tried to do when a great many pieces of upsetting news hit him one after another: he rolled with the punch. He took each fact as it came and let it slip painlessly into the back of his mind, thinking, Okay, okay, I'll think about that one later; and that one; and that one; so that the alert, front part of his mind could remain free enough to keep him in command of the situation. That way, he was able to have the right expression constantly on his face and to say the right things; he could even take pleasure in realizing that at least the party had livened up, at least there was plenty of action now. And he was surprised and proud to see how well Milly was handling the thing.

"Gee, it sounds wonderful, kids," she said when they were finished. "I mean it; it really sounds wonderful. We'll certainly miss you, though—won't we, sweetie? Golly." Her eyes were glistening. "Golly. We're really going to miss you people a lot."

Shep agreed that this was true, and the Wheelers both withdrew into a graceful, polite sentimentality of their own. They would, they said, certainly miss the Campbells too. Very much.

Later, when it was all over and the Wheelers were gone and the house was quiet, Shep carefully allowed a little of the pain to rise up in him—just enough to remind him that his first duty, right now, was to his wife. He could hold the rest of it down for the time being.

"You know what I think, doll?" he began, coming to stand beside her as she rinsed out the glasses and the ash trays at the kitchen sink. "I think this whole thing of theirs sounds like a pretty immature deal." And he could see her shoulders slacken with gratitude.

"Oh, so do I. I mean I didn't want to say anything, but I thought that exact same thing. Immature is exactly the right word. I mean have either of them even stopped for a minute to think of their children?"

"Right," he said. "And that's only one thing. Another thing: what kind of half-assed idea is this about her supporting him?

I mean what kind of a man is going to be able to take a thing like that?"

"Oh, that's so true," she said. "I was thinking that exact same thing. I mean I hate to say this because I really do like them both so much and they're—*you* know, they're really our best friends and everything, but it's true. I kept thinking that exact same— that really is exactly what I thought."

But later still, flat on his back in the darkness upstairs, he was of no use to her at all. He could feel the wide-awake tension of her lying there beside him; he could hear the light rasp of her breathing, with its little telltale quiver near the crest of each inhalation, and he knew that if he so much as touched her—if he so much as turned to her and let her know he was awake— she would be in his arms and sobbing, getting the whole thing out of her system into his neck, while he stroked her back and whispered, "What's the matter, baby? Huh? What's the matter? Tell Daddy."

And he couldn't do it. He couldn't make the effort. He didn't want her tears soaking into his pajama top; he didn't want her warm, shuddering spine in the palm of his hand. Not tonight, anyway; not now. He was in no shape to comfort anybody.

Paris! The very sound of the name of the place had gone straight to the tender root of everything, had taken him back to a time when the weight of the world rode as light and clean as the proud invisible bird whose talons seemed always to grip the place where the lieutenant's bar lay pinned on the shoulder of his Eisenhower jacket. Oh, he remembered the avenues of Paris, and the trees, and the miraculous ease of conquest in the evenings ("You want the big one, Campbell? Okay, you take the big one and I'll take the little one. Hey, Ma'm'selle ... 'Scuse me, Ma'm'selle ...") and the mornings, the lost blue-and-yellow mornings with their hot little cups of coffee, their fresh rolls, and their promise of everlasting life.

And all right, all right; maybe that was kid stuff, soldier stuff, field commission stuff; all right.

But oh God, to be there with April Wheeler. To swing down those streets with April Wheeler's cool fingers locked in his own, to climb the stone stairway of some broken old gray house with her; to sway with her into some high blue room with a red-tiled floor; to have the light husky ripple of her laugh and her voice up there ("*Wouldn't you like to be loved by me?*"); to have the lemon-skin smell of her and the long, clean feel of her when he—when she—oh Jesus.

Oh, Jesus God, to be there with April Wheeler.

THREE

SINCE 1936, WHEN they moved out of the city forever, Mr. and Mrs. Howard Givings had changed their place of residence every two or three years; and they had always explained that this was because Helen had a way with houses. She could buy one in a rundown condition, move in, vigorously improve its value and sell it at a profit, to be invested in the next house. Beginning in Westchester, moving gradually north into Putnam County and then over into Connecticut, she had done that with six houses. But their present house, the seventh, was a different story. They had lived in it for five, almost six years now, and they doubted if they'd ever move away. As Mrs. Givings often said, she had fallen in love with the place.

It was one of the few authentic pre-Revolutionary dwellings left in the district, flanked by two of the few remaining wine-glass elms, and she liked to think of it as a final bastion against vulgarity. The demands of the working day might take her deep into the ever-encroaching swarm of the enemy camp; she might have to stand smiling in the kitchens of horrid little ranch houses and split levels, dealing with impossibly rude people whose children ran tricycles against her shins and spilled Kool-Aid on her dress; she might have to breathe the exhaust fumes and absorb the desolation of Route Twelve, with its supermarkets and pizza joints and frozen custard stands, but these things only heightened the joy of her returning. She loved the last few hundred yards of shady road that meant she was almost there, and the brittle hiss of well-raked gravel under her tires, and the switching-off of the ignition in her neat garage, and the brave, tired walk past fragrant flowerbeds to her fine old Colonial door. And the first clean scent of cedar and floorwax inside, the first glimpse of the Currier and Ives print that hung above the charming old umbrella stand, never failed to fill her with the sentimental tenderness of the word "home."

This had been an especially harrowing day. Saturday was always the busiest day of the real estate week, and this afternoon, on top of everything else, she'd had to drive all the way out to Greenacres—not to visit her son, of course, for she never did that unless her husband was along—but for a conference with his doctor, a thing which always left her feeling soiled. Weren't psychiatrists supposed to be wise, deep-voiced, fatherly sorts of people? Then how could you feel anything but soiled in the presence of a red-eyed, nail-biting little man who used adhesive tape to hold his glasses together and a piece of Woolworth jewelry to keep his tie clamped flat against his white-on-white shirt—who had to thumb moistly through a dozen manila folders before he could remember which of his patients you had come to see him about, and who then said, "Yes; oh yes; and, what was your question?"

But now, by the grace of whichever saint it was that protected weary travelers, she was home. "Hello, dear!" she sang from the vestibule, for her husband was certain to be reading the paper in the living room, and without stopping to chat with him she went directly into the kitchen, where the cleaning woman had left the tea things set out. What a cheerful, comforting sight the steaming kettle made! And how clean and ample this kitchen was, with its tall windows. It gave her the kind of peace she could remember knowing only as a child, gossiping with the maids in the kitchen of her father's wonderful house in Philadelphia. And the funny thing, she often reflected, was that none of her other houses, some of which had been every bit as nice as this, or nicer, had ever made her feel this way.

Well, of course, people do change, she sometimes told herself; I suppose it's simply that I'm getting old and tired. But in her heart, shyly, she cherished quite a different explanation. Her ability to love this house, she truly believed, was only one of many changes in her nature these past few years—deep, positive changes that had brought her to a new perspective on the past.

"Because I love it," she could hear her own voice saying years and years ago, in reply to Howard's exasperated wish to know why she refused to quit her job in the city.

"It certainly can't be very interesting," he would say, "and it certainly isn't as if we needed the money. Why, then?" And her answer had always been that she loved it.

"You love the Horst Ball Bearing Company? You love being a stenographer? How can anybody love things like that?"

"It happens that I do. Besides, you know perfectly well we do need the money, if we're going to keep a full-time servant. And you know I'm not a stenographer." She was an administrative assistant. "Really, Howard, there's no point in discussing this."

And she'd never been able to explain or even to understand that what she loved was not the job—it could have been any job—or even the independence it gave her (though of course that was important for a woman constantly veering toward the brink of divorce). Deep down, what she'd loved and needed was work itself. "Hard work," her father had always said, "is the best medicine yet devised for all the ills of man—*and* of woman," and she'd always believed it. The press and bustle and glare of the office, the quick lunch sent up on a tray, the crisp handling of papers and telephones, the exhaustion of staying overtime and the final sweet relief of slipping off her shoes at night, which always left her feeling drained and pure and fit for nothing but two aspirins and a hot bath and a light supper and bed—that was the substance of her love; it was all that fortified her against the pressures of marriage and parenthood. Without it, as she often said, she would have gone out of her mind.

When she did quit the job and move to the country to break into real estate, it had been a difficult transition. There simply wasn't enough work in the real estate business. Not many people were buying property in those days, and there was a limit to the amount of time she could spend on the study of mortgage law and building codes; there were whole days together with nothing to do but rearrange the papers on her rosewood desk and wait for the phone to ring, with her nerves so taut she was ready to scream, until she discovered that her passion could find release in the improvement of the things around her. With her own hands she scraped layers of wallpaper and plaster away to disclose original oak paneling; she installed a new banister on the staircase, took out the ordinary window sashes and put in small-paned, Colonial-looking ones instead; she drew the blueprints and closely supervised the building of a new terrace and a new garage; she cleared and filled and rolled and planted a hundred square feet of new lawn. Within three years she had added five thousand dollars to the market value of the place, had persuaded Howard to sell it and buy another, and had made a good start on improving the second one. Then came the third one and the fourth, and so on, with her real estate business growing all the time, so that during one peak year she had been able to work eighteen hours a day—ten on business and eight on the house. "Because I *love* it," she had insisted, crouching far into the night over the endless tasks of chipping and hammering and varnishing and repair, "I *love* doing this kind of work—don't you?"

And hadn't she been silly? In the sense of calm and well-being that suffused her now, as she arranged the tea things on their tray, Mrs. Givings breathed a tolerant sigh at the thought of how silly, how wrong and foolish she had been in those years. Oh, she had changed, there was no doubt of it. People did change, and a change could be a bloom as well as a withering, couldn't it? Because that was what it seemed to be: a final bloom, a long-delayed emergence into womanliness.

Oh, the growth of her feeling for this house and the dwindling of her fixation on work were only the smallest, the most superficial symptoms of it; there were deeper things as well— disturbing, oddly pleasurable things; physical things. Sometimes a soaring phrase of Beethoven on the kitchen radio could make her want to weep with the pain of gladness. Sometimes, chatting with Howard, she would feel stirrings of—well, of desire: she would want to take him in her arms and press his dear old head to her breast.

"I thought we'd just have the plain tea today," she said, carrying the tray into the living room. "I hope you don't mind. The point is, if we fill up now we won't be hungry for dinner, and we'll be having a very early dinner you see because I'm expected over at the Wheelers' at eight. Rather awkward timing all around, I'm afraid." She set the tray gently on an antique coffee table whose surface was faintly scarred with glue, showing the places where it had split when John threw it across the room on the awful night the State Police came.

"Oh, isn't it lovely to sit *down*," Mrs. Givings said. "Is there anything nicer than sitting down after a hard day?"

It wasn't until she fixed his tea the way he liked it, with three sugars, and held it out for him to take, that she looked up to make sure her husband was there. And it wasn't until that instant, suddenly smelling the tea and seeing her, that Howard Givings realized she was home. His hearing aid had been turned off all afternoon. The shock of it made his face flinch like a startled baby's, but she didn't notice. She went on talking while he put down his *Herald Tribune*, fumbled at the dial of the hearing aid with one unsteady hand and reached out the other to take the cup and saucer, which chattered in his grip.

Howard Givings looked older than sixty-seven. His whole adult life had been spent as a minor official of the seventh largest life insurance company in the world, and now in retirement it seemed that the years of office tedium had marked him as vividly as old seafaring men are marked by wind and sun. He was very white and soft. His face, instead of wrinkling or sinking with age, had puffed out into the delicate smoothness of infancy, and his hair was like a baby's too, as fine as milkweed silk. He had never been a sturdy man, and now his frailty was emphasized by the spread of a fat belly, which obliged him to sit with his meager knees wide apart. He wore a rather natty red-checked shirt, gray flannel trousers, gray socks, and an old pair of black, high-cut orthopedic shoes that were as infinitely wrinkled as his face was smooth.

"Isn't there any cake?" he inquired, after clearing his throat. "I thought we still had some of the cocoanut cake."

"Well yes, dear, but you see I thought we'd just have the plain tea today because we'll be having such an early dinner . . ." She explained all over again about her engagement with the Wheelers, only dimly aware of having told him before, and he nodded, only dimly aware of what she was saying. As she talked she stared in absent-minded fascination at the way the dying sun shone crimson through her husband's earlobe and made his dandruff into flakes of fire, but her thoughts were hurrying ahead to the evening.

This would be no ordinary visit to the Wheelers'; it would, in fact, be the first careful step in fulfilling a plan that had come to her in a kind of vision, weeks and weeks ago. At twilight one evening, taking a stroll to calm her nerves in the blue depths of her back lawn, she had found it peopled in her mind's eye with a family gathering. April Wheeler was there, seated in a white wrought-iron chair and turning her pretty head to smile with affection at some wise and fatherly remark by Howard Givings, who sat beside her near a white wrought-iron table set with ice and cocktail mixings. Across from them, standing and leaning slightly forward with a glass in his hand, Frank Wheeler was engaged in one of his earnest conversations with John, who was reclining in dignified convalescence on a white wrought-iron chaise longue. She could see John smile, composed and courteous, begging to differ with Frank on some minor point of politics or books or baseball or whatever it was that young men talked about, and she could see him turn his head to look up at her and say:

"Mother? Won't you join us?"

The picture kept recurring for days until it was as real as a magazine illustration, and she kept improving on it. She even found a place in it for the Wheelers' children: they could be playing quietly in the shadows behind the rosebushes, dressed in white shorts and tennis shoes, catching fireflies in Mason jars. And the more vivid it grew, the less fault she was able to find with its plausibility. Wouldn't it do John a world of good to recuperate among a few sensitive, congenial people of his own age? And there need be no question of altruism on the Wheelers' part: hadn't they all but told her, time and again, how starved they were for friends of their own kind? Surely the tiresome couple on the Hill (Crandall? Campbell?) couldn't offer them much in the way of—well, of good conversation and so on. And goodness only knew that John, whatever else he might or might not be, was an intellectual.

Oh, it was the right thing for all of them; she knew it; she knew it. But she knew too that it couldn't be hurried. She had known from the start that it would have to be undertaken slowly, a step at a time.

For the past several visiting days, she and Howard had been

allowed to take him for an hour's drive outside the hospital grounds on what was called a trial basis. "I don't think any home visits would be wise at this time," the doctor had said last month, hideously cracking his ink-stained knuckles, one after another, on his desk blotter. "There still does seem to be a good deal of hostility concerning the, ah, home atmosphere and whatnot. Be better just to limit him to these preliminary outings for the present. Later on, depending how things work out, you might try taking him to the home of some close friend, where he'd feel more or less on neutral ground; that would be the next logical step. You can use your own judgment on that."

She had talked it over with Howard—she had even mentioned it discreetly to John a few times, during their drives—and last week her own judgment, carefully weighing the factors, had decided that the time for this next logical step was at hand. She had arranged the conference with the doctor today simply to announce her decision, and to ask one small piece of advice. How much, in his opinion, should she tell the Wheelers about the nature of John's illness? The doctor, as she should have predicted, was no help at all—she could, he said, use her own judgment on that too—but at least he hadn't raised any objections, and all that remained now was to put the question to the Wheelers. It would have been ever so much more comfortable and gracious to have the talk here, as she'd planned, over a candlelit dinner table; but that couldn't be helped.

"I do hope it doesn't seem an imposition," she whisperingly rehearsed as she rinsed out the tea things in the kitchen, "but I was wondering if I could ask a great favor. It's about my son John . . ." Oh, it didn't matter how she phrased it; she would find the right words when the time came, and she knew the Wheelers would understand. Bless them; bless them; she knew they would understand.

She could think of nothing else as she hurried through the preparation and the serving and the washing-up of the early dinner; and when she was ready, when she paused in the hall to freshen her lipstick and to call "I'll see you later, then, dear" before setting off, she was as excited as a girl.

But the moment she walked chatting and laughing into the

Wheelers' living room her excitement changed to a kind of panic. She felt like an intruder.

She had expected to find them as tense and disorganized as ever—both talking at once, bobbing and darting around her, getting in each other's way as they sprang to remove a sharp toy from the chair she was about to sit down on—but instead their welcome was serene. April didn't have to insist that the house was in a terrible mess, because it wasn't; Frank didn't have to blurt "Get you a drink" and go lunging off to wrestle and bang at the refrigerator, because the drinks were there, nicely arranged on the coffee table. The Wheelers had, apparently, been quietly drinking and talking together here for some time before her arrival; they were cordially glad to see her, but if she hadn't come they would have gone on together in perfect self-sufficiency.

"Oh, just a tiny dollop for me, thanks, that's wonderful," Mrs. Givings heard herself saying, and "Oh, isn't it lovely to sit down," and "My, doesn't your house look nice," and a number of other things; and then: "I do hope it doesn't seem an imposition, but I was wondering if I could ask a great favor. It's about my son John."

The muscular contraction in both the Wheelers' faces was so slight that the subtlest camera in the world couldn't have caught it, but Mrs. Givings felt it like a kick. They knew! It was the one possibility she had completely overlooked. Who had told them? How much did they know? Did they know about the smashing of the house and the cutting of the phone wires and the State Police?

But she had to go through with it. Actually, her voice was telling them now, he hadn't been at all well. What with overwork and one thing and another, he'd had what amounted to a complete nervous breakdown. Fortunately he was back in this vicinity for a time—she'd have hated the thought of his being ill so far from home—but all the same it was worrying, to his father and to her. His doctors had thought it wise for him to have a complete rest, so just for the present he was—"—well, actually, just for the present he's at Greenacres." Her voice had become the only living thing in Mrs. Givings; all the rest was numb.

And actually, her voice assured them, they'd be surprised at what a really excellent place Greenacres was, from the standpoint of—oh, of facilities and staff and so on; much better, for instance, than most of the private rest homes and whatnot in the area.

The voice went on and on, steadily weakening, until it came at last to its point. Some Sunday soon—oh, not right away, of course, but some Sunday in the future—would the Wheelers mind very much if . . .

"Why, of course not, Helen," April Wheeler was saying. "We'd love to meet him. It's very nice of you to think of us." And Frank Wheeler, refilling her glass, said that he certainly did sound like an interesting guy.

"How about next Sunday, then?" April said. "If that suits you."

"Next Sunday?" Mrs. Givings pretended to calculate. "Well, let's see: I'm not sure if—All right, fine, then." She knew she ought to feel pleasure at this—it was, after all, exactly what she'd come for—but all she wanted was to get out of here and go home. "Well, of course it's nothing urgent. If next Sunday's inconvenient or anything we can always make it some oth—"

"No, Helen. Next Sunday's fine."

"Well," she said. "Fine, then. Oh goodness, look at the time. I'm afraid I'd better be—oh, but you had something to ask *me* about, didn't you. And here I've done all the talking, as usual." When she took a sip of her drink she discovered that her mouth was very dry. It felt swollen.

"Well, actually, uh, Helen," Frank Wheeler began, "we have some pretty important news . . ."

Half an hour later, driving home, Mrs. Givings held her eyebrows high in astonishment all the way. She could hardly wait to tell her husband about it.

She found him still in his armchair in the yellow lamplight, sitting beside the perfectly priceless grandfather clock she had picked up at an auction before the war. He had finished with the *Herald Tribune* now and was making his way through the *World-Telegram and Sun*.

"Howard," she said. "Do you know what those children told me?"

"What children, dear?"

"The Wheelers. *You* know, the people I went to see? The couple in the little Revolutionary Road place? The people I thought John might like?"

"Oh. No; what?"

"Well, first of all I happen to know they're not at all well-fixed financially; they had to borrow the whole down payment on the house, for one thing, and that was only two years ago. In the second place . . ."

Howard Givings tried to listen, but his eyes kept drifting down the newspaper in his lap. A twelve-year-old boy in South Bend, Indiana, had applied for a twenty-five-dollar bank loan to buy medicine for his dog, whose name was Spot, and the bank manager had personally co-signed the note.

". . . so I said, 'But why *sell*? Surely you'll want to have the place when you come *back*.' And do you know what he said? He looked at me in this very guarded way and said, 'Well, that's the point, you see. We won't be coming back.' I said, 'Oh, have you taken a job there?' 'Nope,' he said—just like that. 'Nope. No job.' I said, 'Will you be staying with relatives, then, or friends, or something?' 'Nope.' " And Mrs. Givings bugged her eyes to impersonate the zenith of irresponsibility. " 'Nope—don't know a soul. We're just going, that's all.' Really, Howard, I can't tell how embarrassing it was. Can you imagine it? I mean, isn't it all sort of—unsavory, somehow? The whole thing?"

Howard Givings touched his hearing aid and said, "How do you mean, unsavory, dear?" He guessed he had lost the thread. It had started out to be something about somebody going to Europe, but now it was evidently about something else.

"Well, isn't it?" she asked. "People practically without a dollar to their name, with children just coming into school age? I mean people don't *do* things like that, do they? Unless they're—well, running away from something, or something? And I mean I'd hate to think there's anything—well, I don't know *what* to think; that's the point. And they always seemed such a steady, settled sort of couple. Isn't it queer? And the awkward thing, you see, is that I'd already committed myself on the John business before they came out with all this; now I suppose we'll have to go through with it, though there hardly seems much point to it any more."

"Go through with what, dear? I don't quite see what you're—"

"Well, with taking him there for a *visit*, Howard. Haven't you been listening to any of this?"

"Oh; yes, of course. What I mean is, why doesn't there seem much point to it?"

"Well, *because*," she said impatiently. "What's the *value* of introducing them to John, if they're going to disappear in the fall?"

"The 'value'?"

"Well, I simply mean—*you* know. He needs *permanent* people. Oh, of course I suppose there's no harm in having him meet them, taking him there once or twice before they—it's just that I'd been thinking in terms of a much more long-range sort of thing, somehow. Oh, dear, isn't it all confusing? Why *do* you suppose people can't be more—" She wasn't quite sure what she was saying now, or what she meant to say, and she found with surprise that she'd been twisting her handkerchief into a tight, moist rope the whole time she was talking. "Still, I suppose one never—can—tell about people," she concluded, and then she turned, left the room, and fled lightly upstairs to change into something comfy.

Passing the shadowed mirror on the landing, she noticed with pride that her own image, at least when seen fleetingly from the corner of an eye, was still that of a swift, lithe girl in a well-appointed house; and on the ample carpet of her bedroom, where she quickly stripped off her jacket and stepped out of her skirt, it was almost as if she were back in her father's house, hurrying to dress for a tea dance. Her blood seemed to race with the emergency of last-minute details (Which kind of perfume? Oh, quick—which kind?) and she very nearly ran out to the banister to call, "Wait! I'm coming! I'll be right down!"

It was the sight and the feel of her old flannel shirt and baggy slacks, hanging from their peg in the closet, that steadied her. Silly, silly, she scolded herself; I *am* getting scatty. But the real shock came when she sat on the bed to take off her stockings, because she had expected her feet to be slim and white with light blue veins and straight, fragile bones. Instead, splayed on the carpet like two toads, they were tough and knuckled with bunions, curling to hide their corneous toenails. She stuffed them quickly into her bright Norwegian slipper-socks (really the nicest things in the world for knocking around the house) and sprang up to pull the rest of her simple, sensible country clothes into place, but it was too late, and for the next five minutes she had to stand there holding on to the bedpost with both hands and keeping her jaws shut very tight because she was crying.

She cried because she'd had such high, high hopes about the Wheelers tonight and now she was terribly, terribly, terribly disappointed. She cried because she was fifty-six years old and her feet were ugly and swollen and horrible; she cried because none of the girls had liked her at school and none of the boys had liked her later; she cried because Howard Givings was the only man who'd ever asked her to marry him, and because she'd done it, and because her only child was insane.

But soon it was over; all she had to do was go into the bathroom and blow her nose and wash her face and brush her hair. Then, refreshed, she walked jauntily and soundlessly downstairs in her slipper-socks and returned to sit in the ladder-back rocker across from her husband, turning out all but one of the lights in the room as she came.

"There," she said. "That's much cozier. Really, Howard, my nerves were just like *wires* after that business with the Wheelers. You can't imagine how it upset me. The point is I'd always thought they were such *solid* young people. I thought *all* the young married people today were supposed to be more settled. Wouldn't you think they ought to be, especially in a community like this? Goodness knows, all *I* hear about is young couples *dying* to come and settle here, and raise their children . . ."

She went on talking and talking, moving around and around the room; and Howard Givings timed his nods, his smiles, and his rumblings so judiciously that she never guessed he had turned his hearing aid off for the night.

FOUR

"FLY THE COOP," Jack Ordway said, stirring his coffee. "Kick over the traces. Take off. Pretty nifty, Franklin."

They were sitting at a ketchup-stained table for two in the dark corner of the Nice place, and Frank was beginning to regret having told Ordway about Europe. A clown, a drunk, a man unable to discuss anything at all except in the elaborately derisive tone he used for talking about himself—wasn't this the desirable kind of confidant to have in a thing like this? But he'd told him, nevertheless, because in the past few weeks it had become more and more difficult to carry his secret alone through the office day. Sitting attentively in staff conferences while Bandy outlined things to be done "in the fall" or "first of the year," accepting Sales Promotion assignments that would theoretically take him months to complete, he would sometimes find his mind sliding readily into gear with the slow machinery of Bandy's projects before it occurred to him to think: No, wait a minute—I won't even be *here* then. At first these little shocks had been fun, but the fun of them had worn off and soon they had become distinctly troubling. It was getting on for the middle of June. In another two and a half months (eleven weeks!) he would be crossing the ocean, never to be concerned with Sales Promotion again, yet the reality of that fact had still to penetrate the reality of the office. It was a perfectly, inescapably real fact at home, where nobody talked of anything else; it was real on the train each morning and again on the train each night, but for the eight hours of his working day it remained as insubstantial as a half-remembered, rapidly fading dream. Everyone and everything in the office conspired against it. The stolid or tired or mildly sardonic faces of his colleagues, the sight of his IN basket and his current work pile, the sound of his phone or of the buzzer that meant he was wanted in Bandy's cubicle—all these seemed constantly to tell him he was destined to stay here forever.

The hell I am! he felt like saying twenty times a day. You just wait and see. But his defiance lacked weight. The bright, dry, torpid lake of this place had contained him too long and too peacefully to be ruffled by any silent threat of escape; it was all too willing to wait and see. This was intolerable; the only way to put an end to it was to speak out and tell somebody; and Jack Ordway was, after all, the best friend he had in the office. Today they had managed to avoid Small and Lathrop and Roscoe for lunch, and had started it off with a couple of weak but adequate martinis; and now the story was out.

"There's one small point I don't quite grasp, though," Ordway was saying. "I don't mean to be dense, but what exactly will you be doing? I don't see you languishing indefinitely at sidewalk cafés while your good frau commutes to the embassy or whatever—but that's the point, you see. I don't quite know what I *do* see you doing. Writing a book? Painting a—"

"Why does everybody think in terms of writing books and painting pictures?" Frank demanded, and then, only partly aware that he was quoting his wife, he said, "My God, are artists and writers the only people entitled to lives of their own? Look. The only reason I'm here in this half-assed job is because—well, I suppose there's a lot of reasons, but here's the point. If I started making a list of all the reasons, the one reason I damn sure couldn't put down is that I like it, because I don't. And I've got this funny feeling that people are better off doing some kind of work they like."

"Fine!" Ordway insisted. "Fine! Fine! Don't let's get all defensive and riled up, please. My only simple-minded question is this: What kind do you like?"

"If I knew that," Frank said, "I wouldn't have to be taking a trip to find out."

Ordway thought this over, tilting his handsome head to one side, lifting his brows and curling out his underlip, which looked unpleasantly pink and slick. "Well, but don't you think," he said, "I mean to say, assuming there is a true vocation lurking in wait for you, don't you think you'd be just as apt to discover it here as there? I mean, isn't that possible?"

"No. I don't think it is. I don't think it's possible for anybody to discover anything on the fifteenth floor of the Knox Building, and I don't think you do either."

"Mm. Must say that sounds like a good point, Franklin. Yes indeed." He drank off the last of his coffee and sat back, smiling quizzically across the table. "And when did you say this noble experiment is going to begin?"

For a second Frank wanted to turn the table over on him, to see the helpless fright in his face as his chair went over backwards and the whole mess of dishes went up and over his head. "Noble experiment"! What kind of supercilious crap was that?

"We're going in September," he said. "Or October at the outside."

Ordway nodded five or six times, gazing at the congealed smears of meat and potato on his plate. He didn't look supercilious now; he looked old and beaten and wistfully envious; and Frank, watching him, felt his own resentment blurring into an affectionate pity. The poor, silly old bastard, he thought. I've spoiled his lunch; I've spoiled his day. He almost wished he could say, "It's all right, Jack, don't worry; it may never happen"; instead he took refuge from his own confusion in a burst of heartiness.

"Tell you what, Jack," he said. "I'll buy you a brandy for old times."

"No, no, no, no," Ordway said, but he looked as pleased as a stroked spaniel when the waiter cleared the plates away and set the rich little cognac glasses in their place; and later, when they'd paid their checks and walked upstairs into the sunlight, he was all smiles.

It was a clear, warm day, with a sky as clean and deep as laundry blueing above the buildings, and it was also payday, time for the traditional after-lunch stroll to the bank.

"Needless to say I'll keep this strictly *entre nous*, old scout," Ordway said as they walked. "I don't suppose you want it noised around. How much notice you planning to give Bandy?"

"Couple of weeks, I guess. Haven't really thought about it."

The sun was pleasingly warm. In another few days it would be hot, but it was perfect now. In the cool marble depths of the bank, whose Muzac system was playing "Holiday for Strings," he entertained himself by pretending it was the last time he would ever stand in line here, the last time he would ever shift his feet and finger his paycheck as he and Ordway waited their turns at one of the ten tellers' windows that were reserved at lunchtime, twice a month, for Knox employees. "You ought to see us shuffling around that damned bank," he had told April years ago. "We're like a litter of suckling pigs waiting for a free tit. Oh, of course we're all very well-mannered, very refined little pigs; we all stand very suavely and try not to jostle each other too much, and when each guy gets up close to the window he takes out his check and sort of folds it in his fingers or palms it or finds some other way of hiding it without seeming to. Because it's very important to be casual, you see, but the really important thing is to make damn sure nobody else sees how much you're getting. Jesus!"

"Gentlemen," said Vince Lathrop, at Frank's shoulder. "Shall we take the air?" He and Ed Small and Sid Roscoe were pocketing their passbooks and their wallets, their tongues still sucking random shreds of Awful place food from the crevices of their teeth, and this was an invitation to join them in a digestive stroll around the block.

He pretended it was the last time he would ever do this, too; the last time he would ever join this slow promenade of office people in the sunshine, the last time the approach of his own polished shoes would ever cause these wobbling pigeons to take fright and skitter away across the spit and peanut shells of the sidewalk, to flap and climb until they were wheeling high over the towers with alternately black and silver wings.

It was better to have told somebody; it had made a difference. He was able to glance around at the talking faces of these four men and feel truly detached from them. Ordway, Lathrop, worried little Ed Small, pretentious, boring old Sid Roscoe—he knew now that he would soon be saying goodbye to all of them and that in another year he'd have trouble remembering their names. In the meantime, and this was the best part, in the meantime it was no longer necessary to dislike them. They weren't such bad guys. He could even join happily in their laughter at some mild joke of Ordway's, and when they turned the last corner and headed back to the Knox Building he could take pleasure in the comradely way they spread out five abreast across the sidewalk, inspired by the sun to step out briskly and swing their arms with all the apparent "unit pride" of soldiers from the same platoon on pass (What *out*fit, Mac? Sales Promotion, Fifteenth Floor, Knox Business Machines).

And Goodbye, goodbye, he could say in his heart to everyone they passed—a chattering knot of stenographers clutching packages from the dimestore, a cynical, heavy-smoking group of young clerks who leaned against a building front in their shirt-sleeves—goodbye to the whole sweet, sad bunch of you. I'm leaving.

It was a splendid sense of freedom, and it lasted until he was back at his desk, where the buzzer that meant he was wanted in Bandy's cubicle was mournfully bleating.

Ted Bandy never looked his best in fine weather; he was an indoor man. His thin gray body, which seemed to have been made for no other purpose than to fill the minimum requirements of a hard-finish, double-breasted business suit, and his thin gray face were able to relax only in the safety of winter, when the office windows were shut. Once, when he'd been assigned to accompany a group of prize-winning salesmen on a trip to Bermuda, Roscoe's *Knox Knews* had carried a photograph of the whole party lined up and grinning on the beach in their swimming trunks; and Roscoe's secretly made enlargement of one section of that picture, showing Bandy doing his best to smile under the weight of two great, hairy arms that had been flung around his neck from either side, had enjoyed weeks of furtive circulation among the cubicles of the Fifteenth Floor, where everyone pronounced it the funniest damn thing they'd ever seen.

Bandy was wearing something of that same expression now, and at first Frank thought it was only because the June breeze from the window had comically dislodged some of the long side hairs that were supposed to be combed across his baldness. But he discovered with a start, on entering the cubicle, that the main cause of Bandy's uneasiness was the presence there of a rare and august visitor.

"Frank, you know Bart Pollock, of course," he said, getting

to his feet, and then with an apologetic nod he said, "Frank Wheeler, Bart."

A massive figure in tan gabardine rose up before him, a big tan face smiled down, and his right hand was enveloped in a warm clinch. "Don't guess we've ever been formally introduced," said a voice deep enough to make the glassware tremble on a speaker's rostrum. "Glad to know you, Frank."

This man, who in any other corporation would have been called "Mr." rather than "Bart," was general sales manager for the Electronics Division, a man from whom Frank had never received anything more than an occasional vague nod in the elevator, and whom he had despised from a distance for years. "I mean he'd be perfect Presidential timber in the worst sense," he had told April once. "He's one of these big calm father-image bastards with a million-dollar smile and about three pounds of muscle between the ears; put him on television and the other party'd never have a chance." And now, feeling his own face twitch into a grimace of servility, feeling a drop of sweat creep out of his armpit and run down his ribs, he tried to atone for this uncontrollable reaction by planning how he would describe it to April tonight. "And I suddenly caught myself sort of *melting* in front of him—isn't that funny? I mean *I* know he's a horse's ass; *I* know he's got nothing to do with anything that matters in my life, and all the same he almost had me cowed. Isn't that the damnedest thing?"

"Pull up a chair, Frank," said Ted Bandy, smoothing the hairs back across his head, and when he sat down again he shifted his weight uncomfortably from one buttock to the other, the gesture of a man with hemorrhoids. "Bart and I've been going over some of the reports on the NAPE conference," he began, "and Bart asked me to call you in on it. It seems . . ."

But Frank couldn't follow the rest of Bandy's sentence because all his attention was fixed on Bart Pollock. Leaning earnestly forward in his chair, Pollock waited until Bandy had finished talking; then he rapped the back of his free hand smartly across the paper he was holding, which turned out to be a copy of *Speaking of Production Control*, and said:

"Frank, this is a crackerjack. They're just tickled to death in Toledo."

"And I mean isn't that the damnedest thing?" he demanded of April that evening, laughing and talking at the same time, following her around the kitchen with a drink in his hand while she got the dinner ready to serve. "I mean isn't it ironic? I do this dumb little piece of work to get myself off the hook with Bandy, and this is what happens. You should've heard old Pollock go on about it—all these years he hasn't known I'm alive, and suddenly I'm his favorite bright young man. Old Bandy sitting there trying to decide whether to be pleased or jealous, me sitting there trying to keep from laughing myself to death—Jesus!"

"Marvelous," she said. "Would you mind carrying these in, darling?"

"And then it turns out he's got this big—What? Oh, sure, okay." He put down his glass, took the plates she handed him and followed her into the other room, where the children were already seated at the table. "And then it turns out he's got this big idea; Pollock, that is. He wants me to do a whole series of the crazy things. *Speaking of Inventory Control, Speaking of Sales Analysis, Speaking of Cost Accounting, Speaking of Payroll*—he's got it all mapped out. I'm supposed to go out to—"

"Excuse me a sec, Frank. Michael, you sit up straight, now, or there's going to be trouble. I mean it. And don't take such big bites. I'm sorry; go on."

"I'm supposed to go out to lunch with him next week and talk it over. Won't that be a riot? Course, if it gets too thick I'll have to tell him I'm leaving the company in the fall. No, but I mean the whole thing's pretty funny, isn't it? After all these—"

"Why not tell him anyway?"

"—years of doping along in the damn job and never—What?"

"I said why don't you tell him anyway? Why not tell the whole pack of them? What can they do?"

"Well," he said, "it's hardly a question of their 'doing' anything; it'd just be—you know, a little awkward, that's all. I mean I certainly don't see the point of saying anything until it's time to give them my formal notice, that's all." He forked a piece of pork chop into his mouth so angrily that he bit the fork as well as the meat, and as he chewed with all the strength of his jaws, exhaling a long breath through his nostrils to show how self-controlled he was, he realized that he didn't quite know what he was angry about.

"Well," she said placidly, without looking up. "Of course that's entirely up to you."

The trouble, he guessed, was that all the way home this evening he had imagined her saying: "And it probably *is* the best sales promotion piece they've ever seen—what's so funny about that?"

And himself saying: "No, but you're missing the point—a thing like this just proves what a bunch of idiots they are."

And her: "I don't think it proves anything of the sort. Why do you always undervalue yourself? I think it proves you're the kind of person who can excel at anything when you want to, or when you have to."

And him: "Well, I don't know; maybe. It's just that I don't *want* to excel at crap like that."

And her: "Of course you don't, and that's why we're leaving. But in the meantime, is there anything so terrible about accepting their recognition? Maybe you don't want it or need it, but that doesn't make it contemptible, does it? I mean I think you ought to feel good about it, Frank. Really."

But she hadn't said anything even faintly like that; she hadn't even looked as if thoughts like that could enter her head. She was sitting here cutting and chewing in perfect composure, with her mind already far away on other things.

"I'M GOING TO take my dollhouse," Jennifer said that Saturday afternoon, "and my doll carriage and my bear and my three Easter rabbits and my giraffe and all my dolls and all my books and records, and my drum."

"That sounds like quite a lot, doesn't it, sweetie?" April said, frowning over her sewing machine. She had decided to spend the weekend sorting out winter clothes, discarding some things and repairing others, concentrating on the simple, sturdy kind of clothes they would need for Europe. Jennifer was sitting at her feet, playing aimlessly with torn-out linings and bits of thread.

"Oh, and my tea set too, and my rock collection and all my games, and my scooter."

"Well, but sweetie, don't you think that's quite a lot to take? Aren't you planning to leave anything behind?"

"No. Maybe I'll throw my giraffe away; I haven't quite decided."

"Your giraffe? No, I wouldn't do that. We'll have plenty of room for all the animals and dolls and the other small things. It's just some of the big things I was worried about—the dollhouse, for instance, and Mike's rocking horse. That kind of thing's very difficult to pack, you see. But you won't have to throw away the dollhouse; you could give it to Madeline."

"To keep?"

"Well, of course to keep. That's better than throwing it away, isn't it?"

" 'Kay," Jennifer said, and then, after a minute: "I know what I'll do. I'll give Madeline my dollhouse and my giraffe and my carriage and my bear and my three Easter rabbits and my—"

"Just the *big* things, I said. Didn't you understand me? I just finished explaining all that. Why can't you listen?" April's voice

154

was rising and flattening out with exasperation, and then she sighed. "Look. Wouldn't you rather go outside and play with Michael?"

"No. I don't feel much like it."

"Oh. Well, I don't feel much like explaining everything fifteen times to somebody who's too bored and silly to pay attention, either. So that's that."

Frank was glad when their voices stopped. He was on the sofa trying to read the introduction to a book of elementary French, which he'd bought to replace the "Brighter" one, and their talking had kept him going over and over the same paragraph.

But half an hour later, when the only sound in the room for that long had been the faint irregular whir of the sewing machine, he looked up uneasily to find that Jennifer was gone.

"Where'd she go, anyway?" he said.

"Out with Michael, I guess."

"No she didn't. I know she didn't go outside."

They got up and went together to the children's room, and there she was, lying down and staring at nothing, with her thumb in her mouth.

April sat on the edge of the bed and laid her palm against Jennifer's temple, and then, apparently feeling no fever, she began stroking her hair. "What's the matter, baby?" She made her voice very gentle. "Can you tell Mommy what's the matter?"

Watching from the doorway, Frank's eyes grew as round as his daughter's. He swallowed, and so did she, first removing her thumb from her mouth.

"Nothing," she said.

April took hold of her hand to prevent the thumb from going back in, and in opening the small fist she discovered that a length of green thread had been wound tightly and many times around her index finger. She began to unwind it. It was so tight that the tip of the finger was plum-colored and the moist skin beneath it was wrinkled and bloodless.

"Is it about moving to France?" April asked, still working on the thread. "Are you feeling sort of bad about that?"

Jennifer didn't answer until the last of the thread was removed. Then she gave a small, barely discernible nod and wrenched herself awkwardly around so that her head could be buried in her mother's lap as she started to cry.

"Oh," April said. "I thought that might be it. Poor old Niffer." She stroked her shoulder. "Well, listen, baby, you know what? There isn't anything to feel bad about."

But it was impossible for Jennifer to stop, now that she'd started. Her sobs grew deeper.

"Remember when we moved out here from the city?" April asked. "Remember how sad it seemed to be leaving the park and everything? And all your friends at nursery school? And remember what happened? It wasn't more than about a week before Madeline's mommy brought her over to meet you, and then you met Doris Donaldson, and the Campbell boys, and pretty soon you started school and met all your other friends, and there wasn't anything to feel bad about any more. And that's just the way it's going to be in France. You'll see."

Jennifer raised her congested face and tried to say something, but it took her several seconds to get the words out between the convulsions of her breath. "Are we going to live there a long time?"

"Of course. Don't you worry about that."

"Forever and ever?"

"Well," April said, "maybe not forever and *ever*, but we'll certainly live there a good long time. You shouldn't worry so much, sweetie. I think it's mostly just from sitting around indoors on such a nice day. Don't you? Let's go wash your face, now, and then you run along outside and see what Michael's doing. Okay?"

When she was gone, Frank took up a slumped, standing position behind his wife at the sewing machine. "Gee," he said. "That really gave me a turn. Didn't it you?"

She didn't look up. "How do you mean?"

"I don't know. It's just that this does seem a pretty inconsiderate thing to be doing, when you think about it, from the kids' point of view. I mean, let's face it: it's going to be pretty rough on them."

"They'll get over it."

"Of course they'll 'get over it,' " he said, trying to make the phrase sound heartless. "We could trip them up and break their arms, and they'd 'get over' that too; that's hardly the point. The point is—"

"Look, Frank." She had turned to face him with her little flat-lipped smile, her tough look. "Are you suggesting we call the whole thing off?"

"No!" He moved away from her to pace the carpet. "Of course I'm not." For all his annoyance, he found it good to be up and talking again after his long silence of faulty concentration with the French book on the sofa. "Of *course* I'm not. Why do you have to start—"

"Because if you're not, then I really don't see any point in discussing this. It's a question of deciding who's in charge and sticking to it. If the children are to be in charge, then obviously we must do what they think is best, which means staying here until we rot. On the other hand—"

"No! Wait a minute; I never said—"

"You wait a minute, please. On the other hand, if we're to be in charge—and I really think we ought to be, don't you? If only because we're about a quarter of a century older than they are? Then that means going. As a secondary thing it also means doing all we can to make the transition as easy as possible for them."

"That's all I'm saying!" He waved his arms. "What're you getting all excited about? Make the transition as easy as pos-sible—that's absolutely all I'm saying."

"All right. The point is I think we're doing that, and I think we'll continue to do it to the best of our ability until they do get over it. In the meantime I'm afraid I don't see any point in hold-ing our heads and moaning about how miserable they're going to be, or talking about tripping them up and breaking their arms. Frankly, I think that's a lot of emotionalistic nonsense and I wish you'd cut it out."

It was the closest thing to a fight they'd had in weeks; it left them on edge and unnecessarily polite for the rest of the day, and caused them to shy away from each other at bedtime. And in the morning they awoke to the sound of rain and the uncomfortable knowledge that this was the Sunday they had arranged to meet John Givings.

Milly Campbell had volunteered to take the children off their hands for the afternoon, "because I mean you probably won't want them around when he's there, will you? In case he turns out to be a real nut or anything?" April had declined; but this morning, as the time of the visit drew near, she had second thoughts about it.

"I think we'll take you up on that after all, Milly," she said into the telephone, "if the offer still goes. I guess you were right—it does seem a weird sort of thing to expose them to." And she drove them to the Campbells' an hour or two earlier than necessary.

"Gosh," she said, sitting down with Frank in the scrubbed kitchen when she returned. "This is sort of nervous-making, isn't it? I wonder what he'll be like? I don't think I've ever met an insane person before, have you? A real certified insane person, I mean."

He poured out two glasses of the very dry sherry he liked on Sunday afternoons. "How much you want to bet," he said, "that he turns out to be pretty much like all the uncertified insane people we know? Let's just relax and take him as he comes."

"Of course. You're right." And she favored him with a look that made yesterday's unpleasantness seem years in the past. "You always do have the right instincts about things like this. You're really a very generous, understanding person, Frank."

The rain had stopped but it was still a wet, gray day and good to be indoors. The radio was dimly playing Mozart and a gentle, sherry-scented repose settled over the kitchen. This was the way he had often wished his marriage could always be—unexcited, companionable, a mutual tenderness touched with romance— and as they sat there quietly talking, waiting for the sight of the Givingses' station wagon to appear through the dripping trees, he shivered pleasurably once or twice as a man who has been out since before dawn will shiver at the feel of the first faint warmth of sun on his neck. He felt himself at peace; and by the time the car did come, he was ready for it.

Mrs. Givings was the first one out, aiming a blind, brilliant smile toward the house before she turned back to deal with the coats and bundles in the back seat. Howard Givings emerged from the driver's side, ponderously wiping his misted spectacles, and behind him came a tall, narrow, red-faced young man wearing a cloth cap. It wasn't the kind of jaunty little back-belted cap that had lately become stylish; it was wide, flat, old-fashioned and cheap, and the rest of his drab costume was equally suggestive of orphanage or prison: shapeless twill work pants and a dark brown button-front sweater that was too small for him. From a distance of fifty feet, if not fifty yards, you could tell he was dressed in items drawn from state institutional clothing supplies.

He didn't look up at the house or at anything else. Lagging behind his parents, he stood with his feet planted wide apart on the wet gravel, slightly pigeon-toed, and gave himself wholly to the business of lighting a cigarette—tamping it methodically on his thumbnail, inspecting it with a frown, fixing it carefully in his lips, hunching and cupping the match to it, and then taking the first deep pulls as intently as if the smoke of this particular cigarette were all he would ever have or expect of sensual gratification.

Mrs. Givings had time to chatter several whole sentences of greeting and apology, and even her husband was able to get a few words in, before John moved from his cigarette-lighting place in the driveway. When he did, he was very quick: he walked springingly on the balls of his feet. Seen at close range, his face proved to be big and lean, with small eyes and thin lips, and its frown was the look of a man worn down by chronic physical pain.

"April . . . Frank," he said in reply to his mother's introduction, almost visibly committing both names to memory. "Glad to meetcha. Heard a lot aboutcha." Then his face burst into an astonishing grin. His cheeks drew back in vertical folds, two perfect rows of big, tobacco-stained teeth sprang out between his whitening lips, and his eyes seemed to lose their power of sight. For a few seconds it seemed that his face might be perma-nently locked in this monstrous parody of a friend-winning, people-influencing smile, but it dwindled as the party moved deferentially into the house.

April explained (too pointedly, Frank thought) that the children were away at a birthday party, and Mrs. Givings began telling of how perfectly frightful the traffic had been on Route Twelve, but her voice trailed off when she found that John had claimed the Wheelers' whole attention. He was making a slow, stiff-legged circuit of the living room, still wearing his cap, examining everything.

"Not bad," he said, nodding. "Not bad. Very adequate little house you got here."

"Won't you all sit down?" April asked, and the elder Givingses obeyed her. John removed his cap and laid it on one of the bookshelves; then he spread his feet and dropped to a squat, sitting on his heels like a farmhand, bouncing a little, reaching down between his knees to flick a cigarette ash neatly into the cuff of his work pants. When he looked up at them now his face was free of tension; he had assumed a kind of pawky, Will Rogers expression that made him look intelligent and humorous.

"Old Helen here's been talking it up about you people for months," he told them. "The nice young Wheelers on Revolutionary Road, the nice young revolutionaries on Wheeler Road—got so I didn't know what she was talking about half the time. Course, that's partly because I didn't listen. You know how she is? How she talks and talks and talks and never says anything? Kind of get so you quit listening after a while. No, but I got to hand it to her this time; this isn't what I pictured at all. This is nice. I don't mean 'nice' the way she means 'nice,' either; don't worry. I mean nice. I like it here. Looks like a place where people live."

"Well," Frank said. "Thank you."

"Would anyone like some sherry?" April inquired, twisting her fingers at her waist.

"Oh no, please don't bother, April," Mrs. Givings was saying. "We're fine; please don't go to any trouble. Actually, we can only stay a min—"

"Ma, how about doing everybody a favor," John said. "How about shutting up a little while. Yes, I'd like some sherry, thanks. Bring some for the folks too, and I'll drink Helen's if she doesn't beat me to it. Oh, hey, listen, though." All the wit vanished from his face as he leaned forward in his squat and extended one gesturing hand toward April like a baseball coach wagging instructions to the infield. "You got a highball glass? Well, look. Take a highball glass, put a couple-three ice cubes in it, and pour the sherry up to the brim. That's the way I like it."

Mrs. Givings, sitting tense as a coiled snake on the edge of the sofa, gently closed her eyes and wanted to die. Sherry in a high-ball glass! His cap on the bookshelf—oh, and those *clothes*. Week after week she brought him clothes of his own to wear—good shirts and trousers, his fine old tweed jacket with the leather elbows, his cashmere sweater—and still he insisted on dressing up in these hospital things. He did it for spite. And this dreadful rudeness! And why was Howard always, always so useless at times like this? Sitting there smiling and blinking in the corner like an old—oh God, why didn't he *help*? "Oh, this is lovely, April, thanks so much," she said, tremulously lifting a sherry glass from the tray. "Oh, and look at this magnificent *food*!" She drew back in mock disbelief at the platter of small, crustless sandwiches that April had made and cut that morning. "You *really* shouldn't have gone to all this bother for us." John Givings took two sips of his drink and left it standing on the bookcase for the rest of the visit. But he ate half the plate of sandwiches as he restlessly patrolled the room, taking three or four at a time and wolfing them down while breathing audibly through his nose. Mrs. Givings managed to hold the floor for a few minutes, talking steadily, making such smooth elisions between one sentence and the next as to leave no opening for interruption. She was trying to filibuster the afternoon away. Had the Wheelers heard the latest ruling of the zoning board? Personally she considered it an outrage; still, she supposed it would ultimately bring the tax rate down, and that was always a blessing . . .

Howard Givings, sleepily nibbling a sandwich, kept a watchful eye on his son's every action during this monologue; he might have been a benign old nursemaid in the park, making sure the youngster stayed out of mischief.

John watched his mother, head cocked to one side, and when he had swallowed his last mouthful he cut her off in mid-sentence.

"You a lawyer, Frank?"

"Me? A lawyer? No. Why?"

"Hoping you might be, is all. I could use a lawyer. Whaddya do, then? Advertising man, or what?"

"No. I work for Knox Business Machines."

"Whaddya do there? You design the machines, or make them, or sell them, or repair them, or what?"

"Sort of help sell them, I guess. I don't really have much to do with the machines themselves; I work in the office. Actually it's sort of a stupid job. I mean there's nothing—you know, interesting about it, or anything."

" 'Interesting'?" John Givings seemed offended by the word. "You worry about whether a job is 'interesting' or not? I thought only women did that. Women and boys. Didn't have you figured that way."

"Oh, *look*, the sun's coming out!" Mrs. Givings cried. She jumped up, went to the picture window and peered through it, her back very rigid. "Maybe we'll see a rainbow. Wouldn't that be lovely?"

The skin at the back of Frank's neck was prickling with annoyance. "All I meant," he explained, "is that I don't like the job and never have."

"Whaddya do it for, then? Oh, okay, okay—" John Givings ducked his head and weakly raised one hand as if in a hopeless attempt to ward off the bludgeon of public chastisement. "Okay; I know; it's none of my business. This is what old Helen calls Being Tactless, Dear. That's my trouble, you see; always has been. Forget I said it. You want to play house, you got to have a job. You want to play very *nice* house, very *sweet* house, then you got to have a job you don't like. Great. This is the way ninety-eight-point-nine per cent of the people work things out, so believe me buddy you've got nothing to apologize for. Anybody comes along and says 'Whaddya do it for?' you can be pretty sure he's on a four-hour pass from the State funny-farm; all agreed. Are we all agreed there, Helen?"

"Oh look, there *is* a rainbow," Mrs. Givings said, "—or no, wait, I guess it isn't—oh, but it's perfectly lovely in the sunshine. Why don't we all take a walk?"

"As a matter of fact," Frank said, "you've pretty well put your finger on it, John. I agree with everything you said just now. We both do. That's why I'm quitting the job in the fall and that's why we're taking off."

John Givings looked incredulously from Frank to April and

back again. "Yeah? Taking off where? Oh, hey, yeah, wait a minute—she did say something about that. You're going to Europe, right? Yeah, I remember. She didn't say why, though; she just said it was 'very strange.'" And all at once he split the air—very nearly split the house, it seemed—with a bray of laughter. "Hey, how about that, Ma? Still seem 'very strange' to you? Huh?"

"Steady down, now," Howard Givings said gently from his corner. "Steady down, son."

But John ignored him.

"Boy!" he shouted. "Boy, I bet this whole conversation seems very, *very* strange to you, huh, Ma?"

They had grown so used to the bright, chirping sound of Mrs. Givings's voice that day that her next words came as a shock, addressed to the picture window and spoken in a wretchedly tight, moist whimper: "Oh John, please stop."

Howard Givings got up and shuffled across the room to her. One of his white, liver-spotted hands made a motion as if to touch her, but he seemed to think better of it and the hand dropped again. They stood close together, looking out the window; it was hard to tell whether they were whispering together or not. Watching them, John's face was still ebullient with the remnants of his laughter.

"Look," Frank said uneasily, "maybe we *ought* to take a walk or something." And April said, "Yes, let's."

"Tell you what," John Givings said. "Why don't the three of us take a walk, and the folks can stay here and wait for their rainbow. Ease the old tension all around."

He loped across the carpet to retrieve his cap, and on the way back he veered sharply with an almost spastic movement to the place where his parents stood, his right fist describing a wide, rapid arc toward his mother's shoulder. Howard Givings saw it coming and his glasses flashed in fright for an instant, but there was no time to interfere before the fist landed—not in a blow but in a pulled-back, soft, affectionate cuffing against the cloth of her dress.

"See you later, then, Ma," he said. "Stay as sweet as you are."

Up in the woods behind the house, steaming in the sun, the

newly rainwashed earth gave off an invigorating fragrance. The Wheelers and their guest, relaxing in an unexpected sense of camaraderie, had to walk single file on the hill and pick their way carefully among the trees; the slightest nudge of an overhanging branch brought down a shower of raindrops, and the glistening bark of passing twigs was apt to leave grainy black smears on their clothing. After a while they quit the woods and walked slowly around the back yard. The men did most of the talking; April listened, staying close to Frank's arm, and more than once he noticed, glancing down at her, that her eyes were bright with what looked like admiration for the things he was saying.

The practical side of the Europe plan didn't seem to interest John Givings, but he was full of persistent questions about their reasons for going; and once, when Frank said something about "the hopeless emptiness of everything in this country," he came to a stop on the grass and looked thunderstruck.

"Wow," he said. "Now you've said it. The hopeless emptiness. Hell, plenty of people are on to the emptiness part; out where I used to work, on the Coast, that's all we ever talked about. We'd sit around talking about emptiness all night. Nobody ever said 'hopeless,' though; that's where we'd chicken out. Because maybe it does take a certain amount of guts to see the emptiness, but it takes a whole hell of a lot more to see the hopelessness. And I guess when you do see the hopelessness, that's when there's nothing to do but take off. If you can."

"Maybe so," Frank said. But he was beginning to feel uncomfortable again; it was time to change the subject. "I hear you're a mathematician."

"You hear wrong. Taught it for a while, that's all. Anyway, it's all gone now. You know what electrical shock treatments are? Because you see, the past couple months I've had thirty-five—or no, wait—thirty-seven—" He squinted at the sky with a vacant look, trying to remember the number. In the sunlight, Frank noticed for the first time that the creases in his cheeks were really the scars of a surgeon's lancet, and that other areas of his face were blotched and tough with scar tissue. At one time in his life his face had probably been a mass of boils or cists. "—thirty-seven electrical shock treatments. The idea is to jolt all the emotional problems out of your mind, you see, but in my case they had a different effect. Jolted out all the God damned mathematics. Whole subject's a total blank."

"How awful," April said.

" '*How awful*.' " John Givings mimicked her in a mincing, effeminate voice and then turned on her with a challenging smirk. "Why?" he demanded. "Because mathematics is so 'interesting'?"

"No," she said. "Because the shocks must be awful and because it's awful for anybody to forget something they want to remember. As a matter of fact I think mathematics must be very dull."

He stared at her for a long time, and nodded with approval. "I like your girl, Wheeler," he announced at last. "I get the feeling she's female. You know what the difference between female and feminine is? Huh? Well, here's a hint: a feminine woman never laughs out loud and always shaves her armpits. Old Helen in there is feminine as hell. I've only met about half a dozen females in my life, and I think you got one of them here. Course, come to think of it, that figures. I get the feeling you're male. There aren't too many males around, either."

Mrs. Givings, covertly watching them from the house, didn't quite know what to think. She was still shaken—the beginning of the afternoon had been worse than the worst of her fears— but she had to admit that John had seldom looked happier and more relaxed than he did now, strolling and chatting in the Wheelers' back yard. And the Wheelers looked comfortable too, which was even more surprising.

"They do seem to—to like him, don't they?" she said to Howard, who was picking through the Wheelers' Sunday *Times*.

"Mm," he said. "You shouldn't get so nervous about these things, Helen. Why don't you just relax when they come back, and let them do the talking?"

"Oh, I know," she said. "I know, you're right. That's what I ought to do."

And she did, and it worked. For the last hour of the visit, while everyone but John had another glass of wine, she scarcely said a word. She and Howard sat benignly in the background of the young people's conversation, a peaceful medley of voices in which John's voice was never once more raucous than the others. They were reminiscing about the children's radio programs of the nineteen-thirties.

"'Bobby Benson,'" Frank was saying. "Bobby Benson of the H-Bar-O Ranch; I always liked him. I think he came on just before 'Little Orphan Annie.'"

"Oh, and 'Jack Armstrong,' of course," April said, "and 'The Shadow,' and that other mystery one—something about a bee? 'The Green Hornet.'"

"No, but 'The Green Hornet' was later," John said. "That was still going in the forties. I mean the real way-back ones; 'thirty-five and -six, along in there. Remember the one about the naval officer? What was his name? Used to come on right about this time? On week days?"

"Oh yes," April said. "Wait a minute—'Don Winslow.'"

"Right! 'Don Winslow of the United States Navy.'"

It wasn't at all the kind of topic Mrs. Givings would have thought they'd discuss, but they all seemed to enjoy it; the sound of their easy, nostalgic laughter filled her with pleasure, and so did the taste of her sherry, and so did the sherry-colored squares of sunset on the wall, each square alive with the nodding shadows of leaves and branches stirred by the wind.

"Oh, this has been such fun," she said when it was time to go, and for a second she was afraid John might turn on her and say something awful, but he didn't. He was talking and shaking hands with Frank, and the party broke up in the driveway with a chorus of regrets and good wishes and promises to see each other soon.

"You were wonderful," April said when the car had disappeared. "The way you handled him! I don't know what I'd ever have done if you hadn't been here."

Frank reached for the sherry bottle, but changed his mind and got out the whiskey instead. He felt he deserved it. "Hell, it wasn't a question of 'handling' him," he said. "I just treated him like anyone else, is all."

"But that's what I mean—that's what was so wonderful. I would've treated him like an animal in the zoo or something, the way Helen does. Wasn't it funny how much more sane he seemed once we got him away from her? And he's sort of nice, isn't he? *And* intelligent. I thought some of the things he said were sort of brilliant."

"Mm."

"He certainly did seem to sort of approve of us, didn't he? Wasn't that nice about 'male' and 'female'? And do you know something, Frank? He's the first person who's really seemed to know what we're talking about."

"That's true." He took a deep drink, standing at the picture window and watching the last of the sunset. "I guess that means we're as crazy as he is."

She came up close behind him and put her arms around his chest, nestling her head against his shoulder blade. "I don't care if we are," she said. "Do you?"

"No."

But he had begun to feel depressed in a way that couldn't be attributed to ordinary Sunday-evening sadness. This odd, exhilarating day was over, and now in the fading light he could see that it had only been a momentary respite from the tension that had harried him all week. He could feel the resumption of it now, despite the reassurance of her clinging at his back—a dread, a constricting heaviness of spirit, a foreboding of some imminent, unavoidable loss.

And he was gradually aware that she felt it too: there was a certain stiffness in the way she was holding him, a suggestion of effort to achieve the effect of spontaneity, as though she knew that a nestling of the shoulder blade was in order and was doing her best to meet the specifications. They stood that way for a long time.

"Wish I didn't have to go to work tomorrow," he said.

"Don't, then. Stay home."

"No. I guess I've got to."

SIX

"NOW TED BANDY'S a nice fella," Bart Pollock said as they walked rapidly uptown, "and he's a good department head, but I'll tell you something." He smiled down along his gabardine shoulder into Frank's attentive face. "I'll tell you something. I'm a little sore at him for the way he's kept you under a bushel all these years."

"Well, I wouldn't say that, Mr.—Bart." Frank felt his features jump into a bashful smile. "But thanks anyway." ("I mean what the hell else could I say?" he would explain to April later, if necessary. "What else can you *say* to a thing like that?") He had to skip and quicken his step to keep up with Pollock's long stride, and he was uncomfortably aware that these little hurrying motions, combined with the way his fingers were fussing to keep his tie from slipping out of his jacket, must make him look the picture of an underling.

"This place okay with you?" Pollock swept him into the lobby and then into the restaurant of a big hotel, a place that bustled with heavy-laden, rubber-heeled waiters and throbbed with executive shoptalk under the clash of knives and forks. When they were settled at a table Frank took a sip of ice water and glanced around the room, wondering if this was the same place he had come with his father that other day for the lunch—the luncheon—with Mr. Oat Fields. He couldn't be sure—there were several hotels of this size and kind in the neighborhood—but the possibility was strong enough to please his sense of ironic coincidence. "Isn't that the damnedest thing?" he would demand of April tonight. "Exactly the same room. Same potted palms, same little bowls of oyster crackers—Jesus, it was like something in a dream. I sat there feeling ten years old."

It was a relief, at any rate, to be sitting down. It made Pollock less tall and allowed Frank to conceal, under the table, the fact

168

that he was picking and tearing at a loose strip of skin along his left thumbnail while Pollock talked. Was Frank married? Children? Where did he live? Well, it certainly was wise to live in the country when you had kids; but how did Frank feel about commuting? It was almost exactly like Oat Fields wishing to know how he felt about school and baseball.

"You know what impressed me most about that piece of yours?" Pollock asked over his martini, the stemmed glass of which looked very fragile in his hand. "The logic and the clarity of it. You hit each point in the right place and you drove it home. To me it wasn't like a piece of reading matter at all. It was like a man talking."

Frank ducked his head. "Well, as a matter of fact, that's what it was. I just talked it into the Dictaphone, you see. Actually the whole thing was more or less an accident. Our department isn't supposed to handle the creative end or the production end of these things, you see; that's the agency's job. All we're supposed to do is control the distribution of their stuff to the field."

Pollock nodded, chewing on his gin-soaked olive. "Let me tell you something. I'm having another of these, you with me? Good. Let me tell you something, Frank. I'm not interested in creative ends or production ends or who's supposed to control the distribution of what. I'm interested in one thing, and one thing only: selling the electronic computer to the American businessman. Frank, a lot of people tend to look down on plain old-fashioned selling today, but I want to tell you something. Back when I was first breaking into the selling field a very wise and wonderful older man told me something I've never forgotten. He said to me, 'Bart, *everything* is selling.' He said, 'Nothing happens in this world, nothing comes *into* this world, until somebody makes a sale.' He said, 'You don't believe me? All right, look at it this way.' He said, 'Bart, where the hell do you think *you'd* be if your father hadn't sold your mother a bill of goods?' "

"And I kept sitting there getting drunk and thinking 'What the hell does this guy *want* from me?' " he would tell April tonight. "Of course I kept thinking none of it matters a damn, but still; he really had me guessing. And it's true about these big, bluff, rough-diamond types, you know it? They do have a certain personal magnetism. He does, anyway."

"Now of course, good selling today consists of many things, the combining of many forces, and as you know this is particularly true when you've got an idea to sell instead of just a product. Take a job like ours, introducing a whole new concept of business control, and hell, it gets so you can't hardly see the woods for the trees. You got your market research people, you got your advertising and your whaddyacallit, your public relations people; you got to coordinate all these forces into one basic, overall selling effort. I like to think of it as building a bridge." He squinted and used one forefinger to describe a slow aerial arc between the ash tray and the celery-and-olives dish. "A bridge of understanding, a bridge of communication between the science of electrox—" he hiccupped—"Excuse me. The science of electronics and the practical, everyday world of commercial management. Now, you take a company like Knox." He looked regretfully into the empty glass of his second, or possibly his third, martini. "Very old, very slow, very conservative—hell, you know this as well as I do: our whole operation's geared to selling typewriters and file cabinets and clankety-clank old punched-card machines, and half the old farts on the payroll think McKinley's in the White House. On the other hand—you want to order now, or wait a while? All right, sir, let's have a look. The ragout's very tasty here and so's the smoked salmon and so's the mushroom omelet and so's the lemon sole. Fine and dandy, make it two. Couple more of these things too, while you're at it. Right. Now, you might say this company's like some real old, tired old man. On the other hand—" He shot his cuffs and leaned massively on the table, eyes bulging. Beads of sweat had begun to appear among the big tan freckles of his head. "On the other hand, here comes this whole revolutionary concept of electronic data processing, and Frank, let's face it: this is a newborn baby." He cradled an imaginary infant in both hands, and then he shook them quickly as if to rid his fingers of a glutinous fluid. "I mean it's still *wet*! I mean they just now hauled it out and turned it over and slapped its ass and by Jesus its belly button's still hangin' out sore as a boil! You follow me? All right; you take this little-biddy newborn baby and you give it to this old, old man, or this old woman, let's say, these old married folks, and whaddya think's gunna happen? Why, they're gunna let it shrivel up and die, that's what. They're gunna take it and lay it away in a dresser drawer someplace and give it sour old milk to suck and never change its pants, and are you tryna tell me that baby'll ever grow up healthy and strong? Why hell that baby's got no more chance 'n a fiddler's bitch. Let me give an example."

And he gave one example after another, while Frank did his best to follow him. After a while he stopped to blot his head with a handkerchief, looking bewildered. "And that's the problem," he said. "That's pretty much what we're up against." Sighting grimly and carefully on the last of his drink, he downed it in a swallow and fell to work on his cooling food, which seemed to sober him. He went on talking as he ate but he was quieter now and more dignified, using words like "obviously" and "furthermore" instead of "fart" and "belly button." His eyes no longer protruded; he had left off being the backwoods tycoon and was resuming his customary role as balanced, moderate executive. Had Frank considered the tremendous effect of the computer on the business life of the future? It was, Bart Pollock could assure him, food for thought. And he went on and on, modestly confessing his ignorance of technicalities, disparaging his right to speak as a prophet, earnestly losing his way in the labyrinthine structure of his sentences.

Watching him and trying to listen, Frank found that his own three martinis (or was it four?) had amplified the sounds of the restaurant into a sea of noise that jammed his eardrums, and had caused a dark mist to close in on all four sides of his vision so that only the things coming directly before him could be seen at all, and they with a terrible clarity: his food, the bubbles in his glass of ice water, Bart Pollock's tirelessly moving mouth. He used the full power of this pinpoint scrutiny to watch Bart Pollock's table manners, to see if he would leave white curds on the rim of his glass or soak his roll in the gravy boat, and he felt enormously, drunkenly gratified on being able to establish that Bart Pollock did neither of those things. Before long Pollock subsided, with visible relief, into a conversational vein that had less to do with abstractions than with company personalities, and that was when Frank felt it safe to bring up the topic nearest his heart.

"Bart," he said. "Do you happen to remember a man here in the Home Office named Otis Fields?"

Pollock blew a long jet of cigarette smoke and watched it fade. "No, I don't believe I—" he began, but then he blinked happily to attention. "Oh, *Oat* Fields. Oh, hell, yes, many years ago. Oat Fields was one of our general sales managers back in—Lord, this goes back a good many—hey, hold on, though. You couldn't 've been around then."

And Frank, surprised at the fluency of his own voice, gave a brief account of the last time he'd sat at a luncheon table very much like this one.

"Earl Wheeler," Pollock said, leaning back to squint in the effort of memory. "Earl Wheeler. Newark, you said? Wait a second. I do remember a Wheeler and I *think* he had a name like Earl—no, but that was in Harrisburg, or Wilmington, and anyway, he was a much older man."

"Harrisburg, that's right. That was later, though. Harrisburg was the last place he worked. The Newark job was earlier, back around 'thirty-five or -six. Then he also worked in Philadelphia a while, and Providence—pretty much all over the Eastern Region. That's why I grew up in about fourteen different places, you see." And he was startled to hear a note of self-pity creeping into his voice: "Never did get much of a chance to feel at home anywhere."

"Earl Wheeler," Pollock was saying. "Why hell, of course I remember him. And you see the reason I didn't connect him with Newark is because that was before *my* time. But I do recall Earl Wheeler very clearly in Harrisburg; only thing is I had the impression he was more of an elderly man. I'm probably—"

"You're right. He was. He already had two full-grown kids by the time I was born, you see—" and he almost caught himself saying, "I was the accident, you see; I was the one they didn't want." Hours later, sobering up and trying to remember this part of the talk, he couldn't be sure that he *hadn't* said that; he couldn't even be sure that he hadn't broken into a wild shout of laughter and said, "You see? You see, Bart? They laid me away in a dresser drawer and gave me sour old milk to suck—" and that he and Bart Pollock hadn't risen up to punch each other's arms at the hilarity of this joke and laughed and laughed until they cried and fell into the coffee cups.

But that didn't happen. What happened instead was Bart Pollock's shaking his head in wonderment and saying, "Isn't that something? And imagine your remembering this restaurant all these years; even remembering old Oat Fields's name."

"Well, it's not too surprising. It was the only time my father ever took me to New York, for one thing; besides, a hell of a lot depended on that day. He really thought Fields was going to give him a Home Office job, you see. He and my mother had the whole thing planned, the house in Westchester and all the rest of it. I don't think he ever did get over it."

Pollock respectfully lowered his eyes. "Well, of course that's— that's the breaks in this business." And then he hurried on to more cheerful aspects of the story. "No, but this is really interesting, Frank. I had no idea you were the son of a Knox man. Funny Ted didn't mention it."

"I don't think Ted knows it. It wasn't a thing I featured when I took the job."

And now Bart Pollock was frowning and smiling at the same time. "Hold on here a second. You mean to say your dad sold for us all his life and you never even let on?"

"Well yes, actually, that's right. I didn't. He was retired then, and I just—I don't know; anyway, I didn't. It seemed important not to at the time."

"I'll tell you something, Frank. I admire that. You didn't want anybody giving you a special break here and a special break there; you wanted to make good on your own. Right?"

Frank shifted uncomfortably in his chair. "No, it wasn't exactly that. I don't know. It was pretty complicated."

"A thing like that *is* complicated," Bart Pollock said with solemnity. "Many people wouldn't understand a thing like that, Frank, but I'll tell you something. I admire it. I bet your dad did too. Didn't he? Or no, wait a minute." He leaned back, smiling and cannily narrowing his eyes. "Wait a minute. Let me see how good a judge of character I am. I bet I know what happened. This is just a guess, now." He winked. "An educated guess. I bet you went ahead and let your dad think his name had helped you get the job, just to please him. Am I right?"

And the disturbing fact of the matter was that he was. On an autumn day of that year, feeling stiff and formal in a new serge suit, Frank had taken his wife to visit his parents; and all the way out to Harrisburg he'd planned to be elaborately, sophisticatedly offhand in the announcing of his double piece of news, the baby and the job. "Oh, and by the way, I've got a steadier kind of job now, too," he had planned to say, "kind of a stupid job, nothing I'm interested in, but the money's nice." And then he would let the old man have it.

But when the moment came, in that overstuffed Harrisburg living room with its smell of weakness and medicine and approaching death, with his father doing his best to be benign, his mother doing her best to be tearfully pleased about the baby and April doing her best to be sweetly and shyly proud—when all the lying tenderness of that moment came it had robbed him of his nerve, and he'd blurted it out—a job in the Home Office!—like a little boy come home with a good report card.

"Who'd you see there?" Earl Wheeler had demanded, looking ten years younger than he'd looked ten minutes before. "Ted who? Bandy? Don't believe I know him; course, I've forgotten a lot of the names. He knew me, though, I guess, didn't he?"

And "*Oh* yes," Frank had heard himself saying over a preposterous swelling in his throat. "*Oh* yes, certainly. He spoke very highly of you, Dad."

And it wasn't until they were on the train again, going back to New York, that he'd regained enough composure to pound his fist on his knee and say, "He beat me! Isn't that the damnedest thing? The old bastard beat me again."

"I knew it," Bart Pollock was saying now, his eyes twinkling and suffused with heart-warmth. "I'll tell you something, Frank: I'm seldom wrong in my hunches about people. Care for a little cordial or a little B and B or something with your dessert?"

"And do you mean to say you sat through the whole lunch," April might well ask tonight, "and told him your whole life story, and never even got around to telling him you're leaving the company in the fall? Whatever was the point of that?"

But Pollock was making it impossible, now, to get a word in edgewise. He was getting down, at last, to business. Who was going to nurse that baby? Who was going to build that bridge?

". . . Your public relations expert? Your electronics engineer? Your management consultant? Well, now, certainly, all of them are going to play important roles in the overall picture; each of them is going to offer very valuable specialized knowledge in their respective fields. But here's the point. No single one of them has the right background or the right qualifications for the job. Frank, I've talked to some of the top advertising and promotion men in the business. I've talked to some of the top technical men in the computer field and I've talked to some of the top business administration men in the country, and we've all of us pretty much come to this conclusion: it's a completely new kind of job, and we're going to have to develop a completely new kind of talent to do it.

"Now, the past six months or so I've been going around sounding men out, inside the company and outside too. So far I've got my eye on half a dozen young men with various backgrounds, and I hope to line up half a dozen more. You see what I'm doing? I'm recruiting myself a team. Now let me"—he held up a thick hand to ward off any interruptions—"let me be more specific. These little pieces you're doing for us now are only the beginning. I want you to finish that series the way we mapped it out the other day in Ted's office; that's fine; but what I'm driving at now goes way beyond that. As I say, this whole project's still taking shape, nothing's definite yet, but this'll show you the direction of my thinking. I've got a hunch you're the kind of a fella I could send out to groups of people all over the country—civic groups, business seminars, groups of our own field sales people as well as customers and prospects, and all you'd do is stand up in front of those groups and talk. You'd talk computers, chapter and verse; you'd answer questions; you'd put the electronic data processing story over in the kind of language a businessman can understand. Frank, maybe it's the old-time salesman in me, but I've always had one conviction, and that's this: when you're trying to sell an idea, I don't care how complicated or what it may be, you'll never find a more effective instrument of persuasion than the living human voice."

"Well, Bart, before you go any further, there's something I—" He felt tight in the chest and short of breath. "I mean I couldn't very well say this in Ted's office the other day because I haven't told him about it yet, but the thing is I'm planning to leave the company in the fall. I guess I should've made that clear earlier; now I feel sort of—I mean I really am sorry if this conflicts with your—"

"You mean to say you *apologized* to him?" April might ask. "As if you had to ask his permission to leave, or something?"

"No!" he would insist. "Of course I didn't apologize to him. Will you give me a chance? I *told* him, that's all. Naturally it was a little awkward; it was bound to be awkward after the way he'd been talking; can't you see that?"

"Well, now I *am* sore at Bandy," Pollock was saying. "Let a man of your caliber go to waste for seven years and then lose you to another outfit." He shook his head.

"Oh, it's not to another *outfit*—I mean *you* know; it's not anything else in the business machine field."

"Well, I'm glad of that, anyway. Frank, you've been aboveboard with me and I appreciate it; now I'll be aboveboard with you. I don't want to pry into things that're none of my business, but can you tell me this? Can you tell me how definite a commitment you've made on this other thing?"

"Well—pretty definite, I'm afraid, Bart. It's kind of hard to—well, yes. Quite definite."

"Because here's my point. If it's a question of money, there's certainly no reason why we can't get together on a satisfactory..."

"No. I mean I appreciate your saying that, but it's not really a question of money at all. It's more of a personal thing."

And that seemed to settle it. Pollock began to nod slowly and steadily, to show his infinite understanding of personal things.

"I mean it won't affect the series I'm working on now," Frank told him. "I'll have plenty of time to finish that; it's just that anything beyond that is—*you* know, pretty much out of the question."

Pollock's nodding continued for a while. Then he said, "Frank, let me put it to you this way. Nothing's ever so definite a man can't change his mind. All I'm asking is, I'd like you to give a little thought to this chat we've had today. Sleep on it a while; talk it over with your wife—and that's always the main thing, isn't it? Talking it over with your wife? Where the hell would any of us be without 'em? And I'd like you to feel free to come to me at any time and say, 'Bart, let's have another chat.' Will you do that? Can we leave it that way? Fine. And remember, this thing I'm talking about would amount to a brand-new job for you. Something that could turn into a very challenging, very satisfying career for any man. Now I'm sure this other thing looks very desirable to you right now"—he winked—"you'll never catch me knocking a competitor; and of course it's entirely your decision. But Frank, in all sincerity, if you do decide for Knox I believe it'll be a thing you'll never regret. And I believe something else, too. I believe—" He lowered his voice. "I believe it'd be a fine memorial and tribute to your dad."

And how could he ever tell April that these abysmally sentimental words had sent an instantaneous rush of blood to the walls of his throat? How could he ever explain, without bringing down her everlasting scorn, that for a minute he was afraid he might weep into his melting chocolate ice cream?

Fortunately, there was no chance to tell her anything that night. She had spent the day at a kind of work she had always hated and lately allowed herself to neglect: cleaning the parts of the house that didn't show. Breathing dust and spitting cobwebs, she had hauled and bumped the screaming vacuum cleaner into all the corners of all the rooms and crawled with it under all the beds; she had cleaned each tile and fixture in the bathroom with a scouring powder whose scent gave her a headache, and she had thrust herself head and shoulders into the oven to swab with ammonia at its clinging black scum. She had torn up a loose flap of linoleum near the stove to reveal what looked like a long brown stain until it came alive—a swarm of ants that seemed still to be crawling inside her clothes for hours afterwards—and she'd even tried to straighten up the dripping disorder of the cellar, where a wet corrugated-paper box of rubbish fell apart in her hands as she lifted it out of a puddle, releasing all its mildewed contents in a splash from which an orange-spotted lizard emerged and sped away across her shoe. By the time Frank came home she was too tired to feel like talking.

She didn't feel like talking the next night, either. Instead they watched a television drama which he found wholly absorbing and she declared was trash.

And it was the next night, or the next—he could never afterwards remember which—that he found her pacing the kitchen in the same tense, high-shouldered way she had paced the stage in the second act of *The Petrified Forest*. From the living room came the muffled strains of horn and xylophone, interspersed with the shrieks of midget voices; the children were watching an animated cartoon on television.

"What's the matter?"

"Nothing."

"I don't believe you. Did something happen today, or what?"

"No." Then the perfection of her curtain-call smile began to blur and moisten into a wrinkled grimace of despair and her breathing became as loud as the boiling vegetables on the stove. "Nothing happened today that I haven't known about for days and days—and oh God, Frank, please don't look so dense; do you really mean you haven't known it too, or guessed it or anything? I'm pregnant, that's all."

"Jesus." His face obediently paled and gaped into the look of a man stunned by bad news, but he knew he wouldn't be able to keep it that way for long: an exultant smile was already struggling up for freedom from his chest; he had to take hold of his mouth to stop it. "Wow," he said quietly through his fingers. "Are you sure?"

"Yes." And she came heavily into his arms as if the act of telling him had taken all her strength away. "Frank, I didn't want to clobber you with it before you've even had a drink or anything; I meant to wait until after dinner but I just—the thing is, I've really been pretty sure all week and today I finally saw the doctor and now I can't even *pretend* it's not true any more."

"Wow." He gave up trying to control his face, which now

hung aching with joy over her shoulder as he pressed and stroked her with both hands, muttering mindless words into her hair. "Oh, listen, it doesn't mean we can't go; listen, it just means we'll have to figure out some other *way* of going, is all."

The pressure was off; life had come mercifully back to normal.

"There isn't any other way," she said. "Do you think I've thought about anything else all week? There *isn't* any other way. The whole *point* of going was to give you a chance to find yourself, and now it's ruined. And it's my fault! My own dumb, careless . . ."

"No, listen to me; nothing's ruined. You're all upset. At the very worst it only means waiting a little while until we can work out some—"

"A little *while*! Two years? Three years? Four? How long do you think it'll *be* before I can take a full-time job? Darling, *think* about it a minute. It's hopeless."

"No, it's not. Listen."

"Not now; don't let's try to talk about it now, okay? Let's at least wait'll the kids are asleep." And she turned back to the stove, wiping the inside of her wrist against one dribbling eye in a childish gesture of shame at being seen in tears.

"Okay."

In the living room, hugging their knees, the children were staring blankly at a cartoon bulldog who brandished a spiked club as he chased a cartoon cat through the wreckage of a cartoon house. "Hi," Frank said, and made his way past them to the bathroom to wash up for dinner, allowing his mind to fill with the rhythm and the song of all the things he would say as soon as he and April were alone. "Listen," he would begin. "Suppose it does take time. Look at it this way . . ." And he would begin to draw the picture of a new life. If there was indeed a two- or three-year span of waiting to be done, wouldn't it be made more endurable by the money from Pollock's job? "Oh, of course it'll be a nothing-job, but the money! Think of the money!" They could get a better house—or better still, if they continued to find the suburbs intolerable, they could move back to town. Oh, not to the dark, roach-infested, subway-rumbling city of the old days, but to a brisk, stimulating, new New York that only money could discover. Who knew how much broader and more interesting their lives might become? And besides ... besides ...

He was washing his hands, breathing the good smell of soap and the aromatic fumes of April's scouring powder, noticing that his face in the mirror looked ruddier and better than he'd seen it look in months—he was thus engaged when the full implication, the full meaning of his "besides" clause broke over him. Besides: why *think* of accepting Pollock's money as a mere compromise solution, an enforced making-the-best-of-things until the renewal of her ability to support him in Paris? Didn't it have the weight and dignity of a plan in its own right? It might lead to almost anything—new people, new places—why, it might even take them to Europe in due time. Wasn't there a good chance that Knox, through Knox International, might soon be expanding its promotion of computers abroad? ("You and Mrs. Wheeler are so very unlike one's preconceived idea of American business people," a Henry James sort of Venetian countess might say as they leaned attractively on a balustrade above the Grand Canal, sipping sweet vermouth ...)

"Well, but what about you?" April would say. "How are you *ever* going to find yourself now?" But as he firmly shut off the hot-water faucet he knew he would have the answer for her:

"Suppose we let that be my business."

And there was a new maturity and manliness in the kindly, resolute face that nodded back at him in the mirror.

When he reached for a towel he found she had forgotten to put one on the rack, and when he went to the linen closet to get one he saw, on the top shelf, a small square package freshly wrapped in drugstore paper. Its newness and the incongruity of its being there among the folded sheets and towels gave it a potent, secret look, like that of a hidden Christmas gift, and it was this as much as his unaccountable, rising fear that made him take it down and open it. Inside the wrapping was a blue cardboard box bearing the Good Housekeeping Seal of Approval, and inside the box was the dark pink bulb of a rubber syringe.

Without giving himself time to think, without even wondering if it mightn't be better to wait till after dinner, he carried the package back through the living room, swiftly past the place where the children watched their cartoon (the cat had turned now and was chasing the dog over acres of cartoon countryside), and into the kitchen. And the way her startled face began to harden when she looked at it, and then up into his eyes, left no doubt at all of her intentions.

"Listen," he said. "Just what the hell do you think you're going to do with this?"

She was backing away through the vegetable steam, not in retreat but in defiant readiness, her hands sliding tensely up and down her hips. "And what do you think *you're* going to do?" she said. "Do you think you're going to stop me?"

PART THREE

ONE

OUR ABILITY TO measure and apportion time affords an almost endless source of comfort.

"Synchronize watches at oh six hundred," says the infantry captain, and each of his huddled lieutenants finds a respite from fear in the act of bringing two tiny pointers into jeweled alignment while tons of heavy artillery go fluttering overhead: the prosaic, civilian-looking dial of the watch has restored, however briefly, an illusion of personal control. Good, it counsels, looking tidily up from the hairs and veins of each terribly vulnerable wrist; fine: so far, everything's happening right on time.

"I'm afraid I'm booked solid through the end of the month," says the executive, voluptuously nestling the phone at his cheek as he thumbs the leaves of his appointment calendar, and his mouth and eyes at that moment betray a sense of deep security. The crisp, plentiful, day-sized pages before him prove that nothing unforeseen, no calamity of chance or fate can overtake him between now and the end of the month. Ruin and pestilence have been held at bay, and death itself will have to wait; he is booked solid.

"Oh, let me see now," says the ancient man, tilting his withered head to wince and blink at the sun in bewildered reminiscence, "my first wife passed away in the spring of—" and for a moment he is touched with terror. The spring of what? Past? Future? What is any spring but a mindless rearrangement of cells in the crust of the spinning earth as it floats in endless circuit of its sun? What is the sun itself but one of a billion insensible stars forever going nowhere into nothingness? Infinity! But soon the merciful valves and switches of his brain begin to do their tired work, and "The spring of Nineteen-Ought-Six," he is able to say. "Or no, wait—" and his blood runs cold again as the galaxies revolve. "Wait! Nineteen-Ought—Four." Now he is sure of it, and a restorative flood of well-being brings his hand involuntarily up to slap his thigh in satisfaction. He may have forgotten the shape of his first wife's smile and the sound of her voice in tears, but by imposing a set of numerals on her death he has imposed coherence on his own life, and on life itself. Now all the other years can fall obediently into place, each with its orderly contribution to the whole. Nineteen-Ten, Nineteen-Twenty—Why, of course he remembers!—Nineteen-Thirty, Nineteen-Forty, right on up to the well-deserved peace of his present and on into the gentle promise of his future. The earth can safely resume its benevolent stillness—Smell that new grass!—and it's the same grand old sun that has hung there smiling on him all these years. "Yes sir," he can say with authority, "Nineteen-Ought-Four," and the stars tonight will please him as tokens of his ultimate heavenly rest. He has brought order out of chaos.

The early summer of 1955 might well have been intolerable for both the Wheelers, and might in the end have turned out very differently, if it hadn't been for the calendar that hung on their kitchen wall. A New Year's gift of A. J. Stolper and Sons, Hardware and Home Furnishings, illustrated with scenes of Rural New England, it was the kind of calendar whose page for each month displays two smaller charts as well, last month and next, so that a quarter of the year can be comprehended in a single searching glance.

The Wheelers were able to fix their date of conception in the latter part of the first week in May—the week after his birthday when they could both remember his whispering, "It feels sort of loose," and her whispering, "Oh no, I'm sure it's all right; don't stop . . ." (she had bought a new diaphragm the following week, just to be sure), and this placed the first week in August, more than four weeks away and clear over on the next page, as the mysterious time "right at the end of the third month" when the school friend, long ago, had said it would be safe to apply the rubber syringe.

Panic had sent her straight to the drugstore the minute she was free of the doctor's office that afternoon; panic had driven him down the hall to confront her with the thing the minute he found it in the closet that evening, and it was panic that held them locked and staring at each other in the vegetable steam, brutally silent, while the cartoon music floated in from the next room. But much later that same night, after each of them furtively and in turn had made studies of the calendar, their panic was drowned in the discovery that row on row of logical, orderly days lay waiting for intelligent use between now and the deadline. There was plenty of time for coming to the right decision on this thing, for working this thing out.

"Darling, I didn't mean to be so awful about it; I wouldn't have been if you hadn't come *at* me with it like that, before either of us had a chance to discuss it in any kind of a rational way."

"I know; I know." And he patted her softly weeping shoulder. These tears didn't mean she was capitulating; he knew that. At best they meant what he'd hopefully suspected from the start, that she halfway wanted to be talked out of it; at worst they meant only that she didn't want to antagonize him, that in drawing her own kind of reassurance from the calendar she had seen the four weeks as a generous opportunity for gradually winning him over. But either way, and this was what filled him with gratitude as he held and stroked her, either way it meant she was considering him; she cared about him. For the time being, that was all that mattered.

"Because I mean we've got to be together in this thing, haven't we?" she asked, drawing back a little in his grip. "Otherwise nothing's going to make any sense. Isn't that right?"

"Of course it is. Can we talk a little now? Because I do have a few things to say."

"Yes. I want to talk too. Only let's both promise not to fight, all right? It's just not a thing we can afford to fight about."

"I know. Listen . . ."

And so the way was cleared for the quiet, controlled, dead-serious debate with which they began to fill one after another of the calendar's days, a debate that kept them both in a fine-drawn state of nerves that was not at all unpleasant. It was very like a courtship.

Like a courtship too it took place in a skillfully arranged

variety of settings; Frank saw to that. Their numberless hundreds of thousands of words were spoken indoors and out, on long drives through the hills at night, in expensive country restaurants, and in New York. They had as many evenings-out in two weeks as they'd had in the whole previous year, and one of the ways he began to suspect he was winning, early in the second week, was that she didn't object to spending so much money; she almost certainly would have done so if she'd still been wholly committed to Europe in the fall.

But by then he was in little need of such minor indications. Almost from the start he had seized the initiative, and he was reasonably confident of victory. The idea he had to sell, after all, was clearly on the side of the angels. It was unselfish, mature, and (though he tried to avoid moralizing) morally unassailable. The other idea, however she might try to romanticize its bravery, was repugnant.

"But Frank, don't you see I only want to *do* it for your sake? Won't you please believe that, or try to believe it?"

And he would smile sadly down at her from his fortress of conviction. "How can it be for my sake," he would ask, "when the very thought of it makes my stomach turn over? Just think a little, April. Please."

His main tactical problem, in this initial phase of the campaign, was to find ways of making his position attractive, as well as commendable. The visits to town and country restaurants were helpful in this connection; she had only to glance around her in such places to discover a world of handsome, graceful, unquestionably worthwhile men and women who had somehow managed to transcend their environment—people who had turned dull jobs to their own advantage, who had exploited the system without knuckling under to it, who would certainly tend, if they knew the facts of the Wheelers' case, to agree with him.

"All right," she would say after hearing him out. "Supposing all this does happen. Supposing a couple of years from now we're both terribly sleek and stimulated and all that, and we have loads of fascinating friends and long vacations in Europe every summer. Do you really think you'd be any happier? Wouldn't you still be wasting the prime of your manhood in a completely empty, meaningless kind of—"

And so she would play straight into his snare:

"Suppose we let that be my business." How much, he would ask her, would his prime of manhood be worth if it had to be made conditional on allowing her to commit a criminal mutilation of herself? "Because that's what you'd be doing, April; there's no getting around it. You'd be committing a crime against your own substance. And mine."

Sometimes, gently, she would charge him with overdramatizing the whole thing. It was a thing women did every day in perfect safety; the girl at school had done it twice at least. Oh, doing it after the third month would be a different story, she granted him that—"I mean it certainly *would* be legitimate to worry, if that were the case. This way, though, being able to time it so closely and everything, it's the safest thing in the world."

But at her every mention of how safe it was he would puff out his cheeks and blow, frowning and shaking his head, as if he'd been asked to agree that an ethical justification could be found for genocide. No. He wouldn't buy it.

Soon there began to be a slight embarrassed hesitation in her voice and a distinct averting of her eyes whenever she spoke of the abortion as "doing this thing," even in the context of a heartfelt statement on how absolutely essential it was that the thing be done, as if the presence of his loving, troubled face had put the matter beyond the limits of conversational decency. Soon too—and this was the most encouraging sign of all—he began to be aware at odd moments that she was covertly watching him through a mist of romantic admiration.

These moments were not always quite spontaneous; as often as not they followed a subtle effort of vanity on his part, a form of masculine flirtation that was as skillful as any girl's. Walking toward or away from her across a restaurant floor, for example, he remembered always to do it in the old "terrifically sexy" way, and when they walked together he fell into another old habit of holding his head unnaturally erect and carrying his inside shoulder an inch or two higher than the other, to give himself more loftiness from where she clung at his arm. When he lit a

cigarette in the dark he was careful to arrange his features in a
virile frown before striking and cupping the flame (he knew,
from having practiced this at the mirror of a blacked-out bathroom years ago, that it made a swift, intensely dramatic portrait),
and he paid scrupulous attention to endless details: keeping his
voice low and resonant, keeping his hair brushed and his bitten
fingernails out of sight; being always the first one athletically up
and out of bed in the morning, so that she might never see his
face lying swollen and helpless in sleep.

Sometimes after a particularly conscious display of this kind,
as when he found he had made all his molars ache by holding
them clamped too long for an effect of grim-jawed determination by candlelight, he would feel a certain distaste with himself
for having to resort to such methods—and, very obscurely, with
her as well, for being so easily swayed by them. What kind of
kid stuff was this? But these attacks of conscience were quickly
allayed: all was fair in love and war; and besides, wasn't she all
too capable of playing the same game? Hadn't she pulled out
everything in her own bag of tricks last month, to seduce him
into the Europe plan? All right, then. Maybe it was sort of ludicrous; maybe it wasn't the healthiest way for grown people to
behave, but that was a question they could take up later. There
was too much at stake to worry about such things now.

And so he freed himself to concentrate on the refinements of
his role. He was particularly careful never to mention his day at
the office or confess to being tired after the train, he assumed a
quiet, almost Continental air of mastery in dealing with waiters
and gas station attendants, he salted his after-theater critiques
with obscure literary references—all to demonstrate that a man
condemned to a life at Knox could still be interesting ("You're
the most interesting person I've ever met"); he enthusiastically
romped with the children, disdainfully mowed the lawn in
record time and once spent the whole of a midnight's drive in
an impersonation of Eddie Cantor singing "That's the Kind of
a Baby for Me" because it made her laugh—all to demonstrate
that a man confronted with this bleakest and most unnatural of
conjugal problems, a wife unwilling to bear his child, could still
be nice ("I love you when you're nice").

His campaign might have been quickly and easily won if he could have arranged for all the hours of the four weeks to be lived at the same pitch of intensity; the trouble was that ordinary life still had to go on.

It was still necessary for him to kill most of each day at the office, where Jack Ordway kept congratulating him on the niftiness of his flying the coop, and for her to spend it imprisoned in the reality of their home.

It was also necessary to deal with Mrs. Givings, who lately had found one excuse after another for calling up and dropping in. Her ostensible purpose was business, which in itself was very trying—there were many details to discuss about putting the house on the market, to which the Wheelers had to listen poker-faced—but her talk kept coming back to John and to "the lovely time we all had that day." Almost before they knew it, they had agreed to a tentative program of future Sunday afternoons "whenever it's convenient, whatever Sundays you're not too busy, between now and the time you leave."

It was necessary to deal with the Campbells, too. One whole Saturday was consumed that way, a picnic and outing at the beach undertaken at the Campbells' insistence—a day of hot dogs and children's tears, of sand and sweat and dazzling confusion—and it left them on the brink of hysteria that night. It was that night, in fact, that the courtship, or the sales campaign, or whatever it was, passed abruptly into its second, nonromantic phase.

"*God*, what a day," April said as soon as she'd shut the children's door, and then she began to move stiffly around the living room in a way that always meant trouble. He had learned early in the courtship, or the campaign, that this room was the worst possible place for getting his points across. All the objects revealed in the merciless stare of its hundred-watt light bulbs seemed to support her argument; and more than once, on hot nights like this, their cumulative effect had threatened to topple the whole intricate structure of his advantage: the furniture that had never settled down and never would, the shelves on shelves of unread or half-read or read-and-forgotten books that had always been supposed to make such a difference and never had; the loathsome, gloating maw of the television set; the forlorn, grubby little heap of toys that might have been steeped in ammonia, so quick was their power to attack the eyes and throat with an acrid pain of guilt and self-reproach ("But I don't think we were ever *meant* to be parents. We're not even *adequate* as parents . . .").

Tonight her forehead, cheekbones and nose were sorely pink with sunburn, and the fact that she'd worn sunglasses all day gave her eyes a white, astonished look. Her hair hung in disorderly strings—she kept having to push out her lower lip to blow it away from her eyes—and her body looked uncomfortable too. She was wearing a damp blouse and a pair of wrinkled blue shorts that were just beginning to be tight across the abdomen. She hated to wear shorts anyway because they called attention to how heavy and soft and vein-shot her thighs had grown in the past few years, though Frank had often told her not to be silly about it ("They're lovely; I like them even better this way; they're a woman's legs now"), and now she seemed almost to be parading them in a kind of spite. All right, look at them, she seemed to be saying. Are they "womanly" enough for you? Is this what you want?

He couldn't, at any rate, take his eyes off them as they ponderously lifted and settled in her walk around the room. He made himself a powerful drink and stood sipping it near the kitchen door, bracing himself.

After a while she sat heavily on the sofa and began a lethargic picking-over of old magazines. Then she dropped them and lay back, setting her sneakered feet on the coffee table, and said, "You really are a much more moral person than I am, Frank. I suppose that's why I admire you." But she didn't look or sound admiring.

He tried to dismiss it with a careful shrug as he took a seat across from her. "I don't know about that. I don't see what any of this has to do with being 'moral.' I mean—*you* know, not in any sense of conventional morality."

She seemed to think this over for a long time as she lay back allowing one knee to sway from side to side, rocking it on the swivel of her ankle. Then: "Is there any other kind?" she asked. "Don't 'moral' and 'conventional' really mean the same thing?"

He could have hit her in the face. Of all the insinuating, treacherous little—Christ! And in any other month of his married life he would have been on his feet and shouting: "*Christ*, when are you going to get over this damn Noël Coward, nineteen-twenties way of denigrating every halfway decent human value with some cute, brittle, snobbish little thing to say? Listen!" he would have raged at her. "Listen! Maybe that's the way *your* parents lived; maybe that's the kind of chic, titillating crap *you* were raised on, but it's about time you figured out it doesn't have a God damned thing to do with the real world." It was his knowledge of the calendar that stopped his mouth. There were twelve days to go. He couldn't afford to take any chances now, and so instead of shouting those things he held his jaws shut and stared at his glass, which he gripped until it nearly spilled with trembling. Without even trying, he had given his most memorable facial performance to date. When the spasm was over he said, very quietly:

"Baby, I know you're tired. We shouldn't be talking about it now. I know you know better than that. Let's skip it."

"Skip what? You know I know better than what?"

"You know. This business about 'moral' and 'conventional.' "

"But I *don't* know the difference." She had come earnestly forward on the sofa, had drawn her sneakers back under it and was leaning toward him with both tense forearms on her knees. Her face was so innocently confused that he couldn't look at it. "Don't you see, Frank? I really *don't* know the difference. Other people seem to; you do; I just don't, that's all, and I don't think I ever really have."

"Look," he said. "First place, 'moral' was your word, not mine. I don't think I've ever held any brief for this thing on moral grounds, conventional or otherwise. I've simply said that under these particular circumstances, it seems pretty obvious that the only mature thing to do is go ahead and have the—"

"But there we are again," she said. "You see? I don't know what 'mature' means, either, and you could talk all night and I still wouldn't know. It's all just *words* to me, Frank. I watch you talking and I think: Isn't that amazing? He really does *think* way; these words really do *mean* something to him. So it seems I've been watching people talk and thinking that all my life"—her voice was becoming unsteady—"and maybe it means there's something awful the matter with me, but it's true. Oh no, stay there. Please don't come and kiss me or anything, or we'll just end up in a big steaming heap and we won't get anything settled. Please stay sitting there, and let's just sort of try to talk. Okay?"

"Okay." And he stayed sitting there. But trying to talk was something else again; all they could do was look at each other, heavy and weak and bright-eyed in the heat.

"All I know," she said at last, "is what I feel, and I know what I feel I've got to do."

He got up and turned off all the lights, murmuring "Cool the place off a little," but the darkness didn't help. This was deadlock. If everything he said was "just words," what was the point of talking? How could any possibility of speech prevail against the weight of a stubbornness as deep as this?

But before long his voice had started to work again; almost independent of his will, it had fallen back and begun to employ his final tactic, the dangerous last-ditch maneuver he had hoped to hold in reserve against the possibility of defeat. It was reckless—there were still twelve days to go—but once he had started he couldn't stop.

"Look," he was saying, "this may sound as if I think there *is* something 'awful' the matter with you; the fact is I don't. I do think, though, that there's one or two aspects to this thing we haven't really touched on yet, and I think we ought to. For instance, I wonder if your real motives here are quite as simple as you think. I mean isn't it possible there are forces at work here that you're not e~ ~ely aware of? That you're not recognizing?"

She d ~ and in the darkness he could only guess at ~ing or not. He took a deep breath. "I mean ~g to do with Europe," he said, "or with ~in yourself, things that have their origin ~—your own upbringing and so on. Emo-

before she said, in a pointedly neutral ~ionally disturbed."

"I didn't say that!" But in the next hour, as his voice went on and on, he managed to say it several times in several different ways. Wasn't it likely, after all, that a girl who'd known nothing but parental rejection from the time of her birth might develop an abiding reluctance to bear children?

"I mean it's always been a wonder to me that you could *survive* a childhood like that," he said at one point, "let alone come out of it without any damage to your—you know, your ego and everything." She herself, he reminded her, had suggested the presence of something "neurotic" in her wish to abort the first pregnancy, on Bethune Street—and all right, all right, of *course* the circumstances were different this time. But wasn't it just possible that something of the same confusion might still exist in her attitude? Oh, he wasn't saying this was the whole story— "I'm not *qualified* to say that"—but he did feel it was a line of reasoning that ought to be very carefully explored.

"But I've *had* two children," she said. "Doesn't that count in my favor?"

He let these words reverberate in the darkness for a while. "The very fact that you put it that way is kind of significant," he said quietly, "don't you think? As if having children were a kind of punishment? As if having two of them could 'count in your favor' as a credit against any obligation to have another? And the way you said it, too—all defensive, all ready to fight. Jesus, April, if you want to talk that way I can come right back at you with another statistic: you've had three pregnancies and you've wanted to abort two of them. What kind of a record is that? Oh, look." He made his voice very gentle, as if he were talking to Jennifer. "Look, baby. All I'm trying to suggest is that you don't seem to be entirely rational about this thing. I just wish you'd think about it a little, that's all."

"All right," her voice said bleakly. "All right, suppose all this is true. Suppose I'm acting out a compulsive behavior pattern, or whatever they call it. So what? I still can't help what I feel, can I? I mean what're we supposed to *do* about it? How am I supposed to get over it? Am I just supposed to Face Up to my Problems and start being a different person tomorrow morning, or what?"

"Oh, baby," he said. "It's so simple. I mean assuming you *are* in some kind of emotional difficulty, assuming there *is* a problem of this sort, don't you see there *is* something we can do about it? Something very logical and sensible that we ought to do about it?" He was weary of the sound of his own voice; he felt he had been talking for years. He licked his lips, which tasted as foreign as the flesh of a dentist's finger in his mouth ("Open wide, now!"), and then he said it. "We ought to have you see a psychoanalyst."

He couldn't see her, but he could guess that her mouth was flattening out and drawing a little to one side, her tough look. "And is Bart Pollock's job going to pay for that too?" she asked.

He issued a sigh. "You see what you're doing, when you say a thing like that? You're fighting with me."

"No, I'm not."

"Yes you are. And what's worse, you're fighting with yourself. This is exactly the kind of thing we've both been doing for years, and it's about time we grew up enough to cut it out. *I* don't know if Pollock's job is going to pay for it; frankly, I couldn't care less whose job pays for what. We're two supposedly adult human beings, and if one or the other of us needs this kind of help we ought to be able to talk it over in an adult way. The question of how it's going to be 'paid for' is the very least important part of it. If it's needed, it'll be paid for. I promise you."

"How nice." It was only by a dim shifting of shadows and a rustling of upholstery that he could tell she was standing up. "Could we sort of stop talking about it now? I'm dead tired."

As he listened to her receding footsteps down the hall, and then to the sounds of her brief preparations for bed, and then to the silence, he finished his drink with a foretaste of defeat. He felt that he had played his last chance, and had almost certainly lost.

But the next day brought fresh reserves of strength to his position from an unexpected source: it was the Sunday of John Givings's second visit.

"Hi!" he called, getting out of the car, and from the moment he ambled pigeon-toed across the driveway with his parents twitching and apologizing around him, it was clear that this would be a different and more difficult afternoon than the last. There would be no strolling companionship today, no fond remembrance of radio shows; he was in a highly agitated state. The sight and the sound of him was so unnerving, at first, that it was some time before Frank began to see how this visit might have a certain beneficial, cautionary effect. Here, after all, was a full-fledged mental case for April to observe and contemplate. Could she still say, after this, that she didn't care if she was crazy too?

"How soon you people taking off?" he demanded, interrupting his mother in the midst of a rapturous sentence about the magnificence of the day. They were sitting out on the back lawn, where April was serving iced tea—or rather, everyone but John was sitting. He was up and walking around, occasionally pausing to stare with narrowed eyes at some point far away in the woods or past the house and down across the road; he looked as if he were turning over grave and secret issues in his mind. "September, did you say? I don't remember."

"It isn't really definite yet," Frank said.

"You'll be around another month or so, though, anyway; right? Because the thing is, I need to ask somebody for a—" He broke off and glanced around the lawn with a puzzled look. "Hey, by the way, where do you people keep your kids? Old Helen keeps telling me about your kids, and I never see 'em. They go to birthday parties every Sunday, or what?"

"They're visiting friends this afternoon," April said.

John Givings looked at her steadily and long, and then at Frank; then he lowered his eyes, squatted, and began to pull blades of grass out of the lawn, "Well, that figures," he said. "I had a paranoid schizophrenic coming to my house, I'd probably get the kids out of the way too. If I had any kids, that is. If I had any house."

"Oh, this is the most wonderful egg *salad*, April," Mrs. Givings said. "You must tell me how you fix it."

"Save it, Ma, okay? She can tell you later. Listen, though, Wheeler. This is important. The thing is, I need to ask somebody for a favor, and as long as you're going to be around for a month I figure I'd like it to be you. Shouldn't take much of your time, and it won't take any of your money. I wonder if you could get me a lawyer."

Howard Givings cleared his throat. "John, don't let's get started again about the lawyer. Steady down, now."

The look on John's face now was that of reasonable patience tried to the breaking point. "Pop," he said, "couldn't you just sit there and eat your wonderful egg salad, and quit horning in? Turn off your hearing aid or something. Come on," he said to Frank. "I guess we'd better make this a private talk. Oh, and bring your wife too." And with an air of tense conspiracy he led them both away to a far corner of the yard. "There isn't any reason why they shouldn't hear this," he explained; "it's just that they'd keep interrupting all the time. Here's the deal. I want to find out if inmates of mental hospitals have any legal rights. You suppose you could find that out for me?"

"Well," Frank said, "offhand, I'm afraid I don't know how I'd—"

"Okay, okay, forget that part of it. In order to find that out you'd probably have to spend money. All I'm asking you to spend is time. Get me the name and address of a good lawyer, and I'll take it from there. The thing is, you see, I've got a good many questions to ask, and I'm willing to pay for the answers. I think I've got a pretty good case, if we can get around this business of the legal rights . . ."

It might have been only that his gaze kept switching back and forth between the Wheelers' faces, with intermittent glances over their shoulders to check on what his parents were doing across the lawn—it might have been only that, in combination with the pallor and dryness of his lips and the fact that his hair stood up and out from his scalp in stiff bristles (he hadn't worn his cap today), but as his monologue in the sun progressed he began to look more and more like the picture of a racked, wild-eyed madman.

". . . Now, I don't need to be told that a man who goes after his mother with a coffee table is putting himself in a weak position legally; that's obvious. If he hits her with it and kills her, that's a criminal case. If all he does is break the coffee table and give her a certain amount of aggravation and she decides to go to court over it, that's a civil case. All right. Either way the man's in a weak position, but here's the point: in neither case is there any question of his own legal rights being jeopardized. Now, supposing the second of these two possibilities takes place. The guy doesn't hit her, does break the coffee table, does give her the aggravation—but the woman, the mother, doesn't exercise her option to take it to court. Supposing what she does instead is to call out the State Troopers. Supposing when she gets hold of the State Troopers she—*Pop!*"

At this apparently meaningless shout he began backing away from them like a cornered fugitive, his face distorted in a mixture of menace and fear; when Frank turned around he saw the reason for this outburst was the slow approach of Howard Givings across the grass.

"*Pop!* I *told* you not to interrupt me, didn't I? Didn't I? I mean it now, Pop. Don't *interrupt* me when I'm *talk*ing."

"Steady down, boy," Howard Givings said. "Let's steady down, now. It's time to go."

"I *mean* it, Pop—" He had backed himself up against the stone wall; he was looking desperately around as if for a weapon, and for a second Frank was afraid he might pick a rock out of the wall and throw it; but Howard Givings continued his steady, mollifying advance. He had only to touch his son softly on the elbow to restore a kind of order: John continued to shout, but he was more like a child in a tantrum now than a maniac. "Don't interrupt me, that's all. You got something to say, you can *save* it till I finish *talk*ing."

"All right, John," Howard Givings murmured, turning and leading him away for a quieting stroll along the edge of the lawn. "All right, now, boy."

"Oh, dear," Mrs. Givings said. "I'm terribly sorry about this. It's his nerves, you see." She was looking up at the Wheelers in an agony of embarrassment, unable to decide what to do with the egg salad sandwich in her hand. "I'm afraid you'll have to— excuse us. We shouldn't have come today."

"Lord," April said, washing out the iced-tea glasses when the visitors had gone. "I wonder what *his* childhood was like."

"Couldn't have been very great, I guess, with a pair of parents like that."

She didn't say anything until she had finished at the sink and hung up the dish towel. Then: "But at least he *had* a pair of parents, so at the very least he must have had more emotional security than me. Is that what you're saying?"

"What *I'm* saying? Jesus, take it easy, will you?"

But she had already gone, banging the screen door behind her, to retrieve the children from the Campbells' house. She seemed calm and aloof through the rest of the evening, moving efficiently through the tasks of the dinner and the children's bedtime, and Frank was careful to keep out of her way. It began to appear that this was to be one of their silent nights, one of the times when they would read the papers in different parts of the room like two discreet, courteous strangers in a hotel lobby; but at ten o'clock, without warning, she broke the truce.

"Sort of a denial of womanhood," she said. "Is that how you'd put it?"

"Is that how I'd put what? What're you talking about?"

She looked faintly annoyed, as if impatient with him for having failed to follow the thread of a continuous discussion. "You know. The psychological thing behind this abortion business. Is that what women are supposed to be expressing when they don't want to have children? That they're not really women, or don't want to be women, or something?"

"Baby, I don't know," he said kindly, while his heart thickened in gratitude. "Believe me, it's a thing about which your guess is as good as mine. It does sound sort of logical, though, doesn't it? I do remember reading somewhere—oh, in Freud or Krafft-Ebing or one of those people; this was back in college—I do remember reading something about a woman with a sort of infantile penis-envy thing that carried over into her adult life; I guess this is supposed to be fairly common among women; I don't know. Anyway, she kept trying to get rid of her pregnancies, and what this particular guy figured out was that she was really trying to sort of open herself up so that the—you know— so that the penis could come out and hang down where it belonged. I'm not sure if I have that right; I read it a long time ago, but that was the general idea." He wasn't, in fact, quite sure if he'd read it at all (though where could it have come from if he hadn't?), and he was not at all sure it had been a wise thing to relate at this particular time.

But she seemed able to absorb the information with no particular surprise. She was looking off into space with her chin in her two cupped hands and both elbows on her knees. She looked perplexed; that was all.

"In any case," he went on, "I'm sure it's probably a mistake to try and draw your own conclusions from the things you read in books. Who knows?" He decided he ought to stop there and let her talk for a while, but she didn't say anything, and the silence seemed to demand to be filled.

"I think we *can* assume, though," he said, "just on the basis of common sense, that if most little girls do have this thing about wanting to be boys, they probably get over it in time by observing and admiring and wanting to emulate their mothers—I mean *you* know, attract a man, establish a home, have children and so on. And in your case, you see, that whole side of life, that whole dimension of experience was denied you from the start. I don't know; all these things are very obscure and hard to—hard to get hold of, I guess."

She got up and walked away to stand near the bookcase, with her back to him, and he was reminded of the way he had first seen her, long ago, across that roomful of forgotten talkers in Morningside Heights—a tall, proud, exceptionally first-rate girl.

"How do you suppose we'd go about finding one?" she asked. "A psychiatrist, I mean. Aren't a lot of them supposed to be quacks? Well, but still, I guess that isn't really much of a problem, is it."

He held his breath.

"Okay," she said. Her eyes were bright with tears as she turned around. "I guess you're right. I guess there isn't much more to say, then, is there?"

He knew, as he lay awake between fitful spells of sleep beside her, later in the night, that the campaign was by no means over. There were still eleven days before the deadline, in any one of which she might violently change her mind. For eleven more days, whenever he was with her, he would have to keep all the forces of his argument marshaled and ready for instant, skillful use.

His job now was to consolidate this delicate victory in as many ways as possible, to hold the line. It would be best, he decided, to lose no time in letting everyone know about their change of plans—the Campbells, everyone—so that the whole question of the Wheelers going to Europe could quickly be relegated to the past tense; and meanwhile he must allow no hint of complacency to undermine his position. He would have to be constantly on hand as a source of reassurance until the danger period was over. For a start, he decided he would stay home from work today.

TWO

"WE'RE NOT?" Jennifer said that afternoon. She and Michael were standing in their bathing suits on the living room carpet, with towels drawn around their shoulders like cloaks. They'd been playing in the lawn sprinkler, and their mother had called them indoors ostensibly to "dry off for a minute and have some milk and cookies," but also, as it turned out, to hear a formal announcement, from both parents, that they weren't going to France after all. "We're not? How come?"

"Because Daddy and Mommy have decided it would be better not to just now," April said. They had settled on this answer a few minutes before (there was no point in telling them about the baby yet) and the words had a stiff, made-up sound which she tried to counteract by adding, very gently, "That's how come."

"Oh." The total neutrality of expression on both children's faces was emphasized by the fact that their eyes were still sun-dazed and their lips, under smiling spoors of milk, were blue from having stayed in the water too long. Jennifer lifted one bare foot and used it to scratch a mosquito bite on the ankle of her other leg.

"Is that all you've got to say?" Frank demanded, with a little more heartiness than he'd planned. "Not even 'Hurray' or anything? We thought you'd be pleased."

The children looked briefly at one another and performed bashful smiles. It had become increasingly hard, lately, for either of them to know what was expected. Jennifer wiped away her milk mustache. "Are we going to France later, then, or what?"

"Well," her mother said. "Maybe. We'll see. But we certainly won't be going for a long time, so it's nothing you need to be thinking about any more."

"So we'll be staying here," Jennifer said helpfully, "but not forever and ever."

"That's about right, Niffer. Give Mommy a kiss now, and then how about both of you going out and getting some sun? And try staying out of the water for a while, okay? Your lips are all blue. You can each have a couple more cookies, if you want."

"Know what we can do, Niffer?" Michael said as soon as they were outside again. "Know that place up in the woods where the big tree's fallen over and it's got this little branch you can sit on and make a pretend soda fountain? We can take our cookies up there and you can be the lady coming into the soda fountain and I can be the soda fountain man."

"I don't feel like it."

"Come on. And I'll say 'What would you like to eat today?' And you'll say 'A cookie, please,' and I'll say—"

"I don't *feel* like it, I said. It's too hot." And she sat well away from him on the scorched grass. Why was it "better not to just now"? And why had her mother looked so funny and sad when she said "That's about right"? And why had her father stayed home from work when he wasn't even sick?

When Michael finished eating he ran crazily out along the crest of the front-yard slope, flailing his arms. "Look at me, Niffer, look at me, look at me—I'm falling down dead!" He wobbled and fell, rolled over a few times and lay very flat and still in the grass, giggling to himself at how funny it must have looked. But she wasn't watching. She had walked up close to the picture window and was peeking inside.

They were still sitting on the sofa, leaning a little toward each other, and her mother was nodding and her father was talking. It was funny to see his hands making little gestures in the air and his mouth, moving and moving, with no sound coming out. After a while her mother went away to the kitchen and her father went on sitting there alone. Then he got up and went down to the cellar and came outdoors with his shovel, to work on the stone path.

"Oh, I don't know whether to be sad or glad," said Milly Campbell a few nights later, squirming deep into the sofa cushions. "I mean it's a darn shame and everything for *you* folks, I guess you're awfully disappointed, but I mean personally I'm just as pleased as I can be. Aren't you, sweetie?"

And Shep, after a tremulous sip of gin and tonic that brought the ice cubes clicking painfully against his front teeth, said he sure was.

But the truth was that he wasn't sure of anything. For weeks now, in an effort to put April Wheeler out of his mind, he had drawn solace from a daydream in which ten years had passed: the Wheelers were coming back from Europe, the Campbells were meeting the boat, and from the moment April came down the gangplank he saw that she'd grown thick and stumpy from her decade of breadwinning. Her cheeks had sagged into jowls, she stood and moved like a man and talked in a sarcastic, squint-eyed way with a cigarette wagging in her lips. Whenever this vision faltered he contented himself with a single-minded cataloguing of her present imperfections (She *was* too heavy across the beam; her voice *did* get too shrill when she was tense; there *was* something nervous and artificial about her smile), and every time he saw a pretty girl, on the beach or at traffic lights on his daily drive to Stamford and back, he would use her to strengthen his belief that the world was full of better-looking, more intelligent, finer and more desirable women than April Wheeler. Throughout this period too he had schooled himself to be more than ordinarily fond of Milly. He had paid her numberless little courtly attentions; once he had picked out an expensive blouse at the best shop in Stamford and brought it home to her ("What do you mean, what for? Because you're my girl, that's what for . . ."), and he had enjoyed the impression that she was flowering into a new serenity at his touch.

And now it was all shot to hell. The Wheelers weren't going anywhere. Milly was sitting here chattering about pregnancy and babies, with her new blouse already missing a button and gray around the armpits; April Wheeler was as cool and beautiful as ever. He cleared his throat. "So you figure you'll be staying on here indefinitely, then?" he asked. "Or will you be getting a bigger house, or what?"

"Ah," said Jack Ordway. "So. Foiled by faulty contraception. Well, Franklin, I can't say I'm sorry. You'd have been sorely missed here in the old cubicle, I can promise you that. Besides which—" he leaned elegantly back in his creaking swivel chair and threw one ankle over his knee—"apart from which, if you'll forgive me, the whole European scheme did sound a bit—a tiny bit unrealistic, sort of. None of my business, I'm sure."

"Pull up a chair, uh, Frank," said Bart Pollock. "What's on your mind?"

It was the hottest day of the year, the kind of a day when everyone on the Fifteenth Floor discussed how scandalous it was that a company the size of Knox did not have air conditioning, yet Frank had expected that Pollock's private office, here on the Twentieth, would somehow be cooler. He had imagined too that Pollock would greet him standing up, perhaps striding across the carpet with hand outstretched, and that as soon as the formalities were out of the way ("Frank, I'm tickled to death . . .") they might adjourn to do business over a brace of Tom Collinses in some air-conditioned cocktail lounge. Instead they were sitting stiff and damp under the irritating buzz of an electric fan. The room was smaller than it looked from the outside, and Pollock, wearing a surprisingly cheap summer shirt through which the outlines of his soaked undershirt were clearly visible, looked more like an exhausted salesman than a top executive. His desk, though appropriately wide and glass-topped, bore as many disorderly piles of paper as Frank's own. Its only ornament suggesting the luxury of rank was a cork-and-silver tray that held a stout little thermos jug for ice water and a tumbler, and a careful inspection of this display revealed that all its elements were finely coated with dust.

"Mm," he said when Frank had finished. "Well, that's fine. I'm personally very glad you've come to this decision. Now of course, as I've told you—" He closed his bulbous eyes and tenderly rubbed their lids. This didn't mean he had forgotten anything; Frank could see that. Everything was all right. It was just that no man could be jubilant in a room like this, on a day like this; and besides, what they were talking about was, after all, a matter of business. "As I mentioned that day at lunch, this whole project's still in the development stage. I'll be calling you in for conferences from time to time as the thing shapes up; meanwhile

I'd suggest you keep on with these whaddyacallits, these promotion pieces of yours. I'll give Ted a buzz and tell him you're working on something for me. That's all he'll need to know for the time being. Right?"

"Changed your what?" said Mrs. Givings, frowning fearfully into the black perforations of her telephone. She was nearing the end of a bleak and very trying day, the whole afternoon of which had been spent at Greenacres—first sitting for unendurable lengths of time on various benches in the waxed and disinfected corridor, waiting for an appointment with John's doctor, then sitting in wretched politeness beside the doctor's desk while he told her that John's behavior in the past several weeks had been "not very encouraging, I'm afraid," and that "I think we'd better call a halt to these outings of his for a while, say five or six weeks."

"But he's been perfectly fine with us," she had lied. "That's what I was going to tell you. Oh, things did get a little out of hand this last time, as I said, but in general he's seemed *very* relaxed. *Very* cheerful."

"Yes. Unfortunately, we can only proceed on the basis of our own, ah, our own observations here in the ward. Tell me, what does his attitude seem to be at the conclusion of the visits? How does he seem to feel about coming back to the hospital each time?"

"He *couldn't* be sweeter about it. Really, Doctor, he's just as willing and cooperative as a lamb."

"Yes." And the doctor had fingered his loathsome tie clasp. "Well, actually, you see, it would probably be a healthier sign if he showed some reluctance. Let's say"—he frowned at his calendar—"let's say at least until the first Sunday in September. Then we might try again."

He might as well have said never. By the first Sunday in September, in all probability, the Wheelers would be on their way to the other side of the world. Now, feeling enormously tired, she had called the Wheelers to cancel the next date they had made—she would have to find other excuses for the other Sundays from now on—and April Wheeler, whose voice sounded small and very far away, was trying to tell her that something was changed. Why did everything always change, when all you wanted, all you had ever humbly asked of whatever God there might be, was that certain things be allowed to remain the same?

"Changed your what? . . ." Then all at once Mrs. Givings was aware of the blood in her veins. ". . . Oh, changed your *plans*. Oh, then you're *not* ready to sell . . ." and her pencil began to draw a row of black, five-pointed stars across the top of her scratch pad—to draw them with such furious pressure that their joyful shapes were embossed on all the pages underneath. "Oh, I *am* so glad to hear that, April. Really, this is the best news I've had in I don't know how long. So you'll be staying here with us, then . . ." She was afraid she might begin to cry; but luckily April was apologizing now for "all the trouble you've gone to about putting the house on the market," which allowed her to retreat into the protection of a cool, tolerant businesswoman's chuckle. "Oh, no, please don't mention that. Really, it's been no trouble at all. . . . All right, then . . . Fine, then, April . . . Good. We'll be in touch."

When she put the receiver back it was as if she were returning a rare and exquisite jewel to its velvet case.

A bad dream or a shrill bird, or both, woke him much too early in the morning and filled him with a sense of dread—a feeling that his next breath and blink of wakefulness would recall him to the knowledge of a grief, a burden of bad news from yesterday that sleep had only temporarily eased. It took him at least a minute to remember that it was good news, not bad: yesterday had been the last of the first week in August. The deadline had come and gone. The debate was over, and he had won.

He raised himself on one elbow to look at her in the blue light—she was turned away from him with her face hidden under a tangle of hair—and nestled close to her back with his arm around her. He arranged his face in a smile of contentment and his limbs in an attitude of total peace, but it didn't work. Half an hour later he was still awake, wanting a cigarette and watching the sky turn to morning.

The peculiar thing was that in the past week or so they hadn't mentioned it. Each afternoon he had come home ready to intercept whatever last-minute points of argument she might raise—he had even cut down on his drinking, so that his head would be clear for discussion—but each evening they had either talked of other things or hadn't talked at all. Last night she had set up the ironing board in front of the television set and worked there, glancing up every few seconds from the steaming whisk and glide of the iron to peer, frowning, at whatever mottled image was cavorting on the screen.

What do you want to talk for? her profile seemed to be saying, in reply to his uneasy gaze from across the room. What is there to talk about? Haven't we done enough talking?

When she turned off the television and folded up the ironing board at last, he went over and touched her arm.

"You know what this is?"

"What what is? What do you mean?"

"Today. It's the last day of the—you know. If you'd gone ahead with that business, this would've been your last day for doing it."

"Oh. Yes, I suppose that's true."

He patted her shoulder, feeling clumsy. "No regrets?"

"Well," she said, "I guess I'd better not have any, had I? Be a little late for them now, wouldn't it?" She carried the ironing board awkwardly away, one of its legs dangling, and she was all the way to the kitchen door before it occurred to him to help her. He sprang to her side.

"Here, let me take that."

"Oh. Thank you."

And in bed, without a word, they made a sensible, temperate, mature kind of love. The last thing he said before falling asleep was, "Listen. We're going to be all right."

"I hope so," she whispered. "I hope so; very much."

Then he had slept, and now he was awake.

He got up and went padding through the silent house. The kitchen was alight with all the colors of the sunrise—it was a beautiful morning—and the calendar had lost its power. There it hung, through the courtesy of A. J. Stolper and Sons, a document useful only in the paying of bills and the making of dental appointments. Days and weeks could pass now without anyone's caring; a month might vanish before anyone thought to tear away the page for the month before.

Franklin H. Wheeler poured himself a glass of ice-cold orange juice, the color of the sun, and sipped it slowly at the kitchen table, afraid it would sicken him to take it all at once. He had won but he didn't feel like a winner. He had successfully righted the course of his life but he felt himself more than ever a victim of the world's indifference. It didn't seem fair.

Only very gradually, there at the table, was he able to sort out and identify what it was that had haunted him on waking, that had threatened to make him gag on his orange juice and now prevented his enjoyment of the brilliant grass and trees and sky beyond the window.

It was that he was going to have another child, and he wasn't at all sure that he wanted one.

"Knowing what you've got, comma," said the living human voice in the playback of the Dictaphone, "knowing what you need, comma, knowing what you can do without, dash. That's inventory control.

"Paragraph . . ."

It was suddenly past the middle of August, and two weeks had elapsed since his last talk with Pollock, or possibly three; time, now that he'd overcome the need to measure and apportion it, had again begun to slip away from him. "You mean to say it's Friday already?" he was apt to demand on what he'd thought was Tuesday or Wednesday, and it wasn't until lunchtime today, when he passed a store window featuring a display of autumn leaves and the words back to school, that he realized the summer was over. Very soon now it would be time for topcoats, and then it would be Christmas.

"The main thing I have to do now," he had recently explained to April, "is to finish this Speaking-of series. I mean I can't very well expect to talk money with him until I've done that, can I?"

"No; I suppose not. You know best."

"Well, I can't. I mean we can't expect any miraculous changes overnight in a thing like this; it's the kind of a thing that can't be rushed."

"Do I seem to be rushing you? Really, Frank; how many ways can I say it? It's entirely up to you."

"I know," he said. "I know, of course I know that. Anyway, I do want to get the damn series done as soon as possible. I'll probably stay in late a couple of nights this week to work on it."

And he'd taken to staying in late nearly every night since then. He rather enjoyed having dinner alone in town and taking walks through the city at evening before catching the late train. It gave him a pleasant sense of independence, of freedom from the commuter's round; and besides, it seemed a suitable practice for the new, mature, non-sentimental kind of marriage that was evidently going to be their way from now on.

The only trouble was that this second Speaking-of piece had turned out to be much harder than the first. He had finished it twice now, and each time had discovered gaping errors of logic or emphasis that seemed to demand a total revision.

The office clock read five-forty-five as he listened to the play-back of his third and final revision, and the silence beyond his cubicle proved that even the last and most drearily conscientious people on the Fifteenth Floor had gone home; soon the platoons of scrubwomen would arrive with mops and buckets. When the recording had droned to its conclusion he felt nicely exhilarated. It wasn't very good, but it would do. Now he could take off uptown and have a couple of drinks before dinner.

He was in the act of leaning over to shut off the machine when the click, click, click of a woman's heels came delicately up the aisle outside. He knew at once that it was Maureen Grube, that she had purposely stayed late in order to be alone with him, and that he was going to take her out tonight. It seemed important not to look openly into the aisle as she passed; instead he remained hunched over the Dictaphone, peeking at the doorway from cover. It was Maureen, all right; the quick glimpse he caught of her was more than enough to confirm that. It was enough to show him that an inch of petticoat was switching nicely through a vent in the hem of her skirt with every step and that her face, as subtly averted as his own, had not quite dared to glance in at him.

Her footsteps receded, and as he waited confidently for their return he reset the machine to the "start" position and leaned back in his chair to listen. That way he could be staring frankly into the aisle, yet quite legitimately occupied with business, when she came by again.

"Copy for Veritype," the Dictaphone said. "Title: Speaking of Inventory Control, parenthesis, revision three. Paragraph. Knowing what you've got, comma, knowing what you need, comma, knowing what you can do without, dash. That's—"

"Oh." She had stopped directly in his line of vision, and her careful expression of surprise was somewhat vitiated by the deep, permanent-looking blush that had suffused her face and neck. "Hello, Frank. Working late?"

He shut off the machine and got slowly to his feet, moving toward her with the loose, almost sleepy gait of a man who knows exactly what he's doing.

"Hi," he said.

THREE

EVERY FRIDAY AND Saturday night, "For Your Dancing Pleasure," the Steve Kovick Quartet played at Vito's Log Cabin, on Route Twelve, and on those two nights (as Steve himself liked to say, winking over the rim of his rye-and-ginger) the joint really jumped.

Piano, bass, tenor sax and drums, they prided themselves on versatility. They could play anything, in any style you wanted to name, and to judge from the delight that swam in their eyes they had no idea of what inferior musicians they were. In the three supporting members of the Quartet this lack of discernment could be excused on the grounds of inexperience or amateurism or both, but it was harder to condone in their leader, who played the drums. A thick, blunt, blue-jawed man, getting on for forty now, he had been a professional for twenty years without ever quite learning his craft. Artistically awakened and nourished by the early recordings and movies of Gene Krupa, he had spent the only happy hours of his youth in a trance of hero-worshiping imitation—first intently slapping telephone books and overturned dishpans, later using a real set of drums in the sweat and liniment smells of the high-school gym—until one June night in his senior year when the rest of the band stopped playing, the hundreds of couples stood still, and Steve Kovick felt the weight of all their rapture on his wagging, chewing head while he beat it out for three solid minutes. But the splendid crash of cymbals with which he ended that performance marked the pinnacle and ruin of his talent. He would never drum that well again, he would never again kindle that much admiration, nor would he ever again lose his frantic grip on the conviction that he was great and getting better all the time. Even now, at a rundown beer-and-pizza joint like Vito's Log Cabin, there was a negligent grandeur in the way he took the stand, the way he frowned over the arrangement of sticks and brushes and hi-hat cymbals and then peered out, beetle-browed, to ask if the spotlight could be adjusted a fraction of an inch before he settled down; and there was elaborate condescension in the way he whisked and thumped through preliminary fox trots or handled the gourds for Latin-American interludes; anyone could tell he was only marking time, waiting for the moment when he could tell the boys to cut loose on one of the old-time Benny Goodman jump numbers.

Only then, once or twice an hour, did he give himself wholly to his work. Socking the bass drum as if to box the ears of every customer in the house, doing his damnedest on snare and tom-tom, he would take off in a triumph of misplaced virtuosity that went relentlessly on and on until it drenched his hair with sweat and left him weak and happy as a child.

The patrons of the Log Cabin on dance nights were mostly high-school seniors (it was the corniest band in the world but the only live music for miles around; besides, there wasn't any cover and they'd serve you without proof of age and the big parking lot was nice and dark) and a smattering of local storekeepers and contractors who sat in a state of constant laughter with their arms around their wives, remarking on how young it made them feel to watch these kids enjoying themselves. There was an occasional tough element, too, boys in black leather jackets and boots who slouched in the urine-smelling corner near the men's room with their thumbs in their jeans, watching the girls with menacingly narrow eyes and taking repeated trips to the toilet to comb and recomb their hair; and there were the regulars, lonely and middle-aged and apparently homeless, the single or inadequately married people who came to the Log Cabin every night, music or not, to drink and sentimentalize under the fly-blown, joke-hung mirror of its rustic bar.

Not infrequently, over the past two years, the dance night crowd had included a party of four intensely humorous young adults who belonged to no discernible group at all: the Campbells and the Wheelers. Frank had discovered the place soon after moving to the country—had discovered it in search of drunkenness one night after a quarrel with his wife, and been quick to bring her back for dancing as soon as things were happier.

"You people ever been to the Log Cabin?" he had asked the Campbells early in their acquaintance, and April had said, "Oh *no*, darling; they'd hate it. It's terrible." The Campbells had looked from one to the other of their faces with uncertain smiles, ready to hate it or love it or espouse whatever other opinion of it might please the Wheelers most.

"No, I don't think they'd hate it," Frank had insisted. "I bet they'd like it. It takes a special kind of taste, is all. I mean the thing about the Log Cabin, you see," he explained to them at last, "is that it's so awful it's kind of nice."

At first, through the spring and summer of 1953, the four of them had come here only once in a while, as a kind of comic relief from more ambitious forms of entertainment; but by the following summer they had fallen into it like a cheap, bad habit, and it was their awareness of this particular degeneration, as much as any other, that had made the idea of the Laurel Players uncommonly attractive last winter. When *The Petrified Forest* went into rehearsal their attendance at the Log Cabin dwindled sharply (there were other, quieter places to stop for drinks on the way home from the school), and in the long uneasy time since the failure of the play they had not come here at all—almost as if to do so would have constituted an admission of moral defeat.

But "What the hell," Frank had said this evening, after every conversational attempt in the Campbells' living room had petered out and died, "why don't we all break down and go to the Log Cabin?"

And here they were, a quiet foursome ordering round after round of drinks, getting up and coupling off to dance, coming back and sitting silent under the blast of the jump numbers. But for all its awkwardness the evening was oddly free of tension, or so at least it seemed to Frank. April was as aloof and enigmatic, as far away from the party as she'd ever been in the worst of the old days, but the difference was that now he refused to worry about it. In the old days he might have talked and laughed himself sick trying to win an affectionate smile from her, or trying by sheer vivacity to make up for her rudeness to the Campbells (because that was what it did amount to, sitting there like some long-necked, heavy-lidded queen among commoners—plain damn rudeness); instead he was content to relax in his chair, one hand lightly tapping the table to Steve Kovick's beat, and perform the minimal pleasantries while thinking his own thoughts.

Was his wife unhappy? That was unfortunate, but it was, after all, her problem. He had a few problems too. This crisp way of thinking, unencumbered by guilt or confusion, was as new and as comfortable as his lightweight autumn suit (a wool gabardine in a pleasingly dark shade of tan, a younger and more tasteful, junior-executive version of the suit Bart Pollock wore). The resumption of the business with Maureen had helped him toward a renewal of self-esteem, so that the face he saw in passing mirrors these days gave him back a level, unembarrassed glance. It was hardly a hero's face but neither was it a self-pitying boy's or a wretchedly anxious husband's; it was the steady, controlled face of a man with a few things on his mind, and he rather liked it. The business with Maureen would have to be brought to a graceful conclusion soon—it had served its purpose—but in the meantime he felt he was entitled to savor it. That, in fact, was what he was doing now, allowing the erotic thump of Steve Kovick's tom-tom to remind him of her hips, gazing wryly off into the swirl of dancers as he gave in to voluptuous memories.

For the last three times, evenings when they couldn't use her apartment because her roommate was home, she had agreed with surprising alacrity to let him take her to a hotel. Anonymous and safe behind a double-locked door in an air-conditioned tower, they had dined on room-service lamb chops and wine while the sound of midtown traffic floated up from twenty stories below; they had reveled in the depths of a long, wide bed and lathered themselves clean in a steaming palace of a bathroom stocked with acres of towels; and each time, when he'd handed her into a taxi at last and turned alone toward Grand Central, he had wanted to laugh aloud at having so perfectly fulfilled the standard daydream of the married man. No fuss, no complications, everything left behind in a tumbled room under somebody else's name, and all of it wound up in time to catch the ten-seventeen. It was too good to be true, like the improbable stories that older, more experienced soldiers had once told him of three-day passes with Red Cross girls. It couldn't go on much longer, of course, and it wouldn't. In the meantime . . .

In the meantime, all during the next slow tune and the one after that, he cordially danced with Milly Campbell. She made a damp, untidy package in his arms and she talked inanely ("Gosh, you know something, Frank? I don't think I've had this much to drink in years and years and years . . ."), but he was afraid that if he danced with April now she would only say, "This is horrible; please let's go home," and he didn't feel like it. He wouldn't have minded going home alone, if such a thing were possible (he had a pleasant vision of himself preparing neatly for bed with book and nightcap, bachelor style); otherwise he was happy enough to stay in this jumbled, lively place where the drinks were cheap and the band was loud and he could feel the inner peace that comes from knowing that all your clothes are new and perfectly fitted.

"Gosh. Gee, Frank, I'm afraid I'm not very—excuse me a second." Milly lurched pathetically away toward the ladies' room, which gave him an opportunity to have a dignified drink alone at the bar. When she came out, a long time later, she looked exhausted and gray under the blue lights. "Gosh." She tried to smile, giving off a faint scent of vomit. "I guess Shep and I'd better sort of go home, Frank. I think I must be sick or something. I guess I'm being an awful party-poop; you must think I'm—"

"No, don't be silly. Just hold on a second and I'll get Shep." He peered dizzily into the swaying roomful of dancers until he picked out Campbell's big red neck and April's small head moving along the far wall; he gave them an urgent beckoning signal, and soon they were all four crunching in the gravel outside, wandering lost in a dark sea of automobiles.

"Which way . . .?"

"This way . . . Over here . . ."

"You okay, honey?"

"It's so *dark* . . ."

The slick, chin-high tops of the cars made an undulating surface that stretched away into the darkness in all directions;

beneath it stood endless shadowy ranks of fenders and fins, of intricately bulbous bumpers and grills alive with numberless points of reflected neon. Once, when Frank bent over to strike a match for guidance, the flame caused a writhing recoil of human flesh only inches away from his face—he had startled a pair of lovers in one of the cars—and he hurried into the darkness of the next aisle, saying, "Where the hell *did* we leave the damn cars, then? Does anybody remember?"

"Here," Shep called. "Over here in the last row. Oh, but Jesus, look. Mine's blocked in." He had backed his big Pontiac against a tree, hours before. Now two other cars stood directly in front of it and there was no room for maneuvering on either side.

"Lord, what a mess . . ."

"Of all the inconsiderate . . ."

"Damn that tree . . ."

"Well, look, though," Frank said. "We've still got one car free; we could run Milly home and bring Shep back, and maybe by that time the car'll be—"

"But it might take *hours*," Milly said weakly, "and meantime your sitter'll be costing you a fortune. Oh dear."

"No, hold it," Shep said. "We can all go home in your car; then I'll borrow your car and come back and—or no, wait—"

"Oh, look." April's voice cut through the confusion with such sober authority that they all stopped talking. "It's perfectly simple. You take Milly home, Frank, and go on home yourself— that takes care of both sitters—and Shep and I can wait till the other car's free. That's the only logical way."

"Fine," Frank said, moving away with his car keys out and ready. "All agreed, then?"

The next thing Shep Campbell knew, the taillights of the Wheelers' car were winking away down Route Twelve and he was walking back toward the Log Cabin (which throbbed now to a slow, sentimental waltz) with April's slender elbow in his hand. In all his guilty fantasies he could never have plotted a better way of finding himself alone with her, and the funny part was that he hadn't even had to arrange it: it had happened because it was the only logical—or no, wait a minute. His fuddled mind worked hard to sort it out as they mounted the steps under red and blue lights. Wait a minute—why couldn't *she* have taken Milly home, and left Frank behind? Wouldn't that have been logical too?

By the time he'd worked it out that far they were back on the brink of the dance floor; she had turned to him gravely with her eyes fixed on his right lapel, and the only thing to do was take her lightly around the waist and go on dancing. He couldn't ask her if she'd planned it this way without being a fool, and he couldn't assume she had without being a bigger one. Allowing his fingers to spread out very shyly on the small of her back and his hot cheek to rest against her hair, he moved to the music and was humbly grateful that the thing had happened; never mind how.

It was like the other time here last summer, but it was much, much better. The other time she'd been drunk, for one thing, and he had known even as he miserably pressed and mauled her that it was strictly a one-way deal: she'd been too far gone to know how much she was giving him, and the proof of it was the way she'd kept arching back her neck to talk and chatter in his face as if they were sitting across a bridge table or some damn thing, instead of locked as tight as lovers from the collarbone down. This time she was sober, she hardly talked at all, and she seemed as sensitive as he was to every tactile subtlety, every tentative seeking and granting and shy withdrawal and seeking again; it was almost more than his bashful heart could stand.

"Feel like another drink?"

"All right."

But as they stood at the bar, self-consciously sipping and puffing cigarettes among the regulars, he couldn't think of anything to say. He felt like a boy on his first date, crippled by the secret, ignorant desire of virginity; he was sweating.

"Tell you what," he said at last, almost roughly. "I'll go check the car." And he promised himself that if she gave the slightest hint, if she smiled and said, "What's your hurry, Shep?" or anything like that, he would forget everything—his wife, his fear, everything—and go for her all the way.

There was nothing in her gray eyes to suggest complicity: they were the eyes of a pleasant, tired young suburban matron who'd been kept up past her bedtime, that was all. "Yes, all right," she said. "Why don't you?"

Stumbling down the wooden steps and out into the darkness, grinding the pebbles fiercely under his heels, he felt all the forces of the plausible, the predictable and the ordinary envelop him like ropes. Nothing was going to happen; and the hell with her. Why wasn't she home where she belonged? Why couldn't she go to Europe or disappear or die? The hell with this aching, suffering, callow, half-assed delusion that he was in "love" with her. The hell with "love" anyway, and with every other phony, time-wasting, half-assed emotion in the world. But by the time he'd reached the last row he was jelly-kneed and trembling in a silent prayer: Oh God, please don't let the car be free.

And it wasn't. The other cars still held it fast against the tree. As he whirled back to face the building its lights careened in his head and he nearly keeled over. He was loaded. That last drink must have really—Wow. His lungs felt very shallow, and he knew that unless something could be done at once to stop the lights from sliding around that way he would be sick. He began running in place, pumping his fists and bringing his knees up high, his shoes making brisk, athletic sounds in the gravel. He did that until he'd counted a hundred, taking deep breaths, and when he was finished the lights held still. He felt chastened and full of blood as he walked back to the Log Cabin, where the Quartet had broken into its own crude version of one of the old-time, big-band numbers—"One O'Clock Jump" or "String of Pearls" or something, the kind of music that always took him back to basic training.

She had left the bar for one of the dark leatherette booths nearby; she was sitting very straight in its deep seat, partly turned around to watch for him through the smoke, and she greeted him with a shyly welcoming smile.

"Still blocked in, I'm afraid," he said.

"Oh, well. Come and sit a minute. I don't really mind, do you?"

He could have crawled across the leatherette seat and buried his head in her lap. What he did instead was to slide in as close beside her as he dared and begin to tear up a cardboard match in the ash tray, splitting it at the base with his thumbnail and carefully peeling it down in strips, frowning as intently as a watchmaker over his work.

She was gazing off into the blur of the dance floor, moving her uptilted head very slightly to the rhythm of the band. "This is the kind of music that's supposed to make everybody our age very nostalgic," she said. "Does it you?"

"I don't know. Not really, I guess."

"It doesn't me, either. I'd like it to, but it doesn't. It's supposed to remind you of all your careless teen-age raptures, and the trouble is I never had any. I never even had a real date until after the war, and by then nobody played this kind of music any more, or if they did I was too busy being blasé to notice it. That whole big-band swing period was a thing I missed out on. Jitterbugging. Trucking on down. Or no, that was earlier, wasn't it? I think people talked about trucking on down when I was in about the sixth grade, at Rye Country Day. At least I remember writing 'Artie Shaw' and 'Benny Goodman' all over the sides of my schoolbooks without quite being sure who they were, because some of the older girls used to have those names on their books and it seemed a terribly sophisticated thing to do, like putting dabs of nail polish on your ankles to hold your bobby socks up. God, how I wanted to be seventeen when I was twelve. I used to watch the seventeen-year-olds getting into cars and riding away with boys after school, and I was absolutely certain they had the answers to everything."

Shep was watching her face so closely that everything else vanished from his consciousness. It didn't even matter what she was saying, nor did he care that she was talking to herself as much as to him.

"And then by the time I turned seventeen I was shut up in this very grim boarding school, and the only times I ever really jitterbugged were with another girl, in the locker room. We'd play Glenn Miller records on this old portable Victrola she had, and we'd practice and practice by the hour. And that's all this kind of music can ever really remind me of—bouncing around in my horrible gym suit in that sweaty old locker room and being convinced that life had passed me by."

"That's hard to believe."

"What is?"

"That you never had any dates or anything, all that time."

"Why?"

He wanted to say, "Oh God, April, you know why. Because you're lovely; because everyone must have loved you, always," but he lacked the courage. Instead he said, "Well, I mean, hell; didn't you ever have fun on vacations?"

"Fun on vacations," she repeated dully. "No. I never did. And now you see you've put your finger on it, Shep. I can't very well blame boarding school for that, can I? No, all I ever did on vacations was read and go to movies by myself and quarrel with whichever aunt or cousin or friend of my mother's it was who happened to be stuck with me that summer, or that Christmas. It all does tend to sound pretty maladjusted, doesn't it? So you're quite right. It wasn't boarding school's fault and it wasn't anyone else's fault, it was my own Emotional Problem. And there's a fairly good rule-of-thumb for you, Shep: take somebody who worries about life passing them by, and the chances are about a hundred-and-eight to one that it's their own Emotional Problem."

"I didn't mean anything like that," Shep said uncomfortably. He didn't like the sardonic lines that had appeared at the pulled-down corner of her mouth, or the way her voice had flattened out, or the way she clawed a cigarette out of the pack and stuck it in her lips—these things were too close to the cruel image he had projected of her ten years from now. "I just meant, I never would've pictured you being that lonely."

"Good," she said. "Bless you, Shep. I always hoped people wouldn't picture me being that lonely. That was really the best thing about being in New York after the war, you see. People didn't."

Now that she'd mentioned her life in New York he was yearning to ask a question that had morbidly haunted him as long as he'd known her: had she still been a virgin when she met Frank? If not, it would somehow lessen his envy; if so, if he had to think of Frank Wheeler as her first lover as well as her husband, he felt it would make his envy too great to be borne. This was the closest he had ever come to an opportunity for finding out, but if words existed to make the question possible they had hopelessly eluded him. He would never know.

". . . Oh, it was fun, I suppose, those years," she was saying. "I always think of that as a happy, stimulating time, and I suppose it was, but even so." Her voice wasn't flat any more. "I still felt—I don't know."

"You still felt that life was passing you by?"

"Sort of. I still had this idea that there was a whole world of marvelous golden people somewhere, as far ahead of me as the seniors at Rye when I was in sixth grade; people who knew everything instinctively, who made their lives work out the way they wanted without even trying, who never had to make the best of a bad job because it never occurred to them to do anything less than perfectly the first time. Sort of heroic super-people, all of them beautiful and witty and calm and kind, and I always imagined that when I did find them I'd suddenly know that I belonged among them, that I was one of them, that I'd been meant to be one of them all along, and everything in the meantime had been a mistake; and they'd know it too. I'd be like the ugly duckling among the swans."

Shep was looking steadily at her profile, hoping the silent force of his love would move her to turn and face him. "I think I know that feeling," he said.

"I doubt it." She didn't look at him, and the little lines had appeared again around her mouth. "At least I hope you don't, for your sake. It's a thing I wouldn't wish on anybody. It's the most stupid, ruinous kind of self-deception there is, and it gets you into nothing but trouble."

He let all the air out of his lungs and subsided against the back of the seat. She didn't really want to talk; not to him, anyway. All she wanted was to sound off, to make herself feel better by playing at being wistful and jaded, and she had elected him as her audience. He wasn't expected to participate in this discussion, and he certainly wasn't to go getting any ideas; his role was to be big, dumb, steady old Shep until the car was free, or until she'd gotten all the gratification there was to be had from the sound of her own voice. Then he'd drive her home and she'd make a few more worldly-wise pronouncements on the way; she might even lean over and give him a sisterly peck on the cheek before she slithered out of the car and slammed the door and went inside to get into bed with Frank Wheeler. And what the hell else did he expect? When the hell was he ever going to grow up?

"Shep?" Both of her slim, cool hands had reached out and grasped one of his on the table, and her face, pressing toward him, was transformed into a mischievous smile. "Oh, Shep— let's do it."

He thought he was going to faint. "Do what?"

"Jitterbug. Come on."

Steve Kovick was nearing the climax of his evening. It was almost closing time; most of the people had gone home, the manager was counting his money, and Steve, no less than the hero of every Hollywood movie ever made about jazz, knew that this was the approach of what was supposed to be his finest hour.

Shep had never really learned to dance, let alone to abandon himself to this kind of dancing, but no power on earth could have stopped him now. Turning, clumsily hopping and shuffling in the enchanted center of that dizzy room, he allowed the noise and the smoke and the lights to revolve and revolve around him because he was wholly certain of her now. As long as he lived he would never see anything more beautiful than the way she reeled away as far as their joined hands would allow and did a quick little bobbing, hip-switching curtsy out there before she came twisting back. Oh, look at her! his heart sang, Look at her! Look at her! He knew that when the music stopped she would fall laughing in his arms, and she did. He knew, leading her tenderly away to the bar, that she would allow his arm to stay close around her while they had another drink, and she did that too. As they talked there in suggestively low voices he no longer cared what he was saying—what did it matter? What did words amount to, anyway?—because he was full of delirious plans. A motel sprang up in his mind's eye: he saw himself filling out the registry form in the glare of its clapboard office ("Thank *you*, sir. That'll be six-fifty, Number Twelve . . .") while she sat waiting in the car outside; he pictured the abrupt, shockingly total privacy of the cabin with its maple chair and desk and staring double bed, and here he was briefly troubled: Could you really take a girl like April Wheeler to a motel? But why not? And besides, a motel wasn't the only possibility. Miles and miles of open country lay waiting in all directions; the night was warm and he had an old army poncho in the car; they could climb to some gentle pasture high out of sight and sound and make their bed among the stars.

It started in the parking lot, in the darkness less than ten yards away from the red- and blue-lighted steps. He stopped and let her turn against him in his arms, and then her crushed lips were opening under his mouth and her hands slid up and around his neck as he pressed her back against the fender of a parked car. They broke apart and came together again; then he led her swaying and stumbling out across the lot—it was nearly empty now—to the place where the chromework of his Pontiac, all alone, caught faint glimmers of starlight under the whispering black trees. He found the right-hand door and helped her in; then he walked in a correct, unhurried way around the hood to the driver's side. The door slammed behind him and there were her arms and her mouth again, there was the feel and the taste of her, and his fingers were finding miraculous ways to unfasten her clothing, and there was her rising breast in his hand. "Oh, April. Oh my God, I—Oh, April . . ."

The noise of their breathing had deafened them to all other sounds: the loud insects that sang near the car, the drone of traffic on Route Twelve and the fainter sounds from the Log Cabin— a woman's shrieking laugh dissolving into the music of horn and piano and drums.

"Honey, wait. Let me take you somewhere—we've got to get out of—"

"No. Please," she whispered. "Here. Now. In the back seat."

And the back seat was where it happened. Cramped and struggling for purchase in the darkness, deep in the mingled scents of gasoline and children's overshoes and Pontiac upholstery, while a delicate breeze brought wave on wave of Steve Kovick's final drum solo of the night, Shep Campbell found and claimed the fulfillment of his love at last.

"Oh, April," he said when he was finished, when he had tenderly disengaged and rearranged her, when he had helped her to lie small and alone on the seat with his wadded coat for a pillow and bunched himself into an awkward squat on the floor boards, holding both her hands, "Oh, April, this isn't just a thing that happened. Listen. This is what I've always—I love you."

"No. Don't say that."

"But it's true. I've always loved you. I'm not just being—listen."

"Please, Shep. Let's just be quiet for a minute, and then you can take me home."

With a little shock he thought of what he'd steadfastly put out of his mind all evening, what had occurred to him briefly and not at all as a deterrent in the heat of his desire, and now for the first time began to take on an oppressive moral weight: she was pregnant. "Okay," he said, "I'm not forgetting anything." He freed one of his hands to rub his eyes and his mouth with vigor, and then he sighed. "I guess you must think I'm kind of an idiot or something."

"Shep, it's not that."

There was just enough light to show him where her face was, not enough for him to see its expression or even to tell whether it had any expression at all.

"It's not that. Honestly. It's just that I don't know who you are."

There was a silence. "Don't talk riddles," he whispered.

"I'm not. I really don't know who you are."

If he couldn't see her face, at least he could touch it. He did so with a blind man's delicacy, drawing his fingertips from her temple down into the hollow of her cheek.

"And even if I did," she said, "I'm afraid it wouldn't help, because you see I don't know who I am, either."

FOUR

WALKING AWAY FROM the hiss and whine of a Sixth Avenue bus, three or four days later, Frank Wheeler moved with a jaunty resignation toward Maureen Grube's street. He didn't especially feel like seeing her tonight, and this, he knew, was as it should be. The purpose of this visit was to break the thing off, and any impulsive eagerness for the sight of her would have been disconcerting. It always surprised and pleased him when his mood coincided with the nature of the thing he had to do, and this rare state had lately become almost habitual. He had been able, for instance, to wrap up all the rest of his Speaking-of series in little more than a day's work apiece. *Speaking of Sales Analysis, Speaking of Cost Accounting*, and *Speaking of Payroll*—all now lay safely finished along with *Production* and *Inventory Control*, in a handsome cardboard folder on Bart Pollock's desk.

"Well, Frank, these are fine," Pollock had said yesterday, riffling the folder with his thumb. "And fortunately, I've got some good news for you this morning." The good news, which Frank was able to receive with perfect composure, was that plans for Pollock's project had now been "finalized." There would be an "informal shakedown conference" next Monday, at which Frank would join his new colleagues in helping to "block out a few objectives," and after which he could consider himself no longer a member of Bandy's staff. Meanwhile, it was now "time for the two of us to get together here on the matter of salary." No nervous sweat broke out inside Frank's shirt as they got together on it, and no ludicrous ghost of Earl Wheeler hung over the proceedings. His eyes never strayed in dismal aesthetic searching among Pollock's office fixtures, nor was he plagued with cautionary thoughts of what April might say. It was strictly business. He was richer by three thousand a year after shaking Pollock's thick hand that morning—a sound, satisfactory amount that would provide, among other things, a comfortable fund against which to draw for the costs of obstetrics and psycho-analysis.

"Good," April said on hearing the figure. "That's about what you expected, isn't it?"

"Just about, yes. Anyway, it's nice to have the thing settled."

"Yes. I imagine it must be."

And now, having so competently arranged his business affairs, he could give his full attention to personal matters—which did, at the moment, need considerable straightening out. For the past two nights, or three, his marriage had taken that technical turn for the worse which, in the old days, would have filled him with anguish: April had begun to sleep in the living room again. But these, thank God, were not the old days. This time it hadn't come about as the result of a fight, for one thing, and it wasn't accompanied by any apparent rancor on her part.

"I haven't been sleeping at all well," she had announced the first night, "and I think I'd be more comfortable alone."

"Okay." He had assumed, though, that it was an arrangement for that night only, and he was nettled the following evening, when she again came trudging from the linen closet with an armload of bedclothes and began making the sofa into a bed.

"What's the deal?" he asked mildly, leaning against the kitchen doorjamb with a drink in his hand while she flapped and spread the sheets. "You sore at me, or what?"

"No. Of course I'm not 'sore' at you."

"You planning to go on doing this indefinitely, or what?"

"I don't know. I'm sorry if it upsets you."

He took his time in replying, first lazily dunking the ice cubes in his glass with a forefinger, then licking the finger, then moving away from the door with a luxuriantly tired shrug. "No," he said. "It doesn't upset me. I'm sorry you're not sleeping well."

And that, of course, was the other, the really important difference: it *didn't* upset him. It annoyed him slightly, but it didn't upset him. Why should it? It was her problem. What boundless reaches of good health, what a wealth of peace there was in this new-found ability to sort out and identify the facts of their separate personalities—this is my problem, that's your problem. The pressures of the past few months had brought them each through a kind of crisis; he could see that now. This was their time of convalescence, during which a certain remoteness from each other's concerns was certainly natural enough, and probably a good sign. He knew, sympathetically, that in her case the adjustment must be especially hard; if it caused her periods of moodiness and insomnia, that was perfectly understandable. In any case, the time was now at hand when he could, in the only mature sense, be of help to her. Next week, or as soon as possible, he would take whatever steps were necessary in lining up a reputable analyst; and he could already foresee his preliminary discussions with the man, whom he pictured as owlish and slow-spoken, possibly Viennese ("I think your own evaluation of the difficulty is essentially correct, Mr. Wheeler. We can't as yet predict how extensive a course of therapy will be indicated, but I can assure you of this: with your continued cooperation and understanding, there is every reason to hope for rapid . . .").

In the meantime, the main task before him was to put an end to the business with Maureen. He would much rather have been able to do it in a bar or a coffee shop uptown; that was what he'd had in mind this morning, when he'd cornered her in an alcove of the central file to make this date, but, "No, come to my place," she had whispered over the spread folder they were using as camouflage. "Norma's leaving early, and I'll fix supper for us."

"No, really," he said. "I'd rather not. The thing is—" He would have said, "The thing is I want to have a talk with you," but her eyes frightened him. What if she should begin to cry or something, right here in the office? Instead he said, "I don't want you to go to any trouble," which was true too; but in the end he had agreed.

The scene of the talk probably didn't matter; the important thing was the talk itself, and the only really important thing about that was to make it definite and final. There was, he assured himself for the hundredth time, nothing to be apologetic about. It depressed him to consider how much energy he had wasted, over the years, in the self-denying posture of apology. From now on, whatever else his life might hold, there would be no more apologies.

"Excuse me," called a woman's voice from the curb. "You're Mr. Frank Wheeler, aren't you?" She was coming toward him across the sidewalk, carrying a small suitcase, and he knew at once who she was from the predatory quality of her smile. She had caught him with his foot on the first of the pink stone steps of Maureen's building.

"I'm Norma Townsend, Maureen's roommate. I wonder if I could have a word with you."

"Sure." He didn't budge. "What can I do for you?"

"Please." She tilted her head slightly to one side as if to reprove a sullen child. "Not here." And she moved past him toward an arty little espresso lounge two doors away. There was nothing to do but follow her, but he atoned for his meekness by staring critically at her tense, quivering buttocks. She was solid and duck-footed, wearing a modishly tubular dress, a "sheath," in defiance of the fact that it emphasized her breadth and muscularity, and she trailed a perfume that had probably been described as Dark and Exciting in its point-of-sale display at Lord and Taylor's.

"I won't keep you a minute," she said when she had him cornered at a small marble-topped table, when she'd arranged the suitcase at her feet, ordered a sweet vermouth, and put her hands through the series of clicking, snapping and organizing motions required in the job of removing a pack of cigarettes from her complicated handbag. "I've just time for an *apéritif*, and then I must run. I'm off to the Cape for two weeks. Maureen *was* coming with me, but she's changed her plans. She now intends to spend her entire vacation here, as I expect you know. *I* didn't know until last night, which I'm afraid does put me in a rather awkward position with the friends we were to visit. Are you sure you won't have a drink?"

"No thanks." He had to admit, watching her, that she wasn't unattractive. If she could loosen her hair instead of skinning it back, if she could take off a little weight through the cheeks ... but then he decided she would have to do more than that. She would have to learn not to move her eyebrows so much when she talked, and she would certainly have to get over saying things like "I've just time for an *apéritif*" and "I'm off to the Cape."

"I happen to be very annoyed with Maureen at the moment," she was saying. "This vacation mix-up is only the latest in a long line of foolishness, but that's beside the point. The main thing—" and here she looked at him keenly—"the important thing, is that I'm very deeply concerned about her too. I've known her a good deal longer and I believe I know her better than you do, Mr. Wheeler. She's a very young, very insecure, very sweet kid, and she's gone through a lot of hell in the past few years. Right now she needs guidance and she needs friendship. On the face of it—and I hope you'll forgive my speaking plainly—on the face of it, the one thing she definitely does not need is to get involved in a pointless affair with a married man. Mind you, I'm not—please don't interrupt. I'm not interested in moralizing. I'd much rather feel that you and I can discuss this thing as civilized adults. But I'm afraid I must begin with an awkward question. Maureen appears to be under the impression that you're in love with her. Is this true?"

The answer was so classically simple that the framing of it filled him with pleasure. "I'm afraid I don't think that's any of your business."

She leaned back and smiled at him in a canny, speculative way, letting little curls of smoke dribble out of her nostrils, picking a flake of cigarette paper from her lip with the lacquered nails of little-finger and thumb. He was reminded of Bart Pollock at lunch saying, "Let me see how good a judge of character I am," and he wanted to reach across the table and strangle her.

"I think I like you, Frank," she said at last. "May I call you that? I think I even like your getting angry; it shows integrity." She came forward again, took a coquettish sip of her drink, and propped one elbow on the table. "Oh, look, Frank," she said. "Let's try to understand each other. I think you're probably a very good, serious boy with a nice wife and a couple of nice kids out there in Connecticut, and I think possibly all that's happened here is that you've gone and gotten yourself involved in a very human, very understandable situation. Doesn't that about sum it up?"

"No," he said. "It doesn't even come close. Now I'll try, okay?"

"Okay."

"Okay. I think you're probably a meddling, tiresome woman, possibly a latent lesbian, and very definitely"—he laid a dollar bill on the table—"very definitely a pain in the ass. Have a nice vacation."

And in four headlong strides, one of which nearly sent an effeminate waiter sprawling with a tray of demi-tasse cups, he was out of the place. All the way up the pink stone steps he felt he couldn't contain the giant sobs of laughter that heaved in his chest—the look on her face!—but in the vestibule, where he leaned against a row of polished brass mailboxes to let it all come out of him, he found that instead of guffaws he was capable only of a self-stifling, whimpering giggle that came in uncontrollable spasms, using only the top part of his lungs and making his diaphragm ache. He couldn't breathe.

When it was over, or nearly over, he crept back to the front door, pushed aside the dusty net curtain that covered its glass and peered down, just in time for a rear view of Norma out on the curb, wagging her handbag for a taxi. Her back was stiff with anger and there was something extremely pathetic about her suitcase, which looked expensive and brand-new. She had probably spent days buying it and weeks shopping for the things that would ride in its silken depths today—new bathing suits, slacks, sun lotion, a new camera—all the fussy, careful apparatus of a girlish good time. With the odd whimpering sounds still bubbling up from his rib cage he felt an incongruous wave of tenderness go out to her, as she climbed into the cab and rolled away.

He was sorry. But he would have to pull himself together now; it was time to deal with Maureen. He took several deep breaths and pressed the bell, and when the answering buzzer let him into the hallway he was careful not to take the stairs too fast. He didn't want to be short of breath when he got there; everything depended on his being calm.

The door was on the latch. He knocked once or twice and then heard her voice, apparently coming from the bedroom. "Frank? Is that you? Come on in. I'll be right out."

The apartment was scrupulously clean, as if in readiness for a

party, and a faint scent of simmering meat came from the kitchenette. Only now, strolling around the carpet, did he notice
that a phonograph was playing the music he was dimly aware of
having heard all the way upstairs, a smooth Viennese waltz done
with many violins, the kind of thing known as cocktail music.

"There's some drinks and stuff on the coffee table," Maureen's
voice called. "Help yourself."

He did, gratefully making a stiff one, and tried to relax by
sitting well back in the deep sofa.

"Did you close the door?" she called. "And lock it?"

"I think so, yes. What's all the—"

"And are you sure you're alone?"

"Sure I'm sure. What's all the mystery about?"

She threw open the bedroom door and stood smiling there on
tiptoe, nude. Then she began an undulant dance around the
room, in waltz time, waving and rippling her wrists like an amateur ballerina, blushing and trying mightily not to giggle as she
whirled for him to the soaring strings. He barely managed to put
his drink on the table, spilling part of it, before she came falling
heavily into his arms and knocked the wind out of him. She
was drenched in the same perfume as Norma's, and when she
enveloped his head in a welcoming kiss he saw, at startlingly close
range, that she was wearing even more eye make-up than usual.
Each of her lashes was as thick and ragged as a spider's leg on her
cheek. Released from her mouth at last, he tried to ease himself
into a more upright sitting position, to shift her weight off his
belly, but it wasn't easy because her arms were still locked around
his neck, and in the effort his coat and shirt were dragged painfully tight across his back and chest. Finally he was able to free
one hand to tear open his choking collar, and he tried to smile.

"Hello," she murmured huskily, and kissed him again, filling
his mouth with her tongue.

This time there was the desperation of a drowning man in his
upward struggle; when he'd made it, she drew back and looked
at him in dismay, her breasts wagging like little startled faces. He
couldn't speak for a minute until he'd regained his breath; then
instead of looking at her he gazed down at his own hands, which
were clasping the heavy sprawl of her thighs across his lap. He

released his grip, spread his fingers and lightly tapped the upper thigh, as if it were the edge of a conference table.

"Look, Maureen," he said. "I think we ought to have a talk."

What happened after that, even while it was happening, was less like reality than a dream. Only a part of his consciousness was involved; the rest of him was a detached observer of the scene, embarrassed and helpless but relatively confident that he would soon wake up. The way her face clouded over when he began to talk, the way she sprang off his lap and fled for her dressing gown, which she clutched around her throat as tightly as a raincoat in a downpour as she paced the carpet—"Well; in that case there really isn't anything more to say, is there? There really wasn't any point in your coming over today, was there?"— these seemed to exist as rankling memories even before they were events: so did the way he followed her around the room, abjectly twisting one hand in the other as he apologized and apologized.

"Maureen, look; try to be reasonable about this. If I've ever given you cause to believe that I—that we—that I'm not happily married or anything, well, I'm sorry. I'm sorry."

"And what about me? How am I supposed to feel? Have you thought about what kind of position this puts me in?"

"I'm sorry. I—"

And this was the final vignette: Maureen hunched in the belching black smoke of the kitchenette while her veal scallopini burned to a crisp.

"It's not too bad, Maureen. I mean we can still eat it, if you like."

"No. It's ruined. Everything's ruined. You'd better go now."

"Oh, look. There's no reason why we have to be—"

"I said please *go*."

No amount of drink in the Grand Central bars was able to blur those images, and all the way home, hungry and drunk and exhausted on the train, he sat with round, imploring eyes and moving lips, still trying to reason with her.

His dread of seeing her in the office the next day was so intense that he was in the act of stepping off the elevator before he remembered that she wouldn't be there. She was on vacation.

Would she follow Norma to the Cape? No; more likely she would use her two weeks to look for another job; in either case he could be fairly certain he would never see her again. And his relief on realizing this soon turned, perversely, into a worried kind of dismay. If he never saw her again, how would he ever have a chance to—well, to explain things to her? To tell her, in a level, unapologetic voice, all the level, unapologetic things he had to say?

Anxious thoughts of Maureen (Should he call her up? Should he write her a letter?) still preoccupied him on Saturday, while he labored at his stone path in the dizzying heat or invented little errands that would take him away from home, allowing him to cruise aimlessly down back roads in his station car, mumbling to himself. It wasn't until early Sunday afternoon, when he'd gone out in the station car to get the papers and ended up driving for miles, that the words "Forget it" rose to his lips.

It was a beautiful day. He was driving over the sunny crest of a long hill, past a thicket of elms whose leaves were just beginning to turn, when he suddenly began to laugh and to pound the old cracked plastic of the steering wheel with his fist. Forget it! What the hell was the point of thinking about it? The whole episode could now be dismissed as something separate and distinct from the main narrative flow of his life—something brief and minor and essentially comic. Norma humping out to the curb with her suitcase, Maureen leaping naked from his lap, himself padding after her through the smoke of the burning meat, wringing his hands—all now seemed as foolish as the distorted figures in an animated cartoon at the moment when the bouncing, tinny music swells up and the big circle begins to close in from all sides, rapidly enclosing the action within a smaller and smaller ring, swallowing it up until it's nothing more than a point of jiggling light that blinks out altogether as the legend "That's All, Folks!" comes sprawling happily out across the screen.

He stopped the car on the side of the road until his laughter had subsided; then, feeling much better, he made a U-turn and headed for home. Forget it! On the way back to Revolutionary Road he allowed his mind to dwell only on good things: the beauty of the day, the finished job of work on Pollock's desk, the three thousand a year, even the "shakedown conference" that was scheduled for tomorrow morning. It hadn't been such a bad summer after all. Now, rolling home, he could look forward to the refreshment of taking a shower and getting into clean clothes; then he would sip sherry (his lips puckered pleasurably at the thought of it) and drowse over the *Times* for the rest of the afternoon. And tonight, if everything went well, would be the perfect time for a rational, common-sense discussion with April about this annoying business of the sofa. Whatever was bothering her could be fixed, could probably have been fixed days ago, if he'd taken the trouble to sit down with her and talk things out.

"Look," he would begin. "This has been kind of a crazy summer, and I know we've both been under a strain. I know you're feeling sort of lonely and confused just now; I know things look pretty bleak, and believe me I—"

The house looked very neat and white as it emerged through the green and yellow leaves; it wasn't such a bad house after all. It looked, as John Givings had once said, like a place where people lived—a place where the difficult, intricate process of living could sometimes give rise to incredible harmonies of happiness and sometimes to near-tragic disorder, as well as to ludicrous minor interludes ("That's All, Folks!"); a place where it was possible for whole summers to be kind of crazy, where it was possible to feel lonely and confused in many ways and for things to look pretty bleak from time to time, but where everything, in the final analysis, was going to be all right.

April was working in the kitchen, where the radio was blaring.

"Wow," he said, laying the heavy Sunday papers on the table. "Is this ever a beautiful day."

"Yes; it's lovely."

He took a long, voluptuously warm shower and spent a long time brushing and combing his hair. In the bedroom, he inspected three shirts before deciding on the one he would wear with his tight, clean khakis—an expensive cotton flannel in a dark green-and-black plaid—and he tried several ways of wearing it before he settled on folding its cuffs back twice, turning its collar up in back and leaving it unbuttoned halfway down his chest. Crouching at the mirror of April's dressing table, he used her hand mirror to check the way the collar looked from the side and to test the effect, in profile, of his tightening jaw muscle.

Back in the kitchen, looking over the papers and loosely snapping his fingers in time to the jazz on the radio, he had to glance at April twice before he realized what was different about her: she was wearing one of her old maternity dresses.

"That looks nice," he said.

"Thank you."

"Is there any sherry?"

"I don't think so, no. I think we've used it up."

"Damn. Guess there isn't any beer either, is there." He considered having whiskey instead, but it was too early in the day.

"I've made some iced tea, if you'd like that. It's in the icebox."

"Okay." And he poured himself a glass without really wanting it. "Where are the kids, anyway?"

"Over at the Campbells'."

"Oh; too bad. I thought I'd read them the funnies."

He continued to finger through the papers for a few minutes, while she worked at the sink; then, because there was nothing else to do, he moved up close behind her and took hold of her arm, which caused her to stiffen.

"Look," he began. "This has been kind of a crazy summer, and I know you're—I know we've both been under a strain. I mean I know you're—"

"You know I'm not sleeping with you and you want to know why," she said, pulling away from his hand. "Well, I'm sorry, Frank, I don't feel like talking about it."

He hesitated, and then, to establish a better mood for communication, he kissed the back of her head with reverence. "Okay," he said. "What do you feel like talking about, then?"

She had finished with the dishes and let the water out of the sink; now she was rinsing the dishrag, and she didn't speak again until she had wrung it out, hung it on its hook, and moved away from the sink to turn and look at him, for the first time. She looked frightened. "Would it be all right if we sort of didn't talk about anything?" she asked. "I mean couldn't we just sort of take each day as it comes, and do the best we can, and not feel we have to talk about everything all the time?"

He smiled at her like a patient psychiatrist. "I don't think I suggested that we 'talk about everything all the time,' " he said. "I certainly didn't mean to. All I meant to sug—"

"All right," she said, backing away another step. "It's because I don't love you. How's that?"

Luckily the bland psychiatrist's smile was still on his face; it saved him from taking her seriously. "That isn't much of an answer," he said kindly. "I wonder what you really feel. I wonder if what you're really doing here isn't sort of trying to evade everything until you're—well, until you're in analysis. Sort of trying to resign from personal responsibility between now and the time you begin your treatment. Do you suppose that might be it?"

"No." She had turned away from him. "Oh, I don't know; yes. Whatever you like. Put it whichever way makes you the most comfortable."

"Well," he said, "it's hardly a question of making me comfortable. All I'm saying is that life does have to go on, analysis or not. Hell, *I* know you're having a bad time just now; it *has* been a tough summer. The point is we've both been under a strain, and we ought to be trying to help each other as much as we can. I mean God knows my own behavior has been pretty weird lately; matter of fact I've been thinking it might be a good idea for me to see the headshrinker myself. Actually—" He turned and stood looking out the window, tightening his jaw. "Actually, one of the reasons I've been hoping we could get together again is because there's something I'd like to tell you about: something kind of—well, kind of neurotic and irrational that happened to me a few weeks ago."

And almost, if not quite, before he knew what his voice was up to, he was telling her about Maureen Grube. He did it with automatic artfulness, identifying her only as "a girl in New York, a girl I hardly even know," rather than as a typist at the office, careful to stress that there had been no emotional involvement on his part while managing to imply that her need for him had been deep and ungovernable. His voice, soft and strong with an occasional husky falter or hesitation that only enhanced its rhythm, combined the power of confession with the narrative grace of romantic storytelling.

"And I think the main thing was simply a case of feeling that my—well, that my masculinity'd been threatened somehow by all that abortion business; wanting to prove something; I don't know. Anyway, I broke it off last week; the whole stupid business. It's over now; really over. If I weren't sure of that I guess I could never've brought myself to tell you about it."

For half a minute, the only sound in the room was the music on the radio.

"Why did you?" she asked.

He shook his head, still looking out the window. "Baby, I don't know. I've tried to explain it to you; I'm still trying to explain it to myself. That's what I meant about its being a neurotic, irrational kind of thing. I—"

"No," she said. "I don't mean why did you have the girl; I mean why did you tell me about it? What's the point? Is it supposed to make me jealous, or something? Is it supposed to make me fall in love with you, or back into bed with you, or what? I mean what am I supposed to say?"

He looked at her, feeling his face blush and twitch into an embarrassed simper that he tried, unsuccessfully, to make over into the psychiatric smile. "Why don't you say what you feel?"

She seemed to think this over for a few seconds, and then she shrugged. "I have. I don't feel anything."

"In other words you don't care what I do or who I go to bed with or anything. Right?"

"No; I guess that's right; I don't."

"But I *want* you to care!"

"I know you do. And I suppose I would, if I loved you; but you see I don't. I don't love you and I never really have, and I never really figured it out until this week, and that's why I'd just as soon not do any talking right now. Do you see?" She picked up a dust cloth and went into the living room, a tired, competent housewife with chores to do.

"And listen to this," said an urgent voice on the radio. "Now, during the big Fall Clearance, you'll find Robert Hall's *entire stock* of men's walk shorts and sport jeans drastically reduced!"

Standing foursquare and staring down at his untouched glass of iced tea on the table, he felt his head fill with such a dense morass of confusion that only one consecutive line of thought came through: an abrupt remembrance of what Sunday this was, which explained why the kids were over at the Campbells', and which also meant there wasn't much time left for talking.

"Oh, now listen," he said, wheeling and following her into the living room with decisive, headlong strides. "You just put down that God damn rag a minute and listen. *Listen* to me. In the first place, you know God damn well you love me."

FIVE

"OH, IT'S SUCH a lovely luxury just to ride instead of driving," Mrs. Givings said, holding fast to the handle of the passenger's door. Her husband always drove on these trips to the hospital, and she never failed to remark on how relaxing a change it made for her. When one drove a car all day and every day, she would point out, there was no more marvelous vacation in the world than sitting back and letting someone else take over. But the force of habit was strong: she continued to watch the road as attentively as if she were holding the wheel, and her right foot would reach out and press the rubber floor mat at the approach of every turn or stop signal. Sometimes, catching herself at this, she would force her eyes to observe the passing countryside and will the sinews of her back to loosen and subside into the upholstery. As a final demonstration of self-control she might even uncoil her hand from the door handle and put it in her lap.

"My, isn't this a marvelous day?" she asked. "Oh, and look at the beautiful leaves, just beginning to turn. Is there anything nicer than the beginning of fall? All the wonderful colors and the crispness in the air; it always takes me back to dear look OUT!"

Her shoe slapped the floor mat and her body arched into a frantic posture of bracing against the impact of collision: a red truck was turning out of a side road, straight ahead.

"I see it, dear," Howard Givings said, smoothly applying the brakes so that the truck had ample room to pass, and afterwards, easing down on the accelerator again, he said: "You just relax, now, and let me worry about the driving."

"Oh, I know; I will. I'm sorry. I know I'm being silly." She took several deep breaths and folded her hands on her thigh, where they rested as tentatively as frightened birds. "It's just that I always do get such awful butterflies in my stomach on these visiting days, especially when it's been so long."

"Patient's name?" asked the painfully thin girl at the visitors' desk.

"John Givings," Mrs. Givings said with a polite dip of her head, and she watched the girl's chewed pencil proceed down a mimeographed list of names until it stopped at Givings, John.

"Relationship?"

"Parents."

"Sign here please and take this slip. Ward Two A, upstairs and to your right. Have the patient back by five p.m."

In the outer waiting room of Ward Two A, after they had pressed the bell marked RING FOR ATTENDANT, Mr. and Mrs. Givings shyly joined a group of other visitors who were inspecting an exhibition of patients' artwork. The pictures included a faithfully rendered likeness of Donald Duck, in crayon, and an elaborate purple-and-brown crucifixion scene in which the sun, or moon, was done in the same crimson paint as the drops of blood that fell at precisely measured intervals from the wound in the Savior's ribs.

In a minute they heard a dim thudding of rubber heels and a jingle of keys behind the locked door; then it opened on a heavy, bespectacled young man in white who said, "May I have your slips, please?" and allowed them to pass, two at a time, into the inner waiting room. This was a large, dimly lighted place containing bright plastic-topped tables and chairs for the visitors of patients not on the privilege list. Most of the tables were occupied, but there was very little sound of conversation. At the table nearest the door a young Negro couple sat holding hands, and it wasn't easy to identify the man as a patient until you noticed that his other hand was holding the chromium leg of the table in a yellow-knuckled grip of desperation, as if it were the rail of a heaving ship. Farther away, an old woman was combing the tangled hair of her son, whose age could have been anything between twenty-five and forty; his head wobbled submissively under her strokes as he ate a peeled banana.

The attendant, hooking his ring of keys to a clip against his hip pocket, struck off down the corridor of the ward and began sonorously calling out names from the slips he had collected. Looking after him down the mouth of the corridor, which was filled with the sound of many radios tuned to different stations, all you could see was a long expanse of waxed linoleum and the corners of several steel hospital beds.

After a while the attendant came back, walking neat and white at the head of a small, shabby parade. John Givings brought up the rear, tall and pigeon-toed, buttoning his sweater with one hand and carrying the twill workman's cap in the other.

"Well," he said, greeting his parents. "They letting the prisoners out in the sunshine today? Big deal." He carefully placed the cap dead-center on his head, and the picture of the public charge was complete. "Let's go."

No one spoke in the car until they were clear of the hospital grounds, past the ranks of long brick ward buildings, past the administration building and the softball diamond, out around the well-tended circle of grass that enclosed the twin white shafts of the State and American flags, and on up the long blacktop road that led to the highway. Mrs. Givings, riding in the back seat (she usually found it more comfortable there when John was in front), tried to gauge his mood by studying the back of his neck. Then she said: "John?"

"Mm?"

"We have some good news. You know the Wheelers, that you liked so much? They've very kindly asked us to drop by again today, by the way, if you'd like to; that's one thing; but the really good news is that they've decided to stay. They're not going to Europe after all. Isn't that lovely?" And with an uneasy smile she watched him slowly turn around to face her over the seat back.

"What happened?" he said.

"Well, I'm sure I don't—how do you mean, what happened, dear? I don't suppose anything necessarily 'happened'; I imagine they simply talked it over and changed their minds."

"You mean you didn't even ask? People're all set to do something as big as that and then they drop the whole idea, and you don't even ask what the deal is? Why?"

"Well, John, I suppose because I didn't feel it was my *business* to ask. One doesn't in*quire* into these things, dear, unless the other person wishes to volunteer the infor*mation*." In an effort to still the rising cautionary note in her voice, which was almost certain to antagonize him, she forced the skin of her forehead and mouth to assume the shape of a jolly smile. "Can't we just be pleased that they're staying, without inquiring into the why of it? Oh, look at that lovely old red silo. I've never noticed that one before, have you? That must be the tallest silo for miles around."

"It's a lovely old silo, Ma," John said. "And it's lovely news about the Wheelers, and you're a lovely person. Isn't she, Pop? Isn't she a lovely person?"

"All right, John," Howard Givings said. "Let's steady down, now."

Mrs. Givings, whose fingers were grinding and tearing a book of matches into moist shreds, closed her eyes and tried to fortify herself for what would almost certainly be an awkward afternoon.

Her anxiety was compounded at the Wheelers' kitchen door. They were home—both cars were there—but the house had a strangely unwelcoming look, as if they weren't expecting visitors. There was no answer to her very light knock on the glass pane of the door, which gave back a vivid reflection of sky and trees, of her own craning face and the faces of Howard and John behind her. She knocked again, and this time she made a visor of one hand and pressed it to the pane, to see inside. The kitchen was empty (she could see what looked like a glass of iced tea on the table) but just then Frank Wheeler came lunging in from the living room, looking awful—looking as if he were about to scream or to weep or to commit violence. She saw at once that he hadn't heard her knock and didn't know she was there: he hadn't come to answer the door but in desperate escape from the living room, possibly from the house itself. And there wasn't time for her to step back before he saw her—caught her crouched and peering into his very eyes—which made him start, stop, and arrange his features into a smile that matched her own.

"Well," he said, opening the door. "Hi, there. Come on in."

Then they were moving sociably into the living room, where April was, and April looked awful too: pale and haggard, twisting her fingers at her waist. "Nice to see you all," she was saying faintly. "Won't you sit down? I'm afraid the house is in a terrible mess."

"Are we awfully early?" Mrs. Givings asked.

"Early? No, no; we were just—would anyone like a drink? Or some—iced tea, or something?"

"Oh, nothing at all, thanks. Actually we can only stay a minute; we just dropped by to say hello."

The party fell into an odd, uncomfortable grouping: the three Givingses seated in a row; the two Wheelers standing backed up against the bookcase, restlessly shifting toward and then apart from each other as they made conversation. Only now, watching them, was Mrs. Givings able to hazard a guess at the cause of their constraint: they must have been quarreling.

"Listen," John said, and all the other talk stopped dead. "What's the deal, anyway? I mean I hear you people changed your minds. How come?"

"Well," Frank said, and chuckled in embarrassment. "Well, not exactly. You might say our minds were sort of—forcibly changed for us."

"How come?"

Frank made a little sidling skip to stand close to his wife, edging behind her. "Well," he said. "I should've thought that was fairly obvious by now." And Mrs. Givings's eyes were drawn, for the first time, to notice what April was wearing. Maternity clothes!

"Oh, *April!*" she cried. "Why, this is perfectly marvelous!" She wondered what one was expected to do on such occasions: should she get up and—well, kiss her, or something? But April didn't look like a girl who wanted to be kissed. "Oh, I think this is terribly exciting," Mrs. Givings went on, and "I can't tell you how pleased I am," and "Oh, but I expect you'll be needing a bigger house, now, won't you?" and through it all she hoped against hope that John would keep still. But:

"Hold it a second, Ma," he said, standing up. "Hold it a second. I don't get this." And he fixed on Frank the stare of a prosecuting attorney. "What's so obvious about it? I mean okay, she's pregnant; so what? Don't people have babies in Europe?"

"Oh John, really," said Mrs. Givings. "I don't think we need to—"

"Ma, will you keep out of this? I'm asking the man a question. If he doesn't want to give me the answer, I'm assuming he'll have sense enough to tell me so."

"Of course," Frank said, smiling down at his shoes. "Suppose we just say that people anywhere aren't very well advised to have babies unless they can afford them. As it happens, the only way we can afford this one is by staying here. It's a question of money, you see."

"Okay." John nodded in apparent satisfaction, looking from one of the Wheelers to the other. "Okay; that's a good reason." They both looked relieved, but Mrs. Givings went tight all over because she knew, from long experience, that something perfectly awful was coming next.

"Money's always a good reason," John said. He began to move around the carpet, hands in his pockets. "But it's hardly ever the real reason. What's the real reason? Wife talk you out of it, or what?" And he turned the full force of his dazzling smile on April, who had moved across the room to stab out her cigarette in an ash tray. Her eyes looked briefly up at him and then down again.

"Huh?" he persisted. "Little woman decide she isn't quite ready to quit playing house? Nah, nah, that's not it. I can tell. She looks too tough. Tough and female and adequate as hell. Okay, then; it must've been you." And he swung around to Frank. "What happened?"

"John, please," Mrs. Givings said. "You're being very—" But there was no stopping him now.

"What happened? You get cold feet, or what? You decide you like it here after all? You figure it's more comfy here in the old Hopeless Emptiness after all, or—Wow, that did it! Look at his face! What's the matter, Wheeler? Am I getting warm?"

"John, you're being impossibly rude. Howard, please—"

"All right, son," Howard Givings said, getting to his feet. "I think we'd better be—"

"Boy!" John broke into his braying laugh. "Boy! You know something? I wouldn't be surprised if you knocked her up on purpose, just so you could spend the rest of your life hiding behind that maternity dress."

"Now, *look*," said Frank Wheeler, and to Mrs. Givings's shocked surprise his fists were clenched and he was trembling from head to foot. "I think that's just about *enough* outa you. I mean who the hell do you think you are? You come in here and say whatever crazy God damn thing comes into your head, and I think it's about time somebody told you to keep your God damn—"

"He's not *well*, Frank," Mrs. Givings managed to say, and then she bit the inside of her lip in consternation.

"Oh, not well my ass. I'm sorry, Mrs. Givings, but I don't give a damn if he's well or sick or dead or alive, I just wish he'd keep his God damn opinions in the God damn insane asylum where they belong."

During the painful silence that followed this, while Mrs. Givings continued to chew her lip, they all stood grouped in the middle of the room: Howard intently folding a light raincoat over his arm; April staring red-faced at the floor; Frank still trembling and audibly breathing, with a terrible mixture of defiance and humiliation in his eyes. John, whose smile was now serene, was the only one of them who seemed at peace.

"Big man you got here, April," he said, winking at her as he fitted the workman's cap on his head. "Big family man, solid citizen. I feel sorry for you. Still, maybe you deserve each other. Matter of fact, the way you look right now, I'm beginning to feel sorry for him, too. I mean come to think of it, you must give him a pretty bad time, if making babies is the only way he can prove he's got a pair of balls."

"All right, John," Howard was murmuring. "Let's get on out to the car now."

"April," Mrs. Givings whispered. "I can't tell you how sorry I—"

"Right," John said, moving away with his father. "Sorry, sorry, sorry. Okay Ma? Have I said 'Sorry' enough times? I *am* sorry, too. Damn; I bet I'm just about the sorriest bastard I know. Course, get right down to it, I don't have a whole hell of a lot to be glad about, do I?"

And at least, Mrs. Givings thought, if nothing else could be salvaged from this horrible day, at least he was allowing Howard to lead him away quietly. All she had to do now was to follow them, to find some way of getting across this floor and out of this house, and then it would all be over.

But John wasn't finished yet. "Hey, I'm glad of one thing, though," he said, stopping near the door and turning back, beginning to laugh again, and Mrs. Givings thought she would die as he extended a long yellow-stained index finger and pointed it at the slight mound of April's pregnancy. "You know what I'm glad of? I'm glad I'm not gonna be that kid."

SIX

THE FIRST THING Frank did when the Givingses were out of the house was to pour himself three fingers of bourbon and drink it down.

"Okay," he said, turning on his wife. "Okay, don't tell me." The ball of whiskey in his stomach made him cough with a convulsive shudder. "Don't tell me; let me guess. I made a Disgusting Spectacle of Myself. Right? Oh, and another thing." He followed her closely through the kitchen and into the living room, glaring in shame and anger and miserable supplication at the smooth back of her head. "Another thing: Everything That Man Said Is True. Right? Isn't that what you're going to say?"

"Apparently I don't have to. You're saying it for me."

"Oh, but April, don't you see how wrong that is? Don't you see how terribly, God-awfully wrong it is, if that's what you think?"

She turned around and faced him. "No. Why is it wrong?"

"Because the man is insane." He put down his drink on the window sill, to free both hands, and used them to make a gesture of impassioned earnestness, clawing upward and outward from his chest with all ten of his spread fingers and gathering them into quivering fists, which he shook beneath his chin. "The man," he said again, "is insane. Do you know what the definition of insanity is?"

"No. Do you?"

"Yes. It's the inability to relate to another human being. It's the inability to love."

She began to laugh. Her head went back, the two perfect rows of her teeth sprang forth, and her eyes were brilliantly narrowed as peal after peal of her laughter rang in the room. "The in," she said; "the in; the inabil; the inability to—"

She was hysterical. Watching her as she swayed and staggered from the support of one piece of furniture to another and then to the wall and back again, laughing and laughing, he wondered what he ought to do. In the movies, when women got hysterical like this, men slapped them until they stopped; but the men in the movies were always calm enough themselves to make it clear what the slapping was for. He wasn't. He wasn't, in fact, able to do anything at all but stand there and watch, foolishly opening and shutting his mouth.

Finally she sank into a chair, still laughing, and he waited for what he guessed would be a transition from laughter to weeping—that was what usually happened in the movies—but instead her subsiding was oddly normal, more like a recovery from a funny joke than from hysteria.

"Oh," she said. "Oh, Frank, you really are a wonderful talker. If black could be made into white by talking, you'd be the man for the job. So now I'm crazy because I don't love you—right? Is that the point?"

"No. Wrong. You're not crazy, and you do love me; *that's* the point."

She got to her feet and backed away from him, her eyes flashing. "But I don't," she said. "In fact I loathe the sight of you. In fact if you come any closer, if you touch me or anything I think I'll scream."

Then he did touch her, saying, "Oh baby, lis—" and she did scream.

It was plainly a false scream, done while she looked coldly into his eyes, but it was high, shrill, and loud enough to shake the house. When the noise of it was over he said:

"God damn you. God damn all your snotty, hateful little— Come *here*, God damn it—"

She switched nimbly past him and pulled a straight chair around to block his path; he grabbed it and slung it against the wall and one of its legs broke off.

"And what're you going to do now?" she taunted him. "Are you going to hit me? To show how much you love me?"

"No." All at once he felt massively strong. "Oh, no. Don't worry. I couldn't be bothered. You're not worth the trouble it'd *take* to hit you. You're not worth the powder it'd take to blow you *up*. You're an *empty*—" He was aware, as his voice filled out, of a sense of luxurious freedom because the children weren't here. Nobody was here, and nobody was coming; they had this whole reverberating house to themselves. "You're an *empty, hol-low fucking shell* of a woman . . ." It was the first opportunity for a wide-open, all-out fight they'd had in months, and he made the most of it, stalking and circling her as he shouted, trembling and gasping for breath. "What the hell are you living in my *house* for, if you hate me so much? *Huh? Will* you answer me that? What the hell are you carrying my *child* for?" Like John Givings, he pointed at her belly. "Why the hell *didn't* you get rid of it, when you had the chance? Because listen. Listen: I got news for you." The great pressure that began to be eased inside him now, as he slowly and quietly intoned his next words, made it seem that this was a cleaner breakthrough into truth than any he had ever made before: "I wish to God you'd done it."

It was the perfect exit line. He lunged past her and out of the room, down the swaying, tilting hall and into the bedroom, where he kicked the door shut behind him, sat bouncingly on the bed and drove his right fist into the palm of his left hand. Wow!

What a thing to say! But wasn't it true? Didn't he wish she'd done it? "Yes," he whispered aloud. "Yes, I do. I do. I do." He was breathing fast and heavily through his mouth, and his heart was going like a drum; after a while he closed his dry lips and swallowed, so that the only sound in the room was the rasp of air going in and out of his nose. Then this subsided, very gradually, as his blood slowed down, and his eyes began to take in some of the things around him: the window, whose glass and curtains were ablaze with the colors of the setting sun; the bright, scented jars and bottles on April's dressing table; her white nightgown hanging from a hook inside the open closet, and her shoes lined up neatly along the closet floor: three-inch heels, ballet shoes, soiled blue bedroom slippers.

Everything was quiet now; he was beginning to wish he hadn't shut himself in here. For one thing, he wanted another drink. Then he heard the kitchen door being closed and the screen being clapped behind it, and the old panic rose up: she was leaving him.

He was up and running soundlessly back through the house, intent on catching her and saying something—anything—before she got the car started; but she wasn't in the car, or anywhere near it. She was nowhere. She had disappeared. He ran all the way around the outside of the house, looking for her, his loose cheeks jogging, and he had started mindlessly to run around it again when he caught sight of her up in the woods. She was climbing unsteadily up the hill, looking very small among the rocks and trees. He sprinted out across the lawn, took the low stone wall in a leap and went stumbling up through the brush, after her, wondering if she really had gone crazy this time. What the hell was she wandering around up there for? Would she, when he caught up with her and took hold of her arm and turned her around, would she have the vacant, smiling stare of lunacy?

"Don't come any closer," she called.

"April, listen, I—"

"Don't come any *closer*. Can't I even get away from you in the *woods*?"

He stopped, panting, ten yards below her. At least she was all right; her face was clear. But they couldn't fight up here—they were well within sight and earshot of houses down on the road.

"April, listen, I didn't mean that. Honestly; I didn't mean that about wishing you'd done it."

"Are you still talking? Isn't there any way to stop your talking?" She was bracing herself against a tree trunk, looking down at him.

"Please come down. What're you doing up—"

"Do you want me to scream again, Frank? Because I will, if you say another word. I mean it."

And if she screamed here on the hillside they would hear her in every house on Revolutionary Road. They would hear her all over the top of the Hill, too, and in the Campbells' house. There was nothing for him to do but to go back alone, down through the woods to the lawn, and then indoors.

Once he was back in the kitchen he gave all his attention to the grim business of keeping watch on her through the window, standing—or crouching, and finally sitting on a chair—

far enough back in the shadows so that she wouldn't be able to see him.

She didn't seem to be doing anything up there: she continued to stand leaning against the tree, and as twilight closed in it became difficult to make her out. Once there was a yellow flare as she lit a cigarette, and then he watched the tiny red coal of it move in the slow arcs of her smoking; by the time it went out the woods were in total darkness.

He went on doggedly watching the same place in the trees until the pale shape of her surprised him at much closer range: she was walking home across the lawn. He barely managed to get out of the kitchen before she came in. Then, hiding in the living room, he listened to her pick up the phone and dial a number.

Her voice was normal and calm. "Hello, Milly? Hi. . . . Oh yes, they left a little while ago. Listen, though, I was wondering if I could ask a favor. The thing is, I'm not feeling very well; I think I may be getting the flu or something, and Frank's tired out. Would you awfully much mind keeping the kids for the night? . . . Oh, that's wonderful, Milly, thanks. . . . No, don't bother, they both had their baths last night. . . . Well, I know they'll enjoy it too. They always have a wonderful time at your place. . . . All right, fine, then. I'll call you in the morning."

Then she came into the living room and turned on the lights, and the exploding glare caused them both to blink and squint. What he felt, above all, was embarrassment. She looked embarrassed too, until she walked across the room and lay down on the sofa with her face out of sight.

It was at times something like this, in the past, that he'd gone out and wrenched the car into gear and driven for miles, stopping at one blue- and red-lighted bar after another, spilling his money on wet counters, morosely listening to the long, fuddled conversations of waitresses and construction workers, playing clangorous jukebox records and then driving again, speeding, eating up the night until he could sleep.

But he wasn't up to that tonight. The trouble was that there had never, in the past, been a time exactly like this. He was physically incapable of going out and starting the car, let alone of driving. His knees had turned to jelly and his head rang, and he was meekly grateful for the protective shell of the house around him; it was all he could do to make his way to the bedroom again and shut himself inside it, though this time, for all his despair, he was sensible enough to take the bottle of whiskey along with him.

There followed a night of vivid and horrible dreams, while he sprawled sweating on the bed in his clothes. Sometimes, either waking or dreaming that he was awake, he thought he heard April moving around the house; then once, toward morning, he could have sworn he opened his eyes and found her sitting close beside him on the edge of the bed. Was it a dream, or not?

"Oh, baby," he whispered through cracked and swollen lips. "Oh, my baby, don't go away." He reached for her hand and held it. "Oh, please stay."

"Sh-sh-sh. It's all right," she said, and squeezed his fingers. "It's all right, Frank. Go to sleep." The sound of her voice and the cool feel of her hand conveyed such a miracle of peace that he didn't care if it was a dream; it was enough to let him sink back into a sleep that was mercifully dreamless.

Then came the bright yellow pain of his real awakening, alone; and he'd scarcely had time to decide that he couldn't possibly go to work today before he remembered that he had to. It was the day of the shakedown conference. Trembling, he forced himself up and into the bathroom, where he put himself tenderly through the ordeals of a shower and a shave.

An illogical, unreasoning hope began to quicken his heart as he dressed. What if it hadn't been a dream? What if she really had come and sat there on the bed and spoken to him that way? And when he went into the kitchen it seemed that his hope was confirmed. It was astonishing.

The table was carefully set with two places for breakfast. The kitchen was filled with sunlight and with the aromas of coffee and bacon. April was at the stove, wearing a fresh maternity dress, and she looked up at him with a shy smile.

"Good morning," she said.

He wanted to go down on his knees and put his arms around her thighs; but he held back. Something told him—possibly the very shyness of her smile—that it would be better not to try anything like that; it would be better just to join her in the playing of this game, this strange, elaborate pretense that nothing had happened yesterday. "Good morning," he said, not quite meeting her eyes.

He sat down and unfolded his napkin. It was incredible. No morning after a fight had ever been as easy as this—but still, he thought as he unsteadily sipped at his orange juice, no fight had ever been as bad as that. Could it be that they'd fought themselves out at last? Maybe this was what happened when there was really and truly nothing more to say, either in acrimony or forgiveness. Life did, after all, have to go on.

"It certainly is a—nice morning out, isn't it?" he said.

"Yes; it is. Would you like scrambled eggs, or fried?"

"Oh, it doesn't really mat—well, yes; scrambled, I guess, if it's just as easy."

"Fine. I'll have scrambled too."

And soon they were sitting companionably across from each other at the bright table, whispering little courtesies over the passing of buttered toast. At first he was too bashful to eat. It was like the first time he'd ever taken a girl out to dinner, at seventeen, when the idea of actually loading food into his mouth and chewing it, right there in front of her, had seemed an unpardonably coarse thing to do; and what saved him now was the same thing that had saved him then: the surprising discovery that he was uncontrollably hungry.

Between swallows he said: "It's sort of nice, having breakfast without the kids for a change."

"Yes." She wasn't eating her eggs, and he saw that her fingers were shaking a little as she reached for her coffee cup; otherwise she looked completely self-possessed. "I thought you'd probably want a good breakfast today," she said. "I mean it's kind of an important day for you, isn't it? Isn't this the day you have your conference with Pollock?"

"That's right, yes." She had even remembered that! But he covered his delight with the deprecating, side-of-the-mouth smile he had used for years in telling her about Knox, and said: "Big deal."

"Well," she said, "I imagine it *is* a pretty big deal; for them, anyway. What exactly do you think you'll be doing? Until they start sending you out on the trips, I mean. You never have told me much about it."

Was she kidding, or what? "Haven't I?" he said. "Well, of course I don't really know much yet myself; that's the thing. I guess it'll mostly be just a matter of what Pollock calls 'blocking out objectives'—sitting around letting him talk, I guess. Acting like we know something about computers. And of course the main reason for this whole thing, at least I *think* it's the main reason, is that Knox may be getting ready to buy up one of these really big computers, bigger than the '500.' Did I tell you about that?"

"No, I don't believe you did." And the remarkable thing was that she looked as though she'd like to hear about it.

"Well, *you* know—one of these monstrous great things like the Univac; the kind of machine they use to forecast the weather and predict elections and all that. And I mean those jobs *sell* for a couple of million dollars apiece, you see; if Knox went into production on one they'd have to organize a whole new promotion program around it. I think that may be what's going on."

He had the odd sensation that his lungs were growing deeper, or that the air was growing richer in oxygen. His shoulders, which had been tight and high, came gradually to rest against the back of the chair. Was this the way other men felt, telling their wives about their work?

". . . Basically it's just a terrifically big, terrifically fast adding machine," he was saying, in reply to her sober wish to know how a computer really worked. "Only instead of mechanical parts, you see, it's got thousands of little individual vacuum tubes . . ." And in a minute he was drawing for her, on a paper napkin, a diagram representing the passage of binary digit pulses through circuitry.

"Oh, *I* see," she said. "At least I think I see; yes. It's really sort of—interesting, isn't it?"

"Oh, well, I don't know, it's—yeah, I guess it *is* sort of interesting, in a way. Of course I don't really know much about it, beyond the basic idea of the thing."

"You always say that. I bet you really know a lot more about it than you think. You certainly do explain it well, anyway."

"Oh?" He felt his smiling cheeks get warm as he lowered his eyes and put the pencil back inside his crisp gabardine suit. "Well, thanks." He finished the last of his second cup of coffee and stood up. "Guess I'd better be getting started."

She stood up too, smoothing her skirt.

"Listen, though, April; this was really nice." The walls of his throat closed up. He felt he was about to cry, but he managed to hold it back. "I mean it was a swell breakfast," he said, blinking. "Really; I don't know when I've ever had a—a nicer breakfast."

"Thank you," she said. "I'm glad; I enjoyed it too."

And could he just walk out now? Without saying anything? Looking at her as they moved toward the door, he wondered if he ought to say "I can't tell you how awful I feel about yesterday," or "I do love you," or something like that; or would it be better not to risk starting things up again? He hesitated, turning to face her, and felt his mouth go into an awkward shape.

"Then you don't really—" he began. "You don't really hate me, or anything?"

Her eyes looked deep and serious; she seemed to be glad he had asked her that question, as if it were one of the few questions in the world she could answer with authority. She shook her head. "No; of course I don't." And she held the door open for him. "Have a good day."

"I will. You too." And then it was easy to decide what to do next: without touching her he began as slowly as any movie actor, to bend toward her lips.

Her face, as it came up close, betrayed an instant's surprise or hesitation, but then it softened; she half closed her eyes and made it clear that this, however brief, would be a mutually willing, mutually gentle kiss. Only after the kiss was completed did he touch her with his hand, on the arm. She was, after all, a damned good-looking girl.

"Okay, then," he said huskily. "So long."

SEVEN

APRIL JOHNSON WHEELER watched her husband's face withdraw, she felt the light squeeze of his hand on her arm and heard his words, and smiled at him.

"So long," she answered.

She followed him outside to stand on the kitchen steps and watch, hugging her arms against the morning chill, while he started up the station car and brought it rumbling out into the sunshine. His flushed profile, thrust out and facing the rear as the car moved past, revealed nothing but the sobriety of a man with a pardonable pride in knowing how to back a car efficiently down a hill. She walked out to a sunny place in front of the carport to see him off, watching the crumpled shape of the old Ford get smaller and smaller. At the end of the driveway, as he backed it out and around into the road, a gleam of sun on the windshield eclipsed his face. She held up her hand and waved anyway, in case he was looking, and when he came into view again as the car straightened out it was clear that he'd seen her. He was bending and grinning up at her, neat and happy in his gabardine suit, his blazing white shirt and dark tie, answering her wave with a small, jaunty wave of his own; then he was gone.

Her smile continued until she was back in the kitchen, clearing away the breakfast dishes into a steaming sinkful of suds; she was still smiling, in fact, when she saw the paper napkin with the diagram of the computer on it, and even then her smile didn't fade: it simply spread and trembled and locked itself into a stiff grimace while the spasms worked at her aching throat, again and again, and the tears broke and ran down her cheeks as fast as she could wipe them away.

She got some music on the radio, to steady her nerves, and by the time she'd finished washing the dishes she was all right again. Her gums were sore from too many cigarettes during the night, her hands were inclined to shake and she was more aware of her heartbeats than usual; otherwise she felt fine. It was a shock, though, when the radio announcer said "Eight forty-five"; it seemed like noon, or early afternoon. She washed her face in cold water and took several deep breaths, trying to slow her heart down; then she lit a cigarette and composed herself at the telephone.

"Hello, Milly?...Hi. Everything all right?...My voice sounds what?...Oh. Well, no, actually, I'm *not* feeling any better; that's really why I called.... Are you sure you don't mind? I mean it may not be for the whole night again; maybe Frank'll want to come over and get them this evening, depending how things work out; but I guess we'd better leave it open, just in case.... Well, that's really wonderful of you, Milly, I do appreciate it.... Oh no, I'm sure it's nothing serious; it's just—you know, one of those things.... All right, then. Give them a kiss for me, and tell them one or the other of us'll be stopping by to pick them up, either tonight or tomorrow.... What?...Oh, well—no, not if they're outdoors playing. Don't call them in." The cigarette broke and shredded in her fingers; she let it drop into the ash tray and used both hands to grip the telephone. "Just give them—you know; give them each a kiss for me, and give them my love, and tell them—*you* know.... All right, Milly. Thanks."

And she barely managed to get the phone back in its cradle before she was crying again. To control herself she lit another cigarette, but it gagged her and she had to go to the bathroom and stand there for a long time, retching dryly even after she'd lost what little breakfast she'd managed to eat. Afterwards, she washed her face again and brushed her teeth, and then it was time to get busy.

"Have you thought it through, April?" Aunt Claire used to say, holding up one stout, arthritic forefinger. "Never undertake to do a thing until you've thought it through; then do the best you can."

The first thing to do was to straighten up the house, and in particular to straighten up the desk, where the hours and hours of her trying to think it through, last night, had left a mess of remnants. The heaped-up ash tray was there, and the opened bottle of ink surrounded by spilled ashes, and the coffee cup containing a dried brown ring. She had only to sit down at the desk and switch on its lamp to bring back the harsh, desolate flavor of the small hours.

In the wastebasket, lumped and crumpled, lay all the failures of the letter she had tried to write. She picked one of them out and opened it and spread it flat, but at first she couldn't read it: she could only marvel at how cramped and black and angry the handwriting looked, like row on row of precisely swatted mosquitos. Then part of it, halfway down the page, came into focus:

> ... your cowardly self-delusions about "love" when you know as well as I do that there's never been anything between us but contempt and distrust and a terrible sickly dependence on each other's weakness—that's why. That's why I couldn't stop laughing today when you said that about the Inability to Love, and that's why I can't stand to let you touch me, and that's why I'll never again believe in anything you think, let alone in anything you say ...

She didn't want to read the rest because she knew it wasn't worth reading. It was weak with hate, like all the other abortive letters on all the other crumpled papers; all of them would have to be burned.

It wasn't until five this morning—and could that really have been only four hours ago?—that she'd finally stopped trying to write the letter. She had forced herself up from the desk then, aching with tiredness, and gone in to take a deep, warm bath, lying very still under the still water for a long time, like a patient in therapy. Afterwards, feeling absent-minded and greatly calmed, she had gone into the bedroom to get dressed; and there he was, on his back.

The sight of him, in the early blue light, sprawled out and twisted in his wrinkled Sunday sports clothes, had been as much of a shock as if she'd found a stranger in the bed. When she sat down in the reek of whiskey to get a closer look at his flushed, sleeping face, she began to understand the real cause of her shock: it was much more than the knowledge that she didn't love him. It was that she didn't, she couldn't possibly hate him. How could anyone hate him? He was—well, he was *Frank*.

Then he'd made a little snoring moan and his lips had begun to work as he groped for her hand. "Oh, baby. Oh, my baby, don't go away . . ."

"Sh-sh-sh. It's all right. It's all right, Frank. Go to sleep."

And that was when she'd thought it through.

So it hadn't been wrong or dishonest of her to say no this morning, when he asked if she hated him, any more than it had been wrong or dishonest to serve him the elaborate breakfast and to show the elaborate interest in his work, and to kiss him goodbye. The kiss, for that matter, had been exactly right—a perfectly fair, friendly kiss, a kiss for a boy you'd just met at a party, a boy who'd danced with you and made you laugh and walked you home afterwards, talking about himself all the way.

The only real mistake, the only wrong and dishonest thing, was ever to have seen him as anything more than that. Oh, for a month or two, just for fun, it might be all right to play a game like that with a boy; but all these years! And all because, in a sentimentally lonely time long ago, she had found it easy and agreeable to believe whatever this one particular boy felt like saying, and to repay him for that pleasure by telling easy, agreeable lies of her own, until each was saying what the other most wanted to hear—until he was saying "I love you" and she was saying "Really, I mean it; you're the most interesting person I've ever met."

What a subtle, treacherous thing it was to let yourself go that way! Because once you'd started it was terribly difficult to stop; soon you were saying "I'm sorry, of course you're right," and "Whatever you think is best," and "You're the most wonderful and valuable thing in the world," and the next thing you knew all honesty, all truth, was as far away and glimmering, as hopelessly unattainable as the world of the golden people. Then you discovered you were working at life the way the Laurel Players worked at *The Petrified Forest*, or the way Steve Kovick worked at his drums—earnest and sloppy and full of pretension and all wrong; you found you were saying yes when you meant no, and "We've got to be together in this thing" when you meant the very opposite; then you were breathing gasoline as if it were flowers and abandoning yourself to a delirium of love under the weight of a clumsy, grunting, red-faced man you didn't even like—Shep Campbell!—and then you were face to face, in total darkness, with the knowledge that you didn't know who you were.

And how could anyone else be blamed for that?

When she'd straightened up the desk and made Frank's bed, with fresh sheets, she carried the wastebasket outdoors and around to the back yard. It was an autumnal day, warm but with a light sharp breeze that scudded stray leaves over the grass and reminded her of all the brave beginnings of childhood, of the apples and pencils and new woolen clothes of the last few days before school.

She took the wastebasket out across the lawn to the incinerator drum, dumped the papers in it and set a match to them. Then she sat down on the edge of the sun-warmed stone wall to wait for their burning, watching the all but invisible flame crawl slowly and then more rapidly up and around them, sending out little waves of heat that shimmered the landscape. The sounds of bird song and rustling trees were faintly mingled with the faraway cries of children at play; she listened carefully but couldn't make out which were Jennifer's and Michael's voices and which were the Campbell boys'—or even, with certainty, whether the voices were coming from the Campbells' part of the Hill.

From a distance, all children's voices sound the same.

"And listen! Listen!—you know what else she brought me, Margie? *Listen!* I'm trying to *tell* you something."

"*Wha*-ut?"

Margie Rothenberg and her little brother George and Mary Jane Crawford and Edna Slater were there, fooling around at the place by the hedge where all the grass was worn away, the place with the little cave and the flat rock where they kept their collection of Dixie Cup lids.

"I said you know what else she brought me? My mother? She brought me this beautiful blue cashmere sweater, for school, and socks that match, and this beautiful little perfume atomizer? This little bottle with a thing that you squeeze? With real perfume in it? Oh, and we drove into White Plains with Mr. Minton, that's my mother's friend, and we went to the movies and had ice cream and everything, and I stayed up till ten minutes after eleven."

"How come she was only here two days?" Margie Rothenberg inquired. "You said she was staying a week. George, you *quit* that now!"

"I did not; I said she *might* stay a week. Next time she probably will, or maybe I'll go and stay a week with her, and if I do that—"

"George! The very next time you pick your nose and eat it I'm gonna tell! I mean it!"

"—and if I do that, you know what? If I do that I won't have to go to school or anything for a whole week; ha, ha. Hey Margie? You want to come home and see my sweater and stuff?"

"I can't. I have to get home in time for 'Don Winslow.'"

"We can hear 'Don Winslow' in my house. Come on."

"I can't. I have to get home. Come on, Georgie."

"Hey Edna? Hey Mary Jane? Know what my mother brought me? She brought me this beautiful—Hey, listen Edna. Listen . . ." There was the sound of an upstairs window rattling open, and she knew that if she turned around she would see the dim shape of Aunt Claire peering out through the copper screen.

"*Aay*-prul!"

"She brought me this beautiful blue sweater, it's cashmere, and this beautiful—"

"*Aay*-prul!"

"What? I'm over here."

"Why didn't you *an*swer, then? I want you to come in this instant and get washed and changed. Your father just called. He's driving out and he'll be here in fifteen minutes."

And she ran for the house so fast that her sneakers seemed hardly to touch the ground. Nothing like this had ever, ever happened before: two whole days with her mother, and then, now, the very next day . . .

She took the stairs two at a time and flew to her room and began to undress in such haste that she popped a button off her blouse, saying, "When did he call? What did he say? How long is he staying?"

"I don't know, dear; he said he's on his way up to Boston. You certainly don't need to tear your clothes. There's plenty of time."

Then she was out on the front porch in her party dress, watching down the street for the first glimpse of his long, high-wheeled, beautiful touring car. When it did come into sight, two blocks away, she forced herself not to start running down the path; she waited until it pulled up and stopped in front of the house, so she could watch him get out.

And oh, how tall, how wonderfully slender and straight he was! How golden the sunlight shone on his hair and his laughing face—"Daddy!"—and then she was running, and then she was in his arms.

"How's my sweetheart?" He smelled of linen and whiskey and tobacco; the short hairs at the back of his neck were bristly to the touch and his jaw was like a warm pumice stone. But his voice was the best of all: as deep and thrilling as blowing across the mouth of an earthen jug. "Do you know you've grown about three feet? I don't know if I can *handle* a girl as big as you. Can't carry you, anyway; I know that much. Let's go on in and see your Aunt Claire. How's everything? How're all your boy friends?"

In the living room, talking with Aunt Claire, he was marvelous. His slim ankles, beneath trouser cuffs that had been raised to just the right height, were clad in taut socks of fluted black wool; his dark brown shoes were so shapely and so gracefully arranged on the carpet, one a little forward and one back, that she felt she ought to study them for a long time, to commit them to memory as the way a man's feet ought to look. But her gaze kept straying upward to his princely knees, to his close-fitting vest with its fine little drape of watch chain, to the way he held himself in his chair and to his white-cuffed wrists and hands, one holding a highball glass and the other making slow, easy gestures in the air, and to his brilliant face. There was too much of him for the eye to behold all at once.

He was finishing a joke: ". . . so Eleanor drew herself up and said, 'Young man, you're drunk.' The fellow looked at her and he said, 'That's true, Mrs. Roosevelt, I am.' He said, 'But here's the difference, Mrs. Roosevelt: *I'll* be all *right* in the morning.'"

Aunt Claire's thick torso doubled over into her lap and April pretended to think it was unbearably funny too, though she hadn't heard the first part and wasn't sure if she would have understood it anyway. But the laughter had scarcely died in the room before he was getting up to leave.

"You mean you're—you mean you're not even staying for dinner, Daddy?"

"Sweetie, I'd love to, but I've got these people waiting in Boston and they're going to be very, very angry with your Daddy if he doesn't get up there in a hurry. How about a kiss?"

And then, hating herself for it, she began acting like a baby. "But you've only stayed about an *hour*. And you—you didn't even bring me a present or anything and you—"

"Oh, *Ape*-rull," Aunt Claire was saying. "Why do you want to go and spoil a nice visit?"

But at least he wasn't standing up any more: he had squatted nimbly beside her and put his arm around her. "Sweetie, I'm afraid you're right about the present, and I feel like a dog about it. Listen, though. Tell you what. Let's you and I go out to the car and rummage through my stuff, and maybe we can find something after all. Want to try?"

Darkness was falling as they left Aunt Claire and walked together down the path, and the silent interior of the car was filled with a thrilling sense of latent power and speed. When he turned on the dashboard lights it was like being in a trim, leathery home of their own. Everything they would ever need for living together was here: comfortable places to sit, a means of travel, a lighter for his cigarettes, a little shelf on which she could spread a napkin for the sandwiches and milk that would comprise their meals on the road; and the front and back seats were big enough for sleeping.

"Glove compartment?" he was saying. "Nope; nothing in here but a lot of old maps and things. Well, let's try the suitcase." He twisted around and reached into the back seat, where he unfastened the clasps of a big Gladstone. "Let's see, now. Socks; shirts; that's no good. Gee, this is quite a problem. You know something? A man ought never to travel without a fresh supply of bangles and spangles; can't ever tell when he might come across a pretty girl. Oh, look. Wait a second, here's something. Not *much*, of course, but something." He drew out a long brown bottle with the picture of a horse and the words "White Horse" on its label. Something very small was attached to its neck by a ribbon, but he concealed it from view until he opened his penknife and cut it free. Then, holding it by the ribbon, he laid it delicately in her hand—a tiny, perfect white horse.

"There you are, my darling," he said. "And you can keep it forever."

The fire was out. She prodded the blackened lumps of paper with a stick to make sure they had burned; there was nothing but ashes.

The children's voices faintly followed her as she carried the wastebasket back across the lawn; only by going inside and closing the door was she able to shut them out. She turned off the radio too, and the house became extraordinarily quiet.

She put the wastebasket back in its place and sat down at the desk again with a fresh sheet of paper. This time the letter took no time at all to write. There was only one big, important thing to say, and it was best said in a very few words—so few as to allow no possible elaborations or distortions of meaning.

Dear Frank,
    Whatever happens please don't
blame yourself.

From old, insidious habit she almost added the words *I love you*, but she caught herself in time and made the signature plain: *April*. She put it in an envelope, wrote *Frank* on the outside, and left it on the exact center of the desk.

In the kitchen she took down her largest stewing pot, filled it with water and set it on the stove to boil. From storage cartons in the cellar she got out the other necessary pieces of equipment: the tongs that had once been used for sterilizing formula bottles, and the blue drugstore box containing the two parts of the syringe, rubber bulb and long plastic nozzle. She dropped these things in the stewing pot, which was just beginning to steam.

By the time she'd made the other preparations, putting a supply of fresh towels in the bathroom, writing down the number of the hospital and propping it by the telephone, the water was boiling nicely. It was wobbling the lid of the pot and causing the syringe to nudge and rumble against its sides.

It was nine-thirty. In another ten minutes she would turn off the heat; then it would take a while for the water to cool. In the meantime there was nothing to do but wait.

"Have you thought it through, April? Never undertake to do a thing until you've—"

But she needed no more advice and no more instruction. She was calm and quiet now with knowing what she had always known, what neither her parents nor Aunt Claire nor Frank nor anyone else had ever had to teach her: that if you wanted to do something absolutely honest, something true, it always turned out to be a thing that had to be done alone.

EIGHT

AT TWO O'CLOCK that afternoon, Milly Campbell had just completed her housework. She was resting on the television hassock, addled with the smells of dust and floorwax and with the noise of the children outside (six kids were really too many for one person to handle, even for a couple of days) and she always said afterwards that she had "this very definite sense of foreboding" for at least a minute before hearing the sound that confirmed it.

It was a sound of emergency—of Fire, Murder, Police—the deep, shockingly loud purr that an automobile siren makes when the driver has just gotten started and has had to slow down for a turn before opening up to full speed. She got to the window in the nick of time to see it, down over the tops of the trees below the lawn: the long shape of an ambulance turning out of Revolutionary Road, catching the sun in a quick, brilliant reflection as it straightened out and pulled away down Route Twelve with its siren mounting higher and higher into a sustained, unbearable shriek that hung in the air long after the ambulance itself had vanished in the distance. It left her chewing her lips with worry.

"I mean I knew there were plenty of other people on that road," she said afterwards. "It could've been anybody, but I just had this feeling it was April. I started to call her but then I stopped because I knew it would sound silly, and I thought she might be sleeping."

So she sat uneasily at the telephone until it suddenly burst into ringing. It was Mrs. Givings, making the receiver vibrate painfully against Milly's ear.

"Do you know what's happened at the Wheelers'? Because I was just going past their place and there was an ambulance coming out of their drive, and I'm terribly alarmed. And now I've been trying to call them and there's no answer . . ."

"I almost died," Milly explained later. "After she hung up

I just sat there feeling sick, and then I did what I always do when something horrible happens. I called Shep."

Slowly rubbing the back of his neck as he stood looking out a window of the Allied Precision Laboratories, Inc., Shep Campbell was lost in a muddled reverie. For a week now, ever since the incredible night at the Log Cabin, he hadn't been of much use to Allied Precision, to Milly or to himself. On the first day, like any lovesick kid, he had called her up from a phone booth and said, "April, when can I see you?" and she'd made it clear, in so many words, that he couldn't see her at all and that he should have known better than to ask. The memory of this had rankled him all that night and the next day—God, what a loutish, unsophisticated clown she must have thought him—and caused him to spend many hours in whispered rehearsal of the cool, mature, understanding things he would say when he called her again. But when he got into the phone booth again he loused everything up. All the carefully practiced lines came out wrong, his voice was shaking like a fool's and he started saying he loved her again, and the whole thing ended with her saying, kindly but firmly: "Look Shep; I really don't want to hang up on you, but I'm afraid I'll have to unless you hang up first."

He had seen her only once. Yesterday, when she brought her kids over to the house, he had hidden trembling in the bedroom and peeked down through the dimity curtains to watch her getting out of her car—a tired, pregnant woman—and he couldn't see her steadily for the beating of his heart.

"Phone, Mr. Campbell," one of the girls called, and as he moved to pick it up at his desk he wondered, against all reasonable logic, if it might be April. It wasn't.

"Hi, baby—what? Listen, now, calm down. *Who's* in the hospital? When? Oh Jesus."

But the remarkable thing was that for the first time all week he felt a sense of competence. His rump dropped lightly to the felt pad of his chair, his legs flexed under it in a kind of squat, and he nestled the phone at his cheek with one hand and held his mechanical pencil poised in the other—a tense, steady paratrooper, ready for action.

"Calm *down* a second," he told her. "Have you called the hospital yet? Honey, that's the *first* thing we ought to do, before we start calling Frank. . . . Okay, okay, I know you're all upset. I'll call them and find out, and then I'll call him. Now listen, you take it easy, hear me?" His pencil made a number of resolutely parallel lines on a scratch pad. "Okay," he said. "And for God's sake don't let on to the kids that anything's wrong—our kids *or* their kids. . . . Okay. . . . Okay, right. I'll call you."

Then he had the hospital on the phone and he was briskly cutting through all the confusion of the switchboard, dismissing the voices that couldn't help him and taking just the right tone of quick, commanding inquiry with those that could.

". . . undergoing emergency what? . . . Well, but I mean treatment for *what?* . . . Oh. You mean she had a miscarriage. Well, look: can you tell me how she is? . . . I see. And do you know how long that'll be? . . . Doctor what?" His pencil jumped and wiggled as he wrote down the name. "Okay. One more thing: has anyone notified her husband yet? . . . Okay. Thanks."

Hunching still lower over the phone, he put through a call to Knox Business Machines in New York.

"Mr. Frank Wheeler, please. . . . He's where?. . .Well, get him *out* of conference, then. This is an emergency." And only then, while he waited, did his guts begin to tighten with anxiety.

Then Frank was on the phone, saying "Oh my God" in a shocked, insubstantial voice.

"No, wait, listen, Frank: take it easy, boy. Far as I know she's all right. That's absolutely all they'd tell me. Now listen. Grab the first train you can to Stamford, I'll meet you there and we'll be at the hospital in five minutes. . . . Right. I'm checking out of here right now. Okay, Frank."

Out in the parking lot, running at full tilt for his car and pulling on his flapping jacket as he ran, Shep felt his exhilaration returning with the fresh air that whistled in his ears. It was the old combat feeling, the sense of doing exactly the right thing, quickly and well, when all the other elements of the situation were out of control.

At the station, waiting for the train, he used the time to call Milly again (she had calmed down) and to call the hospital (there was no news); then he walked up and down the platform in the afternoon sun, jingling coins in his pocket and saying, under his breath, "Come *on*; come *on*." This incongruously peaceful lull was like the war too—hurry up and wait. But suddenly the train was on him, shuddering the platform, and Frank was a frantic figure clinging to its side, dropping off and nearly falling on his face and then sprinting toward Shep with wild eyes and a flying necktie.

"Okay, Frank—" They were running side by side to the parking lot even before the train had stopped. "Car's right here."

"Is she—are they still—?"

"Same as when I called you."

They didn't talk on the short, slow ride through traffic to the hospital, and Shep wasn't sure his voice would have worked if he'd tried to use it. The way Frank's eyes looked, and the way he huddled and trembled in the seat beside him, had filled him with fear. He knew now that all his opportunities for action would soon be over; when he had steered up this final hill to this ugly brown building, he would pass into an area of total helplessness.

As they bolted through the whispering doors marked VISITORS' ENTRANCE, as they paused to husk and stutter at an information desk and then struck off down the corridor with the intense, swift heel-and-toe of competitors in a walking race, Shep's mind went mercifully out of focus in the way that it had always done, sooner or later, in combat: a dim, protective inner voice said, This isn't really happening; don't believe any of this.

"Mrs. who? Mrs. Wheeler?" said a plump freckled nurse near the end of the corridor, blinking over the rim of her sterile mask. "You mean the emergency? Well I don't *know*, offhand. I'm afraid I can't—" she glanced uneasily at a closed door over which a red light shone, and Frank made a lunge for it. She skittered in his path as if to stop him by force, if necessary, but Shep grabbed his arm and held him back.

"Can't he go in? He's her husband."

"No, he certainly can't," she said, her eyes growing wide with a sense of responsibility. But at last she agreed, reluctantly, to go inside herself and speak to the doctor. A minute later he came out, a slight, embarrassed-looking man in a wrinkled surgical gown.

"Which is Mr. Wheeler?" he asked, and then he took Frank by the arm and led him away for a private talk.

Shep, respectfully keeping his distance, allowed the inner voice to assure him that she couldn't possibly be dying. People didn't die this way, at the end of a drowsing corridor like this in the middle of the afternoon. Why, hell, if she was dying that janitor wouldn't be pushing his mop so peacefully across the linoleum, and he certainly wouldn't be humming, nor would they let the radio play so loud in the ward a few doors away. If April Wheeler was dying they certainly wouldn't have this bulletin board here on the wall, with its mimeographed announcement of a staff dance ("Fun! Refreshments!") and they wouldn't have these wicker chairs arranged this way, with this table and this neat display of magazines. What the hell did they expect you to do? Sit down and cross your legs and flip through a copy of *Life* while somebody died? Of course not. This was a place where babies were born or where simple, run-of-the-mill miscarriages were cleaned up in a jiffy; it was a place where you waited and worried until you'd made sure everything was all right, and then you walked out and had a drink and went home.

Experimentally, he sat down in one of the wicker chairs. One of the magazines was *U.S. Camera*, and he toyed with a temptation to pick it up and look through it for photographs of women in the nude; but instead he sprang to his feet again and walked a few steps one way and a few steps another. The trouble was that he had to go to the bathroom. The pain in his bladder was abrupt and keen, and he wondered how long it would take him to find his way to a toilet and back.

But the doctor had gone back inside now and Frank was standing there alone, rubbing his temple with the heel of his hand. "Jesus, Shep, I couldn't even *understand* half the things he told me. He said the fetus was out before they got her here. He said they had to operate to take out the whaddyacallit, the placenta, and they did, only now she's still bleeding. He said she lost a lot of blood even before the ambulance came, and now they're trying to stop it, and he said a whole lot of things I didn't get, about capillaries, and he said she's unconscious. Jesus."

"How about sitting down a minute, Frank?"

"That's what he said too. What the hell do I want to sit down for?"

So they continued to stand, listening to the janitor's low humming and to the rhythmic thud of his mop against the wall, and to the occasional rubber-heeled thump and rustle of a nurse walking by. Once Frank's eyes came into focus long enough for him to accept a cigarette, which Shep offered in a little excess of friendliness and courtesy—"Cigarette, fella? Atta boy. Here, I got the match—" and then, encouraged by the good cheer in his own voice, he said: "Tell you what, Frank. I'll go get us a cup of coffee."

"No."

"No, that's all right. I won't be a minute." And he escaped down the hall and around the corner and down another hall until he found the men's room, where he stood trembling and very nearly whimpering as the pressure on his bladder was slowly relieved. Afterwards he went out in the hall again and asked directions until he found the canteen, which was hundreds of yards away at the other end of the building and was called the Hospitality Shop. He hurried through its toys and cupcakes and magazines to order two containers of coffee; then, holding the hot paper cups gingerly to keep from scalding his fingers, he started back to the emergency area. But he was lost. All the corridors looked alike, and he got all the way to the end of one of them before discovering he was going in the wrong direction. It took him a long time to find his way back, and he would always remember that this was what he was doing—mincing down hallways carrying two containers of coffee, wearing a silly, inquiring smile—this was what he was doing when April Wheeler died.

He knew it had happened as soon as he'd turned the last corner, into the long hall with the red-lighted door at the end. Frank had disappeared; that whole part of the hall was empty. He was still fifty yards away when he saw the door open and a number of nurses come spilling out and hurrying efficiently off in all directions; behind them, slowly, came not one but three or four doctors, two of them supporting Frank like polite, solicitous waiters helping a drunk out of a saloon.

Shep looked frantically around for a place to put the coffee down; squatting, he set both containers on the floor against the wall and then broke into a run, and then he was in the midst of the doctors, aware of them only as a mass of white clothing and bobbing pink faces and a discord of voices:

". . . terrible shock, of course . . ."

". . . hemorrhaging was much too severe to . . ."

". . . here, look, try to sit down and . . ."

". . . capillaries . . ."

". . . actually she held on for a remarkably . . ."

". . . no, look, sit down and . . ."

". . . these things happen, there's really . . ."

They were trying to make Frank sit down in one of the wicker chairs, which squeaked and skidded under their efforts, but he remained stubbornly on his feet, silent and expressionless, breathing rapidly, his head wobbling a little with each breath as he stared at nothing.

The sequence of events after that would remain forever uncertain in Shep's memory. Hours must have passed because it was night before they got home, and they must have covered many miles because he was driving the whole time, but he had no real idea of where they traveled. Once, in some town, he stopped at a package store and bought a pint of bourbon, which he tore open while the engine idled at the curb. He handed it to Frank— "Here, fella—" and watched him suck at its mouth with lips as loose as a baby's. Somewhere else—or was it the same place?— he went to a roadside phone booth and called Milly, and when she said "Oh God! No!" he told her to for Christ's sake shut up before the children heard her. He had to stay on the phone until she'd pulled herself together, keeping an eye on Frank's unmoving head in the car outside. "Now, listen," he told her. "I can't bring him home until the kids are asleep; what you've got to do is get them in bed as soon as you can, and for God's sake try to act natural. Then I'll bring him home to our place for the night. I mean we sure as hell can't let him go home to *his* house . . ."

The rest of the time they were on the road, going nowhere.

He remembered the trip only as a succession of traffic lights and electrical wires and trees, of houses and shopping centers and endless rolling hills under the pale sky, and of Frank either silent or making faint little moans or mumbling this phrase, over and over:

". . . and she was so damn nice this morning. Isn't that the damnedest thing? She was so damn *nice* this morning . . ."

Once, and Shep could never remember whether it was early or late in the ride, he said, "She did it to herself, Shep. She killed herself."

And Shep's mind performed its trick of rolling with the punch: he would think about this one later. "Frank, take it easy," he said. "Don't talk crap. These things happen, that's all."

"Not this one. This one didn't happen. She wanted to do it last month and it would've been safe then. It would've been safe then and I talked her out of it. I talked her out of it and then we had a fight yesterday and now she—Oh Jesus. Oh Jesus. And she was so damn *nice* this morning."

Shep kept his eyes on the road, grateful that there was plenty to occupy the alert, front part of his mind. Because how would he ever know, now, how much or little truth there was in this? And how would he ever know how much or little it had to do with himself?

Alone in her darkened living room, much later, Milly sat chewing her handkerchief and feeling like a terrible coward. She'd done pretty well up to a point; she had managed to do a good job of acting with the children and to get them all in bed an hour early, well before Shep's arrival; she had made some sandwiches and set them out in the kitchen, in case anyone got hungry later ("Life goes on," her mother had always said, making sandwiches on the day of a death); she had even found time to call Mrs. Givings, whose reaction to the news was to say "Oh, oh, oh," over and over again; and she'd done her very best to be ready for the ordeal of confronting Frank. She'd been ready to sit up all night with him and—well, read to him from the Bible, or something; ready to hold him and let him weep on her breast; anything.

But nothing had prepared her for the awful blankness of his eyes when Shep brought him up the kitchen steps. "Oh Frank," she'd said, and started to cry, and run for the living room with her handkerchief in her mouth, and ever since then she'd been completely useless.

She'd done nothing but sit here and listen to the dim sounds the two of them made in the kitchen (a scraping chair, a clink of bottle on glass, and Shep's voice: "Here, fella. Drink it up, now . . ."), trying to work up the courage to go back. Once Shep had tiptoed in, smelling of whiskey, to consult with her.

"Oh, sweetie, I'm sorry," she had whispered against his shirt. "I know I'm not being any help, but I *can't*. I can't stand the way he *looks*."

"Okay. That's okay, honey. You take it easy; I'll look after him. He's sort of in a state of shock, is all. Jesus, what a thing." He sounded a little drunk. "Jesus, what an awful thing. You know what he told me in the car? He said she did it to herself. You believe that?"

"She *what*?"

"Gave herself an abortion; or tried to."

"Oh," she whispered, shuddering. "Oh, how awful. You think she did? But why would she do that?"

"How the hell do I know? Am I supposed to know everything? I'm just telling you what he *said*, for Christ's sake." He rubbed his head with both hands. "Hell, I'm sorry, honey."

"All right. You better get back. I'll come out and sit with him in a little while, and you can get some rest. We'll take turns."

"Okay."

But more than two hours had passed since then, and still she hadn't found the strength to carry out her promise. All she could do was to sit here and dread it. There had been no sounds in the kitchen for a long time now. What were they *doing* in there? Just sitting, or what?

And so in the end it was curiosity as much as courage that helped her to her feet and across the room and down the hall to the brilliant kitchen doorway. She hesitated, taking a deep breath, squinting her eyes in preparation for the glare of the lights, and then she went in.

Shep's head was in his arms on the kitchen table, an inch away from the untouched plate of sandwiches; he was sound asleep and faintly snoring. Frank wasn't there.

The Revolutionary Hill Estates had not been designed to accommodate a tragedy. Even at night, as if on purpose, the development held no looming shadows and no gaunt silhouettes. It was invincibly cheerful, a toyland of white and pastel houses whose bright, uncurtained windows winked blandly through a dappling of green and yellow leaves. Proud floodlights were trained on some of the lawns, on some of the neat front doors and on the hips of some of the berthed, ice-cream colored automobiles.

A man running down these streets in desperate grief was indecently out of place. Except for the whisk of his shoes on the asphalt and the rush of his own breath, it was so quiet that he could hear the sounds of television in the dozing rooms behind the leaves—a blurred comedian's shout followed by dim, spastic waves of laughter and applause, and then the striking-up of a band. Even when he veered from the pavement, cut across someone's back yard and plunged into the down-sloping woods, intent on a madman's shortcut to Revolutionary Road, even then there was no escape: the house lights beamed and stumbled happily along with him among the twigs that whipped his face, and once when he lost his footing and fell scrabbling down a rocky ravine, he came up with a child's enameled tin beach bucket in his hand.

As he clambered out onto asphalt again at the base of the Hill he allowed his dizzy, jogging mind to indulge in a cruel delusion: it had all been a nightmare; he would round this next bend and see the lights blazing in his own house; he would run inside and find her at the ironing board, or curled up on the sofa with a magazine ("What's the *matter*, Frank? Your *pants* are all muddy! Of *course* I'm all right . . .").

But then he saw the house—really saw it—long and milk-white in the moonlight, with black windows, the only darkened house on the road.

She had been very careful about the blood. Except for a tidy trail of drops leading out to the telephone and back, it had all been confined to the bathroom, and even there it had mostly been flushed away. Two heavy towels, soaked crimson, lay lumped in the tub, close to the drain. "I thought that would be the simplest way to handle it," he could hear her saying. "I thought you could just wrap the towels up in newspaper and put them in the garbage, and then give the tub a good rinsing out. Okay?" On the floor of the linen closet he found the syringe in its pot of cold water; she had probably put it there to hide it from the ambulance crew. "I mean I just thought it would be best to get it out of sight; I didn't want to have to answer a lot of dumb questions."

And his head continued to ring with the sound of her voice as he set to work. "There; now that's done," it said when he pressed the newspaper bundles deep into the garbage can outside the kitchen door, and when he returned to fall on his knees and scrub at the trail of drops it was still with him. "Try a damp sponge and a little dry detergent, darling—it's there in the cabinet under the sink. That ought to take it up. There, you see? That's fine. I didn't get any on the rug, did I? Oh, good."

How could she be dead when the house was alive with the sound of her and the sense of her? Even when he had finished the cleaning, when there was nothing to do but walk around and turn on lights and turn them off again, even then her presence was everywhere, as real as the scent of her dresses in the bedroom closet. It was only after he'd spent a long time in the closet, embracing her clothes, that he went back to the living room and found the note she had left for him on the desk. And he barely had time to read it, and to turn the light off again, before he saw the Campbells' Pontiac slowing down for the turn into the driveway. He went quickly back to the bedroom and shut himself inside the closet, among the clothes. From there he heard the car rumble to a stop outside; then the kitchen door opened and there were several faltering footsteps.

"Frank?" Shep called hoarsely. "Frank? You here?"

He heard him walking through the rooms, stumbling and cursing as he felt along the walls for light switches; finally he heard him leave, and when the sound of the car had faded away he came out of hiding, carrying his note, and sat in the darkness by the picture window.

But after that interruption, April's voice no longer spoke to him. He tried for hours to recapture it, whispering words for it to say, going back to the closet time and again and into the drawers of her dressing table and into the kitchen, where he thought the pantry shelves and the racked plates and coffee cups would surely contain the ghost of her, but it was gone.

NINE

ACCORDING TO Milly Campbell, who told the story many, many times in the following months, everything worked out as well as could be expected. "I mean," she would always add, and here she would give a little shudder, "I mean, considering it was just about the most horrible thing we've ever been through in our lives. Wasn't it, sweetie?"

And Shep would agree that it certainly was. His role during these recitals was to sit and stare gravely at the carpet, occasionally shaking his head or flexing his bite, until she cued him to make certain small corroborations. He was glad enough to let her do most of the talking—or rather, he was glad of it in the beginning, throughout the fall and winter of the year. By spring, he had begun to wish she would find other things to talk about.

And his annoyance grew all but intolerable one Friday evening in May, when she was going over the whole business with some new acquaintances named Brace—the very couple who had recently moved into the Wheelers' house. The trouble was partly just that: it seemed a betrayal and a sacrilege, somehow, to be telling the story to people who would go home and talk it over in that particular house; and it was partly that the Braces made such a dull audience, nodding and shaking their polite, bridge-playing heads in remorse for people they had never known. But mostly it was that Milly's voice had taken on a little too much of a voluptuous narrative pleasure. She's *enjoying* this, he thought, watching her over the rim of his highball glass as she came to the part about how awful it had been the next day. By God, she's really getting a kick out of it.

"... and I mean Shep and I were just about out of our minds by morning," she was saying. "We didn't have the faintest idea where Frank was; we kept calling the hospital to see if they'd heard from him; and then we had to go through this horrible thing with the kids of pretending everything was fine. They knew something was the matter, though; you know how kids are. They sensed it. When I was giving them breakfast Jennifer looked at me and said, 'Milly? Is Mommy going to come and pick us up today, or what?' And she was sort of smiling, you know? As if she knew it was a silly question but she'd promised her brother she'd ask it? I almost died. I said, 'Well, dear, I don't know what your mommy's plans are, exactly.' Wasn't that awful? But I didn't know what else to say.

"Then about two o'clock we called the hospital and they said Frank had just left: he'd gone in and signed all the papers, or whatever it is you have to do when somebody dies; and a little later he came driving up here. The minute he came in I said, 'Frank, is there anything we can do? Because,' I said, 'if there's anything at all we can do, just say so.'

"He said no, he thought he'd taken care of everything. He said he'd called his brother in Pittsfield—he's got this much older brother, you see; actually he's got two of them, but he never used to mention them; I'd forgotten he *had* any family—and he said the brother and his wife were coming down the next day, to help out with the kids and everything, and the funeral. So I said, 'All right, but please stay here with us tonight.' I said, 'You can't take the kids back to your house alone.' He said okay, he would; but he said first he wanted to take them out for a drive somewhere, and break the news to them. And that's what he did. He went out in the yard and they saw him and came running over, and he said 'Hi!' and picked them up and put them in the car and drove away. I really think it was the saddest thing I've ever seen in my life. And I'll never forget what Jennifer said when he brought them back that night. It was past their bedtime and they were both kind of sleepy, and I was helping Jennifer get ready for bed and she said, 'Milly? You know what?' She said, 'My mommy's in Heaven and we had dinner in a restaurant.'"

"God!" said Nancy Brace. "But I mean how did things work out finally?" She was a sharp-faced, bespectacled girl who had worked before her marriage as a buyer for one of the top New York specialty shops. She liked her stories neat, with points, and she clearly felt there were too many loose ends in this one. "Did his relatives stay on here a while? And then what?"

"Oh, no," Milly explained. "Right after the funeral they took the kids back up to Pittsfield with them, and Frank went along for a few days, to help them make the adjustment; then he moved into the city and started going up there for weekends, and that's the way things are now. I guess it's more or less a permanent arrangement. They're very nice, the brother and his wife—wonderful people, really, and very good with the kids; of course they're, *you* know, a lot older and everything.

"And then I guess we didn't see anything more of Frank after that until March, or whenever it was, when he came out to see about closing the sale of the house. And of course that's when you folks met him. He spent a couple of days with us then, and we had a long talk. That was when he told us about finding the note she'd left him. That was when he said that if it hadn't been for that note he thought he would've killed himself that night."

Warren Brace cleared the phlegm from his throat and swallowed it. A slow-spoken, pipe-clenching man with thinning hair and incongruously soft, childish lips, he was employed in the city by a firm of management consultants, a kind of work he described as well suited to what he called his analytical turn of mind. "You know?" he said. "This is the kind of thing that really—" He paused, examining the wisp of smoke that curled from his wet pipestem. "Really makes you stop and think."

"Well, but how did he seem otherwise?" Nancy Brace inquired. "I mean did he seem to've made a—a fairly good adjustment?"

Milly sighed, tugging down her skirt and curling her feet up into the chair cushion in a single quick, awkward gesture. "Well, he'd lost a lot of weight," she said, "but I guess he looked well enough, except for that. He said being in analysis was helping him a lot; he talked a little about that. And he talked about his job—he's got this different kind of job now? I mean he's still sort of vaguely working for Knox, but it's under a new setup, or something? I didn't quite understand that part of it. What's the name of his new company, sweetie?"

"Bart Pollock Associates."

"*Oh* yes," said Warren Brace. "They're up at Fifty-ninth and Madison. Very interesting new firm, as a matter of fact. Sort of industrial public relations in the electronics field. They started out with the Knox account, and now I believe they've got a couple of others. They ought to be really going places in the next few years."

"Well," Milly went on, "anyway, he seemed to be keeping busy. And he seemed—oh, I guess 'cheerful' is the wrong word, but that's sort of what I mean. I really felt his attitude was—well, courageous. Very courageous."

On the mumbled pretext of refilling their glasses, Shep made his way out to the kitchen, where he banged and clattered a tray of ice cubes in the sink to drown out her voice. Why did she have to make such a God damn soap opera out of it? If she couldn't tell it the way it really was, to people who really wanted to listen, why the hell tell it at all? Courageous! Of all the asinine, mean-ingless . . .

And forgetting his guests, or rather coming to the abrupt decision that they could damn well get their own God damn drinks, he poured himself a stiff one and took it out to the darkness of the back yard, letting the door close behind him with a little slam.

Courageous! What kind of bullshit was that? How could a man be courageous when he wasn't even alive? Because that was the whole point; that was the way he'd seemed when he came to call that March afternoon: a walking, talking, smiling, life-less man.

At first sight, getting out of his car, he had looked pretty much the same as ever except that his jacket hung a little looser on him and he'd taken to wearing it with the top button fastened as well as the middle one, to gather up some of the slack. But after you'd heard his voice—"Hi, Milly; good to see you, Shep"—and felt the light, dry press of his handshake, you began to see how the life had gone out of him.

He was so damned mild! He sat there arranging the crease of his pants over his knees and brushing little flecks of ash off his lap and holding his drink with his pinkie hooked around under-neath the glass, for safety. And he had a new way of laughing: a soft, simpering giggle. You couldn't picture him really laughing, or really crying, or really sweating or eating or getting drunk or getting excited—or even standing up for himself. For Christ's sake, he looked like somebody you could walk up to and take a swing at and knock down, and all he'd do would be to lie there and apologize for getting in your way. So that when he finally did come out with that business about finding the note—"I honestly think I'd have killed myself, if it hadn't been for that"—it was all you could do to keep from saying, Oh, bullshit! You're a lying bastard, Wheeler; you'd never have had the nerve.

And it was even worse than that: he was boring. He must have spent at least an hour talking about his half-assed job, and God only knew how many other hours on his other favorite subject: "my analyst this"; "my analyst that"—he had turned into one of these people that want to tell you about their God damned analyst all the time. "And I mean I think we're really getting down to some basic stuff; things I've never really faced before about my relationship with my father . . ." Christ! And that was what had become of Frank; that was what you'd have to know about, if you wanted to know how things had really worked out.

He took a gulp of whiskey, seeing a quick blur of stars and moon through the wet dome of his glass. Then he started back for the house, but he didn't make it; he had to turn around again and head out to the far border of the lawn and walk around out there in little circles; he was crying.

It was the smell of spring in the air that did it—earth and flowers—because it was almost exactly a year now since the time of the Laurel Players, and to remember the Laurel Players was to remember April Wheeler's way of walking across the stage, and her smile, and the sound of her voice (*"Wouldn't you like to be loved by me?"*), and in remembering all this there was nothing for Shep Campbell to do but walk around on the grass and cry, a big wretched baby with his fist in his mouth and the warm tears spilling down his knuckles.

He found it so easy and so pleasant to cry that he didn't try to stop for a while, until he realized he was forcing his sobs a little, exaggerating their depth with unnecessary shudders. Then, ashamed of himself, he bent over and carefully set his drink on the grass, got out his handkerchief and blew his nose.

The whole point of crying was to quit before you cornied it

up. The whole point of grief itself was to cut it out while it was still honest, while it still meant something. Because the thing was so easily corrupted: let yourself go and you started embellishing your own sobs, or you started telling about the Wheelers with a sad, sentimental smile and saying Frank was courageous, and then what the hell did you have?

Milly was still talking, still embellishing, when he went back indoors to pass around the fresh highballs. She had reached her summing-up now, leaning earnestly forward with her elbows on her slightly spread, wrinkled knees.

"No, but I really do think it was an experience that's brought us closer together," she was saying. "Shep and me, I mean. Don't you, sweetie?"

And both the Braces turned to stare at him in mute reiteration of her question. Did he? Well, didn't he?

The only thing to say, of course, was, "Yeah, that's so; it really has."

And the funny part, he suddenly realized, the funny part was that he meant it. Looking at her now in the lamplight, this small, rumpled, foolish woman, he knew he had told the truth. Because God damn it, she was alive, wasn't she? If he walked over to her chair right now and touched the back of her neck, she would close her eyes and smile, wouldn't she? Damn right, she would. And when the Braces went home—and with God's help they would soon be getting the hell on their way—when the Braces went home she would go in and bustle clumsily around the kitchen, washing the dishes and talking a mile a minute ("Oh I like them *so* much; don't you?"). Then she would go to bed, and in the morning she'd get up and come humping downstairs again in her torn dressing gown with its smell of sleep and orange juice and cough syrup and stale deodorants, and go on living.

For Mrs. Givings, too, the time after April's death followed a pattern of shock, pain, and slow recovery.

At first she could think of it only in terms of overwhelming personal guilt, and so was unable to discuss it at all, even with Howard. She knew that Howard or anyone else would only insist it had been an accident, that no one could be held responsible, and the last thing she wanted was to be comforted. The memory of that ambulance backing down out of the Wheelers' drive, at the very moment when she'd come bringing well-rehearsed apologies ("April, about yesterday; you've both been wonderful but I'll never ask you to go through that sort of thing again; Howard and I have agreed now that John's difficulties are quite beyond our . . ."), and then of little Mrs. Campbell's voice on the phone that same afternoon, telling her the news, had filled her with a self-reproach so deep and pure it was almost pleasurable. She was physically sick for a week.

This, then, was what came of good intentions. Try to love your child, and you helped to bring about another mother's death.

"And I know you'll say there was probably no connection," she explained to John's psychiatrist, "but frankly, Doctor, I'm not asking your opinion. I'm simply saying that it's quite out of the question for us ever to think in terms of bringing him into contact with outside people again. Quite out of the question."

"Mm," the doctor said. "Yes. Well, of course, matters of this sort are entirely up to you and Mr.—ah, Mr. Givings to decide."

"I know he's ill," she went on, and here she had to sniffle back an alarming threat of tears, "I know he's ill and he's much to be pitied, but he's also very destructive, Doctor. Impossibly destructive."

"Mm. Yes . . ."

After that they confined their weekly visits to the inner waiting room of John's ward. He didn't seem to mind. He would ask about the Wheelers from time to time, but of course they told him nothing. By Christmas they had slipped into the habit of allowing two or three weeks to elapse between visits; then they tapered off to once a month.

Little things make a difference. One sleeting January day, at the shopping center, her eye was caught and held by a small, brown, mixed-breed spaniel puppy in the pet-shop window. Feeling absurd—she had never done anything quite so silly and impulsive in her life—she went in and bought him on the spot and took him home.

And what a pleasure he was! Oh, he was troublesome too— paper-training and housebreaking and worms and so on; it takes a lot of plain, hard work to make a good pet—but he was worth it.

"*Roll* over!" she would say, sitting cross-legged on the carpet in her slipper-socks. "*Roll* over, boy!" Then she would knead his fuzzy little ribs and belly with her fingers while he squirmed on his spine, his four paws waving in the air and his black lips drawn back from his teeth in giggling ecstasy.

"*Oh*, you're such a good little dog! *Oh*, you're such a good little wet-nosed sweetie-pie—aren't you? Aren't you? Yes you *are*! Oh, yes you *are*!" It was the puppy, more than anything or anyone else, that made her winter endurable.

Business began to pick up with the coming of spring, which never failed to give her a sense of life beginning all over again; but one ordeal remained to be survived: the selling of the Wheelers' house. Her dread of the inevitable meeting with Frank in the lawyer's office, at the closing, was so intense that she hardly slept at all the night before. It turned out, though, to be much less awkward than she'd feared. He was cordial and dignified—"Good to see you, Mrs. Givings"—they talked only of business matters, and he left as soon as the papers were signed. Afterwards, it was as if she'd closed a door forever on the whole experience.

The next two months kept her exhaustingly, deliriously busy: more of the sweet old houses coming on the market, more of the more presentable new ones being built, more and more of the right sort of people coming out from the city—people who wanted and deserved something really nice, and who didn't care about haggling for bargains. It soon developed into the best real estate spring of her career, and she took a craftsman's pride in it. The days were long and often very difficult, but that only made the shrunken evenings more exquisitely restful.

Between playing with the puppy and chatting with Howard, she found any number of simple, constructive little tasks to do around the house.

"Isn't this cozy?" she asked one fine May evening as she crouched on spread newspapers to varnish a chair. Howard, bored with the *World-Telegram*, was sitting with folded hands and looking out the window; the puppy was curled up asleep on his little rug nearby, sated with happiness. "It's wonderful just to let yourself unwind after a hard day," she said. "Would you like some more coffee, dear? Or some more cake?"

"No, thanks. I may have a glass of milk later on."

Turning the chair carefully on its spattered papers and seating herself on the floor to reach its underside, she went on talking as her brush trailed back and forth.

". . . I simply can't tell you how pleased I am about the little Revolutionary Road place, Howard. Remember how dreary it looked all winter? All cold and dark and—well, spooky. Creepy-crawly. And now whenever I drive past it gives me such a lift to see it all perked up and spanking clean again, with lights in the windows. Oh, and they're delightful young people, the Braces. She's very sweet and fun to talk to; he's rather reserved. I think he must do something very brilliant in town. He said to me, 'Mrs. Givings, I can't thank you enough. This is just the kind of home we've always wanted.' Wasn't that a sweet thing to say? And do you know, I was just thinking. I've loved that little house for years, and these are the first really suitable people I've ever found for it. Really nice, congenial people, I mean."

Her husband stirred and shifted the placement of his ortho-pedic shoes. "Well," he said, "except for the Wheelers, you mean."

"Well, but I mean *really* congenial people," she said. "*Our* kind of people. Oh, I was very fond of the Wheelers, but they always were a bit—a bit whimsical, for my taste. A bit neurotic. I may not have stressed it, but they were often very trying people to deal with, in many ways. Actually, the main reason the little house has been so hard to *sell* is that they let it depreciate so dreadfully. Warped window frames, wet cellar, crayon marks on the walls, filthy smudges around all the doorknobs and fixtures—really careless, destructive things. And that awful stone path going half-way down the front lawn and ending in a mud puddle—can you imagine anyone defacing a property like that? It's going to cost Mr. Brace a small fortune to get it cleared away and replanted. No, but it was more than that. The kind of thing I mean goes deeper than that."

She paused to press the excess varnish from her brush against the side of the can, frowning, working her lips in an effort to find words for the kind of thing she meant.

"It's just that they *were* a rather strange young couple. Irresponsible. The guarded way they'd look at you; the way they'd talk to you; unwholesome, sort of. Oh, and another thing. Do you know what I came across in the cellar? All dead and dried out? I came across an enormous box of sedum plantings that I must have spent an entire day collecting for them last spring. I remember very carefully selecting the best shoots and very tenderly packing them in just the right kind of soil—*that's* the kind of thing I mean, you see. Wouldn't you think that when someone goes to a certain amount of trouble to give you a perfectly good plant, a living, growing thing, wouldn't you think the very least you'd do would be to—"

But from there on Howard Givings heard only a welcome, thunderous sea of silence. He had turned off his hearing aid.

THE EASTER PARADE

a novel

To Gina Catherine

PART ONE

ONE

NEITHER OF THE Grimes sisters would have a happy life, and looking back it always seemed that the trouble began with their parents' divorce. That happened in 1930, when Sarah was nine years old and Emily five. Their mother, who encouraged both girls to call her "Pookie," took them out of New York to a rented house in Tenafly, New Jersey, where she thought the schools would be better and where she hoped to launch a career in suburban real estate. It didn't work out—very few of her plans for independence ever did—and they left Tenafly after two years, but it was a memorable time for the girls.

"Doesn't your father ever come home?' other children would ask, and Sarah would always take the lead in explaining what a divorce was.

"Do you ever get to see him?"

"Sure we do."

"Where does he live?"

"In New York City."

"What does he do?"

"He writes headlines. He writes the headlines in the New York *Sun*." And the way she said it made clear that they ought to be impressed. Anyone could be a flashy, irresponsible reporter or a steady drudge of a rewrite man; but the man who wrote the headlines! The man who read through all the complexities of daily news to pick out salient points and who then summed everything up in a few well-chosen words, artfully composed to fit a limited space—there was a consummate journalist and a father worthy of the name.

Once, when the girls went to visit him in the city, he took them through the *Sun* plant and they saw everything.

"The first edition's ready to run," he said, "so we'll go down to the pressroom and watch that; then I'll show you around upstairs." He escorted them down an iron stairway that smelled of ink and newsprint, and out into a great underground room where the high rotary presses stood in ranks. Workmen hurried everywhere, all wearing crisp little squared-off hats made of intricately folded newspaper.

"Why do they wear those paper hats, Daddy?" Emily asked.

"Well, they'd probably tell you it's to keep the ink out of their hair, but I think they just wear 'em to look jaunty."

"What does 'jaunty' mean?"

"Oh, it means sort of like that bear of yours," he said, pointing to a garnet-studded pin in the form of a teddy bear that she'd worn on her dress that day and hoped he might notice. "That's a very jaunty bear."

They watched the curved, freshly cast metal page plates slide in on conveyor rollers to be clamped into place on the cylinders; then after a ringing of bells they watched the presses roll. The steel floor shuddered under their feet, which tickled, and the noise was so overwhelming that they couldn't talk: they could only look at each other and smile, and Emily covered her ears with her hands. White streaks of newsprint ran in every direction through the machines, and finished newspapers came riding out in neat, overlapped abundance.

"What'd you think of that?" Walter Grimes asked his daughters as they climbed the stairs. "Now we'll take a look at the city room."

It was an acre of desks, where men sat hammering typewriters. "That place up front where the desks are shoved together is the city desk," he said. "The city editor's the bald man talking on the telephone. And the man over there is even more important. He's the managing editor."

"Where's your desk, Daddy?" Sarah asked.

"Oh, I work on the copy desk. On the rim. See over there?" He pointed to a big semicircular table of yellow wood. One man sat at the hub of it and six others sat around the rim, reading or scribbling with pencils.

"Is that where you write the headlines?"

"Well, writing heads is part of it, yes. What happens is, when the reporters and rewrite men finish their stories they give them to a copy boy—that young fellow there is a copy boy—and he brings them to us. We check them over for grammar and spelling and punctuation, then we write the heads and they're ready to go. Hello, Charlie," he said to a man passing on his way to the water cooler. "Charlie, I'd like you to meet my girls. This is Sarah and this is Emily."

"Well," the man said, bending down from the waist. "What a pair of sweethearts. How do you do?"

Next he took them to the teletype room, where they could watch wire-service news coming in from all over the world, and then to the composing room where everything was set into type and fitted into page forms. "You ready for lunch?" he inquired. "Want to go to the ladies' room first?"

As they walked out across City Hall Park in the spring sunshine he held them both by the hand. They both wore light coats over their best dresses, with white socks and black patent-leather shoes, and they were nice-looking girls. Sarah was the dark one, with a look of trusting innocence that would never leave her; Emily, a head shorter, was blond and thin and very serious.

"City Hall doesn't look like much, does it?" Walter Grimes said. "But see the big building over there through the trees? The dark red one? That's the *World*—was, I should say; it folded last year. Greatest daily newspaper in America."

"Well, but the *Sun*'s the best now, right?" Sarah said.

"Oh, no, honey; the *Sun* isn't really much of a paper."

"It isn't? Why?" Sarah looked worried.

"Oh, it's kind of reactionary."

"What does that mean?"

"It means very, very conservative; very Republican."

"Aren't we Republicans?"

"I guess your mother is, baby. I'm not."

He had two drinks before lunch, ordering ginger ale for the girls; then, when they were tucking into their chicken à la king and mashed potatoes, Emily spoke up for the first time since they'd left the office. "Daddy? If you don't like the *Sun*, why do you work there?"

His long face, which both girls considered handsome, looked tired. "Because I need a job, little rabbit," he said. "Jobs are getting hard to find. Oh, I suppose if I were very talented I might move on, but I'm just—you know—I'm only a copy-desk man."

It wasn't much to take back to Tenafly, but at least they could still say he wrote headlines.

". . . And if you think writing headlines is easy, you're wrong!" Sarah told a rude boy on the playground after school one day.

Emily, though, was a stickler for accuracy, and as soon as the boy was out of earshot she reminded her sister of the facts. "He's only a copy-desk man," she said.

Esther Grimes, or Pookie, was a small, active woman whose life seemed pledged to achieving and sustaining an elusive quality she called "flair." She pored over fashion magazines, dressed tastefully and tried many ways of fixing her hair, but her eyes remained bewildered and she never quite learned to keep her lipstick within the borders of her mouth, which gave her an air of dazed and vulnerable uncertainty. She found more flair among rich people than in the middle class, and so she aspired to the attitudes and mannerisms of wealth in raising her daughters. She always sought "nice" communities to live in, whether she could afford them or not, and she tried to be strict on matters of decorum.

"Dear, I *wish* you wouldn't do that," she said to Sarah at breakfast one morning.

"Do what?"

"Dunk your toast crusts in your milk that way."

"Oh." Sarah drew a long, soaked crust of buttered toast out of her milk glass and brought it dripping to her reaching mouth. "Why?" she asked after she'd chewed and swallowed.

"Just because. It doesn't *look* nice. Emily's four whole years younger than you, and *she* doesn't do baby things like that."

And that was another thing: she always suggested, in hundreds of ways, that Emily had more flair than Sarah.

When it became clear that she would not succeed in Tenafly real estate she began to make frequent all-day trips to other towns, or into the city, leaving the girls with other families. Sarah didn't seem to mind her absences, but Emily did: she didn't like the smells of other people's homes; she couldn't eat; she would worry all day, picturing hideous traffic accidents, and if Pookie was an hour or two late in coming to get them she would cry like a baby.

One day in the fall they went to stay with a family named Clark. They brought their paper dolls along in case they were left to themselves, which seemed likely—all three of the Clark children were boys—but Mrs. Clark had admonished her oldest son Myron to be a good host, and he took his duties seriously. He was eleven, and spent most of the day showing off for them.

"Hey, watch," he kept saying. "Watch this."

There was a horizontal steel pipe supported by steel stanchions at the far end of the Clarks' back yard, and Myron was very good at skinning-the-cat. He would run for the bar, his shirttail flapping beneath his sweater, seize it in both hands, swing his heels up under and over it and hang by the knees; then he'd reach up, turn himself inside out and drop to the ground in a puff of dust.

Later he led his brothers and the Grimes girls in a complicated game of war, after which they went indoors to examine his stamp collection, and when they came outside again there was nothing much to do.

"Hey, look," he said. "Sarah's just tall enough to go under the bar without touching it." It was true: the top of her head cleared the bar by about half an inch. "I know what let's do," Myron said. "Let's have Sarah run at the bar as fast as she can and she'll go skimming right under it, and it'll look really neat."

A distance of some thirty yards was established; the others stood on the sidelines to watch, and Sarah started to run, her long hair flying. What nobody realized was that Sarah running would be taller than Sarah standing still—Emily realized it a fraction of a second too late, when there wasn't even time to cry out. The bar caught Sarah just above the eye with a sound Emily would never forget—*ding!*—and then she was writhing and screaming in the dirt with blood all over her face.

Emily wet her pants as she raced for the house with the Clark boys. Mrs. Clark screamed a little too when she saw Sarah; then she wrapped her in a blanket—she had heard that accident victims sometimes go into shock—and drove her to the hospital, with Emily and Myron in the back seat. Sarah had stopped crying by then—she never cried much—but Emily had only begun. She cried all the way to the hospital and in the hall outside the emergency room from which Mrs. Clark emerged three times to say "No fracture" and "No concussion" and "Seven stitches."

Then they were all back at the house—"I've never seen *anyone* bear pain so well," Mrs. Clark kept saying—and Sarah was lying on the sofa in the darkened living room with most of her face swollen purple and blue, with a heavy bandage blinding one eye and a towelful of ice over the bandage. The boys were out in the yard again, but Emily wouldn't leave the living room.

"You must let your sister rest," Mrs. Clark told her. "Run along outside, now, dear."

"That's okay," Sarah said in a strange, distant voice. "She can stay."

So Emily was allowed to stay, which was probably a good thing because she would have fought and kicked if anyone had tried to remove her from where she stood on the Clarks' ugly carpet, biting her wet fist. She wasn't crying now; she was only watching her prostrate sister in the shadows and feeling wave on wave of a terrible sense of loss.

"It's okay, Emmy," Sarah said in that faraway voice. "It's okay. Don't feel bad. Pookie'll come soon."

Sarah's eye wasn't damaged—her wide, deep brown eyes remained the dominant feature in a face that would become beautiful—but for the rest of her life a fine little blue-white scar wavered down from one eyebrow into the lid, like the hesitant stroke of a pencil, and Emily could never look at it without remembering how well her sister had borne pain. It reminded her too, time and again, of her own susceptibility to panic and her unfathomable dread of being alone.

TWO

IT WAS SARAH who gave Emily her first information about sex. They were eating orange popsicles and fooling around a broken hammock in the yard of their house in Larchmont, New York— that was one of the other suburban towns they lived in after Tenafly—and as Emily listened her mind filled with confused and troubling images.

"And you mean they put it up in*side* you?"

"Yup. All the way. And it hurts."

"What if it doesn't fit?"

"Oh, it fits. They make it fit."

"And then what?"

"Then you have a baby. That's why you don't do it until after you're married. Except you know Elaine Simko in the eighth grade? She did it with a boy and started having a baby, and that's why she had to leave school. Nobody even knows where she is now."

"You sure? Elaine Simko?"

"Positive."

"Well, but why would she want to do a thing like that?"

"The boy seduced her."

"What does that mean?"

Sarah took a long, slow suck of her popsicle. "You're too young to understand."

"I am not. But you said it *hurts*, Sarah. If it hurts, why would she—"

"Well, it hurts, but it feels good too. You know how some-times when you're taking a bath, or maybe you put your hand down there and kind of rub around, and it feels—"

"Oh." And Emily lowered her eyes in embarrassment. "I see."

She often said "I see" about things she didn't wholly under-stand—and so, for that matter, did Sarah. Neither of them understood why their mother found it necessary to change homes so often, for example—they'd be just beginning to make friends in one place when they'd move to another—but they never questioned it.

Pookie was inscrutable in many ways. "I tell my children everything," she would boast to other adults; "we don't have any secrets in this family"—and then in the next breath she would lower her voice to say something the girls weren't supposed to hear.

In keeping with the terms of the divorce agreement, Walter Grimes came out to visit the girls two or three times a year in whatever house they were renting, and sometimes he would spend the night on the living-room sofa. The year Emily was ten she lay awake for a long time on Christmas night, listening to the unaccustomed sound of her parents' voices downstairs—they were talking and talking—and because she had to know what was going on she acted like a baby: she called out for her mother.

"What is it, dear?" Pookie turned on the light and bent over her, smelling of gin.

"My stomach's upset."

"Do you want some bicarbonate?"

"No."

"What do you want, then?"

"I don't know."

"You're just being silly. Let me tuck you in, and you just think about all the nice things you got for Christmas and go to sleep. And you mustn't call me again; promise?"

"Okay."

"Because Daddy and I are having a very important talk. We're talking over a lot of things we should have discussed a long, long time ago, and we're coming to a new—a new understanding."

She gave Emily a wet kiss, turned out the light and hurried back downstairs, where the talking went on and on, and Emily lay waiting for sleep in a warm flush of happiness. Coming to a new understanding! It was like something a divorced mother in the movies might say, just before the big music comes up for the fadeout.

But the next morning unfolded like all the other last mornings of his visits: he was as quiet and polite as a stranger at breakfast, and Pookie avoided his eyes; then he called a taxi to take him to the train. At first Emily thought maybe he had only gone back to the city to get his belongings, but that hope evaporated in the days and weeks that followed. She could never find the words to ask her mother about it, and she didn't mention it to Sarah.

Both girls had what dentists call an overbite and children call buck teeth, but Sarah's condition was the worse: by the time she was fourteen she could scarcely close her lips. Walter Grimes agreed to pay for orthodontia, and this meant that Sarah rode the train into New York once a week to spend the afternoon with him, and to have her braces adjusted. Emily was jealous, both of the orthodontia and the city visits, but Pookie explained that they couldn't afford treatment for both girls at once; her turn would come later, when she was older.

In the meantime Sarah's braces were terrible: they picked up unsightly white shreds of food, and someone at school called her a walking hardware store. Who could imagine kissing a mouth like that? Who, for that matter, could bear to be close to her *body* for any length of time? Sarah washed her sweaters very carefully in an effort to keep the dyed color alive in their armpits, but it didn't work: a navy blue sweater would bleach to robin's-egg blue under the arms, and a red one to yellowish pink. Her strong sweat, no less than her braces, seemed a curse.

Another curse fell, for both girls, when Pookie announced that she'd found a wonderful house in a wonderful little town called Bradley, and that they'd be moving there in the fall. They had almost lost track of the number of times they'd moved.

"Well, it wasn't so bad, was it?" Pookie asked them after their first day of school in Bradley. "Tell me about it."

Emily had endured a day of silent hostility—one of the only two new girls in the whole sixth grade—and said she guessed it had been all right. But Sarah, a high-school freshman, was bubbling over with news of how fine it had been.

"They had a special assembly for all the new girls," she said, "and somebody played the piano and all the old girls stood up and sang this song. Listen:

How do you do, new girls, how do you do?
Is there anything that we can do for you?
We are glad that you are here
For you always bring good cheer
How do you do, new girls, how do you do?"

"Well!" Pookie said happily. "Wasn't that nice."

And Emily could only turn her face away in a spasm of disgust. It may have been "nice," but it was treacherous; *she* knew the treachery implicit in a song like that.

The grade school and high school were in the same big building, which meant that Emily could catch occasional glimpses of her sister, if she was lucky, during the day; it also meant they could walk home together every afternoon. The arrangement was that they would meet in Emily's classroom after school.

But one Friday during football season Emily found herself waiting and waiting in the empty classroom, with no sign of Sarah, until her stomach began to knot with anxiety. When Sarah did arrive at last she looked funny—she had a funny smile and behind her lumbered a frowning boy.

"Emmy, this is Harold Schneider," she said.

"Hi."

"Hi." He was big and muscular and pimple-faced.

"We're going to the game over in Armonk," Sarah explained. "Just tell Pookie I'll be home for dinner, okay? You won't mind walking home by yourself, will you?"

The trouble was that Pookie had gone into New York that morning, after saying, at breakfast, "Well, I *think* I'll get home before you do, but I'd better not promise." That meant not only walking home alone but letting herself into the empty house alone to stare for hours at the naked furniture and the ticking clock, waiting. And if her mother ever did come home— "Where's Sarah?"—how could she ever tell her that Sarah had gone off with a boy named Harold to a town called Armonk? It was out of the question.

"How're you gonna get there?" she inquired.

"In Harold's car. He's seventeen."

"I don't think Pookie'd like that, Sarah. And I think you know she wouldn't like it. You better come on home with me."

Sarah turned helplessly to Harold, whose big face had twitched into a half-smile of incredulity, as if to say he'd never met such a bratty little kid in his life.

"Emmy, don't *be* this way," Sarah implored, with a quaver that proved she was losing the argument.

"Be *what* way? I'm only saying what you know."

And in the end Emily won. Harold Schneider slouched away down the hall, shaking his head (he could probably find another girl before game time), and the Grimes sisters walked home together—or rather in single file, with Emily in the lead.

"Damn you, damn you, damn you," Sarah said behind her on the sidewalk. "I could *kill* you for this—" and she took three running steps and kicked her little sister solidly on one buttock, causing Emily to fall on her hands and spill all her school-books, the loose-leaf binder breaking open and scattering its pages. "—I could *kill* you for ruining everything."

It turned out, ironically, that Pookie was home when they got there. "What's the *matter*?" she asked, and when Sarah had told the whole story, crying—it was one of the very few times Emily had ever seen her cry—it became clear that all the mistakes of the afternoon had been Emily's.

"And were there a lot of people going to the game, Sarah?" Pookie inquired.

"Oh, yes. All the seniors and *ev*erybody . . ."

Pookie looked less bewildered than usual. "Well, Emily," she said sternly. "That wasn't good at all, what you did. Do you understand that? It wasn't good at all."

There were better times in Bradley. That winter Emily made a few friends with whom she fooled around after school, which tended to make her worry less about whether Pookie would be home or not; and during that same winter Harold Schneider began taking Sarah to the movies.

"Has he kissed you yet?" Emily inquired after their third or fourth date.

"None of your business."

"Come on, Sarah."

"Oh, all right. Yes. He has."

"What's it like?"

"It's about like what you'd imagine."

"Oh." And Emily wanted to say *Doesn't he mind your braces?* but thought better of it. Instead she said "What do you see in Harold, anyway?"

"Oh, he's—very nice," Sarah said, and went back to washing her sweater.

There was another town after Bradley, and then still another; in the last town Sarah graduated from high school with no particular plans for college, which her parents couldn't have afforded anyway. Her teeth were straight now and the braces had come off; she seemed never to sweat at all, and she had a lovely full-breasted figure that made men turn around on the street and made Emily weak with envy. Emily's own teeth were still slightly bucked and would never be corrected (her mother had forgotten her promise); she was tall and thin and small in the chest. "You have a coltish grace, dear," her mother assured her. "You'll be *very* attractive."

In 1940 they moved back to the city, and the place Pookie found for them was no ordinary apartment: it was a once-grand, shabby old "floor through" on the south side of Washington Square, with big windows facing the park. It cost more than Pookie could afford, but she scrimped on other expenses; they bought no new clothes and ate a great deal of spaghetti. The kitchen and bathroom fixtures were rusty antiques, but the ceilings were uncommonly high and visitors never failed to remark that the place had "character." It was on the ground floor, which meant that passengers on the double-decked Fifth Avenue buses could peer into it as they made their circuit of the park on the way uptown, and there seemed to be a certain amount of flair in this for Pookie.

Wendell L. Willkie was the Republican candidate for President that year, and Pookie sent the girls uptown to work as volunteers in the national headquarters of something called Associated Willkie Clubs of America. She thought it might be good for Emily, who needed something to do; more importantly, she thought it would give Sarah a chance to "meet people," by which she meant suitable young men. Sarah was nineteen, and none of the boys she'd liked so far, from Harold Schneider on, had struck her mother as suitable at all.

Sarah did meet people at the Willkie Clubs; within a few weeks she brought home a young man named Donald Clellon. He was pale and very polite, and dressed so carefully that the first thing you noticed about him was his clothes: a pinstripe suit, a black Chesterfield with a velvet collar, and a black derby. The derby was a little odd—they hadn't been in style for years—but he wore it with such authority as to suggest that the fashion might be coming back. And he spoke in the same meticulous, almost fussy way he dressed: instead of saying "something like that" he always said "something of that nature."

"What do you see in Donald, anyway?" Emily asked.

"He's very mature and very considerate," Sarah said. "And he's very—I don't know, I just like him." She paused and lowered her eyes like a movie star in a close-up. "I think I may be in love with him."

Pookie liked him well enough too, at first—it was charming for Sarah to have such an attentive suitor—and when they solemnly asked her permission to become engaged she cried a little but raised no objection.

It was Walter Grimes, to whom the engagement was presented as an accomplished fact, who asked all the questions. Who exactly *was* this Donald Clellon? If he was twenty-seven, as he claimed, what business or profession had he been in before the Willkie campaign? If he was as well-educated as his manner implied, where had he gone to college? Where, for that matter, was he from?

"Why didn't you just ask him, Walter?"

"I didn't want to grill the kid over a lunch table, with Sarah sitting there; I thought you'd probably have the answers."

"Oh."

"You mean you've never asked him anything either?"

"Well, he's always seemed so—no; I haven't."

There followed several tense interviews, usually late at night after Pookie had waited up for them, with Emily listening just outside the living-room door.

". . . Donald, there's something I've never quite understood. Where exactly are you from?"

"I've told you, Mrs. Grimes. I was born here in Garden City but my parents moved around quite a lot. I was raised chiefly in the Middle West. Various parts of the Middle West. After my father died my mother moved to Topeka, Kansas; that's where she makes her home now."

"And where did you go to college?"

"I thought I'd told you that too, when we first met. The fact is I haven't been to college; we couldn't afford it. I was fortunate enough to find work in a law firm in Topeka; then after Mr. Willkie's nomination I worked for the Willkie Club out there until I was transferred here."

"Oh. I see."

And that seemed to take care of it for one night, but there were others.

". . . Donald, if you only worked in the law office for three years, and if you went there right after high school, then how can you be—"

"Oh, it wasn't right after high school, Mrs. Grimes. I held a number of other jobs first. Construction work, heavy laboring jobs, things of that nature. Anything I could get. I had my mother to support, you see."

"I see."

In the end, after Willkie had lost the election and Donald was working at some vague job with a brokerage house downtown, he contradicted himself enough times to reveal that he wasn't twenty-seven; he was twenty-one. He'd been exaggerating his age for some time because he'd always *felt* older than his contemporaries; everyone in the Willkie Clubs had thought he was twenty-seven, and when he'd met Sarah he'd said "twenty-seven" automatically. Couldn't Mrs. Grimes understand an indiscretion like that? Couldn't Sarah understand?

"Well, but Donald," Pookie said, while Emily strained to hear every nuance of the talk, "if you haven't told the truth about that, how can we trust you about anything else?"

"How can you trust me? Well, you know I love Sarah; you know I have a good future in the brokerage business—"

"How do we know that? No, Donald, this won't do. It won't do at all . . ."

After their voices stopped, Emily risked a peek into the living room. Pookie looked righteous and Sarah looked stricken; Donald Clellon sat alone with his head in his hands. There was a little ridge around the crown of his well-combed, brilliantined hair, marking the place where his derby had been.

Sarah didn't bring him home again, but she continued to meet and go out with him several times a week. The heroines of all the movies she had ever seen made clear that she couldn't do otherwise; besides, what about all the people to whom she'd introduced him as "my fiancé"?

". . . He's a liar!" Pookie would shout. "He's a child! We don't even know what he is!"

"I don't *care*," Sarah would shout back. "I love Donald and I'm going to marry him!"

And there would be nothing for Pookie to do but flap her hands and cry. The quarrels usually ended with both of them collapsed in tears in different parts of the musty, elegant old apartment, while Emily listened and sucked her knuckles.

But everything changed with the coming of the new year: a family moved in upstairs that Pookie found immediately interesting. Their name was Wilson, a middle-aged couple with a grown son, and they were English war refugees. They had been through the London Blitz (Geoffrey Wilson was too reserved to talk much about it, but his wife Edna could tell dreadful stories), and they'd escaped to this country with only the clothes on their backs and whatever they could carry in their suitcases. That was all Pookie knew about them at first, but she was careful to linger around the mailboxes in the hope of striking up further conversations, and it wasn't long before she knew more.

"The Wilsons aren't really English at all," she told her daughters. "You'd never guess it from their accents, but they're Americans. He's from New York—he comes from an old New York family—and she's a Tate from Boston. They went to England many years ago for his business—she was the British representative for an American firm—and Tony was born there and went to an English public school. That's what the English call their private boarding schools, you know. I just knew he'd been to an English public school because of the delightful way he talks—he says 'I say,' and 'Oh, rot,' and things like that. Anyway, they're wonderful people. Have you talked to them yet, Sarah? Have you, Emmy? I *know* you'd both love them. They're so— I don't know, so wonderfully *English*."

Sarah listened patiently enough, but she wasn't interested. The strain of her engagement to Donald Clellon was beginning to show: she was very pale, and she'd lost weight. Through people in the Willkie campaign she had found work for a token salary in the offices of United China Relief; she was called Chairman of the Debutante Committee, a title Pookie loved to pronounce, and her job was to supervise the rich girls who volunteered to collect nickels and dimes along Fifth Avenue to help the Chinese multitudes in their war against the Japanese. The work wasn't hard but she came home exhausted every night, sometimes too tired even to go out with Donald, and she spent much of her time in a brooding silence that neither Pookie nor Emily could penetrate.

And then it happened. Young Tony Wilson came hurrying downstairs one morning, his fine English shoes barely touching the tread of each warped step, just as Sarah walked out into the vestibule, and they almost collided.

"Excuse me," she said.

"Excuse *me*. Are you Miss Grimes?"

"Yes. And you're—"

"Tony Wilson; I live upstairs."

Their talk couldn't have lasted more than three or four minutes before he excused himself again and left the house, but it was enough to bring Sarah sleepwalking back into the apartment, allowing herself to be late for work. The debutantes and the Chinese multitudes could wait. "Oh, Emmy," she said, "have you *seen* him?"

"I've passed him in the hall occasionally."

"Well, isn't he something? Isn't he just about the most—the most beautiful person you've ever—"

Pookie came into the living room, her eyes wide and her uncertain lips glistening with breakfast bacon grease. "Who?"

she said. "You mean Tony? Oh, I'm so glad; I knew you'd like him, dear."

And Sarah had to sit down in one of their moth-eaten easy chairs to catch her breath. "Oh, Pookie," she said. "He looks— he looks just like Laurence *Oliv*ier."

That was true, though Emily hadn't thought of it before. Tony Wilson was of medium height, broad-shouldered and well-built; his wavy brown hair was carelessly arranged across the forehead and around the ears; his mouth was full and humorous and his eyes seemed always to be laughing at some subtle private joke that he might tell you when you got to know him better. He was twenty-three years old.

A very few days later he knocked on the door to ask if he might have the pleasure of Sarah's company for dinner some evening soon, and that was the end of Donald Clellon.

Tony didn't have much money—"I'm a laborer," he said, which meant that he worked at a big naval aircraft plant on Long Island and very likely did something of Top Secret importance— but he owned a 1929 Oldsmobile convertible and drove it with flair. He would take Sarah on drives into the far reaches of Long Island or Connecticut or New Jersey, where they'd have dinner at what she always described as "wonderful" restaurants, and they'd always be back in time for a drink at a "wonderful" bar called Anatole's, which Tony had discovered on the upper East Side.

"Now, *this* fellow's a different story entirely," Walter Grimes said on the telephone. "I like him; you can't help liking him . . ."

"Our young people seem to be getting on rather well, Mrs. Grimes," Geoffrey Wilson said one afternoon, with his wife smiling beside him. "Perhaps it's time for *us* to get better acquainted."

Emily had often seen her mother flirt with men before, but never quite so openly as the way she flirted with Geoffrey Wilson. "Oh, that's *mar*velous!" she would cry at his every minor witticism, and then she'd dissolve into peals of deep-throated laughter, pressing her middle finger coquettishly against her upper lip to conceal the fact that her gums were shrinking and her teeth going bad.

And Emily thought the man *was* funny—it wasn't so much what he said, she decided, as the way he said it—but she was embarrassed by Pookie's enthusiasm. Besides, a little too much of Geoffrey Wilson's humor depended on his strange delivery, in which the heavy English accent seemed compounded by a speech impediment: he talked as though he held a billiard ball in his mouth. His wife Edna was pleasant and plump and drank a good deal of sherry.

Emily was always included in her mother's afternoons and evenings with the Wilsons—she would sit quietly and nibble salted crackers through their talk and laughter—but she would much rather have been out with Sarah and Tony, riding in that splendid old car with her hair blowing attractively in the wind, strolling with them along some deserted beach and then coming back to Manhattan at midnight and sitting in their special booth at Anatole's while the pianist played their song.

"Do you and Tony have a song?" she asked Sarah.

"A song?" Sarah was painting her fingernails, and she was in a hurry because Tony would call for her in fifteen minutes. "Well, Tony likes 'Bewitched, Bothered and Bewildered,' but I sort of like 'All the Things You Are.'"

"Oh," Emily said, and now she had music to accompany her fantasies. "Well, they're both good songs."

"And you know what we do?"

"What?"

"Well, when we're having our first drink we kind of hook our arms around each other's like this—here, I'll show you. Careful of my nails." And she slipped her wrist through the crook of Emily's elbow and brought an imaginary glass to her own lips. "Like that. Isn't that nice?"

It certainly was. Everything about Sarah's romance with Tony was almost too nice to be borne.

"Sarah?"

"Mm?"

"Would you go all the way with him if he asked you to?"

"You mean before we're married? Oh, Emily, don't be ridiculous."

So it wasn't quite as profound a romance as some she'd read about, but even so it was very, very nice. That night Emily lay steaming in her bath for a long time, and when she'd gotten out and dried herself, with the bathwater slowly draining away, she stood posing naked at the mirror. Because her breasts were so meager she concentrated on the beauty of her shoulders and her neck. She pouted and parted her lips very slightly, the way girls did in the movies when they were just about to be kissed.

"Oh, you're lovely," said a phantom young man with an English accent, just out of camera range. "I've wanted to say this for days, for weeks, and now I must: it's you I love, Emily."

"I love you too, Tony," she whispered, and her nipples began to harden and rise of their own accord. Somewhere in the background a small orchestra played "All the Things You Are."

"I want to hold you. Oh, let me hold you and I'll never let you go."

"Oh," she whispered. "Oh, Tony."

"I need you, Emily. Will you—will you go all the way with me?"

"Yes. Oh, yes, Tony, I will. I will . . ."

"Emmy?" her mother called from outside the locked door. "You've been in that bathroom over an *hour*. What're you *doing* in there?"

At Easter time Sarah's employers lent her an expensive dress of heavy silk, said to be a model of the kind of clothes worn by aristocratic Chinese ladies before the war, and a broad-brimmed hat of closely woven straw. Her assignment was to mingle with the fashionable crowds on upper Fifth Avenue and to get her picture taken by a photographer from the public relations office.

"Oh, you look stunning, dear," Pookie said on Easter morning. "I've never seen you look so lovely."

But Sarah only frowned, which made her all the lovelier. "I don't *care* about the silly Easter parade," she said. "Tony and I were planning to drive out to Amagansett today."

"Oh, please," Pookie said. "It'll only be for an hour or two; Tony won't mind."

Then Tony came in and said "Oh, I say. Smashing." And after looking at Sarah for a long time he said "Look; I've an idea. Can you wait five minutes?"

They heard him charge upstairs, seeming to shake the old house, and when he came back he was wearing an English cutaway, complete with flowing ascot, dove-gray waistcoat and striped trousers.

"Oh, Tony," Sarah said.

"It wants a pressing," he said, turning around for their admiration and shooting his cuffs, "and one really ought to have a gray topper, but I think it'll do. Ready?"

Emily and Pookie watched from the windows as the open car rolled past on its way uptown—Tony turning briefly from the wheel to smile at them, Sarah holding her hat in place with one hand and waving with the other—and then they were gone.

The public relations photographer did his job well, and so did the editors of the rotogravure section of *The New York Times*. The picture came out the following Sunday in a pageful of other, less striking photographs. The camera had caught Sarah and Tony smiling at each other like the very soul of romance in the April sunshine, with massed trees and a high corner of the Plaza hotel just visible behind them.

"I can get eight-by-ten glossies from the office," Sarah said.

"Oh, wonderful," Pookie said. "Get as many as you can. And let's get more newspapers, too. Emmy? Get some money out of my purse. Run down to the newsstand and get four more papers. Get six."

"I can't carry that many."

"Of course you can."

And whether she was annoyed or not as she left the house, Emily knew how important it was to have as many copies as possible. It was a picture that could be mounted and framed and treasured forever.

THREE

THEY WERE MARRIED in the fall of 1941, in a small Episcopal church of Pookie's choosing. Emily thought the wedding was nice enough, except that the dress she had to wear as bridesmaid seemed contrived to call attention to her small breasts, and also that her mother wept throughout the ceremony. Pookie had spent a lot of money on her own dress and rich little hat, both in a new shade called Shocking Pink, and she'd spent many days regaling anyone who would listen with the same weak joke. "How would *that* look in the newspapers?" she asked time and again, pressing her middle finger to her upper lip. "The bride's mother wore Shocking Pink!" She drank too much at the reception, too, and when the time came for her to dance with Geoffrey Wilson she batted her eyelids and sank as dreamily into his arms as if it were he and not his son who looked like Laurence Olivier. He was visibly embarrassed and tried to loosen his hold on her back, but she clung to him like a slug.

Walter Grimes kept mostly to himself at the party; he stood nursing his scotch, ready to smile at Sarah whenever she smiled at him.

Sarah and Tony went to Cape Cod for a week, while Emily lay worrying about them. (What if Sarah was too nervous to do it right the first time? And if it wasn't right the first time, what could you possibly talk about while you waited to try again? And if it became a matter of trying, wouldn't that spoil everything?) Then they settled into what Pookie described as a "wretched little apartment" near the Magnum Aircraft plant.

"But that's only temporary," she would tell her friends on the telephone. "In a few months they'll be moving into the Wilsons' estate. Have I told you about the Wilsons' estate?"

Geoffrey Wilson had inherited, from his father, eight acres of land in the hamlet of St. Charles, on the North Shore of

Long Island. The place had a fourteen-room main house (Pookie always described it as "a wonderful old house," though she hadn't yet seen it); that was where Geoffrey and Edna would live as soon as the present tenants' lease expired next year. And there was a separate cottage on the property that would be perfect for Sarah and Tony; didn't that sound like the ideal arrangement?

Pookie talked so much about the Wilsons' estate all winter that she seemed scarcely to realize the war had started, but Emily realized almost nothing else. Tony was an American citizen, after all; he would probably be drafted and trained and sent somewhere to have his handsome head blown off.

"Tony says it's nothing to worry about," Sarah assured her, one day when Emily and Pookie went out to visit the "wretched" apartment. "Even if he *is* drafted he's pretty sure the higher-ups at Magnum will arrange to get him assigned back to the plant as enlisted naval personnel. Because Tony doesn't just *work* at Magnum; he's practically an engineer. He had almost three years' apprenticeship with an engineering firm in England—that's the way they do it over there, you see, they have apprenticeships instead of engineering school—and the people at Magnum realize that. He's a valuable man."

He didn't look very valuable when he came home from the plant that afternoon, wearing green work clothes with an employee identification badge clipped over his heart, carrying his tin lunch box under his arm, but despite that costume he managed to radiate the old elegant vigor and charm. Maybe Sarah was right.

"I say," he said. "Won't you join us for a drink?"

He and Sarah sat close together on the sofa and carefully went through the ritual from Anatole's, entwining their arms to take the first sip.

"Do you always do that?" Emily inquired.

"Always," Sarah said.

That spring Emily was awarded a full scholarship to Barnard College.

"Wonderful!" Pookie said. "Oh, darling, I'm so proud of you.

Just think: you'll be the first member of our family with a college education."

"Except for Daddy, you mean."

"Oh. Well, yes, I suppose that's right; but I meant *our* family. Anyway, it's just wonderful. Tell you what let's do. Let's call Sarah right away and tell her, and then you and I'll get all dolled up and go out and celebrate."

They did call Sarah—she said she was very pleased—and then Emily said "I'm going to call Daddy now, okay?"

"Oh. Well, all right, certainly, if you want to."

". . . A *full* scholarship?" he said. "Wow. You must have really impressed those people . . ."

She arranged to meet him for lunch the following day, in one of the dark basement restaurants he liked near City Hall. She got there first and waited near the coatroom, and she thought he looked surprisingly old as he came down the steps, wearing a raincoat that wasn't quite clean.

"Hello, honey," he said. "My God, you're getting tall. We'd like a booth for two, George."

"Certainly, Mr. Grimes."

And maybe he was only a copy-desk man, but the headwaiter knew his name. The waiter knew him too—knew just which kind of whiskey to bring and set before him.

"That's really great about Barnard," he said. "It's the best news I've had in I don't know how long." Then he coughed and said "Excuse me."

The drink brightened him—his eyes shone and his mouth tightened pleasantly—and he had a second one before the food arrived.

"Did you go through Syracuse on a scholarship, Daddy?" she asked, "Or did you pay your way?"

He looked puzzled. " 'Go through Syracuse'? Honey, I didn't 'go through.' I only went to Syracuse for a year, then I started working on the town paper up there."

"Oh."

"You mean you thought I was a college graduate? Where'd you get that idea? Your mother?"

"I guess so, yes."

"Well, your mother has her own way of dealing with information."

He didn't eat all of his lunch, and when the coffee came he peered down at it as if it didn't appeal to him either. "I wish Sarah could have gone to college," he said. "Of course it's fine that she's happily married, and all that, but still. Education is a wonderful thing." Then the cough hit him again. He had to turn away from the table and press a handkerchief to his mouth and nose, and a small vein stood out in his temple as he coughed and coughed. When it was over, or nearly over, he reached for his water glass and took a sip. That seemed to help—he was able to take several deep breaths—but then his breath caught and he was coughing again.

"You do have a bad cold," she said when he'd recovered.

"Oh, it's only partly the cold; it's mainly the damn cigarettes. You know something? Twenty years from now cigarettes'll be against the law. People'll have to get them from bootleggers, the way we did with liquor during Prohibition. Have you thought about what you'll major in?"

"English, I think."

"Good. You'll read a lot of good books. Oh, you'll read some that aren't so good, too, but you'll learn to distinguish between them. You'll live in the world of ideas for four whole years before you have to concern yourself with anything as trivial as the demands of workaday reality—that's what's nice about college. Would you like some dessert, little rabbit?"

When she got home that day she thought of facing down her mother with the truth about Syracuse, but decided against it. There was no hope of changing Pookie.

Nor was there any hope, it seemed, of changing the way they had come to spend their evenings together since Sarah's marriage. Occasionally the Wilsons would invite them upstairs, or come down; more often the two of them sat reading magazines in the living room, while cars and Fifth Avenue buses droned past the windows. One or the other of them might make a plate of fudge, more to kill time than to satisfy any real craving, and on Sundays there were good programs on the radio, but for the most part they were as idle as if they had nothing to do but wait for the telephone to ring. And what could be less likely than that? Who would want to call up an aging divorcée with rotten teeth, or a plain, skinny girl who moped around feeling sorry for herself all the time?

One night Emily spent half an hour watching her mother turn the pages of a magazine. Pookie would slowly, absently wipe her thumb against her moist lower lip and then wipe the thumb against the lower right-hand corner of each page, for easier turning; it left the corners of all the pages wrinkled and faintly smeared with lipstick. And tonight she had eaten fudge, which meant there would be traces of fudge as well as lipstick on the pages. Emily found she couldn't watch the process without grinding her teeth. It made her scalp prickle too, and made her squirm in her chair. She got up.

"I think I'll go to a movie," she said. "There's supposed to be a fairly good one at the Eighth Street Playhouse."

"Oh. Well, all right, dear, if you want to."

She escaped to the bathroom to comb her hair, and then she was free of the house, walking out into Washington Square, taking deep breaths of the gentle air and taking a small but honest pride in the fit and hang of her almost-new yellow dress. It was just after dark and the park lamps were glowing in the trees.

"Excuse me, miss," said a tall soldier walking beside her. "Can you tell me where Nick's is? The jazz place?"

And she stopped in perplexity. "Well, I know where it is— I mean I've been there a few times—but it's sort of hard to tell you how to get there from here. I guess the best thing would be to go down Waverly to Sixth Avenue, no, Seventh Avenue, and then turn left—I mean right—and go uptown about four or five—no, wait; your quickest way would be to go down Eighth Street to Greenwich Avenue; that'll take you . . ."

And the whole time she was babbling that way, waving her hands to make inaccurate directions, he stood smiling patiently down at her. He was a homely boy with kind eyes, and he looked very trim in his bright tan summer uniform.

"Thanks," he said when she was finished. "But I got a better idea. How'd you like to take a ride on a Fifth Avenue bus?"

Climbing the steep, curved staircase of an open-topped

double-decker had never before seemed the beginning of a peril-ous adventure, nor had it ever made her aware of the pump of her heart. When they rode past her house she shrank away from the railing and averted her face in case Pookie happened to be looking out the window.

One lucky thing was that the soldier did most of the talking. His name was either Warren Maddock or Warren Maddox—she would have to ask him to clear that up later. He was on a three-day pass from Camp Croft, South Carolina, where he had completed infantry training, and he would soon be "shipped out to a division," whatever that meant. His home was a small town in Wisconsin; he was the oldest of four brothers, and his father was in the roofing business. This was his first visit to New York.

"You lived here all your life, Emily?"

"No; I lived mostly in the suburbs."

"I see. Must be funny for a person to live here all their life, never get a chance to get out and run or anything. I mean it's a great city, don't get me wrong; I just mean I think the country's better for growing up. You in high school?"

"Not any more. I'm going to Barnard College in the fall." After a moment she added "I have a scholarship there."

"A scholarship! Hey, you must be smart. I better watch my step around a girl like you." And with that he let his hand slip from the wooden back of the seat to hold her shoulder; his big thumb began massaging the flesh near her collarbone as he talked.

"What kind of work's your dad do?"

"He's a newspaperman."

"Oh yeah? Is that the Empire State Building up ahead?"

"Yes."

"I thought so. Funny, I've seen pictures of it, but you don't really get the idea how big it is. You've got nice hair, Emily. I never have much liked curly hair on a girl; straight hair's a lot nicer..."

Somewhere above Forty-second Street he kissed her. It wasn't the first time she'd been kissed—not even the first time she'd been kissed on top of a Fifth Avenue bus; one of the boys in high school had been that brave—but it was the first kiss of its kind, ever.

At Fifty-ninth he mumbled "Let's take a walk," and helped her down the rumbling stairs; then they were in Central Park, and his arm was still around her. This part of the park was crawling with soldiers and girls: they sat necking on benches, and they walked in groups or in couples with their arms around each other. Some of the walking girls had let their fingers slip into their soldiers' hip pockets; others held them higher, up under the ribcage. She wondered if she was expected to put her arm around Warren Maddock, or Maddox, but it seemed too early in their acquaintance for that. Still, she had kissed him: could "early" or "late" be said to matter any more?

He was still talking. "No, but it's funny: sometimes you meet a girl and it doesn't seem right at all; other times it does. Like, I've only known you for about half an hour, and now we're old friends . . ."

He steered her down a path where there didn't seem to be any lights at all. As they walked he dropped his hand from her shoulder and worked it up under her arm to cradle one breast. His thumb began to stroke her erect, extraordinarily sensitive nipple, which weakened her knees, and her arm went around his back as a matter of course.

". . . A lot of guys just want one thing from a girl, especially after they're in the Army; I don't understand that. I like to get to *know* a girl—get to know her whole personality, you know what I mean? You're nice; Emily; I always have liked skinny girls—I mean *you* know, slender girls . . ."

Only when she felt grass and earth underfoot did she realize they had left the path. He was leading her out across a small meadow, and when they came into near-total darkness under a rustling tree there was nothing awkward about the way they sank to the ground together: it was as smooth as a maneuver on a dance floor, and it seemed dictated by his thumb on her nipple. For a little while they lay writhing together and kissing; then his big hand was moving high up her thigh and he was saying "Oh, let me, Emily, let me . . . It's okay, I've got something . . . Just let me, Emily . . ."

She didn't say yes, but she certainly didn't say no. Everything he did—even when he helped her to free one foot from her

underpants—seemed to happen because it was urgently necessary: she was helpless and he was helping her, and nothing else
mattered in the world.

She expected pain but there wasn't time to brace herself
before it was there—it took her by surprise—and with it there
began an insistent pleasure, building to what gave every promise
of ecstasy before it dwindled and died. He slipped out of her,
sank one knee into the grass beside her leg and rolled away,
breathing hard; then he rolled back and took her in his arms.
"Oh," he said. "Oh." He smelled pleasantly of fresh sweat and
starched cotton.

She felt sore and moist and thought she might be bleeding,
but the worst thing was being afraid they would find nothing to
talk about. What *did* you talk about, after something like this?
When they were back under a park lamp she said "Is my dress
dirty?" and after he had put on his overseas cap with great care
he fell a step behind her to look.

"Naw, it's fine," he said. "You didn't even get any grass stains.
Want to go for a malted or something?"

He took her in a taxi to Times Square, where they drank
big chocolate malteds at a stand-up counter and didn't talk at
all. Her stomach seemed to constrict on receiving the stuff—she
knew she would be sick—but she drank it anyway because it was
better than standing there with nothing to say. By the time she'd
finished it her nausea was so acute she didn't know if she could
make it all the way home before vomiting.

"Ready?" he said, wiping his mouth, and guided her out to
the crowded sidewalk by one elbow. "Now you tell me where
you live, and we'll see if we can find it on the subway."

Everyone they passed looked grotesque, like figures in a fever
dream: a leering, bespectacled sailor, a drunken Negro in a
purple suit, a muttering old woman carrying four greasy shopping bags. There was a wire-mesh municipal trash container on
the corner and she ran for it and made it just in time. He came
up behind her and tried to hold her arms during the seizure but
she shook free of him: she wanted to go through this bleak,
humiliating business alone. When the spasms were over, even the
dry ones, she found some Kleenex in her purse and cleaned her

mouth, but the taste of vomited chocolate malted was still rich in her throat and nose.

"You okay, Emily?" he inquired. "Want me to get you a drink of water?"

"No, that's all right. I'm fine. I'm sorry."

On the downtown IRT local he sat reading the advertisements or inspecting the faces of passengers across the aisle, saying nothing. Even if she'd known how to start a conversation the train was too loud—they would have had to shout—and soon another, more dismal thought occurred to her: now that she'd vomited, he wouldn't want to kiss her goodnight. When they got off the train the fresh air felt good, but their silence continued all the way to Washington Square and to the approximate place in the park where they'd met.

"Where's your home, Emily?"

"Oh, you'd better not take me home. I'll just say goodnight here."

"You sure? Will you be okay?"

"Sure. I'm fine."

"Okay, then." And sure enough, all he did was squeeze her arm and give her a little kiss on the cheek. "Take care, now," he said.

Only after turning back to watch him walk away did she realize how much was wrong: they hadn't exchanged addresses and promises to write; she wasn't even sure of his last name.

"Emmy?" Pookie called from her bed. "How was the movie?"

A week later Pookie answered a ringing telephone at ten o'clock in the morning. ". . . Oh; yes, hello . . . He *what*? Oh my God . . . When? . . . I see . . . God . . . Oh, God . . ."

And when she'd hung up the phone she said "Your father died this morning, dear."

"He did?" Emily sat down in a creaking straight chair with her hands in her lap, and she would always remember that on first hearing the news she felt nothing at all.

Pookie said "God" a few more times, as if waiting for it to sink in, and then she began to weep. When her sobs had abated she said "It was pneumonia. He'd been sick for over a week and the doctor was trying to treat him at home, but you know Daddy."

"What do you mean, I 'know' him?"

"I mean *you* know; as long as he was in his own apartment he had his scotch and his cigarettes. Then finally he agreed to go into the hospital yesterday, but it was too late."

"Who called you? The hospital?"

"Mrs. Hammond. *You* know. Irene Hammond, your father's friend."

But Emily didn't know—she'd never heard of Irene Hammond—and now as it occurred to her that Irene Hammond had probably been much more than a friend she began to feel something for the first time. It wasn't grief, exactly; it was more like regret.

"Oh, how I dread calling Sarah," Pookie said. "She's always been her father's baby."

When she did call her, Emily could tell just from hearing Pookie's end of the talk that Sarah's grief was immediate and profound. But if Sarah had always been her father's baby, whose baby was Emily?

At the mortuary they had laid Walter Grimes out to look much younger than his fifty-six years; they'd given him pink cheeks and lips, and Emily didn't want to look at him. But Sarah leaned over and kissed the corpse on the forehead; then Pookie kissed it on the mouth, which made Emily shudder.

Irene Hammond turned out to be a trim, nice-looking woman in her forties. "I've heard *so* much about you girls," she said, and when she shook Tony Wilson's hand she said she'd heard a lot about him too. Then she turned back to Emily and said "I can't tell you how pleased your father was about that scholarship."

The crematory was somewhere in Westchester County, and they rode out there in the limousine following the hearse—Sarah and Tony on the jump seats, Pookie and Emily in back. Behind them came another car carrying Irene Hammond and the few of Walter Grimes's relatives who'd been able to come down from upstate, and then came other cars bringing employees of the New York *Sun*.

There wasn't much of a ceremony at the chapel. An electric

organ played, a tired-looking man read a few non-denomina-
tional prayers, the casket was removed, and it was over.

"Wait," Sarah said as they filed outside, and she hurried back
to her pew and crouched alone to let a last convulsion of sobbing
overcome her. It was as if all her mourning in the past few days
had not been quite enough—it was required that her bowed face
crumple and her shoulders shake one final time.

And Emily had yet to shed a single tear. It troubled her all the
way back to the city, and she rode with one hand sandwiched
between her cheek and the cool, shuddering glass of the limousine window, as if that might help. She tried whispering "Daddy"
to herself, tried closing her eyes and picturing his face, but it
didn't work. Then she thought of something that made her
throat close up: she might never have been her father's baby, but
he had always called her "little rabbit." And she was crying easily
now, causing her mother to reach over and squeeze her hand;
the only trouble was that she couldn't be sure whether she cried
for her father or for Warren Maddock, or Maddox, who was back
in South Carolina now being shipped out to a division.

But she stopped crying abruptly when she realized that even
that was a lie: these tears, as always before in her life, were wholly
for herself—for poor, sensitive Emily Grimes whom nobody
understood, and who understood nothing.

FOUR

SARAH GAVE BIRTH to three sons in three years, and the way Emily could always keep track of their ages was by thinking: Tony Junior was born in my freshman year; Peter in my sophomore year; Eric when I was a junior.

"Oh dear, the way they're *breeding*," Pookie said on hearing of the third pregnancy. "I thought only Italian *peasants* did things like that."

The third pregnancy turned out to be the last—the boys would remain a family of three—but Pookie always managed to suggest, with a rueful little rolling of the eyes, that three was plenty.

Even the news of the first pregnancy had seemed to upset her. "Well, of *course* I'm pleased," she'd told Emily. "It's just that Sarah's so *young*." Pookie had given up the place on Washington Square; she'd found modest employment in a Greenwich Village real estate office and moved into a small walk-up just off Hudson Street. Emily had come down from Barnard to spend a weekend with her, and Pookie was fixing sardine sandwiches for lunch. She pried the last oily shred of sardine from the can with two fingers. "Besides," she said, and sucked the fingers. "Besides, can you imagine me as a grandmother?"

Emily wanted to say I can't even imagine you as a mother, but controlled herself. The important thing on these weekends was to survive them; and tomorrow they were going out to St. Charles, Long Island, for Emily's first pilgrimage to the Wilsons' estate.

"*How* far, did you say?"

"Oh, I forget the exact number of miles," Pookie said, "but it's only a couple of hours on the train. It's really quite a pleasant trip, if you take along something to read."

Emily took along one of her freshman English texts, but she'd

326

scarcely settled down with it before the conductor punched their tickets and said "Change a jamake."

"What did he say?"

"You always have to change at Jamaica for the St. Charles train," Pookie explained. "It doesn't take long."

But it did: they stood for half an hour on the windy Jamaica platform before their train came clattering in, and that was only the beginning of the journey. Were all Long Island trains this loud and dirty and badly in need of repair, or only those going to St. Charles?

When they got off at the tiny station at last Pookie said "There aren't any taxis, of course, because of the war, but it's only a short walk. Aren't the trees beautiful? Smell this fresh air!"

On the short main street of St. Charles they passed a liquor store and a hardware store and a grubby little store offering BLOOD AND SAND WORMS; then they were on a country road, and the heels of Emily's spectator pumps kept turning under her as she walked. "Is it much farther?" she asked.

"Just beyond this next field. Then we go past a wooded area that's part of the estate, and then we're there. I can't get over how beautiful everything is."

And Emily was willing to acknowledge that the place was nice. Overgrown, but nice. A driveway led off the road into the trees and the high, rustling hedges; where it forked Pookie said "The main house is over there—you can just see a corner of it, but we'll see it later—and Sarah's cottage is this way."

It was a bungalow of white clapboard with a little lawn, and Sarah came out to greet them on the lawn. "Hi," she said. "Welcome to the House at Pooh Corner." She said that as if she'd rehearsed it, and the way she was dressed showed considerable preparation too: bright, fresh maternity clothes that might have been bought for the occasion. She looked lovely.

She served a lunch that was almost as inadequate as one of Pookie's meals; then the problem was that the conversation kept petering out. Sarah wanted to hear "everything" about Barnard, but when Emily began to talk she saw her sister's eyes glaze over in smiling boredom. Pookie said "Isn't this nice? Just the three of us together again?" But it wasn't really very nice at all, and for most of the afternoon they sat around the sparsely furnished living room in attitudes of forced conviviality, Pookie smoking many cigarettes and dropping ashes on the rug, three women with nothing much to say to one another. Color illustrations of Magnum Navy fighter planes in action occupied one wall; on another was the framed Easter photograph of Sarah and Tony.

Geoffrey Wilson had invited them over to the main house for a drink, and Pookie kept watching the clock: she didn't want to be late.

"You two go ahead," Sarah said. "If Tony gets home in time we'll join you, but he probably won't; he's been putting in a lot of overtime lately."

So they went to the main house without her. It was built of white clapboard too, and it was long and ugly—three stories high in some places and two in others, with black-roofed gables jutting into the trees. The first thing that hit you when you went inside was the smell of mildew. It seeped from the brown oil paintings in the vestibule, from the creaking floor and carpets and walls and gaunt furniture of the long, dark living room.

"... It's an old house," Geoffrey Wilson was saying as he poured a shot of whiskey for Pookie, "and it's too big to manage without servants, but we try to cope. Will you have scotch too, Emily, or will you join Edna in some sherry?"

"Sherry, please."

"And the worst problem is the heating," he went on. "My father built it as a summer place, you see, and there's never been a proper heating system. One of the tenants did put in an oil burner that looks *vaguely* adequate, but I imagine we'll have to shut off most of the rooms this winter. Well. Cheers."

"*I* think it's a *charming* house," Pookie said, settling down to enjoy the cocktail hour. "I won't hear a word against it. Look, Emmy, see the lovely old portraits? They're some of Geoffrey's ancestors. There are stories connected with every single thing in this room."

"Mostly ve'y dull stories, I'm afraid," Geoffrey Wilson said.

"Fascinating stories," she insisted. "Oh, Geoffrey, I can't tell you how I've come to love it out here—all the lovely meadows and the woodland, and Sarah's cottage, and this wonderful old house. It has such—I don't know; such flair. Does it have a name?"

"A name?"

"You know, the way estates have names. Like 'Jalna,' or 'Green Gables.' "

Geoffrey Wilson pretended to think it over. "The way it looks now," he said, "I suppose we might call it 'Overgrown Hedges.' "

And Pookie didn't realize he was kidding. "Oh, I *like* that," she said. "Not 'Overgrown,' though, that's not quite right. What about"—she worked her lips—"what about 'Great Hedges'?"

"Mm," he said kindly. "Yes; rather nice."

"That's what *I'm* going to call it, anyway," she announced. " 'Great Hedges,' St. Charles, Long Island, New York."

"Well." He turned to Emily. "How are you finding your— college?"

"Oh, it's very—interesting." Emily took a sip and sat back to watch her mother get drunk. She knew it wouldn't take long. With the second drink Pookie began to monopolize the talk, telling long pointless anecdotes about houses she'd lived in, hunching forward in her deep chair with her elbows on her slightly parted knees. Emily, sitting across from her, could watch her face loosen as she talked and drank, watch her knees move farther apart until they revealed the gartered tops of her stockings, the shadowed, sagging insides of her naked thighs and finally the crotch of her underpants.

". . . No, but the *nicest* house I ever had was in Larchmont. Remember Larchmont, dear? We had real casement windows and a real slate roof; of course we couldn't afford it, but the minute I saw it I said *That's* where I want to live, and I went right in and signed the lease, and the girls loved it. I'll never forget how—Oh, *thank* you, Geoffrey; just one more and then we've really got to be . . ."

Why couldn't she get drunk quietly, with her legs curled up in the cushions, like Edna Wilson?

"A little more sherry, Emily?"

"No thanks. I'm fine."

". . . And of course the schools were wonderful in Larchmont; that's one reason I wish we could have stayed; still, I've always thought it did the girls a world of good to move around to different places, and then of course . . .''

By the time she was ready to leave at last Geoffrey Wilson had to help her to the door. It was getting dark. Emily took her arm—it felt soft and weak—and they made their way past trees and overgrown shrubbery toward the long road to the railroad station. She knew Pookie would sleep on the train—she hoped she would, anyway; it would be better than if she stayed awake and talked—and their dinner, if they had any, would be a hot dog and coffee in Penn Station. But she didn't mind: the weekend was almost over, and in a matter of hours she'd be back in school.

School was the center of her life. She had never heard the word "intellectual" used as a noun before she went to Barnard, and she took it to heart. It was a brave noun, a proud noun, a noun suggesting lifelong dedication to lofty things and a cool disdain for the commonplace. An intellectual might lose her virginity to a soldier in the park, but she could learn to look back on it with wry, amused detachment. An intellectual might have a mother who showed her underpants when drunk, but she wouldn't let it bother her. And Emily Grimes might not be an intellectual yet, but if she took copious notes in even the dullest of her classes, and if she read every night until her eyes ached, it was only a question of time. There were girls in her class, and even a few Columbia boys, who thought of her as an intellectual already, just from the way she talked.

"It's not just a bore," she said once of a tiresome eighteenth-century novel, "it's a *pernicious* bore." And she couldn't help noticing that several other girls made liberal use of the word "pernicious" around the dormitory during the next few days.

But there was more to being an intellectual than a manner of speaking, more even than making the dean's list every semester, or spending all your free time at museums and concerts and the kind of movies called "films." There was learning not to be stricken dumb when you walked into a party full of older, certified intellectuals—and not to make the opposite mistake of talking your head off, saying one inane or outrageous thing after another in a hopeless effort to atone for whatever inane or out-rageous thing you'd said two minutes before. And if you did make a fool of yourself at parties like that, you had to learn not to writhe in bed afterwards in an agony of chagrin.

You had to be serious, but—this was the maddening para-dox—you had to seem never to take anything very seriously.

"I thought you did very well," said a rumpled man at a party during her sophomore year.

"I what? What do you mean?"

"Just now, when you were talking to Lazlow. I was listening."

"Talking to who?"

"You didn't even know who he is? Clifford Lazlow, political science. He a tiger."

"Oh."

"Anyway, you did very well. You weren't intimidated and you weren't aggressive either."

"But he's just a funny little man in bifocals."

"That's funny." And he shook his plump shoulders to simulate a spasm of laughter. "That's really funny. A funny little man in bifocals. Can I get you a drink?"

"No, actually, I—well, all right."

His name was Andrew Crawford and he was a graduate assistant in philosophy. His damp hair hung in his eyes as he talked, and she wanted to comb it back with her fingers. He wasn't really as pudgy as he'd seemed at first glance; he was attractive in his own way, especially when he was tense with talking, but he looked as though he ought to spend more time outdoors. When he got his doctorate, he said, he would continue to teach—"if the Army doesn't get me, and there's not much chance of that; I'm a physical wreck"—and he would also travel. He wanted to see whatever would be left of Europe, and he wanted to go to Russia too, and China. The world would be made over again in unforeseeable ways, and he didn't want to miss any of it. Essentially, though, he wanted to teach. "I like the classroom," he said. "I know it sounds stuffy, but I like the academic life. What's your field?"

"Well, I'm only a sophomore; I'm an English major, but I don't really—"

"Really? You look older than that. I mean you don't look

older, but you *seem* older. The way you move around; the way you handled old Lazlow. I could've sworn you were a grad student. You have a very—I don't know. You seem very sure of yourself. In a good way, I mean. These parties get a little thick after a while, don't you think? Everybody shouting each other down, everybody trying to score points. It's all ego, ego, ego. You ready for a refill?"

"No; I'd better be going."

"Where do you live? I'll take you home."

"No, actually, I'm with someone."

"Who?"

"You wouldn't know him; Dave Ferguson. He's over there by the door; the tall one."

"Him? But he's only about fifteen years *old*."

"That's silly. He's twenty-one."

"Why isn't he in the Army? Strapping youth like that."

"He has a bad knee."

"A 'trick knee,' right?" Andrew Crawford said. "A 'football knee.' Oh, yes, dear God, I know the type."

"Well, I don't know what you're implying, but I—"

"Not implying anything at all. I never imply. Always say exactly what I mean."

"Anyway, I have to go."

"Wait." And he started after her through the crowd. "Could I call you sometime? Can I have your number?"

As she wrote down the number she wondered why she was doing it. Wouldn't it have been perfectly easy to say no to Andrew Crawford? But that was the trouble: it *wouldn't* have been easy. There was something about him—his eyes, his mouth, his soft-looking shoulders—that suggested he'd be hurt beyond all reason if you said no.

"Thank you," he said, putting her number in his pocket, and he looked as pleased as a child singled out for praise. "Oh, thank you."

"Who was the little fat guy?" Dave Ferguson inquired when they were out on the street.

"I don't know. A graduate student in philosophy. I wouldn't exactly call him fat." After a while she said "Arrogant, though."

And then she was troubled again: you couldn't exactly call him arrogant, either.

"He sure had the hots for you."

"You say that about everybody."

It was a clear night, and she enjoyed walking with Dave Ferguson. He held her close but not in the clutching, almost desperate way some boys did; his legs matched her stride perfectly, and their heels made a sharp, invigorating cadence on the street.

"Can I come up?" he asked at her doorstep. She had her own apartment in "approved student housing" now; she had let him "come up" three or four times, and twice he had stayed all night.

"I don't think so tonight, Dave," she said, not quite meeting his eyes. "I'm really very—"

"What's the matter? You sick?"

"No; it's just that I'm so tired I want to go right to sleep. And I've got that awful Chaucer exam tomorrow."

After turning back to watch him retreat up the sidewalk, hunched in his raincoat, she wondered why she had sent him away. Life was confusing.

One distressing thing Emily learned in college was to feel more intelligent than her sister. She had felt more intelligent than her mother for years, but that was different; when it happened with Sarah she felt she had betrayed a trust.

She began to notice it when she and Pookie went out to St. Charles soon after Sarah's second boy was born. Tony Junior was standing now, drooling and clinging to his mother's leg as they peered into the crib at the small new face.

"Oh, I think Peter's a lovely name," Pookie said. "And you're right, Sarah, he is different. He and little Tony have whole different personalities. Don't they, Emmy?"

"Mm."

With the inspection over and the babies asleep, they sat around the living room and Sarah poured three glasses of sherry. She had evidently picked up sherry from Edna Wilson.

"*Oh*, it feels so good to sit down," she said, and she did look tired; but she began to look refreshed as she talked. There were times, especially with a little alcohol in her veins, when Sarah could be almost as much of a talker as Pookie.

"... I couldn't help thinking of Daddy back in August or whenever it was, when Italy surrendered. Did you see the papers that day? The headlines? Well, the *News*—that's the only paper we get; Tony likes it—the *News* headline was 'ITALY QUITS'; but I happened to be down in the village that day so I saw all the other papers. The *Times* and the *Tribune* said 'ITALY SURRENDERS,' or something like that, and so did most of the others. But do you know what the *Sun* said? Daddy's paper? The dear old *Sun*'s headline was 'ITALY CAPITULATES.' Can you imagine? Can you imagine *Daddy* writing a headline like that, or ever allowing it to be written? He would have died. I mean," she added quickly, "he never would've let it happen." And she took a deep drink.

"I don't get it," Emily said.

"Oh, Emmy," Sarah said. "How many people know what 'capitulate' means?"

"Do you know what it means?"

Sarah blinked. "Well, but I mean how many *other* people do? And for a daily newspaper that's supposed to reach millions of people—I don't know; I thought it was funny, that's all."

"Marvelous," Pookie said.

Sarah sat back in the sofa, tucking her ankles up beneath her —had she copied that gesture from Edna Wilson too?—and launched into her next monologue with the zest of a performer who knows her audience will be enthralled. "Oh, I *must* tell you this," she began. "First of all, I got a letter from Donald Clellon last year, and he—"

"Donald Clellon?" Emily said. "Did you really?"

"Oh, just sort of a sad little letter; that's not important. He said he was in the army now and he often thought of me— *you* know—and he said he was out here at Camp Upton. So anyway—"

"How long ago was that?"

"I don't know; a year or so ago. Anyway, last month we had an air-raid scare out here—did you hear about that?"

"Oh, *no*," Pookie said, looking concerned.

"Well, it was nothing, of course, that's the whole point. It only lasted a few hours. *I* wasn't frightened, but some of the little townspeople were—they talked about it for days afterwards. *Any*way, they announced on the radio that one of the soldiers at Camp Upton had turned in the alarm by mistake, and I said—I told this to Tony and he couldn't stop laughing—I said 'I bet it was Donald Clellon.'"

Pookie threw back her head for peal after peal of hearty laughter, showing her bad teeth, and Sarah was helpless with laughter too.

"Well, but wait," Emily said while her mother and sister were recovering. "Camp Upton is only an induction center; they only stay there a few days before they go to other camps for basic training, and then they're shipped out to divisions. If it was a year ago that Donald wrote you, he's probably overseas by now." And she would have added He might even be dead, but didn't want to overdo it.

"Oh?" Sarah said. "Well, I didn't know that, but even so."

"Oh, Emmy," Pookie said. "Don't spoil the story. Where's your sense of humor?" And she repeated the punch line, to savor it. " 'I bet it was Donald Clellon.'"

Emily didn't know where her sense of humor was, but she knew it wasn't here—nor would it be in the main house, later this afternoon, when she and Pookie went over there for their ritual visit with the elder Wilsons. She guessed she had left it, along with everything else that mattered, back at school.

For a little while she expected Andrew Crawford to call her any day; then she stopped thinking about it, and more than a whole year went by before he did—the year she became a junior.

She had broken off with Dave Ferguson and spent six romantic, melancholy weeks with a boy named Paul Resnick who was waiting to be drafted; he later wrote her a long letter from Fort Sill, Oklahoma, explaining that he loved her but didn't want to be tied down. She worked that summer in an upper-Broadway bookstore—"English majors make good booksellers," the manager told her; "I'll take an English major every time"—and then the following winter, out of the blue, Andrew Crawford called her.

"I wasn't at all certain you'd remember me," he said as they settled into a booth in a Greek restaurant near the Columbia campus.

"Why did you wait so long to call?"

"I was shy," he said, opening his napkin. "I was shy and also I was miserably involved with a young lady whose name shall not be mentioned here."

"Oh. What do people call you, anyway? Andy?"

"Oh, Lord, no. 'Andy' suggests some devilish, hell-for-leather sort of fellow; not my type at all, I'm afraid. I've always been called Andrew. A little hard to get your mouth around, I'll admit—sort of like Ernest or Clarence—but I'm used to it."

From the way he ate she could tell he liked his food—he *was* a little chubby—and he didn't say much until he was full, by which time there was a faint shine of grease around his mouth. Then he began to talk as if talking were another sensual pleasure, using words like "tangential" and "reductive." He talked of the war not as a cataclysm that might soon swallow him up—he said for the second time that he was a physical wreck—but as a complex and fascinating international game; he went on to talk of books she'd never read and authors she'd never heard of, and then he was talking about classical music, of which she knew almost nothing. ". . . And as you may know, the piano part in that sonata is one of the most difficult pieces in the world. Technically, I mean."

"Are you a musician, too?"

"Used to be, sort of. I studied piano and clarinet for many years—you know, I was one of these tiresome little creatures called 'gifted children'—then when it turned out I didn't have the talent to perform I tried composing. Studied composition at Eastman until it was clear I didn't have much talent for that either; then I gave up music altogether."

"It must be very—painful to give up something like that."

"Oh, it broke my heart. But then, back in those days my heart was getting broken on an average of about once a month, so it was only a matter of degree. What would you like for dessert?"

"How often does your heart get broken now?"

"Mm? Oh, somewhat less frequently. Perhaps two or three

times a year. What about dessert? They have marvelous baklava here."

She decided she liked him. She didn't much like the grease around his mouth, but he wiped that away before digging into his baklava, and she liked everything else. No other boy she'd known had such a wide general knowledge and so many well-reasoned opinions—he *was* an intellectual—nor had any other boy had the maturity to be self-deprecating. But that was the point: he wasn't a boy. He was thirty. He had come to terms with the world.

She allowed herself to nestle close to his arm as they walked, and when they came to her doorway she said "Would you like to come up for some coffee?"

He backed two steps away on the sidewalk, looking surprised. "No," he said, "no, really; thanks very much; some other time." And he didn't even kiss her; all he did was smile and make an awkward little wave of the hand as he turned away. Upstairs, she walked the floor for a long time with one knuckle in her mouth, trying to figure out what she'd done wrong.

But he did call her again a few days later. This time they went to a Mozart concert, and when they got back to her place he said he thought a little coffee might be pleasant.

He sat on the sofa-bed her mother had helped her buy at the Salvation Army outlet, and as she fussed around the kitchenette she didn't know whether to sit beside him or in the chair across the coffee table. She chose to sit beside him, but he seemed not to notice it. When she leaned back he leaned forward, stirring his coffee, and when she leaned forward he leaned back. All this time he was talking, first about the concert and then about the war and the world and himself.

She reached for a cigarette (she needed something to do with her hands) and she had just lighted it when he made a lunge for her. Sparks flew into her hair and down the front of her dress; she was on her feet, brushing herself off, and he was all apologies. "God, I'm sorry; that was clumsy; I'm always doing things like— you must think I'm—"

"It's all right," she told him. "You startled me, that's all."

"I know; I—I'm terribly sorry."

"No, really; it's all right." She got rid of the cigarette and sat down with him again, and this time his reaching arms went smoothly around her. His face was pink when he kissed her, and she noticed too that he didn't grope for her breasts and her thighs right away, as boys usually did; he seemed to enjoy just hugging and kissing, which he accompanied with soft little moans.

After a while he pulled away from her mouth and said "When's your first class in the morning?"

"Oh, it doesn't matter."

"It does, though. Look at the time. Really, I'd better go."

"No; stay. Please. I want you to stay."

And only then did he begin making love to her. Moaning, he tore off his coat and tie and dropped them on the floor; then he urgently helped her to unfasten her dress. In a few quick, awkward motions she made the sofa into a bed and they were deep inside it, writhing and gasping and clinging together. His warm, heavy torso was soft to the touch, but he was strong.

"Oh," he said. "Oh, Emily, I love you."

"No, no; don't say that."

"But it's true; I have to say it. I love you."

He lay mouthing and sucking one of her nipples for a while, stroking her with his hands; then his mouth went to the other one. After a long time he rolled partly away from her and said "Emily?"

"Yes?"

"I'm sorry, it's—I can't. This happens to me sometimes. I can't."

"Oh."

"I can't tell you how sorry I am; it's just one of those—Does it make you hate me?"

"No, of course not, Andrew."

With a great deflating sigh he heaved himself up and sat on the edge of the bed, and he looked so dejected that she put her arms around him from behind.

"Good," he said. "That's nice. I like to have you hold me that way. And it's true: I do love you. You're delightful. You're sweet and healthy and kind and I love you. It's just that I can't seem to—demonstrate it tonight."

"Sh-sh. It's all right."

"Tell me the truth. Has this ever happened to you before? Has a man ever failed you this way before?"

"Sure."

"You'd say that even if it wasn't true. Ah, God, you're a nice girl. Listen, though, Emily: it's a thing that only happens to me sometimes. Do you believe that?"

"Of course."

"The rest of the time I'm fine. My God, sometimes I can screw and screw until—"

"Sh-sh. It's all right. It was just tonight. There'll be other nights."

"Do you promise? Do you promise me that?"

"Of course."

"That's marvelous," he said, and turned around to take her in his arms.

But for a week, including several afternoons as well as nights and mornings, they tried and tried again without success. Afterwards, what she remembered best about that week was the heat and sweat of their struggle and the smell of the bed.

Several times she said "It must be my fault," and he told her if she talked that way it would only make things worse.

Once he almost accomplished it: he worked his way inside her, and she could feel him. "There!" he said. "Oh, God, there; there—" but it wasn't long before he slipped out and lay heavily on her, panting or sobbing in defeat. "I lost it," he said. "I lost it."

She stroked his damp hair. "It was wonderful for a minute."

"That's kind of you, but I know it wasn't 'wonderful.' It was only the beginning."

"Well, it was the beginning, Andrew. We'll do better next time."

"God. That's what I always say. Every time I leave you and go back into that miserable, brutal, screaming world I think 'I'll do better next time.' And it's always the same—always, always the same."

"Sh-sh. Let's just sleep now. Then maybe in the morning we'll—"

"No. It's even worse in the morning. You know that."

During a warm February thaw he called her to announce he had made a decision. It couldn't be discussed on the phone; could she meet him at the West End at four-thirty?

She found him alone at the bar with a stein of beer, one foot cocked on the rail, and he walked with long strides as he led her to a booth, carrying his shoulders in an easy slouch. That was something she'd noticed before: when she met him somewhere, in a bar or on a street corner, he always moved with the demeanor of an athlete at rest.

He sat close beside her in the booth, holding one of her hands between the beers, and told her he had decided to see a psychoanalyst. He had gotten the man's name from someone "in the department"; he had arranged for his first session and was willing to go as often as necessary—twice, three times a week; he didn't care. It would take all of his savings and much of his salary—he might even have to borrow money—but there was no other way.

"Well, that's—very brave of you, Andrew."

He squeezed her hand. "It's not brave; it's an act of desperation. It's something I probably should have done long ago. And Emily, this is the difficult part: I don't think we ought to see each other while I'm in therapy. Let's say for at least a year. Then I'll look you up again, and of course you'll probably be involved with another man; I can only hope you'll still be free. Because the point is I want to marry you, Emily, and I—"

"You want to *marry* me? But you haven't even—"

"Please," he said, closing his eyes as if in pain. "I know what I haven't even done."

"I wasn't going to say that. I was only going to say you haven't even proposed to me yet."

"You're the sweetest, healthiest, kindest girl I've ever met," he said, and put his arm around her. "Of course I haven't—how could I, under the circumstances? But as soon as this year is over, as soon as I'm—you know—I'll come back and offer you the most heartfelt proposal of marriage you've ever heard. Do you understand, Emily?"

"Well, yes. Except that I—well, yes. Sure, I understand."

"That's marvelous. Now let's get out of here before I burst into tears."

It was a pleasant day—young couples crowded the sidewalk, out to enjoy the false spring—and he led her quickly to a florist's shop on the corner.

"I'm going to put you in a cab and send you home," he said, "but first I'm going to buy you flowers."

"No, that's silly; I don't want any flowers."

"Yes you do. Wait." He came out of the shop with a dozen yellow roses and pressed them into her hands. "Here. Put them in water; then you'll remember me at least until they die. Emily? Will you miss me?"

"Of course."

"Just pretend I've gone off to war, like all the other, better men you've known. All right. No long goodbyes." He kissed her cheek; then he loped into the street, still moving in the athletic way that wasn't natural to him; he flagged down a taxicab and stood there holding the door open for her, smiling with bright eyes that looked a little out of focus.

As the cab pulled away she turned around in the heavy scent of roses to see if he would wave, but she caught only a glimpse of his back heading into the sidewalk crowd.

Except that she wanted to cry, she didn't really know what she felt. She tried to figure it out all the way home until she discovered, climbing the stairs, that she felt a great sense of relief.

Soon after the war ended in Europe, a young merchant seaman came into the bookstore and began talking to her as if he'd known her all her life. His fingernails were broken and black, but he could recite long passages of Milton and Dryden and Pope from memory without seeming to show off: there was, he said, plenty of time for reading aboard ship. He wore a black sweater that looked too warm for the season, and he had a big, blond, handsome head that she described to herself as "Nordic." He stood talking, shifting his weight from one foot to the other, holding a stack of books against his hip, and she felt a powerful urge to put her hands on him. She was afraid he might leave the store without asking her for a date, and he almost did—he said "Well; see you," and started to turn away, but then he turned back and said "Hey, listen: what time do you get off work?"

He was staying in a rundown hotel in Hell's Kitchen—she soon came to know everything about that hotel, from the smells of piss and disinfectant in the lobby to the slow cage of the elevator to the raddled green carpet in his room—and his ship was undergoing extensive repairs in the Brooklyn Navy Yard, which meant he would be in New York all summer. His name was Lars Ericson.

He was as hard and smooth as ivory, and beautifully proportioned; at first she thought she could never get enough of him. She liked to lie in his bed and watch him move naked around the room: he reminded her of Michelangelo's *David*. There were small carbuncular knobs on the back of his neck and out across his shoulders, but if she squinted very slightly she didn't see them.

". . . And you've really had no education at all?"

"Of course I have. I've told you; I went through the eighth grade."

"And you really speak four languages?"

"I never told you that. I'm only fluent in French and Spanish. My Italian's very sketchy, very primitive."

"Ah, God, you're wonderful. Come over here . . ."

She hoped he might want to be a writer or a painter—she had a vision of him working in a windswept beach cottage, like Eugene O'Neill, while she waded thigh-deep to gather clams and mussels for their supper and the wheeling gulls screamed overhead—but he was perfectly content to be a seaman. He said he liked the freedom it gave him.

"Well, but I mean, freedom to do what?"

"Not necessarily to 'do' anything. Freedom to be."

"Oh. I see. At least I think I see."

She thought she saw a great many things in that voluptuous, invigorating summer with Lars Ericson. She thought she saw that her time in college was a waste. Maybe *anybody's* time in college was a waste. And maybe that had something to do with the tragedy of a man like Andrew Crawford: he had given his life to academia—not just his mind, but his life—and it had shriveled his manhood.

In any case, there was certainly nothing wrong with Lars Ericson's manhood. It grew from him like the sturdy limb of a tree; it prodded and thrusted and plunged in her; it drove her slowly and steadily into a long-sustained delirium for which the only possible expression was a scream; it left her weak and panting and feeling like a woman, waiting for more.

One night as they lay exhausted in his bed there was a knock on the door, and the voice of an adolescent boy called "Lars? You home?"

"I'm home," he called back, "but I'm busy. I have a guest."

"Oh."

"I'll see you tomorrow, Marvin," he said. "Or maybe not tomorrow, but you know; I'll see you around."

"Okay."

"Who was that?" she asked when the footsteps went away.

"Just a kid from the ship. He likes to come in and play chess sometimes. I feel kind of sorry for him: he's all alone here, doesn't have much to do."

"He ought to get out and find a girl."

"Oh, I think he's too shy for that. He's only seventeen."

"I'll bet *you* weren't too shy at that age. Or no, wait—I'll bet you were shy, but the girls wouldn't leave you alone. Not just girls—older women. Chic, sophisticated older women with penthouses. Right? And they'd get you up in their penthouses and take off all your clothes with their teeth, and they'd run their tongues all over your chest, and they'd go down on their knees and beg for you. Right? Isn't that the way it was?"

"I don't know, Emily. You've got quite an imagination."

"You *kindle* my imagination; you *feed* my imagination. Oh, feed me. Feed me."

One afternoon he showed up at her apartment wearing a cheap new gas-blue suit with padded shoulders—no Columbia boy would be caught dead in a suit like that, but that only added to its charm—and said he'd borrowed a car for the evening. Would she like to drive out to Sheepshead Bay and have a shore dinner?

"That'd be lovely. Who'd you borrow the car from?"

"Oh, a friend. Man I know."

On the long drive through Brooklyn he seemed preoccupied. He steered with one hand and used the other to play with his mouth, repeatedly pulling out his lower lip and letting it go back against his teeth, and he scarcely talked to her at all. She had hoped they might sit side by side in the restaurant, so he could put his arm around her and they could murmur and laugh together throughout the meal; instead they were across from each other at a big table in the middle of the sawdust-sprinkled floor.

"Is there a place out here," she inquired, "where we could go dancing after dinner?"

"Not that I know of," he said around a mouthful of lobster.

The food rode heavily in her stomach all the way home—there had been too much grease on the fried potatoes—and Lars didn't break his silence until he'd found a parking space near her building. Then, sitting in the stilled car and looking straight through the windshield, he said "Emily, I don't think we ought to see each other any more."

"You don't? Why?"

"Because I have to be true to my own nature. You're very nice and we've had some good times, but I have to think of my own needs."

"I'm not tying you down, Lars. You're as free as—"

"I didn't *say* you were tying me down. I simply said I have to be true to my own—Emily, the point is there's someone else."

"Oh? What's she like?"

"It isn't a girl," he said as if that would make it easier, "it's a man. I happen to be bisexual, you see."

All the moisture went out of her mouth. "You mean homosexual?"

"Of course not; you ought to know better than that. I said *bi*sexual."

"Doesn't that amount to the same thing?"

"No; not at all."

"But you like men better than women."

"I like both. I've enjoyed one kind of experience with you; now I feel I'm ready for the other."

"I see," she said. And when would she ever learn to stop saying "I see" about things she didn't see at all?

He walked her to her door and they stood facing each other on the sidewalk, a few feet apart.

"I'm sorry it has to end this way," he said. He put one hand low on his hip and gazed off down the street in order to let her admire his profile, and he looked more than ever like Michelangelo's *David*, even in that awful suit.

"So long, Lars," she said.

There would be no more sex, she promised herself as she drove her fist repeatedly into the pillow upstairs. She would meet men, she would go out with them and laugh and dance and do all the other things you were supposed to do, but there would be no more sex until—well, until she was absolutely sure of what she was doing.

She broke her promise in November with a haggard law student who said he was a communist, and broke it again in February with a witty boy who played the drums in a jazz combo. The law student stopped calling her because he said she was "ideologically impure," and it turned out that the drummer had three other girls.

Then it was spring again. She was about to graduate from college with no idea of what to do with her life, and it was almost time for Andrew Crawford to end his psychoanalytical exile.

"Emily?" he said on the telephone one evening. "Are you alone?"

"Yes. Hello, Andrew."

"I can't tell you how many times I've started to dial this number and quit on the seventh digit. But you're really there, aren't you. I'm really talking to you. Listen: before I go any further I've got to know this. Are you—do you have a man?"

"No."

"That's almost too good to be—I hardly dared hope for that."

She met him at the West End the following afternoon. "Two beers," he told the waiter. "Or no, wait. Two very dry, extra dry martinis."

He looked about the same—maybe a little heavier; she couldn't be sure—and his face was bright with nervous tension.

". . . Nothing's more boring than hearing about someone else's analysis," he was saying, "so I'll spare you that. Let me just say it's been a tremendous experience. Difficult, painful—God, you can't imagine how painful—but a tremendous experience.

It may go on for several more years, but I've turned the first corner. I *feel* so much better. The world isn't filled with terrors for me any more. I feel I know who I am for the first time in my life."

"Well, that's wonderful, Andrew."

He took a greedy sip of his martini and settled back in the booth with a sigh, dropping one hand to her thigh. "And how about you?" he said. "How was your year?"

"Oh, I don't know. All right."

"I vowed I wouldn't ask you this," he said, "but now that I have your marvelous thigh in my hand I've got to know. How many affairs have you had?"

"Three."

He winced. "God. Three. I was afraid you might say eight or ten, but in a way three is worse. Three suggests real, important affairs. It suggests you've been in love with three different men."

"I don't know what love is, Andrew. I've told you that."

"You told me that last year. And you still don't know? Well, good; that's something, anyway. Because you see I *do* know what love is, and I'm going to work on you and work on you until you do too. Oh, listen to me—'work on you.' That sounds as if I meant—God, I'm sorry."

"You don't have to apologize."

"I know. That's what Dr. Goldman keeps telling me. He says I've spent my life apologizing."

There were more martinis at the Greek restaurant, and wine with dinner, and when they started home to her place he seemed a little drunk. She didn't know whether that was a good sign or a bad one.

"This is taking on all the aspects of a major sporting event," he said as they approached her steps. "A championship fight, or something. The contender's been in training for a year; can he make it this time? Stay tuned for Round One, after this word from—"

"Don't, Andrew." She settled her arm around his broad back. "It's not like that at all. We'll just go upstairs and make love to each other."

"Ah, you're so sweet. You're so sweet and healthy and kind."

They tried for hours—they tried everything—and it was no better than the best of their times last year. In the end he sat slumped on the edge of the bed as if on a prizefighter's stool, his head hanging.

"So," he said. "A technical knockout in the fourth round. Or was it only the third? You're the winner and still champion."

"Don't, Andrew."

"Why not? I'm only trying to make light of it. At least the sportswriters will be able to say I was graceful in defeat."

And the following night he scored a victory. It wasn't perfect—in its climactic moments she failed to respond as fully as she knew she should—but it was what the author of any sex manual would have called an adequate performance.

". . . Oh, Emily," he said when he'd recovered his breath, "oh, if only this had happened the first time, last year, instead of all those miserable nights of—"

"Sh-sh." She stroked his shoulder. "That's all in the past now."

"Right," he said. "All in the past. Now let's think about the future."

They were married soon after her graduation, in a civil ceremony at the Municipal Building. The only attendants, or witnesses, were a young married couple of Andrew's acquaintance named Kroll. When they walked out across City Hall Park afterwards for what Mrs. Kroll insisted on calling "the wedding breakfast," Emily found herself in one of the busy lunchtime restaurants she had come to with her father long ago.

They told their mothers first. Pookie wept into the telephone, as Emily had known she would, and made them promise to come and visit her the next night. Andrew's mother, who lived in Englewood, New Jersey, invited them for the following Sunday.

". . . Oh, he's nice, dear," Pookie said when she'd cornered Emily in the cramped kitchen downtown, while Andrew sat sipping coffee in the next room. "I was a little—well, frightened of him at first, but when you get to know him he's really awfully nice. And I love the sort of formal way he talks; he must be *very* intelligent . . ."

Andrew's mother was older than Emily had expected, a blue-haired, wrinkled and powdered woman wearing knee-length elastic stockings. She sat on a chintz-covered sofa with three white Persian cats, in a room that smelled of recent vacuum cleaning, and she blinked at Emily repeatedly as if having to remind herself that Emily was there. In a bright, airless sun porch called "the music room" there was an upright piano, and there was a framed studio photograph of Andrew at the age of eight or nine, dressed in a sailor suit, seated on the piano bench with a clarinet across his chubby lap. Mrs. Crawford opened the keyboard and looked imploringly at her son. "Play something for us, Andrew," she said. "Has Emily heard you play?"

"Oh, Mother, please. You know I don't play any more."

"You play like an angel. Sometimes when there's Mozart or Chopin on the radio I just close my eyes"—she closed her eyes—"and picture you here—right here at this piano . . ."

In the end he gave in: he played a short selection from Chopin, and even Emily could tell he was hurrying through it, seeming to play sloppily on purpose.

"God!" he said when they were back on the train for New York. "Every time I go out there it takes me days to recover—whole days just to get to the point where I can *breathe* again . . ."

Only one visit remained to be made—to Sarah and Tony in St. Charles—and they put it off until the end of the summer, when Andrew had bought a used car.

"So," he said as they sped along the wide Long Island highway. "At last I get to meet your beautiful sister and your dashing, romantic brother-in-law. I feel as if I'd known them for years."

He was in a sour, touchy mood, and she knew why. His sexual performance had been adequate all summer, with occasional lapses, but just lately—in the past week or so—he had fallen back into the old habit of failure. Last night he had suffered a premature ejaculation against her leg, and afterwards he had wept in her arms.

"Was he in the service?"

"Who?"

"Laurence Olivier. Who'd you think I meant?"

"I've told you," she said. "He was drafted into the Navy, but they assigned him back to Magnum as naval personnel."

"Well, at least he didn't storm the beaches at Normandy," Andrew said, "and win the Silver Star with fourteen Oakleaf Clusters—we'll be spared *that* kind of an evening."

It wasn't easy to find St. Charles from the spidery lines on the road map, but once they were in the village she saw enough landmarks (BLOOD AND SAND WORMS) to guide Andrew out to the Wilsons' place. Beside the driveway was a small hand-lettered sign reading GREAT HEDGES, and she recognized the lettering as Sarah's.

The young Wilsons sat on a blanket on their front lawn with their three sons toddling and chirping around them in the afternoon sunshine; they were so absorbed in each other that they didn't see their guests arrive.

"I wish I had a camera," Emily called. "You make a lovely picture."

"Emmy!" Sarah sprang to her feet and came forward across the bright grass with both arms held out. "And you're Andrew Crawford—it's *so* nice to meet you."

Tony's greeting was less effusive—his smiling eyes, crinkled at the corners, seemed more amused than pleased, as if he were thinking Must I really put myself out for this fellow? Just because he's married to my wife's little sister?—but he shook Andrew's hand firmly enough and managed to mumble appropriate things.

"I didn't know even *Eric* was on his feet now," Emily said.

"Certainly," Sarah told her. "He's almost eighteen months old. And that's Peter there, the one with the cookie crumbs on his face, and the big one's Tony Junior. He's three and a half. What do you think of them?"

"They're beautiful, Sarah."

"We just came out here to get the last of the sun," Sarah said, "but let's go inside. It's cocktail time. Darling? Would you shake out the blanket, please? It's all cookie crumbs."

Cocktail time, in the carefully cleaned-up living room, meant that the Crawfords had to sit and watch with fixed smiles while the Wilsons went through the old Anatole's business of entwining arms for the first sip. For what seemed a long time after that the party failed to ignite. Shadows lengthened on the floor and the west windows turned bright gold, and still the four of them were stiff and shy. Even Sarah was less talkative than usual: she told no rambling anecdotes, and except for a few awkwardly phrased questions about Andrew's work she seemed constrained in his presence, as if afraid she might appear trivial to such a learned man.

"Philosophy," Tony said, swirling the ice cubes in his empty glass. "I'm afraid that whole field's rather a mystery to me. Must be ve'y difficult to read, let alone teach. How does one go about teaching it?"

"Oh, well," Andrew said, "you know; we get up there and try to educate the little bastards."

Tony chuckled approvingly, and Sarah turned her laughing face on him as if to say You see? You see? I *told* you Emmy wouldn't marry a creep.

"I say, are we ever going to eat?" Tony inquired.

"I'll have just one more cigarette," Sarah said. "Then I'll get the boys to bed, and then we'll have dinner."

The small roast was badly overcooked and so were the vegetables, but Andrew had been warned not to expect very much in the way of food. It began to seem that the visit might be a success after all, for all of them, until they moved back into the living room after coffee.

There were more drinks then, in taller glasses, and the trouble might have been partly that: Andrew wasn't used to drinking that much, and he grew a little over-earnest in recommending a Jugoslavian movie, or "film," that he and Emily had seen. ". . . I don't see how anyone could fail to be moved by it," he concluded, "anyone with any belief in humanity."

Tony had looked sleepy through most of the recital, but the last line brought him awake. "Oh, I believe in humanity," he said. "Humanity's perf'ly all right with me." Then his mouth went into a subtle shape of wit, suggesting that his next remark would bring down the house. "I like everyone but coons, kikes, and Catholics."

Sarah had started to laugh in anticipation of whatever he might say, but when she heard it she cut her laughter short and lowered her eyes, displaying the fine little blue-white scar of the gymnastics bar long ago. There was an uneasy silence.

"Is that something you learned in your English public school?" Andrew inquired.

"Mm?"

"I said is that something they taught you in your English public school? How to say something like that?"

Tony blinked in bewilderment; then he mumbled something inaudible—it might have been "Oh, I say" or "Sorry" or it might have been neither—and stared at his glass with a jaded little smile to show that he for one had had quite enough of this tiresome nonsense.

Somehow a measure of decorum was restored. They managed to labor through a ceremony of small talk and smiles and good-nights, and then they were free.

"The Country Squire," Andrew said, gripping the steering wheel tight in both hands as they droned along the highway toward home. "He was raised with the English upper-middle class. He's 'practically an engineer.' He lives in a place called Great Hedges. He's sired three sons out of his beautiful wife; and he comes up with a remark like that. He's a Neanderthal. He's a pig."

"It was inexcusable," Emily said. "Wholly inexcusable."

"Oh, and by the way, it's true what you told me," Andrew went on, "they *do* read nothing but the *Daily News*. When I went out to the bathroom I passed a stack of *Daily News*es about three feet high—the only bona-fide reading matter in that whole lovey-dovey little house."

"I know."

"Ah, but you love him, don't you?"

"What? What do you mean? I don't 'love' him."

"You've told me," Andrew said. "You can't take it back now. You've told me that when they were first engaged you had fantasies about him. You had fantasies that you were the one he really loved."

"Oh, come on, Andrew."

"And I can imagine what you did to support those fantasies— to flesh them out, so to speak. I'll bet you masturbated over him.

Didn't you? Oh, I'll bet you tickled your little nipples until they came up hard, and then you—"

"Stop it, Andrew."

"—and then you went to work on your clitoris—picturing him all the time, imagining what he'd say and how he'd feel and what he'd do to you—and then you spread your legs and shoved a couple of fingers up your—"

"I want you to *stop* this, Andrew. If you don't stop it I'll open this door and get out of this car and—"

"All *right*."

She thought his rage would make him drive too fast, but he was carefully holding the car under the speed limit. His profile, in the dim blue light of the dashboard, was clenched in the look of a man controlling himself against impossible odds. She turned away from him and stared out the window for a long time, watching the slow movement of endless dark, flat land and the red throbbing of radio-tower lights high in the distance. Did women ever divorce their husbands after less than a year of marriage?

He didn't speak again until after they'd crossed the Queensboro Bridge, until after they'd crawled through traffic to the West Side and turned uptown, heading home. Then he said "Do you want to know something, Emily? I hate your body. Oh, I suppose I love it too, at least God knows I try to, but at the same time I hate it. I hate what it put me through last year—what it's putting me through now. I hate your sensitive little tits. I hate your ass and your hips, the way they move and turn; I hate your thighs, the way they open up. I hate your waist and your belly and your great hairy mound and your clitoris and your whole slippery cunt. I'll repeat this exact statement to Dr. Goldman tomorrow and he'll ask me why I said it, and I'll say 'Because I *had* to say it.' So do you see, Emily? Do you understand? I'm saying this because I *have* to say it. I hate your body." His cheeks were quivering. "I hate your body."

PART TWO

ONE

FOR A FEW YEARS after she divorced Andrew Crawford, Emily worked as a librarian in a Wall Street brokerage house. Then she got another job: she joined the editorial staff of a biweekly trade journal called *Food Field Observer*. It was pleasant, undemanding work, writing news and feature stories for the grocery industry; sometimes when she composed a headline quickly and well, so that the spaces counted out right the first time—

> "HOTEL BAR" BUTTER
> HITS SALES PEAK;
> MARGARINES FADE

—she would think of her father. There was always a dim chance that the job could lead to employment on a real magazine, which might be fun; besides, college had taught her that the purpose of a liberal-arts education was not to train but to free the mind. It didn't matter what you did for a living; the important thing was the kind of person you were.

And most of the time she thought of herself as a responsible, well-rounded person. She lived in Chelsea now, in a place with tall windows facing a quiet street. It could easily have been made into an "interesting" apartment, if she'd cared enough to bother about such things; in any case it was big enough to give parties in, and she liked parties. It also made a snug little temporary home for two, and during that time there were a good many men.

In the space of two years she had two abortions. The first would have been the child of a man she didn't like very much, and the central problem with the second was that she couldn't be sure whose child it would have been. After that second abortion she stayed home from the office for a week, lying around the apartment alone or taking hesitant, painful walks along the empty streets. She thought of going to a psychiatrist—some of the people she knew went to psychiatrists—but it would cost too much and might not be worth the effort. Besides, she had a healthier idea. On a low, sturdy table in her apartment she set up the portable typewriter her father had given her as a high school graduation present and began work on a magazine article.

ABORTION: A WOMAN'S VIEW

She liked the tentative title, but couldn't settle on an opening sentence, or what she had learned to call a "lead."

It is painful, dangerous, "immoral" and illegal, yet every year more than _____ million women get abortions in America.

That had a nice ring to it, but it set her up for a kind of hortatory stance she would somehow have to maintain throughout the article.

She tried another attack.

Like many girls of my age, I had always assumed that abortion is a dreadful thing—to be approached, if at all, with the fear and trembling one reserves for a descent into the outer circles of hell.

That sounded better, but even after she'd changed "girls" to "women" it failed to please her. Something was wrong.

She decided to skip the lead for now and plunge into the body of the article. For many hours she wrote many paragraphs, smoking many cigarettes that she was unaware either of lighting or of putting out. Then she went over it with a pencil, scribbling revisions in the margins and sometimes on whole new pages ("Rev. A, pgh. 3, p. 7"), feeling a heady sense of having found her vocation. But the messy stack of manuscript was there waiting for her in the morning, after a fitful sleep; and she had to acknowledge, with an editor's gelid eye, that it didn't read well at all.

When her week of sick leave was over she went back to the office, grateful for the orderly rhythm of an eight-hour day. For several evenings and most of one weekend she worked on the abortion article, but in the end she stowed it in a cardboard box that she called "my files," and put the typewriter away. She would need the table for parties.

Then suddenly it was 1955, and she was thirty years old.

"... And of course if you want to be a career girl that's fine," her mother said on one of the rare and dreaded evenings when Emily went down to her place for dinner. "I only wish *I'd* found a satisfying career when I was your age. It's just that I do feel—"

"It's not a 'career'; it's only a job."

"Well, all the more reason, then. It's just that I do feel it's time for you to—oh, I won't say 'settle down'; Lord knows I never settled down; I just mean—"

"Get married again. Have children."

"Well, is that so strange? Don't you know *any* young man you'd like to marry? Sarah told me she and Tony *loved* the last man you brought out there; what was his name? Fred something?"

"Fred Stanley." He had come to bore her beyond endurance after a few months; she had taken him to St. Charles only on a whim, because he was so presentable.

"Oh, I know, I know," Pookie said with a world-weary smile, digging into her cool spaghetti; she had a full set of false teeth now, which greatly improved her smile. "It's none of my business." Her business came up later that night, after she'd had too much to drink: it was a grievance Emily had heard many times before. "Do you know it's been more than six *months* since I was out at St. Charles? Sarah never invites me. Never invites me. And she *knows* how I love it out there, how I love to spend time with the children. I call up every Sunday and she says 'Well, I guess you'd like to talk to the boys now,' and of course I *love* talking to them, hearing their voices—especially Peter, he's my favorite—and then when we're finished she comes back on and says 'This is costing you a fortune, Pookie, we'd better think about your phone bill.' And I say 'Never *mind* the phone bill, I want to talk to *you*,' but she never invites me. And the few times, the very few times I've suggested it myself she says 'I'm afraid next weekend wouldn't be convenient, Pookie.' Ha. 'Convenient'..."

There was a dribble of spaghetti sauce on her mother's chin, and Emily had to fight an impulse to get up and wipe it off.

"... And when I *think*; when I *think* of the weeks and weeks

I spent out there when Tony was gone in the Navy and all three
of those babies were in diapers, how I cooked and scrubbed and
the furnace didn't work half the time or the pump either, and
we had to carry water from the main house—did anyone ever
ask if that was 'convenient' for *me*?" To emphasize her point she
shook the long ash of her cigarette defiantly on the floor and
took another drink of her cloudy, fingerprinted highball. "Oh,
I suppose I could always call Geoffrey; *he* understands. He and
Edna'd probably invite me, but still—"

"Why don't you?" Emily said, inspecting her watch. "Call
Geoffrey, and maybe he'll ask you out for a weekend."

"Ah, well, you're looking at your watch. All right. All right.
I know. You have to get back to your job and your parties and
your men and whatever else it is you do. I know. Go ahead." And
Pookie waved her moist cigarette in dismissal. "Go ahead," she
said. "Go ahead; run along."

The following spring the job of managing editor on *Food Field
Observer* fell vacant, and for a few days Emily thought she might
be promoted, but instead they hired a man of about forty named
Jack Flanders. He was very tall and spare with a sad, sensitive
face, and Emily found she couldn't keep her eyes off him. His
office was separated from hers by a glass partition: she could
watch him frown over his pencil or his typewriter, watch him
talk on his telephone, watch him get up and stand gazing out his
window as if lost in thought (and he couldn't have been thinking
about the job). He reminded her a little of her father, long ago.
Once when he was on the phone she saw his long face break into
a smile of such pure delight that he could only have been talking
to a woman, and she felt an irrational twinge of jealousy.

He had a deep, resonant voice, and he was very courteous. He
always said "Thanks, Emily," or "That's fine, Emily" when she
brought him something in the line of duty, and once he said
"That's a pretty dress," but he never seemed to meet her eyes.

On the day of a deadline, when everyone was tired and over-
worked, she opened a manila envelope to find six glossy photographs, each of what looked like a shallow box or tray made of
porous white cardboard. Each box was of different proportions
and each picture taken from a different angle, with different

lighting, to emphasize a separate aspect of its design. The press release that came with them was breathless with phrases like "revolutionary concept" and "bold new approach," but she distilled from it the information that this was how fresh cuts of meat might now be packaged for sale in supermarkets. She wrote a story long enough to fill half a column, with a two-column head; then she marked up four of the pictures for single-column cuts, wrote short captions for them and took the finished job to Jack Flanders.

"Why so many pictures?" he inquired.

"They sent six; I only used four."

"Mm," he said, frowning. "Wonder why they didn't put any meat in 'em? Couple of pork chops or something. Or show a guy's hand holding the box, so you'd get an idea of the size."

"Mm."

He scrutinized the four photographs for a long time. Then he said "You know something, Emily?" And he looked at her with the beginnings of the same smile she'd seen him submit to on the phone that other day. "There are times when a word—one word—is worth a thousand pictures."

Remembering it later she was able to agree with him that it hadn't really been all that funny, but at the time—and maybe it was just the way he said it—her laughter was overwhelming. She couldn't stop; she was weak; she had to lean against his desk for support. When it was over she found him looking at her with a shy, happy face.

"Emily?" he said. "Think you might come out for a drink with me after work tonight?"

He had been divorced for six years. He had two children who lived with their mother, and he wrote poetry.

"Published?" she asked.

"Three times."

"In magazines, you mean?"

"No, no; books. Three books."

He lived in one of the drab blocks of the West Twenties, just off Fifth Avenue, where random residential buildings are pressed in among the lofts, and his apartment was what she guessed could be called Spartan—no rug, no curtains, no television.

After their fine first night together, when it seemed abundantly clear that this particular long, skinny man was exactly the kind she had always wanted, she prowled along his bookshelves, wearing his bathrobe, until she came to three slim volumes with the name John Flanders on their spines. He was out in the kitchen making coffee.

"My God, Jack," she called. "You were a Yale Younger Poet."

"Yeah, well, it's kind of a lottery," he said. "They have to give it to somebody every year." But his self-effacement didn't quite ring true: she could tell how pleased he was that she'd found the book—he almost certainly would have showed it to her if she hadn't.

She turned it over and read one of the endorsements aloud: "'In John Flanders we have an authentic new voice, rich in wisdom, passion, and perfect technical control. Let us rejoice in his gift.' Wow."

"Yeah," he said in the same proud-bashful way. "Big deal, huh? You can take that home with you, if you'd like. Fact, I'd like you to. The second book's okay too; probably not as good as the first. Only for Christ's sake don't mess with the third one. It's lousy. You wouldn't believe how lousy. Sugar and milk?"

While they sat sipping coffee, looking out at the tan-and-green loft buildings, she said "What are you doing on a *trade* paper?"

"Got to have some kind of a job. And the point is it's easy; I can do it with my left hand and forget it when I come home."

"Don't poets usually work in universities?"

"Ah, I've had that. Did it for more years than I can count. Kissing ass with the department chairman, sweating out tenure, fending off hordes of solemn, dense little faces all day and having them haunt you all night—and the worst part is you end up writing academic *poetry*. No, baby, believe me, *Food Field Observer* is a better deal."

"Why don't you apply for a whaddyacallit? A Guggenheim?"

"Had it. Had the Rockefeller, too."

"Can you tell me why the third book is lousy?"

"Ah, my whole life was a mess then. I'd just been divorced,

I was drinking too much; guess I thought I knew what I was doing in those poems, but I didn't know my ass from third base. Sentimental, self-indulgent, self-pitying—miserable stuff. The last time I saw Dudley Fitts he barely nodded to me."

"And how's your life now?"

"Oh, still pretty much of a mess, I guess, except I've found that sometimes"—he worked his hand up inside the sleeve of the bathrobe to her elbow, which he fondled as if it were an erogenous zone—"sometimes, if you play your cards right, you get to meet a nice girl."

For a week they were never apart—they spent the nights either at his place or at hers—and she never had enough solitude to read his first book, until she took a day off from work for that purpose.

It wasn't easy. She had read a lot of contemporary poetry at Barnard and always done well enough in her "explications," but she never read it for pleasure. She went through the early poems too quickly, getting only impressions of their ideas; then she had to go back and study each one to appreciate how it was made. The later poems were richer, though they retained the quality of seeming to have been spoken in Jack's voice, and almost the whole of the final section of the book was devoted to a single long poem, so intricate and containing what she guessed were so many levels of meaning that she had to read it three times. It was almost five o'clock before she was able to call him at the office and say she thought the book was great.

"Honest to God?" She could almost see the delight in his face. "You wouldn't bullshit me, would you, Emily? Which ones you like best?"

"Oh, I liked them all, Jack. Really. Let me think. I loved the one called 'A Celebration'; it almost made me cry."

"Oh?" He sounded disappointed. "Well, yeah, that's a pleasant little formal lyric, but it hasn't got much meat on its bones. What about the war poem, the one called 'Hand Grenade'?"

"Oh, yes, that one too. It has a nice—acidity to it."

"Acidity; good word. That's exactly what it was supposed to have. And of course I guess the only important question is what did you think of the last one. The big one."

"I was coming to that. It's beautiful, Jack. It's very, very moving. Hurry and come home."

Early in the summer he was invited to teach for two years in the Writers' Workshop at the State University of Iowa.

"You know something, baby?" he said when they'd both read the letter. "Might be kind of a mistake to turn this down."

"I thought you hated teaching."

"Well, but Iowa's different. The way I understand it, this 'Workshop' is wholly separate from the English department. It's a graduate program, kind of a professional school. The kids are carefully chosen—they're not really students at all, they're young writers—and the only 'teaching' I'd have to do would be four or five hours a week. Because the idea is, see, the teachers are supposed to produce their own stuff while they're out there, so they give you plenty of time. And I mean Christ, if I can't get this book wrapped up in two years there's something *really* the matter with me. Besides," he said, shyly rubbing his chin with his thumb, and she could tell that this next consideration would be the clincher of his argument. "Besides—oh, I know this sounds dumb, but it's kind of an honor to be invited out there. Must mean somebody doesn't think my last book sank me forever."

"Well, all right, Jack, but the honor's still there whether you accept the invitation or not. So think about it: do you really want to go to *Iowa*?"

They were both on their feet and pacing the floor of his apartment, as they'd been doing since he opened the letter. He walked over to her across the bare boards, put his arms around her and bent down to hide his face against her hair. "I do want to go," he said, "but I'll only go on one condition."

"What's that?"

"If you come with me," he said huskily, "and stay with me, and be my girl."

In August they both quit their jobs on *Food Field Observer*, and on the last weekend before they left for Iowa she took him out to St. Charles.

"...Oh, I *like* him," Sarah said when she and Emily were alone in the sun-shot kitchen. "I really like him a lot—and Tony does too, I can tell." She paused to lick a fragment of liver paste from her finger. "You know what *I* think you ought to do?"

"What?"

"Marry him."

"What do you mean, 'marry' him? You're always telling me to 'marry' people, Sarah. You say that about every man I bring *out* here. Is marriage supposed to be the answer to everything?"

Sarah looked hurt. "It's the answer to an awful lot of things."

And Emily almost said How would *you* know? but caught herself in time. Instead she said "Well, we'll see," and they carried plates of sloppily made hors d'oeuvres back into the living room.

"Well, of course, my war was a pretty dismal business," Jack was saying, "crawling around Guam with a radio on my back, but I do remember those sleek little Magnum Navy fighters. I used to wonder what it must be like to be up there in one of them, tooling around."

"You ought to see the ones we're turning out now," Tony said. "Jet fighters. Strap yourself into one of those jobs and *Shoom!*" He made a kind of salute, knifing the upright flat of his hand straight ahead from his temple to suggest the speed of the takeoff.

"Yeah," Jack said. "Yeah, I can imagine."

When the boys came in, out of breath, Emily tried not to be too effusive about how much they'd grown since her last visit, but the changes were remarkable. Tony Junior was fourteen now and big for his age, already built like his father. He was a nice-looking kid but there was something a little vacant about his smile, admitting at least the possibility that he might grow up to be an amiable fool; and Eric, the youngest, had developed a guarded look that was more sullen than shy. Only Peter, the middle one, the one Pookie always called her favorite, held her attention. He was thin and tense as a whippet; he had his mother's large brown eyes, and he looked intelligent even while chewing bubble gum.

"Hey, Aunt Emmy?" he said around his chewing. "Remember the Presidents you gave me when I was ten?"

"The present? What present?"

"No, the Presidents."

And finally she did remember. Every Christmas she spent too

many hours buying stuff for the boys; she would wade grudgingly through department stores on sore feet, breathing stale air and quarreling with exhausted clerks, and one year she had settled on what she could only hope was a suitable gift for Peter: a flat cardboard box containing white plastic statuettes of every American President through Eisenhower. "Oh, the *Presidents*," she said.

"Right. Anyway, I really enjoyed them."

"Oh, *did* he," Sarah said. "You know what he did? He made this big excavation out in the yard, like a park, with lawns and groves of trees and a river running through it, and bridges over the river, and he set up all the Presidents in different places, each with a different sized pedestal according to his reputation. He gave Lincoln the highest pedestal because he was the greatest, and he put the ones like Franklin Pierce and Millard Fillmore very low—oh, and he gave William Howard Taft a very wide pedestal because he was the fattest, and he—"

"Okay, Mom," Peter said.

"No, but really," she went on. "I wish you could've seen it. And you know what he did with Truman? At first he couldn't decide what to do with Truman, and then he—"

"I think you've about covered it, dear," Tony said with a barely perceptible wink at their guests.

"Oh," she said. "Well, all right." And she quickly took a drink to hide her mouth. That mannerism had never changed: whenever Sarah was embarrassed, after she'd told a joke and was waiting for the laughter, or when she was afraid she'd talked too much, she would go for her mouth as if to cover nakedness— with Cokes or popsicles as a child, with drinks or cigarettes now. Maybe all the years of splayed, protruding teeth, and then of braces, had made her mouth the most vulnerable part of her for life.

Later that afternoon the boys began wrestling on the floor until they knocked over a small table, and their father said "All right, men. Shape up." It was his standard, all-purpose admonition for them; evidently it was something he'd learned in the Navy.

"There's nothing for them to *do* in here, Tony," Sarah said.

"Let them go back outside, then."

"No," she said, "I've got a better idea." And she turned to Emily. "This is something you've *got* to see. Peter? Get the guitars."

Eric folded his arms across his chest to show he didn't mind being left out, and the older boys clambered into another room and came back with two cheap guitars. When they were sure their audience was ready they stood in the middle of the floor, filling the small house with sound, and gave an impersonation of the Everly Brothers:

> Bye bye, love
> Bye bye, happiness . . .

Tony Junior was only hitting a couple of simple chords and chanting the words; Peter did all the difficult finger-work, and he seemed to be putting his heart into the song.

"They're great kids, Sarah," Emily said when they'd gone outside again. "That Peter's really something."

"Have I told you what he wants to be when he grows up?"

"What—President?"

"No," Sarah said, as if that might be one of several viable alternatives. "No, you'd never guess. He wants to be an Episcopalian priest. I took them to the Easter service at the little church here in town a few years ago, and Peter never got over it. Now he gets me up to take him to church every Sunday, or else he hitch-hikes in."

"Oh, well," Emily said, "I imagine that's something he'll probably outgrow."

"Not if I know Peter."

At the dinner table, exhilarated by his afternoon of showing off, Peter interrupted the adults with so many silly remarks that Tony told him to shape up twice. The third time, when he put his napkin on his head, Sarah assumed command. "Peter," she said. "Shape up." She glanced quickly at Tony to see if she'd said it right, then at Emily to see if it had sounded funny, and then she hid her mouth in her glass.

"I understand you're on the radio," Jack Flanders said to Sarah later that evening, when the adults were alone in the living room.

"Oh, not any more," she said, looking pleased. "That's all

over now." In the early fifties she had served as "hostess" for a Saturday morning housewives' program on the local Suffolk County radio station—Emily had heard it once, and thought she did very well—but the program had expired after eighteen months. "It was only a little local station," Sarah explained, "but I did enjoy it—especially writing the scripts. I love to write."

And that led her into a subject she had clearly wanted to bring up for hours: she was writing a book. One of Geoffrey Wilson's ancestors on his mother's side, a New York man named George Fall, had been a Western pioneer. Together with a small group of other Easterners he had helped to clear and settle part of what was now Montana. Little was known about George Fall, but he had written many letters home during his adventures, and one of his nephews had transcribed them into the form of a pamphlet, privately printed, a copy of which had come into Geoffrey Wilson's possession.

"It's fascinating stuff," Sarah said. "Of course, it's pretty hard to read—it's all in this very quaint, old-fashioned style, and you have to use your imagination to fill in the gaps—but the material's all there. I figured somebody's got to do a book on this; it might as well be me."

"Well, that's—quite an undertaking, Sarah," Emily said, and Jack said it certainly did sound interesting.

Oh, the project was still in the very early stages, she assured them, as if to minimize their envy; she had made a rough outline, finished the Introduction and done a first draft of the opening chapter, but the chapter still needed work. She didn't even have a title yet, though she was thinking of calling it *George Fall's America*, and she would have to do a lot of library research on the period as she went along. The book would take time, but she loved doing it—and it was a wonderful feeling just to be *doing* something again.

"Mm," Emily said. "I can imagine."

"Might even be a little money in it," Tony said, chuckling. "*That*'d cert'ly be a wonderful feeling."

Sarah looked shy, and then suddenly bold. "Would you like to hear my Introduction?" she asked. "It isn't often I have an audience of two real writers. Darling?" she said to her husband.

"Why don't you fix us all another drink, and then I'll read my Introduction."

With her shoes off and her ankles snug beneath her buttocks, holding her trembling manuscript high in one hand and allowing her voice to fill out to the timbre appropriate for a small lecture hall, Sarah began to read aloud.

The Introduction told of how George Fall's letters had been preserved, and of how they had provided the basis for this book. There followed a brief summary of his travels that included many dates and place-names, and even that was easy to listen to: Emily was surprised at how well the sentences flowed; but then, Sarah's radio script had surprised her too.

Tony looked sleepy during the reading—he had probably heard it before—and his tolerant downcast smile, as he stared at his drink, seemed to say that if this sort of thing gave the little woman pleasure, well and good.

Sarah had reached her conclusion:

"George Fall was in many ways a noble man, but he was not unique. In his time there were countless others like him —men who dared, who gave up comfort and security to confront a wilderness, to face adversity against seemingly hopeless odds, to conquer a continent. In a very real sense, then, the story of George Fall is the story of America."

She put the manuscript down, looking shy again, and took a deep drink of whiskey and water.

"That's excellent, Sarah," Emily said. "Really excellent." And Jack said something polite to show he was in total agreement.

"Well, it probably needs work," Sarah said, "but that's the general idea."

". . . Your sister's very sweet," Jack Flanders said when he and Emily were on the train going home. "And she *does* write well; I wasn't just saying that."

"I wasn't just saying it either. I know she does. I can't get over how soft and dumpy she's getting, though. She used to have the most beautiful figure I've ever seen."

"Yeah, well, that happens to a lot of full-blown women," he

said. "That's why I like 'em skinny. No, but I see what you mean about your brother-in-law; he *is* kind of a boor."

"I always get the most terrible *headaches* when I go out there," Emily said. "I don't know why, but it never fails. Could you sort of rub the back of my neck?"

TWO

IOWA CITY WAS a pleasant town, built in the shadow of the university along a slow river. Some of the straight, tree-lined, sun-splashed residential streets reminded Emily of illustrations in *The Saturday Evening Post*—was this what America really did look like?—and she wanted to live in one of their ample old white houses; but then they discovered a small, odd-looking stone bungalow on a dirt road in the country, four miles out of town. It had been built as an artist's studio, the real estate lady explained; that accounted for the outsized living room and the tall picture window. "It wouldn't be at all practical for people with children," she said, "but for just the two of you it might be fun."

They bought a cheap used car and spent several evenings exploring the countryside, which turned out to be far less monotonous than they'd expected. "I thought it'd be all cornfields and prairies," Emily said, "didn't you? And here are all these rolling hills and woods—oh, and doesn't the air smell wonderful?"

"Mm. Yeah."

And it was always a pleasure to come home to the little house.

Soon there was a staff meeting from which Jack returned in an exultant mood. "I don't mean to depart from my customary boyish modesty, baby," he said, pacing the floor with a drink in his hand, "but I happen to be the best poet they've got out here. Maybe the *only* one. Jesus, you ought to meet these other clowns —you ought to *read* them."

She didn't read them, but she met them, at several raucous and confusing parties.

"I liked the older man," she told Jack as they drove home one night. "What's his name? Hugh Jarvis?"

"Yeah, well, Jarvis is okay, I guess. He wrote some good stuff twenty years ago, but he's washed up now. What'd you think of that little bastard Krueger?"

"He seemed very shy. I liked his wife, though; she's—interesting. She's somebody I'd like to get to know."

"Mm," he said. "Well, if that means having the Kruegers out for dinner, or anything like that, you'd better forget about it right now. I don't want that phony little son of a bitch in my house."

And so there was no one in the house but themselves. They were isolated. Jack had set up his work table in a corner of the main room and he sat there for most of the day, hunched over his pencil.

"You ought to use the *little* room for working," she said. "Wouldn't that be better?"

"No. I like being able to look up and see you. Moving in and out of the kitchen, hauling the vacuum cleaner, whatever the hell you're doing. Lets me know you're really here."

One morning, when the housework was done, she brought out her portable typewriter and set it up as far as possible across the room from him.

A NEW YORKER DISCOVERS THE MIDDLE WEST
Except for parts of New Jersey, and maybe Pennsylvania, I had always pictured everything between the Hudson River and the Rockies as a wasteland.

"Writing a letter?" Jack inquired.

"No; something else. Just a sort of idea I have. Does the typewriter bother you?"

" 'Course not."

The idea had been simmering in her mind for days, complete with that title and that lead; now she settled down to work.

There was Chicago, of course, a gritty and inadequate oasis to the north, and there were isolated spots like Madison, Wisconsin, renowned for their quaintly charming imitations of Eastern culture, but for the most part there was nothing to be found "out there" but vast reaches of corn and wheat and stifling ignorance. The cities bustled with people like George F. Babbitt; the numberless small towns were haunted by what F. Scott Fitzgerald called "their interminable inquisitions that spared only the children and the very old."

Was it any wonder that all the famous writers born in the Middle West had fled it as soon as they could? Oh, they might indulge themselves in sad rhapsodies about it afterwards, but that was only nostalgia; you never heard of them going back there to live.

As an Easterner, born in New York itself, I greatly enjoyed showing stray, bewildered Middle Western visitors through my part of the world. Here, I would explain; this is the way we

"Is this idea of yours a big secret?" Jack called from across the room, "Or can you tell me about it?"

"Oh, it's just—I don't know exactly what it is. It might turn into a magazine piece or something."

"Oh?"

"I don't know. I'm just fooling around."

"Good," he said. "That's what I'm doing, too."

On Mondays and Thursdays he disappeared into the campus, and when he came back he was always on edge—either chagrined or exhilarated, depending on how his class had gone.

"Ah, these kids," he grumbled once, pouring himself a drink, "these fucking kids. Give 'em half a chance and they'll eat you alive."

He drank too much on the good days, too, but he was better company: "Hell, this job's a breeze, baby, if you don't try too hard. Walk in there and talk about what you know, and they lap it up as if they'd never heard it before."

"Maybe they never *have* heard it before," she said. "I imagine you must be a very good teacher. You've certainly taught me a lot."

"Yeah?" He looked shy and greatly pleased. "About poetry, you mean?"

"About everything. About the world. About life."

And that night they could scarcely wait to be finished with their cooling dinner before they fell into bed.

"Oh, Emily," he said, stroking and fondling her. "Oh, baby, you know what you are? I keep saying 'You're great' and 'You're perfect' and 'You're tremendous,' but none of those words are right. You know what you are? You're magic. You're magic."

He told her she was magic so many times, on so many nights, that she finally said "Jack, I wish you'd stop saying that."

"Why?"

"Just because. It's getting a little old."

" 'Old,' huh? Okay." And he seemed hurt.

But she had never seen him happier than when he came home three hours late on one of his class days, a week or so later. "Sorry, sweetheart," he said. "I got to drinking with some of the kids after school. Did you eat?"

"Not yet; it's all in the oven."

"Damn. I would've called you, but I wasn't watching the time."

"That's all right."

As they ate dried-out pork chops, which he washed down with bourbon and water, he couldn't stop talking. "The damnedest thing: there's this kid Jim Maxwell—have I told you about him?"

"I don't think so."

"Big, burly guy; comes from some godforsaken place in south Texas, wears cowboy boots and all that. He always scares me in class because he's so tough—*and* so smart. Damn good poet, too, at least he will be soon. Anyway, tonight he waited until all the other kids'd left the bar, so it was just the two of us having one last round, and he gave me this very squinty look and said he had something to tell me. Then he said—damn, baby, this is too much—he said that when he read my first book it changed his life. Isn't that the God damnedest thing?"

"Well," she said. "That's a great compliment."

"No, but I mean I can't get over it. Can you imagine me writing anything that could change the life of some total stranger in south *Texas*?" And he forked a slice of pork chop into his mouth and chewed it mightily, savoring his pleasure.

By November he had come to admit, or rather to insist, that his own work wasn't going well at all. He would get up from his desk many times a day to stalk the floor, flipping cigarette butts into the fireplace (the bed of ashes in the fireplace became so choked with cigarette butts that only a roaring log fire would burn them out), and saying things like "Who the hell ever said I was supposed to be a poet anyway?"

"Can I read some of what you've been working on?" she asked once.

"No. You'd only lose what little respect for me you have left. You know what it's like? It's like bad light verse. Not even *good* light verse. Dum de dum de dum, and dum de diddly poo. I should've been a songwriter in the nineteen thirties, only I probably would've failed even at that. It'd take about twenty-seven of me to make an Irving Berlin." He stood slumped and staring out the big window at the yellowed grass and naked trees. "I read an interview with Irving Berlin once," he said. "The guy asked him what his greatest fear was, and he said 'Some day I'm going to reach for it, and it isn't going to be there.' Well, that's me, baby. I know I had it—I could feel it, the way you feel blood in your veins—and now I reach for it and reach for it, and it isn't there."

Then the long white Middle Western winter settled in. Jack went back to New York to visit his children over Christmas, and she had the little house to herself. It was lonely at first, until she found she rather enjoyed being alone. She tried working on her magazine article, but its dense, clotted paragraphs seemed to be getting nowhere; then on the third day she received an ebullient Christmas letter from her sister. She had been exclusively concerned with Jack Flanders for so long that it was oddly refreshing to sit down with this letter and remember who she was.

> . . . All is well at Great Hedges, and all send their love. Tony has been putting in much overtime, so we rarely get to see him. The boys are thriving . . .

Sarah's handwriting was still the neat, girlish script she had taught herself in junior high school. ("Well, it's sweet handwriting, dear," Pookie had told her, "but it's a little affected. Never mind, though; it'll develop more sophistication as you get older.") Emily skimmed through the inconsequential parts of the letter until she came to the meat of it:

As you may know, Pookie has lost her job—the real estate agency went bankrupt—and naturally we've been very concerned about her. But Geoffrey has come up with a very generous solution. He is fixing up the apartment over the garage into a nice little home for her, where she can live rent-free. She is eligible for Social Security. Tony feels it may be a little awkward having her here, and I agree—not that I don't love her, but you know what I mean—but I'm sure we'll all manage.

Now for the other big news: we are about to inherit the Main House! Geoffrey and Edna will be moving back to New York in the spring—she hasn't been at all well, & he is tired of the long commute & wants to be closer to his office. When they move out, we'll move in, and rent out the cottage for some badly needed income. Can you picture me taking care of that enormous place?

I have shelved *George Fall* because it turned out that I couldn't proceed very far without doing research in Montana. Can you imagine me ever getting to Montana? I am still writing, though, planning a series of humorous sketches about family life—the kind of thing Cornelia Otis Skinner does so well. I admire her work tremendously.

There was more—Sarah always ended her letters on a cheerful note, even if she had to force it—but the essential sadness of the message from St. Charles was clear.

When Jack got home he was filled with high purpose. No more fooling around, he announced. No more drinking too much every night. Above all, no more letting the students' work take up so much of his time. Did she realize he'd let things slide to the point where he was working on student manuscripts almost every day? What kind of nonsense was that?

"... Because here's the thing, Emily: I did a lot of thinking on this trip. Did me good to get away and kind of put things in perspective. The point is I think I do have a book. And the only thing that stands in the way of getting it done by summer—the *only* thing—is my own half-assedness. If I'm careful, and lucky—you have to be lucky as well as careful—I can bring it off."

"Well," she said. "That's wonderful, Jack."

The winter seemed to go on forever. The furnace broke down twice—they had to huddle at the fireplace all day wearing sweaters and coats, with blankets around their shoulders—and the car broke down three times. Even when both were in working order there was a pattern of bleak discomfort to the days. Going into town meant putting on heavy socks and boots, wrapping a muffler up to your chin and shivering until the car heater blew warm, gasoline-scented air in your face, then driving the four treacherous miles on ice and snow, under a sky as close and white as the snow itself.

One day when Emily was finished at the supermarket—she had learned how not to be stultified by the supermarket, how to deal with it in quick, competent movements that brought results—she sat for a long time in the steaming brilliance of the laundromat. She watched the whirl of suds and soaked cloth in the porthole of her machine; then she watched the other customers, trying to guess which were students and which were faculty and which were people from the town. She bought a chocolate bar and it tasted surprisingly good—as if, without her knowing it, sitting here and eating this chocolate was the one thing she had wanted to do all day. Waiting for the drying cycle to end she began to feel a vague dread, but it wasn't until she was at the warm, lint-speckled folding table that she figured it out: she didn't want to go home. And it wasn't the drive through snow and ice she dreaded, it was going home to Jack.

"Ah, that fucking Krueger," he said on slamming into the house one evening in February. "I'd like to kick his balls in, if he has any."

"Bill Krueger, you mean?"

"Yeah, yeah, 'Bill.' The cutesy-poo little bastard with the dimpled chin and the charming wife and the three cutesy-poo little girls." And that was all he said until he'd made himself a drink and finished half of it. Then, with one thumb at his temple and his hand spanning his brow, as if he were afraid to let her see his eyes, he said "Here's the thing, baby. Try to understand. I'm what the kids here call 'traditional.' I like Keats and Yeats and Hopkins and—shit, you know what I like. And Krueger's what they call 'experimental'—he's thrown everything overboard. His favorite critical adjective is 'audacious.' Some kid'll get stoned on pot and scribble out the first thing that comes into his head, and Krueger'll say 'Mm, that's a very audacious line.' His students are all alike, the snottiest, most irresponsible kids in town. They think the way to be a poet is to wear funny clothes and write sideways on the page. Krueger's published three books, got another one coming out this year, and he's in all the fucking magazines all the fucking time. You can't even pick *up* a magazine without finding William Fucking Krueger, and baby here's the kicker—here's the punch line: the little cocksucker is nine years younger than me."

"Oh. Well, so anyway, what happened?"

"Shit. This afternoon was what they call Valentine's Day. That means they pass out 'preference sheets' and the kids all write down which teacher they want for next semester; then the teachers get together afterwards and sort them out. You're not supposed to care about it, of course, and everybody acts very nonchalant, but my God you ought to see the red faces and the trembling hands. Anyway, I lost four of my kids to Krueger. Four. And one of them was Harvey Klein."

"Oh." She didn't know who Harvey Klein was—there were evenings when she didn't listen very carefully—but this was plainly an occasion for solace. "Well, Jack, I can certainly see how that would make you feel bad, but the point is it shouldn't. If I were a student in a place like this, *I'd* want to work with as many different teachers as I could. Doesn't that sound logical?"

"Not very."

"And besides, you didn't come out here to waste your energy hating Krueger—or even teaching Harvey Klein. You came here to get your own work done."

He took his hand away from his forehead, squeezed it into a fist and socked the table, which made her jump. "Right," he said. "Emily, you are absolutely right about that. The damn book is *all* that ought to concern me, every day. Even at this very minute, if I have half an hour before dinner I ought to be over there at the desk working, instead of bleeding on you with a lot of trivial, invidious shit like this. You're right, baby; you're right. I want to thank you for bringing it to my attention."

But he spent the rest of the evening in a silent, impenetrable gloom. It was either that night or a very few nights later that she woke up at three to find him gone from the bed. Then she heard him moving around in the kitchen, dropping ice cubes into a glass. The air around the bed was heavy with smoke, as if he'd lain here smoking for hours.

"Jack?" she called.

"Yeah. Sorry I woke you up."

"That's all right. Come on back to bed."

And he did, but he didn't get in. He sat slumped in his bathrobe in the darkness, drinking, and for a long time the only sound in the house was his occasional hacking cough.

"Oh, this isn't me, baby," he said at last. "This isn't me."

"What do you mean, it isn't you? It seems pretty much like you to me."

"I mean I wish to God you could've known me when I was working on my first book, or even my second. *That* was me. I was stronger then. I knew what the hell I was doing and I did it, and everything else fell into place around that. I didn't snivel and snarl and shout and retch and puke all the time. I didn't walk around like a man without skin, without flesh, worrying about what people *thought* of me. I wasn't—" He lowered his voice to show that this next point would be the most telling and damning of all—"I wasn't forty-three years old."

The coming of spring made everything a little better. For many days there was a warm, deep blue sky; the snow shriveled on the fields and even in the woods, and one morning on his way to school Jack came bursting back into the house to announce that he'd found a crocus in the yard.

They began taking long walks every afternoon, down the dirt road, out across the meadows and under the big trees. They didn't talk much—Jack usually walked with his head down and his hands in his pockets, brooding—but their time outdoors soon became the high point of Emily's day. She looked forward to it as eagerly as Jack looked forward to the drinks they had when they got home. Each afternoon she waited with growing impatience for the hour when she could put on her suede jacket, go over to his desk and say "Want to take a walk?"

"A walk," he would say, throwing down his pencil as if delighted to be rid of it. "By God, that's a great idea."

And the walks were even better after they inherited a dog from some neighbors down the road, a tan-and-white mongrel terrier named Cindy. She would lope along beside them or prance in circles around them, showing off, or go racing into the fields to burrow.

"Look, Jack," Emily said once, clutching his arm. "She's going into that pipe under the road—she wants to go through the whole thing and come out the other *side*." And when the dog emerged muddy and trembling from the far end of the pipe she called "Wonderful, Cindy! Oh, good dog! Good dog!" She clapped her hands. "Wasn't that neat, Jack?"

"Yeah. Sure was."

Their most memorable walk was on a breezy afternoon in April. They had gone farther than usual that day, and heading home across a great rutted field, tired but invigorated, they came to a solitary oak tree that seemed to reach into the sky like an enormous wrist and hand. It compelled them to silence as they stood in its shadow looking up through its branches, and they would both remember that Emily got the idea first. She took off her suede jacket and dropped it on the ground. Then she smiled at him—she thought he looked quite handsome with the wind blowing his hair flat against his forehead—and began unfastening the buttons of her blouse.

In no time at all they were naked and embracing on their knees; then he helped her to lie back on the moist earth, saying "Oh, baby; oh, baby . . ." And they both knew that Cindy would almost certainly begin to bark if anyone dared to approach this sacred place.

Half an hour later, back in the house, he looked up bashfully from his whiskey and said "Wow. Oh, wow. That was really— that was really something."

"Well," she said, lowering her eyes, and she could feel herself blushing, "what's the point of living in the country if you can't do things like that occasionally?"

It rained almost steadily for the next month. Dead earthworms littered the muddy walk from the door to the car, and last year's leaves were blown flat against the picture window to slide down in its streams. Emily took to spending hours at that window, sometimes reading but more often not, staring out into the rain.

"What do you *see* out there, anyway?" Jack asked her.

"Nothing much. Just thinking, I guess."

"What're you thinking about?"

"I don't know. I ought to take the laundry in."

"Ah, come on; the laundry can wait. All I mean is, if something's troubling you I'd like to know about it."

"No, no," she said. "Nothing's troubling me." And she went to get the laundry together.

When she passed his desk again on her way to the door, hauling the heavy denim bag, he looked up and said "Emily?"

"Mm?"

He was forty-three years old, but at that moment his half-smiling face looked as helpless as a child's. "You still like me?" he asked.

"Oh, of course," she told him, and busied herself with her raincoat.

Near the end of the spring semester he said he thought his book was substantially finished. But it wasn't a triumphant announcement, or even a happy one. "The thing is," he explained, "I don't feel ready to send it off yet. The important work is done, I think, but it needs cutting and pruning and fixing. I think it might be smart to hold it back for the summer. Set a deadline for myself in September and have the whole summer to go over it."

"Well," she said. "Good. You'll have three months without classes."

"I know; but I don't want to stay here. It'll get hot as a bitch and it'll be dead. Besides, do you realize how much money we've got in the bank? We could go damn near anywhere."

She had two quick visions—one of heavy surf crashing on rocks and white sand, East Coast or West, and one of purple, cloud-hung mountain ranges. Would love on a beach or love in the mountains be better than this? "Well," she said, "where do you want to go?"

"That's what I've been leading up to, baby." And the way he looked now reminded her of her father long ago on Christmas morning, when she and Sarah would tear into the wrappings of gifts that turned out to be exactly what they wanted. "How'd you like to go to Europe?"

They flew well ahead of the earth's turning; Heathrow Airport caught them dazed and trembling and gritty-eyed from lack of sleep at seven o'clock in the morning. There wasn't much to see on the ride into London—it seemed not very different than riding into New York from St. Charles—and the cheap hotel recommended by the travel agency was filled with wary, disoriented tourists like themselves.

Jack Flanders had lived in London with his wife soon after the war, and now he kept remarking on how much everything had changed. "The whole town's so American-looking," he said. "I guess we'll find that pretty much all over." But he insisted that the Underground was great—Wait'll you see how much better it is than the subways in New York"—and took her out to what he called his old neighborhood, where South Kensington and Chelsea are divided by the Fulham Road.

The bartender at his old pub failed to recognize him, until after Jack had spoken his name and shaken his hand; then he became very hearty, but it was clear from the way he didn't quite meet Jack's eyes that he was pretending.

"The point is I'm too *old* to care whether some half-assed bartender remembers me," Jack said as they drank warm beer at a corner table, well away from the dart game. "And besides, I've always hated Americans who come back from England with corny stories about marvelous little pubs. Let's get out of here."

He took her up a side street to the darkened house whose basement flat he had once occupied, and he drew away from her to stare at it, slumped and brooding, for a very long time. Emily stood near the curb looking idly up and down the street, which was so quiet she could hear the whir and click of the mechanism for changing the traffic light on the corner. She knew it was silly to be impatient—he might be working on an idea for a poem—but that didn't help increase her patience.

"Son of a bitch," he said quietly on turning away from the building at last. "Memories, memories. This was a mistake, baby, coming to this house; it's really shot me down. Let's get a drink. A real drink, I mean."

But the pubs were closed. "It's okay," he assured her. "There's a little club around this next corner called the Apron Strings; I used to be a member; I think they'll let us in. Might even run into some people I used to know." Instead they ran into a stone-faced West Indian doorman who denied them admission; the club had changed management since Jack's time.

They got into a taxicab and Jack leaned earnestly forward to address the driver. "Can you take us someplace where we can get a drink? I don't mean some clip joint; I mean a decent place where we can get a drink." And when he'd settled back beside Emily for the ride he said "I know you think this is dumb, baby, but if I don't get some whiskey in me tonight I'll *never* get to sleep."

They were greeted in an anteroom by a man in a tuxedo who looked Egyptian or Lebanese. "Is very expensive here," he told them with a kindly, confidential smile. "I would not recommend it." But Jack's thirst won out, and they sat in a dim carpeted cellar where an effeminate young Negro played sloppy cocktail piano, and where the bill for two drinks came to twenty-two dollars.

"Probably one of the all-time dumbest things I've ever done in my life," Jack said as they rode back to the hotel, and when they walked into the lobby they found the bar very much open for business. "Oh, *Jesus,*" he said, smiting his temple with the heel of his hand, "that's right—I'd forgotten. Hotel bars stay open late too. Isn't this the God damnedest thing? Well; guess we might as well have a nightcap."

Sipping whiskey she didn't want, hearing the strident dissonance of British and American voices—one handsome young Englishman at the bar reminded her of the way Tony Wilson had looked in 1941—Emily knew she was going to cry. She tried to avert it with a childhood trick that had sometimes worked before—pressing both thumbnails hard into the tender flesh beneath the nails of her index fingers, so that the self-inflicted pain might be greater than the ache of her swelling throat—but it was no use.

"You okay, baby?" Jack inquired. "You look—Oh, Jesus, you look like you're just about to—Wait. Wait'll I pay the check, and we'll—Can you hold it till we get upstairs?"

In their room she cried and cried, while he put his arms around her and stroked her and kissed her shuddering head, saying "Oh, baby, come on, now. I know it was awful, but it was all my fault; besides, it's only twenty-two dollars."

"It isn't the twenty-two dollars," she said.

"Well, the whole lousy evening, then. The way I dragged you out to see that house and went into one of my big self-indulgent depressions; the way I—"

"It isn't you; why do you always think everything's you? It's just—it's just that this is my first night in a foreign country and it's made me feel so—vulnerable." And that was true enough, she decided as she got up from the bed to blow her nose and wash her face, but it was only part of the truth. The rest of it was that she didn't want to travel with a man she didn't love.

Paris was better: everything looked just like the photographs of Paris she had studied all her life, and she wanted to walk for hours. "Aren't you getting tired?" Jack would say, lagging behind. He had lived here too, in the old days, but now as he trudged along with a look of petulant bewilderment in his eyes he was the picture of a bumbling American tourist. When they walked into the vast silence of Notre Dame she had to thrust two fingers in the back of his belt to restrain him from walking right into the little cluster of chairs where people were praying.

They had planned on an extended stay in Cannes, so that Jack could work. He said he'd done some of the best work of his life in Cannes; it held a sentimental attraction for him. Besides, it would be practical: she could be out at the beach all day while he secluded himself.

And she did enjoy the beach. She loved to swim, and she was willing to admit she liked the stares of approval she received from suntanned Frenchmen at the way she looked in her bikini.

Thin, yes, they seemed to say; small-breasted, certainly; but nice. Very nice.

When her day was over she would go back to the hotel and find their room blue and acrid with cigarette smoke. "How'd it go?" she would ask.

"Terrible." He'd be up and pacing, looking haggard. "You know something? A book of poems is no stronger than its weakest poem. And some of these—five or six of them—are so weak they're going to drag the others down. The whole damn book's going to sink like a stone."

"Take a day off. Come to the beach tomorrow."

"No, no; that won't help."

Nothing would help, and for days he fussed and grumbled. At last he said "It's too expensive here anyway; we're spending a fortune. We could try Italy, or Spain."

And they tried both.

She liked the architecture and sculpture of Florence—she kept seeing things she'd learned about in art-history classes long ago—and in the shops and stalls around the covered bridge she bought small gifts for Pookie and Sarah and the boys; but Rome was hot enough to melt your eyeballs. She almost fainted on her way to visit the Sistine Chapel: she had to sway and stagger into an unfriendly cafe for a glass of water; she had to sit staring into a Coca-Cola for a long time before she gathered strength to go back to the stifling hotel, where Jack was waiting with a pencil behind his ear and another one clamped in his teeth.

They both insisted they liked Barcelona—it had trees and sea breezes; they found a cool room within their price range, and there were good places to sit and have a beer in the afternoons—but Madrid was as inscrutable and unyielding as London. The only good thing about Madrid, Jack said, was the bar at their hotel, where you always got a generous shot-and-a-half in your glass when you ordered "whiskey escoso."

Then they were in Lisbon, and it was time to go home.

Nothing had changed in Iowa City. The sight of their little house, and then of the big room inside it, called up vivid memories of the year before: it was as if they had never been away.

Emily drove off to pick up Cindy from the house where they'd boarded her, and when the dog recognized her, wagging and quivering and showing her teeth, she realized she'd been looking forward to this moment all summer.

In October Jack said "Remember I said I'd set a September deadline for myself? That ought to teach you to trust me and my half-assed deadlines."

"Why don't you send it off the way it is?" she said. "A good editor could help you weed out the weak poems; maybe he could even help you make them better."

"Nah, nah, no editor's that good. Anyway it isn't just a few poems that're weak; the whole book has a sickly, neurotic cast to it. If I had the guts to let you read it you'd see what I mean. I'm going to do *one* thing you suggested, though. I'm going to move my stuff into the little room, and work there."

That was an improvement: she no longer had to feel he was watching her all day.

Soon after he started working in the little room she went in there to clean up, while he was gone at school, and tried to shift the placement of a heavy cardboard box containing winter clothes. It tipped and came open, and she found a fifth of bourbon, half full, that had lain hidden in the folds of an overcoat. She considered taking it out and putting it among the official bottles in the kitchen cabinet, but in the end she laid it carefully back where it seemed to belong.

She resurrected the manuscript of *A New Yorker Discovers the Middle West* and worked fairly steadily on it for some days, but she couldn't make it cohere. The trouble, she decided, was that the essential point of the article was a lie: she *hadn't* discovered the Middle West, any more than she had discovered Europe.

One Sunday morning she sat in the rocking chair in her robe, with Cindy sprawled across her lap. She held her breakfast coffee mug in one hand, stroking Cindy's bristly fur with the other, and she sang a childhood song in a small voice, scarcely aware of singing at all:

> How do you do, my Cindy?
> How do you do today?

Won't you be my partner?
I will show you the way.

"Know what?" Jack said, smiling at her from the breakfast table. "The way you carry on with that dog, anybody'd say you want a baby."

She was startled. "A baby?"

"Sure." He got up and came to stand beside her, and his fingers began to play with a lock of her hair. "Doesn't every woman want a baby sometime?"

The advantage of being seated, while he stood over her, was that she didn't have to meet his eyes. "Oh, I don't know," she said. "Sure, I guess so; sometime."

"It might be pointed out," he said, "that you're not getting any younger."

"What's all this *about*, Jack?"

"Let Cindy get down. Stand up. Come and give me a hug. Then I'll tell you." He wrapped her close in his arms and she put her head against his chest, so that it still was not required to look at his eyes. "Listen," he said. "When I got married I didn't know what I was doing; did it for all the wrong reasons; and for years now, ever since the divorce, I've been saying I'd never do it again. But the point is you've changed all that, Emily. Listen. Not now—oh, not now, baby, but soon—as soon as the damn book's done—do you think you might consider marrying me?"

He took both her hands and held her at arms' length. His eyes were shining, and his mouth was curling into a shape of shyness and pride like that of a boy who's just stolen his first kiss. There was a tiny trickle of egg yolk on his chin.

"Well, I don't know, Jack," she said. "It's a thing I'd have to think about, I guess."

"Okay." He looked hurt. "Okay; I know I'm no prize package."

"It isn't you; it's me. I just don't know if I'm ready for—"

"*Okay*, I said." And after a while he went into the little room and shut the door.

They still took walks nearly every afternoon—the country was rich with autumn foliage—but now it was Emily who tended to walk with her head down, keeping her own counsel, looking at her shoes. Without saying anything about it, they avoided the route that led past the solitary oak tree.

In November she made up her mind to leave him. She would go back to New York but not to *Food Field Observer*; she would find a better job, and a better apartment too; she would embark on a new and better life, and she would be free.

All that remained was breaking the news. She formed the opening phrases in her mind and rehearsed them several times: "Things aren't right, Jack. I think we both know that. I've decided the best thing to do, for both of us, is to . . ." And she sat waiting for him outside the closed door of the little room.

When he came out he moved as if he'd been shot in the back. He sank into the sofa across from her, and she looked at him closely for signs that he might have been nipping from the secret bottle, but he was sober. His eyes were as round as an actor's in the final moments of a tragedy.

"I can't," he announced, barely above a whisper, and she was reminded of the way Andrew Crawford had said "I can't" in bed, years ago.

"Can't what?"

"Can't write."

She had comforted him so often at times like this that now she was empty of all consolation and reassurance; she could only tell him what was true. "I wish you wouldn't say that," she said.

"You do? Well, so do I. I wish a lot of things."

It was clear that she couldn't tell him now. She waited two or three days, until she was damned if she'd wait any longer, and then she said it. "Things aren't right; I think we both know that. I've decided the best thing to do . . ."

She could never afterwards remember how she finished that sentence, or what reply he made to it, or what she said next. She remembered only his brief show of raffish indifference and then his rage, when he shouted and threw a whiskey glass against the wall—he seemed to feel he might get her to stay if only they had a loud enough quarrel—and then his collapse into pleading: "Oh, baby, don't do this; please don't do this to me . . ."

It was two in the morning before she could make a bed for herself on the sofa.

With the fall chilling rapidly into winter, she went back to New York alone.

THREE

SHE KNEW SHE was awake because she could see morning light in the pale floating shape of a closed Venetian blind, far away. It wasn't a dream: she was lying naked in bed with a strange man, in a strange place, with no memory of the night before. The man, whoever he was, had a heavy arm and leg flung around her, clamping her down, and in her struggle to free herself she knocked over a bedside table that fell with a crash of broken glass. It didn't wake him, but he groaned and turned away from her; that made it easy to crawl down to the foot of the bed and get out, avoiding the glass, and feel her way along the wall for a light switch. She didn't panic: nothing like this had ever happened to her before, but that didn't mean it would ever happen again. If she could find her clothes and get out of here and get a cab and go home it might still be possible to put the world in order.

When she found the switch the apartment sprang into existence around her, but she didn't recognize it. She still didn't recognize the man, either. He was facing away from her but she could see his profile; she studied it as carefully as if she were making a drawing from life, but it meant nothing. The only familiar things in the room were her clothes, draped over the back of a corduroy armchair not far from where the man's shoes and pants and shirt and underwear lay strewn on the floor. The word "sordid" came into her mind; this was sordid.

She got dressed quickly and found the bathroom, and while combing her hair at the mirror she realized that getting out of here wasn't absolutely essential; there was another alternative. She could take a hot shower and go to the kitchen and make coffee and wait for him to wake up; she could greet him with a pleasant morning smile—a slightly reserved, sophisticated smile—and as they talked she'd be sure to remember everything she had to know: who he was, how they'd met, where she'd

been last night. It would all come back, and she might easily
decide she liked him. He might make Bloody Marys to ease
their hangovers, and take her out for breakfast, and it might
turn out to be—

But this was the counsel of irresponsibility, of promiscuity, of
sordidness, and she quickly decided against it. Back in the room
where he slept she righted the spindly table that had fallen with
its load of bottles and glasses. She found a sheet of paper and
wrote a note for him, which she propped on the table:

> Be careful:
> Broken glass on floor.
>   E.

Then she let herself out of the apartment and was free. It wasn't
until she was on the street—it turned out to be Morton Street,
near Seventh Avenue—that she felt the weight of all the unaccustomed drinking she must have done last night. The sun assaulted
her, sending yellow streaks of pain deep into her skull; she could
barely see, and her hand shook badly in trying to open the door
of a taxicab. But riding home, inhaling the hot wind that came
in through the cab window, she began to feel better. It was
Saturday—how could she be so sure it was Saturday when she'd
forgotten everything else?—and that gave her two full days of
recuperation before she had to go back to work.

It was the summer of 1961, and she was thirty-six.

Soon after coming back from Iowa she'd been hired as a copywriter for a small advertising agency, and she'd become something of a protégée to the woman who ran it. It was a good job,
though she would rather have been in journalism, and the best
part of it was that she could live in a high, spacious apartment
near Gramercy Park.

"Morning, Miss Grimes," said Frank, at the desk. There was
nothing in his face to suggest that he might have guessed how
she'd spent the night, but she couldn't be sure: she walked
through the lobby with a bearing of unusual severity, in case he
was following her with his eyes.

The wallpaper of the hallway was patterned in a yellow-on-
gray design of rearing horses; she had passed it hundreds of times

without a glance, but now the first thing she saw on getting off the elevator was that someone had penciled a long, thick penis jutting out from between one of the horses' hind legs, with big testicles slung beneath it. Her first impulse was to find a pencil eraser and rub it out, but she knew that wouldn't work: it would have to be obliterated with new paper.

Alone and safe behind her own locked door, she took pleasure in finding that everything in her home was clean. She spent half an hour soaping and scrubbing herself in the shower, and while there she began to remember the events of the night. She had gone to the apartment of a married couple she scarcely knew, in the East Sixties, and it had turned out to be a bigger, noisier party than she'd expected—that accounted for the nervousness that had made her drink too fast. She closed her eyes under the pelting of hot water and recalled a sea of talking, laughing people out of which several strangers' faces came up close: a jolly bald man who said the whole preposterous idea of Kennedy for President had been a triumph of money and public relations; a thin, dapper fellow in an expensive suit who said "I understand you're in the ad game too"; and the man who was probably the one she'd slept with, whose earnest voice had talked to her for what seemed like hours and whose plain, heavy-browed face was very likely the face she had studied this morning. But she couldn't remember his name. Ned? Ted? It was something like that.

She put on clean, comfortable clothes and drank coffee—she would have loved a beer but was afraid to open one and was just beginning to enjoy a sense of her life's coming back to solidity when the telephone rang. He had struggled awake; he had groaned through his own morning ablutions and guzzled a beer; he had found the number she'd probably given him and prepared a courtly little greeting for her, a mixture of apology and reawakened desire. Now he would ask her out for breakfast, or lunch, and she would have to decide what to say. She bit her lip and let the phone ring four times before she picked it up. "Emmy?" It was her sister Sarah's voice, and it sounded like that of a shy, serious child. "Look, it's about Pookie, and I'm afraid it's bad news."

"Is she dead?"

"No; but she's very—Let me start at the beginning, okay? I hadn't seen her for four or five days, which was sort of strange because she's usually—you know—over here quite a lot, so this morning I sent Eric over to the garage apartment to sort of check on her, and he came running back and said 'Mom, you better get over there.' She was lying on the living-room floor without any clothes on, and at first I thought she *was* dead: I couldn't even tell if she was breathing, but I was pretty sure I could feel a very faint pulse. Another thing: she'd gone to the—Can I be basic?"

"You mean she'd emptied her bowels?"

"That's right."

"Well, Sarah, people do that when they're—"

"I know, but there was a pulse. Anyway, as luck would have it our own doctor is on vacation, and the man filling in for him is this kind of rude young guy I'd never seen before; he examined her and said she was alive but in a coma, and he asked me how old she was and I couldn't tell him—*you* know how Pookie's always been about her age—and he looked around and saw all these empty whiskey bottles and he said 'Well, Mrs. Wilson, nobody lives forever.' "

"Is she in the hospital now?"

"Not yet. He said he'd make arrangements but it might take time. He said we could expect the ambulance some time this afternoon."

It still hadn't come by the time Emily eased herself off the sweltering train at St. Charles, where Sarah met her in the old Plymouth she shared with her sons. "*Oh*, I'm so glad you're here, Emmy," she said. "I feel better about everything already." And driving very slowly, puzzling over the gearshift and the floor pedals as if she'd never quite mastered the knack of them, she began to take her sister home.

"It's funny," Emily said as they passed a giant pink-and-white shopping center. "When I first came out here this was all open country."

"Things change, dear," Sarah said.

But nothing was changed about the old Wilson place, except that tall weeds had long eclipsed the little GREAT HEDGES sign.

Tony's maroon Thunderbird stood glistening in the driveway. He bought himself a new one every other year, and nobody else was allowed to drive it; Sarah had explained once that this was his sole extravagance.

"Is Tony home?" Emily asked.

"No; he went off fishing for the day with some of the guys from Magnum. He doesn't even know about any of this yet." Then, after she'd parked at a respectful distance from the Thunderbird and gotten out to stand frowning over the car keys in her hand, she said "Look, Emmy, I know you must be starving but I think we ought to look in on Pookie first. I mean I don't want to have her just *lying* there, okay?"

"Sure," Emily said. "Sure; of course." And they walked on crunching gravel to the sunbaked box of the "garage," whose garage space was too narrow for modern automobiles. Emily had visited her mother in the upstairs apartment several times— listening to her talk for hours under the close beaverboard ceiling, staring at photographs of herself and Sarah as children on the smudged beaverboard walls, waiting for the first possible chance of escape—but nothing prepared her for what she found now at the top of the creaking stairs.

The naked old woman lay face down, as if she'd tripped on the rug and fallen forward. The heat of the place was all but unbearable—she might easily have collapsed from the heat alone —and it was true about the whiskey bottles: there were six or eight of them around the room, all "Bellows Partners' Choice" and all empty. (Had she been embarrassed to put so many bottles into the trash for one of the boys to remove?)

"Girls, I'm terribly sorry about all this," she seemed to be saying. "Isn't there something we can do?"

"Do you think we could get her into bed?" Sarah said. "For when the ambulance comes?"

"Right. Good idea."

First they prepared the bedroom. The tangled sheets looked as if they hadn't been changed for many weeks, and Sarah couldn't find clean ones, but they did their best to make the bed presentable; then they went back to get her. They were both sweating freely by this time and breathing hard. Crouching, they eased her over on her back. Emily took her under the armpits and Sarah under the knees, and they carried her. She was small but very heavy.

"Careful of this door frame," Sarah said, "it's narrow."

They sat her on the bed and held her upright while Sarah worked with a comb at her sparse hair.

"Never mind that, dear," she seemed to say as her loose head wobbled under the comb. "I can do that later. Just cover me. Cover me."

"There," Sarah said. "That's a little better. Now, if you can sort of turn her, I'll bring her feet up and we'll—that's it—easy; easy—there."

She was lying face-up with her head on the pillow, and her daughters stood back from the ugly old body with a sense of relief and accomplishment.

"You know something?" Sarah said brightly. "I'd give a lot to have that good a figure when *I'm* her age."

"Mm. Does she have a nightgown or something?"

"I don't know; let's look."

All they could find was a light summer robe that was almost clean. Stooping and jostling each other, they worked a sleeve of it up one soft arm and stuffed the flimsy cloth under her back to bring the other sleeve into place; when the robe was finally closed and fastened their mother was dressed, and they drew the top sheet up to her chin.

"Well, I can tell you it hasn't been easy," Sarah said as they went back into the living room to gather up the whiskey bottles. "It hasn't been easy having her here over the past—what's it been now, four years?"

"I can imagine."

"I mean *look* at this place." Holding three or four bottles in one arm, she used her free hand to gesture around the apartment. Every surface in sight was filmed with grime. The ashtrays were heaped to overflowing with very short cigarette butts. "And come here; look at this." She led Emily into the bathroom and pointed down the toilet bowl, which was brown both above and below the water-line. "*Oh*, if only she could have stayed in the city," Sarah said, "with things to do and people to see. Because the thing is there was never anything for her to *do* out here. She'd always be over at the house, and she wouldn't watch television; she wouldn't let us watch television; she'd talk and talk and talk until Tony was nearly out of his mind, and she'd—she'd—"

"I know, baby," Emily said.

They went downstairs—the fresh air felt good, even in the heat —and carried their armloads of whiskey bottles to the kitchen door of the main house, where they pressed them deep into a garbage can that was crawling with flies.

"You know what I think?" Sarah said as they sat exhausted at the kitchen table. "I think we both deserve a drink."

The ambulance arrived in midafternoon—four quick, vigorous young men in gleaming white who seemed to enjoy their work. They strapped the old woman into an aluminum stretcher, brought her downstairs with swift delicacy, shoved her inside their vehicle and slammed its doors and were gone.

That evening Sarah drove Emily to the hospital, where a tired-looking doctor explained the nature of a cerebral hemorrhage. Their mother might die in the next day or so, he said, or she might live for a good many years with severe brain damage. In the latter case, she would probably have to be institutionalized.

". . . And of course institutions cost money," Sarah said as they rode slowly homeward through the clean new suburbs, "and we haven't *got* any money."

EAT, said a big electric sign just ahead; beneath it, in smaller letters, was the word COCKTAILS, and Sarah steered the old Plymouth into the parking lot.

"I didn't feel like going home just yet anyway," she said, "did you?" When they were settled in a slick booth inside she said "I really wanted the air conditioning more than the drink; doesn't it feel wonderful?" Then she raised her glass for a toast, looking suddenly very young, and said "Here's to Pookie's making a full recovery."

"Well," Emily said, "I don't think we'd better count on anything like that, Sarah. The doctor said—"

"I know what he said," she insisted, "but I know Pookie, too. She's a remarkable woman. She's tough. *I* bet she bounces back from this. Just wait and see."

There was no point in arguing; Emily agreed that they would wait and see. For a little while there was no talk at all, and Emily used the silence to dwell with bewilderment and chagrin on the way she had woken up this morning. Ned? Ted? Would she ever figure it out? Had she had what drunks call a blackout?

When she came into focus on her sister's face again it was bright with proud talk about Peter, who would be starting college in the fall, and who viewed college only as a necessary preparation for being accepted into General Theological Seminary.

"... All these years, and his ambition hasn't wavered once. That's what he wants to do, and he's going to do it. He's a remarkable boy."

"Mm. And how about Tony Junior? He must've finished high school last year."

"That's right; except the thing is he didn't graduate."

"Oh? You mean his grades weren't good enough?"

"That's right. Oh, he *could* have graduated, but he spent practically the whole year running around with this—haven't I told you about that?"

"A girl, you mean?"

"She's not a girl, that's the whole point. She's thirty-five years *old*. She's divorced and she's rich and she's ruining him. Ruining him. I can't even talk to him any more, and neither can his father. Even Peter can't talk to him."

"Oh, well," Emily said, "a lot of boys go through things like that. I imagine he'll be all right. Probably be a good thing for him, in the long run."

"That's what his father says." Sarah looked pensively into her glass. "And Eric—well, Eric's sort of like Tony Junior. Sort of like his father, too, I suppose. Never been a student; all he cares about is cars."

"Are you—getting any writing done, Sarah?"

"Oh, not really. I've more or less given up on the humorous family-life sketches. I did four of them, but Tony said they weren't funny. He said they were good—well-written, good details, held your interest and all that—but he said they weren't funny. Maybe I was trying too hard."

"Could I read them sometime?"

"Sure, if you want to. Only you probably won't think they're funny either. I don't know. Humor is a lot harder than—you know—serious stuff. Harder for me, anyway."

And Emily's mind went away again, thinking of her own troubles; she returned only when she realized that Sarah had brought the conversation around to money.

". . . And have you any idea what Tony's take-home pay from Magnum is?" she was saying. "Wait, look; here, I'll show you." She rummaged in her purse. "Here's the stub from his last pay-check. Just look."

Emily had expected it wouldn't be much, but even so she was surprised: it was a little less than she earned at the advertising agency.

"And he's worked there twenty-one years," Sarah said. "Can you imagine? It's that old, old, stupid old business of the college degree, you see. All the men his age with engineering degrees are in top management now. Of course Tony has a supervisory position too, but it's much lower down in the—you know—in the organization. Our only other income is the rent from the cottage, and most of that goes into upkeep. And have you any idea of the *taxes* we pay?"

"I guess I've always thought old Geoffrey helped you out to some extent."

"Geoffrey's poorer than we are, dear. That little import office barely pays their rent in the city, and Edna's been very sick."

"So there isn't any—inheritance, or anything."

"Inheritance? Oh, no. There's never been anything like that."

"Well, Sarah, how do you manage?"

"Oh, we do. Just barely, but we manage. On the first of every month I sit down at the dining-room table—and I make the boys sit down with me too, at least I did when they were younger; it's been good for them to learn about handling money—and I divide everything into accounts. First and foremost is the G.H. account. That covers—"

" 'G.H.'?"

"Great Hedges," Sarah said.

"Why do you call the place that?"

"What do you mean? It's *al*ways been called—"

"Pookie gave it that name, baby. I was there when she thought it up."

"She did?" And Sarah looked so stunned that Emily was sorry she'd said it. They both reached for their drinks.

"Look, Sarah," Emily began. "It's probably none of my business, but why don't you and Tony sell that place? The houses wouldn't be worth anything, but think of the land. You've got eight acres in one of the fastest-growing parts of Long Island. You could probably get—"

Sarah was shaking her head. "No; no, that's out of the question. We couldn't do that; it wouldn't be fair to the boys. They love the place, you see. It's their home. It's the only home they've ever known. Remember how awful it was when we were little? Never having a—"

"But the boys are *grown*," Emily said, and the alcohol was beginning to work in her: she spoke more sharply than she'd meant to. "They'll all be leaving soon. Isn't it time for you and Tony to think of yourselves? The point is you could get a good, efficient modern house for *half* what you're spending on—"

"That's another thing," Sarah said. "Even if it weren't for the boys, I can't quite picture Tony and me in some pedantic little—"

" 'Pedantic'?"

"*You* know, some conventional little ranch house like all the others."

"That isn't what 'pedantic' means."

"It isn't? I thought it meant conventional. Anyway, I don't see how we could ever do a thing like that."

"Why not?"

The argument went on for half an hour, going over and over the same ground, until in the end, when they were getting up to go back to the car. Sarah suddenly gave in. "Oh, you're right, Emmy," she said. "It *would* be good for us to sell the place. Good for the boys, too. There's just one hitch."

"What's that?"

"You'd never convince Tony."

Back at the house they walked through the garbage-smelling kitchen, through the dining room, across the musty, creaking living room—where Emily always expected to find old Edna curled up and smiling on the sofa—and into what Sarah called the den, where Tony and Peter were watching television.

"Hi, Aunt Emmy," Peter said in a manly voice, getting to his feet.

Tony rose slowly, as if reluctant to leave the screen, and came forward with a can of beer in his hand. He was still in his fishing clothes, speckled with bait stains, and his face was bright with sunburn. "I say," he said. "I'm ve'y sorry about Pewkeh."

Peter turned off the booming television and Sarah gave them a full report on what the doctor had said, concluding with her own fact-defying prognosis: "*I* bet she bounces back."

"Mm," Tony said.

For hours that night—long after Tony and Peter had gone to bed, long after Eric and even Tony Junior had come slouching in with mumbled greetings for their aunt and mumbled expressions of sorrow about their grandmother—the Grimes sisters stayed up to talk and drink. They started out in the den and later moved into the living room, which Sarah said was cooler. There Emily sat cross-legged on the floor, for easy access to the liquor on the coffee table, and Sarah sank into the sofa.

"... And I'll never forget Tenafly," Sarah was saying. "Remember when we lived in Tenafly? In that sort of stucco house with the bathroom on the ground floor?"

"Sure I remember."

"I was nine then and you must have been about five; it was the first place we lived after the divorce. Anyway, Daddy came out to visit us there once, and after you were in bed he took me out for a walk. We went to the drugstore and had black-and-white ice-cream sodas. And on the way home—I can still remember that street, the way it curved around—on the way home he said 'Baby, can I ask you a question?' Then he said 'Who do you love more, your mother or me?' "

"My God. Did he really say that? And what did you say?"

"I told him—" Sarah sniffled. "I told him I'd have to think it over. Oh, I knew, of course"—her voice wavered out of control, but she recovered it—"I knew I loved him much, much more than Pookie, but it seemed terribly disloyal to Pookie to come right out and say it. So I said I'd think it over and tell him the next day. He said 'You promise? If I call you on the telephone tomorrow, will you tell me then?' And I promised. I remember not being able to look Pookie in the face that night and not sleeping very well, but when he called up I told him. I said 'You, Daddy,' and I thought he was going to cry, right there on the phone. He used to cry a lot, you know."

"He did? I never saw him cry."

"Well, he did. He was a very emotional man. Anyway, he said 'That's wonderful, sweetheart,' and I remember being relieved that he wasn't crying. Then he said 'Listen. As soon as I can arrange a few things I'm going to have you come and live with me. It might not be right away but it'll be soon, and we'll be together always.'"

"God," Emily said. "And then of course he never did anything about it."

"Oh, I stopped expecting it to happen after a while; I stopped thinking about it."

"And you had to go on living with Pookie and me." Emily fumbled for a cigarette. "I had no idea you went through anything like that."

"Oh, don't misunderstand," Sarah said. "He loved you too; he always used to ask me about you, especially later, when you were growing up—what you were like, what you'd like for your birthday—*you* know. It's just that he never really got to know you very well."

"I know." Emily took a drink, finding her keen sense of melancholy enhanced by the way the alcohol seemed to go straight from the roof of her mouth into her veins. She had a story of her own to tell now; it might not be as sad a story as Sarah's, but it would do. "Remember Larchmont?" she began.

"Sure."

"Well, when Daddy came out for Christmas that year . . ." She told of how she'd lain awake to hear her parents talking and talking downstairs and how she'd called out for her mother, who had come up smelling of gin and said they were "coming to a new understanding," and how all hope had been lost the next day.

Sarah was nodding in corroboration. "I know," she said. "I remember that night. I was awake too. I heard you call out."

"You did?"

"And I heard Pookie come up. I was as excited as you were. And then a little later, maybe half an hour later, I got up and went downstairs."

"You went downstairs?"

"And there wasn't much light in the living room, but I could see them lying together on the sofa."

Emily swallowed. "You mean they were—getting laid?"

"Well, there wasn't much light, but he was on top and it was —you know—it was a very passionate embrace." And Sarah brought her glass up quickly to hide her mouth.

"Oh," Emily said. "I see."

They were both silent for a while. Then Emily said "I wish you'd told me that a long time ago, Sarah. Or no, come to think of it, I guess I'm glad you didn't. Tell me something else. Have you ever understood why they got divorced? Oh, I know *her* version—she felt 'stifled'; she wanted freedom; she always used to compare herself with the woman in *A Doll's House*."

"*A Doll's House*, right. Well, it was partly that; but then a couple of years after the divorce she decided she wanted to come back to him, and he wouldn't have her."

"You sure?"

"Positive."

"Why?"

"Well, think about it, Emmy. If you were a man, would you have taken her back?"

Emily thought about it. "No. But then, why did he ever marry her in the first place?"

"Oh, he loved her; don't worry about that. He told me once she was the most fascinating woman he'd ever met."

"You're kidding."

"Well, maybe he didn't say 'fascinating.' But he said she cast a spell."

Emily studied the drink in her hand. "When did you *have* all these talks with him, anyway?"

"Oh, mostly during the time I had braces. I didn't *have* to go into the city once a week, you see—the dentist only wanted to see me once a month. That once-a-week story was something Daddy and I made up, so we'd have more time together. Pookie never did figure it out."

"Neither did I." And even now, at thirty-six, Emily was jealous. "And who was Irene Hammond?" she asked. "The lady I met at Daddy's funeral?"

"Oh, Irene Hammond was only around in the last few years, toward the end of his life. There were others."

"There were? Did you meet them?"

"Some of them. Two or three of them."

"Were they nice?"

"One of them I didn't like at all; the others were all right."

"Why do you suppose he never married again?"

"I don't know. He said once—this was when I was engaged to Donald Clellon—he said that a man ought to be happy in his work before he got married, and maybe it was partly that. He was never happy in his work, you see. I mean, he'd wanted to be a great reporter, somebody like Richard Harding Davis, or Heywood Broun. I don't think he ever understood why he was only—you know—only a copy-desk man."

And that did it. They had been holding back tears all evening, all night, but that phrase was too much. Sarah started crying first and Emily got up from the floor to take her in her arms and comfort her, until it was clear that she couldn't comfort anyone because she was crying too. With their mother lying in a coma twenty miles away, they clung together drunkenly and wept for the loss of their father.

Pookie didn't die the next day, or the day after that. By the end of the third day it was assumed that her condition was "stabilized," and Emily decided to go home. She wanted to be back in her air-conditioned apartment, where nothing smelled of mildew and everything was clean, and she wanted to get back to work.

"Pity we don't see more of you, Emmy," Tony said as he drove her swiftly to the station in his Thunderbird. When he parked near the platform to wait for the train, she realized she might never have a better chance than this for bringing up the question of selling the place. She tried to do it tactfully, making clear that she knew it was none of her business, implying that it must surely be something he'd thought about before.

"Oh, God, yes," he said as they heard the sound of the approaching train. "I'd love to be rid of it all. Let them take a bulldozer and bury it. If it were up to me I'd—"

"You mean it *isn't* up to you?"

"Oh, no, pet; it's Sarah, you see. She'd never hear of it."

"But Sarah says she *wants* to do it. She told me *you* were the one who didn't."

"Oh?" he said, looking bemused. "That so?"

The train was on them with an overwhelming noise; there was nothing for Emily to do but say goodbye.

When she got off the elevator at her floor—the great cock and balls still protruded from the wallpaper horse—she was almost too tired to stand. The apartment was as cool and welcoming as she'd known it would be, and she sank into a deep chair with her heels sliding straight out on the floor. This was fatigue. Tomorrow she would ride uptown to Baldwin Advertising, she would do her job with all the intelligence and efficiency they had come to expect of her, and she would drink nothing for a week except a beer or a glass of wine after work each day. In no time at all she would be herself again.

But meanwhile it was only eight o'clock in the evening; there was nothing in the place she wanted to read; nothing to watch on television; nothing to do but sit here and go over and over the time in St. Charles in her mind. After a while she was up and pacing the floor with her fist in her mouth. Then her telephone rang.

"Emily?" said a man's voice. "Oh, wow, are you really there? I've been calling you and calling you."

"Who's this?"

"It's Ted; Ted Banks—Friday night, remember? I've been calling you since Saturday morning—three, four times a day, and you were never home. Are you okay?"

Hearing his voice and his last name brought it all back. She could see his plain, heavy-browed face now and remember the shape and the weight and the feel of him; she could remember everything. "I was out of town for a few days," she said. "My mother was very ill."

"Oh? How is she now?"

"She's—better."

"Good. Look, Emily, first of all I want to apologize—I haven't had that much to drink in years and years. I'm not used to it."

"I'm not either."

"So if I made a total fool of myself I'm terribly—"

"That's okay; we were both pretty foolish." She wasn't tired any more, except in a pleasant, well-earned way. She felt good.

"Well, listen: do you think I could see you again?"

"Sure, Ted."

"Oh, great; that's great. Because I really—When? How soon?"

She looked with pleasure around her apartment. Everything was clean; everything was ready. "Well," she said, "almost anytime, Ted. Why not tonight? Give me half an hour to wash up and change, and then—you know—come on over."

FOUR

THE NURSING HOME, a modest Episcopalian retreat at which the Grimes sisters shared the cost of their mother's care, lay roughly halfway between the city and St. Charles. At first Emily went out there once a month; later she cut it down to three or four times a year. Her first visit, in the autumn after Pookie's collapse, was the most memorable.

"Emmy!" the old woman cried, lying half-raised in her hospital bed. "I *knew* you'd come today!"

At first glance she looked startlingly well—her eyes gleamed and her false teeth were bared in a triumphant smile—but then she began to talk. Her wet mouth labored, slurring syllables in a slow parody of the way she'd talked all her life.

"... And isn't it wonderful how everything's worked out so well for us? Just imagine! Sarah's a real princess, and look at *you*. I always knew there was something special about our family."

"Mm," Emily said. "Well, you're looking fine. How do you feel?"

"Oh, I'm a little tired, but I'm just so happy—so happy and so proud of you both. Especially you, Emmy. Lots of girls marry into European royalty—only, you know something funny? I still haven't learned to pronounce his last name!—but how many ever get to be First Lady?"

"Are you—comfortable here?"

"Oh, it's nice enough—of course I knew it'd be nice, built right into the White House—but I'll tell you something, dear." She lowered her voice to an urgent stage whisper. "Some of these nurses don't know how to behave when they're dealing with the President's mother-in-law. Anyway—" She settled back on her pillow. "Anyway, I know you must be terribly busy; I won't keep you. *He* stopped by to see me the other day."

"He did?"

404

"Oh, just for a few minutes, after his press conference, and he called me Pookie and gave me a little kiss. Such a handsome figure of a man, with that beautiful smile. He has such—such flair. Just imagine! The youngest man ever elected President in American history."

Emily planned her next sentence carefully. "Pookie," she said, "have you been having a lot of dreams?"

The old woman blinked several times. "Dreams, oh, yes. Sometimes—" She looked suddenly frightened. "Sometimes I have bad dreams, terrible dreams about all kinds of terrible things, but I always wake up." Her face relaxed. "And when I wake up everything's wonderful again . . ."

On her way out of the place, passing the open doors of many murmurous rooms filled with beds and wheelchairs, occasionally glimpsing an ancient person's head, she found a nurses' station where two thick-legged young women in white were drinking coffee and reading magazines.

"Excuse me. I'm Mrs. Grimes's daughter—Mrs. Grimes in Two-F."

One of the nurses said "Oh, you must be Mrs. Kennedy"; the other, with a tired little smile to show she was only kidding, said "Can I have your autograph?"

"That's what I wanted to ask about. Is she always this way?"

"Sometimes; not always."

"Does her doctor know about it?"

"Well, you'd have to ask him. Doctor's only here Tuesday and Friday mornings."

"I see," Emily said. "Well, look: is it better to sort of play along with her in something like this, or to try and—"

"Doesn't make much difference, one way or the other," the nurse said. "I wouldn't worry about it, Mrs. —?"

"Grimes; I'm not married."

The delusion didn't last long. Throughout the winter Pookie seemed to know who she was, most of the time, but her talk was much less coherent. She was able to sit in her chair and even to walk around, though once she splattered the floor with urine. By spring she had turned morose and silent, speaking only to complain of her failing eyesight and the nurses' neglect and the shortage of cigarettes. Once, having demanded that a nurse bring her a lipstick and a mirror, she studied her frowning reflection and daubed a full, crimson mouth on the surface of the mirror.

During that year Emily was promoted to "copy supervisor" of Baldwin Advertising. Hannah Baldwin, a trim and vigorous "gal" in her fifties who liked to have it known that hers was one of the only three agencies in New York run by a woman, told her she had a real future in the business. "We love you, Emily," she said more than once, and Emily had to admit it was reciprocated. Oh, not love, exactly—surely not love on either side—more of a mutual respect and satisfaction. She enjoyed her work.

But she enjoyed her leisure a great deal more. Ted Banks lasted only a few months; the trouble was mainly that they both felt an irresistible urge to drink too much when they were together, as if they didn't want to touch each other sober.

Things were on a much more intelligent footing with Michael Hogan. He was a rugged, energetic, surprisingly gentle man; he ran a small public relations firm, but talked so little about his work that she sometimes forgot what he did for a living, and the best thing about him was that he made almost no emotional demands on her. It couldn't even be said that they were close friends: whole weeks might pass without her hearing from him, or caring, and when he did call ("Emily? Feel like having dinner?") it was as if they'd never been apart. They both liked it that way.

"You know something?" she told him once. "There aren't very many people you can enjoy spending Sunday with."

"Mm," he said. He was shaving, standing just inside the open door of his bathroom; she lay propped on pillows in his big double bed, leafing through his copy of *The New York Times Book Review.*

She turned a page and a photograph of Jack Flanders jumped out at her, looking much older and even sadder than when she'd seen him last. There were pictures of three other men in the same full-page review, which ran under the heading "A Spring Poetry Roundup"; she skimmed the columns quickly and found the part about Jack.

In middle age, the once volatile John Flanders has settled into an amiable acceptance of things as they are—pierced, time and again, by a sharp regret for things lost. *Days and Nights*, his fourth book, displays the careful craftsmanship we have come to expect of him, but too frequently there is too little else to admire. Are acceptance and regret enough? For daily living, perhaps—not, one suspects, for the higher demands of art. This reader misses the old Flanders fire.

Some of the love poems are affecting, particularly "Iowa Oak Tree," with its strong, erotic final stanza, and "Proposal of Marriage," with its curious opening lines "I watch you fooling with the dog and wonder / What does this girl want from me?" Elsewhere, however, one is tempted to dismiss poem after poem as commonplace or sentimental.

The long final poem should probably have been cut from the manuscript before it went to the printer. Even its title is awkward—"Remembering London Revisited"—and the work itself performs a bewildering exercise in double flashback: the poet regrets a time when he stood at a London doorway regretting still another, earlier time. How much chagrin can a single poem bear without becoming ludicrous?

One closes this slim volume with something of the poet's own regret-within-regret malaise, and with all too little of his hope.

Turning to the brilliant, audacious new work of William Krueger, we find what can only be called an embarrassment of poetic riches . . .

The buzz of Michael Hogan's electric razor had stopped some time ago; she looked up and found him peering over her shoulder.

"What's the deal?" he asked her.

"Nothing; just something here about a man I used to know."

"Yeah? Which one?"

There were four photographs on the page, she could easily have pointed to one of the others—even Krueger—and Michael

Hogan would never know, or care, but she felt a stirring of old loyalty. "Him," she said, touching her forefinger to Jack's face.

"Looks like he just lost his last friend," Michael Hogan said.

One Friday morning Sarah called Emily at the office to inquire, happily, if she was free for lunch.

"You mean you're in town?"

"That's right."

"Fine," Emily said. "What's the occasion?"

"Well, Tony had to come in for a business meeting today, that's part of it, but the main thing is we've got tickets to see Roderick Hamilton in *Come Home, Stranger* tonight, and afterwards we're going backstage to *meet* him."

Roderick Hamilton was a famous English actor whose new play had recently opened in New York. "That's wonderful," Emily said.

"He and Tony went to school together in England, you see— have I ever told you that?"

"Yes, I believe you have."

"And at first Tony was too shy to write to him, but I made him do it, and we got back this really nice, really charming letter saying of course he remembered Tony and wanted to see him again, and wanted to meet me. Isn't that exciting?"

"It certainly is."

"So look. We're staying at the Roosevelt, and Tony'll be gone all day. Why don't you come up here for lunch? They have this really nice place called the Rough Rider Room."

"Well," Emily said. "That sounds appropriate for a couple of old rough riders like you and me."

"What, dear?"

"Never mind. Would one o'clock suit you?"

When she first walked into the restaurant she thought Sarah hadn't arrived yet—all the tables were filled with strangers—but then she saw that a plump little overdressed matron, sitting alone, was smiling at her.

"Come sit down, dear," Sarah said. "You look wonderful."

"So do you," Emily said, but it wasn't true. In St. Charles, wearing country clothes, Sarah might still look her age—which

Emily quickly calculated was forty-one—but here she looked older. Her eyes were lined and shadowed and she had a double chin. She was slump-shouldered. She had evidently been undecided about which of several pieces of bright costume jewelry to wear with her cheap beige suit, and had solved the problem by wearing them all. In the past year her teeth had developed heavy brown stains.

"Something from the bar, ladies?" the waiter inquired.

"Oh, yes," Sarah said. "I'd like an extra dry martini, straight up, with a lemon twist."

Emily ordered a glass of white wine ("I have to work this afternoon") and they both tried to relax.

"Do you know," Sarah said, "I was just thinking. This is the first time I've been to New York in nine years. It's funny how everything's changed."

"You ought to get in more often."

"I know; I'd love to; it's just that Tony hates it so. He hates the traffic, and he says everything's too expensive."

"Mm."

"Oh!" Sarah said, brightening again. "Did I tell you we heard from Tony Junior?" Some months ago, having concluded his affair with the divorcée (she had found an older man), Tony Junior had gone off to enlist in the Marine Corps. "He's at Camp Pendleton, California, and he sent us a nice long letter," Sarah said. "Of course Tony's still furious with him—he's even threatened to disin*herit* him—"

"Disinherit him from what?"

"—Well, you know, disown him; but I think the experience'll do him a world of good."

"And how are the other boys?"

"Oh, Peter's busy at college, on the dean's list *every* semester, and Eric—well, it's hard to tell with Eric. He's still mad about cars."

Then the talk turned to their mother, whom Emily hadn't visited for some time. The social worker at the nursing home, Sarah said, had called her to report that Pookie was becoming a discipline problem.

"How do you mean, a discipline problem?"

"Well, he said she does things that upset the other patients. One night about four in the morning she went into some old man's room and said 'Why aren't you ready? Have you forgotten this is our wedding day?' And apparently she went on and on like that, until the old man had to call the nurses to come and take her back."

"Oh, my God."

"No, but he was very nice about it—the social worker, I mean. He just said that if that kind of behavior continues we'll have to take her out of there."

"Well, but where would we—I mean where would we *put* her?"

Sarah was lighting a cigarette. "Central Islip, I guess," she said, exhaling smoke.

"What's that?"

"The State Hospital. It's free. Oh, but I understand it's very nice."

"I see," Emily said.

Over her second martini Sarah made a shy announcement. "I suppose I really shouldn't have this," she said. "My doctor told me I drink too much."

"He did?"

"Oh, it wasn't a grim warning or anything; he just told me to cut down. He said my—you know—my liver's enlarged. I don't know. Let's not talk about sad things any more. I hardly ever get to see you, Emmy, and I want to hear all about your job and your love life and everything. Besides, I'm going to meet Roderick *Ham*ilton tonight, and I want—to be in a good mood. Let's enjoy ourselves."

But a few minutes later she was gazing wistfully around the room. "It's nice here, isn't it," she said. "This is one of the places Daddy used to take me to, just before he'd put me on the train. Sometimes we'd go to the Biltmore, too, or the Commodore, but this is the place I remember best. The waiters knew him here, and they knew me too. They'd always bring me a double scoop of ice cream, while Daddy had his double scotch, and we'd talk and talk . . ."

Afterwards, Emily couldn't remember whether Sarah drank

three martinis or four at that lunch in the Rough Rider Room; she remembered only that she herself was fuddled with wine by the time their chicken à la king arrived, and that Sarah ate very little of her portion. She didn't drink her coffee, either.

"Oh, dear, Emmy," she said. "I guess I'm a little drunk. Isn't that ridiculous? I don't know why I—oh, but it's okay. I can have a little nap upstairs. I'll have plenty of time before Tony gets back; then we'll have dinner and go to the theater and I'll be fine."

She needed help in getting out of her chair. She needed help in walking across the floor, too—Emily held her high and firmly under one soft arm—and in walking down the corridor to the elevators.

"It's okay, Emmy," she kept saying. "It's okay. I can manage." But Emily didn't let go until they were up in the room, where Sarah tottered a few steps forward and collapsed on the double bed. "I'm fine," she said. "I'll just get a little sleep now, and I'll be fine."

"Don't you want to take your clothes off?"

"That's okay. Don't worry about it. I'll be fine."

And Emily went back to the office for a distracted afternoon's work. It wasn't until nearly five o'clock that she began to feel a guilty pleasure: now that she had seen her sister, it might be many months—maybe years—before she would have to see her again.

This would be an evening alone; and sometimes, when she planned things right, she found she didn't mind being alone at all. First she changed into comfortable clothes and got the materials for her light supper started in the kitchenette, then she fixed herself a drink—never more than two—and watched the *CBS Evening News*. Later, after she'd eaten and washed the dishes, she would sit in her deep chair or lie on her sofa with a book, reading, and the hours would pass uncounted until it was time to go to bed.

When the telephone rang at nine o'clock it startled her, and the weak, plaintive sound of Sarah's voice—"Emmy?"—brought her quickly to her feet. "Look," Sarah said. "I hate to ask you this, but do you think you could come up here? To the hotel?"

"What's the matter? Why aren't you at the theater?"

"I—didn't go. I'll explain it when I see you, okay?"

All the way uptown, in a cab that kept getting caught in traffic jams, Emily tried to keep her mind empty; she was still trying to keep her mind empty when she walked down the long carpeted corridor to Sarah's door, which was an inch or two ajar. She thought of pushing it open, but knocked instead.

"Anthony?" Sarah called in a shy, hopeful voice.

"No, baby, it's me."

"Oh. Come on in, Emmy."

Emily went inside the dark room and let the door click shut behind her. "Are you all right?" she said. "Where's the light?"

"Don't turn it on yet. Let's talk a minute first, okay?"

In the dim blue light of the window Emily could see that Sarah was lying on the bed, the way she'd left her this afternoon, except that now the bed was unmade and she appeared to be wearing only her slip.

"I'm awfully sorry about this, Emmy; I probably shouldn't have called you, but the thing is—well, I'll start at the beginning, okay? When Tony got back here I was still—You know—still drunk, I guess, and we had a terrible fight about it and he said he wasn't going to take me to the play, and he—anyway, he went to the play alone."

"He went to the play alone?"

"That's right. Oh, you can't blame him; I *wasn't* in any condition to meet Roderick Hamilton; that part of it's all my fault. But I just—the point is, you and I had such good talks last summer, and I just called you up because I sort of need someone to talk to."

"I see. Well, I'm glad you did call. Can I turn the light on now?"

"I guess you might as well."

Emily felt along the wall for the light switch, and when she found it the room exploded into clarity. There was blood on the tangled sheets and on the pillow; there was blood down the front of Sarah's slip and all over her swollen, wincing face, and in her hair.

Emily sat down in a chair and shaded her eyes with one hand. "I don't believe this," she said. "I don't believe this for a minute. You mean he *beat* you?"

"That's right. Could I have a cigarette, dear?"

"Well, but Sarah, are you badly hurt? Let me look at you."

"No, don't. Don't come any closer, okay? I'll be all right. If I can just get up and wash my face I'll be—I should've done this before you came." She struggled to her feet and went unsteadily into the bathroom, from which came the sound of water running in the sink. "God," she called back. "Can you imagine *this* face being introduced to Roderick Hamilton backstage?"

"Sarah, look," Emily said when they were together in the bedroom again. "You're going to have to tell me a few things. Has this happened before?"

Sarah had managed to get her face almost clean; she was wearing a robe and smoking a cigarette. "Oh, sure," she said. "Happens all the time. I guess it's been happening once or twice a month for about—well, twenty years. It's not usually as bad as this."

"And you've never told anyone."

"I almost told Geoffrey once, years ago. He saw a bruise on my face and asked me about it and I almost told him, but I thought, No, that would only make *more* trouble. I don't know; I guess I probably would've told Daddy about it, if he'd lived. The boys have seen it happen a few times. Tony Junior told him once if he ever saw him do it again he'd kill him. He said that to his own father."

There were liquor bottles and an ice bucket on a low cabinet against the wall, and Emily looked at them with longing. All she had to do was make herself a drink—and she wanted a strong one—but she willed herself to stay in her chair, still shading her eyes with her hand as if unable to look her sister full in the face. "Oh, Sarah," she said. "Oh, Sarah. Why do you put up with it?"

"It's a marriage," Sarah said. "If you want to stay married, you learn to put up with things. Besides, I love the guy."

"What do you mean, 'I love the guy'? That sounds like a line out of some corny—How can you 'love' someone who treats you like—"

A key scraped and turned in the lock, and Emily stood up to face him. She had her opening words prepared and ready.

He came in blinking in surprise at seeing her. His expressionless face looked a little drunk, and he was dressed for the evening in a dark summer suit that Sarah had probably picked out in some cheap suburban department store.

"How was the play, you son of a bitch?" Emily asked him.

"Don't, Emmy," Sarah said.

"Don't *what*? Isn't it about time somebody talked straight around here? How was Roderick Hamilton, you bullying, wife-beating bastard?"

Tony ignored her, moving past her with the look of a despised little boy ignoring his tormentors, but the room was so small that he had to brush against her on his way to the liquor cabinet. He set out three generous, hotel-room water tumblers and began pouring whiskey.

His silence didn't faze her, and she decided that if he handed her a drink she would throw it in his face, but first she had a few more things to say. "You're a Neanderthal," she told him, remembering what Andrew Crawford had called him long ago. "You're a pig. And I swear—are you listening to me? I swear to God if you ever touch my sister again I'll—" There was no way to finish that sentence except to repeat Tony Junior's threat, and she repeated it: "I'll kill you."

She drank—apparently he *had* handed her a drink, and apparently she'd accepted it without thinking—and only now, with the alcohol spreading warm through her chest and down her arms, did she begin to realize how much she was enjoying herself. It was fine to be passionately in the right on so clear an issue—the scrappy kid sister as avenging angel; she wanted this exhilaration to go on and on. Glancing over at Sarah, though, she wished Sarah hadn't washed her face and covered her slip and straightened up the bedclothes to hide the bloodstains; it would have made a more dramatic picture the other way.

"It's okay, Emmy," Sarah said in the same calming, under-standing way she had always said it in childhood when Emily was out of control. Sarah had a drink in her hand now too; for a moment Emily was afraid she might have to stand here and watch while Tony sat down on the bed beside his wife and they per-formed the old smiling, arm-entwining ritual from Anatole's, but that didn't happen.

Tony seemed to draw composure from Sarah's "It's okay,

Emmy"; he looked into Emily's eyes for the first time, with an infuriating suggestion of a smile, and said "Not really ve'y much one can say, is there? Won't you sit down?"

"I will *not* sit down," she answered, and immediately spoiled the effect of that line by taking another long drink from her glass. The high pleasure of the confrontation was gone. She felt like a strident intruder in something that was none of her business. She managed to get off a few more plangent statements before leaving—things she couldn't remember afterwards, probably repeating her own and Tony Junior's hollow threat of murder—and she asked Sarah several times, with what sounded like fake solicitude, if she was sure she'd be "all right"; then she was out in the elevator and then she was home, feeling like a fool.

It took a great effort of will to keep from calling Michael Hogan ("It's just that I feel I *can't* be alone tonight," she would have said, "and there's a whole *week*end to get through..."); instead she had a few more drinks by herself and went to bed.

The phone rang late the next morning and she was almost sure it would be Michael Hogan ("Feel like having dinner?") but it wasn't.

"Emmy?"

"Sarah? Are you all right? Where are you?"

"Downtown—I'm in a phone booth. Tony drove on back, but I told him I wanted to stay in the city. I wanted to sort of think things over. I've been sitting in the park and—"

"Sitting in the park?"

"Washington Square. It's funny how everything's changed. I didn't know our old house was gone."

"That whole block was torn down years ago," Emily said, "when they built the Student Center."

"Oh. Well, I didn't know that. Anyway, if you don't have any special plans I thought maybe you might come down and meet me here. We could have breakfast, or brunch or something."

"Well," Emily said, "sure. Where will I find you?"

"I'll be in the park, okay? On one of the benches right near where the old house used to be. You don't have to hurry; take your time."

On the way downtown Emily weighed the possibilities. If Sarah had left her husband she might want to stay with her sister for a while—maybe a long while—which would inconvenience Michael Hogan. Still, Michael did have an apartment of his own; they could work something out. On the other hand, maybe she *was* only "thinking things over"; maybe she would go back to St. Charles tonight.

The park was filled with baby carriages and with laughing, athletic young men throwing frisbees. Its whole design had changed—the paths ran in different directions now—but Emily had no trouble remembering, in passing, the approximate place where Warren Maddock, or Maddox, had picked her up.

Sarah looked as pathetic on her bench as Emily had expected —small and dowdy in her wrinkled beige, lifting her soft, bruised face to the sun and almost visibly savoring visions of another time.

Emily took her to a cool, decent coffee shop (she knew that if they went to a real restaurant there would be irresistible Bloody Marys, or beers) and for an hour or two they talked in circles.

". . . We're not getting anywhere, Sarah," she said at last. "You say you know you ought to leave him; you even say you *want* to leave him, and then when we start going into the practical aspects of that you come back to this business of 'I love the guy.' We're talking in circles."

Sarah looked down at the congealed remains of egg and sausage on her plate. "I know," she said. "I always talk in circles, and you always talk in a straight line. I wish I had your mind."

"It isn't a question of 'mind,' Sarah, it's just—"

"Yes it is. We're a lot different, you and me. I'm not saying one way of looking at things is better than the other, it's just that I've always thought of marriage as being—well, sacred. I don't expect other people to feel that way, but it's the way I am. I was a virgin when I got married and I've been a virgin ever since. I mean," she added quickly, "*you* know—I've never played around or anything." With the words "played around or anything" she brought her cigarette quickly to her lips and squinted over it, either to hide embarrassment or to suggest a veiled sophistication.

"Well, fine," Emily said. "But even if marriage is sacred,

doesn't that imply that both parties ought to agree on it? What's sacred about the way Tony treats you?"

"He does the best he can, Emmy. I know that may sound funny, but it's true."

Emily exhaled a great cloud of smoke and sat back to look around the coffee shop. In a booth across the aisle a couple of young lovers were murmuring, side by side, the girl's fingers tracing little elliptical patterns on the inner thigh of the boy's tight, well-faded blue jeans.

"Listen, Sarah," she said. "Let's take this whole discussion back to where we were a few minutes ago. You can stay at my place as long as you like. We can work together at finding you a place of your own, and a job. And you don't have to think of it as a permanent separation; think of it as—"

"I know, dear, and it's very sweet of you, but there are so many complications. For one thing, what could I possibly *do*?"

"There's any *number* of things you could do," Emily said, though the only thing she could picture was Sarah working as a receptionist in some doctor's or dentist's office. (Where *did* all those pleasant, inefficient middle-aged ladies come from, and how had they gotten their jobs?) "*That's* not important," she hurried on. "The only important thing now is to make up your mind. Either go back to St. Charles, or start a new life for yourself here."

Sarah was silent, as if pretending to think it over for the sake of appearances; then she said "I'd better go back," as Emily had known she would. "I'll take the train back this afternoon."

"Why?" Emily said. "Because he 'needs' you?"

"We need each other."

So it was settled: Sarah would go back; all of Emily's days and nights would be free for Michael Hogan, and for whatever man might follow him in the long succession. She had to admit she was relieved, but it was a relief that couldn't be shown. "And what you're really afraid of," she said, intending it as a kind of taunt, "what you're really afraid of is that Tony might leave *you*."

Sarah lowered her eyes, displaying the fine little blue-white scar. "That's right," she said.

PART THREE

ONE

WHENEVER EMILY THOUGHT about her sister over the next few years—and it wasn't often—she reminded herself that she'd done her best. She had spoken her mind to Tony, and she'd offered Sarah sanctuary. Could anyone have done more than that?

Sometimes she found that Sarah made an interesting topic of conversation with men.

"I have a sister whose husband beats her all the time," she would say.

"Yeah? Really beats her?"

"Really beats her. Been beating her for twenty years. And do you know a funny thing? I know this sounds awful, talking about my own sister, but I think she sort of enjoys it."

"Enjoys it?"

"Well, maybe she doesn't enjoy it, exactly, but she takes it in stride. She believes in marriage, you see. She said to me once 'I was a virgin when I got married and I've been a virgin ever since.' Isn't that the damnedest statement you've ever heard?"

When she talked that way with a man—usually half drunk, usually late at night—she would regret it profoundly afterwards; but it wasn't hard to assuage her guilt by vowing that she wouldn't do it again.

Besides, there wasn't time for anxiety. She was busy. Early in 1965 Baldwin Advertising obtained what Hannah Baldwin called a dream account: National Carbon, whose new synthetic fiber Tynol seemed almost certain to revolutionize the fabric industry. "Think what nylon did!" Hannah exulted. "The sky's the limit on this thing, and we've lucked in on the ground floor."

Emily developed a series of ads introducing the fiber, and Hannah loved them. "I think you've got it licked, honey," she said. "We'll knock their eyes out."

But instead there was a troublesome hitch. "I can't imagine

what's wrong," Hannah told Emily. "National Carbon's legal counsel just called me; he wants you to go in and talk to him about the campaign. He wouldn't say anything on the phone, but he sounded very grim. His name's Dunninger."

She found him high in a great steel-and-glass tower, alone in his carpeted office. He was big and sturdy, with a heavy jaw and a voice that made her want to curl up and ride in his pocket like a kitten.

"Let me take your coat, Miss Grimes," he said. "Sit down— no, come around here and sit beside me; then we can go over the material together. In general I think it's fine," he began, and as he talked she looked beyond the layouts and pages of copy to explore the whole ample surface of his desk. Its only ornament was a photograph of a lovely dark-haired girl, probably his daughter; they probably lived in Connecticut, and when he got home every day he would play a few fast sets of tennis with her before they went in to shower and change and join Mrs. Dunninger for cocktails in the library. And what would Mrs. Dunninger be like?

". . . There's just one point," he was saying. "One phrase, and unfortunately it's a phrase that appears over and over in your, uh, copy. You say Tynol has 'the natural elegance of wool.' That could easily be construed as misrepresentation, you see, when we're talking about a synthetic. I'm afraid if we let it go we'll have the F.T.C. on our necks."

"I don't get it," Emily said. "If I say 'You have the patience of a saint,' it certainly doesn't mean you *are* one."

"Ah." He leaned back in his chair, smiling at her. "But if I say 'You have the eyes of a strumpet,' there might conceivably be room for doubt."

They sat laughing and talking for longer than their business required, and she couldn't help noticing that he seemed to be happily taking stock of her legs and her body and her face. She was thirty-nine, but his eyes made her feel much younger.

"Is that your daughter?" she said of the photograph.

He looked embarrassed. "No, it's my wife."

And she couldn't say "I'm sorry" or anything like that without making it worse. "Oh," she said. "She's lovely." Then she mumbled that she'd better be going, and stood up.

"I think you'll find 'natural' is the offending word," he said, walking her to the door. "If you can get around that I don't think there'll be any problem."

She told him she would do her best, and as the elevator dropped her back to reality she revised her fantasies: he didn't live in Connecticut; he lived in an East Side penthouse where that beautiful girl pouted and preened in mirrors all day, waiting for him to come home.

"Miss Grimes?" he said on the telephone a very few days later. "Howard Dunninger. I just wondered if you might have lunch with me."

Almost the first thing he told her, as they sipped wine in what she described to herself as a "wonderful" French restaurant, was that he wasn't really married at all: he and his wife had separated three months ago.

"Well, 'separated' is a euphemism," he said. "The fact is she left me. Not for another man; just because she was tired of me—I imagine she'd been tired of me for some time—and she wanted to see what freedom is like. Oh, it's understandable, I suppose. I'm fifty; she's twenty-eight. When we started living together I was forty-two and she was twenty."

"Isn't it a little romantic to keep her picture on your desk?"

"Pure cowardice," he said. "It's been there so long I thought people in the office might think it looked funny if I put it away."

"Where is she now?"

"California. She wanted to put the greatest possible distance between us, you see."

"Do you have any children?"

"Only from my first marriage; that was a long time ago. Two boys. They're grown now."

Chewing fresh French bread and salad, glancing around at the well-dressed, sophisticated-looking people at other tables, Emily realized it would be easy to make love with Howard Dunninger this very afternoon. Hannah wouldn't care if she didn't show up at the office, and surely the general counsel for National Carbon could set his own schedule. They had both outlived the time of trivial responsibilities.

"What time do you want to get back, Emily?" he asked as the waiter set a gleaming little cognac glass beside her coffee.

"Oh, it doesn't matter; no special time."

"Good." His thin lips curled into a shape of shyness. "I've done so damn much of the talking I've hardly gotten to know you. Tell me about yourself."

"Well, there's not really much to tell."

But there was: her autobiography, edited and heightened here and there for dramatic effect, seemed impossible to conclude. She was still talking when he guided her out across the blazing sidewalk and into a taxicab, and when the cab let them off at his apartment building. She stopped talking finally in the elevator— not because she was finished but only because it seemed important to be quiet here.

It wasn't a penthouse, and it wasn't nearly as grand as she'd imagined. It was blue and brown and white and smelled of leather; it was almost ordinary, and its floor seemed to tilt at dangerous angles as he went about the courtly preliminaries: ". . . Can I get you a drink? Sit down over here . . ." No sooner had he sat close beside her on the sofa than they were all over each other, and the sounds of the city nineteen floors below were overwhelmed by the greater sounds of their breathing; when he helped her into the bedroom it was like a long-awaited, well-deserved passage into light and air.

Howard Dunninger filled her life. He was as appealing as Jack Flanders, with none of Jack's terrible dependency; he seemed to make as few demands on her as Michael Hogan; and when she sought comparisons for the way he made her feel in bed, night after night, she had to go all the way back to Lars Ericson.

After the first few weeks they stopped using his apartment—he said he didn't want to be constantly reminded of his wife—and started using hers. That made it easier for her to get to work on time in the morning, and there was another, subtler advantage: when she was a guest in his place there seemed to be a tentative, temporary quality to the thing; when he came to hers it implied a greater commitment. Or did it? The more she thought about this the more she realized that the argument might easily be reversed: when he was the visitor he could always get up and go away.

In any case, her apartment became their home. He was shy at first about moving his things in, but soon one of her bureau drawers was packed with his laundered shirts, and there were three dark suits and a bright cluster of neckties hanging in the closet. She liked to run her hand down the length of those ties, as if they were a heavy silken rope.

Howard owned a Buick convertible, which he kept in a garage uptown, and in good weather they took drives into the country. Once, having started out for Vermont on a Friday afternoon, they drove all the way up to Quebec City, where they checked into the Château Frontenac as if it were a motel; and Sunday night, on the long trip home, they drank French champagne out of Styrofoam cups.

They went to the theater sometimes, and to small drinking places that she'd only read about before, but most evenings they stayed home, as quiet and gentle with each other as people who'd been peacefully married for years. As she often told him—and she knew it might have been wiser not to tell him at all—she had never enjoyed herself so much with anyone.

The trouble was that he was still in love with his wife.

"There!" he said once, when she hadn't even known he was looking at her. "What you did just then—the way you held your hair back with one hand and bent over the coffee table to pick up that glass—that could have been Linda."

"I don't see how I can possibly remind you of her," she said. "After all, she's a young girl and I'm practically forty."

"I know; and you really don't look anything alike, except that she's small-breasted too and you have the same kind of legs, but just once in a while, some of your mannerisms—it's uncanny."

Another time, when he'd come home in a sour mood and drunk a lot of wine with dinner, he sat nursing a bourbon and water for a long time, silent, until he began to talk in a way that suggested he would never stop.

"... No, but you have to understand about Linda," he said. "It wasn't just that she was my wife; she was all I'd ever wanted in a woman. She was—how can I explain it?"

"You don't have to explain it."

"Yes I do. Have to get it straight in my own mind or I'll *never* get over her. Listen. Let me tell you how I met her. Try to understand this, Emily. I was forty-two years old but I felt older. I'd been married and divorced, I'd had what seemed any number of girls; I guess I felt I'd pretty well exhausted my possibilities. I was out in East Hampton for a couple of weeks and somebody asked me to a party. A lighted swimming pool, Japanese lanterns in the trees, Sinatra records piped out from the house—that kind of thing. A mixed crowd: there were a lot of actors who made television commercials, a couple of children's-book illustrators, a couple of writers, a few business types trying to look arty in their burgundy Bermuda shorts. And son of a bitch, Emily, I turned around and there was this creature lying on this white chaise longue. I'd never seen skin like that, or eyes like that, or lips like that. She was wearing—"

"Are you really going to tell me what she was *wearing*?"

"—wearing a simple, short black dress, and I took a big drink for courage and went over to her and said 'Hi. Are you somebody's wife?' And she looked up at me—she was too shy or I guess too reserved to smile—and she—"

"Oh, Howard, this is silly," Emily said. "You're just going to get yourself all worked up. You really are a terrible romantic."

"All right, I'll keep it as brief as I can. I don't want to bore you."

"You're not 'boring' me; it's just that you're—"

"All right. The point is, the very next night she was in my bed, and every other night after that; when we got back to town she moved all her stuff into my apartment. She was still in college— she went to Barnard, same as you—and when her classes were over every day she'd hurry down to my place in order to be there when I got home. I can't begin to tell you how sweet that was. I'd go home bracing myself, thinking No, it's too good to be true; she won't be there—and she always was. I look back on that time, that first year and a half, as the God damned happiest time of my life."

He was up and walking the floor now with his drink in his hand, and Emily knew better than to interrupt him.

"Then we got married, and I guess that did take the edge off it a little—for her, I think, more than for me. I was still—well, I hate to keep saying 'happy,' but that's the only word for it. Proud, too; enormously proud. I'd take her places, people would congratulate me, and I remember I'd say 'I don't believe her; I don't believe any of this yet.' Then of course after a while I did start to believe her; I started taking her for granted in ways that nobody should ever take *any*body for granted. In the early years she used to say I never bored her, and I took it as a great compliment, but I don't remember her ever saying that toward the end. I'd probably begun to bore the hell out of her with my vanity and my posturings and my—I don't know. My self-pity. And I think that's when she started getting restless, along about the time I started boring her. God damn it, Emily, how can I make you understand how nice she was? It's a thing that can't be described. Tender, loving, and at the same time she was tough. I don't mean 'tough' in any pejorative sense, I mean resilient, courageous; she had a wholly unsentimental way of looking at the world. Intelligent! Jesus, it was almost frightening sometimes how she'd go straight to the heart of some elusive, complicated thing with an intuitive insight. She was funny, too—oh, she didn't sit around getting off paralyzing one-liners, it's just that she had a very sharp eye for the absurdity behind anything pretentious. She was a great companion. Why do I keep saying 'was'? It's not as if she were dead. She was a great companion for me and now she'll be a great companion for some other man—or men. I imagine she'll try out quite a few men before she settles down again."

He sank heavily into an armchair, closing his eyes, and began massaging the thin bridge of his nose with thumb and forefinger. "And sometimes now when I think of her in that particular context," he said in a flat, almost dead voice, "when I picture her out there with some other man, opening her—opening her legs for him and—"

"Howard I'm not going to let you do this," Emily said, standing up for emphasis. "It's maudlin. You're acting like a lovesick little boy, and it's very unbecoming. Besides, it's not very—" She wasn't at all sure if she should finish this sentence, but she did "—not very considerate of me."

That brought his eyes open, but he closed them again. "I thought you and I were friends," he said. "I thought the idea was, you were supposed to be able to talk freely with a friend."

"Hasn't it occurred to you that I might be a little jealous?"

"Mm," he said. "No, as a matter of fact that hadn't occurred to me. I don't get it. How can you be jealous of something that's in the past?"

"Oh, *How*ard. Come on, now. What if I spent whole evenings going over all the wonderful, wonderful qualities of different men I've known?" But that question answered itself: she could tell Howard Dunninger anything about any of her men, or all of them, and he wouldn't care.

In December of that year, National Carbon assigned him to California for two weeks.

"And I suppose you'll see Linda out there, won't you?" she said when he was getting ready to leave.

"I don't see how," he said. "I'll be in Los Angeles; she's 'way up north of San Francisco. It's a big state. Besides, I—"

"Besides you what?"

"Besides I what nothing. I can't seem to get this God damned suitcase shut."

It was a bad two weeks—he called her only twice, toward the end—but she survived it; and he really did come home.

Then in February, late one night when they were about to go to bed, Sarah called.

"Emmy? Are you alone?"

"Well, no, actually, I'm—"

"Oh, you're not. I see. I was hoping you would be." The rhythm and texture of Sarah's voice evoked a sharp sense of that terrible old house in St. Charles—the mildew, the chill, the ancestors staring from the walls, the smell of garbage in the kitchen.

"What's the matter, Sarah?"

"Let's put it this way. To quote John Steinbeck, this is the winter of our discontent."

"I don't think that was original with Steinbeck, baby," Emily said. "Has Tony been—?"

"That's right. And I've made a decision, Emmy. I'm not staying here any more. I want to come and stay with you."

"Well, Sarah, the thing is—I'm afraid that wouldn't be possible." She glanced at Howard, who stood in his bathrobe a few feet away, listening and looking interested. She had told him about her sister. "The thing is, I'm not living alone now."

"Oh. You mean you have a—I see. Well, that does complicate things, but I don't care. I'm leaving anyway. I'll stay in an inexpensive hotel or something. Listen, though: do you think you could help me find a job? *I* can write advertising copy too. *I've* always been able to—you know—turn a phrase."

"There's a little more to it than that," Emily said. "It takes quite a few years to get a job like mine. I really think you'd be better off looking for some other kind of work."

"What kind?"

"Well, maybe working as a receptionist, or something like that." There was a pause. "Look, Sarah, are you absolutely sure you want to do this?" Emily held the phone in both hands and chewed her lip, trying to figure out her motives. Not very long ago she had urged her sister to leave home; now she was urging her to stay.

"Oh, I don't know, Emmy," Sarah said. "I guess I'm not absolutely sure of anything. Everything's so—so mixed up."

"Is Tony there?" Emily asked. "Can I talk to him?" And when Tony came on with a drunken-sounding grunt she felt a fine, swift return of the exhilaration she'd known that night in the hotel room. "Listen, Wilson," she began. "I want you to leave my sister alone, is that clear?" As her voice rose and flattened out she understood why she was doing this: she was showing off for Howard. This would prove she wasn't always tender and loving; she could be tough, resilient, courageous; she had a wholly unsentimental way of looking at the world. ". . . I want you to keep your big—your big fucking hands to yourself," she said, "and if I were a man I'd come out there tonight and make you wish you never *had* any hands. Is that clear? Put Sarah back on."

There were muffled scraping sounds, as if heavy furniture had to be moved before Sarah could come back to the telephone. When she did, it was clear at once that she'd changed her mind.

"I'm sorry to bother you with all this, Emmy," she said. "I probably shouldn't have called in the first place. I'll be all right."

"No, listen," Emily said, feeling greatly relieved. "Call me anytime. Please feel free to call me anytime, and meanwhile I'll keep an eye on the 'Help Wanted' ads in the *Times*, okay? It's just that I don't think you'd be very wise to come right *now*, is all."

"No; I don't either. All right, Emmy. Thanks."

When the phone was back in its cradle, Howard handed her a drink and said "That's terrible. That must've been very hard on you."

"It's just that there isn't anything I can *do*, Howard," she said. She wanted him to take her in his arms, so she could cry against his shoulder, but he made no move toward her.

"Well," he said, "actually, you could let her have this apartment for a while; we could stay up at my place."

"I know; that did occur to me; but the point is the apartment's only the beginning. You have no *idea* how helpless she is— a funny little middle-aged woman with terrible clothes and bad teeth and without a skill to her name—she can't even *type* except with two fingers."

"Oh, well, I imagine there are things she could do. I might even be able to help her find something at National Carbon."

"And she'd be around our necks," Emily said with more bitterness than she'd intended. "We'd never be free of her for a minute if she were here. I don't *want* her, Howard. I know it may sound awful, but I don't *want* her dragging down my life. If you can't understand that I guess it's just too—too complicated to explain."

"Okay," he said, smiling and frowning at the same time. "Okay. Just take it easy."

Several weeks went by before the next call, at about the same time of night, and this time it was Tony who called. He sounded drunk again, and she could hardly hear him because of other slurred male voices in the background, which she realized after a second were the sound of television turned up too loud.

". . . Your sister's in the hospital," Tony's voice said, trying for as neutral a tone as that of a gruff policeman reporting to the victim's next of kin.

"The hospital? What hospital?"

"Central Islip," the voice said; then it added "where she belongs," and the silence was filled only with the muffled boom and rumble of the television voices.

"Oh my God, Howard," Emily said when she'd hung up the phone. "She's in Central Islip."

"What's that?"

"It's where my mother is. The state hospital. The insane asylum."

"Well, Emily, listen," Howard said gently. "Her husband couldn't have just *put* her there. If she's been committed there it can only be because some doctor decided to send her in for treatment. This isn't the Nineteenth Century; nobody says 'insane asylum' any more. It's a modern psychiatric hospital, and it's—"

"You don't *know* what it is, Howard. I do. I've been out there to see my mother. It's twenty or maybe fifty enormous brick buildings; even when you're out there you can't comprehend how big it is because there are so many trees. You walk along those paths thinking This isn't so bad, and then two more buildings come up at you through the trees, and two more, and two more. And they have bars on the windows, and sometimes you can hear a person screaming in there."

"Don't make a melodrama out of it, Emily," Howard said. "The first thing to do is call the hospital and find out what she was admitted for."

"It's eleven o'clock at night. Besides, they'd never tell me— a strange voice on the phone. They must have rules about that. You'd have to be a doctor to—"

"Or a lawyer, maybe," he said. "Sometimes being a lawyer comes in handy. I'll find out what her diagnosis is tomorrow, and I'll tell you tomorrow night. Okay? Now come on to bed and stop acting like an actress."

When he came home the following night he said " 'Acute alcoholism.' " Then he said "Oh, come on, Emily, that's not so bad. All she has to do is dry out and they'll let her go. It isn't as if it were 'paranoid schizophrenia,' or something like that."

That was a Monday. It was Saturday before Emily was free to ride the train out to Central Islip bringing two cartons of cigarettes (one for her sister and one for her mother); on the platform she nodded to one of the scruffy-looking cab drivers who clamored around her—they seemed to make a nice business out of one-dollar fares to the hospital and back—and then she was in that bewildering maze of trees and buildings.

Sarah's building was one of the older ones—it had a turn-of-the-century look—and Emily found her on a heavily screened upstairs verandah, sitting deep in conversation with another woman of about her own age. They both wore printed house-coats and cotton slippers, and the whole of Sarah's scalp was wrapped in something white that looked at first like a turban—the kind that had been stylish in the early forties—but proved to be a bandage.

"Emmy!" she cried. "Mary Ann, I want you to meet my bril-liant sister—the one I was just telling you about. Emmy, this is my very best friend, Mary Ann Polchek."

And Emily smiled at a faded, frightened little face.

"Let's sit over here where we can talk," Sarah said, moving slowly as she led Emily to a couple of vacant chairs in the after-noon shadows. "*Gee*, it's nice of you to come all the way out here. Oh, and you've brought cigarettes, too; aren't you sweet."

"You mean that lady's your best friend from home?" Emily asked when they were settled. "Or just here?"

"Just here. She's a wonderful person. You really shouldn't have made this long trip, dear; I'll be getting out of here in a couple of weeks."

"You will?'

"Well, three weeks at the most, my doctor says. I just needed a little rest. Actually, all I care about is getting out before the first, when Tony Junior comes home. Did I tell you his medical discharge came through?" Tony Junior had injured his hip in a jeep accident, which kept him away from Vietnam; the other recent news about him was that he was married to a California girl. "I can't wait to see him," Sarah said. "He's decided to settle in St. Charles with his family."

"His family?"

"Well, the girl he married has two children, you see."

"Oh. And what will he do?"

"Go back to work for the garage, I guess. They love him there."

"I see. Listen, Sarah, tell me about yourself. How're you feeling?"

"Fine." Sarah's smile seemed determined to prove there was nothing wrong, and Emily noticed that her teeth were white: she must have had them repaired and cleaned.

One important question had to be asked, in spite of the smile, and Emily asked it. "How did you hurt your head?"

"Oh, that was just stupid," Sarah said. "*All* my own fault. One night I got up in the middle of the night because I couldn't sleep, and I went downstairs to get a glass of milk. And on the way back I was *al*most to the top of the stairs when I slipped and fell all the way down. Wasn't that stupid?"

And Emily felt her own mouth spread in what she guessed might pass for a smile of agreement on how stupid it was. "Were you badly hurt?"

"No, no, it was nothing." Sarah vaguely indicated the head bandage with one hand. "This is nothing."

It wasn't nothing; they must have had to shave her head before the bandage went on—it was that closely wrapped—and Emily almost said Did they shave your head? but thought better of it. "Well," she said instead. "It's good to see you looking so well."

For a while they just sat smoking, smiling whenever they met each other's eyes to show that everything was all right. Sarah didn't know that Emily knew of the "acute alcoholism" diagnosis; Emily wondered if there might be any tactful way to bring it up, and decided there wasn't. It became clear as they sat there that Sarah would keep her troubles to herself from now on. There would be no more confidences now, no more telephone calls and no more requests for help.

"Do you—think things'll be all right when you go home?" Emily said.

"How do you mean?"

"You think you still might want to come to New York?"

"*Oh*, no." Sarah looked embarrassed. "That was just silly. I'm sorry I called you that night. I was just—you know—tired and upset. Those things pass. I needed a good rest, that's all."

"Because I *have* been following the 'Help Wanted' ads," Emily said, "and I have a friend who thinks you might find something at National Carbon. And there's no reason why you couldn't stay at my place for a while, until you get settled."

Sarah was shaking her head. "No, Emmy. All that's past now. Let's just forget it, okay?"

"Okay. Except that I—well, okay."

"Are you going to visit Pookie while you're here?"

"I thought I would, yes. Do you know how to get to her building?" And Emily instantly realized what a foolish question that was. How could Sarah know the location of any other building when she was locked into this one? "It doesn't matter," she said quickly. "I'll find it."

"Well," Sarah said, getting slowly to her feet. "I guess you'd better be on your way. Thanks *so* much for coming, dear; it was wonderful to see you. Give my love to Pookie."

Out under the trees again, Emily walked a long way before realizing that she couldn't remember whether the man at the door had said three buildings down and four to the right or four buildings down and three to the right, and there was no one else to ask. A sign at one intersection said E-4 to E-9, which was no help, and another sign beneath it said MORGUE. In the distance, twin smokestacks rose against the gray sky. It was probably only the power plant—she knew that—but she wondered if it might be a crematory.

"Excuse me, sir," she said to an old man sitting on a bench. "Can you tell me where—"

"Don't mess with me, lady," he said, and then, placing his thumb against one nostril, he leaned forward and blew a bright stream of snot out of the other. "Don't mess with me."

She kept walking, trying not to think of the old man, until a taxicab slowed down at the curb and the driver stuck his head out and said "Taxi?"

"Yes," she said. "Thank you."

And it really didn't matter, she assured herself as the cab pulled away toward the train station. Old Pookie would only have lain silent with a look of terminal petulance on her face; she would have extended one hand to receive the cigarettes but wouldn't have smiled, wouldn't have talked, probably wouldn't have given any sign that she knew who Emily was.

Back in the city, she waited well over three weeks before calling St. Charles to find out if Sarah was home. She did it from the office, late on a weekday morning, so that Tony wouldn't be there.

". . . Oh, hi, Emmy . . . Oh, sure, I've been home for days . . . How's who?"

"I said how's everything?"

"Everything's fine. Tony Junior's here, with his wife and her children, so the place is something of a madhouse. She's very nice and very pregnant. They're staying here for a while, and we're helping them find a house of their own."

"I see. Well, be sure to keep in touch, Sarah. Let me know if there's anything I can—you know—anything I can do."

And Sarah did keep in touch, though not by telephone. Some time later she sent Emily a letter. The envelope was addressed in the old pert, debutantish handwriting, but the letter itself was typed, with a good many corrections marked in ballpoint pen.

Dear Emmy:

I am writing you instead of calling because I want to try out the typewriter Peter gave me for my birthday. It is an Underwood portable, second-hand, and it has a few faults here and there, but it types! With a little cleaning and re-adjustment, I'll be wearing it like a glove in no time.

It's a boy! Eight pounds seven ounces. And he looks just like his grandfather, my husband. (This makes my husband very angry, because it makes him tend to feel like a grandfather, and he doesn't care for the idea.) I have just finished building a bassinette. Never again! I began with a large clothes basket, some foam rubber, some padded plastic-coated fabric, some sheeting, some thumbtacks, and endless yards of blue ribbon. It was a brave beginning, and eventually a week later it reached fruition. Triumph-ant, but exhausted, I drove it down to Tony Junior's house, but nobody was home. The darned thing rode around in my station wagon for two days before it finally came to roost.

I am up to my ears in blackberries this week. Our pasture contains a full quarter acre of huge berries just screaming to be picked. So far I have picked, washed, syruped and frozen 30 pints, and made 20 jars of jelly, and I still can't keep ahead of them. Personally, I hate blackberries. I do this, remembering what the man said when asked why he wanted to climb Mt. Everest—"Because it's there."

I have not been to see Pookie for two very valid reasons. First, my driving is limited to strictly local stuff, at least until I gain a little more self-confidence and grow a little more hair. And second, because I almost never have the use of a car. Tony drives his T-bird to Magnum, Eric drives *his* T-bird to the motorcycle shop where he works, and Peter drives my station wagon to his summer job in Setauket.

Must say goodbye now and beat-feet back to the black-berry patch. Take care of yourself.

Love, Sarah

"What do you make of it?" Emily asked Howard when he'd read the letter.

"What do you mean, 'make of it'? Just a cheerful little letter, that's all."

"But that's the point, Howard—it's *too* cheerful. Except for that one reference to growing her hair you'd think she was the happiest, most contented little housewife in the world."

"Maybe that's the way she likes to see herself."

"Well, but the thing is I know better—and she *knows* I know better."

"Oh, come on," Howard said, getting up from his chair to move impatiently around the room. "What do you *want* from her? You want her opening her heart to you every five minutes? Telling you how many times he's beaten her this month? When she *does* that, you say you 'don't want her dragging down your life.' You're a funny girl, Emily."

And much later that night, as they lay drained of passion in her bed, she hesitantly touched his arm and said "Howard?"

"Mm?"

"If I ask you something, will you promise to tell me the truth?"

"Mm."

"Do you really think I'm a funny girl?"

In the summer of 1967 they spent their vacations at Howard's old place in East Hampton, where he hadn't been since the final year of his marriage. She liked the brightness and the roominess and the sandy, grassy smell of the house—after the city it was like breathing pure oxygen—and she liked its weathered cedar shingles, which shone almost silver in the sun. The word "delightful" kept occurring to her ("We had a delightful time," she would say to anyone who asked, when they got back to New York). She liked the surf, and the way Howard would wade out into it and jump with each breaking wave; she liked the way his prick would shrivel up and turn purple and blue from wind and water, so that only her lips and tongue, tasting salt, could restore it to weight.

"Howard?" she said on their final morning, which was Sunday. "I was thinking I might call my sister. Maybe we could sort of make a detour and stop off to see her on our way home."

"Sure," he said. "Nice idea."

"But I mean are you sure you don't mind? It's really 'way out of our way, and we'll probably just stumble into some dreadful, squalid scene."

"Christ's sake, Emily, of course I don't mind. I've always wanted to meet your sister."

And so she made the call. A man answered, but it wasn't Tony. "She's resting now," he said. "Can I take a message?"

"Well, no, I just—who's this? Is this Tony Junior?"

"No, it's Peter."

"Oh, *Peter.* Well, I just—this is Emily. Emily Grimes."

"Aunt Emmy!" he said. "I *thought* that sounded like your voice . . ."

It was arranged that they would stop by between two and three o'clock that afternoon. "You'd better brace yourself, Howard," she said when they'd found their way into St. Charles at last. "This'll be perfectly awful."

"Don't be silly," he told her.

She had hoped Peter might answer the door—then there would be an embrace and a courteous handshake ("How do you do, sir?") before they moved laughing into the living room—but instead it was Tony. He opened the door only a few inches and stood ready to slam it, like a man intent on protecting the sanctity of his home. When he saw who it was he blinked and stepped back, opening it wider, and Emily wondered how she could possibly greet him, after calling him a bastard and a son of a bitch and threatening his life. "Hello, Tony," she said. "This is Howard Dunninger; Tony Wilson."

He moved his mouth a little to mumble that he was pleased to meet Howard, and ushered them through the vestibule.

Sarah sat curled up on the sofa, the way old Edna Wilson used to sit, smiling vaguely. Emily looked into that smile for at least a second before realizing what was wrong with it: the lower half of Sarah's face was collapsed.

"Oh, Emmy," she wailed, trying ineffectually to hide her mouth with one hand, "I forgot to put my *teef* in."

"That's all right," Emily said. "Sit still." But it was clear that Sarah had been sitting still all day; she might not have been able to get up if she'd wanted to.

"Come sit beside me, Emmy," she said when the introductions were over. "It's so wonderful to *see* you." And she took both of Emily's hands in a surprisingly strong grip. Emily found it awkward to sit there, reaching sideways to allow her hands to be squeezed and fondled in her sister's lap; the only thing to do was move in closer, until their thighs touched, and when she did that she came into the zone of a heavy, fruity smell of alcohol.

". . . My very own baby sister," Sarah was saying while Emily tried not to look at her dark, grinning gums. "Do all you people realize this is my very own baby sister?"

Tony sat stolidly in a chair across from the sofa, wearing paint-stained dungarees and looking like an exhausted laborer. Beside him, Howard Dunninger smiled uneasily. The only self-assured member of the group was Peter, who had turned into a striking young man. He was dressed in spattered work clothes too—he and his father had been painting the house before their guests arrived—and Emily liked his looks. He wasn't tall and he wasn't quite handsome, but he moved around in a graceful way and there was something humorous and wise about his face.

"Have you finished at the seminary yet, Peter?" she asked him.

"One more year to go," he said. "It starts next week."

"How was your summer?"

"Oh, okay, thanks. I was in Africa for a while."

"In Africa? Really?"

And he held the floor for a few minutes, mercifully saving everyone else from conversational effort, while he described Africa as a sleeping giant "just beginning to stretch." When he said that he raised and spread both shapely arms, fists clenched, in a sleepy stretching motion, and it occurred to Emily that there must be any number of young girls who thought Peter Wilson was a dreamboat.

"Oh, Emmy," Sarah said. "My brilliant little baby sister— I love you."

"Well," Emily said. "That's nice." And she realized at once, if only because Tony was looking at her narrowly, that it had been the wrong thing to say. "I mean," she amended, "*you* know; I love you too."

"Isn't she marvelous?" Sarah asked the company. "Isn't my little sister marvelous? What do you think, Howie? Is it all right to call you Howie?"

"Sure," Howard said kindly. "I think she's marvelous."

It had been over a year now since Sarah's head was shaved, but her hair still had a cropped, untidy look, and it was lusterless. The rest of her, beneath that half-collapsed face, was all sag and bloat: she looked a great deal older than her age. Soon the others began to talk among themselves, leaving the sisters alone on the sofa, and Emily used the opportunity to say "I didn't know you'd lost your teeth, Sarah. When did that happen?"

"Oh, I don't know; couple of years ago," Sarah said in the same embarrassed, pointedly offhand way she'd dismissed her head wound as "nothing" in Central Islip, and Emily realized too late that it hadn't been a very tactful question. To atone for it she squeezed the pale hands that were squeezing her own and said "You're looking very well."

"Peter!" Sarah called sharply, and Emily thought she might say "Shape up," but instead she said "Tell the story about the old Negro priest you met in Africa."

"Never mind that now, Mom," he said.

"Oh, please. Come on, Peter."

"Mom, I'd really rather not, okay? It isn't a 'story' anyway."

"Of course it is," she insisted. "When Peter was in Africa he met this wonderful old Negro priest, and he—"

"Mom, will you cut it out?" he said, smiling to show he wasn't really annoyed with her, and only then did she leave him alone. Still smiling, he puckered his lips very slightly as if to blow her a kiss. Then he turned to Howard and said "What kind of legal work do you do, sir?"

A little later the kitchen door slammed and a hulking, squint-eyed youth came in, wearing a studded leather jacket and motorcycle boots, looking as if he meant harm to them all; it took Emily a moment to realize that this was Sarah's third son, Eric. He dipped his head politely at Emily and shook hands with Howard; then he drew his father and brother aside for a long mumbled conference that seemed to be about the workings of an automobile, and when their business was concluded he slouched outdoors again.

It was a bright September afternoon. Trees stirred in the wind beyond the windows, and mottled shadows moved on the dusty floor. No one could think of anything to talk about.

"Anthony?" Sarah said quietly, as if reminding her husband of some private duty.

"Mm," he replied, and went out to the kitchen. When he came back he carried what looked like a glass of orange juice, but there was nothing festive in his way of bringing it to her: the glass hung from his fingers, close to one thigh of his jeans, and he seemed to sneak it into her waiting hand. She took the first few swallows slowly and solemnly enough to make clear that it contained vodka or gin.

"Anyone like some—coffee or something?" Tony Wilson asked his guests.

"No, thanks," Emily said. "Actually, we'd better be going; it's a long drive."

"Oh, you *can't* go," Sarah told her. "You only just got here. I won't *let* you go." Then, as her drink began to take effect, she brightened with a new idea. "Peter," she said. "Will you do me a favor? One little favor?"

"What's that?"

She paused for dramatic effect. "Get the guitar."

He looked mortified. "Oh, no, Mom," he said, and one of his hands, hanging from his knee as he sat, made a little negative gesture to show it was out of the question.

"Please, Peter."

"No."

But Sarah wouldn't take no for an answer. "All you have to do," she explained, "is go out to your car and get it, and bring it back in here, and play 'Where Have All the Flowers Gone.'"

In the end it was Tony who broke the deadlock. "He doesn't want to, dear," he told his wife.

Then Emily got to her feet, smiling, to prove she'd meant it when she'd said that she and Howard had better be going.

Sarah, looking bewildered on the sofa, did not get up to wish them goodbye.

There were no more letters from Sarah, and no telephone calls. At Christmastime the Wilsons' card was signed hastily by Tony, rather than in Sarah's jubilant hand, and this was briefly disturbing.

"Do you think I ought to call her?" Emily asked Howard.

"What for? Just because of the Christmas card? No, honey. If she's in any kind of trouble she'll call you."

"Okay. I suppose you're right."

And then late one night in May of 1968—three months, as Emily figured out later, before Sarah's forty-seventh birthday—the ringing phone brought Emily stumbling out of bed.

"Aunt Emily?"

"Peter?"

"No, it's Tony—Tony Junior . . . I'm afraid your sister passed away today."

And the first thing that occurred to her, even before the news sank in, was that it was just like Tony Junior to have said "passed away" instead of "died."

"What did she—die of?" she inquired after a moment.

"She'd been suffering from a liver ailment for a long time," he said huskily, "so it was mostly that, complicated by a fall she took in the house."

"I see." And Emily heard her own voice sink to the hushed solemnity with which people receive the news of death in the movies. None of this seemed real. "How's your father taking it?"

"Oh, he's—holding up pretty well."

"Well," she said, "give him my—you know—give him my love."

TWO

HOWARD'S CAR WAS being repaired, so they had to go out to the funeral on the train.

"Change a jamake," the conductor told them.

All the way to St. Charles, staring through a dirty window at the slowly wheeling suburbs, Emily gave herself over to memories of her sister. Sarah at twenty, elegantly dressed in borrowed clothes and complaining that she didn't care about the silly Easter parade; Sarah at sixteen with braces on her teeth, bending over the sink each night to wash her sweaters; Sarah at twelve; Sarah at nine.

At nine or ten, Sarah had been much the more imaginative of the girls. She could take a ten-cent book of Woolworth paper dolls, cut out the dolls and their tabbed clothing without ever going over the lines, and invest each dressed doll with a personality of its own. She would decide which of the girl dolls was the prettiest and most popular (and if she felt her dress wasn't nice enough she would design and make a better one, using crayons or watercolor paints); then she would fold all the other dolls forward at the hips to make them sit down as an audience; she would hold the performer upright, make her tremble very slightly the way real singers do, and have her sing "Welcome, Sweet Springtime" or "Look for the Silver Lining," to both of which she knew all the words.

"You okay, Emily?" Howard asked, touching her arm.

"Sure," she said. "I'm fine."

Young Eric met them at the station, wearing mirror sunglasses and dressed in a cheap dark suit from which his big wrists hung like slabs of meat.

"Is Peter here yet?" she asked him.

"Everybody's here," he said as he steered them expertly through traffic.

This was going to be awful. The only thing to do was get through it, get it over with somehow, and try to remember that Howard Dunninger was there with her. He rode alone in the back seat of Eric's car, but by turning her head very slightly she could see the well-pressed Oxford-gray flannel of his trousers, and that was comforting.

"There isn't gonna be a real funeral," Eric said at the wheel. "We're just gonna have a little service at the—you know—at the graveside."

Then they were all walking on fresh grass among tombstones, under a blue sky, and it occurred to Emily that the Wilsons must really have been an important family after all, if they had a private burial plot in one of the most crowded sections of Long Island. Sarah's open grave was covered with a gray tarpaulin. Her closed coffin, lying on the contraption that would lower it into the earth, looked quite small—she had never been very big except in childhood memories. Not far away, one of the newer-looking tombstones read "Edna; beloved wife of Geoffrey," and that was the first Emily knew that old Edna had died: it was funny Sarah hadn't told her. She made a mental note to ask Sarah about it after the ceremony, before it struck her that she could never ask Sarah anything again. Very shyly, like a child seeking her father's forgiveness, she put her fingers through Howard's arm. She could almost hear Sarah's voice saying "It's okay, Emmy. It's okay."

To their left a big, soft-looking man stood weeping, or rather working his lips in an effort at self-control and blinking his red eyes; close beside him was a matronly young woman with a toddling infant and an older boy and girl clinging to her skirt. It was Tony Junior with his wife and baby and stepchildren. The minister was there too, clasping his small prayer book while they waited for the other mourners to arrive.

Several car doors slammed in the distance and soon a cluster of men appeared, walking quickly. Tony was in the middle, in animated conversation with another man. He seemed to be laughing and talking at the same time, and he repeatedly made the same gesture he had used years ago in telling Jack Flanders about the takeoff speed of Magnum jet fighters ("Shoom!")—

knifing the flat of his hand straight ahead from his temple. The man beside him smiled and nodded, and once he cuffed Tony's shoulder with his fist. From their clothes and bearing—starchy and solid, lower middle class—Emily assumed that these other men were some of Tony's co-workers at the Magnum plant; behind them came Peter and another group, solemn young men of about his own age who looked like graduate students.

Tony was still talking when he came up to where Emily and Howard stood. "... Straight ahead, right?" he demanded of the man beside him. "No looking back"—he made the hand-and-temple gesture—"everything straight ahead."

"Right, Tony," the man said. "That's it."

"Oh, I say," Tony said, blinking. "Hello, Emmy." The hollows of his eyes were red and swollen, as if he'd vigorously ground his fists into them for a long time.

"Hello, Tony."

Then he saw Howard and shook hands with him. "Nice to see you, Mr. Howinger. I say, one of our men went over to your firm last month; I told him 'I know the *legal* counsel there; might be useful for you.' P'raps you'll run into him; hell of a nice chap named—or no, wait. That was Union Carbide."

"Well," Howard said, "they're pretty much the same thing."

And Tony turned his inflamed eyes on Emily again. He seemed to be trying to tell her something for which he lacked the words. "I say," he said, bringing the flat of his hand up beside one eye. "Straight ahead. No looking back; no looking sideways—" The hand shot forward. "Straight ahead."

"Right, Tony," she said.

When the ceremony began the Magnum men and the graduate students stood back at a respectful distance. Peter, whose eyes and mouth looked free of any emotion but concern, led his father off to one side of the grave and held him firmly by the upper arm as if to keep him from falling. As the minister's voice intoned the ecclesiastical words Tony's jaws fell open and several strands of spittle clung and trembled between his lips.

"... Earth to earth," the minister was saying, "ashes to ashes, dust to dust ..." and he crumbled a handful of dirt on the top of Sarah's coffin to symbolize her burial.

Then it was over, and they were all walking out of the cemetery. Peter had turned his father over to the Magnum men; now he fell into step with Emily and Howard and said "You're coming back to the house with us for a while, aren't you? Here, we'll go in my car."

Except that his hands shook a little on the ignition key and the steering wheel, he seemed wholly in control of himself. "Those younger guys are friends of mine from the seminary," he said as he drove. "I didn't ask them to come; they found out about it and came out on their own. It always surprises me how kind people are."

"Mm," Emily said. She wanted to say How did she die, Peter? Tell me the truth; instead she turned her head to watch the bright supermarkets and filling stations slide past. "Peter," she said after a while. "Is your grandfather well?"

"Oh, he's fine, Aunt Emmy. He wanted to come out today, but he didn't feel up to it. He's been in a nursing home for some time, you see."

The old house looked even more gaunt and forbidding than Emily had remembered it. One of Tony Junior's stepchildren opened the door for them, giggled, and ran away to hide in the musty living room; the rest of the party was assembled around the dining-room table, which was strewn with sandwich makings and with bottles of beer and soda. It was a noisy gathering.

"...And *this* guy," one of the Magnum men was saying, punching Tony heartily on the shoulder, "this guy catches one measly little blowfish, and he makes such a big deal out of it I thought he's gonna tip the *boat* over."

Tony, his eyes still swollen, rolled with the punch in a spasm of laughter and raised a can of beer to his lips.

"Can I get you something, Aunt Emmy?" Peter asked.

"No, thanks. Well, yes—I'll take a beer, if you have enough."

"You, sir?"

"Nothing for now, thanks," Howard said. "I'm fine."

"No, but I'll never forget this *one* time we went out," the man from Magnum said. Flushed with the success of his first fishing story, he launched into another without seeming to notice that he'd lost most of his audience. "Who-all was with us that time, Tony? You, me, Fred Slovick—I forget. Anyway, we . . ."

"Anybody else on the liverwurst?" Tony Junior inquired. He was taking sandwich orders. "You want the regular mustard on that, or the baby-shit?" His wife, who had apparently put the baby down for a nap, was trying to wipe spilled Coca-Cola from the dress of a peevish five-year-old.

"Tell me one thing, though." One of the seminary students, a pleasant-looking boy with a Southern accent, directed a shy smile at Tony Junior. "One thing I don't understand. How come you didn't beat up on your brother more when you were kids?"

"Oh, I tried," Tony Junior said, spreading mayonnaise on rye bread. "I tried plenty of times, but it wasn't easy. I mean he's little, but he's wiry."

". . . So I says 'I got five bucks,' " the Magnum man was shouting. "I got *five bucks* says Wilson don't catch nothin' all day."

"Ah, Christ, Marty," Tony said, laughing and shaking his head in happy exasperation, "You'll be telling that story when we're *all* dead."

Peter went to answer the phone; when he came back he said "It's for you, Dad."

Still glowing in the aftermath of Marty's story (of which the punch line was that he'd caught more blowfish than anyone else in the boat that day), Tony narrowed his eyes over a shot glass of whiskey and said "Who is it, Pete?"

"It's Sergeant Ryan. You know; over at the station."

Tony knocked back his whiskey and grimaced at the sweet pain of its taste. "Police," he muttered, getting to his feet. "Damned police think I killed my wife."

"Oh, now, Dad, come on," Peter said in a mollifying way as he followed his father out of the room. "You know better than that. I've told you and told you, it's only a routine investigation."

Tony's talk with Sergeant Ryan didn't last long; when he rejoined the party he had another drink—two bottles of whiskey were being passed around the table now—and the shouts and laughter went on far into the late afternoon.

Dark blue shadows filled the house when Emily got up to make her way to the bathroom. In the hallway she stumbled and nearly fell; righting herself, she found she had collided with a small cabinet bearing old copies of the *Daily News* stacked three feet high. On the way back she passed a framed photograph, the picture of Tony and Sarah on Easter Sunday of 1941. It was hanging awry, as if from the impact of some heavy blow that had shuddered the wall. Carefully, with unsteady fingers, she reached up and straightened it.

Lights were being turned on against the heavily gathering dusk.

"... No, but what *I* want to know," the Magnum man was saying to Tony Junior, "what *I* want to know is what kind of a job you guys can do for me."

"The best, Marty," Tony Junior assured him. "You can ask anybody: we're the best mechanics in this part of Suffolk County."

"Because I mean from *my* standpoint of view," Marty persisted, "from *my* standpoint of view that's the only—you know —the only consideration."

"Ma," one of the children whined. "Hey, Ma, c'we go home now?"

"I say, come and have a drink," Tony said to a hesitant group of seminary students. "Don't you chaps ever drink?"

"Thank you, sir," one of them said. "A little bourbon and water."

"Are you all right, Emily?" Howard inquired, looking up from his conversation with another of the Magnum men.

"I'm fine. Can I get you a drink?"

"I've got one, thanks."

Through it all Eric stood leaning alone against the kitchen doorjamb, silent and inscrutable behind his mirror sunglasses, like a young security guard hired to keep the party from getting out of hand.

Tony Junior's wife took the children home without saying goodbye to anyone; not long after that the seminary students left, and then all the Magnum men but Marty made their departure.

"... Listen, Tony," Marty said. "You gotta eat, right? Let's everybody go grab a steak at Manny's."

And in several cars, after some drink-fuddled preliminary

bickering about who would ride with whom, the mourners roared down the highway to a floodlit California-style restaurant called Manny Feldon's Chop House.

It was so dark inside the place that they could scarcely see across the table as they raised their heavy cocktail glasses. Peter was sober: he sat close beside his father, as if this ceremony too, like the one in the graveyard, might require his assistance. Marty and Tony Junior were once again deep in their talk of business, though now it seemed to have taken a philosophical turn. There was no substitute for honest workmanship in any field, Marty was saying, while Tony Junior nodded slowly and steadily to show he couldn't agree more. "I mean *any* field, whether it's mechanics or carpentry or shoemaking or you name it. Am I right?"

Emily held her edge of the table firmly in both hands because it had become the only steady surface in sight: everything else was shifting and turning. Beside her in the deep upholstery against the wall—and the wall was unsteady too—Howard was putting away enough liquor to suggest that this might be the third or fourth night since she'd known him that he would go to bed drunk.

Eric sat close to no one, and he was the only one who ate heartily when the giant steaks arrived. He ate with the rhythmic passion of a starving man, hunched over his plate as if to guarantee that it wouldn't be snatched away.

"... No, but the older I get," Marty was saying "—and mind you, I figure I've only got maybe fifteen years tops—the older I get the more I stop and think. I mean you see these kids today running around with their long hair and their crummy jeans and their crazy ideas, and what do *they* know? Am I right? I mean what do *they* know?"

In the end Howard proved sober enough to fish the timetable out of his pocket, study it in the wavering glow of his cigarette lighter and determine that they had fifteen minutes to catch the last train.

"Keep in touch, Aunt Emmy," Peter said, rising to wish them goodbye, and he shook hands with Howard. "Thanks for coming out, sir."

Tony struggled out of his chair, swaying. He mumbled something inaudible to Howard, wiped his mouth and looked undecided about whether to give Emily a kiss on the cheek. Instead he held her hand for a second, not quite looking her in the eyes; then he let go, brought his own hand slowly up to his temple and shot it forward. "Straight ahead," he said.

It took Emily a long time to realize that Sarah was dead. Sometimes, waking from a dream of childhood filled with Sarah's face and Sarah's voice, she would go and study her own face in the bright bathroom mirror until she found assurance that it was still the face of Sarah's sister, and that it didn't look old.

"Howard?" she said once when they were lying in bed, waiting for sleep. "Do you know something? I really wish you could have known Sarah in the old days, before everything went to pieces. She was lovely."

"Mm," he said.

"Lovely and bright and full of life—and this may sound silly, but I think if you'd known her then it might've helped you to know me better."

"Oh, I don't know. I think I know you pretty well."

"No you don't," she said.

"Mm?"

"You don't really. We hardly ever talk."

"Are you kidding? We talk all the damn time, Emily."

"You never want to hear about my childhood or anything."

"Sure I do. I know all about your childhood. Besides, everybody's childhood is pretty much alike."

"How can you *say* that? Only the most obtuse, insensitive person in the *world* could say a thing like that."

"Okay, okay, okay," he said sleepily. "Tell me a story about your childhood. Make it heartbreaking."

"*Ugh!*" And she rolled away from him. "You're impossible. You're a Neanderthal."

"Mm."

Another time, when they were coming back from a drive in the country at dusk, she said "How can you be so sure it was cirrhosis, Howard?"

"I'm not sure; I just said it was most likely, considering the way she drank."

"But then there's that fishy business of the 'fall she took in the house.' And the police calling up, and Tony saying 'The police think I killed my wife.' I'll bet he did, Howard. I'll bet he flew into a drunken rage and hit her with a chair or something."

"They didn't arrest him, did they? If they'd had any evidence they'd have arrested him."

"Well, but he and the boys could've *concealed* the evidence."

"Honey, we've been over all this a hundred times. It's just one of those things you'll never know. Life is full of things like that."

Three or four old barns went by, and then any number of suburban developments, and then the beginnings of the Bronx; they were all the way to the Henry Hudson Bridge before she said "You're right."

"Right about what?"

"Life *is* full of things like that."

There were things she would never know about Howard, too, however much she might love him. Sometimes it seemed that she scarcely knew him at all.

Things weren't going very well at work. Hannah Baldwin seldom asked Emily out to lunch any more—she had taken to having lunch with one of the younger women in Emily's department—and she seldom called her "honey," nor did she often come out of her private office to place one stout, well-clad haunch on the edge of Emily's desk and waste whole hours with idle chatter in the middle of a working day. She had begun to give her what Emily described to Howard as "funny looks"— speculative, not very friendly looks—and she found things to criticize in the way Emily did her job.

"This copy's flat," she said once of something on which Emily had worked for many days. "It just lies there. Isn't there some way you can breathe a little life into it?"

When the name of a Swedish importer came out in print without the umlaut over one of its vowels, Hannah heavily implied that it was all Emily's fault. And when Emily let a National

Carbon ad go through production without noticing that the words "patent pending" did not appear after "Tynol," Hannah behaved as if it were a calamity. "Have you any idea what the *legal* implications are in a thing like this?" she demanded.

"Hannah, I'm sure it'll be all right," Emily said. "I *know* the legal counsel for National Carbon."

Hannah blinked and squinted. "You 'know' him? What do you mean, you 'know' him?"

Emily felt blood in her face. "I mean we're friends."

There was a pause. "Well," Hannah said at last, "it's nice to have friends, but it doesn't have much to do with the business world."

That night Emily told Howard about it, at dinner, and he said "Sounds to me like she's going through menopause. Not a hell of a lot you can do about that." He sliced off a piece of steak and chewed it thoroughly before swallowing. Then he said "Why don't you quit the damn job, Emily? You don't have to work. We don't need the money."

"No, no," she said quickly. "It's not that bad; I'm not ready to do anything like that." But later, standing at the sink to wash the dishes while he fixed himself an after-dinner drink, she felt a powerful urge to cry. She wanted to go to him and weep attractively against his shirt. He had said "We don't need the money," just as if they were married.

One evening, a year after Sarah's death, a tired woman's voice identifying itself as Central Islip State Hospital called up to say "We regret to inform you of the death of Esther Crimes."

"Oh," Emily said. "I see. Well, can you tell me what the procedure is?"

"The procedure?"

"I mean—you know—about funeral arrangements."

"That's entirely up to you, Miss Grimes."

"I know it's up to me. All I mean is—"

"If you wish a private funeral, we can recommend several funeral homes in this area."

"Just recommend one, okay?"

"My instructions are to recommend several."

"Oh. Well, okay, wait—let me get a pencil." And as she passed Howard's chair on her way from the phone she said "My mother's dead. Whaddya know about that?"

When her business was concluded Howard said "Emily? Would you like me to go along with you out there tomorrow?"

"Oh, no," she told him. "It'll just be an awful little ceremony at the whaddyacallit, the mortuary. I can handle it myself."

All three of Pookie's grandsons were waiting under the Central Islip trees when Emily's taxi pulled up outside the mortuary the next afternoon. They were the only people there. Peter left his brothers and came forward to help her out of the cab, smiling. "Good to see you, Aunt Emmy," he said. He was wearing a clerical collar; he had been ordained. "Normally they send a priest over from the hospital to perform these services," he said, "but I asked if I could do it and they said okay."

"Well, that's—that's fine, Peter," she said. "That's very nice."

The dim chapel smelled of dust and varnish. Emily, Eric and Tony Junior sat in the front pew, facing the altar where Pookie's closed coffin lay between two candlesticks. Then Peter came in through a side door, wearing some kind of Episcopalian stole, and began to read aloud from his prayer book.

" . . . We brought nothing into this world, and it is certain we can take nothing out. The Lord gave, and the Lord hath taken away; blessed be the name of the Lord . . ."

When it was over, Emily went out to the office and up to a cashier's window, where a man gave her an itemized invoice and accepted her check in payment, after asking to see her driver's license. "You may accompany the remains to the crematory," he said, "but I wouldn't recommend it. There's nothing to see."

"Thank you," she said, remembering the twin smokestacks on the Central Islip horizon.

"Thank *you*."

The three Wilson boys were waiting for her. "Aunt Emmy?" Peter said. "I know my father'd like to see you. Can I drive you over there, just for a few minutes?"

"Well, I—all right, sure."

"How about you guys?"

But it turned out that both his brothers had to get back to their jobs, and after they'd mumbled goodbye their cars roared away in different directions.

"My father's married again," Peter said as he drove her down a long straight road. "Did you know that?"

"No; no, I didn't."

"Best thing in the world for him. He married a very nice lady who owns a restaurant in St. Charles, a widow. They'd been friends for years."

"I see. And do they live in the old—"

"Oh, no; Great Hedges is long gone. He sold it to a developer soon after my mother died. There's nothing out there now but dirt and bulldozers. No, he moved in with his new wife—her name's Vera—in an apartment over the restaurant. It's very nice. And he's retired from Magnum—did you know that?"

"No."

"Well, he was in a bad car accident about six months ago, suffered a bad head injury and broke his shoulder, so he took his retirement early. Now he's just sort of recuperating and taking things easy; I imagine when he's ready to work again he'll go partners with Vera in the restaurant business."

"I see." After a while it occurred to her to ask about old Geoffrey. "How's your grandfather, Peter?"

"Oh, he died, Aunt Emmy. He died last year."

"Well, I'm—very sorry to hear that."

The fields on either side of the road gave way to dense masses of houses, and to shopping centers with acres of parked cars. "Tell me about yourself, Peter," she said. "Where are you located now?"

"I lucked into a terrific job," he said, glancing briefly away from the wheel. "I'm assistant chaplain at Edwards College, up in New Hampshire. Have you heard of Edwards?"

"Certainly."

"I couldn't have asked for a better situation in a first job," he went on. "My boss is a fine man, a fine priest, and we seem to think alike. The work is very challenging and very gratifying. Besides, I like working with young people."

"Mm," she said. "Well, that's fine. Congratulations."

"What about you, Aunt Emmy?"

"Oh, things are pretty much the same with me."

There was a long pause. Then, staring meditatively at the road ahead, he said "You know something? I've always admired you, Aunt Emmy. My mother used to say 'Emmy's a free spirit.' I didn't know what that meant when I was little, so I asked her once. And she said 'Emmy doesn't care what anybody thinks. She's her own person and she goes her own way.'"

The walls of Emily's throat closed up. When she felt it was safe to speak she said "Did she really say that?"

"As nearly as I can remember, that's exactly what she said."

They were traveling now through suburban streets so thickly populated that he had to keep braking for stop-lights. "It's not much farther," he said. "Right around this next corner... Here."

The restaurant's sign promised STEAK and LOBSTERS and COCKTAILS, but it had a dreary look: the paint was flaking off its white clapboard front, and its windows were too small. It was the kind of place that a hungry man and woman in a car might spend several minutes considering ("Whaddya think?" "Well, I don't know; it looks sort of awful. Maybe there'll be a better place further on." "Honey, I've told you: there won't be anything else for miles." "Oh, well, in that case—sure; what the hell.")

Peter parked in the weed-grown gravel of its parking lot and led Emily around behind the building to a wooden staircase that led up to a second-story door.

"Dad?" he called. "You home?"

And there was Tony Wilson, looking like an aging, bewildered Laurence Olivier as he opened the flimsy door and let them in. "I say," he said. "Hello, Emmy."

The small apartment had a makeshift look—it reminded Emily of Pookie's old apartment over the garage at Great Hedges—and it contained too much furniture. Two of Tony's ancestors stared from the cluttered walls; the other pictures were the kind that come with picture frames purchased in a five- and ten-cent store. Vera came bustling in from the kitchen, all smiles, a vigorous big-boned woman in her forties, wearing shorts.

"I hope you won't think my legs are always this heavy," she said. "I have these terrible allergies, and sometimes they make my legs swell up." And she struck her fist against one quivering thigh to indicate the excess flesh. "Can you find a place to sit down? Peter, move that box out of the blue chair so she can sit down."

"Thank you," Emily said.

"We were so sorry to hear about your mother," Vera said in a lowered voice, sitting beside Tony on a small sofa that Emily recognized from the old house. "You only get one mother."

"Well, she'd been—very sick for a long time."

"I know. My mother went the same way. Five years in and out of the hospital, in constant pain. Cancer of the pancreas. My first husband, too—cancer of the colon. He died in agony. And *this* one." She nudged Tony heavily in the upper arm. "*God*, what a scare he gave me. Did Peter tell you about the accident? Oh, I forgot to offer you something. Would you care for some coffee? Or some tea?"

"No, thanks; neither one. I'm fine."

"Have a cookie, anyway; they're good." She pointed to a plate of chocolate-chip cookies on the coffee table. Peter reached over and took one, which he munched while she went on talking. "*Any*way," she said, "the Highway Patrol called me at five-thirty in the afternoon, and I got over to the hospital before they started working on him. They had him lying on a stretcher in the emergency room, unconscious, blood all over the place, and I swear to God I thought he was dead. His brains were spilling out."

"Okay, Vera," Peter said around a mouthful of cookie.

She turned on him, her eyes round with innocence and indignation. "You don't believe me? You don't believe me? I swear to God. I swear to God, Peter, the man's brains were spilling out in his *hair*."

Peter swallowed. "Well," he said, "at least they managed to patch him up." And he turned to his father. "Dad, here's the piece I was telling you about, the one I thought you might like to read." From the inside pocket of his coat he drew a folded brochure, handsomely printed on rich tan paper, with an old-English kind of crest and the words "Edwards College" as part of its heading.

"What's this?" Vera demanded, still bridling over his disbelief of the brains in the hair. "A sermon or something?"

"Oh, come on, Vera," Peter said. "You know I don't give you sermons. It's just a bulletin my church puts out."

"Mm," Tony said. He pulled a pair of reading glasses from his shirt pocket, put them on and peered through them at the brochure, blinking several times.

"That first article is by my boss," Peter explained. "You might enjoy reading that too. My own piece is on the inside page."

"Mm." Tony carefully put the brochure away in his shirt pocket, along with his glasses and his pack of cigarettes, and said "Ve'y good, Pete."

"Oh, this Peter," Vera confided to Emily. "Isn't he too much? Isn't he gonna make some girl happy one of these days?"

"He certainly is."

"Tony Junior and I have our problems," she said, "and Eric— well, I don't know about Eric; but this Peter. He really is too much. Only you know what, though? They're spoiling him, all those women up at Edwards College. Spoiling him rotten. They *feed* him; they make his *bed* for him; they take out his *laundry* for him—"

"Okay, Vera," Peter said, and then he inspected his watch. "I guess we'd better be getting started, Aunt Emmy, if we want to make that train."

Once during the following winter Howard had to go to Los Angeles again—the seventh or eighth such trip he'd made since she'd known him.

"I won't *need* all this heavy stuff," he said when she was helping him to pack. "You don't understand how warm it is out there."

"Oh," she said. "That's right, I forgot." And she let him do the rest of the packing by himself.

She went into the kitchen to make coffee, but changed her mind and fixed herself a drink instead. These departures were always upsetting. She was determined not to ask him if he intended to see Linda: the last time she'd asked him that, on his third or fourth trip, it had brought on what almost amounted to a fight. Besides, she assured herself as the alcohol warmed her blood, it wasn't really very likely. He and Linda had been separated for almost six years now—six *years*, for God's sake—and though he sometimes still talked about her in the old infuriating way, it certainly ought to be clear by now that the marriage was dissolved.

But that brought up the insidious question that had nagged her from the beginning, threatening time and again to make her fly at him with shrill and redundant demands for an answer: if the marriage was dissolved, why didn't they get a divorce?

"What's the deal?" Howard said, smiling in the kitchen doorway. "You drinking alone?"

"Sure. I always drink alone when you go on these trips. I'm getting in practice for when you disappear to California for good. Give me a few years and I'll be one of these terrible old ladies you see on the street with four shopping bags, picking through trash cans and talking to themselves."

"Cut it out, Emily. You mad at me? What're you mad about?"

"Of course I'm not 'mad' at you. Would you like a drink?"

That particular California trip gave her no cause for worry. He called her four times while he was gone, and the fourth time, when he said he was tired, she said "Listen, Howard: don't go through that awful business of taking a cab home from the airport. I'll drive the car out and meet you."

"No, no," he said. "You don't have to do that."

"I know I don't have to. It's just a thing I'd like to do."

There was a pause while he seemed to think it over. Then he said "Okay, good. You're a sweetheart, Emily."

She wasn't used to driving his big, quiet car, especially at night and in the rain. Its power and fluidity frightened her—she applied the brakes more often than necessary, causing drivers behind her to sound their horns—but she enjoyed the rich, massive feel of it and the way the dark, dark green of its broad hood was pearled with trembling raindrops.

Howard looked drawn and exhausted as he emerged from the plane ramp—he looked old—but when he caught sight of her his face glowed in a way that was almost boyish. "Damn," he said. "It sure is nice to find you waiting here."

Less than a year later he went to California again—and this time his absence was filled with silence and dread. She couldn't even plan to meet him with the car because she wasn't sure which day or night he'd come home, let alone on which flight. All she could do was wait—trying to appease Hannah Baldwin's disgruntlement through the working hours, trying to suppress a keen temptation to drink herself to sleep in the evenings.

Once during that time, walking back to the office after lunch, she saw a haggard, petulant woman's face—a face that anyone would have said was aging badly (lined and deeply shadowed eyes; a weak, self-pitying mouth)—and found with a shock that it was herself, caught unawares in the reflection of a plate-glass window. That night, alone at the bathroom mirror, she tried any number of ways to make the face look better: crinkling its eyes in a subtle smile and then in a wider smile of pure delight, tightening and loosening its lips to varying degrees, using a hand mirror to gauge the effects of its profile from different angles, experimenting tirelessly with new ways of enhancing its shape through different arrangements of her hair. Then, in front of the full-length mirror in the vestibule, she took off all her clothes and scrutinized her body under bright lights. Her belly had to be sucked flat before it looked right, but having small breasts was almost an advantage now; there wasn't much that age could do to them. Turning away, she peered over her shoulder to confirm the knowledge that her buttocks were underslung and the backs of her thighs wrinkled; but in general, she decided, facing the mirror again, she wasn't bad at all. She paced off a distance of ten feet, until she stood on the living-room carpet, and there she went through a series of the steps and positions she had learned in a modern dance class at Barnard. It was good exercise, and it gave her a proudly erotic feeling. The distant mirror showed a slim, lithe girl in effortless motion, until she put a foot wrong and froze into awkwardness. She was breathing hard and beginning to sweat. This was silly.

The thing to do was take a shower. But when she walked into the bathroom the medicine-cabinet mirror caught her as cruelly as the window on the street that day, and there it was again: the face of a middle-aged woman in hopeless and terrible need.

Howard came home two nights after the night she stopped expecting him, and she knew the moment she saw him, if not from the very sound of his key in the lock, that it was all over.

"... I would've called you," he explained, "but I didn't see any point in waking you up just to say I'd be a little late. How've you been?"

"All right. How was your trip?"

"Oh, it was—quite a trip. Let me get us both a drink, and then we'll talk." From the kitchen, over the sounds of ice cubes and glassware, he called "Actually, Emily, there's quite a lot to talk about," and he came back to her with two clicking highballs. He looked guilty. "First of all," he began after the heavy sigh that followed his first few sips, "I don't suppose it's really news to you that I've seen Linda occasionally on some of these trips over the past—however long it's been."

"No," she said. "That's not really news."

"Sometimes I'd finish work a day or two ahead of time," he went on, sounding encouraged, "and I'd fly up to San Francisco and we'd have dinner together. Nothing more than that. She'd tell me about how she was doing—and actually she's doing very well: she and another girl have their own business, designing clothes—and I'd just sit there acting sort of like her father. Once or twice I'd ask her if she'd met any nice guys, and then when she'd tell me about men she'd been 'seeing' or 'dating' I'd feel my heart start to pound like some crazy—I don't know. I'd feel the blood racing all the way down to my fingertips. I'd feel—"

"Get to the point, Howard."

"All right." He drank off nearly all of his bourbon-and-water and then he sighed again, as if in relief that the hard part was over. "The point is there wasn't really any National Carbon business on this trip," he said. "I did lie to you on that score, Emily, and I'm sorry. I hate lying. I spent the whole time with Linda. She's almost thirty-five now—nobody can call her an impressionable kid any more—and she's decided she wants to come back to me."

For weeks and months afterwards, Emily thought of many passionate, well-worded rejoinders she might have made to that statement; at the time, though, all she could muster was the weak, meek little phrase she had hated herself for using since childhood: "I see."

It took only a couple of days for Howard to move his belongings out of the apartment. He was very apologetic about everything. Only once, when he flicked the heavy silken rope of his neckties out of the closet, was there any kind of a scene, and that turned into such a dreadful, squalid scene—it ended with her falling on her knees to embrace his legs and begging him, begging him to stay—that Emily did the best she could to put it out of her mind.

There were worse things in the world than being alone. She told herself that every day as she went efficiently about the business of getting ready for work, of enduring her eight hours in Baldwin Advertising and of conquering the evenings until she could sleep.

There was no longer any listing for Michael Hogan in the Manhattan Telephone Directory, or any listing for his public relations firm. He had always talked of moving to Texas, which was his home; probably he'd made the move.

Ted Banks was still listed, at his old address, but when she called him he explained with what seemed an excessive amount of embarrassment that he was married to a wonderful person.

She tried others—it had always seemed that her life was filled with men—but none came through.

There was no Flanders, John; and when she tried Flanders, J., on West End Avenue, it turned out to be a woman.

For a year she found an exquisite pain—almost pleasure—in facing the world as if she didn't care. Look at me, she would say to herself in the middle of a trying day. Look at me: I'm surviving; I'm coping; I'm in control of all this.

But some days were worse than others; and one afternoon, a few days before her forty-eighth birthday, turned out to be especially bad. She had carried a batch of finished copy and layouts uptown for a client's approval, and on coming back she was all the way into Hannah Baldwin's office before discovering that she'd left it all on the seat of the taxicab.

"Oh, my God!" Hannah cried, reeling back on the casters of her desk chair as if she'd been shot through the heart. Then she came forward again, placed both elbows on the desk and held her head with all ten fingers, messing up her careful hair. "You've gotta be kidding," she said. "That was *finished* copy. That was *approved* copy. It had the client's *signature* on it..."

And Emily stood watching her, realizing at last how much she had always disliked her, knowing this was probably the last time she would ever face this humiliation.

"... Total, utter carelessness," Hannah was saying. "Any *child* could've been trusted with a thing like this, and it's so *typical* of you, Emily. And it isn't as if you hadn't been warned; I've given you every chance. I've been carrying you—I've been carrying you for years—and I simply can't afford it any longer."

"I have several things to tell *you*, Hannah," Emily said, proud that she was shaking only a little and that her voice came out almost steady, "and the first is that I've worked here too long to be 'fired.' I want to resign as of today."

Hannah took her hands away from her disheveled hair and looked up into Emily's eyes for the first time. "Oh, Emily, you *are* a child. Don't you see I'm trying to do you a favor? If you resign you'll have nothing. If you let me fire you, you can draw Unemployment. Don't you even know that? Were you born yesterday?"

THREE

ON THE DOLE—A WOMAN'S STORY

IF YOU'RE FIRED from a job in New York, you can receive unemployment compensation checks for fifty-two weeks. After that, if you still haven't found work, your only recourse is to go on Welfare. There are more than one and a half million people on Welfare in the metropolitan area.

I am white, Anglo-Saxon, Protestant, and a college graduate. I have always earned my living in "professional" fields—as a librarian, as a journalist, and finally as an advertising copywriter. I am now in my ninth month of unemployment status, with nothing but Welfare in sight. My employment counsellors, public and private, have done their best; they tell me there simply aren't any jobs.

Perhaps no one can fully explain this predicament, but at the risk of displaying an easy and all too fashionable self-pity, I will hazard a guess: I am a woman, and I am no longer young.

That was as far as Emily's article went. It had been rolled into her typewriter for weeks; now the paper was curled and sun-bleached and gathering dust.

She was in the eleventh month of her unemployment status when she began to fear that she might be losing her mind. She had given up the old apartment and moved into a smaller, cheaper place in the West Twenties, not far from where Jack Flanders had once lived. Watching the early morning light filter down among the loft buildings across the street, she often thought of Jack Flanders fondling her elbow inside his bathrobe and saying "Sometimes, if you play your cards right, you get to meet a nice girl." But that was part of the trouble: she lived in memories all the time. No sight or sound or smell in the whole of New York was free of old associations; wherever she walked, and she sometimes walked for hours, she found only the past.

Hard liquor frightened her, but she drank enough beer to help her sleep in the afternoons—it was a good way to kill time—and it was on waking from one of these naps, sitting on the bed and staring at four empty beer cans on the floor, that she had her first intimations of madness. If anyone had asked her what day or month or year it was she would have had to say "Wait—let me think," and she didn't know whether the gray beyond her windows was dawn or dusk. Worse still, her dreams had been filled with clamorous voices from the past, and now the voices were still talking. She ran for the door to make sure it was locked—Good; nobody could get in; she was alone and safe in her own private place—and after standing there for a long time with her fist in her mouth she got the telephone book and fumbled through the "New York—City of" listings until she found "Mental Health Information Service." But when she tried to call that number it rang eleven times with no answer. Then she remembered it was Sunday; she would have to wait.

"You ought to get out and *meet* people, Emily," Grace Talbot often told her. Grace Talbot had worked at Baldwin Advertising too, until she found a better job with a bigger agency, and lately had become Emily's only friend. She was wry and hawk-faced and not very likable, but once a week, when they met for a restaurant dinner together, she seemed better than nothing.

And she was certainly better than nothing now. Emily was halfway through the dialing of her number before she realized she didn't know what to say. She couldn't say "Grace, I think I'm going crazy" without sounding like a fool.

"Hello?"

"Hi, Grace, it's Emily. I just called for—you know—no very good reason, except to talk."

"Oh. Well, that's—nice. How've you been?"

"Oh, okay, I guess, except that Sundays in New York can be pretty awful."

"Really? God, I *love* Sundays. I luxuriate in bed for hours with the *Times*, and with cinnamon toast and cups upon cups of tea, and then in the afternoon I take a walk in the park, or sometimes friends drop over, or sometimes I go to a film. It's the only day of the week when I really feel like myself."

There was a pause during which Emily regretted having called at all. Then she said "What'd you do this afternoon?"

"Oh, I had a drink with some friends, George and Myra Fox. *I've* told you about them: he writes blurb copy for paperback books; she's a commercial artist. They're delightful people."

"Oh. Well, I just thought I'd check in with you and—you know—see what you were up to." Everything she said made her hate herself more and more. "I'm sorry if I bothered you in the middle of something, or anything like that."

And there was another pause. "Emily?" Grace Talbot said at last. "You know something? I wish you'd quit kidding me, and quite kidding yourself. *I* know how lonely you are; it's a *crime* for anyone to be that lonely. Listen: George and Myra are having a few people over next Friday evening. How about coming along with me? . . ."

A party. It would be the first party in longer than she wanted to remember, and Friday was only five days away.

All week she could think of nothing else; then Friday was upon her, and all that mattered in the world was getting her clothes and her hair right. She settled on a simple black dress (she couldn't help remembering how Howard Dunninger had said, of Linda, "She was wearing a simple, short black dress . . .") and a hair style that left one lock attractively low over the eye. She looked good. There might easily be a man there, a graying, pleasant-looking man of her own age or older, who would say "Tell me about yourself, Emily . . ."

But it wasn't really a party at all. The eight or ten people in the Foxes' living room never left their seats to get up and move around; they all seemed to know each other, and they sat in attitudes of exhaustion, with sardonic faces, sipping at tiny glasses of cheap red wine. There were no unattached men. Emily and Grace, sitting well apart from the main group, were wholly excluded from the talk until Myra Fox bustled over to their rescue, bringing the expectant listening looks of several other guests in her wake.

"Have I told you about Trudy?" she demanded of Grace. "Our neighbor on this floor? She said she might drop in later, so you may meet her, but you really ought to *know* about her first. She's really something. She's—"

And here George Fox, standing with a wine bottle poised for pouring, interrupted his wife in a voice loud enough to address the group. "Trudy runs a women's masturbation clinic," he said.

"Oh, George, it's not a 'clinic.' It's a studio."

"A studio, right," George Fox said. "She gets women of all ages—mostly sort of middle-aged, I gather—and she charges quite a hefty fee. The classes meet in her studio and go through a warm-up of modern dance routines—in the nude, of course—and then they get down to the well, they get down to the business at hand, you might say. Because Trudy doesn't believe in masturbation as a poor substitute for the real thing, you see; she believes in masturbation as a way of life. Sort of the ultimate in radical feminism. Who needs men?"

"I don't believe it," somebody said.

"You don't believe it? Stick around. You'll meet her. Ask her yourself. And she likes nothing better than to show visitors through the studio."

Trudy did drop in later—or rather, she made an entrance. The most startling thing about her was that her head was shaved—she looked like a handsome, totally bald man of forty or so—and then you noticed her clothes: a man's purple undershirt through which the nipples of her small breasts jutted, and a pair of well-bleached blue jeans whose crotch had been appliquéd in the pattern of a big yellow butterfly. She mingled with the company for a while, drawing deeply on a cigarette in a way that emphasized her hollow cheeks and prominent cheekbones; then, when some of the guests were beginning to leave, she said "Would anyone care to see my studio?"

First came an entrance hall with many coat hooks on its walls and a sign above its archway reading PLEASE REMOVE YOUR CLOTHES. "You can ignore that," Trudy said, "but please do take off your shoes," and she led her stockinged visitors into the big, deeply carpeted main room.

On one wall was a huge, anatomically perfect drawing of

a woman reclining naked with her legs apart, fondling one breast with one hand and applying an electric vibrator to her crotch with the other. On another wall, bathed in a spotlight from the ceiling, was what looked like a sculptured sunburst of many podlike aluminum shapes. Close up, the pods proved to be precise life-sized renderings of open vaginas—some considerably larger than others, all with intricately different kinds of outer and inner labia. Emily was inspecting the display when Trudy came up to stand at her shoulder.

"These are some of my students," she explained. "A sculptor friend of mine modeled them in wax, then they were cast into aluminum."

"I see," Emily said. "Well, that's very—interesting." The glass of wine was warm and sticky in her fingers, and her spine ached with tiredness. She had a presentiment that if she didn't get out of here at once, Trudy would invite her to enroll in her classes.

Trying not to hurry, she excused herself and went back to the entrance hall where her shoes lay, and then back to the Foxes' apartment where several people were agreeing with each other that Trudy's studio was the God damnedest thing they had ever seen.

"I *told* you," George Fox kept saying. "You wouldn't believe me, but I *told* you . . ."

Then the party was over and she was out on the sidewalk saying goodnight to Grace Talbot, who insisted several times that the evening had been "fun," and then she was on her way home.

There were no more parties, and she got out of the habit of taking walks. She left her apartment only to buy food ("TV dinners" and other cheap, processed food, easy to prepare and quick to eat), and there were many days when she didn't even do that. Once, having willed herself out on the street and into a corner delicatessen, she had selected her purchases from the shelves and the freezer and placed them near the cash register when she looked up and found the proprietor smiling into her eyes. He was a soft, stout man in his sixties, with coffee stains on his apron, and in none of the times she'd dealt with him before had he ever smiled like that, or even spoken to her.

"You know something?" he said, as shyly as if he were about to make a declaration of love. "If all my customers were like you, my life would be a great deal happier."

"Mm?" she said. "Why is that?"

"Because you help yourself," he said. "You pick everything out for yourself and you bring it up here. That's wonderful. Most people—especially the women—come in here and say 'Box of Wheaties.' I go all the way back to where the cereal's kept, bring it all the way back up, and they say 'Oh, I forgot—a box of Rice Krispies, too.' So for thirty-nine cents I'm getting a heart attack. Not you. Not you, ever. You're a pleasure to do business with."

"Well," she said. "Thank you." And her fingers trembled as she counted out the dollar bills. It was the first time in nearly a week that she'd heard the sound of her own voice, and it had been much, much longer than that since anyone—anyone—had said something nice to her.

Several times she started to dial the number for Mental Health Information Service, but couldn't make herself complete the call. Then once she did complete it and was referred to another number, at which a woman with a heavy Spanish accent, speaking carefully, explained the procedure: Emily could go to Bellevue Hospital any weekday morning before ten, go down to the basement level and look for a sign reading WALK-IN CLINIC. There she would be interviewed by a social worker, and an appointment with a psychiatrist would be arranged for her at a later date.

"Thank you very much," Emily said, but she never went. The prospect of going down into the bowels of Bellevue in search of the Walk-in Clinic seemed almost as bereft of hope as that of walking into Trudy's studio.

One afternoon she was returning from a long walk to the Village that she'd forced herself to take—a visit seething with memories of the dead—when she came to a stop on the sidewalk and felt her blood quicken with the beginnings of a new idea. She hurried home then, and once she was alone behind her locked door she dragged a heavy, dusty cardboard box out of its storage place and into the middle of the floor. It was a box of old letters—she had never been able to throw a letter away—and she went through many thick handfuls of shifting, sliding envelopes, all of them hopelessly out of chronological order, before she found one of the two she was looking for:

Mr. and Mrs. Martin S. Gregory
Have the honor to announce the marriage of their daughter
Carol Elizabeth
to
The Reverend Peter J. Wilson
On Friday, the eleventh of October, nineteen sixty-nine
St. John's Church
Edwardstown, New Hampshire

She remembered being slightly hurt at not having been invited to the wedding, but Howard had said "Oh, that's silly; nobody gives big, fancy weddings any more." She had sent an expensive silver gift and received a nice, touchingly young-sounding note of thanks from Peter's bride, written in a bold little private-school hand.

It took what seemed hours to find the second item, which was a good deal more recent.

The Reverend and Mrs. Peter J. Wilson
Announce the birth of a daughter
Sarah Jane
Seven pounds, six ounces
December third, nineteen seventy

"Oh, look, Howard," she had said. "They named her after Sarah. Isn't that nice?"

"Mm," he'd said. "Very nice."

But now that she had the two announcements she wasn't certain what to do with them. To hide the uncertainty from herself she spent a long time cleaning up the spilled, strewn letters on the floor and stuffing them back into the box, which she heaved and skidded back into the shadows where it belonged. Then she washed the dust off her hands and sat quiet with a cold can of beer, trying to think.

It was four or five days before she worked up the courage to place a person-to-person call to the Reverend Peter J. Wilson in Edwardstown, New Hampshire.

"Aunt Emmy!" he said. "Wow, it's good to hear from you. How've you been?"

"Oh, I've been—all right, thanks. And how are all of you? How's the little girl?"

And they went on that way, talking of nothing at all, until he said "You still at the advertising agency?"

"No, I—actually, I haven't been doing that for some time. Actually, I'm not working at all now." She was keenly aware of having said "actually" twice, and it made her bite her lip. "I'm just sort of living alone now, and I've got a lot of time on my hands, which I guess is why"—she tried a little laugh—"which I guess is why I just decided to call you up out of the blue."

"Well, great," he said, and the way he said "great" made it clear that he'd understood what "just sort of living alone now" meant. "That's great. You ever get up this way?"

"What's that?"

"Do you ever get up this way? New England? New Hampshire? Because I mean we'd love to see you. Carol's always wanted to meet you. Maybe you could come up for a weekend or something. Wait, listen: *I've* got an idea. How about *next* weekend?"

"Oh, Peter—" Her heart was beating rapidly. "—Now it sounds like I've invited myself."

"No, no," he insisted. "Don't be silly—it doesn't sound like that at all. Listen. We've got plenty of room; you'd be perfectly comfortable—and it doesn't have to be just for the weekend, either; you can stay as long as you like . . ."

It was arranged. She would ride up to Edwardstown on the bus the following Friday—it was a six-hour trip, with an hour's layover in Boston—and Peter would meet her at the station.

For the next few days she moved with a new authority, a sense of herself as someone important, someone to be reckoned with, someone to love. Clothes were a problem: she had so few that were suitable for New England in the spring that she toyed with the idea of buying more, but that was silly; she couldn't afford it. On the night before her journey she stayed up late to wash out all her underwear and pantyhose under the weak yellow light of the bathroom (the landlord had economized by installing twenty-five-watt bulbs in all the bathrooms) and after that she couldn't sleep. She was still frazzled with lack of sleep when she carried her small suitcase into the raucous labyrinth of the Port Authority Bus Terminal, early Friday morning.

She had thought she might sleep on the bus, but for a long time all she could do was smoke many cigarettes and stare through her blue-tinted window at the passing landscape. It was a brilliant April day. Then a spasm of sleep took her by surprise in the early afternoon; she awoke with a cramp in one arm, with her dress badly wrinkled and her eyeballs feeling as if they'd been sprinkled with sand. The bus was only a few minutes from Edwardstown.

Peter's greeting was enthusiastic. He grabbed up her suitcase as if the sight of her carrying such a load offended him, and led her off toward his car. It was a pleasure to walk beside him: he moved in an easy, athletic stride and held her elbow with his free hand. He was wearing his clerical collar—she thought he must be a very high-church Episcopalian, if he wore it all the time—with a rather natty light gray suit.

"The country's beautiful up here," he said as he drove. "And you really picked a beautiful day to arrive."

"Mm. It's lovely. It certainly was—nice of you to ask me."

"It was nice of you to come."

"Is your house far from here?"

"Only a few miles." After a while he said "You know something, Aunt Emmy? I've thought of you often since this Women's Lib movement began. You've always struck me as the original liberated woman."

"Liberated from what?"

"Well, you know—from all the old, outmoded sociological concepts of what a woman's role should be."

"Jesus, Peter. I hope you do better than *that* in your sermons."

"Better than what?"

"Using phrases like 'outmoded sociological concepts.' What are you—one of these 'hip' priests?"

"Oh, I guess I'm fairly hip, yes. You have to be, if you're working with young people."

"How old are you now, Peter? Twenty-eight? Twenty-nine?"

"You *are* out of touch, Aunt Emmy. I'm thirty-one."

"And how old is your daughter?"

"Going on four."

"I was—very pleased," she said, "that you and your wife named your daughter after your mother."

"Good," he said, pulling out into the passing lane to overtake a fuel truck. When he'd drawn back into the driving lane he said "I'm glad you were pleased. And I'll tell you what: we're hoping for a boy next time, but if we have another girl we might name her after you. What would you think of that?"

"Well, I'd be very—that would be very—" But she couldn't finish because she was collapsed and crying against the passenger's door, hiding her face with both hands.

"Aunt Emmy?" he inquired shyly. "Aunt Emmy? You okay?"

This was humiliating. She hadn't been with him ten minutes, and already she had let him see her cry. "I'm fine," she said as soon as she could speak. "I'm just—tired, is all. I didn't get much sleep last night."

"Well, you'll sleep tonight. The air is very thin and very pure up here; people say it makes them sleep like the dead."

"Mm." And she busied herself with lighting a cigarette, the ritual she had relied on all her life to restore an illusion of composure.

"My mother used to have trouble sleeping," he said. "I remember when we were kids we were always saying 'Be quiet. Mom's trying to sleep.' "

"Yes," Emily said. "I know she had trouble sleeping." She was keenly tempted to say How did she die? but controlled herself. Instead she said "What's your wife like, Peter?"

"Well, you'll meet her soon enough. You'll get to know her."

"Is she pretty?"

"Oh, wow, is she ever. She's beautiful. I guess like most men I've always had fantasies of beautiful women, but this girl's a fantasy come to life. Wait'll you see her."

"All right. I'll wait. And what do you do, the two of you? Do you sit around talking about Jesus all the time?"

"Do we what?"

"Do you stay up late talking about Jesus and resurrection and stuff like that?"

He glanced briefly at her, looking puzzled. "I don't see what you're getting at."

"I'm only trying to get some picture of your—of how you—of the way you spend your time with your fantasy come to life." She could hear hysteria rising in her voice. She rolled down the partly opened window and snapped her cigarette away into the windstream, and all at once she felt strong and exhilarated, the way she'd felt in confronting Tony. "So all right, Mr. Wonderful," she said, "let's come clean. How did she die?"

"I don't even know what you're—"

"Peter, your father used to beat your mother all the time. That's a thing I happen to know, and I know you know it too. She told me all three of you boys knew it. Don't lie to me; how did she die?"

"My mother died of a liver ailment—"

"—'complicated by a fall she took in the house.' Oh, I've heard that song and dance before. You kids must've really memorized that line. Well, it's the *fall* I want to hear about. How did she fall? How was she hurt?"

"I wasn't there, Aunt Emmy."

"Christ, what a cop-out. You weren't there. And you never even asked?"

"Of course I asked. Eric was there; he told me she stumbled over a chair in the living room and struck her head."

"And do you really think that's enough to kill somebody?"

"It could be, sure, if the person falls badly."

"All right. Tell me about the police investigation. I happen to know there was a police investigation, Peter."

"There's *always* an investigation in a case like that. They didn't find anything; there was nothing to find. You sound like some kind of—why're you grilling me, Aunt Emmy?"

"Because I want to know the truth. Your father is a very brutal man."

Trees and neat white houses streamed past the car window, with a blue-green range of mountains high in the distance, and

Peter took his time in answering her—so much time that she began to be afraid he was looking for a place to turn the car around, so he could drive her back to the bus station and send her home.

"He's a limited man," he said at last, speaking carefully, "and in many ways an ignorant man, but I wouldn't call him brutal."

"Brutal," she insisted, trembling badly now. "He's brutal and stupid and he killed my sister—he killed her with twenty-five years of brutality and stupidity and neglect."

"Come on, Aunt Emmy; cut it out. My father's always done the best he could. Most people do the best they can. When terrible things happen, there usually isn't anyone to blame."

"What's *that*, for God's sake? Is that something you learned in your seminary, along with 'Turn the other cheek'?"

He had slowed down and signaled to make a turn, and now she saw a short concrete driveway, a neat lawn, and a small two-story house of exactly the kind she had imagined. They were here. The inside of the garage, where he brought the car to a stop, was tidier than most people's garages. Leaning against the wall were two bicycles, one with a padded baby seat attached behind its saddle.

"So you bicycle!" she called to him across the top of the car. She had gotten out quickly, still trembling, and snatched her suitcase from the back seat; then, because a good loud sound was needed to punctuate her rage, she slammed the car door with all her strength. "*That's* what you do. Oh, and what a lovely sight it must be, the two of you out bicycling with little what's-her-name on a Sunday afternoon, all tanned and leggy in your sexy little cut-off jeans—you must be the envy of all New Hampshire. . . ." She had started around the back of the car to join him, but he was only standing there and looking at her, blinking.

". . . And then you come home and take showers—do you take showers together?—and maybe you play a little grab-ass in the kitchen while you're fixing drinks, and then you have dinner and put the baby to bed and sit around talking about Jesus and resurrection for a while, and then comes the main event of the day, right? You and your wife go into the bedroom and shut the door, and you help each other take off all your clothes, and then oh, Lord God—talk about fantasies coming to *life*—"

"Aunt Emmy," he said, "that's out of line."

Out of line. Breathing hard, with her jaws clenched tight, she carried her suitcase down the driveway toward the street. She didn't know where she was going and she knew she looked ridiculous, but it was impossible to walk in any other direction.

At the foot of the driveway she stopped, not looking back, and after a while she heard a jingle of pocketed coins or keys and a rubber-heeled tread; he was coming down to get her.

She turned around. "Oh, Peter, I'm sorry," she said, not quite looking at him. "I can't—I can't tell you how sorry I am."

He seemed very embarrassed. "You don't have to apologize," he said, taking the suitcase from her hand. "I think you're probably very tired and need some rest." He was looking at her in a detached, speculative way now, more like an alert young psychiatrist than a priest.

"Yes, I'm tired," she said. "And do you know a funny thing? I'm almost fifty years old and I've never understood anything in my whole life."

"All right," he said quietly. "All right, Aunt Emmy. Now. Would you like to come on in and meet the family?"

ELEVEN KINDS OF
LONELINESS

DOCTOR JACK-O'-LANTERN

ALL MISS PRICE had been told about the new boy was that he'd spent most of his life in some kind of orphanage, and that the gray-haired "aunt and uncle" with whom he now lived were really foster parents, paid by the Welfare Department of the city of New York. A less dedicated or less imaginative teacher might have pressed for more details, but Miss Price was content with the rough outline. It was enough, in fact, to fill her with a sense of mission that shone from her eyes, as plain as love, from the first morning he joined the fourth grade.

He arrived early and sat in the back row—his spine very straight, his ankles crossed precisely under the desk and his hands folded on the very center of its top, as if symmetry might make him less conspicuous—and while the other children were filing in and settling down, he received a long, expressionless stare from each of them.

"We have a new classmate this morning," Miss Price said, laboring the obvious in a way that made everybody want to giggle. "His name is Vincent Sabella and he comes from New York City. I know we'll all do our best to make him feel at home."

This time they all swung around to stare at once, which caused him to duck his head slightly and shift his weight from one buttock to the other. Ordinarily, the fact of someone's coming from New York might have held a certain prestige, for to most of the children the city was an awesome, adult place that swallowed up their fathers every day, and which they themselves were permitted to visit only rarely, in their best clothes, as a treat. But anyone could see at a glance that Vincent Sabella had nothing whatever to do with skyscrapers. Even if you could ignore his tangled black hair and gray skin, his clothes would have given him away: absurdly new corduroys, absurdly old sneakers and a yellow sweatshirt, much too small, with the shredded remains of a Mickey Mouse design stamped on its chest. Clearly, he was from the part of New York that you had to pass through on the train to Grand Central—the part where people hung bedding over their windowsills and leaned out on it all day in a trance of boredom, and where you got vistas of straight, deep streets, one after another, all alike in the clutter of their sidewalks and all swarming with gray boys at play in some desperate kind of ball game.

The girls decided that he wasn't very nice and turned away, but the boys lingered in their scrutiny, looking him up and down with faint smiles. This was the kind of kid they were accustomed to thinking of as "tough," the kind whose stares had made all of them uncomfortable at one time or another in unfamiliar neighborhoods; here was a unique chance for retaliation.

"What would you like us to call you, Vincent?" Miss Price inquired. "I mean, do you prefer Vincent, or Vince, or—or what?" (It was purely an academic question; even Miss Price knew that the boys would call him "Sabella" and that the girls wouldn't call him anything at all.)

"Vinny's okay," he said in a strange, croaking voice that had evidently yelled itself hoarse down the ugly streets of his home.

"I'm afraid I didn't hear you," she said, craning her pretty head forward and to one side so that a heavy lock of hair swung free of one shoulder. "Did you say 'Vince'?"

"Vinny, I said," he said again, squirming.

"Vincent, is it? All right, then, Vincent." A few of the class giggled, but nobody bothered to correct her; it would be more fun to let the mistake continue.

"I won't take time to introduce you to everyone by name, Vincent," Miss Price went on, "because I think it would be simpler just to let you learn the names as we go along, don't you? Now, we won't expect you to take any real part in the work for the first day or so; just take your time, and if there's anything you don't understand, why, don't be afraid to ask."

He made an unintelligible croak and smiled fleetingly, just enough to show that the roots of his teeth were green.

"Now then," Miss Price said, getting down to business. "This is Monday morning, and so the first thing on the program is reports. Who'd like to start off?"

Vincent Sabella was momentarily forgotten as six or seven hands went up, and Miss Price drew back in mock confusion. "Goodness, we do have a lot of reports this morning," she said. The idea of the reports—a fifteen-minute period every Monday in which the children were encouraged to relate their experiences over the weekend—was Miss Price's own, and she took a pardonable pride in it. The principal had commended her on it at a recent staff meeting, pointing out that it made a splendid bridge between the worlds of school and home, and that it was a fine way for children to learn poise and assurance. It called for intelligent supervision—the shy children had to be drawn out and the show-offs curbed—but in general, as Miss Price had assured the principal, it was fun for everyone. She particularly hoped it would be fun today, to help put Vincent Sabella at ease, and that was why she chose Nancy Parker to start off; there was nobody like Nancy for holding an audience.

The others fell silent as Nancy moved gracefully to the head of the room; even the two or three girls who secretly despised her had to feign enthrallment when she spoke (she was that popular), and every boy in the class, who at recess liked nothing better than to push her shrieking into the mud, was unable to watch her without an idiotically tremulous smile.

"Well—" she began, and then she clapped a hand over her mouth while everyone laughed.

"Oh, *Nancy*," Miss Price said. "You *know* the rule about starting a report with 'well.'"

Nancy knew the rule; she had only broken it to get the laugh. Now she let her fit of giggles subside, ran her fragile forefingers down the side seams of her skirt, and began again in the proper way. "On Friday my whole family went for a ride in my brother's new car. My brother bought this new Pontiac last week, and he wanted to take us all for a ride—you know, to try it out and everything? So we went into White Plains and had dinner in a restaurant there, and then we all wanted to go see this movie, *Doctor Jekyll and Mr. Hyde*, but my brother said it was too horrible and everything, and I wasn't old enough to enjoy it—oh, he made me so mad! And then, let's see. On Saturday I stayed home all day and helped my mother make my sister's wedding dress. My sister's engaged to be married, you see, and my mother's making this wedding dress for her? So we did that, and then on Sunday this friend of my brother's came over for dinner, and then they both had to get back to college that night, and I was allowed to stay up late and say goodbye to them and everything, and I guess that's all." She always had a sure instinct for keeping her performance brief—or rather, for making it seem briefer than it really was.

"Very good, Nancy," Miss Price said. "Now, who's next?"

Warren Berg was next, elaborately hitching up his pants as he made his way down the aisle. "On Saturday I went over to Bill Stringer's house for lunch," he began in his direct, man-to-man style, and Bill Stringer wriggled bashfully in the front row. Warren Berg and Bill Stringer were great friends, and their reports often overlapped. "And then after lunch we went into White Plains, on our bikes. Only we saw *Doctor Jekyll and Mr. Hyde.*" Here he nodded his head in Nancy's direction, and Nancy got another laugh by making a little whimper of envy. "It was real good too," he went on, with mounting excitement. "It's all about this guy who—"

"About a *man* who," Miss Price corrected.

"About a man who mixes up this chemical, like, that he drinks? And whenever he drinks this chemical, he changes into this real monster, like? You see him drink this chemical, and then you see his hands start to get all scales all over them, like a reptile and everything, and then you see his face start to change into this real horrible-looking face—with fangs and all? Sticking out of his mouth?"

All the girls shuddered in pleasure. "Well," Miss Price said, "I think Nancy's brother was probably wise in not wanting her to see it. What did you do *after* the movie, Warren?"

There was a general "*Aw-w-w!*" of disappointment—everyone wanted to hear more about the scales and fangs—but Miss Price never liked to let the reports degenerate into accounts of movies. Warren continued without much enthusiasm: all they had done after the movie was fool around Bill Stringer's yard until suppertime. "And then on Sunday," he said, brightening again, "Bill Stringer came over to *my* house, and my dad helped us rig up this old tire on this long rope? From a tree? There's this steep hill down behind my house, you see—this ravine, like?—and we hung this tire so that what you do is, you take the tire and run a little ways and then lift your feet, and you go swinging way, way out over the ravine and back again."

"That sounds like fun," Miss Price said, glancing at her watch.

"Oh, it's *fun*, all right," Warren conceded. But then he hitched up his pants again and added, with a puckering of his forehead, " 'Course, it's pretty dangerous. You let go of that tire or anything, you'd get a bad fall. Hit a rock or anything, you'd probably break your leg, or your spine. But my dad said he trusted us both to look out for our own safety."

"Well, I'm afraid that's all we'll have time for, Warren," Miss Price said. "Now, there's just time for one more report. Who's ready? Arthur Cross?"

There was a soft groan, because Arthur Cross was the biggest dope in class and his reports were always a bore. This time it turned out to be something tedious about going to visit his uncle on Long Island. At one point he made a slip—he said "botor-moat" instead of "motorboat"—and everyone laughed with the particular edge of scorn they reserved for Arthur Cross. But the laughter died abruptly when it was joined by a harsh, dry croaking from the back of the room. Vincent Sabella was laughing too, green teeth and all, and they all had to glare at him until he stopped.

When the reports were over, everyone settled down for school. It was recess time before any of the children thought much about Vincent Sabella again, and then they thought of him only to make sure he was left out of everything. He wasn't in the group of boys that clustered around the horizontal bar to take turns at skinning-the-cat, or the group that whispered in a far corner of the playground, hatching a plot to push Nancy Parker in the mud. Nor was he in the larger group, of which even Arthur Cross was a member, that chased itself in circles in a frantic variation of the game of tag. He couldn't join the girls, of course, or the boys from other classes, and so he joined nobody. He stayed on the apron of the playground, close to school, and for the first part of the recess he pretended to be very busy with the laces of his sneakers. He would squat to undo and retie them, straighten up and take a few experimental steps in a springy, athletic way, and then get down and go to work on them again. After five minutes of this he gave it up, picked up a handful of pebbles and began shying them at an invisible target several yards away. That was good for another five minutes, but then there were still five minutes left, and he could think of nothing to do but stand there, first with his hands in his pockets, then with his hands on his hips, and then with his arms folded in a manly way across his chest.

Miss Price stood watching all this from the doorway, and she spent the full recess wondering if she ought to go out and do something about it. She guessed it would be better not to.

She managed to control the same impulse at recess the next day, and every other day that week, though every day it grew more difficult. But one thing she could not control was a tendency to let her anxiety show in class. All Vincent Sabella's errors in schoolwork were publicly excused, even those having nothing to do with his newness, and all his accomplishments were singled out for special mention. Her campaign to build him up was painfully obvious, and never more so than when she tried to make it subtle; once, for instance, in explaining an arithmetic problem, she said, "Now, suppose Warren Berg and Vincent Sabella went to the store with fifteen cents each, and candy bars cost ten cents. How many candy bars would each boy have?" By the end of the week he was well on the way to becoming the worst possible kind of teacher's pet, a victim of the teacher's pity.

On Friday she decided the best thing to do would be to speak to him privately, and try to draw him out. She could say something about the pictures he had painted in art class—that would do for an opening—and she decided to do it at lunchtime.

The only trouble was that lunchtime, next to recess, was the most trying part of Vincent Sabella's day. Instead of going home for an hour as the other children did, he brought his lunch to school in a wrinkled paper bag and ate it in the classroom, which always made for a certain amount of awkwardness. The last children to leave would see him still seated apologetically at his desk, holding his paper bag, and anyone who happened to straggle back later for a forgotten hat or sweater would surprise him in the middle of his meal—perhaps shielding a hard-boiled egg from view or wiping mayonnaise from his mouth with a furtive hand. It was a situation that Miss Price did not improve by walking up to him while the room was still half full of children and sitting prettily on the edge of the desk beside his, making it clear that she was cutting her own lunch hour short in order to be with him.

"Vincent," she began, "I've been meaning to tell you how much I enjoyed those pictures of yours. They're really very good."

He mumbled something and shifted his eyes to the cluster of departing children at the door. She went right on talking and smiling, elaborating on her praise of the pictures; and finally, after the door had closed behind the last child, he was able to give her his attention. He did so tentatively at first; but the more she talked, the more he seemed to relax, until she realized she was putting him at ease. It was as simple and as gratifying as stroking a cat. She had finished with the pictures now and moved on, triumphantly, to broader fields of praise. "It's never easy," she was saying, "to come to a new school and adjust yourself to the— well, the new work, and new working methods, and I think you've done a splendid job so far. I really do. But tell me, do you think you're going to like it here?"

He looked at the floor just long enough to make his reply— "It's awright"—and then his eyes stared into hers again.

"I'm so glad. Please don't let me interfere with your lunch, Vincent. Do go ahead and eat, that is, if you don't mind my sitting here with you." But it was now abundantly clear that he didn't mind at all, and he began to unwrap a bologna sandwich with what she felt sure was the best appetite he'd had all week. It wouldn't even have mattered very much now if someone from the class had come in and watched, though it was probably just as well that no one did.

Miss Price sat back more comfortably on the desk top, crossed her legs and allowed one slim stockinged foot to slip part of the way out of its moccasin. "Of course," she went on, "it always does take a little time to sort of get your bearings in a new school. For one thing, well, it's never too easy for the new member of the class to make friends with the other members. What I mean is, you mustn't mind if the others seem a little rude to you at first. Actually, they're just as anxious to make friends as you are, but they're shy. All it takes is a little time, and a little effort on your part as well as theirs. Not too much, of course, but a little. Now for instance, these reports we have Monday mornings—they're a fine way for people to get to know one another. A person never feels he has to make a report; it's just a thing he can do if he wants to. And that's only one way of helping others to know the kind of person you are; there are lots and lots of ways. The main thing to remember is that making friends is the most natural thing in the world, and it's only a question of time until you have all the friends you want. And in the meantime, Vincent, I hope you'll consider *me* your friend, and feel free to call on me for whatever advice or anything you might need. Will you do that?"

He nodded, swallowing.

"Good." She stood up and smoothed her skirt over her long thighs. "Now I must go or I'll be late for *my* lunch. But I'm glad we had this little talk, Vincent, and I hope we'll have others."

It was probably a lucky thing that she stood up when she did, for if she'd stayed on that desk a minute longer Vincent Sabella would have thrown his arms around her and buried his face in the warm gray flannel of her lap, and that might have been enough to confuse the most dedicated and imaginative of teachers.

At report time on Monday morning, nobody was more surprised than Miss Price when Vincent Sabella's smudged hand was among the first and most eager to rise. Apprehensively she considered letting someone else start off, but then, for fear of hurting his feelings, she said, "All right, Vincent," in as matter-of-fact a way as she could manage.

There was a suggestion of muffled titters from the class as he walked confidently to the head of the room and turned to face his audience. He looked, if anything, too confident: there were signs, in the way he held his shoulders and the way his eyes shone, of the terrible poise of panic.

"Saturday I seen that pitcha," he announced.

"Saw, Vincent," Miss Price corrected gently.

"That's what I mean," he said; "I sore that pitcha. *Doctor Jack-o'-Lantern and Mr. Hide.*"

There was a burst of wild, delighted laughter and a chorus of correction: "Doctor *Jekyll!*"

He was unable to speak over the noise. Miss Price was on her feet, furious. "It's a *perfectly natural mistake!*" she was saying. "There's no reason for any of you to be so rude. Go on, Vincent, and please excuse this very silly interruption." The laughter subsided, but the class continued to shake their heads derisively from side to side. It hadn't, of course, been a perfectly natural mistake at all; for one thing it proved that he was a hopeless dope, and for another it proved that he was lying.

"That's what I mean," he continued. "*Doctor Jackal and Mr Hide.* I got it a little mixed up. Anyways, I seen all about where his teet' start comin' outa his mout' and all like that, and I thought it was very good. And then on Sunday my mudda and fodda come out to see me in this car, they got. This Buick. My fodda siz, 'Vinny, wanna go for a little ride?' I siz, 'Sure, where yiz goin'?' He siz, 'Anyplace ya like.' So I siz, 'Let's go out in the country a ways, get on one of them big roads and make some time.' So we go out—oh, I guess fifty, sixty miles—and we're cruisin' along this highway, when this cop starts tailin' us? My fodda siz, 'Don't worry, we'll shake him,' and he steps on it, see? My mudda's gettin' pretty scared, but my fodda siz, 'Don't worry, dear.' He's tryin' to make this turn, see, so he can get off the highway and shake the cop? But just when he's makin' the turn, the cop opens up and starts shootin', see?"

By this time the few members of the class who could bear to look at him at all were doing so with heads on one side and mouths partly open, the way you look at a broken arm or a circus freak.

"We just barely made it," Vincent went on, his eyes gleaming, "and this one bullet got my fodda in the shoulder. Didn't hurt him bad—just grazed him, like—so my mudda bandaged it up for him and all, but he couldn't do no more drivin' after that, and we had to get him to a doctor, see? So my fodda siz, 'Vinny, think you can drive a ways?' I siz, 'Sure, if you show me how.'

So he showed me how to work the gas and the brake, and all like that, and I drove to the doctor. My mudda siz, 'I'm prouda you, Vinny, drivin' all by yourself.' So anyways, we got to the doctor, got my fodda fixed up and all, and then he drove us back home." He was breathless. After an uncertain pause he said, "And that's all." Then he walked quickly back to his desk, his stiff new corduroy pants whistling faintly with each step.

"Well, that was very—entertaining, Vincent," Miss Price said, trying to act as if nothing had happened. "Now, who's next?" But nobody raised a hand.

Recess was worse than usual for him that day; at least it was until he found a place to hide—a narrow concrete alley, blind except for several closed fire-exit doors, that cut between two sections of the school building. It was reassuringly dismal and cool in there—he could stand with his back to the wall and his eyes guarding the entrance, and the noises of recess were as remote as the sunshine. But when the bell rang he had to go back to class, and in another hour it was lunchtime.

Miss Price left him alone until her own meal was finished. Then, after standing with one hand on the doorknob for a full minute to gather courage, she went in and sat beside him for another little talk, just as he was trying to swallow the last of a pimento-cheese sandwich.

"Vincent," she began, "we all enjoyed your report this morning, but I think we would have enjoyed it more—a great deal more—if you'd told us something about your real life instead. I mean," she hurried on, "for instance, I noticed you were wearing a nice new windbreaker this morning. It *is* new, isn't it? And did your aunt buy it for you over the weekend?"

He did not deny it.

"Well then, why couldn't you have told us about going to the store with your aunt, and buying the windbreaker, and whatever you did afterwards. That would have made a perfectly good report." She paused, and for the first time looked steadily into his eyes. "You do understand what I'm trying to say, don't you, Vincent?"

He wiped crumbs of bread from his lips, looked at the floor, and nodded.

"And you'll remember next time, won't you?"

He nodded again. "Please may I be excused, Miss Price?"

"Of course you may."

He went to the boys' lavatory and vomited. Afterwards he washed his face and drank a little water, and then he returned to the classroom. Miss Price was busy at her desk now, and didn't look up. To avoid getting involved with her again, he wandered out to the cloakroom and sat on one of the long benches, where he picked up someone's discarded overshoe and turned it over and over in his hands. In a little while he heard the chatter of returning children, and to avoid being discovered there, he got up and went to the fire-exit door. Pushing it open, he found that it gave onto the alley he had hidden in that morning, and he slipped outside. For a minute or two he just stood there, looking at the blankness of the concrete wall; then he found a piece of chalk in his pocket and wrote out all the dirty words he could think of, in block letters a foot high. He had put down four words and was trying to remember a fifth when he heard a shuffling at the door behind him. Arthur Cross was there, holding the door open and reading the words with wide eyes. "Boy," he said in an awed half-whisper. "Boy, you're gonna get it. You're really gonna *get* it."

Startled, and then suddenly calm, Vincent Sabella palmed his chalk, hooked his thumbs in his belt and turned on Arthur with a menacing look. "Yeah?" he inquired. "Who's gonna squeal on me?"

"Well, nobody's gonna *squeal* on you," Arthur Cross said uneasily, "but you shouldn't go around writing—"

"Arright," Vincent said, advancing a step. His shoulders were slumped, his head thrust forward and his eyes narrowed, like Edward G. Robinson. "Arright. That's all I wanna know. I don't like squealers, unnastand?"

While he was saying this, Warren Berg and Bill Stringer appeared in the doorway—just in time to hear it and to see the words on the wall before Vincent turned on them. "And that goes fa you too, unnastand?" he said. "Both a yiz."

And the remarkable thing was that both their faces fell into the same foolish, defensive smile that Arthur Cross was wearing.

It wasn't until they had glanced at each other that they were able to meet his eyes with the proper degree of contempt, and by then it was too late. "Think you're pretty smart, don'tcha, Sabella?" Bill Stringer said.

"Never mind what I think," Vincent told him. "You heard what I said. Now let's get back inside."

And they could do nothing but move aside to make way for him, and follow him dumfounded into the cloakroom.

It was Nancy Parker who squealed—although, of course, with someone like Nancy Parker you didn't think of it as squealing. She had heard everything from the cloakroom; as soon as the boys came in she peeked into the alley, saw the words and, setting her face in a prim frown, went straight to Miss Price. Miss Price was just about to call the class to order for the afternoon when Nancy came up and whispered in her ear. They both disappeared into the cloakroom—from which, after a moment, came the sound of the fire-exit door being abruptly slammed—and when they returned to class Nancy was flushed with righteousness, Miss Price very pale. No announcement was made. Classes proceeded in the ordinary way all afternoon, though it was clear that Miss Price was upset, and it wasn't until she was dismissing the children at three o'clock that she brought the thing into the open. "Will Vincent Sabella please remain seated?" She nodded at the rest of the class. "That's all."

While the room was clearing out she sat at her desk, closed her eyes and massaged the frail bridge of her nose with thumb and forefinger, sorting out half-remembered fragments of a book she had once read on the subject of seriously disturbed children. Perhaps, after all, she should never have undertaken the responsibility of Vincent Sabella's loneliness. Perhaps the whole thing called for the attention of a specialist. She took a deep breath.

"Come over here and sit beside me, Vincent," she said, and when he had settled himself, she looked at him. "I want you to tell me the truth. Did you write those words on the wall outside?"

He stared at the floor.

"Look at me," she said, and he looked at her. She had never looked prettier: her cheeks slightly flushed, her eyes shining and her sweet mouth pressed into a self-conscious frown. "First of all," she said, handing him a small enameled basin streaked with poster paint, "I want you to take this to the boys' room and fill it with hot water and soap."

He did as he was told, and when he came back, carrying the basin carefully to keep the suds from spilling, she was sorting out some old rags in the bottom drawer of her desk. "Here," she said, selecting one and shutting the drawer in a businesslike way. "This will do. Soak this up." She led him back to the fire exit and stood in the alley watching him, silently, while he washed off all the words.

When the job had been done, and the rag and basin put away, they sat down at Miss Price's desk again. "I suppose you think I'm angry with you, Vincent," she said. "Well, I'm not. I almost wish I could be angry—that would make it much easier—but instead I'm hurt. I've tried to be a good friend to you, and I thought you wanted to be my friend too. But this kind of thing— well, it's very hard to be friendly with a person who'd do a thing like that."

She saw, gratefully, that there were tears in his eyes. "Vincent, perhaps I understand some things better than you think. Perhaps I understand that sometimes, when a person does a thing like that, it isn't really because he wants to hurt anyone, but only because he's unhappy. He knows it isn't a good thing to do, and he even knows it isn't going to make him any happier afterwards, but he goes ahead and does it anyway. Then when he finds he's lost a friend, he's terribly sorry, but it's too late. The thing is done."

She allowed this somber note to reverberate in the silence of the room for a little while before she spoke again. "I won't be able to forget this, Vincent. But perhaps, just this once, we can still be friends—as long as I understand that you didn't mean to hurt me. But you must promise me that you won't forget it either. Never forget that when you do a thing like that, you're going to hurt people who want very much to like you, and in that way you're going to hurt yourself. Will you promise me to remember that, dear?"

The "dear" was as involuntary as the slender hand that reached out and held the shoulder of his sweatshirt; both made his head hang lower than before.

"All right," she said. "You may go now."

He got his windbreaker out of the cloakroom and left, avoiding the tired uncertainty of her eyes. The corridors were deserted, and dead silent except for the hollow, rhythmic knocking of a janitor's push-broom against some distant wall. His own rubber-soled tread only added to the silence; so did the lonely little noise made by the zipping-up of his windbreaker, and so did the faint mechanical sigh of the heavy front door. The silence made it all the more startling when he found, several yards down the concrete walk outside, that two boys were walking beside him: Warren Berg and Bill Stringer. They were both smiling at him in an eager, almost friendly way.

"What'd she do to ya, anyway?" Bill Stringer asked.

Caught off guard, Vincent barely managed to put on his Edward G. Robinson face in time. "Nunnya business," he said, and walked faster.

"No, listen—wait up, hey," Warren Berg said, as they trotted to keep up with him. "What'd she do, anyway? She bawl ya out, or what? Wait up, hey, Vinny."

The name made him tremble all over. He had to jam his hands in his windbreaker pockets and force himself to keep on walking; he had to force his voice to be steady when he said, "Nunnya *business*, I told ya. Lea' me alone."

But they were right in step with him now. "Boy, she must of given you the works," Warren Berg persisted. "What'd she say, anyway? C'mon, tell us, Vinny."

This time the name was too much for him. It overwhelmed his resistance and made his softening knees slow down to a slack, conversational stroll. "She din say nothin'," he said at last; and then after a dramatic pause he added, "She let the ruler do her talkin' for her."

"The *ruler*? Ya mean she used a *ruler* on ya?" Their faces were stunned, either with disbelief or admiration, and it began to look more and more like admiration as they listened.

"On the knuckles," Vincent said through tightening lips. "Five times on each hand. She siz, 'Make a fist. Lay it out here on the desk.' Then she takes the ruler and *Whop! Whop! Whop!* Five times. Ya think that don't hurt, you're crazy."

Miss Price, buttoning her polo coat as the front door whispered shut behind her, could scarcely believe her eyes. This couldn't be Vincent Sabella—this perfectly normal, perfectly happy boy on the sidewalk ahead of her, flanked by attentive friends. But it was, and the scene made her want to laugh aloud with pleasure and relief. He was going to be all right, after all. For all her well-intentioned groping in the shadows she could never have predicted a scene like this, and certainly could never have caused it to happen. But it was happening, and it just proved, once again, that she would never understand the ways of children.

She quickened her graceful stride and overtook them, turning to smile down at them as she passed. "Goodnight, boys," she called, intending it as a kind of cheerful benediction; and then, embarrassed by their three startled faces, she smiled even wider and said, "Goodness, it *is* getting colder, isn't it? That windbreaker of yours looks nice and warm, Vincent. I envy you." Finally they nodded bashfully at her; she called goodnight again, turned, and continued on her way to the bus stop.

She left a profound silence in her wake. Staring after her, Warren Berg and Bill Stringer waited until she had disappeared around the corner before they turned on Vincent Sabella.

"Ruler, my eye!" Bill Stringer said. "Ruler, my eye!" He gave Vincent a disgusted shove that sent him stumbling against Warren Berg, who shoved him back.

"Jeez, you lie about *everything*, don'tcha, Sabella? You lie about *everything*!"

Jostled off balance, keeping his hands tight in the windbreaker pockets, Vincent tried in vain to retain his dignity. "Think *I* care if yiz believe me?" he said, and then because he couldn't think of anything else to say, he said it again. "Think *I* care if yiz believe me?"

But he was walking alone. Warren Berg and Bill Stringer were drifting away across the street, walking backwards in order to look back on him with furious contempt. "Just like the lies you told about the policeman shooting your father," Bill Stringer called.

"Even *movies* he lies about," Warren Berg put in; and suddenly doubling up with artificial laughter he cupped both hands to his mouth and yelled, "Hey, Doctor Jack-o'-Lantern!"

It wasn't a very good nickname, but it had an authentic ring to it—the kind of a name that might spread around, catch on quickly, and stick. Nudging each other, they both took up the cry:

"What's the matter, Doctor Jack-o'-Lantern?"

"Why don'tcha run on home with Miss Price, Doctor Jack-o'-Lantern?"

"So long, Doctor Jack-o'-Lantern!"

Vincent Sabella went on walking, ignoring them, waiting until they were out of sight. Then he turned and retraced his steps all the way back to school, around through the playground and back to the alley, where the wall was still dark in spots from the circular scrubbing of his wet rag.

Choosing a dry place, he got out his chalk and began to draw a head with great care, in profile, making the hair long and rich and taking his time over the face, erasing it with moist fingers and reworking it until it was the most beautiful face he had ever drawn: a delicate nose, slightly parted lips, an eye with lashes that curved as gracefully as a bird's wing. He paused to admire it with a lover's solemnity; then from the lips he drew a line that connected with a big speech balloon, and in the balloon he wrote, so angrily that the chalk kept breaking in his fingers, every one of the words he had written that noon. Returning to the head, he gave it a slender neck and gently sloping shoulders, and then, with bold strikes, he gave it the body of a naked woman: great breasts with hard little nipples, a trim waist, a dot for a navel, wide hips and thighs that flared around a triangle of fiercely scribbled pubic hair. Beneath the picture he printed its title: "Miss Price."

He stood there looking at it for a little while, breathing hard, and then he went home.

NOBODY EXPECTED GRACE to do any work the Friday before her wedding. In fact, nobody would let her, whether she wanted to or not.

A gardenia corsage lay in a cellophane box beside her type-writer—from Mr. Atwood, her boss—and tucked inside the envelope that came with it was a ten-dollar gift certificate from Bloomingdale's. Mr. Atwood had treated her with a special courtliness ever since the time she necked with him at the office Christmas party, and now when she went in to thank him he was all hunched over, rattling desk drawers, blushing and barely meeting her eyes.

"Aw, now, don't mention it, Grace," he said. "Pleasure's all mine. Here, you need a pin to put that gadget on with?"

"There's a pin that came with it," she said, holding up the corsage. "See? A nice white one."

Beaming, he watched her pin the flowers high on the lapel of her suit. Then he cleared his throat importantly and pulled out the writing panel of his desk, ready to give the morning's dicta-tion. But it turned out there were only two short letters, and it wasn't until an hour later, when she caught him handing over a pile of Dictaphone cylinders to Central Typing, that she realized he had done her a favor.

"That's very sweet of you, Mr. Atwood," she said, "but I do think you ought to give me all your work today, just like any oth—"

"Aw, now, Grace," he said. "You only get married once."

The girls all made a fuss over her too, crowding around her desk and giggling, asking again and again to see Ralph's photo-graph ("Oh, he's *cute!*"), while the office manager looked on, nervously, reluctant to be a spoilsport but anxious to point out that it was, after all, a working day.

Then at lunch there was the traditional little party at Schrafft's —nine women and girls, giddy on their unfamiliar cocktails, letting their chicken à la king grow cold while they pummeled her with old times and good wishes. There were more flowers and another gift—a silver candy dish for which all the girls had whisperingly chipped in.

Grace said "Thank you" and "I certainly do appreciate it" and "I don't know what to say" until her head rang with the words and the corners of her mouth ached from smiling, and she thought the afternoon would never end.

Ralph called up about four o'clock, exuberant. "How ya doin', honey?" he asked, and before she could answer he said, "Listen. Guess what I got?"

"I don't know. A present or something? What?" She tried to sound excited, but it wasn't easy.

"A bonus. Fifty dollars." She could almost see the flattening of his lips as he said "fifty dollars" with the particular earnestness he reserved for pronouncing sums of money.

"Why, that's lovely, Ralph," she said, and if there was any tiredness in her voice he didn't notice it.

"Lovely, huh?" he said with a laugh, mocking the girlishness of the word. "Ya *like* that, huh, Gracie? No, but I mean I was really surprised, ya know it? The boss siz, 'Here, Ralph,' and he hands me this envelope. He don't even crack a smile or nothin', and I'm wonderin', what's the deal here? I'm getting fired here, or what? He siz, 'G'ahead, Ralph, open it.' So I open it, and then I look at the boss and he's grinning a mile wide." He chuckled and sighed. "Well, so listen, honey. What time ya want me to come over tonight?"

"Oh, I don't know. Soon as you can, I guess."

"Well listen, I gotta go over to Eddie's house and pick up that bag he's gonna loan me, so I might as well do that, go on home and eat, and then come over to your place around eight-thirty, nine o'clock. Okay?"

"All right," she said. "I'll see you then, darling." She had been calling him "darling" for only a short time—since it had become irrevocably clear that she was, after all, going to marry him—and the word still had an alien sound. As she straightened the stacks of stationery in her desk (because there was nothing else to do), a familiar little panic gripped her: she couldn't marry him—she hardly even *knew* him. Sometimes it occurred to her differently, that she couldn't marry him because she knew him too well, and either way it left her badly shaken, vulnerable to all the things that Martha, her roommate, had said from the very beginning.

"Isn't he funny?" Martha had said after their first date. "He says 'terlet.' I didn't know people really said 'terlet.'" And Grace had giggled, ready enough to agree that it *was* funny. That was a time when she had been ready to agree with Martha on practically anything—when it often seemed, in fact, that finding a girl like Martha from an ad in the *Times* was just about the luckiest thing that had ever happened to her.

But Ralph had persisted all through the summer, and by fall she had begun standing up for him. "What don't you *like* about him, Martha? He's perfectly nice."

"Oh, everybody's perfectly nice, Grace," Martha would say in her college voice, making perfectly nice a faintly absurd thing to be, and then she'd look up crossly from the careful painting of her fingernails. "It's just that he's such a little—a little *white worm*. Can't you see that?"

"Well, I certainly don't see what his *complexion* has to do with—"

"Oh God, *you* know what I mean. Can't you see what I *mean*? Oh, and all those friends of his, his Eddie and his Marty and his George with their mean, ratty little clerks' lives and their mean, ratty little . . . It's just that they're all *alike*, those people. All they ever say is 'Hey, wha' happen t'ya Giants?' and 'Hey, wha' happen t'ya Yankees?' and they all live way out in Sunnyside or Woodhaven or some awful place, and their mothers have those damn little china elephants on the mantelpiece." And Martha would frown over her nail polish again, making it clear that the subject was closed.

All that fall and winter she was confused. For a while she tried going out only with Martha's kind of men—the kind that used words like "amusing" all the time and wore small-shouldered flannel suits like a uniform; and for a while she tried going out with no men at all. She even tried that crazy business with Mr.

Atwood at the office Christmas party. And all the time Ralph kept calling up, hanging around, waiting for her to make up her mind. Once she took him home to meet her parents in Pennsylvania (where she never would have dreamed of taking Martha), but it wasn't until Easter time that she finally gave in.

They had gone to a dance somewhere in Queens, one of the big American Legion dances that Ralph's crowd was always going to, and when the band played "Easter Parade" he held her very close, hardly moving, and sang to her in a faint, whispering tenor. It was the kind of thing she'd never have expected Ralph to do—a sweet, gentle thing—and it probably wasn't just then that she decided to marry him, but it always seemed so afterwards. It always seemed she had decided that minute, swaying to the music with his husky voice in her hair:

> "I'll be all in clover
> And when they look you over
> I'll be the proudest fella
> In the Easter Parade. . . ."

That night she had told Martha, and she could still see the look on Martha's face. "Oh, Grace, you're not—surely you're not *serious*. I mean, I thought he was more or less of a *joke*—you can't really mean you want to—"

"Shut up! You just shut up, Martha!" And she'd cried all night. Even now she hated Martha for it; even as she stared blindly at a row of filing cabinets along the office wall, half sick with fear that Martha was right.

The noise of giggles swept over her, and she saw with a start that two of the girls—Irene and Rose—were grinning over their typewriters and pointing at her, "*We* saw ya!" Irene sang. "*We* saw ya! Mooning again, huh Grace?" Then Rose did a burlesque of mooning, heaving her meager breasts and batting her eyes, and they both collapsed in laughter.

With an effort of will Grace resumed the guileless, open smile of a bride. The thing to do was concentrate on plans.

Tomorrow morning, "bright and early," as her mother would say, she would meet Ralph at Penn Station for the trip home. They'd arrive about one, and her parents would meet the train.

"Good t'see ya, Ralph!" her father would say, and her mother would probably kiss him. A warm, homely love filled her: *they* wouldn't call him a white worm; *they* didn't have any ideas about Princeton men and "interesting" men and all the other kinds of men Martha was so stuck-up about. Then her father would probably take Ralph out for a beer and show him the paper mill where he worked (and at least Ralph wouldn't be snobby about a person working in a paper mill, either), and then Ralph's family and friends would come down from New York in the evening.

She'd have time for a long talk with her mother that night, and the next morning, "bright and early" (her eyes stung at the thought of her mother's plain, happy face), they would start getting dressed for the wedding. Then the church and the cere-mony, and then the reception (Would her father get drunk? Would Muriel Ketchel sulk about not being a bridesmaid?), and finally the train to Atlantic City, and the hotel. But from the hotel on she couldn't plan any more. A door would lock behind her and there would be a wild, fantastic silence, and nobody in all the world but Ralph to lead the way.

"Well, Grace," Mr. Atwood was saying, "I want to wish you every happiness." He was standing at her desk with his hat and coat on, and all around her were the chattering and scraping-back of chairs that meant it was five o'clock.

"Thank you, Mr. Atwood." She got to her feet, suddenly surrounded by all the girls in a bedlam of farewell.

"All the luck in the world, Grace."

"Drop us a card, huh Grace? From Atlantic City?"

"So long, Grace."

"G'night, Grace, and listen: the best of everything."

Finally she was free of them all, out of the elevator, out of the building, hurrying through the crowds to the subway.

When she got home Martha was standing in the door of the kitchenette, looking very svelte in a crisp new dress.

"Hi, Grace. I bet they ate you alive today, didn't they?"

"Oh no," Grace said. "Everybody was—real nice." She sat down, exhausted, and dropped the flowers and the wrapped candy dish on a table. Then she noticed that the whole apart-ment was swept and dusted, and the dinner was cooking in the kitchenette. "Gee, everything looks wonderful," she said. "What'd you do all this for?"

"Oh, well, I got home early anyway," Martha said. Then she smiled, and it was one of the few times Grace had ever seen her look shy. "I just thought it might be nice to have the place looking decent for a change, when Ralph comes over."

"Well," Grace said, "it certainly was nice of you."

The way Martha looked now was even more surprising: she looked awkward. She was turning a greasy spatula in her fingers, holding it delicately away from her dress and examining it, as if she had something difficult to say. "Look, Grace," she began. "You do understand why I can't come to the wedding, don't you?"

"Oh, sure," Grace said, although in fact she didn't, exactly. It was something about having to go up to Harvard to see her brother before he went into the Army, but it had sounded like a lie from the beginning.

"It's just that I'd hate you to think I—well, anyway, I'm glad if you do understand. And the other thing I wanted to say is more important."

"What?"

"Well, just that I'm sorry for all the awful things I used to say about Ralph. I never had a right to talk to you that way. He's a very sweet boy and I—well, I'm sorry, that's all."

It wasn't easy for Grace to hide a rush of gratitude and relief when she said, "Why, that's all right, Martha, I—"

"The chops are on fire!" Martha bolted for the kitchenette. "It's all right," she called back. "They're edible." And when she came out to serve dinner all her old composure was restored. "I'll have to eat and run," she said as they sat down. "My train leaves in forty minutes."

"I thought it was *tomorrow* you were going."

"Well, it was, actually," Martha said, "but I decided to go tonight. Because you see, Grace, another thing—if you can stand one more apology—another thing I'm sorry for is that I've hardly ever given you and Ralph a chance to be alone here. So tonight I'm going to clear out." She hesitated. "It'll be a sort of wedding gift from me, okay?" And then she smiled, not shyly this time but in a way that was more in character—the eyes subtly averted after a flicker of special meaning. It was a smile that Grace—through stages of suspicion, bewilderment, awe, and practiced imitation—had long ago come to associate with the word "sophisticated."

"Well, that's very sweet of you," Grace said, but she didn't really get the point just then. It wasn't until long after the meal was over and the dishes washed, until Martha had left for her train in a whirl of cosmetics and luggage and quick goodbyes, that she began to understand.

She took a deep, voluptuous bath and spent a long time drying herself, posing in the mirror, filled with a strange, slow excitement. In her bedroom, from the rustling tissues of an expensive white box, she drew the prizes of her trousseau—a sheer nightgown of white nylon and a matching negligee—put them on, and went to the mirror again. She had never worn anything like this before, or felt like this, and the thought of letting Ralph see her like this sent her into the kitchenette for a glass of the special dry sherry Martha kept for cocktail parties. Then she turned out all the lights but one and, carrying her glass, went to the sofa and arranged herself there to wait for him. After a while she got up and brought the sherry bottle over to the coffee table, where she set it on a tray with another glass.

When Ralph left the office he felt vaguely let down. Somehow, he'd expected more of the Friday before his wedding. The bonus check had been all right (though secretly he'd been counting on twice that amount), and the boys had bought him a drink at lunch and kidded around in the appropriate way ("Ah, don't feel too bad, Ralph—worse things could happen"), but still, there ought to have been a real party. Not just the boys in the office, but Eddie, and *all* his friends. Instead there would only be meeting Eddie at the White Rose like every other night of the year, and riding home to borrow Eddie's suitcase and to eat, and then having to ride all the way back to Manhattan just to see Gracie for an hour or two. Eddie wasn't in the bar when he arrived, which sharpened the edge of his loneliness. Morosely he drank a beer, waiting.

Eddie was his best friend, and an ideal best man because he'd been in on the courtship of Gracie from the start. It was in this very bar, in fact, that Ralph had told him about their first date last summer: "Ooh, Eddie—what a paira *knockers*!"

And Eddie had grinned. "Yeah? So what's the roommate like?"

"Ah, you don't want the roommate, Eddie. The roommate's a dog. A snob too, I think. No, but this *other* one, this little *Gracie*—boy, I mean, she is *stacked*."

Half the fun of every date—even more than half—had been telling Eddie about it afterwards, exaggerating a little here and there, asking Eddie's advice on tactics. But after today, like so many other pleasures, it would all be left behind. Gracie had promised him at least one night off a week to spend with the boys, after they were married, but even so it would never be the same. Girls never understood a thing like friendship.

There was a ball game on the bar's television screen and he watched it idly, his throat swelling in a sentimental pain of loss. Nearly all his life had been devoted to the friendship of boys and men, to trying to be a good guy, and now the best of it was over.

Finally Eddie's stiff finger jabbed the seat of his pants in greeting. "Whaddya say, sport?"

Ralph narrowed his eyes to indolent contempt and slowly turned around. "Wha' happen ta you, wise guy? Get lost?"

"Whaddya—in a hurry a somethin'?" Eddie barely moved his lips when he spoke. "Can't wait two minutes?" He slouched on a stool and slid a quarter at the bartender. "Draw one, there, Jack."

They drank in silence for a while, staring at the television. "Got a little bonus today," Ralph said. "Fifty dollars."

"Yeah?" Eddie said. "Good."

A batter struck out; the inning was over and the commercial came on. "So?" Eddie said, rocking the beer around in his glass. "Still gonna get married?"

"Why not?" Ralph said with a shrug. "Listen, finish that, willya? I wanna get a move on."

"Wait awhile, wait awhile. What's ya hurry?"

"C'mon, willya?" Ralph stepped impatiently away from the bar. "I wanna go pick up ya bag."

"Ah, bag schmagg."

Ralph moved up close again and glowered at him. "Look, wise guy. Nobody's gonna *make* ya loan me the goddamn bag, ya know. I don't wanna break ya *heart* or nothin'—"

"Arright, arright, arright. You'll getcha bag. Don't worry so much." He finished the beer and wiped his mouth. "Let's go."

Having to borrow a bag for his wedding trip was a sore point with Ralph; he'd much rather have bought one of his own. There was a fine one displayed in the window of a luggage shop they passed every night on their way to the subway—a big, tawny Gladstone with a zippered compartment on the side, at thirty-nine ninety-five—and Ralph had had his eye on it ever since Easter time. "Think I'll buy that," he'd told Eddie, in the same offhand way that a day or so before he had announced his engagement ("Think I'll marry the girl"). Eddie's response to both remarks had been the same: "Whaddyacrazy?" Both times Ralph had said, "Why not?" and in defense of the bag he had added, "Gonna get married, I'll *need* somethin' like that." From then on it was as if the bag, almost as much as Gracie herself, had become a symbol of the new and richer life he sought. But after the ring and the new clothes and all the other expenses, he'd found at last that he couldn't afford it; he had settled for the loan of Eddie's, which was similar but cheaper and worn, and without the zippered compartment.

Now as they passed the luggage shop he stopped, caught in the grip of a reckless idea. "Hey wait awhile, Eddie. Know what I think I'll do with that fifty-dollar bonus? I think I'll buy that bag right now." He felt breathless.

"Whaddya—crazy? Forty bucks for a bag you'll use maybe one time a year? Ya crazy, Ralph. C'mon."

"Ah—I dunno. Ya think so?"

"Listen, you better *keep* ya money, boy. You're gonna *need* it."

"Ah—yeah," Ralph said at last. "I guess ya right." And he fell in step with Eddie again, heading for the subway. This was the way things usually turned out in his life; he could never own a bag like that until he made a better salary, and he accepted it—

just as he'd accepted without question, after the first thin sigh, the knowledge that he'd never possess his bride until after the wedding.

The subway swallowed them, rattled and banged them along in a rocking, mindless trance for half an hour, and disgorged them at last into the cool early evening of Queens.

Removing their coats and loosening their ties, they let the breeze dry their sweated shirts as they walked. "So what's the deal?" Eddie asked. "What time we supposed to show up in this Pennsylvania burg tomorra?"

"Ah, suit yourself," Ralph said. "Any time in the evening's okay."

"So whadda we do then? What the hell can ya do in a hillbilly town like that, anyway?"

"Ah, I dunno," Ralph said defensively. "Sit around and talk, I guess; drink beer with Gracie's old man or somethin'; I dunno."

"Jesus," Eddie said. "Some weekend. Big, big deal."

Ralph stopped on the sidewalk, suddenly enraged, his damp coat wadded in his fist. "Look, you bastid. Nobody's gonna *make* ya come, ya know—you or Marty or George or any a the rest of 'em. Get that straight. You're not doin' *me* no favors, unnastand?"

"Whatsa matta?" Eddie inquired. "Whatsa matta? Can'tcha take a joke?"

"Joke," Ralph said. "You're fulla jokes." And plodding sullenly in Eddie's wake, he felt close to tears.

They turned off into the block where they both lived, a double row of neat, identical houses bordering the street where they'd fought and loafed and played stickball all their lives. Eddie pushed open the front door of his house and ushered Ralph into the vestibule, with its homely smell of cauliflower and overshoes. "G'wan in," he said, jerking a thumb at the closed living-room door, and he hung back to let Ralph go first.

Ralph opened the door and took three steps inside before it hit him like a sock on the jaw. The room, dead silent, was packed deep with grinning, red-faced men—Marty, George, the boys from the block, the boys from the office—everybody, all his friends, all on their feet and poised motionless in a solid mass. Skinny Maguire was crouched at the upright piano, his spread fingers high over the keys, and when he struck the first rollicking chords they all roared into song, beating time with their fists, their enormous grins distorting the words:

> "Fa he's a jally guh fella
> Fa he's a jally guh fella
> Fa he's a jally guh fell-ah
> That nobody can deny!"

Weakly Ralph retreated a step on the carpet and stood there wide-eyed, swallowing, holding his coat. "*That nobody can deny!*" they sang, "*That nobody can deny!*" And as they swung into the second chorus Eddie's father appeared through the dining-room curtains, bald and beaming, in full song, with a great glass pitcher of beer in either hand. At last Skinny hammered out the final line:

"*That—no—bod—dee—can—dee—nye!*"

And they all surged forward cheering, grabbing Ralph's hand, pounding his arms and his back while he stood trembling, his own voice lost under the noise, "Gee, fellas—thanks. I—don't know what to—thanks, fellas...."

Then the crowd cleaved in half, and Eddie made his way slowly down the middle. His eyes gleamed in a smile of love, and from his bashful hand hung the suitcase—not his own, but a new one: the big, tawny Gladstone with the zippered compartment on the side.

"*Speech!*" they were yelling. "*Speech! Speech!*"

But Ralph couldn't speak and couldn't smile. He could hardly even see.

At ten o'clock Grace began walking around the apartment and biting her lip. What if he wasn't coming? But of course he was coming. She sat down again and carefully smoothed the billows of nylon around her thighs, forcing herself to be calm. The whole thing would be ruined if she was nervous.

The noise of the doorbell was like an electric shock. She was halfway to the door before she stopped, breathing hard, and composed herself again. Then she pressed the buzzer and opened the door a crack to watch for him on the stairs.

When she saw he was carrying a suitcase, and saw the pale seriousness of his face as he mounted the stairs, she thought at first that he knew; he had come prepared to lock the door and take her in his arms. "Hello, darling," she said softly, and opened the door wider.

"Hi, baby." He brushed past her and walked inside. "Guess I'm late, huh? You in bed?"

"No." She closed the door and leaned against it with both hands holding the doorknob at the small of her back, the way heroines close doors in the movies. "I was just—waiting for you."

He wasn't looking at her. He went to the sofa and sat down, holding the suitcase on his lap and running his fingers over its surface. "Gracie," he said, barely above a whisper. "Look at this."

She looked at it, and then into his tragic eyes.

"Remember," he said, "I told you about that bag I wanted to buy? Forty dollars?" He stopped and looked around. "Hey, where's Martha? She in bed?"

"She's gone, darling," Grace said, moving slowly toward the sofa. "She's gone for the whole weekend." She sat down beside him, leaned close, and gave him Martha's special smile.

"Oh yeah?" he said. "Well anyway, listen. I said I was gonna borrow Eddie's bag instead, remember?"

"Yes."

"Well, so tonight at the White Rose I siz, 'C'mon, Eddie, let's go home pick up ya bag.' He siz, 'Ah, bag schmagg.' I siz, 'Whatsa matta?' but he don't say nothin', see? So we go home to his place and the living-room door's shut, see?"

She squirmed closer and put her head on his chest. Automatically he raised an arm and dropped it around her shoulders, still talking. "He siz, 'G'ahead, Ralph, open the door.' I siz, 'Whatsa deal?' He siz, 'Never mind, Ralph, open the door.' So I open the door, and oh Jesus." His fingers gripped her shoulder with such intensity that she looked up at him in alarm.

"They was all there, Gracie," he said. "All the fellas. Playin' the piana, singin', cheerin'—" His voice wavered and his eyelids fluttered shut, their lashes wet. "A big surprise party," he said, trying to smile. "Fa me. Can ya beat that, Gracie? And then— and then Eddie comes out and—Eddie comes out and hands me this. The very same bag I been lookin' at all this time. He bought it with his own money and he didn't say nothin', just to give me a surprise. 'Here, Ralph,' he siz. 'Just to let ya know you're the greatest guy in the world.'" His fingers tightened again, trembling. "I cried, Gracie," he whispered. "I couldn't help it. I don't think the fellas saw it or anything, but I was cryin'." He turned his face away and worked his lips in a tremendous effort to hold back the tears.

"Would you like a drink, darling?" she asked tenderly.

"Nah, that's all right, Gracie. I'm all right." Gently he set the suitcase on the carpet. "Only, gimme a cigarette, huh?"

She got one from the coffee table, put it in his lips and lit it. "Let me get you a drink," she said.

He frowned through the smoke. "Whaddya got, that sherry wine? Nah, I don't like that stuff. Anyway, I'm fulla beer." He leaned back and closed his eyes. "And then Eddie's mother feeds us this terrific meal," he went on, and his voice was almost normal now. "We had *steaks*; we had French-fried *potatas*"— his head rolled on the sofa-back with each item of the menu —"lettuce-and-tomata *salad, pickles, bread, butter*—everything. The works."

"Well," she said. "Wasn't that nice."

"And afterwards we had ice cream and coffee," he said, "and all the beer we could drink. I mean, it was a real spread."

Grace ran her hands over her lap, partly to smooth the nylon and partly to dry the moisture on her palms. "Well, that certainly was nice of them," she said. They sat there silent for what seemed a long time.

"I can only stay a minute, Gracie," Ralph said at last. "I promised 'em I'd be back."

Her heart thumped under the nylon. "Ralph, do you—do you like this?"

"What, honey?"

"My negligee. You weren't supposed to see it until—after the wedding, but I thought I'd—"

"Nice," he said, feeling the flimsy material between thumb and index finger, like a merchant. "Very nice. Wudga pay fa this, honey?"

"Oh—I don't know. But do you like it?"

He kissed her and began, at last, to stroke her with his hands. "Nice," he kept saying. "Nice. Hey, I like this." His hand hesitated at the low neckline, slipped inside and held her breast.

"I do love you, Ralph," she whispered. "You know that, don't you?"

His fingers pinched her nipple, once, and slid quickly out again. The policy of restraint, the habit of months was too strong to break. "Sure," he said. "And I love you, baby. Now you be a good girl and get ya beauty sleep, and I'll see ya in the morning. Okay?"

"Oh, Ralph. Don't go. Stay."

"Ah, I promised the fellas, Gracie." He stood up and straightened his clothes. "They're waitin' fa me, out home."

She blazed to her feet, but the cry that was meant for a woman's appeal came out, through her tightening lips, as the whine of a wife: "Can't they wait?"

"Whaddya—crazy?" He backed away, eyes round with righteousness. She would have to understand. If this was the way she acted before the wedding, how the hell was it going to be afterwards? "Have a heart, willya? Keep the fellas waitin' tonight? After all they done fa *me*?"

After a second or two, during which her face became less pretty than he had ever seen it before, she was able to smile. "Of course not, darling. You're right."

He came forward again and gently brushed the tip of her chin with his fist, smiling, a husband reassured. "At's more like it," he said. "So I'll see ya, Penn Station, nine o'clock tomorra. Right, Gracie? Only, before I go—" he winked and slapped his belly. "I'm fulla beer. Mind if I use ya terlet?"

When he came out of the bathroom she was waiting to say goodnight, standing with her arms folded across her chest, as if for warmth. Lovingly he hefted the new suitcase and joined her at the door. "Okay, then, baby," he said, and kissed her. "Nine o'clock. Don't forget, now."

She smiled tiredly and opened the door for him. "Don't worry, Ralph," she said. "I'll be there."

JODY ROLLED THE BONES

SERGEANT REECE WAS a slim, quiet Tennessean who always managed to look neat in fatigues, and he wasn't exactly what we'd expected an infantry platoon sergeant to be. We learned soon enough that he was typical—almost a prototype—of the men who had drifted into the Regular Army in the thirties and stayed to form the cadres of the great wartime training centers, but at the time he surprised us. We were pretty naïve, and I think we'd all expected more of a Victor McLaglen—burly, roaring and tough, but lovable, in the Hollywood tradition. Reece was tough, all right, but he never roared and we didn't love him.

He alienated us on the first day by butchering our names. We were all from New York, and most of our names did require a little effort, but Reece made a great show of being defeated by them. His thin features puckered over the roster, his little mustache twitching at each unfamiliar syllable. "Dee—Dee Alice—" he stammered, "Dee Alice—"

"Here," D'Allesandro said, and it went like that with almost every name. At one point, after he'd grappled with Schacht, Scoglio, and Sizscovicz, he came to Smith. "Hey, Smith," he said, looking up with a slow, unengaging grin. "What the hell *yew* doin' heah 'mong all these gorillas?" Nobody thought it was funny. At last he finished and tucked the clipboard under his arm. "All right," he told us. "My name's Sahjint Reece and I'm your platoon sahjint. That means when I say do somethin', do it." He gave us a long, appraising glare. "P'toon!" he snapped, making his diaphragm jump. "Tetch—*hut!*" And his tyranny began. By the end of that day and for many days thereafter we had him firmly fixed in our minds as, to use D'Allesandro's phrase, a dumb Rebel bastard.

I had better point out here that we were probably not very lovable either. We were all eighteen, a confused, platoon-sized bunch of city kids determined to be unenthusiastic about Basic Training. Apathy in boys of that age may be unusual—it is certainly unattractive—but this was 1944, the war was no longer new, and bitterness was the fashionable mood. To throw yourself into Army life with gusto only meant you were a kid who didn't know the score, and nobody wanted to be that. Secretly we may have yearned for battle, or at least for ribbons, but on the surface we were shameless little wise guys about everything. Trying to make us soldiers must have been a staggering job, and Reece bore the brunt of it.

But of course that side of the thing didn't occur to us, at first. All we knew was that he rode us hard and we hated his guts. We saw very little of our lieutenant, a plump collegiate youth who showed up periodically to insist that if we played ball with him, he would play ball with us, and even less of our company commander (I hardly remember what he looked like, except that he wore glasses). But Reece was always there, calm and contemptuous, never speaking except to give orders and never smiling except in cruelty. And we could tell by observing the other platoons that he was exceptionally strict; he had, for instance, his own method of rationing water.

It was summer, and the camp lay flat under the blistering Texas sun. A generous supply of salt tablets was all that kept us conscious until nightfall; our fatigues were always streaked white from the salt of our sweat and we were always thirsty, but the camp's supply of drinking water had to be transported from a spring many miles away, so there was a standing order to go easy on it. Most noncoms were thirsty enough themselves to construe the regulation loosely, but Reece took it to heart. "If yew men don't learn nothin' else about soldierin'," he would say, "you're gonna learn water discipline." The water hung in Lister bags, fat canvas udders placed at intervals along the roads, and although it was warm and acrid with chemicals, the high point of every morning and every afternoon was the moment when we were authorized a break to fill our canteens with it. Most platoons would attack a Lister bag in a jostling wallowing rush, working its little steel teats until the bag hung limp and wrinkled, and a dark stain of waste lay spreading in the dust beneath it. Not us.

Reece felt that half a canteenful at a time was enough for any man, and he would stand by the Lister bag in grim supervision, letting us at it in an orderly column of twos. When a man held his canteen too long under the bag, Reece would stop everything, pull the man out of line, and say, "Pour that out. All of it."

"I'll be *goddamned* if I will!" D'Allessandro shot back at him one day, and we all stood fascinated, watching them glare at each other in the dazzling heat. D'Allessandro was a husky boy with fierce black eyes who had in a few weeks become our spokesman; I guess he was the only one brave enough to stage a scene like this. "Whaddya think I am," he shouted, "a goddamn *camel*, like you?" We giggled.

Reece demanded silence from the rest of us, got it, and turned back to D'Allessandro, squinting and licking his dry lips. "All right," he said quietly, "drink it. All of it. The resta yew men keep away from that bag, keep your hands off your canteens. I want y'all to watch this. Go on, drink it."

D'Allessandro gave us a grin of nervous triumph and began to drink, pausing only to catch his breath with the water dribbling on his chest. "Drink it," Reece would snap each time he stopped. It made us desperately thirsty to watch him, but we were beginning to get the idea. When the canteen was empty Reece told him to fill it up again. He did, still smiling but looking a little worried. "Now drink that," Reece said. "Fast. Faster." And when he was finished, gasping, with the empty canteen in his hand, Reece said, "Now get your helmet and rifle. See that barracks over there?" A white building shimmered in the distance, a couple of hundred yards away. "You're gonna proceed on the double to that barracks, go around it and come back on the double. Meantime your buddies're gonna be waitin' here; ain't none of 'em gonna get nothin' to drink till yew get back. All right, now, move. *Move*. On the *double*."

In loyalty to D'Allessandro none of us laughed, but he did look absurd trotting heavily out across the drill field, his helmet wobbling. Before he reached the barracks we saw him stop, crouch, and vomit up the water. Then he staggered on, a tiny figure in the faraway dust, disappeared around the building, and finally emerged at the other side to begin the long trip back. At last he arrived and fell exhausted on the ground. "Now," Reece said softly. "Had enough to drink?" Only then were the rest of us allowed to use the Lister bag, two at a time. When we were all through, Reece squatted nimbly and drew half a canteen for himself without spilling a drop.

That was the kind of thing he did, every day, and if anyone had suggested he was only doing his job, our response would have been a long and unanimous Bronx cheer.

I think our first brief easing of hostility toward him occurred quite early in the training cycle, one morning when one of the instructors, a strapping first lieutenant, was trying to teach us the bayonet. We felt pretty sure that in the big, modern kind of war for which we were bound we probably would not be called on to fight with bayonets (and that if we ever were it wouldn't make a hell of a lot of difference whether we'd mastered the finer points of parry and thrust), and so our lassitude that morning was even purer than usual. We let the instructor talk to us, then got up and fumbled through the various positions he had outlined.

The other platoons looked as bad as we did, and faced with such dreary incompetence on a company scale the instructor rubbed his mouth. "No," he said. "No, no, you men haven't got the idea at all. Fall back to your places and sit down. Sergeant Reece front and center, please."

Reece had been sitting with the other platoon sergeants in their customary bored little circle, aloof from the lecture, but he rose promptly and came forward.

"Sergeant, I'd like you to show these people what a bayonet is all about," the instructor said. And from the moment Reece hefted a bayoneted rifle in his hands we knew, grudgingly or not, that we were going to see something. It was the feeling you get at a ball game when a heavy hitter selects a bat. At the instructor's commands he whipped smartly into each of the positions, freezing into a slim statue while the officer crouched and weaved around him, talking, pointing out the distribution of his weight and the angles of his limbs, explaining that this was how it should be done. Then, to climax the performance, the instructor sent Reece alone through the bayonet course. He went through it fast, never off balance and never wasting a motion, smashing blocks of wood off their wooden shoulders with his rifle butt, driving his blade deep into a shuddering torso of bundled sticks and ripping it out to bear down on the next one. He looked good. It would be too much to say that he kindled our admiration, but there is an automatic pleasure in watching a thing done well. The other platoons were clearly impressed, and although nobody in our platoon said anything, I think we were a little proud of him.

But the next period that day was close-order drill, at which the platoon sergeants had full command, and within half an hour Reece had nagged us into open resentment again. "What the hell's he think," Schacht muttered in the ranks, "he's some kind of a big deal now, just because he's a hotshot with that stupid bayonet?" And the rest of us felt a vague shame that we had so nearly been taken in.

When we eventually did change our minds about him, it did not seem due, specifically, to any act of his, but to an experience that changed our minds about the Army in general, and about ourselves. This was the rifle range, the only part of our training we thoroughly enjoyed. After so many hours of drill and calisthenics, of droning lectures in the sun and training films run off in sweltering clapboard buildings, the prospect of actually going out and shooting held considerable promise, and when the time came it proved to be fun. There was a keen pleasure in sprawling prone on the embankment of the firing line with a rifle stock nestled at your cheek and the oily, gleaming clips of ammunition close at hand; in squinting out across a great expanse of earth at your target and waiting for the signal from a measured voice on the loudspeaker. "Ready on the right. Ready on the left. Ready on the firing line. . . . The flag is up. The flag is waving. The flag is down. Commence—*fire!*" There would be a blast of many rifles in your ears, a breathless moment as you squeezed the trigger, and a sharp jolt as you fired. Then you'd relax and watch the target slide down in the distance, controlled by unseen hands in the pit beneath it. When it reappeared a moment later a colored disk would be thrust up with it, waved and withdrawn, signaling your score. The man kneeling behind you with the scorecard would mutter, "Nice going" or "Tough," and you'd squirm in the sand and take aim again. Like nothing else we had found in the Army, this was something to rouse a competitive instinct, and when it took the form of wanting our platoon to make a better showing than the others, it brought us as close to a genuine *esprit de corps* as anything could.

We spent a week or so on the range, leaving early every morning and staying all day, taking our noon meal from a field kitchen that was in itself a refreshing change from the mess hall. Another good feature—at first it seemed the best of all—was that the range gave us a respite from Sergeant Reece. He marched us out there and back, and he supervised the cleaning of our rifles in the barracks, but for the bulk of the day he turned us over to the range staff, an impersonal, kindly crowd, much less concerned with petty discipline than with marksmanship.

Still, Reece had ample opportunity to bully us in the hours when he was in charge, but after a few days on the range we found he was easing up. When we counted cadence on the road now, for instance, he no longer made us do it over and over, louder each time, until our dry throats burned from yelling, "HUT, WHO, REEP, HOE!" He would quit after one or two counts like the other platoon sergeants, and at first we didn't know what to make of it. "What's the deal?" we asked each other, baffled, and I guess the deal was simply that we'd begun to do it right the first time, loud enough and in perfect unison. We were marching well, and this was Reece's way of letting us know it.

The trip to the range was several miles, and a good share of it was through the part of camp where marching at attention was required—we were never given route step until after we'd cleared the last of the company streets and buildings. But with our new efficiency at marching we got so that we almost enjoyed it, and even responded with enthusiasm to Reece's marching chant. It had always been his habit, after making us count cadence, to go through one of those traditional singsong chants calling for traditional shouts of reply, and we'd always resented it before. But now the chant seemed uniquely stirring, an authentic piece of folklore from older armies and older wars, with roots deep in the life we were just beginning to understand. He would begin by expanding his ordinary nasal "Left . . . left . . . left" into a mournful little tune: "Oh yew *had* a good *home* and yew *left*—" to which we would answer, "RIGHT!" as our right feet fell. We would go through several variations on this theme:

"Oh yew had a good job and yew left—"

"RIGHT!"

"Oh yew had a good gal and yew left—"

"RIGHT!"

And then he'd vary the tune a little: "Oh Jody rolled the bones when yew left—"

"RIGHT!" we'd yell in soldierly accord, and none of us had to wonder what the words meant. Jody was your faithless friend, the soft civilian to whom the dice-throw of chance had given everything you held dear; and the next verses, a series of taunting couplets, made it clear that he would always have the last laugh. You might march and shoot and learn to perfection your creed of disciplined force, but Jody was a force beyond control, and the fact had been faced by generations of proud, lonely men like this one, this splendid soldier who swung along beside our ranks in the sun and bawled the words from a twisted mouth: "Ain't no use in goin' home—Jody's got your gal and gone. Sound off—"

"HUT, WHO!"

"Sound off—"

"REEP, HOE!"

"Ever' time yew stand Retreat, Jody gets a piece of meat. Sound off—"

"HUT, WHO!"

"Sound off—"

"REEP, HOE!" It was almost a disappointment when he gave us route step on the outskirts of camp and we became individuals again, cocking back our helmets and slouching along out of step, with the fine unanimity of the chant left behind. When we returned from the range dusty and tired, our ears numb from the noise of fire, it was somehow bracing to swing into formal cadence again for the last leg of the journey, heads up, backs straight, and split the cooling air with our roars of response.

A good part of our evenings, after chow, would be spent cleaning our rifles with the painstaking care that Reece demanded.

The barracks would fill with the sharp, good smells of bore cleaner and oil as we worked, and when the job had been done to Reece's satisfaction we would usually drift out to the front steps for a smoke while we waited our turns at the showers. One night a group of us lingered there more quietly than usual, finding, I think, that the customary small talk of injustice and complaint was inadequate, unsuited to the strange well-being we had all begun to feel these last few days. Finally Fogarty put the mood into words. He was a small, serious boy, the runt of the platoon and something of a butt of jokes, and I guess he had nothing much to lose by letting his guard down. "Ah, I dunno," he said, leaning back against the doorjamb with a sigh, "I dunno about you guys, but I like this—going out to the range, marching and all. Makes you feel like you're really soldiering, you know what I mean?"

It was a dangerously naïve thing to say—"soldiering" was Reece's favorite word—and we looked at him uncertainly for a second. But then D'Allessandro glanced deadpan around the group, defying anyone to laugh, and we relaxed. The idea of soldiering had become respectable, and because the idea as well as the word was inseparable in our minds from Sergeant Reece, he became respectable too.

Soon the change had come over the whole platoon. We were working with Reece now, instead of against him, trying instead of pretending to try. We wanted to be soldiers. The intensity of our effort must sometimes have been ludicrous, and might have caused a lesser man to suspect we were kidding—I remember earnest little choruses of "Okay, Sergeant" whenever he dispatched an order—but Reece took it all straight-faced, with that air of unlimited self-assurance that is the first requisite of good leadership. And he was as fair as he was strict, which must surely be the second requisite. In appointing provisional squad leaders, for example, he coolly passed over several men who had all but licked his shoes for recognition, and picked those he knew could hold our respect—D'Allessandro was one, and the others were equally well chosen. The rest of his formula was classically simple: he led by being excellent, at everything from cleaning a rifle to rolling a pair of socks, and we followed by trying to emulate him.

But if excellence is easy to admire it is hard to like, and Reece refused to make himself likable. It was his only failing, but it was a big one, for respect without affection can't last long—not, at least, where the sentimentality of adolescent minds is involved. Reece rationed kindness the way he rationed water: we might cherish each drop out of all proportion to its worth, but we never got enough or anything like enough to slake our thirst. We were delighted when he suddenly began to get our names right at roll call and when we noticed that he was taking the edge of insult off most of his reprimands, for we knew these signs to be acknowledgments of our growth as soldiers, but somehow we felt a right to expect more.

We were delighted too at the discovery that our plump lieutenant was afraid of him; we could barely hide our pleasure at the condescending look that came over Reece's face whenever the lieutenant appeared, or at the tone of the young officer's voice—uneasy, almost apologetic—when he said, "All right, Sergeant." It made us feel close to Reece in a proud soldierly alliance, and once or twice he granted us the keen compliment of a wink behind the lieutenant's back, but only once or twice. We might imitate his walk and his squinting stare, get the shirts of our suntans tailored skintight like his and even adopt some of his habits of speech, Southern accent and all, but we could never quite consider him a Good Joe. He just wasn't the type. Formal obedience, in working hours, was all he wanted, and we hardly knew him at all.

On the rare evenings when he stayed on the post he would sit either alone or in the unapproachable company of one or two other cadremen as taciturn as himself, drinking beer in the PX. Most nights and all weekends he disappeared into town. I'm sure none of us expected him to spend his free time with us—the thought would never have occurred to us, in fact—but the smallest glimpse into his personal life would have helped. If he had ever reminisced with us about his home, for instance, or related the conversations of his PX friends, or told us of a bar he liked in town, I think we would all have been touchingly grateful, but

he never did. And what made it worse was that, unlike him, we
had no real life outside the day's routine. The town was a small,
dusty maze of clapboard and neon, crawling with soldiers, and
to most of us it yielded only loneliness, however we may have
swaggered down its avenues. There wasn't enough town to go
around; whatever delights it held remained the secrets of those
who had found them first, and if you were young, shy, and not
precisely sure what you were looking for anyway, it was a dreary
place. You could hang around the USO and perhaps get to dance
with a girl long hardened against a callow advance; you could
settle for the insipid pleasures of watermelon stands and penny
arcades, or you could prowl aimlessly in groups through the dark
back streets, where all you met as a rule were other groups of
soldiers on the aimless prowl. "So whaddya wanna *do*?" we
would ask each other impatiently, and the only answer was, "Ah,
I dunno. Cruise around awhile, I guess." Usually we'd drink
enough beer to be drunk, or sick, on the bus back to camp, grateful for the promise of an orderly new day.

It was probably not surprising, then, that our emotional life
became ingrown. Like frustrated suburban wives we fed on each
other's discontent; we became divided into mean little cliques
and subdivided into jealously shifting pairs of buddies, and we
pieced out our idleness with gossip. Most of the gossip was
self-contained; for news from the extraplatoon world we relied
largely on the company clerk, a friendly, sedentary man who
liked to dispense rumors over a carefully balanced cup of coffee
as he strolled from table to table in the mess hall. "I got this
from Personnel," he would say in preface to some improbable
hearsay about the distant brass (the colonel had syphilis; the
stockade commander had weaseled out of a combat assignment;
the training program had been cut short and we'd all be overseas
in a month). But one Saturday noon he had something less
remote; he had gotten it from his own company orderly room,
and it sounded plausible. For weeks, he told us, the plump lieutenant had been trying to get Reece transferred; now it appeared
to be in the works, and next week might well be Reece's last as
a platoon sergeant. "His days are numbered," the clerk said
darkly.

"Whaddya mean, transferred?" D'Allessandro asked. "Transferred where?"

"Keep your voice down," the clerk said, with an uneasy glance toward the noncoms' table, where Reece bent stolidly over his food. "I dunno. That part I dunno. Anyway, it's a lousy deal. You kids got the best damn platoon sergeant on the post, if you wanna know something. He's too *damn* good, in fact; that's his trouble. Too good for a half-assed second lieutenant to handle. In the Army it never pays to be that good."

"You're right," D'Allessandro said solemnly. "It never pays."

"Yeah?" Schacht inquired, grinning. "Is that right, Squad Leader? Tell us about it, Squad Leader." And the talk at our table degenerated into wisecracks. The clerk drifted away.

Reece must have heard the story about the same time we did; at any rate that weekend marked a sudden change in his behavior. He left for town with the tense look of a man methodically planning to get drunk, and on Monday morning he almost missed Reveille. He nearly always had a hangover on Monday mornings, but it had never before interfered with his day's work; he had always been there to get us up and out with his angry tongue. This time, though, there was an odd silence in the barracks as we dressed. "Hey, he isn't *here*," somebody called from the door of Reece's room near the stairs. "Reece isn't *here*." The squad leaders were admirably quick to take the initiative. They coaxed and prodded until we had all tumbled outside and into formation in the dark, very nearly as fast as we'd have done it under Reece's supervision. But the night's CQ, in making his rounds, had already discovered Reece's absence and run off to rouse the lieutenant.

The company officers rarely stood Reveille, particularly on Mondays, but now as we stood leaderless in the company street our lieutenant came jogging around the side of the barracks. By the lights of the building we could see that his shirt was half buttoned and his hair wild; he looked puffy with sleep and badly confused. Still running, he called, "All right, you men, uh—"

All the squad leaders drew their breath to call us to attention, but they got no further than a ragged "Tetch—" when Reece emerged out of the gloaming, stepped up in front of the lieutenant, and said, "P'toon! Tetch—*hut!*" There he was, a little winded from running, still wearing the wrinkled suntans of the night before, but plainly in charge. He called the roll by squads; then he kicked out one stiff leg in the ornate, Regular Army way of doing an about-face, neatly executed the turn and ended up facing the lieutenant in a perfect salute. "All presen'accounted for, sir," he said.

The lieutenant was too startled to do anything but salute back, sloppily, and mumble "All right, Sergeant." I guess he felt he couldn't even say, "See that this doesn't happen again," since, after all, nothing very much had happened, except that he'd been gotten out of bed for Reveille. And I guess he spent the rest of the day wondering whether he should have reprimanded Reece for being out of uniform; he looked as if the question was already bothering him as he turned to go back to his quarters. Dismissed, our formation broke up in a thunderclap of laughter that he pretended not to hear.

But Sergeant Reece soon spoiled the joke. He didn't even thank the squad leaders for helping him out of a tight spot, and for the rest of the day he treated us to the kind of petty nagging we thought we had outgrown. On the drill field he braced little Fogarty and said, "When'd yew shave last?"

Like many of our faces, Fogarty's bore only a pale fuzz that hardly needed shaving at all. "About a week ago," he said.

" 'Bout a week ago, *Sah*jint," Reece corrected.

"About a week ago, Sergeant," Fogarty said.

Reece curled back his thin lips. "Yew look lak a mangy ole mungrel bitch," he said. "Doan yew know you're s'posed to shave ever' day?"

"I wouldn't have nothing to *shave* every day."

"Wouldn't have nothin' to shave, *Sah*jint."

Fogarty swallowed, blinking. "Nothing to shave, Sergeant," he said.

We all felt badly let down. "What the hell's he think we are," Schacht demanded that noon, "a bunch of rookies?" And D'Allessandro grumbled in mutinous agreement.

A bad hangover might have excused Reece that day, but it

could hardly have accounted for the next day and the day after that. He was bullying us without reason and without relief, and he was destroying everything he had built up so carefully in the many weeks before; the whole delicate structure of our respect for him crumbled and fell.

"It's final," the company clerk said grimly at supper Wednesday night. "The orders are cut. Tomorrow's his last day."

"So?" Schacht inquired. "Where's he going?"

"Keep your voice down," the clerk said. "Gonna work with the instructors. Spend part of his time out on the bivouac area and part on the bayonet course."

Schacht laughed, nudging D'Allessandro. "Hot damn," he said, "he'll eat that up, won't he? Specially the bayonet part. Bastard'll get to show off every day. He'll like that."

"Whaddya, *kidding*?" the clerk asked, offended. "Like it my ass. That guy loved his job. You think I'm kidding? He *loved* his job, and it's a lousy break. You kids don't know when you're well off."

D'Allessandro took up the argument, narrowing his eyes. "Yeah?" he said. "You think so? You oughta see him out there every day this week. Every day."

The clerk leaned forward so earnestly that some of his coffee spilled. "Listen," he said. "He's known about this all week—how the hellya *want* him to act? How the hell would *you* act if you knew somebody was screwing you out of the thing you liked best? Can'tcha see he's under a strain?"

But that, we all told him with our surly stares, was no excuse for being a dumb Rebel bastard.

"Some of you kids act too big for your pants," the clerk said, and went away in a sulk.

"Ah, don't believe everything you hear," Schacht said. "I'll believe he's transferred when I see it."

But it was true. That night Reece sat up late in his room, drinking morosely with one of his cronies. We could hear their low, blurred voices in the darkness, and the occasional clink of their whiskey bottle. The following day he was neither easy nor hard on us in the field, but brooding and aloof as if he had other things on his mind. And when he marched us back that evening he kept us standing in formation in front of the barracks for a few moments, at ease, before dismissing us. His restless glance seemed to survey all our faces in turn. Then he began to speak in a voice more gentle than any we had ever heard him use. "I won't be seein' yew men any more after today," he said. "I'm bein' transferred. One thing yew can always count on in th' Army, and that is, if yew find somethin' good, some job yew like, they always transfer your ass somewheres else."

I think we were all touched—I know I was; it was the closest he had ever come to saying he liked us. But it was too late. Anything he said or did now would have been too late, and our predominant feeling was relief. Reece seemed to sense this, and seemed to cut short the things he had planned to say.

"I know there ain't no call for me to make a speech," he said, "and I ain't gonna make one. Onliest thing I want to say is—" He lowered his eyes and stared at his dusty service shoes. "I want to wish all yew men a lot of luck. Y'all keep your nose clean, hear? And stay outa trouble?" The next words could scarcely be heard. "And doan let nobody push y'around."

A short, painful silence followed, as painful as the parting of disenchanted lovers. Then he drew himself straight. "P'toon! Tetch—*hut!*" He looked us over once more with hard and glittering eyes. "Dismissed."

And when we came back from chow that night we found he had already packed his barracks bags and cleared out. We didn't even get to shake his hand.

Our new platoon sergeant was there in the morning, a squat jolly cab driver from Queens who insisted that we call him only by his first name, which was Ruby. He was every inch a Good Joe. He turned us loose at the Lister bags every chance he got, and confided with a giggle that, through a buddy of his in the PX, he often got his own canteen filled with Coca-Cola and crushed ice. He was a slack drill-master, and on the road he never made us count cadence except when we passed an officer, never made us chant or sing anything except a ragged version of "Give My Regards to Broadway," which he led with fervor although he didn't know all the words.

It took us a little while to adjust to him, after Reece. Once when the lieutenant came to the barracks to give one of his little talks about playing ball, ending up with his usual "All right, Sergeant," Ruby hooked his thumbs in his cartridge belt, slouched comfortably, and said, "Fellas, I hope yez all listened and gave ya attention to what the lieutenant said. I think I can speak fa yez all as well as myself when I say, Lieutenant, we're *gonna* play ball wit' you, like you said, because this here is one platoon that knows a Good Joe when we see one."

As flustered by this as he had ever been by Reece's silent scorn, the lieutenant could only blush and stammer, "Well, uh—thank you, Sergeant. Uh—I guess that's all, then. Carry on." And as soon as the lieutenant was out of sight we all began to make loud retching noises, to hold our noses or go through the motions of shoveling, as if we stood knee-deep in manure. "Christ, Ruby," Schacht cried, "what the hella *you* buckin' for?"

Ruby hunched his shoulders and spread his hands, bubbling with good-natured laughter. "To stay alive," he said. "To stay alive, whaddya think?" And he defended the point vigorously over the mounting din of our ridicule. "Whatsa matta?" he demanded. "Whatsa matta? Don'tcha think he does it to the captain? Don'tcha think the captain does it up at Battalion? Listen, wise up, will yez? *Evvybody* does it! *Evvybody* does it! What the hellya think makes the Army *go*?" Finally he dismissed the whole subject with cab-driverly nonchalance. 'Arright, arright, just stick around. *Yull* find out. Wait'll you kids got my time in the Army, *then* yez can talk." But by that time we were all laughing with him; he had won our hearts.

In the evenings, at the PX, we would cluster around him while he sat behind a battery of beer bottles, waving his expressive hands and talking the kind of relaxed, civilian language we all could understand. "Ah, I got this brother-in-law, a real smott bastid. Know how *he* got outa the Army? Know how *he* got out?" There would follow an involved, unlikely tale of treachery to which the only expected response was a laugh. "Sure!" Ruby would insist, laughing. "Don'tcha believe me? Don'tcha believe me? And this other guy I know, boy, talk about bein' *smott*—I'm tellin' ya, this bastid's *really* smott. Know how *he* got out?"

Sometimes our allegiance wavered, but not for long. One evening a group of us sat around the front steps, dawdling over cigarettes before we pushed off to the PX, and discussing at length—as if to convince ourselves—the many things that made life with Ruby so enjoyable. "Well yeah," little Fogarty said, "but I dunno. With Ruby it don't seem much like soldiering any more."

This was the second time Fogarty had thrown us into a momentary confusion, and for the second time D'Allessandro cleared the air. "So?" he said with a shrug. "Who the hell wants to soldier?"

That said it perfectly. We could spit in the dust and amble off toward the PX now, round-shouldered, relieved, confident that Sergeant Reece would not haunt us again. Who the hell wanted to soldier? "Not *me*," we could all say in our hearts, "not *this* chicken," and our very defiance would dignify the attitude. An attitude was all we needed anyway, all we had ever needed, and this one would always sit more comfortably than Reece's stern, demanding creed. It meant, I guess, that at the end of our training cycle the camp delivered up a bunch of shameless little wise guys to be scattered and absorbed into the vast disorder of the Army, but at least Reece never saw it happen, and he was the only one who might have cared.

NO PAIN WHATSOEVER

MYRA STRAIGHTENED HERSELF in the backseat and smoothed her skirt, pushing Jack's hand away.

"All right, baby," he whispered, smiling, "take it easy."

"You take it easy, Jack," she told him. "I mean it, now."

His hand yielded, limp, but his arm stayed indolently around her shoulders. Myra ignored him and stared out the window. It was early Sunday evening, late in December, and the Long Island streets looked stale; dirty crusts of snow lay shriveled on the sidewalk, and cardboard images of Santa Claus leered out of closed liquor stores.

"I still don't feel right about you driving me all the way out here," Myra called to Marty, who was driving, to be polite.

" 'S all right," Marty grumbled. Then he sounded his horn and added, to the back of a slow truck, "Get that son of a bitch outa the way."

Myra was annoyed—why did Marty always have to be such a grouch?—but Irene, Marty's wife, squirmed around in the front seat with her friendly grin. "Marty don't mind," she said. "It's good for 'm, getting out on a Sunday insteada laying around the house."

"Well," Myra said, "I certainly do appreciate it." The truth was that she would much rather have taken the bus, alone, as usual. In the four years she had been coming out here to visit her husband every Sunday she had grown used to the long ride, and she liked stopping at a little cafeteria in Hempstead, where you had to change buses, for coffee and cake on the way home. But today she and Jack had gone over to Irene and Marty's for dinner, and the dinner was so late that Marty had to offer to drive her out to the hospital, and she had to accept. And then of course Irene had to come along, and Jack too, and they all acted as if they were doing her a favor. But you had to be polite. "It certainly is nice," Myra called, "to be riding out here in a car, instead of a—*don't* Jack!"

Jack said, "*Sh-h-h*, take it easy, baby," but she threw off his hand and twisted away. Watching them, Irene put her tongue between her teeth and giggled, and Myra felt herself blushing. It wasn't that there was anything to be ashamed of—Irene and Marty knew all about Jack and everything; most of her friends did, and nobody blamed her (after all, wasn't it almost like being a widow?)—it was just that Jack ought to know better. Couldn't he at least have the decency to keep his hands to himself now, of all times?

"There," Marty said. "Now we'll make some time." The truck had turned off and they were picking up speed, leaving the streetcar tracks and stores behind as the street became a road and then a highway.

"Care to hear the radio, kids?" Irene called. She clicked one of the dial tabs and a voice urged everyone to enjoy television in their own homes, now, tonight. She clicked another and a voice said, "Yes, your money buys more in a Crawford store!"

"Turn that son of a bitch off," Marty said, and sounding the horn again, he pulled out into the fast lane.

When the car entered the hospital grounds, Irene turned around in the front seat and said, "Say, this is a beautiful place. I mean it, isn't this a beautiful place? Oh, look, they got a Christmas tree up, with lights and all."

"Well," Marty said, "where to?"

"Straight ahead," Myra told him, "down to that big circle, where the Christmas tree is. Then you turn right, out around the Administration Building, and on out to the end of that street." He made the turn correctly, and as they approached the long, low TB building, she said, "Here it is, Marty, this one right here." He drew up to the curb and stopped, and she gathered together the magazines she had brought for her husband and stepped out on the thin gray snow.

Irene hunched her shoulders and turned around, hugging herself. "Oo-oo, it's *cold* out there, isn't it? Listen, honey, what time is it you'll be through, now? Eight o'clock, is it?"

"That's right," Myra said, "but listen, why don't you people go on home? I can just as soon take the bus back, like I always do."

"Whaddya think I am, crazy?" Irene said. "You think I want to drive all the way home with Jack moping there in the back-seat?" She giggled and winked. "Be hard enough just trying to keep him happy while you're inside, let alone driving all the way home. No, listen, we'll cruise around a little, honey, maybe have a little drink or something, and then we'll come back here for you at eight o'clock sharp."

"Well okay, but I'd really just as soon—"

"Right here," Irene said. "We'll see you right here in front of the building at eight o'clock sharp. Now hurry up and shut the door before we all freeze to death."

Myra smiled as she slammed the door, but Jack, sulking, did not look up to smile back, or wave. Then the car rolled away and she walked up the path and the steps to the TB building.

The small waiting room smelled of steam heat and wet over-shoes, and she hurried through it, past the door marked NURSES' OFFICE—CLEAN AREA and into the big, noisy center ward. There were thirty-six beds in the center ward, divided in half by a wide aisle and subdivided by shoulder-high partitions into open cubicles of six beds each. All the sheets and the hospital pajamas were dyed yellow, to distinguish them from uncontaminated linen in the hospital laundry, and this combined with the pale green of the walls made a sickly color scheme that Myra could never get used to. The noise was terrible too; each patient had a radio, and they all seemed to be playing different stations at once. There were clumps of visitors at some of the beds—one of the newer men lay with his arms around his wife in a kiss—but at other beds the men looked lonely, reading or listening to their radios.

Myra's husband didn't see her until she was right beside his bed. He was sitting up, cross-legged, frowning over something in his lap. "Hello, Harry," she said.

He looked up. "Oh, hi there, honey, didn't see you coming."

She leaned over and kissed him quickly on the cheek. Some-times they kissed on the lips, but you weren't supposed to.

Harry glanced at his watch. "You're late. Was the bus late?"

"I didn't come on the bus," she said, taking off her coat. "I got a ride out. Irene, the girl that works in my office? She and her husband drove me out in their car."

"Oh, that's nice. Whyn't you bring 'em on in?"

"Oh, they couldn't stay—they had someplace else to go. But they both said to give you their regards. Here, I brought you these."

"Oh, thanks, that's swell." He took the magazines and spread them out on the bed: *Life*, *Collier's* and *Popular Science*. "That's swell, honey. Sit down and stay awhile."

Myra laid her coat over the back of the bedside chair and sat down. "Hello there, Mr. Chance," she said to a very long Negro in the next bed who was nodding and grinning at her.

"How're you, Mrs. Wilson?"

"Fine, thanks, and you?"

"Oh, no use complaining," Mr. Chance said.

She peered across Harry's bed at Red O'Meara, who lay listening to his radio on the other side. "Hi there, Red."

"Oh, hi, Mrs. Wilson. Didn't see you come in."

"Your wife coming in tonight, Red?"

"She comes Saturdays now. She was here last night."

"Oh," Myra said, "well, tell her I said hello."

"I sure will, Mrs. Wilson."

Then she smiled at the elderly man across the cubicle whose name she could never remember, who never had any visitors, and he smiled back, looking rather shy. She settled herself on the little steel chair, opening her handbag for cigarettes. "What's that thing on your lap, Harry?" It was a ring of blond wood a foot wide, with a great deal of blue knitting wool attached to little pegs around its edge.

"Oh, this?" Harry said, holding it up. "It's what they call rake-knitting. Something I got from occupational therapy."

"*What*-knitting?"

"Rake-knitting. See, what you do, you take this little hook and kind of pry the wool up and over each peg, like that, and you keep on doing that around and around the ring until you got yourself a muffler or a stocking cap—something like that."

"Oh, *I* see," Myra said. "It's like what we used to do when I was a kid, only we did it with a regular little spool, with nails stuck in it? You wind string around the nails and pull it through the spool and it makes sort of a knitted rope, like."

"Oh, yeah?" Harry said. "With a spool, huh? Yeah, I think my sister used to do that too, now that I think of it. With a spool. You're right, this is the same principle, only bigger."

"What're you going to make?"

"Oh, I don't know, I'm just fooling around with it. Thought I might make a stocking cap or something. I don't know." He inspected his work, turning the knitting-rake around in his hands, then leaned over and put it away in his bed stand. "It's just something to do."

She offered him the pack and he took a cigarette. When he bent forward to take the match the yellow pajamas gaped open and she saw his chest, unbelievably thin, partly caved-in on one side where the ribs were gone. She could just see the end of the ugly, newly healed scar from the last operation.

"Thanks, honey," he said, the cigarette wagging in his lips, and he leaned back against the pillows, stretching out his socked feet on the spread.

"How're you feeling, Harry?" she said.

"Feeling fine."

"You're looking better," she lied. "If you can gain a little weight now, you'll look fine."

"Pay up," said a voice over the din of the radios, and Myra looked around to see a little man coming down the center aisle in a wheelchair, walking the chair slowly with his feet, as all TB patients did to avoid the chest strain of turning the wheels with their hands. He was headed for Harry's bed, grinning with yellow teeth. "Pay up," he said again as the wheelchair came to a stop beside the bed. A piece of rubber tubing protruded from some kind of bandage on his chest. It coiled across his pajama top, held in place by a safety pin, and ended in a small rubber-capped bottle which rode heavily in his breast pocket. "Come on, come on," he said. "Pay up."

"Oh, yeah!" Harry said, laughing. "I forgot all about it,

Walter." From the drawer of his bed stand he got out a dollar bill and handed it to the man, who folded it with thin fingers and put it in his pocket, along with the bottle.

"Okay, Harry," he said. "All squared away now, right?"

"Right, Walter."

He backed the wheelchair up and turned it around, and Myra saw that his chest, back and shoulders were crumpled and mis-shapen. "Sorry to butt in," he said, turning the sickly grin on Myra.

She smiled. "That's all right." When he had gone up the aisle again, she said, "What was that all about?"

"Oh, we had a bet on the fight Friday night. I'd forgotten all about it."

"Oh. Have I met him before?"

"Who, Walter? Sure, I think so, honey. You must've met him when I was over in surgery. Old Walter was in surgery more'n two years; they just brought him back here last week. Kid's had a rough time of it. He's got plenty of guts."

"What's that thing on his pajamas? That bottle?"

"He's draining," Harry said, settling back against the yellow pillows. "Old Walter's a good guy; I'm glad he's back." Then he lowered his voice, confidentially. "Matter of fact, he's one of the few really good guys left in this ward, with so many of the old crowd gone now, or over in surgery."

"Don't you like the new boys?" Myra asked, keeping her own voice low so that Red O'Meara, who was relatively new, wouldn't hear. "They seem perfectly nice to me."

"Oh, they're all right, I guess," Harry said. "I just mean, well, I get along better with guys like Walter, that's all, We been through a lot together, or something. I don't know. These new guys get on your nerves sometimes, the way they talk. For instance, there's not one of them knows anything about TB, and they all of them think they know it all; you can't tell them anything. I mean, a thing like that can get on your nerves."

Myra said she guessed she saw what he meant, and then it seemed that the best thing to do was change the subject. "Irene thought the hospital looked real pretty, with the Christmas tree and all."

"Oh, yeah?" Very carefully, Harry reached over and flicked his cigarette into the spotless ashtray on his bed stand. All his habits were precise and neat from living so long in bed. "How're things going at the office, honey?"

"Oh, all right, I guess. Remember I told you about that girl Janet that got fired for staying out too long at lunch, and we were all scared they'd start cracking down on that half-hour lunch period?"

"Oh, yeah," Harry said, but she could tell he didn't remember and wasn't really listening.

"Well, it seems to be all blown over now, because last week Irene and three other girls stayed out almost two hours and nobody said a word. And one of them, a girl named Rose, has been kind of expecting to get fired for a couple of months now, and they didn't even say anything to her."

"Oh, yeah?" Harry said. "Well, that's good."

There was a pause. "Harry?" she said.

"What, honey?"

"Have they told you anything new?"

"Anything new?"

"I mean, about whether or not you're going to need the operation on the other side."

"Oh, *no*, honey. I told you, we can't expect to hear anything on that for quite some time yet—I thought I explained all that." His mouth was smiling and his eyes frowning to show it had been a foolish question. It was the same look he always used to give her at first, long ago, when she would say, "But when do you *think* they'll let you come home?" Now he said, "Thing is, I've still got to get over this *last* one. You got to do one thing at a time in this business; you need a long postoperative period before you're really in the clear, especially with a record of breakdowns like I've had in the last—what is it, now—four years? No, what they'll do is wait awhile, I don't know, maybe six months, maybe longer, and see how this side's coming along. Then they'll decide about the other side. Might give me more surgery and they might not. You can't count on anything in this business, honey, you know that."

"No, of course, Harry, I'm sorry. I don't mean to ask stupid questions. I just meant, well, how're you feeling and everything. You still have any pain?"

"None at all, any more," Harry said. "I mean, as long as I don't go raising my arm too high or anything. When I do that it hurts, and sometimes I start to roll over on that side in my sleep, and that hurts too, but as long as I stay—you know—more or less in a normal position, why, there's no pain whatsoever."

"That's good," she said, "I'm awfully glad to hear that anyway."

Neither of them spoke for what seemed a long time, and in the noise of radios and the noise of laughing and coughing from other beds, their silence seemed strange. Harry began to riffle *Popular Science* absently with his thumb. Myra's eyes strayed to the framed picture on his bed stand, an enlarged snapshot of the two of them just before their marriage, taken in her mother's backyard in Michigan. She looked very young in the picture, leggy in her 1945 skirt, not knowing how to dress or even how to stand, knowing nothing and ready for anything with a child's smile. And Harry—but the surprising thing was that Harry looked older in the picture, somehow, than he did now. Probably it was the thicker face and build, and of course the clothes helped—the dark, decorated Eisenhower jacket and the gleaming boots. Oh, he'd been good-looking, all right, with his set jaw and hard gray eyes—much better looking, for instance, than a too stocky, too solid man like Jack. But now with the loss of weight there had been a softening about the lips and eyes that gave him the look of a thin little boy. His face had changed to suit the pajamas.

"Sure am glad you brought me this," Harry said of his *Popular Science*. "They got an article in here I want to read."

"Good," she said, and she wanted to say: Can't it wait until I've gone?

Harry flipped the magazine on its face, fighting the urge to read, and said, "How's everything else, honey? Outside of the office, I mean."

"All right," she said. "I had a letter from Mother the other day, kind of a Christmas letter. She sent you her best regards."

"Good," Harry said, but the magazine was winning. He

flipped it over again, opened it to his article and read a few lines very casually—as if only to make sure it was the right article—and then lost himself in it.

Myra lighted a fresh cigarette from the butt of her last one, picked up the *Life* and began to turn the pages. From time to time she looked up to watch him; he lay biting a knuckle as he read, scratching the sole of one socked foot with the curled toe of the other.

They spent the rest of the visiting hour that way. Shortly before eight o'clock a group of people came down the aisle, smiling and trundling a studio piano on rubber-tired casters—the Sunday night Red Cross entertainers. Mrs. Balacheck led the procession; a kindly, heavyset woman in uniform, who played. Then came the piano, pushed by a pale young tenor whose lips were always wet, and then the female singers: a swollen soprano in a taffeta dress that looked tight under the arms and a stern-faced, lean contralto with a briefcase. They wheeled the piano close to Harry's bed, in the approximate middle of the ward, and began to unpack their sheet music.

Harry looked up from his reading. "Evening, Mrs. Balacheck."

Her glasses gleamed at him. "How're you tonight, Harry? Like to hear a few Christmas carols tonight?"

"Yes, ma'am."

One by one the radios were turned off and the chattering died. But just before Mrs. Balacheck hit the keys a stocky nurse intervened, thumping rubber-heeled down the aisle with a hand outstretched to ward off the music until she could make an announcement. Mrs. Balacheck sat back, and the nurse, craning her neck, called, "Visiting hour's over!" to one end of the ward and, "Visiting hour's over!" to the other. Then she nodded to Mrs. Balacheck, smiling behind her sterilized linen mask, and thumped away again. After a moment's whispered counsel, Mrs. Balacheck began to play an introductory "Jingle Bells," her cheeks wobbling, to cover the disturbance of departing visitors, while the singers retired to cough quietly among themselves; they would wait until their audience settled down.

"Gee," Harry said, "I didn't realize it was that late. Here, I'll walk you out to the door." He sat up slowly and swung his feet to the floor.

"No, don't bother, Harry," Myra said. "You lie still."

"No, that's all right," he said, wriggling into his slippers. "Will you hand me the robe, honey?" He stood up, and she helped him on with a corduroy VA bathrobe that was too short for him.

"Goodnight, Mr. Chance," Myra said, and Mr. Chance grinned and nodded. Then she said goodnight to Red O'Meara and the elderly man, and as they passed his wheelchair in the aisle, she said goodnight to Walter. She took Harry's arm, startled at its thinness, and matched his slow steps very carefully. They stood facing each other in the small awkward crowd of visitors that lingered in the waiting room.

"Well," Harry said, "take care of yourself now, honey. See you next week."

"Oo-oo," somebody's mother said, plodding hump-shouldered out the door, "it *is* cold tonight." She turned back to wave to her son, then grasped her husband's arm and went down the steps to the snow-blown path. Someone else caught the door and held it open for other visitors to pass through, filling the room with a cold draft, and then it closed again, and Myra and Harry were alone.

"All right, Harry," Myra said, "you go back to bed and listen to the music, now." He looked very frail standing there with his robe hanging open. She reached up and closed it neatly over his chest, took the dangling belt and knotted it firmly, while he smiled down at her. "Now you go on back in there before you catch cold."

"Okay. Goodnight, honey."

"Goodnight," she said, and standing on tiptoe, she kissed his cheek. "Goodnight, Harry."

At the door she turned to watch him walk back to the ward in the tight, high-waisted robe. Then she went outside and down the steps, turning up her coat collar in the sudden cold. Marty's car was not there; the road was bare except for the dwindling backs of the other visitors, passing under a streetlamp now as they made their way down to the bus stop near the Administration

Building. She drew the coat more closely around her and stood close to the building for shelter from the wind.

"Jingle Bells" ended inside, to muffled applause, and after a moment the program began in earnest. A few solemn chords sounded on the piano, and then the voices came through:

> "Hark, the herald angels sing,
> Glory to the newborn King..."

All at once Myra's throat closed up and the streetlights swam in her eyes. Then half her fist was in her mouth and she was sobbing wretchedly, making little puffs of mist that floated away in the dark. It took her a long time to stop, and each sniffling intake of breath made a high sharp noise that sounded as if it could be heard for miles. Finally it was over, or nearly over; she managed to control her shoulders, to blow her nose and put her handkerchief away, closing her bag with a reassuring, business-like snap.

Then the lights of the car came probing up the road. She ran down the path and stood waiting in the wind.

Inside the car a warm smell of whiskey hung among the cherry-red points of cigarettes, and Irene's voice squealed, "Oo-oo! Hurry up and shut the *door!*"

Jack's arms gathered her close as the door slammed, and in a thick whisper he said, "Hello, baby."

They were all a little drunk; even Marty was in high spirits. "Hold tight, everybody!" he called, as they swung around the Administration Building, past the Christmas tree, and leveled off for the straightaway to the gate, gaining speed. "Everybody hold tight!"

Irene's face floated chattering over the back of the front seat. "Myra, honey, listen, we found the most adorable little place down the road, kind of a roadhouse, like, only real inexpensive and everything? So listen, we wanna take you back there for a little drink, okay?"

"Sure," Myra said, "fine."

"'Cause I mean, we're way ahead of you now anyway, and anyway I want you to see this place... Marty, will you take it *easy!*" She laughed. "Honestly, anybody else driving this car with what he's had to drink in him, I'd be scared to death, you know it? But you never got to worry about old Marty. He's the best old driver in the world, drunk, sober, I don't care *what* he is."

But they weren't listening. Deep in a kiss, Jack slipped his hand inside her coat, expertly around and inside all the other layers until it held the flesh of her breast. "All over being mad at me, baby?" he mumbled against her lips. "Wanna go have a little drink?"

Her hands gripped the bulk of his back and clung there. Then she let herself be turned so that his other hand could creep secretly up her thigh. "All right," she whispered, "but let's only have one and then afterwards—"

"Okay, baby, okay."

"—and then afterwards, darling, let's go right home."

A GLUTTON FOR PUNISHMENT

FOR A LITTLE while when Walter Henderson was nine years old
he thought falling dead was the very zenith of romance, and so
did a number of his friends. Having found that the only truly
rewarding part of any cops-and-robbers game was the moment
when you pretended to be shot, clutched your heart, dropped
your pistol and crumpled to the earth, they soon dispensed with
the rest of it—the tiresome business of choosing up sides and
sneaking around—and refined the game to its essence. It became
a matter of individual performance, almost an art. One of them
at a time would run dramatically along the crest of a hill, and at
a given point the ambush would occur: a simultaneous jerking
of aimed toy pistols and a chorus of those staccato throaty
sounds—a kind of hoarse-whispered *"Pk-k-ew! Pk-k-ew!"*—
with which little boys simulate the noise of gunfire. Then the
performer would stop, turn, stand poised for a moment in graceful agony, pitch over and fall down the hill in a whirl of arms and
legs and a splendid cloud of dust, and finally sprawl flat at the
bottom, a rumpled corpse. When he got up and brushed off his
clothes, the others would criticize his form ("Pretty good," or
"Too stiff," or "Didn't look natural"), and then it would be the
next player's turn. That was all there was to the game, but Walter
Henderson loved it. He was a slight, poorly coordinated boy,
and this was the only thing even faintly like a sport at which he
excelled. Nobody could match the abandon with which he flung
his limp body down the hill, and he reveled in the small acclaim
it won him. Eventually the others grew bored with the game,
after some older boys had laughed at them; Walter turned reluctantly to more wholesome forms of play, and soon he had forgotten about it.

But he had occasion to remember it, vividly, one May afternoon nearly twenty-five years later in a Lexington Avenue office

building, while he sat at his desk pretending to work and waiting to be fired. He had become a sober, keen-looking young man now, with clothes that showed the influence of an Eastern university and neat brown hair that was just beginning to thin out on top. Years of good health had made him less slight, and though he still had trouble with his coordination it showed up mainly in minor things nowadays, like an inability to coordinate his hat, his wallet, his theater tickets and his change without making his wife stop and wait for him, or a tendency to push heavily against doors marked "Pull." He looked, at any rate, the picture of sanity and competence as he sat there in the office. No one could have told that the cool sweat of anxiety was sliding under his shirt, or that the fingers of his left hand, concealed in his pocket, were slowly grinding and tearing a book of matches into a moist cardboard pulp. He had seen it coming for weeks, and this morning, from the minute he got off the elevator, he had sensed that this was the day it would happen. When several of his superiors said, "Morning, Walt," he had seen the faintest suggestion of concern behind their smiles; then once this afternoon, glancing out over the gate of the cubicle where he worked, he'd happened to catch the eye of George Crowell, the department manager, who was hesitating in the door of his private office with some papers in his hand. Crowell turned away quickly, but Walter knew he had been watching him, troubled but determined. In a matter of minutes, he felt sure, Crowell would call him in and break the news—with difficulty, of course, since Crowell was the kind of boss who took pride in being a regular guy. There was nothing to do now but let the thing happen and try to take it as gracefully as possible.

That was when the childhood memory began to prey on his mind, for it suddenly struck him—and the force of it sent his thumbnail biting deep into the secret matchbook—that letting things happen and taking them gracefully had been, in a way, the pattern of his life. There was certainly no denying that the role of good loser had always held an inordinate appeal for him. All through adolescence he had specialized in it, gamely losing fights with stronger boys, playing football badly in the secret hope of being injured and carried dramatically off the field ("You got to hand it to old Henderson for *one* thing, anyway," the high-school coach had said with a chuckle, "he's a real little glutton for punishment"). College had offered a wider scope to his talent—there were exams to be flunked and elections to be lost—and later the Air Force had made it possible for him to wash out, honorably, as a flight cadet. And now, inevitably, it seemed, he was running true to form once more. The several jobs he'd held before this had been the beginner's kind at which it isn't easy to fail; when the opportunity for this one first arose it had been, in Crowell's phrase, "a real challenge."

"Good," Walter had said. "That's what I'm looking for." When he related that part of the conversation to his wife she had said, "Oh, wonderful!" and they'd moved to an expensive apartment in the East Sixties on the strength of it. And lately, when he started coming home with a beaten look and announcing darkly that he doubted if he could hold on much longer, she would enjoin the children not to bother him ("Daddy's very tired tonight"), bring him a drink and soothe him with careful, wifely reassurance, doing her best to conceal her fear, never guessing, or at least never showing, that she was dealing with a chronic, compulsive failure, a strange little boy in love with the attitudes of collapse. And the amazing thing, he thought—the really amazing thing—was that he himself had never looked at it that way before.

"Walt?"

The cubicle gate had swung open and George Crowell was standing there, looking uncomfortable. "Will you step into my office a minute?"

"Right, George." And Walter followed him out of the cubicle, out across the office floor, feeling many eyes on his back. Keep it dignified, he told himself. The important thing is to keep it dignified. Then the door closed behind them and the two of them were alone in the carpeted silence of Crowell's private office. Automobile horns blared in the distance, twenty-one stories below; the only other sounds were their breathing, the squeak of Crowell's shoes as he went to his desk and the creak of his swivel chair as he sat down. "Pull up a chair, Walt," he said. "Smoke?"

"No thanks." Walter sat down and laced his fingers tight between his knees.

Crowell shut the cigarette box without taking one for himself, pushed it aside and leaned forward, both hands spread flat on the plate-glass top of the desk. "Walt, I might as well give you this straight from the shoulder," he said, and the last shred of hope slipped away. The funny part was that it came as a shock, even so. "Mr. Harvey and I have felt for some time that you haven't quite caught on to the work here, and we've both very reluctantly come to the conclusion that the best thing to do, in your own best interests as well as ours, is to let you go. Now," he added quickly, "this is no reflection on you personally, Walt. We do a highly specialized kind of work here and we can't expect everybody to stay on top of the job. In your case particularly, we really feel you'd be happier in some organization better suited to your—abilities."

Crowell leaned back, and when he raised his hands their moisture left two gray, perfect prints on the glass, like the hands of a skeleton. Walter stared at them, fascinated, while they shriveled and disappeared.

"Well," he said, and looked up. "You put that very nicely, George. Thanks."

Crowell's lips worked into an apologetic, regular guy's smile. "Awfully sorry," he said. "These things just happen." And he began to fumble with the knobs of his desk drawers, visibly relieved that the worst was over. "Now," he said, "we've made out a check here covering your salary through the end of next month. That'll give you something in the way of—severance pay, so to speak—to tide you over until you find something." He held out a long envelope.

"That's very generous," Walter said. Then there was a silence, and Walter realized it was up to him to break it. He got to his feet. "All right, George. I won't keep you."

Crowell got up quickly and came around the desk with both hands held out—one to shake Walter's hand, the other to put on his shoulder as they walked to the door. The gesture, at once friendly and humiliating, brought a quick rush of blood to Walter's throat, and for a terrible second he thought he might be going to cry. "Well, boy," Crowell said, "good luck to you."

"Thanks," he said, and he was so relieved to find his voice steady that he said it again, smiling. "Thanks. So long, George."

There was a distance of some fifty feet to be crossed on the way back to his cubicle, and Walter Henderson accomplished it with style. He was aware of how trim and straight his departing shoulders looked to Crowell; he was aware too, as he threaded his way among desks whose occupants either glanced up shyly at him or looked as if they'd like to, of every subtle play of well-controlled emotion in his face. It was as if the whole thing were a scene in a movie. The camera had opened the action from Crowell's viewpoint and dollied back to take the entire office as a frame for Walter's figure in lonely, stately passage; now it came in for a long-held close-up of Walter's face, switched to other brief views of his colleagues' turning heads (Joe Collins looking worried, Fred Holmes trying to keep from looking pleased), and switched again to Walter's viewpoint as it discovered the plain, unsuspecting face of Mary, his secretary; who was waiting for him at his desk with a report he had given her to type.

"I hope this is all right, Mr. Henderson."

Walter took it and dropped it on the desk. "Forget it, Mary," he said. "Look, you might as well take the rest of the day off, and go see the personnel manager in the morning. You'll be getting a new job. I've just been fired."

Her first expression was a faint, suspicious smile—she thought he was kidding—but then she began to look pale and shaken. She was very young and not too bright; they had probably never told her in secretarial school that it was possible for your boss to get fired. "Why, that's *terrible*, Mr. Henderson. I—well, but why would they *do* such a thing?"

"Oh, I don't know," he said. "Lot of little reasons, I guess." He was opening and slamming the drawers of his desk, cleaning out his belongings. There wasn't much: a handful of old personal letters, a dry fountain pen, a cigarette lighter with no flint, and half of a wrapped chocolate bar. He was aware of how poignant each of these objects looked to her, as she watched him sort them out and fill his pockets, and he was aware of the dignity with which he straightened up, turned, took his hat from the stand and put it on.

"Doesn't affect you, of course, Mary," he said. "They'll have a new job for you in the morning. Well." He held out his hand. "Good luck."

"Thank you; the same to you. Well, then, g'night"—and here she brought her chewed fingernails up to her lips for an uncertain little giggle—"I mean, g'bye, then, Mr. Henderson."

The next part of the scene was at the water cooler, where Joe Collins's sober eyes became enriched with sympathy as Walter approached him.

"Joe," Walter said. "I'm leaving. Got the ax."

"No!" But Collins's look of shock was plainly an act of kindness; it couldn't have been much of a surprise. "Jesus, Walt, what the hell's the matter with these people?"

Then Fred Holmes chimed in, very grave and sorry, clearly pleased with the news: "Gee, boy, that's a damn shame."

Walter led the two of them away to the elevators, where he pressed the "down" button; and suddenly other men were bearing down on him from all corners of the office, their faces stiff with sorrow, their hands held out.

"Awful sorry, Walt . . ."

"Good luck, boy . . ."

"Keep in touch, okay, Walt? . . ."

Nodding and smiling, shaking hands, Walter said, "Thanks," and "So long," and "I certainly will"; then the red light came on over one of the elevators with its little mechanical *ding!* and in another few seconds the doors slid open and the operator's voice said, "Down!" He backed into the car, still wearing his fixed smile and waving a jaunty salute to their earnest, talking faces, and the scene found its perfect conclusion as the doors slid shut, clamped, and the car dropped in silence through space.

All the way down he stood with the ruddy, bright-eyed look of a man fulfilled by pleasure; it wasn't until he was out on the street, walking rapidly, that he realized how completely he had enjoyed himself.

The heavy shock of this knowledge slowed him down, until he came to a stop and stood against a building front for the better part of a minute. His scalp prickled under his hat, and his fingers began to fumble with the knot of his tie and the button of his coat. He felt as if he had surprised himself in some obscene and shameful act, and he had never felt more helpless, or more frightened.

Then in a burst of action he set off again, squaring his hat and setting his jaw, bringing his heels down hard on the pavement, trying to look hurried and impatient and impelled by business. A man could drive himself crazy trying to psychoanalyze himself in the middle of Lexington Avenue, in the middle of the afternoon. The thing to do was get busy now, and start looking for a job.

The only trouble, he realized, coming to a stop again and looking around, was that he didn't know where he was going. He was somewhere in the upper Forties, on a corner that was bright with florist shops and taxicabs, alive with well-dressed men and women walking in the clear spring air. A telephone was what he needed first. He hurried across the street to a drugstore and made his way through smells of toilet soap and perfume and ketchup and bacon to the rank of phone booths along the rear wall; he got out his address book and found the page showing the several employment agencies where his applications were filed, then he got his dimes ready and shut himself into one of the booths.

But all the agencies told him the same thing: no openings in his field at the moment; no point in his coming in until they called him. When he was finished he dug for the address book again, to check the number of an acquaintance who had told him, a month before, that there might soon be an opening in his office. The book wasn't in his inside pocket; he plunged his hands into the other pockets of his coat and then his pants, cracking an elbow painfully against the wall of the booth, but all he could find were the old letters and the piece of chocolate from his desk. Cursing, he dropped the chocolate on the floor and, as if it were a lighted cigarette, stepped on it. These exertions in the heat of the booth made his breathing rapid and shallow. He was feeling faint by the time he saw the address book right in front of him, on top of the coin box, where he'd left it. His finger trembled in the dial, and when he started to speak, clawing the collar away from his sweating neck with his free hand, his voice was as weak and urgent as a beggar's.

"Jack," he said. "I was just wondering—just wondering if you'd heard anything new on the opening you mentioned a while back."

"On the which?"

"The opening. You know. You said there might be a job in your—"

"Oh, that. No, haven't heard a thing, Walt. I'll be in touch with you if anything breaks."

"Okay, Jack." He pulled open the folding door of the booth and leaned back against the stamped-tin wall, breathing deeply to welcome the rush of cool air. "I just thought it might've slipped your mind or something," he said. His voice was almost normal again. "Sorry to bother you."

"Hell, that's okay," said the hearty voice in the receiver. "What's the matter, boy? Things getting a little sticky where you are?"

"*Oh* no," Walter found himself saying, and he was immediately glad of the lie. He almost never lied, and it always surprised him to discover how easy it could be. His voice gained confidence. "No. I'm all *right* here, Jack, it's just that I didn't want to—*you* know, I thought it might have slipped your mind, is all. How's the family?"

When the conversation was over, he guessed there was nothing more to do but go home. But he continued to sit in the open booth for a long time, with his feet stretched out on the drugstore floor, until a small, canny smile began to play on his face, slowly dissolving and changing into a look of normal strength. The ease of the lie had given him an idea that grew, the more he thought it over, into a profound and revolutionary decision.

He would not tell his wife. With luck he was sure to find some kind of work before the month was out, and in the meantime, for once in his life, he would keep his troubles to himself. Tonight, when she asked how the day had gone, he would say, "Oh, all right," or even "Fine." In the morning he would leave the house at the usual time and stay away all day, and he would go on doing the same thing every day until he had a job.

The phrase "Pull yourself together" occurred to him, and there was more than determination in the way he pulled himself together there in the phone booth, the way he gathered up his coins and straightened his tie and walked out to the street: there was a kind of nobility.

Several hours had to be killed before the normal time of his homecoming, and when he found himself walking west on Forty-second Street he decided to kill them in the Public Library. He mounted the wide stone steps importantly, and soon he was installed in the reading room, examining a bound copy of last year's *Life* magazines and going over and over his plan, enlarging and perfecting it.

He knew, sensibly, that there would be nothing easy about the day-to-day deception. It would call for the constant vigilance and cunning of an outlaw. But wasn't it the very difficulty of the plan that made it worthwhile? And in the end, when it was all over and he could tell her at last, it would be a reward worth every minute of the ordeal. He knew just how she would look at him when he told her—in blank disbelief at first and then, gradually, with the dawning of a kind of respect he hadn't seen in her eyes for years.

"You mean you kept it to yourself all this *time*? But *why*, Walt?"

"Oh well," he would say casually, even shrugging, "I didn't see any point in upsetting you."

When it was time to leave the library he lingered in the main entrance for a minute, taking deep pulls from a cigarette and looking down over the five o'clock traffic and crowds. The scene held a special nostalgia for him, because it was here, on a spring evening five years before, that he had come to meet her for the first time. "Can you meet me at the top of the library steps?" she had asked over the phone that morning, and it wasn't until many months later, after they were married, that this struck him as a peculiar meeting place. When he asked her about it then, she laughed at him. "Of *course* it was inconvenient—that was the whole point. I wanted to pose up there, like a princess in a castle or something, and make you climb up all those lovely steps to claim me."

And that was exactly how it had seemed. He'd escaped from the office ten minutes early that day and hurried to Grand Central to wash and shave in a gleaming subterranean dressing room;

he had waited in a fit of impatience while a very old, stout, slow attendant took his suit away to be pressed. Then, after tipping the attendant more than he could afford, he had raced outside and up Forty-second Street, tense and breathless as he strode past shoe stores and milk bars, as he winnowed his way through swarms of intolerably slow-moving pedestrians who had no idea of how urgent his mission was. He was afraid of being late, even half afraid that it was all some kind of a joke and she wouldn't be there at all. But as soon as he hit Fifth Avenue he saw her up there in the distance, alone, standing at the top of the library steps—a slender, radiant brunette in a fashionable black coat.

He slowed down, then. He crossed the avenue at a stroll, one hand in his pocket, and took the steps with such an easy, athletic nonchalance that nobody could have guessed at the hours of anxiety, the days of strategic and tactical planning this particular moment had cost him.

When he was fairly certain she could see him coming he looked up at her again, and she smiled. It wasn't the first time he had seen her smile that way, but it was the first time he could be sure it was intended wholly for him, and it caused warm tremors of pleasure in his chest. He couldn't remember the words of their greeting, but he remembered being quite sure that they were all right, that it was starting off well—that her wide shining eyes were seeing him exactly as he most wanted to be seen. The things he said, whatever they were, struck her as witty, and the things she said, or the sound of her voice when she said them, made him feel taller and stronger and broader of shoulder than ever before in his life. When they turned and started down the steps together he took hold of her upper arm, claiming her, and felt the light jounce of her breast on the backs of his fingers with each step. And the evening before them, spread out and waiting at their feet, seemed miraculously long and miraculously rich with promise.

Starting down alone, now, he found it strengthening to have one clear triumph to look back on—one time in his life, at least, when he had denied the possibility of failure, and won. Other memories came into focus when he crossed the avenue and started back down the gentle slope of Forty-second Street: they had come this way that evening too, and walked to the Biltmore for a drink, and he remembered how she had looked sitting beside him in the semidarkness of the cocktail lounge, squirming forward from the hips while he helped her out of the sleeves of her coat and then settling back, giving her long hair a toss and looking at him in a provocative sidelong way as she raised the glass to her lips. A little later she had said, "Oh, let's go down to the river—I love the river at this time of day," and they had left the hotel and walked there. He walked there now, down through the clangor of Third Avenue and up toward Tudor City—it seemed a much longer walk alone—until he was standing at the little balustrade, looking down over the swarm of sleek cars on the East River Drive and at the slow, gray water moving beyond it. It was on this very spot, while a tugboat moaned somewhere under the darkening skyline of Queens, that he had drawn her close and kissed her for the first time. Now he turned away, a new man, and set out to walk all the way home.

The first thing that hit him, when he let himself in the apartment door, was the smell of Brussels sprouts. The children were still at their supper in the kitchen: he could hear their high mumbled voices over the clink of dishes, and then his wife's voice, tired and coaxing. When the door slammed he heard her say, "There's Daddy now," and the children began to call, "Daddy! Daddy!"

He put his hat carefully in the hall closet and turned around just as she appeared in the kitchen doorway, drying her hands on her apron and smiling through her tiredness. "Home on time for once," she said. "How lovely. I was afraid you'd be working late again."

"No," he said. "No, I didn't have to work late." His voice had an oddly foreign, amplified sound in his own ears, as if he were speaking in an echo chamber.

"You do look tired, though, Walt. You look worn out."

"Walked home, that's all. Guess I'm not used to it. How's everything?"

"Oh, fine." But she looked worn out herself.

When they went together into the kitchen he felt encircled and entrapped by its humid brightness. His eyes roamed dolefully over the milk cartons, the mayonnaise jars and soup cans and cereal boxes, the peaches lined up to ripen on the windowsill, the remarkable frailty and tenderness of his two children, whose chattering faces were lightly streaked with mashed potato.

Things looked better in the bathroom, where he took longer than necessary over the job of washing up for dinner. At least he could be alone here, braced by splashings of cold water; the only intrusion was the sound of his wife's voice rising in impatience with the older child: "All right, Andrew Henderson. No story for *you* tonight unless you finish up all that custard *now*." A little later came the scraping of chairs and stacking of dishes that meant their supper was over, and the light scuffle of shoes and the slamming door that meant they had been turned loose in their room for an hour to play before bath time.

Walter carefully dried his hands; then he went out to the living-room sofa and settled himself there with a magazine, taking very slow, deep breaths to show how self-controlled he was. In a minute she came in to join him, her apron removed and her lipstick replenished, bringing the cocktail pitcher full of ice. "Oh," she said with a sigh. "Thank God that's over. Now for a little peace and quiet."

"I'll get the drinks, honey," he said, bolting to his feet. He had hoped his voice might sound normal now, but it still came out with echo-chamber resonance.

"You will not," she commanded. "You sit down. You deserve to sit still and be waited on, when you come home looking so tired. How did the day go, Walt?"

"Oh, all right," he said, sitting down again. "Fine." He watched her measuring out the gin and vermouth, stirring the pitcher in her neat, quick way, arranging the tray and bringing it across the room.

"There," she said, settling herself close beside him. "Will you do the honors, darling?" And when he had filled the chilled glasses she raised hers and said, "Oh, lovely. Cheers." This bright cocktail mood was a carefully studied effect, he knew. So was her motherly sternness over the children's supper; so was the brisk, no-nonsense efficiency with which, earlier today, she had attacked the supermarket; and so, later tonight, would be the tenderness of her surrender in his arms. The orderly rotation of many careful moods was her life, or rather, was what her life had become. She managed it well, and it was only rarely, looking very closely at her face, that he could see how much the effort was costing her.

But the drink was a great help. The first bitter, ice-cold sip of it seemed to restore his calm, and the glass in his hand looked reassuringly deep. He took another sip or two before daring to look at her again, and when he did it was a heartening sight. Her smile was almost completely free of tension, and soon they were chatting together as comfortably as happy lovers.

"Oh, isn't it nice just to sit down and unwind?" she said, allowing her head to sink back into the upholstery. "And isn't it lovely to think it's Friday night?"

"Sure is," he said, and instantly put his mouth in his drink to hide his shock. Friday night! That meant there would be two days before he could even begin to look for a job—two days of mild imprisonment in the house, or of dealing with tricycles and popsicles in the park, without a hope of escaping the burden of his secret. "Funny," he said. "I'd almost forgotten it was Friday."

"Oh, how *can* you forget?" She squirmed luxuriously deeper into the sofa. "I look forward to it all week. Pour me just a tiny bit more, darling, and then I must get back to the chores."

He poured a tiny bit more for her and a full glass for himself. His hand was shaking and he spilled a little of it, but she didn't seem to notice. Nor did she seem to notice that his replies grew more and more strained as she kept the conversation going. When she got back to the chores—basting the roast, drawing the children's baths, tidying up their room for the night—Walter sat alone and allowed his mind to slide into a heavy, gin-fuddled confusion. Only one persistent thought came through, a piece of self-advice that was as clear and cold as the drink that rose again and again to his lips: Hold on. No matter what she says, no matter what happens tonight or tomorrow or the next day, just hold on. Hold on.

But holding on grew less and less easy as the children's splashing bath-noises floated into the room; it was more difficult still by the time they were brought in to say goodnight, carrying their teddy bears and dressed in clean pajamas, their faces shining and smelling of soap. After that, it became impossible to stay seated on the sofa. He sprang up and began stalking around the floor, lighting one cigarette after another, listening to his wife's clear, modulated reading of the bedtime story in the next room ("You may go into the fields, or down the lane, but *don't* go into Mr. McGregor's garden . . .").

When she came out again, closing the children's door behind her, she found him standing like a tragic statue at the window, looking down into the darkening courtyard. "What's the matter, Walt?"

He turned on her with a false grin. "Nothing's the matter," he said in the echo-chamber voice, and the movie camera started rolling again. It came in for a close-up of his own tense face, then switched over to observe her movements as she hovered uncertainly at the coffee table.

"Well," she said. "I'm going to have one more cigarette and then I must get the dinner on the table." She sat down again— not leaning back this time, or smiling, for this was her busy, getting-the-dinner-on-the-table mood. "Have you got a match, Walt?"

"Sure." And he came toward her, probing in his pocket as if to bring forth something he had been saving to give her all day.

"God," she said. "Look at those matches. What *happened* to them?"

"These?" He stared down at the raddled, twisted matchbook as if it were a piece of incriminating evidence. "Must've been kind of tearing them up or something," he said. "Nervous habit."

"Thanks," she said, accepting the light from his trembling fingers, and then she began to look at him with wide, dead-serious eyes. "Walt, there *is* something wrong, isn't there?"

"Of course not. Why should there be anything wr—"

"Tell me the truth. Is it the job? Is it about—what you were afraid of last week? I mean, did anything happen today to make you think they might— Did Crowell say anything? Tell me." The faint lines on her face seemed to have deepened. She looked severe and competent and suddenly much older, not even very pretty anymore—a woman used to dealing with emergencies, ready to take charge.

He began to walk slowly away toward an easy chair across the room, and the shape of his back was an eloquent statement of impending defeat. At the edge of the carpet he stopped and seemed to stiffen, a wounded man holding himself together; then he turned around and faced her with the suggestion of a melancholy smile.

"Well, darling—" he began. His right hand came up and touched the middle button of his shirt, as if to unfasten it, and then with a great deflating sigh he collapsed backward into the chair, one foot sliding out on the carpet and the other curled beneath him. It was the most graceful thing he had done all day. "They got me," he said.

A WRESTLER WITH SHARKS

NOBODY HAD MUCH respect for *The Labor Leader*. Even Finkel and Kramm, its owners, the two sour brothers-in-law who'd dreamed it up in the first place and who somehow managed to make a profit on it year after year—even they could take little pride in the thing. At least, that's what I used to suspect from the way they'd hump grudgingly around the office, shivering the bile-green partitions with their thumps and shouts, grabbing and tearing at galley proofs, breaking pencil points, dropping wet cigar butts on the floor and slamming telephones contemptuously into their cradles. *The Labor Leader* was all either of them would ever have for a life's work, and they seemed to hate it.

You couldn't blame them: the thing was a monster. In format it was a fat biweekly tabloid, badly printed, that spilled easily out of your hands and was very hard to put together again in the right order; in policy it called itself "An Independent Newspaper Pledged to the Spirit of the Trade Union Movement," but its real pitch was to be a kind of trade journal for union officials, who subscribed to it out of union funds and who must surely have been inclined to tolerate, rather than to want or need, whatever thin sustenance it gave to them. The *Leader*'s coverage of national events "from the labor angle" was certain to be stale, likely to be muddled, and often opaque with typographical errors; most of its dense columns were filled with flattering reports on the doings of the unions whose leaders were on the subscription list, often to the exclusion of much bigger news about those whose leaders weren't. And every issue carried scores of simple-minded ads urging "Harmony" in the names of various small industrial firms that Finkel and Kramm had been able to beg or browbeat into buying space—a compromise that would almost certainly have hobbled a real labor paper but that didn't, typically enough, seem to cramp the *Leader*'s style at all.

There was a fast turnover on the editorial staff. Whenever

somebody quit, the *Leader* would advertise in the help-wanted section of the *Times*, offering a "moderate salary commensurate with experience." This always brought a good crowd to the sidewalk outside the *Leader*'s office, a gritty storefront on the lower fringe of the garment district, and Kramm, who was the editor (Finkel was the publisher), would keep them all waiting for half an hour before he picked up a sheaf of application forms, shot his cuffs, and gravely opened the door—I think he enjoyed this occasional chance to play the man of affairs.

"All right, take your time," he'd say, as they jostled inside and pressed against the wooden rail that shielded the inner offices. "Take your time, gentlemen." Then he would raise a hand and say, "May I have your attention, please?" And he'd begin to explain the job. Half the applicants would go away when he got to the part about the salary structure, and most of those who remained offered little competition to anyone who was sober, clean and able to construct an English sentence.

That's the way we'd all been hired, the six or eight of us who frowned under the *Leader*'s sickly fluorescent lights that winter, and most of us made no secret of our desire for better things. I went to work there a couple of weeks after losing my job on one of the metropolitan dailies, and stayed only until I was rescued the next spring by the big picture magazine that still employs me. The others had other explanations, which, like me, they spent a great deal of time discussing: it was a great place for shrill and redundant hard-luck stories.

But Leon Sobel joined the staff about a month after I did, and from the moment Kramm led him into the editorial room we all knew he was going to be different. He stood among the messy desks with the look of a man surveying new fields to conquer, and when Kramm introduced him around (forgetting half our names) he made a theatrically solemn business out of shaking hands. He was about thirty-five, older than most of us, a very small, tense man with black hair that seemed to explode from his skull and a humorless thin-lipped face that was blotched with the scars of acne. His eyebrows were always in motion when he talked, and his eyes, not so much piercing as anxious to pierce, never left the eyes of his listener.

The first thing I learned about him was that he'd never held an office job before: he had been a sheet-metal worker all his adult life. What's more, he hadn't come to the *Leader* out of need, like the rest of us, but, as he put it, out of principle. To do so, in fact, he had given up a factory job paying nearly twice the money.

"What'sa matter, don'tcha believe me?" he asked, after telling me this.

"Well, it's not that," I said. "It's just that I—"

"Maybe you think I'm crazy," he said, and screwed up his face into a canny smile.

I tried to protest, but he wouldn't have it. "Listen, don't worry, McCabe. I'm called crazy a lotta times already. It don't bother me. My wife says, 'Leon, you gotta expect it.' She says, 'People never understand a man who wants something more outa life than just money.' And she's right! She's right!"

"No," I said. "Wait a second. I—"

"People think you gotta be one of two things: either you're a shark, or you gotta lay back and let the sharks eatcha alive—this is the world. Me, I'm the kinda guy's gotta go out and wrestle with the sharks. Why? I dunno why. This is crazy? Okay."

"Wait a second," I said. And I tried to explain that I had nothing whatever against his striking a blow for social justice, if that was what he had in mind; it was just that I thought *The Labor Leader* was about the least likely place in the world for him to do it.

But his shrug told me I was quibbling. "So?" he said. "It's a paper, isn't it? Well, I'm a writer. And what good's a writer if he don't get printed? Listen." He lifted one haunch and placed it on the edge of my desk—he was too short a man to do this gracefully, but the force of his argument helped him to bring it off. "Listen, McCabe. You're a young kid yet. I wanna tellya something. Know how many books I wrote already?" And now his hands came into play, as they always did sooner or later. Both stubby fists were thrust under my nose and allowed to shake there for a moment before they burst into a thicket of stiff, quivering fingers—only the thumb of one hand remained folded down. "Nine," he said, and the hands fell limp on his thigh, to rest until he needed them again. "Nine. Novels, philosophy, political theory—the entire gamut. And not one of 'em published. Believe me, I been around awhile."

"I believe you," I said.

"So finally I sat down and figured: What's the answer? And I figured this: the trouble with my books is, they tell the truth. And the truth is a funny thing, McCabe. People wanna read it, but they only wanna read it when it comes from somebody they already know their name. Am I right? So all right. I figure, I wanna write these books, first I gotta build up a name for myself. This is worth any sacrifice. This is the only way. You know something, McCabe? The last one I wrote took me two years?" Two fingers sprang up to illustrate the point, and dropped again. "Two years, working four, five hours every night and all day long on the weekends. And then you oughta seen the crap I got from the publishers. Every damn publisher in town. My wife cried. She says, 'But why, Leon? Why?'" Here his lips curled tight against his small, stained teeth, and the fist of one hand smacked the palm of the other on his thigh, but then he relaxed. "I told her, 'Listen, honey. You know why.'" And now he was smiling at me in quiet triumph. "I says, 'This book told the truth. That's why.'" Then he winked, slid off my desk and walked away, erect and jaunty in his soiled sport shirt and his dark serge pants that hung loose and shiny in the seat. That was Sobel.

It took him a little while to loosen up in the job; for the first week or so, when he wasn't talking, he went at everything with a zeal and a fear of failure that disconcerted everyone but Finney, the managing editor. Like the rest of us, Sobel had a list of twelve or fifteen union offices around town, and the main part of his job was to keep in touch with them and write up whatever bits of news they gave out. As a rule there was nothing very exciting to write about. The average story ran two or three paragraphs with a single-column head:

PLUMBERS WIN
3¢ PAY HIKE

or something like that. But Sobel composed them all as carefully as sonnets, and after he'd turned one in he would sit chewing his lips in anxiety until Finney raised a forefinger and said, "C'mere a second, Sobel."

Then he'd go over and stand, nodding apologetically, while Finney pointed out some niggling grammatical flaw. "Never end a sentence with a preposition, Sobel. You don't wanna say, 'gave the plumbers new grounds to bargain on.' You wanna say, 'gave the plumbers new grounds on which to bargain.'"

Finney enjoyed these lectures. The annoying thing, from a spectator's point of view, was that Sobel took so long to learn what everyone else seemed to know instinctively: that Finney was scared of his own shadow and would back down on anything at all if you raised your voice. He was a frail, nervous man who dribbled on his chin when he got excited and raked trembling fingers through his thickly oiled hair, with the result that his fingers spread hair oil, like a spoor of his personality, to everything he touched: his clothes, his pencils, his telephone and his typewriter keys. I guess the main reason he was managing editor was that nobody else would submit to the bullying he took from Kramm: their editorial conferences always began with Kramm shouting "Finney! Finney!" from behind his partition, and Finney jumping like a squirrel to hurry inside. Then you'd hear the relentless drone of Kramm's demands and the quavering sputter of Finney's explanations, and it would end with a thump as Kramm socked his desk. "*No*, Finney. No, no, *no*! What's the matter with you? I gotta draw you a picture? All right, all right, get outa here, I'll do it myself." At first you might wonder why Finney took it—nobody could need a job that badly—but the answer lay in the fact that there were only three bylined pieces in *The Labor Leader*: a boiler-plated sports feature that we got from a syndicate, a ponderous column called "LABOR TODAY, by Julius Kramm," that ran facing the editorial page, and a double-column box in the back of the book with the heading:

BROADWAY BEAT

BY WES FINNEY

There was even a thumbnail picture of him in the upper left-hand corner, hair slicked down and teeth bared in a confident smile. The text managed to work in a labor angle here and there—a paragraph on Actors' Equity, say, or the stagehands' union—but mostly he played it straight, in the manner of two or three real Broadway-and-nightclub columnists. "Heard about the new thrush at the Copa?" he would ask the labor leaders; then he'd give them her name, with a sly note about her bust and hip measurements and a folksy note about the state from which she "hailed," and he'd wind it up like this: "She's got the whole town talking, and turning up in droves. Their verdict, in which this department wholly concurs: the lady has class." No reader could have guessed that Wes Finney's shoes needed repair, that he got no complimentary tickets to anything and never went out except to take in a movie or to crouch over a liverwurst sandwich at the Automat. He wrote the column on his own time and got extra money for it—the figure I heard was fifty dollars a month. So it was a mutually satisfactory deal: for that small sum Kramm held his whipping boy in absolute bondage; for that small torture Finney could paste clippings in a scrapbook, with all the contamination of *The Labor Leader* sheared away into the wastebasket of his furnished room, and whisper himself to sleep with dreams of ultimate freedom.

Anyway, this was the man who could make Sobel apologize for the grammar of his news stories, and it was a sad thing to watch. Of course, it couldn't go on forever, and one day it stopped.

Finney had called Sobel over to explain about split infinitives, and Sobel was wrinkling his brow in an effort to understand. Neither of them noticed that Kramm was standing in the doorway of his office a few feet away, listening, and looking at the wet end of his cigar as if it tasted terrible.

"Finney," he said. "You wanna be an English teacher, get a job in the high school."

Startled, Finney stuck a pencil behind his ear without noticing that another pencil was already there, and both pencils clattered to the floor. "Well, I—" he said. "Just thought I'd—"

"Finney, this does not interest me. Pick up your pencils and listen to me, please. For your information, Mr. Sobel is not supposed to be a literary Englishman. He is supposed to be a literate American, and this I believe he is. Do I make myself clear?"

And the look on Sobel's face as he walked back to his own desk was that of a man released from prison.

From that moment on he began to relax; or almost from that moment—what seemed to clinch the transformation was O'Leary's hat.

O'Leary was a recent City College graduate and one of the best men on the staff (he has since done very well; you'll often see his byline in one of the evening papers), and the hat he wore that winter was of the waterproof cloth kind that is sold in raincoat shops. There was nothing very dashing about it—in fact its floppiness made O'Leary's face look too thin—but Sobel must secretly have admired it as a symbol of journalism, or of nonconformity, for one morning he showed up in an identical one, brand new. It looked even worse on him than on O'Leary, particularly when worn with his lumpy brown overcoat, but he seemed to cherish it. He developed a whole new set of mannerisms to go with the hat: cocking it back, with a flip of the index finger as he settled down to make his morning phone calls ("This is Leon Sobel, of *The Labor Leader...*"), tugging it smartly forward as he left the office on a reporting assignment, twirling it onto a peg when he came back to write his story. At the end of the day, when he'd dropped the last of his copy into Finney's wire basket, he would shape the hat into a careless slant over one eyebrow, swing the overcoat around his shoulders and stride out with a loose salute of farewell, and I used to picture him studying his reflection in the black subway windows all the way home to the Bronx.

He seemed determined to love his work. He even brought in a snapshot of his family—a tired, abjectly smiling woman and two small sons—and fastened it to his desktop with cellophane tape. Nobody else ever left anything more personal than a book of matches in the office overnight.

One afternoon toward the end of February, Finney summoned me to his oily desk. "McCabe," he said. "Wanna do a column for us?"

"What kind of a column?"

"Labor gossip," he said. "Straight union items with a gossip or a chatter angle—little humor, personalities, stuff like that.

Mr. Kramm thinks we need it, and I told him you'd be the best man for the job."

I can't deny that I was flattered (we are all conditioned by our surroundings, after all), but I was also suspicious. "Do I get a byline?"

He began to blink nervously. "Oh, no, no byline," he said. "Mr. Kramm wants this to be anonymous. See, the guys'll give you any items they turn up, and you'll just collect 'em and put 'em in shape. It's just something you can do on office time, part of your regular job. See what I mean?"

I saw what he meant. "Part of my regular salary too," I said. "Right?"

"That's right."

"No thanks," I told him, and then, feeling generous, I suggested that he try O'Leary.

"Nah, I already asked him," Finney said. "He don't wanna do it either. Nobody does."

I should have guessed, of course, that he'd been working down the list of everyone in the office. And to judge from the lateness of the day, I must have been close to the tail end.

Sobel fell in step with me as we left the building after work that night. He was wearing his overcoat cloak-style, the sleeves dangling, and holding his cloth hat in place as he hopped nimbly to avoid the furrows of dirty slush on the sidewalk. "Letcha in on a little secret, McCabe," he said. "I'm doin' a column for the paper. It's all arranged."

"Yeah?" I said. "Any money in it?"

"Money?" He winked. "I'll tell y' about that part. Let's get a cuppa coffee." He led me into the tiled and steaming brilliance of the Automat, and when we were settled at a damp corner table he explained everything. "Finney says no money, see? So I said okay. He says no byline either. I said okay." He winked again. "Playin' it smart."

"How do you mean?"

"How do I mean?" He always repeated your question like that, savoring it, holding his black eyebrows high while he made you wait for the answer. "Listen, I got this Finney figured out. *He* don't decide these things. You think he decides anything around that place? You better wise up, McCabe. Mr. *Kramm* makes the decisions. And Mr. Kramm is an intelligent man, don't kid yourself." Nodding, he raised his coffee cup, but his lips recoiled from the heat of it, puckered, and blew into the steam before they began to sip with gingerly impatience.

"Well," I said, "okay, but I'd check with Kramm before you start counting on anything."

"Check?" He put his cup down with a clatter. "What's to check? Listen, Mr. Kramm wants a column, right? You think he cares if I get a byline or not? Or the money, either—you think if I write a good column he's gonna quibble over payin' me for it? Ya crazy. *Finney's* the one, don'tcha see? *He* don't wanna gimme a break because he's worried about losing his *own* column. Get it? So all right. I check with nobody until I got that column written." He prodded his chest with a stiff thumb. "On my own time. Then I take it to Mr. Kramm and we talk business. You leave it to me." He settled down comfortably, elbows on the table, both hands cradling the cup just short of drinking position while he blew into the steam.

"Well," I said. "I hope you're right. Be nice if it does work out that way."

"Ah, it may not," he conceded, pulling his mouth into a grimace of speculation and tilting his head to one side. "You know. It's a gamble." But he was only saying that out of politeness, to minimize my envy. He could afford to express doubt because he felt none, and I could tell he was already planning the way he'd tell his wife about it.

The next morning Finney came around to each of our desks with instructions that we were to give Sobel any gossip or chatter items we might turn up; the column was scheduled to begin in the next issue. Later I saw him in conference with Sobel, briefing him on how the column was to be written, and I noticed that Finney did all the talking: Sobel just sat there making thin, contemptuous jets of cigarette smoke.

We had just put an issue to press, so the deadline for the column was two weeks away. Not many items turned up at first—it was hard enough getting news out of the unions we covered, let alone "chatter." Whenever someone did hand him a note,

Sobel would frown over it, add a scribble of his own and drop it in a desk drawer; once or twice I saw him drop one in the wastebasket. I only remember one of the several pieces I gave him: the business agent of a steamfitters' local I covered had yelled at me through a closed door that he couldn't be bothered that day because his wife had just had twins. But Sobel didn't want it. "So, the guy's got twins," he said. "So what?"

"Suit yourself," I said. "You getting much other stuff?"

He shrugged. "Some. I'm not worried. I'll tellya one thing, though—I'm not using a lotta this crap. This chatter. Who the hell's gonna read it? You can't have a whole column fulla crap like that. Gotta be something to hold it together. Am I right?"

Another time (the column was all he talked about now) he chuckled affectionately and said, "My wife says I'm just as bad now as when I was working on my books. Write, write, write. She don't care, though," he added. "She's really getting excited about this thing. She's telling everybody—the neighbors, everybody. Her brother come over Sunday, starts asking me how the job's going—you know, in a wise-guy kinda way? I just kept quiet, but my wife pipes up: 'Leon's doing a column for the paper now'—and she tells him all about it. Boy, you oughta seen his face."

Every morning he brought in the work he had done the night before, a wad of handwritten papers, and used his lunch hour to type it out and revise it while he chewed a sandwich at his desk. And he was the last one to go home every night; we'd leave him there hammering his typewriter in a trance of concentration. Finney kept bothering him—"How you coming on that feature, Sobel?"—but he always parried the question with squinted eyes and a truculent lift of the chin. "Whaddya worried about? You'll get it." And he would wink at me.

On the morning of the deadline he came to work with a little patch of toilet paper on his cheek; he had cut himself shaving in his nervousness, but otherwise he looked as confident as ever. There were no calls to make that morning—on deadline days we all stayed in to work on copy and proofs—so the first thing he did was to spread out the finished manuscript for a final reading. His absorption was so complete that he didn't look up until

Finney was standing at his elbow. "You wanna gimme that feature, Sobel?"

Sobel grabbed up the papers and shielded them with an arrogant forearm. He looked steadily at Finney and said, with a firmness that he must have been rehearsing for two weeks: "I'm showing this to Mr. Kramm. Not you."

Finney's whole face began to twitch in a fit of nerves. "Nah, nah, Mr. Kramm don't need to see it," he said. "Anyway, he's not in yet. C'mon, lemme have it."

"You're wasting your time, Finney," Sobel said. "I'm waiting for Mr. Kramm."

Muttering, avoiding Sobel's triumphant eyes, Finney went back to his own desk, where he was reading proof on BROADWAY BEAT.

My own job that morning was at the layout table, pasting up the dummy for the first section. I was standing there, working with the unwieldy page forms and the paste-clogged scissors, when Sobel sidled up behind me, looking anxious. "You wanna read it, McCabe?" he asked. "Before I turn it in?" And he handed me the manuscript.

The first thing that hit me was that he had clipped a photograph to the top of page 1, a small portrait of himself in his cloth hat. The next thing was his title:

SOBEL SPEAKING
BY LEON SOBEL

I can't remember the exact words of the opening paragraph, but it went something like this:

> This is the "debut" of a new department in *The Labor Leader* and, moreover, it is also "something new" for your correspondent, who has never handled a column before. However, he is far from being a novice with the written word, on the contrary he is an "ink-stained veteran" of many battles on the field of ideas, to be exact nine books have emanated from his pen.
>
> Naturally in those tomes his task was somewhat different than that which it will be in this column, and yet he hopes

that this column will also strive as they did to penetrate the basic human mystery, in other words, to tell the truth.

When I looked up I saw he had picked open the razor cut on his cheek and it was bleeding freely. "Well," I said, "for one thing, I wouldn't give it to him with your picture that way— I mean, don't you think it might be better to let him read it first, and then—"

"Okay," he said, blotting at his face with a wadded gray hand-kerchief. "Okay, I'll take the picture off. G'ahead, read the rest."

But there wasn't time to read the rest. Kramm had come in, Finney had spoken to him, and now he was standing in the door of his office, champing crossly on a dead cigar. "You wanted to see me, Sobel?" he called.

"Just a second," Sobel said. He straightened the pages of SOBEL SPEAKING and detached the photograph, which he jammed into his hip pocket as he started for the door. Halfway there he remembered to take off his hat, and threw it unsuccess-fully at the hat stand. Then he disappeared behind the partition, and we all settled down to listen.

It wasn't long before Kramm's reaction came through. "*No*, Sobel. No, no, *no*! What *is* this? What are you tryna put *over* on me here?"

Outside, Finney winced comically and clapped the side of his head, giggling, and O'Leary had to glare at him until he stopped.

We heard Sobel's voice, a blurred sentence or two of protest, and then Kramm came through again: " 'Basic human mystery' —this is gossip? This is chatter? You can't follow instructions? Wait a minute—Finney! Finney!"

Finney loped to the door, delighted to be of service, and we heard him making clear, righteous replies to Kramm's inter-rogation: Yes, he had told Sobel what kind of a column was wanted; yes, he had specified that there was to be no byline; yes, Sobel had been provided with ample gossip material. All we heard from Sobel was something indistinct, said in a very tight, flat voice. Kramm made a guttural reply, and even though we couldn't make out the words we knew it was all over. Then they came out, Finney wearing the foolish smile you sometimes see in the crowds that gape at street accidents, Sobel as expressionless as death.

He picked his hat off the floor and his coat off the stand, put them on, and came over to me. "So long, McCabe," he said. "Take it easy."

Shaking hands with him, I felt my face jump into Finney's idiot smile, and I asked a stupid question. "You leaving?"

He nodded. Then he shook hands with O'Leary—"So long, kid"—and hesitated, uncertain whether to shake hands with the rest of the staff. He settled for a little wave of the forefinger, and walked out to the street.

Finney lost no time in giving us all the inside story in an eager whisper: "The guy's *crazy*! He says to Kramm, 'You take this column or I quit'—just like that. Kramm just looks at him and says, 'Quit? Get outa here, you're fired.' I mean, what *else* could he say?"

Turning away, I saw that the snapshot of Sobel's wife and sons still lay taped to his desk. I stripped it off and took it out to the sidewalk. "Hey, Sobel!" I yelled. He was a block away, very small, walking toward the subway. I started to run after him, nearly breaking my neck on the frozen slush. "Hey *Sobel!*" But he didn't hear me.

Back at the office I found his address in the Bronx telephone directory, put the picture in an envelope and dropped it in the mail, and I wish that were the end of the story.

But that afternoon I called up the editor of a hardware trade journal I had worked on before the war, who said he had no vacancies on his staff but might soon, and would be willing to interview Sobel if he wanted to drop in. It was a foolish idea: the wages there were even lower than on the *Leader*, and besides, it was a place for very young men whose fathers wanted them to learn the hardware business—Sobel would probably have been ruled out the minute he opened his mouth. But it seemed better than nothing, and as soon as I was out of the office that night I went to a phone booth and looked up Sobel's name again.

A woman's voice answered, but it wasn't the high, faint voice I'd expected. It was low and melodious—that was the first of my several surprises.

"Mrs. Sobel?" I asked, absurdly smiling into the mouthpiece. "Is Leon there?"

She started to say, "Just a minute," but changed it to "Who's calling, please? I'd rather not disturb him right now."

I told her my name and tried to explain about the hardware deal.

"I don't understand," she said. "What kind of a paper is it, exactly?"

"Well, it's a trade journal," I said. "It doesn't amount to much, I guess, but it's—*you* know, a pretty good little thing, of its kind."

"I see," she said. "And you want him to go in and apply for a job? Is that it?"

"Well I mean, if he *wants* to, is all," I said. I was beginning to sweat. It was impossible to reconcile the wan face in Sobel's snapshot with this serene, almost beautiful voice. "I just thought he might like to give it a try, is all."

"Well," she said, "just a minute, I'll ask him." She put down the phone, and I heard them talking in the background. Their words were muffled at first but then I heard Sobel say, "Ah, I'll talk to him—I'll just say thanks for calling." And I heard her answer, with infinite tenderness, "No, honey, why should you? He doesn't deserve it."

"McCabe's all right," he said.

"No he's not," she told him, "or he'd have the decency to leave you alone. Let me do it. Please. I'll get rid of him."

When she came back to the phone she said, "No, my husband says he wouldn't be interested in a job of that kind." Then she thanked me politely, said goodbye, and left me to climb guilty and sweating out of the phone booth.

FUN WITH A STRANGER

ALL THAT SUMMER the children who were due to start third grade under Miss Snell had been warned about her. "Boy, you're gonna get it," the older children would say, distorting their faces with a wicked pleasure. "You're really gonna *get* it. Mrs. *Cleary's* all right" (Mrs. Cleary taught the other, luckier half of third grade) "—she's *fine*, but boy, that *Snell*—you better watch out." So it happened that the morale of Miss Snell's class was low even before school opened in September, and she did little in the first few weeks to improve it.

She was probably sixty, a big rawboned woman with a man's face, and her clothes, if not her very pores, seemed always to exude that dry essence of pencil shavings and chalk dust that is the smell of school. She was strict and humorless, preoccupied with rooting out the things she held intolerable: mumbling, slumping, daydreaming, frequent trips to the bathroom, and, the worst of all, "coming to school without proper supplies." Her small eyes were sharp, and when somebody sent out a stealthy alarm of whispers and nudges to try to borrow a pencil from somebody else, it almost never worked. "What's the trouble back there?" she would demand. "I mean you, John Gerhardt." And John Gerhardt—or Howard White or whoever it happened to be—caught in the middle of a whisper, could only turn red and say, "Nothing."

"Don't mumble. Is it a pencil? Have you come to school without a pencil again? Stand up when you're spoken to."

And there would follow a long lecture on Proper Supplies that ended only after the offender had come forward to receive a pencil from the small hoard on her desk, had been made to say, "Thank you, Miss Snell," and to repeat, until he said it loud enough for everyone to hear, a promise that he wouldn't chew it or break its point.

With erasers it was even worse because they were more often in short supply, owing to a general tendency to chew them off the ends of pencils. Miss Snell kept a big, shapeless old eraser on her desk, and she seemed very proud of it. "This is *my* eraser," she would say, shaking it at the class. "I've had this eraser for five years. Five years." (And this was not hard to believe, for the eraser looked as old and gray and worn-down as the hand that brandished it.) "I've never played with it because it's not a toy. I've never chewed it because it's not good to eat. And I've never lost it because I'm not foolish and I'm not careless. I need this eraser for my work and I've taken good care of it. Now, why can't you do the same with *your* erasers? I don't know what's the matter with this class. I've never had a class that was so foolish and so careless and so *childish* about its supplies."

She never seemed to lose her temper, but it would almost have been better if she did, for it was the flat, dry, passionless redundance of her scolding that got everybody down. When Miss Snell singled someone out for a special upbraiding it was an ordeal by talk. She would come up to within a foot of her victim's face, her eyes would stare unblinking into his, and the wrinkled gray flesh of her mouth would labor to pronounce his guilt, grimly and deliberately, until all the color faded from the day. She seemed to have no favorites; once she even picked on Alice Johnson, who always had plenty of supplies and did nearly everything right. Alice was mumbling while reading aloud, and when she continued to mumble after several warnings Miss Snell went over and took her book away and lectured her for several minutes running. Alice looked stunned at first; then her eyes filled up, her mouth twitched into terrible shapes, and she gave in to the ultimate humiliation of crying in class.

It was not uncommon to cry in Miss Snell's class, even among the boys. And ironically, it always seemed to be during the lull after one of these scenes—when the only sound in the room was somebody's slow, half-stifled sobbing, and the rest of the class stared straight ahead in an agony of embarrassment—that the noise of group laughter would float in from Mrs. Cleary's class across the hall.

Still, they could not hate Miss Snell, for children's villains must

be all black, and there was no denying that Miss Snell was sometimes nice in an awkward, groping way of her own. "When we
learn a new word it's like making a friend," she said once. "And
we all like to make friends, don't we? Now, for instance, when
school began this year you were all strangers to me, but I wanted
very much to learn your names and remember your faces, and
so I made the effort. It was confusing at first, but before long I'd
made friends with all of you. And later on we'll have some good
times together—oh, perhaps a little party at Christmastime, or
something like that—and then I know I'd be very sorry if I
hadn't made that effort, because you can't very well have fun
with a stranger, can you?" She gave them a homely, shy smile.
"And that's just the way it is with words."

When she said something like that it was more embarrassing
than anything else, but it did leave the children with a certain
vague sense of responsibility toward her, and often prompted
them into a loyal reticence when children from other classes
demanded to know how bad she really was, "Well, not too bad,"
they would say uncomfortably, and try to change the subject.

John Gerhardt and Howard White usually walked home from
school together, and often as not, though they tried to avoid it,
they were joined by two of the children from Mrs. Cleary's
class who lived on their street—Freddy Taylor and his twin
sister Grace. John and Howard usually got about as far as the
end of the playground before the twins came running after
them out of the crowd. "Hey, wait up!" Freddy would call.
"Wait up!" And in a moment the twins would fall into step
beside them, chattering, swinging their identical plaid canvas
schoolbags.

"Guess what we're gonna do next week," Freddy said in his
chirping voice one afternoon. "Our whole class, I mean. Guess.
Come on, guess."

John Gerhardt had already made it plain to the twins once, in
so many words, that he didn't like walking home with a girl,
and now he very nearly said something to the effect that one
girl was bad enough, but two were more than he could take.
Instead he aimed a knowing glance at Howard White and they

both walked on in silence, determined not to answer Freddy's insistent "Guess."

But Freddy didn't wait long for an answer. "We're gonna take a field trip," he said, "for our class in Transportation. We're gonna go to Harmon. You know what Harmon is?"

"Sure," Howard White said. "A town."

"No, but I mean, you know what they *do* there? What they do is, that's where they change all the trains coming into New York from steam locomotives to electric power. Mrs. Cleary says we're gonna watch 'em changing the locomotives and everything."

"We're gonna spend practically the whole day," Grace said.

"So what's so great about that?" Howard White asked. "I can go there *any* day, if I feel like it, on my bike." This was an exaggeration—he wasn't allowed out of a two-block radius on his bike—but it sounded good, especially when he added, "I don't need any Mrs. Cleary to take me," with a mincing, sissy emphasis on the "Cleary."

"On a school day?" Grace inquired. "Can you go on a *school* day?"

Lamely Howard murmured, "Sure, if I feel like it," but it was a clear point for the twins.

"Mrs. Cleary says we're gonna take a lotta field trips," Freddy said. "Later on, we're gonna go to the Museum of Natural History, in New York, and a whole lotta other places. Too bad you're not in Mrs. Cleary's class."

"Doesn't bother me any," John Gerhardt said. Then he came up with a direct quotation from his father that seemed appropriate: "Anyway, I don't *go* to school to fool around. I go to school to work. Come on, Howard."

A day or two later it turned out that both classes were scheduled to take the field trip together; Miss Snell had just neglected to tell her pupils about it. When she did tell them it was in one of her nice moods. "I think the trip will be especially valuable," she said, "because it will be instructive and at the same time it will be a real treat for all of us." That afternoon John Gerhardt and Howard White conveyed the news to the twins with studied carelessness and secret delight.

But the victory was short-lived, for the field trip itself only emphasized the difference between the two teachers. Mrs. Cleary ran everything with charm and enthusiasm; she was young and lithe and just about the prettiest woman Miss Snell's class had ever seen. It was she who arranged for the children to climb up and inspect the cab of a huge locomotive that stood idle on a siding, and she who found out where the public toilets were. The most tedious facts about trains came alive when she explained them; the most forbidding engineers and switchmen became jovial hosts when she smiled up at them, with her long hair blowing and her hands plunged jauntily in the pockets of her polo coat.

Through it all Miss Snell hung in the background, gaunt and sour, her shoulders hunched against the wind and her squinted eyes roving, alert for stragglers. At one point she made Mrs. Cleary wait while she called her own class aside and announced that there would be no more field trips if they couldn't learn to stay together in a group. She spoiled everything, and by the time it was over the class was painfully embarrassed for her. She'd had every chance to give a good account of herself that day, and now her failure was as pitiful as it was disappointing. That was the worst part of it: she was pitiful—they didn't even want to look at her, in her sad, lumpy black coat and hat. All they wanted was to get her into the bus and back to school and out of sight as fast as possible.

The events of autumn each brought a special season to the school. First came Halloween, for which several art classes were devoted to crayoned jack-o'-lanterns and arching black cats. Thanksgiving was bigger; for a week or two the children painted turkeys and horns of plenty and brown-clad Pilgrim Fathers with high buckled hats and trumpet-barreled muskets, and in music class they sang "We Gather Together" and "America the Beautiful" again and again. And almost as soon as Thanksgiving was over the long preparations for Christmas began: red and green predominated, and carols were rehearsed for the annual Christmas Pageant. Every day the halls became more thickly festooned with Christmas trimmings, until finally it was the last week before vacation.

"You gonna have a party in your class?" Freddy Taylor inquired one day.

"Sure, prob'ly," John Gerhardt said, though in fact he wasn't sure at all. Except for that one vague reference, many weeks before, Miss Snell had said or hinted nothing whatever about a Christmas party.

"Miss Snell tell ya you're gonna have one, or what?" Grace asked.

"Well, she didn't exactly *tell* us," John Gerhardt said obscurely. Howard White walked along without a word, scuffing his shoes.

"Mrs. Cleary didn't tell us either," Grace said, "because it's supposed to be a surprise, but we know we're gonna have one. Some of the kids who had her last year said so. They said she always has this big party on the last day, with a tree and everything, and favors and things to eat. You gonna have all that?"

"Oh, I don't know," John Gerhardt said. "Sure, prob'ly." But later, when the twins were gone, he got a little worried. "Hey, Howard," he said, "you think she is gonna have a party, or what?"

"Search *me*," Howard White said, with a careful shrug. "*I* didn't say anything." But he was uneasy about it too, and so was the rest of the class. As vacation drew nearer, and particularly during the few anticlimactic days of school left after the Christmas Pageant was over, it seemed less and less likely that Miss Snell was planning a party of any kind, and it preyed on all their minds.

It rained on the last day of school. The morning went by like any other morning, and after lunch, like any other rainy day, the corridors were packed with chattering children in raincoats and rubbers, milling around and waiting for the afternoon classes to begin. Around the third-grade classrooms there was a special tension, for Mrs. Cleary had locked the door of her room, and the word soon spread that she was alone inside making preparations for a party that would begin when the bell rang and last all afternoon. "I peeked," Grace Taylor was saying breathlessly to anyone who would listen. "She's got this little tree with all blue lights, and she's got the room all fixed up and all the desks moved away and everything."

Others from her class tagged after her with questions—

"*What'd* you see?" "All blue lights?"—and still others jostled around the door, trying to get a look through the keyhole.

Miss Snell's class pressed self-consciously against the corridor wall, mostly silent, hands in their pockets. Their door was closed too, but nobody wanted to see if it was locked for fear it might swing open and reveal Miss Snell sitting sensibly at her desk, correcting papers. Instead they watched Mrs. Cleary's door, and when it opened at last they watched the other children flock in. All the girls yelled, "Ooh!" in chorus as they disappeared inside, and even from where Miss Snell's class stood they could see that the room was transformed. There *was* a tree with blue lights— the whole room glowed blue, in fact—and the floor was cleared. They could just see the corner of a table in the middle, bearing platters of bright candy and cake. Mrs. Cleary stood in the doorway, beautiful and beaming, slightly flushed with welcome. She gave a kindly, distracted smile to the craning faces of Miss Snell's class, then closed the door again.

A second later Miss Snell's door opened, and the first thing they saw was that the room was unchanged. The desks were all in place, ready for work; their own workaday Christmas paintings still spotted the walls, and there was no other decoration except for the grubby red cardboard letters spelling "Merry Christmas" that had hung over the blackboard all week. But then with a rush of relief they saw that on Miss Snell's desk lay a neat little pile of red-and-white-wrapped packages. Miss Snell stood unsmiling at the head of the room, waiting for the class to get settled. Instinctively, nobody lingered to stare at the gifts or to comment on them. Miss Snell's attitude made it plain that the party hadn't begun yet.

It was time for spelling, and she instructed them to get their pencils and paper ready. In the silences between her enunciation of each word to be spelled, the noise of Mrs. Cleary's class could be heard—repeated laughter and whoops of surprise. But the little pile of gifts made everything all right; the children had only to look at them to know that there was nothing to be embarrassed about, after all. Miss Snell had come through.

The gifts were all wrapped alike, in white tissue paper with red ribbon, and the few whose individual shapes John Gerhardt could discern looked like they might be jackknives. Maybe it would be jackknives for the boys, he thought, and little pocket flashlights for the girls. Or more likely, since jackknives were probably too expensive, it would be something well-meant and useless from the dime store, like individual lead soldiers for the boys and miniature dolls for the girls. But even that would be good enough—something hard and bright to prove that she was human after all, to pull out of a pocket and casually display to the Taylor twins. ("Well, no, not a *party*, exactly, but she gave us all these little presents. Look.")

"John Gerhardt," Miss Snell said, "if you can't give your attention to anything but the . . . things on my desk, perhaps I'd better put them out of sight." The class giggled a little, and she smiled. It was only a small, shy smile, quickly corrected before she turned back to her spelling book, but it was enough to break the tension. While the spelling papers were being collected Howard White leaned close to John Gerhardt and whispered, "Tie clips. Bet it's tie clips for the boys and some kinda jewelry for the girls."

"Sh-sh!" John told him, but then he added, "Too thick for tie clips." There was a general shifting around; everyone expected the party to begin as soon as Miss Snell had all the spelling papers. Instead she called for silence and began the afternoon class in Transportation.

The afternoon wore on. Every time Miss Snell glanced at the clock they expected her to say, "Oh, my goodness—I'd almost forgotten." But she didn't. It was a little after two, with less than an hour of school left, when Miss Snell was interrupted by a knock on the door. "Yes?" she said irritably. "What is it?"

Little Grace Taylor came in, with half a cupcake in her hand and the other half in her mouth. She displayed elaborate surprise at finding the class at work—backing up a step and putting her free hand to her lips.

"Well?" Miss Snell demanded. "Do you want something?"

"Mrs. Cleary wants to know if—"

"Must you talk with your mouth full?"

Grace swallowed. She wasn't the least bit shy. "Mrs. Cleary wants to know if you have any extra paper plates."

"I have no paper plates," Miss Snell said. "And will you kindly inform Mrs. Cleary that this class is in session?"

"All right," Grace took another bite of her cake and turned to leave. Her eyes caught the pile of gifts and she paused to look at them, clearly unimpressed.

"You're holding up the class," Miss Snell said. Grace moved on. At the door she gave the class a sly glance and a quick, silent giggle full of cake crumbs, and then slipped out.

The minute hand crept down to two-thirty, passed it, and inched toward two-forty-five. Finally, at five minutes of three, Miss Snell laid down her book. "All right," she said, "I think we may all put our books away now. This is the last day of school before the holidays, and I've prepared a—little surprise for you." She smiled again. "Now, I think it would be best if you all stay in your places, and I'll just pass these around. Alice Johnson, will you please come and help me? The rest of you stay seated." Alice went forward, and Miss Snell divided the little packages into two heaps, using two pieces of drawing paper as trays. Alice took one paperful, cradling it carefully, and Miss Snell the other. Before they started around the room Miss Snell said, "Now, I think the most courteous thing would be for each of you to wait until everyone is served, and then we'll all open the packages together. All right, Alice."

They started down the aisle, reading the labels and passing out the gifts. The labels were the familiar Woolworth kind with a picture of Santa Claus and "Merry Christmas" printed on them, and Miss Snell had filled them out in her neat blackboard lettering. John Gerhardt's read: "To John G., From Miss Snell." He picked it up, but the moment he felt the package he knew, with a little shock, exactly what it was. There was no surprise left by the time Miss Snell returned to the head of the class and said, "All right."

He peeled off the paper and laid the gift on his desk. It was an eraser, the serviceable ten-cent kind, half white for pencil and half gray for ink. From the corner of his eye he saw that Howard White, beside him, was unwrapping an identical one, and a furtive glance around the room confirmed that all the gifts had been the same. Nobody knew what to do, and for what seemed a full minute the room was silent except for the dwindling rustle of tissue paper. Miss Snell stood at the head of the class, her clasped fingers writhing like dry worms at her waist, her face melted into the soft, tremulous smile of a giver. She looked completely helpless.

At last one of the girls said, "Thank you, Miss Snell," and then the rest of the class said it in ragged unison: "Thank you, Miss Snell."

"You're all very welcome," she said, composing herself, "and I hope you all have a pleasant holiday."

Mercifully, the bell rang then, and in the jostling clamor of retreat to the cloakroom it was no longer necessary to look at Miss Snell. Her voice rose above the noise: "Will you all please dispose of your paper and ribbons in the basket before you leave?"

John Gerhardt yanked on his rubbers, grabbed his raincoat, and elbowed his way out of the cloakroom, out of the classroom and down the noisy corridor. "Hey, Howard, wait up!" he yelled to Howard White, and finally both of them were free of school, running, splashing through puddles on the playground. Miss Snell was left behind now, farther behind with every step; if they ran fast enough they could even avoid the Taylor twins, and then there would be no need to think about any of it anymore. Legs pounding, raincoats streaming, they ran with the exhilaration of escape.

THE B.A.R. MAN

UNTIL HE GOT his name on the police blotter, and in the papers, nobody had ever thought much about John Fallon. He was employed as a clerk in a big insurance company, where he hulked among the file cabinets with a conscientious frown, his white shirt cuffs turned back to expose a tight gold watch on one wrist and a loose serviceman's identification bracelet, the relic of a braver and more careless time, on the other. He was twenty-nine years old, big and burly, with neatly combed brown hair and a heavy white face. His eyes were kindly except when he widened them in bewilderment or narrowed them in menace, and his mouth was childishly slack except when he tightened it to say something tough. For street wear, he preferred slick, gas-blue suits with stiff shoulders and very low-set buttons, and he walked with the hard, ringing cadence of steel-capped heels. He lived in Sunnyside, Queens, and had been married for ten years to a very thin girl named Rose who suffered from sinus headaches, couldn't have children, and earned more money than he did by typing eighty-seven words a minute without missing a beat on her chewing gum.

Five evenings a week, Sunday through Thursday, the Fallons sat at home playing cards or watching television, and sometimes she would send him out to buy sandwiches and potato salad for a light snack before they went to bed. Friday, being the end of the workweek and the night of the fights on television, was his night with the boys at the Island Bar and Grill, just off Queens Boulevard. The crowd there were friends of habit rather than of choice, and for the first half hour they would stand around self-consciously, insulting one another and jeering at each new arrival ("Oh Jesus, looka what just come in!"). But by the time the fights were over they would usually have joked and drunk themselves into a high good humor, and the evening would often end in song and staggering at two or three o'clock. Fallon's Saturday, after a morning of sleep and an afternoon of helping with the housework, was devoted to the entertainment of his wife: they would catch the show at one of the neighborhood movies and go to an ice-cream parlor afterwards, and they were usually in bed by twelve. Then came the drowsy living-room clutter of newspapers on Sunday, and his week began again.

The trouble might never have happened if his wife had not insisted, that particular Friday, on breaking his routine: there was a Gregory Peck picture in its final showing that night, and she said she saw no reason why he couldn't do without his prize fight, for once in his life. She told him this on Friday morning, and it was the first of many things that went wrong with his day.

At lunch—the special payday lunch that he always shared with three fellow clerks from his office, in a German tavern down-town—the others were all talking about the fights, and Fallon took little part in the conversation. Jack Kopeck, who knew nothing about boxing (he had called the previous week's perfor-mance "a damn good bout" when in fact it had been fifteen rounds of clinches and cream-puff sparring, with the mockery of a decision at the end), told the party at some length that the best all-around bout he'd ever seen was in the Navy. And that led to a lot of Navy talk around the table, while Fallon squirmed in boredom.

"So here *I* was," Kopeck was saying, jabbing his breastbone with a manicured thumb in the windup of his third long story, "my first day on a new ship, and nothing but these tailor-made dress blues to stand inspection in. Scared? Jesus, I was shakin' like a leaf. Old man comes around, looks at me, says, 'Where d'ya think *you're* at, sailor? A fancy-dress ball?' "

"Talk about inspections," Mike Boyle said, bugging his round comedian's eyes. "Lemme tell ya, *we* had this commander, he'd take this white glove and wipe his finger down the bulkhead? And brother, if that glove came away with a specka dust on it, you were dead."

Then they started getting sentimental. "Ah, it's a good life, though, the Navy," Kopeck said. "A clean life. The best part about the Navy is, you're somebody, know what I mean? Every man's got his own individual job to do. And I mean what the hell, in the Army all you do is walk around and look stupid like everybody else."

"Brother," said little George Walsh, wiping mustard on his knockwurst, "you can say that again. I had four years in the Army and, believe me, you can say that again."

That was when John Fallon's patience ran out. "Yeah?" he said. "What parta the Army was that?"

"What part?" Walsh said, blinking. "Well, I was in the ordnance for a while, in Virginia, and then I was in Texas, and Georgia—how d'ya mean, what part?"

Fallon's eyes narrowed and his lips curled tight. "You oughta tried an infantry outfit, Mac," he said.

"Oh, well," Walsh deferred with a wavering smile.

But Kopeck and Boyle took up the challenge, grinning at him.

"The *infantry*?" Boyle said. "Whadda they got—specialists in the infantry?"

"You betcher ass they got specialists," Fallon said. "Every son of a bitch *in* a rifle company's a specialist, if you wanna know something. And I'll tellya *one* thing, Mac—they don't worry about no silk gloves and no tailor-made clothes, you can betcher ass on that."

"Wait a second," Kopeck said. "I wanna know one thing, John. What was your specialty?"

"I was a B.A.R. man," Fallon said.

"What's that?"

And this was the first time Fallon realized how much the crowd in the office had changed over the years. In the old days, back around 'forty-nine or 'fifty, with the old crowd, anyone who didn't know what a B.A.R. was would almost certainly have kept his mouth shut.

"The B.A.R.," Fallon said, laying down his fork, "is the Browning Automatic Rifle. It's a thirty-caliber, magazine-fed, fully-automatic piece that provides the major firepower of a twelve-man rifle squad. That answer your question?"

"How d'ya mean?" Boyle inquired. "Like a tommy gun?"

And Fallon had to explain, as if he were talking to children or girls, that it was nothing at all like a tommy gun and that its tactical function was entirely different; finally he had to take out his mechanical pencil and draw, from memory and love, a silhouette of the weapon on the back of his weekly pay envelope.

"So okay," Kopeck said, "tell me one thing, John. Whaddya have to know to shoot this gun? You gotta have special training, or what?"

Fallon's eyes were angry slits as he crammed the pencil and envelope back into his coat. "Try it sometime," he said. "Try walkin' twenty miles on an empty stomach with that B.A.R. and a full ammo belt on your back, and then lay down in some swamp with the water up over your ass, and you're pinned down by machine-gun and mortar fire and your squad leader starts yellin', 'Get that B.A.R. up!' and you gotta cover the withdrawal of the whole platoon or the whole damn company. *Try* it sometime, Mac—*you'll* find out whatcha gotta have." And he took too deep a drink of his beer, which made him cough and sputter into his big freckled fist.

"Easy, easy," Boyle said, smiling. "Don't bust a gut, boy."

But Fallon only wiped his mouth and glared at them, breathing hard.

"Okay, so you're a hero," Kopeck said lightly. "You're a fighting man. Tell me one thing, though, John. Did you personally shoot this gun in combat?"

"Whadda you think?" Fallon said through thin, unmoving lips.

"How many times?"

The fact of the matter was that Fallon, as a husky and competent soldier of nineteen, many times pronounced "a damn good B.A.R. man" by the others in his squad, had carried his weapon on blistered feet over miles of road and field and forest in the last two months of the war, had lain with it under many artillery and mortar barrages and jabbed it at the chests of many freshly taken German prisoners; but he'd had occasion to fire it only twice, at vague areas rather than men, had brought down nothing either time, and had been mildly reprimanded the second time for wasting ammunition.

"Nunnya goddamn business how many!" he said, and the others looked down at their plates with ill-concealed smiles. He glared at them, defying anyone to make a crack, but the worst part of it was that none of them said anything. They ate or drank their beer in silence, and after a while they changed the subject.

Fallon did not smile all afternoon, and he was still sullen when he met his wife at the supermarket, near home, for their weekend shopping. She looked tired, the way she always did when her sinus trouble was about to get worse, and while he ponderously wheeled the wire-mesh cart behind her he kept turning his head to follow the churning hips and full breasts of other young women in the store.

"Ow!" she cried once, and dropped a box of Ritz crackers to rub her heel in pain. "Can't you watch where you're *going* with that thing? You better let me push it."

"You shouldn't of stopped so sudden," he told her. "I didn't know you were gonna stop."

And thereafter, to make sure he didn't run the cart into her again, he had to give his full attention to her own narrow body and stick-thin legs. From the side view, Rose Fallon seemed always to be leaning slightly forward; walking, her buttocks seemed to float as an ungraceful separate entity in her wake. Some years ago, a doctor had explained her sterility with the fact that her womb was tipped, and told her it might be corrected by a course of exercises; she had done the exercises halfheartedly for a while and gradually given them up. Fallon could never remember whether her odd posture was supposed to be the cause or the result of the inner condition, but he did know for certain that, like her sinus trouble, it had grown worse in the years since their marriage; he could have sworn she stood straight when he met her.

"You want Rice Krispies or Post Toasties, John?" she asked him.

"Rice Krispies."

"Well, but we just had that last week. Aren't you tired of it?"

"Okay, the other, then."

"What are you mumbling for? I can't hear you."

"Post Toasties, I said!"

Walking home, he was puffing more than usual under the double armload of groceries. "What's the *matter*?" she asked, when he stopped to change his grip on the bags.

"Guess I'm outa shape," he said. "I oughta get out and play some handball."

"Oh, honestly," she said. "You're always saying that, and all you ever do is lie around and read the papers."

She took a bath before fixing the dinner, and then ate with a bulky housecoat roped around her in her usual state of post-bath dishevelment: hair damp, skin dry and porous, no lipstick and a smiling spoor of milk around the upper borders of her unsmiling mouth. "Where do you think you're going?" she said, when he had pushed his plate away and stood up. "Look at that—a full glass of milk on the table. Honestly, John, you're the one that makes me *buy* milk and then when I buy it you go and leave a full glass on the table. Now come back here and drink that up."

He went back and gulped the milk, which made him feel ill.

When her meal was over she began her careful preparations for the evening out; long after he had washed and dried the dishes she was still at the ironing board, pressing the skirt and blouse she planned to wear to the movies. He sat down to wait for her. "Be late to the show if you don't get a move on," he said.

"Oh, don't be silly. We've got practically a whole hour. What's the *matter* with you tonight, anyway?"

Her spike-heeled street shoes looked absurd under the ankle-length wrapper, particularly when she stooped over, splay-toed, to pull out the wall plug of the ironing cord.

"How come you quit those exercises?" he asked her.

"What exercises? What are you talking about?"

"You know," he said. "You know. Those exercises for your tipped utiyus."

"*Uterus*," she said. "You always say 'utiyus.' It's *uterus*."

"So what the hell's the difference? Why'd ya quit 'em?"

"Oh, honestly, John," she said, folding up the ironing board. "Why bring that up *now*, for heaven's sake?"

"So whaddya wanna do? Walk around with a tipped utiyus the resta ya life, or what?"

"Well," she said, "I certainly don't wanna get pregnant, if that's what you mean. May I ask where we'd be if I had to quit my job?"

He got up and began to stalk around the living room, glaring fiercely at the lamp shades, the watercolor flower paintings, and the small china figure of a seated, sleeping Mexican at whose back bloomed a dry cactus plant. He went to the bedroom, where her fresh underwear was laid out for the evening, and picked up a white brassiere containing the foam-rubber cups without which her chest was as meager as a boy's. When she came in he turned on her, waving it in her startled face, and said, "Why d'ya *wear* these goddamn things?"

She snatched the brassiere from him and backed against the doorjamb, her eyes raking him up and down. "Now, *look*," she said. "I've had *enough* of this. Are you gonna start acting decent, or not? Are we going to the movies, or not?"

And suddenly she looked so pathetic that he couldn't stand it. He grabbed his coat and pushed past her. "Do whatcha like," he said. "I'm goin' out." And he slammed out of the apartment.

It wasn't until he swung onto Queens Boulevard that his muscles began to relax and his breathing to slow down. He didn't stop at the Island Bar and Grill—it was too early for the fights anyway, and he was too upset to enjoy them. Instead, he clattered down the stairs to the subway and whipped through the turnstile, headed for Manhattan.

He had set a vague course for Times Square, but thirst overcame him at Third Avenue; he went up to the street and had two shots with a beer chaser in the first bar he came to, a bleak place with stamped-tin walls and a urine smell. On his right, at the bar, an old woman was waving her cigarette like a baton and singing "Peg o' My Heart," and on his left one middle-aged man was saying to another, "Well, my point of view is this: maybe you can argue with McCarthy's methods, but son of a bitch, you can't argue with him on principle. Am I right?"

Fallon left the place and went to another near Lexington, a chrome-and-leather place where everyone looked bluish green in the subtle light. There he stood at the bar beside two young soldiers with divisional patches on their sleeves and infantry braid on the PX caps that lay folded under their shoulder tabs. They wore no ribbons—they were only kids—but Fallon could tell they were no recruits: they knew how to wear their Eisenhower jackets, for one thing, short and skintight, and their combat boots were soft and almost black with polish. Both their heads suddenly turned to look past him, and Fallon, turning too, joined them in watching a girl in a tight tan skirt detach herself from a party at one of the tables in a shadowy corner. She brushed past them, murmuring, "Excuse me," and all three of their heads were drawn to watch her buttocks shift and settle, shift and settle until she disappeared into the ladies' room.

"Man, that's rough," the shorter of the two soldiers said, and his grin included Fallon, who grinned back.

"Oughta be a law against wavin' it around that way," the tall soldier said. "Bad for the troops."

Their accents were Western, and they both had the kind of blond, squint-eyed, country-boy faces that Fallon remembered from his old platoon. "What outfit you boys in?" he inquired. "I oughta reckanize that patch."

They told him, and he said, "Oh, yeah, sure—I remember. They were in the Seventh Army, right? Back in 'forty-four and -five?"

"Couldn't say for sure, sir," the short soldier said. "That was a good bit before our time."

"Where the hellya get that 'sir' stuff?" Fallon demanded heartily. "I wasn't no officer. I never made better'n pfc, except for a couple weeks when they made me an acting buck sergeant, there in Germany. I was a B.A.R. man."

The short soldier looked him over. "That figures," he said. "You got the build for a B.A.R. man. That old B.A.R.'s a heavy son of a bitch."

"You're right," Fallon said. "It's heavy; but, I wanna tellya, its a damn sweet weapon in combat. Listen, what are you boys drinking? My name's Johnny Fallon, by the way."

They shook hands with him, mumbling their names, and when the girl in the tan skirt came out of the ladies' room they all turned to watch her again. This time, watching until she had settled herself at her table, they concentrated on the wobbling fullness of her blouse.

"Man," the short soldier said, "I mean, that's a pair."

"Probably ain't real," the tall one said.

"They're real, son," Fallon assured him, turning back to his beer with a man-of-the-world wink. "They're real. I can spot a paira falsies a mile away."

They had a few more rounds, talking Army, and after a while the tall soldier asked Fallon how to get to the Central Plaza, where he'd heard about the Friday night jazz; then they were all three rolling down Second Avenue in a cab, for which Fallon paid. While they stood waiting for the elevator at the Central Plaza, he worked the wedding ring off his finger and stuck it in his watch pocket.

The wide, high ballroom was jammed with young men and girls; hundreds of them sat listening or laughing around pitchers of beer; another hundred danced wildly in a cleared space between banks of tables. On the bandstand, far away, a sweating group of colored and white musicians bore down, their horns gleaming in the smoky light.

Fallon, to whom all jazz sounded the same, took on the look of a connoisseur as he slouched in the doorway, his face tense and glazed under the squeal of clarinets, his gas-blue trousers quivering with the slight, rhythmic dip of his knees and his fingers snapping loosely to the beat of the drums. But it wasn't music that possessed him as he steered the soldiers to a table next to three girls, nor was it music that made him get up, as soon as the band played something slow enough, and ask the best-looking of the three to dance. She was tall and well-built, a black-haired Italian girl with a faint shine of sweat on her brow, and as she walked ahead of him toward the dance floor, threading her way between the tables, he reveled in the slow grace of her twisting hips and floating skirt. In his exultant, beer-blurred mind he already knew how it would be when he took her home—how she would feel to his exploring hands in the dark privacy of the taxi, and how she would be later, undu-lant and naked, in some ultimate vague bedroom at the end of the night. And as soon as they reached the dance floor, when she turned around and lifted her arms, he crushed her tight and warm against him.

"Now, *look*," she said, arching back angrily so that the cords stood out in her damp neck. "Is that what you call *dancing*?"

He relaxed his grip, trembling, and grinned at her. "Take it easy, honey," he said. "I won't bite."

"Never mind the 'honey,' either," she said, and that was all she said until the dance was over.

But she had to stay with him, for the two soldiers had moved in on her lively, giggling girlfriends. They were all at the same table now, and for half an hour the six of them sat there in an uneasy party mood: one of the other girls (they were both small and blonde) kept shrieking with laughter at the things the short soldier was mumbling to her, and the other had the tall soldier's long arm around her neck. But Fallon's big brunette, who had reluctantly given her name as Marie, sat silent and primly straight beside him, snapping and unsnapping the clasp of the handbag in her lap. Fallon's fingers gripped the back of her chair with white-knuckled intensity, but whenever he let them slip tentatively to her shoulder she would shrug free.

"You live around here, Marie?" he asked her.

"The Bronx," she said.

"You come down here often?"

"Sometimes."

"Care for a cigarette?"

"I don't smoke."

Fallon's face was burning, the small curving vein in his right temple throbbed visibly, and sweat was sliding down his ribs. He was like a boy on his first date, paralyzed and stricken dumb by the nearness of her warm dress, by the smell of her perfume, by the way her delicate fingers worked on the handbag and the way the moisture glistened on her plump lower lip.

At the next table a young sailor stood up and bellowed something through cupped hands at the bandstand, and the cry was taken up elsewhere around the room. It sounded like "We want the saints!" but Fallon couldn't make sense of it. At least it gave him an opening. "What's that they're yellin'?" he asked her.

"The Saints," she told him, meeting his eyes just long enough to impart the information. "They wanna hear 'The Saints.' "

"Oh."

After that they stopped talking altogether for a long time until Marie made a face of impatience at the nearest of her girlfriends. "Let's go, hey," she said. "C'mon. I wanna go home."

"Aw, *Marie*," the other girl said, flushed with beer and flirtation (she was wearing the short soldier's overseas cap now). "Don't be such a stupid." Then, seeing Fallon's tortured face, she tried to help him out. "Are you in the Army too?" she asked brightly, leaning toward him across the table.

"Me?" Fallon said, startled. "No, I—I used to be, though. I been outa the Army for quite a while now."

"Oh, yeah?"

"He used to be a B.A.R. man," the short soldier told her.

"Oh, yeah?"

"We want 'The Saints'!" "We want 'The Saints'!" They were yelling it from all corners of the enormous room now, with greater and greater urgency.

"C'mon, hey," Marie said again to her girlfriend. "Let's go, I'm tired."

"So *go* then," the girl in the soldier's hat said crossly. "*Go* if you want to, Marie. Can'tcha go home by yourself?"

"No, wait, listen—" Fallon sprang to his feet. "Don't go yet, Marie—I'll tell ya what. I'll go get some more beer, okay?" And he bolted from the table before she could refuse.

"No more for me," she called after him, but he was already three tables away, walking fast toward the little ell of the room where the bar was. "Bitch," he was whispering. "Bitch. Bitch." And the images that tortured him now, while he stood in line at the makeshift bar, were intensified by rage: there would be struggling limbs and torn clothes in the taxi; there would be blind force in the bedroom, and stifled cries of pain that would turn to whimpering and finally to spastic moans of lust. Oh, he'd loosen her up! He'd loosen her up!

"C'mon, c'mon," he said to the men who were fumbling with pitchers and beer spigots and wet dollar bills behind the bar.

"We—want—'The Saints'!" "We—want—'The Saints'!" The chant in the ballroom reached its climax. Then, after the drums built up a relentless, brutal rhythm that grew all but intolerable until it ended in a cymbal smash and gave way to the blare of the brass section, the crowd went wild. It took some seconds for Fallon to realize, getting his pitcher of beer at last and turning away from the bar, that the band was playing "When the Saints Go Marching In."

The place was a madhouse. Girls screamed and boys stood yelling on chairs, waving their arms; glasses were smashed and chairs sent spinning, and four policemen stood alert along the walls, ready for a riot as the band rode it out.

> When the saints
> Go marching in
> Oh, when the saints go marching in . . .

Fallon moved in jostled bewilderment through the noise, trying to find his party. He found their table, but couldn't be sure it was theirs—it was empty except for a crumpled cigarette package and a wet stain of beer, and one of its chairs lay overturned on the floor. He thought he saw Marie among the frantic dancers, but it turned out to be another big brunette in the same kind of dress. Then he thought he saw the short soldier gesturing wildly across the room, and made his way over to him, but it was another soldier with a country-boy face. Fallon turned around and around, sweating, looking everywhere in the dizzy crowd. Then a boy in a damp pink shirt reeled heavily against his elbow and the beer spilled in a cold rush on his hand and sleeve, and that was when he realized they were gone. They had ditched him.

He was out on the street and walking, fast and hard on his steel-capped heels, and the night traffic noises were appallingly quiet after the bedlam of shouting and jazz. He walked with no idea of direction and no sense of time, aware of nothing beyond the pound of his heels, the thrust and pull of his muscles, the quavering intake and sharp outward rush of his breath and the pump of his blood.

He didn't know if ten minutes or an hour passed, twenty blocks or five, before he had to slow down and stop on the fringe of a small crowd that clustered around a lighted doorway where policemen were waving the people on.

"Keep moving," one of the policemen was saying. "Move along, please. Keep moving."

But Fallon, like most of the others, stood still. It was the door-way to some kind of lecture hall—he could tell that by the bulletin board that was just visible under the yellow lights inside, and by the flight of marble stairs that led up to what must have been an auditorium. But what caught most of his attention was the picket line: three men about his own age, their eyes agleam with righteousness, wearing the blue-and-gold overseas caps of some veterans' organization and carrying placards that said:

SMOKE OUT THIS FIFTH AMENDMENT COMMIE
PROF. MITCHELL GO BACK TO RUSSIA
AMERICA'S FIGHTING SONS PROTEST MITCHELL

"Move along," the police were saying. "Keep moving."

"Civil rights, my ass," said a flat muttering voice at Fallon's elbow. "They oughta lock this Mitchell up. You read what he said in the Senate hearing?" And Fallon, nodding, recalled a fragile, snobbish face in a number of newspaper pictures.

"Look at there—" the muttering voice said. "Here they come. They're comin' out now."

And they were. Down the marble steps they came, past the bulletin board and out onto the sidewalk: men in raincoats and greasy tweeds, petulant, Greenwich Village-looking girls in tight pants, a few Negroes, a few very clean, self-conscious college boys.

The pickets were backed off and standing still now, hold-ing their placards high with one hand and curving the other around their mouths to call, "Boo-oo! Boo-oo!"

The crowd picked it up: "Boo-oo!" "Boo-oo!" And some-body called, "Go back to Russia!"

"Keep moving," the cops were saying. "Move along, now. Keep moving."

"There he is," said the muttering voice. "There he comes now—that's Mitchell."

And Fallon saw him: a tall, slight man in a cheap double-breasted suit that was too big for him, carrying a briefcase and flanked by two plain women in glasses. There was the snobbish face of the newspaper pictures, turning slowly from side to side now, with a serene, superior smile that seemed to be saying, to everyone it met: *Oh, you poor fool. You poor fool.*

"*KILL that bastard!*"

Not until several people whirled to look at him did Fallon realize he was yelling; then all he knew was that he had to yell again and again until his voice broke, like a child in tears: "*KILL that bastard! KILL 'im! KILL 'im!*"

In four bucking, lunging strides he was through to the front of the crowd; then one of the pickets dropped his placard and rushed him, saying, "Easy, Mac! Take it *easy*—" But Fallon threw him off, grappled with another man and wrenched free again, got both hands on Mitchell's coat front and tore him down like a crumpled puppet. He saw Mitchell's face recoil in wet-mouthed terror on the sidewalk, and the last thing he knew, as the cop's blue arm swung high over his head, was a sense of absolute fulfillment and relief.

A REALLY GOOD JAZZ PIANO

BECAUSE OF THE midnight noise on both ends of the line there was some confusion at Harry's New York Bar when the call came through. All the bartender could tell at first was that it was a long-distance call from Cannes, evidently from some kind of night-club, and the operator's frantic voice made it sound like an emergency. Then at last, by plugging his free ear and shouting questions into the phone, he learned that it was only Ken Platt, calling up to have an aimless chat with his friend Carson Wyler, and this made him shake his head in exasperation as he set the phone on the bar beside Carson's glass of Pernod.

"Here," he said. "It's for you, for God's sake. It's your buddy." Like a number of other Paris bartenders he knew them both pretty well: Carson was the handsome one, the one with the slim, witty face and the English-sounding accent; Ken was the fat one who laughed all the time and tagged along. They were both three years out of Yale and trying to get all the fun they could out of living in Europe.

"Carson?" said Ken's eager voice, vibrating painfully in the receiver. "This is Ken—I knew I'd find you there. Listen, when you coming down, anyway?"

Carson puckered his well-shaped brow at the phone. "You know when I'm coming down," he said. "I wired you, I'm coming down Saturday. What's the matter with you?"

"Hell, nothing's the matter with me—maybe a little drunk is all. No, but listen, what I really called up about, there's a man here named Sid plays a really good jazz piano, and I want you to hear him. He's a friend of mine. Listen, wait a minute, I'll get the phone over close so you can hear. Listen to this, now. Wait a minute."

There were some blurred scraping sounds and the sound of Ken laughing and somebody else laughing, and then the piano came through. It sounded tinny in the telephone, but Carson could tell it was good. It was "Sweet Lorraine," done in a rich traditional style with nothing commercial about it, and this surprised him, for Ken was ordinarily a poor judge of music. After a minute he handed the phone to a stranger he had been drinking with, a farm machinery salesman from Philadelphia. "Listen to this," he said. "This is first-rate."

The farm machinery salesman held his ear to the phone with a puzzled look. "What is it?"

" 'Sweet Lorraine.' "

"No, but I mean what's the deal? Where's it coming from?"

"Cannes. Somebody Ken turned up down there. You've met Ken, haven't you?"

"No, I haven't," the salesman said, frowning into the phone. "Here, it's stopped now and somebody's talking. You better take it."

"Hello? Hello?" Ken's voice was saying. "Carson?"

"Yes, Ken. I'm right here."

"Where'd you go? Who was that other guy?"

"That was a gentleman from Philadelphia named—" he looked up questioningly.

"Baldinger," said the salesman, straightening his coat.

"Named Mr. Baldinger. He's here at the bar with me."

"Oh. Well listen, how'd you like Sid's playing?"

"Fine, Ken. Tell him I said it was first-rate."

"You want to talk to him? He's right here, wait a minute."

There were some more obscure sounds and then a deep middle-aged voice said, "Hello there."

"How do you do, Sid. My name's Carson Wyler, and I enjoyed your playing very much."

"Well," the voice said. "Thank you, thank you a lot. I appreciate it." It could have been either a colored or a white man's voice, but Carson assumed he was colored, mostly from the slight edge of self-consciousness or pride in the way Ken had said, "He's a friend of mine."

"I'm coming down to Cannes this weekend, Sid," Carson said, "and I'll be looking forward to—"

But Sid had evidently given back the phone, for Ken's voice cut in. "Carson?"

"What?"

"Listen, what time you coming Saturday? I mean what train and everything?" They had originally planned to go to Cannes together, but Carson had become involved with a girl in Paris, and Ken had gone on alone, with the understanding that Carson would join him in a week. Now it had been nearly a month.

"I don't know the exact train," Carson said, with some impatience. "It doesn't matter, does it? I'll see you at the hotel sometime Saturday."

"Okay. Oh and wait, listen, the other reason I called, I want to sponsor Sid here for the IBF, okay?"

"Right. Good idea. Put him back on." And while he was waiting he got out his fountain pen and asked the bartender for the IBF membership book.

"Hello again," Sid's voice said. "What's this I'm supposed to be joining here?"

"The IBF," Carson said. "That stands for International Bar Flies, something they started here at Harry's back in—I don't know. Long time ago. Kind of a club."

"Very good," Sid said, chuckling.

"Now, what it amounts to is this," Carson began, and even the bartender, for whom the IBF was a bore and a nuisance, had to smile with pleasure at the serious, painstaking way he told about it—how each member received a lapel button bearing the insignia of a fly, together with a printed booklet that contained the club rules and a listing of all other IBF bars in the world; how the cardinal rule was that when two members met they were expected to greet one another by brushing the fingers of their right hands on each other's shoulders and saying, "*Bzz-z-z, bzz-z-z!*"

This was one of Carson's special talents, the ability to find and convey an unashamed enjoyment in trivial things. Many people could not have described the IBF to a jazz musician without breaking off in an apologetic laugh to explain that it was, of course, a sort of sad little game for lonely tourists, a square's thing really, and that its very lack of sophistication was what made it fun; Carson told it straight. In much the same way he had once made it fashionable among some of the more literary undergraduates at Yale to spend Sunday mornings respectfully absorbed in the funny papers of the *New York Mirror*; more recently the same trait had rapidly endeared him to many chance acquaintances, notably to his current girl, the young Swedish art student for whom he had stayed in Paris. "You have beautiful taste in everything," she had told him on their first memorable night together. "You have a truly educated, truly original mind."

"Got that?" he said into the phone, and paused to sip his Pernod. "Right. Now if you'll give me your full name and address, Sid, I'll get everything organized on this end." Sid spelled it out and Carson lettered it carefully into the membership book, with his own name and Ken's as cosponsors, while Mr. Baldinger watched. When they were finished Ken's voice came back to say a reluctant goodbye, and they hung up.

"That must've been a pretty expensive telephone call," Mr. Baldinger said, impressed.

"You're right," Carson said. "I guess it was."

"What's the deal on this membership book, anyway? All this barfly business?"

"Oh, aren't you a member, Mr. Baldinger? I thought you were a member. Here, I'll sponsor you, if you like."

Mr. Baldinger got what he later described as an enormous kick out of it: far into the early morning he was still sidling up to everyone at the bar, one after another, and buzzing them.

Carson didn't get to Cannes on Saturday, for it took him longer than he'd planned to conclude his affair with the Swedish girl. He had expected a tearful scene, or at least a brave exchange of tender promises and smiles, but instead she was surprisingly casual about his leaving—even abstracted, as if already concentrating on her next truly educated, truly original mind— and this forced him into several uneasy delays that accomplished nothing except to fill her with impatience and him with a sense of being dispossessed. He didn't get to Cannes until the following Tuesday afternoon, after further telephone talks with Ken, and then, when he eased himself onto the station platform, stiff and sour with hangover, he was damned if he knew why he'd come at all. The sun assaulted him, burning deep into his gritty scalp and raising a quick sweat inside his rumpled suit; it struck blinding glints off the chromework of parked cars and motor scooters and made sickly blue vapors of exhaust rise up against pink buildings; it played garishly among the swarm of tourists who jostled him, showing him all their pores, all the tension of their store-new sports clothes, their clutched suitcases and slung cameras, all the anxiety of their smiling, shouting mouths. Cannes would be like any other resort town in the world, all hurry and disappointment, and why hadn't he stayed where he belonged, in a high cool room with a long-legged girl? Why the hell had he let himself be coaxed and wheedled into coming here?

But then he saw Ken's happy face bobbing in the crowd— "Carson!"—and there he came, running in his overgrown fat boy's thigh-chafing way, clumsy with welcome. "Taxi's over here, take your bag—boy, do you look beat! Get you a shower and a drink first, okay? How the hell are you?"

And riding light on the taxi cushions as they swung onto the Croisette, with its spectacular blaze of blue and gold and its blood-quickening rush of sea air, Carson began to relax. Look at the girls! There were acres of them; and besides, it was good to be with old Ken again. It was easy to see, now, that the thing in Paris could only have gotten worse if he'd stayed. He had left just in time.

Ken couldn't stop talking. Pacing in and out of the bathroom while Carson took his shower, jingling a pocketful of coins, he talked in the laughing, full-throated joy of a man who has gone for weeks without hearing his own voice. The truth was that Ken never really had a good time away from Carson. They were each other's best friends, but it had never been an equal friendship, and they both knew it. At Yale Ken would probably have been left out of everything if it hadn't been for his status as Carson's dull but inseparable companion, and this was a pattern that nothing in Europe had changed. What *was* it about Ken that put people off? Carson had pondered this question for years. Was it just that he was fat and physically awkward, or that he could be strident and silly in his eagerness to be liked? But weren't these essentially likable qualities? No, Carson guessed the closest he could come to a real explanation was the fact that when Ken smiled his upper lip slid back to reveal a small moist inner lip that trembled against his gum. Many people with this kind of mouth may find it no great handicap—Carson was willing to admit that—but it did seem to be the thing everyone remembered most vividly about Ken Platt, whatever more substantial-sounding reasons one might give for avoiding him; in any case it was what Carson himself was always most aware of, in moments of irritation. Right now, for example, in the simple business of trying to dry himself and comb his hair and put on fresh clothes, this wide, moving, double-lipped smile kept getting in his way. It was everywhere, blocking his reach for the towel rack, hovering too close over his jumbled suitcase, swimming in the mirror to eclipse the tying of his tie, until Carson had to clamp his jaws tight to keep from yelling, "All *right*, Ken—shut *up* now!"

But a few minutes later they were able to compose themselves in the shaded silence of the hotel bar. The bartender was peeling a lemon, neatly pinching and pulling back a strip of its bright flesh between thumb and knife blade, and the fine citric smell of it, combining with the scent of gin in the faint smoke of crushed ice, gave flavor to a full restoration of their ease. A couple of cold martinis drowned the last of Carson's pique, and by the time they were out of the place and swinging down the sidewalk on their way to dinner he felt strong again with a sense of the old camaraderie, the familiar, buoyant wealth of Ken's admiration. It was a feeling touched with sadness too, for Ken would soon have to go back to the States. His father in Denver, the author of sarcastic weekly letters on business stationery, was holding open a junior partnership for him, and Ken, having long since completed the Sorbonne courses that were his ostensible reason for coming to France, had no further excuse for staying. Carson, luckier in this as in everything else, had no need of an excuse: he had an adequate private income and no family ties; he could afford to browse around Europe for years, if he felt like it, looking for things that pleased him.

"You're still white as a sheet," he told Ken across their restaurant table. "Haven't you been going to the beach?"

"Sure." Ken looked quickly at his plate. "I've been to the

beach a few times. The weather hasn't been too good for it lately, is all."

But Carson guessed the real reason, that Ken was embarrassed to display his body, so he changed the subject. "Oh, by the way," he said. "I brought along the IBF stuff, for that piano player friend of yours."

"Oh, swell." Ken looked up in genuine relief. "I'll take you over there soon as we're finished eating, okay?" And as if to hurry this prospect along he forked a dripping load of salad into his mouth and tore off too big a bite of bread to chew with it, using the remaining stump of bread to mop at the oil and vinegar in his plate. "You'll like him, Carson," he said soberly around his chewing. "He's a great guy. I really admire him a lot." He swallowed with effort and hurried on: "I mean hell, with talent like that he could go back to the States tomorrow and make a fortune, but he likes it here. One thing, of course, he's got a girl here, this really lovely French girl, and I guess he couldn't very well take her back with him—no, but really, it's more than that. People accept him here. As an artist, I mean, as well as a man. Nobody condescends to him, nobody tries to interfere with his music, and that's all he wants out of life. Oh, I mean he doesn't tell you all this—probably be a bore if he did—it's just a thing you sense about him. Comes out in everything he says, his whole mental attitude." He popped the soaked bread into his mouth and chewed it with authority. "I mean the guy's got *authentic* integrity," he said. "Wonderful thing."

"Did sound like a damn good piano," Carson said, reaching for the wine bottle, "what little I heard of it."

"Wait'll you really hear it, though. Wait'll he really gets going."

They both enjoyed the fact that this was Ken's discovery. Always before it had been Carson who led the way, who found the girls and learned the idioms and knew how best to spend each hour; it was Carson who had tracked down all the really colorful places in Paris where you never saw Americans, and who then, just when Ken was learning to find places of his own, had paradoxically made Harry's Bar become the most colorful place of all. Through all this, Ken had been glad enough to follow, shaking his grateful head in wonderment, but it was no small thing to have turned up an incorruptible jazz talent in the back streets of a foreign city, all alone. It proved that Ken's dependence could be less than total after all, and this reflected credit on them both.

The place where Sid played was more of an expensive bar than a nightclub, a small carpeted basement several streets back from the sea. It was still early, and they found him having a drink alone at the bar.

"Well," he said when he saw Ken. "Hello there." He was stocky and well-tailored, a very dark Negro with a pleasant smile full of strong white teeth.

"Sid, I'd like you to meet Carson Wyler. You talked to him on the phone that time, remember?"

"Oh yes," Sid said, shaking hands. "Oh yes. Very pleased to meet you, Carson. What're you gentlemen drinking?"

They made a little ceremony of buttoning the IBF insignia into the lapel of Sid's tan gabardine, of buzzing his shoulder and offering the shoulders of their own identical seersucker jackets to be buzzed in turn. "Well, this is fine," Sid said, chuckling and leafing through the booklet. "Very good." Then he put the booklet in his pocket, finished his drink and slid off the bar stool. "And now if you'll excuse me, I got to go to work."

"Not much of an audience yet," Ken said.

Sid shrugged. "Place like this, I'd just as soon have it that way. You get a big crowd, you always get some square asking for 'Deep in the Heart of Texas,' or some damn thing."

Ken laughed and winked at Carson, and they both turned to watch Sid take his place at the piano, which stood on a low spot-lighted dais across the room. He fingered the keys idly for a while to make stray phrases and chords, a craftsman fondling his tools, and then he settled down. The compelling beat emerged, and out of it the climb and waver of the melody, an arrangement of "Baby, Won't You Please Come Home."

They stayed for hours, listening to Sid play and buying him drinks whenever he took a break, to the obvious envy of other customers. Sid's girl came in, tall and brown-haired, with a bright, startled-looking face that was almost beautiful, and Ken introduced her with a small uncontrollable flourish: "This is Jaqueline." She whispered something about not speaking English very well, and when it was time for Sid's next break—the place was filling now and there was considerable applause when he finished—the four of them took a table together.

Ken let Carson do most of the talking now; he was more than content just to sit there, smiling around this tableful of friends with all the serenity of a well-fed young priest. It was the happiest evening of his life in Europe, to a degree that even Carson would never have guessed. In the space of a few hours it filled all the emptiness of his past month, the time that had begun with Carson's saying, "Go, then. Can't you go to Cannes by yourself?" It atoned for all the hot miles walked up and down the Croisette on blistered feet to peek like a fool at girls who lay incredibly near naked in the sand; for the cramped, boring bus rides to Nice and Monte Carlo and St. Paul-de-Vence; for the day he had paid a sinister druggist three times too much for a pair of sunglasses only to find, on catching sight of his own image in the gleam of a passing shop window, that they made him look like a great blind fish; for the terrible daily, nightly sense of being young and rich and free on the Riviera—the Riviera!—and of having nothing to do. Once in the first week he had gone with a prostitute whose canny smile, whose shrill insistence on a high price and whose facial flicker of distaste at the sight of his body had frightened him into an agony of impotence; most other nights he had gotten drunk or sick from bar to bar, afraid of prostitutes and of rebuffs from other girls, afraid even of striking up conversations with men lest they mistake him for a fairy. He had spent a whole afternoon in the French equivalent of a dime store, feigning a shopper's interest in padlocks and shaving cream and cheap tin toys, moving through the bright stale air of the place with a throatful of longing for home. Five nights in a row he had hidden himself in the protective darkness of American movies, just as he'd done years ago in Denver to get away from boys who called him Lard-Ass Platt, and after the last of these entertainments, back in the hotel with the taste of chocolate creams still cloying his mouth, he had cried himself to sleep. But all this was dissolving now under the fine reckless grace of Sid's piano, under the spell of Carson's intelligent smile and the way Carson raised his hands to clap each time the music stopped.

Sometime after midnight, when everyone but Sid had drunk too much, Carson asked him how long he had been away from the States. "Since the war," he said. "I came over in the Army and I never did go back."

Ken, coated with a film of sweat and happiness, thrust his glass high in the air for a toast. "And by God, here's hoping you never have to, Sid."

"Why is that, 'have to'?" Jaqueline said. Her face looked harsh and sober in the dim light. "Why do you say that?"

Ken blinked at her. "Well, I just mean—you know—that he never has to sell out, or anything. He never would, of course."

"What does this mean, 'sell out'?" There was an uneasy silence until Sid laughed in his deep, rumbling way. "Take it easy, honey," he said, and turned to Ken. "We don't look at it that way, you see. Matter of fact, I'm working on angles all the time to get back to the States, make some money there. We both feel that way about it."

"Well, but you're doing all right here, aren't you?" Ken said, almost pleading with him. "You're making enough money and everything, aren't you?"

Sid smiled patiently. "I don't mean a job like this, though, you see. I mean real money."

"You know who is Murray Diamond?" Jaqueline inquired, holding her eyebrows high. "The owner of nightclubs in Las Vegas?"

But Sid was shaking his head and laughing. "Honey, wait a minute—I keep telling you, that's nothing to count on. Murray Diamond happened to be in here the other night, you see," he explained. "Didn't have much time, but he said he'd try to drop around again some night this week. Be a big break for me. 'Course, like I say, that's nothing to count on."

"Well but *Jesus*, Sid—" Ken shook his head in bafflement; then, letting his face tighten into a look of outrage, he thumped the table with a bouncing fist. "Why prostitute yourself?" he demanded. "I mean damn it, you *know* they'll make you prostitute yourself in the States!"

Sid was still smiling, but his eyes had narrowed slightly. "I guess it's all in the way you look at it," he said.

And the worst part of it, for Ken, was that Carson came so quickly to his rescue. "Oh, I'm sure Ken doesn't mean that the way it *sounds*," he said, and while Ken was babbling apologies of his own ("No, of course not, all I meant was—*you* know . . .") he went on to say other things, light, nimble things that only Carson could say, until the awkwardness was gone. When the time came to say goodnight there were handshakes and smiles and promises to see each other soon.

But the minute they were out on the street, Carson turned on Ken. "Why did you have to get so damned sophomoric about that? Couldn't you see how embarrassing it was?"

"I know," Ken said, hurrying to keep pace with Carson's long legs, "I know. But hell, I *was* disappointed in him, Carson. The point is I never heard him *talk* like that before." What he omitted here, of course, was that he had never really heard him talk at all except in the one shy conversation that had led to the calling-up of Harry's Bar that other night, after which Ken had fled back to the hotel in fear of over-staying his welcome.

"Well but even so," Carson said. "Don't you think it's the man's own business what he wants to do with his life?"

"Okay," Ken said, "*okay*. I *told* him I was sorry, didn't I?" He felt so humble now that it took him some minutes to realize that, in a sense, he hadn't come off too badly. After all, Carson's only triumph tonight had been that of the diplomat, the soother of feelings; it was he, Ken, who had done the more dramatic thing. Sophomoric or not, impulsive or not, wasn't there a certain dignity in having spoken his mind that way? Now, licking his lips and glancing at Carson's profile as they walked, he squared his shoulders and tried to make his walk less of a waddle and more of a headlong, manly stride. "It's just that I can't help how I feel, that's all," he said with conviction. "When I'm disappointed in a person I show it, that's all."

"All right. Let's forget it."

And Ken was almost sure, though he hardly dared believe it, that he could detect a grudging respect in Carson's voice.

*

Everything went wrong the next day. The fading light of after-noon found the two of them slumped and staring in a bleak workingman's café near the railroad station, barely speaking to each other. It was a day that had started out unusually well too—that was the trouble.

They had slept till noon and gone to the beach after lunch, for Ken didn't mind the beach when he wasn't alone, and before long they had picked up two American girls in the easy, graceful way that Carson always managed such things. One minute the girls were sullen strangers, wiping scented oil on their bodies and looking as if any intrusion would mean a call for the police, the next minute they were weak with laughter at the things Carson was saying, moving aside their bottles and their zippered blue TWA satchels to make room for unexpected guests. There was a tall one for Carson with long firm thighs, intelligent eyes and a way of tossing back her hair that gave her a look of real beauty, and a small one for Ken—a cute, freckled good-sport of a girl whose every cheerful glance and gesture showed she was used to taking second best. Ken, bellying deep into the sand with his chin on two stacked fists, smiling up very close to her warm legs, felt almost none of the conversational tension that normally hampered him at times like this. Even when Carson and the tall girl got up to run splashing into the water he was able to hold her interest: she said several times that the Sorbonne "must have been fascinating," and she sympathized with his having to go back to Denver, though she said it was "probably the best thing."

"And your friend's just going to stay over here indefinitely, then?" she asked. "Is it really true what he said? I mean that he isn't studying or working or anything? Just sort of floating around?"

"Well—yeah, that's right." Ken tried a squinty smile like Carson's own. "Why?"

"It's interesting, that's all. I don't think I've ever met a person like that before."

That was when Ken began to realize what the laughter and the scanty French bathing suits had disguised about these girls, that they were girls of a kind neither he nor Carson had dealt with for a long time—suburban, middle-class girls who had duti-fully won their parents' blessing for this guided tour; girls who said "golly Moses," whose campus-shop clothes and hockey-field strides would have instantly betrayed them on the street. They were the very kind of girls who had gathered at the punch bowl to murmur "Ugh!" at the way he looked in his first tuxedo, whose ignorant, maddeningly bland little stares of rejection had poisoned all his aching years in Denver and New Haven. They were squares. And the remarkable thing was that he felt so good. Rolling his weight to one elbow, clutching up slow, hot handfuls of sand and emptying them, again and again, he found his flow of words coming quick and smooth:

". . . no, really, there's a lot to see in Paris; shame you couldn't spend more time there; actually most of the places I like best are more or less off the beaten track; of course I was lucky in having a fairly good grasp of the language, and then I met so many congenial . . ."

He was holding his own; he was making out. He hardly even noticed when Carson and the tall girl came trotting back from their swim, as lithe and handsome as a couple in a travel poster, to drop beside them in a bustle of towels and cigarettes and shuddering jokes about how cold the water was. His only mounting worry was that Carson, who must by now have made his own discovery about these girls, would decide they weren't worth bothering with. But a single glance at Carson's subtly smiling, talking face reassured him: sitting tense at the tall girl's feet while she stood to towel her back in a way that made her breasts sway delightfully, Carson was plainly determined to follow through. "Look," he said. "Why don't we all have dinner together? Then afterwards we might—"

Both girls began chattering their regrets: they were afraid not, thanks anyway, they were meeting friends at the hotel for dinner and actually ought to be starting back now, much as they hated to—"God, look at the time!" And they really did sound sorry, so sorry that Ken, gathering all his courage, reached out and held the warm, fine-boned hand that swung at the small girl's thigh as the four of them plodded back toward the bathhouses. She even squeezed his heavy fingers, and smiled at him.

"Some other night, then?" Carson was saying. "Before you leave?"

"Well, actually," the tall girl said, "our evenings do seem to be pretty well booked up. Probably run into you on the beach again though. It's been fun."

"Goddamn little snot-nosed New Rochelle bitch," Carson said when they were alone in the men's bathhouse.

"*Sh-h-h!* Keep your *voice* down, Carson. They *can* hear you in there."

"Oh, don't be an idiot." Carson flung his trunks on the duck-boards with a sandy slap. "I hope they do hear me—what the hell's the matter with you?" He looked at Ken as if he hated him, "Pair of goddamn teasing little professional virgins. *Christ*, why didn't I stay in Paris?"

And now here they were, Carson glowering, Ken sulking at the sunset through flyspecked windows while a pushing, garlic-smelling bunch of laborers laughed and shouted over the pinball machine. They went on drinking until long past the dinner hour; then they ate a late, unpleasant meal together in a restaurant where the wine was corky and there was too much grease on the fried potatoes. When the messy plates were cleared away Carson lit a cigarette. "What do you want to do tonight?" he said.

There was a faint shine of grease around Ken's mouth and cheeks. "I don't know," he said. "Lot of good places to go, I guess."

"I suppose it would offend your artistic sensibilities to go and hear Sid's piano again?"

Ken gave him a weak, rather testy smile. "You still harping on that?" he said. "Sure I'd like to go."

"Even though he may prostitute himself?"

"Why don't you lay off that, Carson?"

They could hear the piano from the street, even before they walked into the square of light that poured up from the doorway of Sid's place. On the stairs the sound of it grew stronger and richer, mixed now with the sound of a man's hoarse singing, but only when they were down in the room, squinting through the blue smoke, did they realize the singer was Sid himself. Eyes half closed, head turned to smile along his shoulder into the crowd, he was singing as he swayed and worked at the keys.

"Man, she got a pair of eyes. . . ."

The blue spotlight struck winking stars in the moisture of his
teeth and the faint thread of sweat that striped his temple.

> "I mean they're brighter than the summer skies
> And when you see them you gunna realize
> Just why I love my sweet Lorraine. . . ."

"Damn place is packed," Carson said. There were no vacancies at the bar, but they stood uncertainly near it for a while,
watching Sid perform, until Carson found that one of the girls
on the bar stools directly behind him was Jaqueline. "Oh," he
said. "Hi. Pretty good crowd tonight."

She smiled and nodded and then craned past him to watch Sid.

"I didn't know he sang too," Carson said. "This something
new?"

Her smile gave way to an impatient little frown and she put a
forefinger against her lips. Rebuffed, he turned back and moved
heavily from one foot to the other. Then he nudged Ken. "You
want to go or stay? If you want to stay let's at least sit down."

"*Sh-h-h!*" Several people turned in their chairs to frown at
him. "*Sh-h-h!*"

"Come on, then," he said, and he led Ken sidling and stumbling through the ranks of listeners to the only vacant table in
the room, a small one down in front, too close to the music and
wet with spilled drink, that had been pushed aside to make room
for larger parties. Settled there, they could see now that Sid
wasn't looking into the crowd at large. He was singing directly
to a bored-looking couple in evening clothes who sat a few
tables away, a silver-blonde girl who could have been a movie
starlet and a small, chubby bald man with a deep tan, a man so
obviously Murray Diamond that a casting director might have
sent him here to play the part. Sometimes Sid's large eyes would
stray to other parts of the room or to the smoke-hung ceiling,
but they seemed to come into focus only when he looked at
these two people. Even when the song ended and the piano
took off alone on a long, intricate variation, even then he kept

glancing up to see if they were watching. When he finished, to a small thunderclap of applause, the bald man lifted his face, closed it around an amber cigarette holder and clapped his hands a few times.

"Very nice, Sam," he said.

"My name's Sid, Mr. Diamond," Sid said, "but I thank you a lot just the same. Glad y'enjoyed it, sir." He was leaning back, grinning along his shoulder while his fingers toyed with the keys. "Anything special you'd like to hear, Mr. Diamond? Something old-time? Some more of that real old Dixieland? Maybe a little boogie, maybe something a little on the sweet side, what we call a commercial number? Got all kind of tunes here, waitin' to be played."

"Anything at all, uh, Sid," Murray Diamond said, and then the blonde leaned close and whispered something in his ear. "How about 'Stardust,' there, Sid?" he said. "Can you play 'Stardust'?"

"Well, now, Mr. Diamond. If I couldn't play 'Stardust' I don't guess I'd be in business very long, France or any other country." His grin turned into a deep false laugh and his hands slid into the opening chords of the song.

That was when Carson made his first friendly gesture in hours, sending a warm blush of gratitude into Ken's face. He hitched his chair up close to Ken's and began to speak in a voice so soft that no one could have accused him of making a disturbance. "You know something?" he said. "This is disgusting. My God, I don't care if he wants to go to Las Vegas. I don't even care if he wants to suck *around* for it. This is something else. This is something that turns my stomach." He paused, frowning at the floor, and Ken watched the small wormlike vein moving in his temple. "Putting on this phony accent," Carson said. "All this big phony Uncle Remus routine." And then he went into a little popeyed, head-tossing, hissing parody of Sid. "Yassuh, Mr. Dahmon' suh. Wudg'all lak t'heah, Mr. Dahmon' suh? Got awl *kine* a toons heah, jes' waitin' to played, and yok, yok, yok, and shet ma mouf!" He finished his drink and set the glass down hard. "You know damn well he doesn't have to talk that way. You know damn well he's a perfectly bright, educated guy. My God, on the phone I couldn't even tell he was colored."

"Well yeah," Ken said. "It is sort of depressing."

"Depressing? It's degrading." Carson curled his lip. "It's degenerate."

"I know," Ken said. "I guess that may be partly what I meant about prostituting himself."

"You were certainly right, then. This is damn near enough to make you lose faith in the Negro race."

Being told he was right was always a tonic to Ken, and it was uncommonly bracing after a day like this. He knocked back his drink, straightened his spine and wiped the light mustache of sweat from his upper lip, pressing his mouth into a soft frown to show that his faith, too, in the Negro race was badly shaken. "Boy," he said. "I sure had him figured wrong."

"No," Carson assured him, "you couldn't have known."

"Listen, let's go, then, Carson. The hell with him." And Ken's mind was already full of plans: they would stroll in the cool of the Croisette for a long, serious talk on the meaning of integrity, on how rare it was and how easily counterfeited, how its pursuit was the only struggle worthy of a man's life, until all the discord of the day was erased.

But Carson moved his chair back, smiling and frowning at the same time. "Go?" he said. "What's the matter with you? Don't you want to stay and watch the spectacle? I do. Doesn't it hold a certain horrible fascination for you?" He held up his glass and signaled for two more cognacs.

"Stardust" came to a graceful conclusion and Sid stood up, bathed in applause, to take his break. He loomed directly over their table as he came forward and stepped down off the dais, his big face shining with sweat; he brushed past them, looking toward Diamond's table, and paused there to say, "Thank you, sir," though Diamond hadn't spoken to him, before he made his way back to the bar.

"I suppose he thinks he didn't see us," Carson said.

"Probably just as well," Ken said. "I wouldn't know what to say to him."

"Wouldn't you? I think I would."

The room was stifling, and Ken's cognac had taken on a faintly repellent look and smell in his hand. He loosened his collar and tie with moist fingers. "Come on, Carson," he said. "Let's get out of here. Let's get some air."

Carson ignored him, watching what went on at the bar. Sid drank something Jaqueline offered and then disappeared into the men's room. When he came out a few minutes later, his face dried and composed, Carson turned back and studied his glass. "Here he comes. I think we're going to get the big hello, now, for Diamond's benefit. Watch."

An instant later Sid's fingers brushed the cloth of Carson's shoulder. "*Bzz-z-z, bzz-z-z!*" he said. "How're you tonight?"

Very slowly, Carson turned his head. With heavy eyelids he met Sid's smile for a split second, the way a man might look at a waiter who had accidentally touched him. Then he turned back to his drink.

"Oh-oh," Sid said. "Maybe I didn't do that right. Maybe I got the wrong shoulder here. I'm not too familiar with the rules and regulations yet." Murray Diamond and the blonde were watching, and Sid winked at them, thumbing out the IBF button in his lapel as he moved in sidling steps around the back of Carson's chair. "This here's a club we belong to, Mr. Diamond," he said. "Barflies club. Only trouble is, I'm not very familiar with the rules and regulations yet." He held the attention of nearly everyone in the room as he touched Carson's other shoulder. "*Bzz-z-z, bzz-z-z!*" This time Carson winced and drew his jacket away, glancing at Ken with a perplexed little shrug as if to say, Do you know what this man wants?

Ken didn't know whether to giggle or vomit; both desires were suddenly strong in him, though his face held straight. For a long time afterwards he would remember how the swabbed black plastic of the table looked between his two unmoving hands, how it seemed the only steady surface in the world.

"Say," Sid said, backing away toward the piano with a glazed smile. "What *is* this here? Some kinda conspiracy here?"

Carson allowed a heavy silence to develop. Then with an air of sudden, mild remembrance, seeming to say, Oh yes, of course, he rose and walked over to Sid, who backed up confusedly into the spotlight. Facing him, he extended one limp finger and touched him on the shoulder. "Buzz," he said. "Does that take care of it?" He turned and walked back to his seat.

Ken prayed for someone to laugh—anyone—but no one did. There was no movement in the room but the dying of Sid's smile as he looked at Carson and at Ken, the slow fleshy enclosing of his teeth and the widening of his eyes.

Murray Diamond looked at them too, briefly—a tough, tan little face—then he cleared his throat and said, "How about 'Hold Me,' there, Sid? Can you play 'Hold Me'?" And Sid sat down and began to play, looking at nothing.

With dignity, Carson nodded for the check and laid the right number of thousand- and hundred-franc notes on the saucer. It seemed to take him no time at all to get out of the place, sliding expertly between the tables and out to the stairs, but it took Ken much longer. Lurching, swaying in the smoke like a great imprisoned bear, he was caught and held by Jaqueline's eyes even before he had cleared the last of the tables. They stared relentlessly at the flabby quaver of his smile, they drilled into his back and sent him falling upstairs. And as soon as the sobering night air hit him, as soon as he saw Carson's erect white suit retreating several doors away, he knew what he wanted to do. He wanted to run up and hit him with all his strength between the shoulder blades, one great chopping blow that would drop him to the street, and then he would hit him again, or kick him—yes, kick him—and he'd say, goddamn you! goddamn you, Carson! The words were already in his mouth and he was ready to swing when Carson stopped and turned to face him under a streetlamp.

"What's the trouble, Ken?" he said. "Don't you think that was funny?"

It wasn't what he said that mattered—for a minute it seemed that nothing Carson said would ever matter again—it was that his face was stricken with the uncannily familiar look of his own heart, the very face he himself, Lard-Ass Platt, had shown all his life to others: haunted and vulnerable and terribly dependent, trying to smile, a look that said Please don't leave me alone.

Ken hung his head, either in mercy or shame. "Hell, I don't

know, Carson," he said. "Let's forget it. Let's get some coffee somewhere."

"Right." And they were together again. The only problem now was that they had started out in the wrong direction: in order to get to the Croisette they would have to walk back past the lighted doorway of Sid's place. It was like walking through fire, but they did it quickly and with what anyone would have said was perfect composure, heads up, eyes front, so that the piano only came up loud for a second or two before it diminished and died behind them under the rhythm of their heels.

OUT WITH THE OLD

BUILDING SEVEN, THE TB building, had grown aloof from the rest of Mulloy Veterans' Hospital in the five years since the war. It lay less than fifty yards from Building Six, the paraplegic building—they faced the same flagpole on the same windswept Long Island plain—but there had been no neighborliness between them since the summer of 1948, when the paraplegics got up a petition demanding that the TB's be made to stay on their own lawn. This had caused a good deal of resentment at the time ("Those paraplegic bastards think they *own* the goddamn place"), but it had long since ceased to matter very much; nor did it matter that nobody from Building Seven was allowed in the hospital canteen unless he hid his face in a sterile paper mask.

Who cared? After all, Building Seven was different. The hundred-odd patients of its three yellow wards had nearly all escaped the place at least once or twice over the years, and had every hope of escaping again, for good, as soon as their X rays cleared up or as soon as they had recovered from various kinds of surgery; meanwhile, they did not think of it as home or even as life, exactly, but as a timeless limbo between spells of what, like prisoners, they called "the outside." Another thing: owing to the unmilitary nature of their ailment, they didn't think of themselves primarily as "veterans" anyway (except perhaps at Christmastime, when each man got a multigraphed letter of salutation from the President and a five-dollar bill from the *New York Journal-American*) and so felt no real bond with the wounded and maimed.

Building Seven was a world of its own. It held out a daily choice between its own kind of virtue—staying in bed—and its own kind of vice: midnight crap games, AWOL, and the smuggling of beer and whiskey through the fire-exit doors of its two latrines. It was the stage for its own kind of comedy—the night

Snyder chased the charge nurse into the fluoroscopy room with a water pistol, for instance, or the time the pint of bourbon slipped out of old Foley's bathrobe and smashed at Dr. Resnick's feet—and once in awhile its own kind of tragedy—the time Jack Fox sat up in bed to say, "Chrissake, open the *window*," coughed, and brought up the freak hemorrhage that killed him in ten minutes, or the other times, two or three times a year, when one of the men who had been wheeled away to surgery, smiling and waving to cries of "Take it easy!" and "Good luck t'ya, boy!" would never come back. But mostly it was a world consumed by its own kind of boredom, where everyone sat or lay amid the Kleenex and the sputum cups and the clangor of all-day radios. That was the way things were in C Ward on the afternoon of New Year's Eve, except that the radios were swamped under the noise of Tiny Kovacs's laughter.

He was an enormous man of thirty, six and a half feet tall and broad as a bear, and that afternoon he was having a private talk with his friend Jones, who looked comically small and scrawny beside him. They would whisper together and then laugh— Jones with a nervous giggle, repeatedly scratching his belly through the pajamas, Tiny with his great guffaw. After a while they got up, still flushed with laughter, and made their way across the ward to McIntyre's bed.

"Hey, Mac, listen," Jones began, "Tiny'n I got an idea." Then he got the giggles and said, "Tell him, Tiny."

The trouble was that McIntyre, a fragile man of forty-one with a lined, sarcastic face, was trying to write an important letter at the time. But they both mistook his grimace of impatience for a smile, and Tiny began to explain the idea in good faith.

"Listen, Mac, tonight around twelve I'm gonna get all undressed, see?" He spoke with some difficulty because all his front teeth were missing; they had gone bad soon after his lungs, and the new plate the hospital had ordered for him was long overdue. "I'll be all naked except I'm gonna wear this towel, see? Like a diaper? And then look, I'm gonna put this here acrost my chest." He unrolled a strip of four-inch bandage, a yard long, on which he or Jones had written "1951" in big block numerals, with marking ink. "Get it?" he said. "A big fat baby? No teef?

And then listen, Mac, you can be the old year, okay? You can put this here on, and this here. You'll be perfect." The second bandage said "1950," and the other item was a false beard of white cotton wool that they'd dug up from a box of Red Cross supplies in the dayroom—it had evidently belonged to an old Santa Claus costume.

"No, thanks," McIntyre said. "Find somebody else, okay?"

"Aw, jeez, you gotta do it, Mac," Tiny said. "Listen, we thought of evvybody else in the building and you're the only one—don'tcha see? Skinny, bald, a little gray hair? And the best part is you're like me, you got no teef *eiver*." Then, to show no offense was meant, he added, "Well, I mean, at lease you could take 'em out, right? You could take 'em out for a couple minutes and put 'em back in *after*—right?"

"Look, Kovacs," McIntyre said, briefly closing his eyes, "I already said no. Now will the both a you please take off?"

Slowly Tiny's face reshaped itself into a pout, blotched red in the cheeks as if he'd been slapped. "Arright," he said with self-control, grabbing the beard and the bandages from McIntyre's bed. "Arright, the hell wiv it." He swung around and strode back to his own side of the ward, and Jones trotted after him, smiling in embarrassment, his loose slippers flapping on the floor.

McIntyre shook his head. "How d'ya like them two for a paira idiot bastards?" he said to the man in the next bed, a thin and very ill Negro named Vernon Sloan. "You hear all that, Vernon?"

"I got the general idea," Sloan said. He started to say something else but began coughing instead, reaching out a long brown hand for his sputum cup, and McIntyre went to work on his letter again.

Back at his own bed, Tiny threw the beard and the bandages in his locker and slammed it shut. Jones hurried up beside him, pleading. "Listen, Tiny, we'll get another guy, is all. We'll get Shulman, or—"

"Ah, Shulman's too fat."

"Well, or Johnson, then, or—"

"Look, forget it, willya, Jones?" Tiny exploded. "Piss on it. I'm through. Try thinkin' up somethin' to give the guys a little laugh on New Year's, and that's whatcha get."

Jones sat down on Tiny's bedside chair. "Well, hell," he said after a pause, "it's still a good idea, isn't it?"

"Ah!" Tiny pushed one heavy hand away in disgust. "Ya think any a these bastids 'ud appreciate it? Ya think there's one sunuvabitchin' bastid in this building 'ud appreciate it? Piss on 'em all."

It was no use arguing; Tiny would sulk for the rest of the day now. This always happened when his feelings were hurt, and they were hurt fairly often, for his particular kind of jollity was apt to get on the other men's nerves. There was, for instance, the business of the quacking rubber duck he had bought in the hospital canteen shortly before Christmas, as a gift for one of his nephews. The trouble that time was that in the end he had decided to buy something else for the child and keep the duck for himself; quacking it made him laugh for hours on end. After the lights were out at night he would creep up on the other patients and quack the duck in their faces, and it wasn't long before nearly everyone told him to cut it out and shut up. Then somebody—McIntyre, in fact—had swiped the duck from Tiny's bed and hidden it, and Tiny had sulked for three days. "You guys think you're so smart," he had grumbled to the ward at large. "Actin' like a buncha kids."

It was Jones who found the duck and returned it to him; Jones was about the only man left who thought the things Tiny did were funny. Now his face brightened a little as he got up to leave. "Anyway, I got my bottle, Tiny," he said. "You'n *me'll* have some fun tonight." Jones was not a drinking man, but New Year's Eve was special and smuggling was a challenge: a few days earlier he had arranged to have a pint of rye brought in and had hidden it, with a good deal of giggling, under some spare pajamas in his locker.

"Don't tell nobody *else* you got it," Tiny said. "I wouldn't tell these bastids the time a day." He jerked a cigarette into his lips and struck the match savagely. Then he got his new Christmas robe off the hanger and put it on—careful, for all his temper, to arrange the fit of the padded shoulders and the sash just right. It was a gorgeous robe, plum-colored satin with contrasting red lapels, and Tiny's face and manner assumed a strange dignity whenever he put it on. This look was as new, or rather, as seasonal, as the robe itself: it dated back to the week before, when he'd gotten dressed to go home for his Christmas pass.

Many of the men were a revelation in one way or another when they appeared in their street clothes. McIntyre had grown surprisingly humble, incapable of sarcasm or pranks, when he put on his scarcely worn accounting clerk's costume of blue serge, and Jones had grown surprisingly tough in his old Navy foul-weather jacket. Young Krebs, whom everybody called junior, had assumed a portly maturity with his double-breasted business suit, and Travers, who most people had forgotten was a Yale man, looked oddly effete in his J. Press flannels and his button-down collar. Several of the Negroes had suddenly become Negroes again, instead of ordinary men, when they appeared in their sharply pegged trousers, draped coats and huge Windsor knots, and they even seemed embarrassed to be talking to the white men on the old familiar terms. But possibly the biggest change of all had been Tiny's. The clothes themselves were no surprise—his family ran a prosperous restaurant in Queens, and he was appropriately well-turned-out in a rich black overcoat and silk scarf—but the dignity they gave him was remarkable. The silly grin was gone, the laugh silenced, the clumsy movements overcome. The eyes beneath his snap-brim hat were not Tiny's eyes at all, but calm and masterful. Even his missing teeth didn't spoil the effect, for he kept his mouth shut except to mutter brief, almost curt Christmas wishes. The other patients looked up with a certain shy respect at this new man, this dramatic stranger whose hard heels crashed on the marble floor as he strode out of the building—and later, when he swung along the sidewalks of Jamaica on his way home, the crowds instinctively moved aside to make way for him.

Tiny was aware of the splendid figure he cut, but by the time he was home he'd stopped thinking about it; in the circle of his family it was real. Nobody called him Tiny there—he was Harold, a gentle son, a quiet hero to many round-eyed children, a rare and honored visitor. At one point, in the afterglow of a great dinner, a little girl was led ceremoniously up to his chair, where she stood shyly, not daring to meet his eyes, her fingers clasping the side seams of her party dress. Her mother urged her to speak: "Do you want to tell Uncle Harold what you say in your prayers every night, Irene?"

"Yes," the little girl said. "I tell Jesus please to bless Uncle Harold and make him get well again soon."

Uncle Harold smiled and took hold of both her hands. "That's swell, Irene," he said huskily. "But you know, you shunt *tell* Him. You should *ask* Him."

She looked into his face for the first time. "That's what I mean," she said. "I ask Him."

And Uncle Harold gathered her in his arms, putting his big face over her shoulder so she couldn't see that his eyes were blurred with tears. "That's a good girl," he whispered. It was a scene nobody in Building Seven would have believed.

He remained Harold until the pass was over and he strode away from a clinging family farewell, shrugging the great overcoat around his shoulders and squaring the hat. He was Harold all the way to the bus terminal and all the way back to the hospital, and the other men still looked at him oddly and greeted him a little shyly when he pounded back into C Ward. He went to his bed and put down his several packages (one of which contained the new robe), then headed for the latrine to get undressed. That was the beginning of the end, for when he came out in the old faded pajamas and scuffed slippers there was only a trace of importance left in his softening face, and even that disappeared in the next hour or two, while he lay on his bed and listened to the radio. Later that evening, when most of the other returning patients had settled down, he sat up and looked around in the old, silly way. He waited patiently for a moment of complete silence, then thrust his rubber duck high in the air and quacked it seven times to the rhythm of "shave-and-a-haircut, two-bits," while everybody groaned and swore. Tiny was back, ready to start a new year.

Now, less than a week later, he could still recapture his dignity whenever he needed it by putting on the robe, striking a pose and thinking hard about his home. Of course, it was only a question of time before the robe grew rumpled with familiarity, and then it would all be over, but meanwhile it worked like a charm.

Across the aisle, McIntyre sat brooding over his unfinished letter. "I don't know, Vernon," he said to Sloan. "I felt sorry for you last week, having to stay in this dump over Christmas, but you know something? You were lucky. I wish they wouldn't of let me go home either."

"That so?" Sloan said. "How do you mean?"

"Ah, I don't know," McIntyre said, wiping his fountain pen with a piece of Kleenex. "I don't know. Just that it's a bitch, having to come back afterwards, I guess." But that was only part of it; the other part, like the letter he'd been trying to write all week, was his own business.

McIntyre's wife had grown fat and bewildered in the last year or two. On the alternate Sunday afternoons when she came out to visit him she never seemed to have much on her mind but the movies she had seen, or the television shows, and she gave him very little news of their two children, who almost never came out. "Anyway, you'll be seein' them Christmas," she would say. "We'll have a lot of fun. Only listen, Dad, are you sure that bus trip isn't gonna tire you out?"

" 'Course not," he had said, a number of times. "I didn't have no trouble last year, did I?"

Nevertheless he was breathing hard when he eased himself off the bus at last, carrying the packages he had bought in the hospital canteen, and he had to walk very slowly up the snow-crusted Brooklyn street to his home.

His daughter, Jean, who was eighteen now, was not there when he came in.

"Oh, sure," his wife explained, "I thought I told you she'd prob'ly be out tonight."

"No," he said. "You didn't tell me. Where'd she go?"

"Oh, out to the movies is all, with her girlfriend Brenda. I didn't think you'd mind, Dad. Fact, I told her to go. She needs a little night off once in a while. *You* know, she's kind of run-down. She gets nervous and everything."

"What's she get nervous about?"

"Well, *you* know. One thing, this job she's got now's very tiring. I mean she likes the work and everything, but she's not used to the full eight hours a day, you know what I mean? She'll settle down to it. Come on, have a cuppa coffee, and then we'll put the tree up. We'll have a lot of fun."

On his way to wash up he passed her empty room, with its clean cosmetic smell, its ragged teddy bear and framed photographs of singers, and he said, "It sure seems funny to be home."

His boy, Joseph, had still been a kid fooling around with model airplanes the Christmas before; now he wore his hair about four inches too long and spent a great deal of time working on it with his comb, shaping it into a gleaming pompadour with upswept sides. He was a heavy smoker too, pinching the cigarette between his yellow-stained thumb and forefinger and cupping the live end in his palm. He hardly moved his lips when he spoke, and his only way of laughing was to make a brief snuffling sound in his nose. He gave one of these little snorts during the trimming of the Christmas tree, when McIntyre said something about a rumor that the Veterans Administration might soon increase disability pensions. It might have meant nothing, but to McIntyre it was the same as if he had said, "Who you tryna kid, Pop? We know where the money's coming from." It seemed an unmistakable, wise-guy reference to the fact that McIntyre's brother-in-law, and not his pension, was providing the bulk of the family income. He resolved to speak to his wife about it at bedtime that night, but when the time came all he said was, "Don't he ever get his hair cut anymore?"

"All the kids are wearing it that way now," she said. "Why do you have to criticize him all the time?"

Jean was there in the morning, slow and rumpled in a loose blue wrapper. "Hi, sweetie," she said, and gave him a kiss that smelled of sleep and stale perfume. She opened her presents quietly and then lay for a long time with one leg thrown over the arm of a deep upholstered chair, her foot swinging, her fingers picking at a pimple on her chin.

McIntyre couldn't take his eyes off her. It wasn't just that she was a woman—the kind of withdrawn, obliquely smiling woman that had filled him with intolerable shyness and desire in his own youth—it was something more disturbing even than that.

"Whaddya looking at, Dad?" she said, smiling and frowning at once. "You keep *lookin'* at me all the time."

He felt himself blushing. "I always like to look at pretty girls. Is that so terrible?"

" 'Course not." She began intently plucking at the broken edge of one of her fingernails, frowning down at her hands in a way that made her long eyelashes fall in delicate curves against her cheeks. "It's just—you know. When a person keeps looking at you all the time it makes you nervous, that's all."

"Honey, listen." McIntyre leaned forward with both elbows on his skinny knees. "Can I ask you something? What's all this business about being nervous? Ever since I come home, that's all I heard. 'Jean's very nervous. Jean's very nervous.' So listen, will you please tell me something? What's there to be so nervous about?"

"Nothing," she said. "I don't know, Dad. Nothing, I guess."

"Well, because the reason I ask—" he was trying to make his voice deep and gentle, the way he was almost sure it had sounded long ago, but it came out scratchy and querulous, short of breath—"the reason I ask is, if there's something bothering you or anything, don't you think you ought to tell your dad about it?"

Her fingernail tore deep into the quick, which caused her to shake it violently and pop it into her mouth with a little whimper of pain, and suddenly she was on her feet, red-faced and crying. "Dad, willya lea' me alone? Willya just please lea' me *alone*?" She ran out of the room and upstairs and slammed her door.

McIntyre had started after her, but instead he stood swaying and glared at his wife and son, who were examining the carpet at opposite ends of the room.

"What's the matter with her, anyway?" he demanded. "Huh? What the hell's going on around here?" But they were as silent as two guilty children. "C'mon," he said. His head made a slight involuntary movement with each suck of air into his frail chest. "C'mon, goddamn it, *tell* me."

With a little wet moan his wife sank down and spread herself among the sofa cushions, weeping, letting her face melt. "All right," she said. "All right, you asked for it. We all done our best to give you a nice Christmas, but if you're gonna come home and snoop around and drive everybody crazy with your questions, all right—it's your funeral. She's four months pregnant—there, now are you satisfied? Now willya please quit bothering everybody?"

McIntyre sat down in an easy chair that was full of rattling Christmas paper, his head still moving with each breath.

"Who was it?" he said at last. "Who's the boy?"

"*Ask* her," his wife said. "Go on, ask her and see. She won't tell you. She won't tell anybody—that's the whole trouble. She wouldn't even of let on about the *baby* if I hadn't found out, and now she won't even tell her own mother the boy's name. She'd rather break her mother's heart—yes, she would, and her brother's too."

Then he heard it again, a little snuffle across the room. Joseph was standing there smirking as he stubbed out a cigarette. His lower lip moved slightly and he said, "Maybe she don't *know* the guy's name."

McIntyre rose very slowly out of the rattling paper, walked over to his son and hit him hard across the face with the flat of his hand, making the long hair jump from his skull and fall around his ears, making his face wince into the face of a hurt, scared little boy. Then blood began to run from the little boy's nose and dribble on the nylon shirt he had gotten for Christmas, and McIntyre hit him again, and that was when his wife screamed.

A few hours later he was back in Building Seven with nothing to do. All week he ate poorly, talked very little, except to Vernon Sloan, and spent a great deal of time working on a letter to his daughter that was still unfinished on the afternoon of New Year's Eve.

After many false starts, which had ended up among the used Kleenex tissues in the paper bag that hung beside his bed, this was what he had written:

JEAN HONEY,

I guess I got pretty excited and made a lot of trouble when I was home. Baby it was only that I have been away so long it is hard for me to understand that your a grown up woman and that is why I kind of went crazy that day. Now Jean I have done some thinking since I got back here and I want to write you a few lines.

The main thing is try not to worry. Remember your not the first girl that's made a mistake and

(*p.* 2)
gotten into trouble of this kind. Your mom is all upset I know but do not let her get you down. Now Jean it may seem that you and I don't know each other very well any more but this is not so. Do you remember when I first come out of the army and you were about 12 then and we used to take a walk in Prospect Pk. sometimes and talk things over. I wish I could have a talk like that

(*p.* 3)
with you now. Your old dad may not be good for much any more but he does know a thing or two about life and especially one important thing, and that is

That was as far as the letter went.

Now that Tiny's laughter was stilled, the ward seemed unnaturally quiet. The old year faded in a thin yellow sunset behind the west windows; then darkness fell, the lights came on and shuddering rubber-wheeled wagons of dinner trays were rolled in by masked and gowned attendants. One of them, a gaunt, bright-eyed man named Carl, went through his daily routine.

"Hey, you guys heard about the man that ran over himself?" he asked, stopping in the middle of the aisle with a steaming pitcher of coffee in his hand.

"Just pour the coffee, Carl," somebody said.

Carl filled a few cups and started across the aisle to fill a few more, but midway he stopped again and bugged his eyes over the rim of his sterile mask. "No, but listen—you guys heard about the man that ran over himself? This is a new one." He looked at Tiny, who usually was more than willing to play straight man for him, but Tiny was moodily buttering a slice of bread, his cheeks wobbling with each stroke of the knife. "Well, anyways," Carl said at last, "this man says to this kid, 'Hey kid, run acrost the street and get me a packa cigarettes, willya?' Kid says, 'No,' see? So the man ran over *himself*!" He doubled up and pounded his thigh. Jones groaned appreciatively; everyone else ate in silence.

When the meal was over and the trays cleared away, McIntyre tore up the old beginning of page 3 and dropped it in the waste bag. He resettled his pillows, brushed some food crumbs off the bed, and wrote this:

(*p.* 3)
with you now.
So Jean please write and tell me the name of this boy. I promise I

But he threw that page away too, and sat for a long time writing nothing, smoking a cigarette with his usual careful effort to avoid inhaling. At last he took up his pen again and cleaned its point very carefully with a leaf of Kleenex. Then he began new page:

(*p.* 3)
with you now.
Now baby I have got an idea. As you know I am now waiting to have another operation on the left side in February but if all goes well maybe I could take off out of this place by April 1. Of course I would not get a discharge but I could take a chance like I did in 1947 and hope for better luck this time. Then we could go away to the country someplace just you and I and I could take a part time job and we could

The starched rustle and rubber-heeled thump of a nurse made him look up; she was standing beside his bed with a bottle of rubbing alcohol. "How about you, McIntyre?" she said. "Back rub?"

"No thanks," he said. "Not tonight."

"My goodness." She peered just a little at the letter, which he shielded just a little with his hand. "You still writing letters? Every time I come past here you're writing letters. You must have a lot of people to write to. I wish I had the time to catch up on my letters."

"Yeah," he said. "Well, that's the thing, see. I got plenty of time."

"Well, but how can you think of so many things to write about?" she said. "That's my trouble. I sit down and I get all ready to write a letter and then I can't think of a single thing to write about. It's terrible."

He watched the shape of her buttocks as she moved away down the aisle. Then he read over the new page, crumpled it, and dropped it in the bag. Closing his eyes and massaging the bridge of his nose with thumb and forefinger, he tried to remember the exact words of the first version. At last he wrote it out again as well as he could:

(*p.* 3)
with you now.

Baby Jean your old dad may not be good for much any more but he does know a thing or two about life and especially one important thing, and that is

But from there on, the pen lay dead in his cramped fingers. It was as if all the letters of the alphabet, all the combinations of letters into words, all the infinite possibilities of handwritten language had ceased to exist.

He looked out the window for help, but the window was a black mirror now and gave back only the lights, the bright bed-sheets and pajamas of the ward. Pulling on his robe and slippers, he went over to stand with his forehead and cupped hands against the cold pane. Now he could make out the string of highway lights in the distance and, beyond that, the horizon of black trees between the snow and the sky. Just above the horizon, on the right, the sky was suffused with a faint pink blur from the lights of Brooklyn and New York, but this was partly hidden from view by a big dark shape in the foreground that was a blind corner of the paraplegic building, a world away.

When McIntyre turned back from the window to blink in the yellow light, leaving a shriveling ghost of his breath on the glass, it was with an oddly shy look of rejuvenation and relief. He walked to his bed, stacked the pages of his manuscript neatly, tore them in halves and in quarters and dropped them into the waste bag. Then he got his pack of cigarettes and went over to stand beside Vernon Sloan, who was blinking through his reading glasses at *The Saturday Evening Post*.

"Smoke, Vernon?" he said.

"No thanks, Mac. I smoke more'n one or two a day, it only makes me cough."

"Okay," McIntyre said, lighting one for himself. "Care to play a little checkers?"

"No thanks, Mac, not right now. I'm a little tired—think I'll just read awhile."

"Any good articles in there this week, Vernon?"

"Oh, pretty good," he said. "Couple pretty good ones." Then his mouth worked into a grin that slowly disclosed nearly all of his very clean teeth. "Say, what's the matter with you, man? You feelin' good or somethin'?"

"Oh, not too bad, Vernon," he said, stretching his skinny arms and his spine. "Not too bad."

"You finish all your writin' finally? Is that it?"

"Yeah, I guess so," he said. "My trouble is, I can't think of anything to write about."

Looking across the aisle to where Tiny Kovacs's wide back sat slumped in the purple amplitude of the new robe, he walked over and laid a hand on one of the enormous satin shoulders. "So?" he said.

Tiny's head swung around to glare at him, immediately hostile. "So what?"

"So where's that beard?"

Tiny wrenched open his locker, grabbed out the beard and thrust it roughly into McIntyre's hands. "Here," he said. "You want it? Take it."

McIntyre held it up to his ears and slipped the string over his head. "String oughta be a little tighter," he said. "There, how's that? Prob'ly look better when I get my teeth out."

But Tiny wasn't listening. He was burrowing in his locker for the strips of bandage. "Here," he said. "Take this stuff too. I don't want no part of it. You wanna do it, you get somebody else."

At that moment Jones came padding over, all smiles. "Hey, you gonna do it, Mac? You change your mind?"

"Jones, talk to this big son of a bitch," McIntyre said through the wagging beard. "He don't wanna cooperate."

"Aw, *jeez*, Tiny," Jones implored. "The whole *thing* depends on you. The whole *thing* was your idea."

"I already told ya," Tiny said. "I don't want no part of it. You wanna do it, you find some other sucker."

After the lights went out at ten nobody bothered much about hiding their whiskey. Men who had been taking furtive nips in the latrines all evening now drank in quietly jovial groups around the wards, with the unofficial once-a-year blessing of the charge nurse. Nobody took particular notice when, a little before midnight, three men from C Ward slipped out to the linen closet to get a sheet and a towel, then to the kitchen to get a mop handle, and then walked the length of the building and disappeared into the A Ward latrine.

There was a last-minute flurry over the beard: it hid so much of McIntyre's face that the effect of his missing teeth was spoiled. Jones solved the problem by cutting away all of it but the chin whiskers, which he fastened in place with bits of adhesive tape. "There," he said, "that does it. That's perfect. Now roll up your pajama pants, Mac, so just your bare legs'll show under the sheet? Get it? Now where's your mop handle?"

"Jones, it don't *work*!" Tiny called tragically. He was standing naked except for a pair of white woolen socks, trying to pin the folded towel around his loins. "The son of a bitch won't stay *up*!"

Jones hurried over to fix it, and finally everything was ready. Nervously, they killed the last of Jones's rye and dropped the empty bottle into a laundry hamper; then they slipped outside and huddled in the darkness at the head of A Ward.

"Ready?" Jones whispered. "Okay. . . . Now." He flicked on the overhead lights, and thirty startled faces blinked in the glare.

First came 1950, a wasted figure crouched on a trembling staff, lame and palsied with age; behind him, grinning and flexing his muscles, danced the enormous diapered baby of the New Year. For a second or two there was silence except for the unsteady tapping of the old man's staff, and then the laughter and the cheers began.

"*Out wivvie old!*" the baby bellowed over the noise, and he made an elaborate burlesque of hauling off and kicking the old man in the seat of the pants, which caused the old man to stagger weakly and rub one buttock as they moved up the aisle. "*Out wivvie old! In wivva new!*"

Jones ran on ahead to turn on the lights of B Ward, where the ovation was even louder. Nurses clustered helplessly in the doorway to watch, frowning or giggling behind their sterile masks as the show made its way through cheers and catcalls.

"Out wivvie old! In wivva new!"

In one of the private rooms a dying man blinked up through the window of his oxygen tent as his door was flung open and his light turned on. He stared bewildered at the frantic toothless clowns who capered at the foot of his bed; finally he understood and gave them a yellow smile, and they moved on to the next private room and the next, arriving at last in C Ward, where their friends stood massed and laughing in the aisle.

There was barely time for the pouring of fresh drinks before all the radios blared up at once and Guy Lombardo's band broke into "Auld Lang Syne"; then all the shouts dissolved into a great off-key chorus in which Tiny's voice could be heard over all the others:

"Should old acquaintance be forgot
And never brought to mind? . . ."

Even Vernon Sloan was singing, propped up in bed and holding a watery highball, which he slowly waved in time to the music. They were all singing.

"For o-o-old lang syne, my boys,
For o-o-old lang syne . . ."

And when the song was over the handshaking began.
"Good luck t'ya, boy."
"Same to you, boy—hope you make it this year."
All over Building Seven men wandered in search of hands to shake; under the noise of shouts and radios the words were repeated again and again: "Good luck t'ya . . ." "Hope you make it this year, boy . . ." And standing still and tired by Tiny Kovacs's bed, where the purple robe lay thrown in careless wads and wrinkles, McIntyre raised his glass and his bare-gummed smile to the crowd, with Tiny's laughter roaring in his ear and Tiny's heavy arm around his neck.

BUILDERS

WRITERS WHO WRITE about writers can easily bring on the worst kind of literary miscarriage; everybody knows that. Start a story off with "Craig crushed out his cigarette and lunged for the typewriter," and there isn't an editor in the United States who'll feel like reading your next sentence.

So don't worry: this is going to be a straight, no-nonsense piece of fiction about a cab driver, a movie star, and an eminent child psychologist, and that's a promise. But you'll have to be patient for a minute, because there's going to be a writer in it too. I won't call him "Craig," and I can guarantee that he won't get away with being the only Sensitive Person among the characters, but we're going to be stuck with him right along and you'd better count on his being as awkward and obtrusive as writers nearly always are, in fiction or in life.

Thirteen years ago, in 1948, I was twenty-two and employed as a rewrite man on the financial news desk of the United Press. The salary was fifty-four dollars a week and it wasn't much of a job, but it did give me two good things. One was that whenever anybody asked me what I did I could say, "Work for the UP," which had a jaunty sound; the other was that every morning I could turn up at the *Daily News* building wearing a jaded look, a cheap trench coat that had shrunk a size too small for me, and a much-handled brown fedora ("Battered" is the way I would have described it then, and I'm grateful that I know a little more now about honesty in the use of words. It was a handled hat, handled by endless nervous pinchings and shapings and reshapings; it wasn't battered at all). What I'm getting at is that just for those few minutes each day, walking up the slight hill of the last hundred yards between the subway exit and the *News* building, I was Ernest Hemingway reporting for work at the *Kansas City Star.*

Had Hemingway been to the war and back before his twentieth birthday? Well, so had I; and all right, maybe there were no wounds or medals for valor in my case, but the basic fact of the matter was there. Had Hemingway bothered about anything as time-wasting and career-delaying as going to college? Hell, no; and me neither. Could Hemingway ever really have cared very much about the newspaper business? Of course not; so there was only a marginal difference, you see, between his lucky break at the *Star* and my own dismal stint on the financial desk. The important thing, as I knew Hemingway would be the first to agree, was that a writer had to begin somewhere.

"Domestic corporate bonds moved irregularly higher in the moderately active trading today. . . ." That was the kind of prose I wrote all day long for the UP wire, and "Rising oil shares paced a lively curb market," and "Directors of Timken Roller Bearing today declared"—hundreds on hundreds of words that I never really understood (What in the name of God are puts and calls, and what is a sinking fund debenture? I'm still damned if I know), while the teletypes chugged and rang and the Wall Street tickers ticked and everybody around me argued baseball, until it was mercifully time to go home.

It always pleased me to reflect that Hemingway had married young; I could go right along with him there. My wife, Joan, and I lived as far west as you can get on West Twelfth Street, in a big three-window room on the third floor, and if it wasn't the Left Bank it certainly wasn't our fault. Every evening after dinner, while Joan washed the dishes, there would be a respectful, almost reverent hush in the room, and this was the time for me to retire behind a three-fold screen in the corner where a table, a student lamp and a portable typewriter were set up. But it was here, of course, under the white stare of that lamp, that the tenuous parallel between Hemingway and me endured its heaviest strain. Because it wasn't any "Up in Michigan" that came out of my machine; it wasn't any "Three Day Blow" or "The Killers"; very often, in fact, it wasn't really anything at all, and even when it was something Joan called "marvelous," I knew deep down that it was always, always something bad.

There were evenings too when all I did behind the screen was

goof off—read every word of the printing on the inside of a
matchbook, say, or all the ads in the back of the *Saturday Review
of Literature*—and it was during one of those times, in the fall of
the year, that I came across these lines:

> Unusual free-lance opportunity for talented writer. Must
> have imagination. Bernard Silver.

—and then a phone number with what looked like a Bronx
exchange.

I won't bother giving you the dry, witty, Hemingway dialogue
that took place when I came out from behind the screen that
night and Joan turned around from the sink, with her hands dripping soapsuds on the open magazine, and we can also skip my
cordial, unenlightening chat with Bernard Silver on the phone.
I'll just move on ahead to a couple of nights later, when I rode
the subway for an hour and found my way at last to his apartment.

"Mr. Prentice?" he inquired. "What's your first name again?
Bob? Good, Bob, I'm Bernie. Come on in, make yourself
comfortable."

And I think both Bernie and his home deserve a little descrip-
tion here. He was in his middle or late forties, a good deal shorter
than me and much stockier, wearing an expensive-looking pale
blue sport shirt with the tails out. His head must have been half
again the size of mine, with thinning black hair washed straight
back, as if he'd stood face-up in the shower; and his face was one
of the most guileless and self-confident faces I've ever seen.

The apartment was very clean, spacious and cream-colored,
full of carpeting and archways. In the narrow alcove near the coat
closet ("Take your coat and hat; good. Let's put this on a hanger
here and we'll be all set; good"), I saw a cluster of framed photographs showing World War I soldiers in various groupings, but
on the walls of the living room there were no pictures of any
kind, only a few wrought-iron lamp brackets and a couple of
mirrors. Once inside the room you weren't apt to notice the lack
of pictures, though, because all your attention was drawn to a
single, amazing piece of furniture. I don't know what you'd call
it—a credenza?—but whatever it was it seemed to go on forever,
chest-high in some places and waist-high in others, made of at

least three different shades of polished brown veneer. Part of it was a television set, part of it was a radio-phonograph; part of it thinned out into shelves that held potted plants and little figurines; part of it, full of chromium knobs and tricky sliding panels, was a bar.

"Ginger ale?" he asked. "My wife and I don't drink, but I can offer you a glass of ginger ale."

I think Bernie's wife must always have gone out to the movies on nights when he interviewed his writing applicants; I did meet her later, though, and we'll come to that. Anyway, there were just the two of us that first evening, settling down in slippery leatherette chairs with our ginger ale, and it was strictly business.

"First of all," he said, "tell me, Bob. Do you know *My Flag Is Down*?" And before I could ask what he was talking about he pulled it out of some recess in the credenza and handed it over—a paperback book that you still see around the drugstores, purporting to be the memoirs of a New York taxicab driver. Then he began to fill me in, while I looked at the book and nodded and wished I'd never left home.

Bernard Silver was a cab driver too. He had been one for twenty-two years, as long as the span of my life, and in the last two or three of these years he had begun to see no reason why a slightly fictionalized version of his own experiences shouldn't be worth a fortune. "I'd like you to take a look at this," he said, and this time the credenza yielded up a neat little box of three-by-five-inch file cards. Hundreds of experiences, he told me; all different; and while he gave me to understand that they might not all be strictly true, he could assure me there was at least a kernel of truth in every last one of them. Could I imagine what a really good ghostwriter might do with a wealth of material like that? Or how much that same writer might expect to salt away when his own fat share of the magazine sales, the book royalties and the movie rights came in?

"Well, I don't know, Mr. Silver. It's a thing I'd have to think over. I guess I'd have to read this other book first, and see if I thought there was any—"

"No, wait awhile. You're getting way ahead of me here, Bob. In the first place I wouldn't want you to read that book because

you wouldn't learn anything. That guy's all gangsters and dames and sex and drinking and that stuff. I'm completely different."
And I sat swilling ginger ale as if to slake a gargantuan thirst, in order to be able to leave as soon as possible after he'd finished explaining how completely different he was. Bernie Silver was a warm person, he told me; an ordinary, everyday guy with a heart as big as all outdoors and a real philosophy of life; did I know what he meant?

I have a trick of tuning out on people (it's easy; all you do is fix your eyes on the speaker's mouth and watch the rhythmic, endlessly changing shapes of lips and tongue, and the first thing you know you can't hear a word), and I was about to start doing that when he said:

"And don't misunderstand me, Bob. I never yet asked a writer to do a single word for me on spec. You write for me, you'll be paid for everything you do. Naturally it can't be very big dough at this stage of the game, but you'll be paid. Fair enough? Here, let me fill up your glass."

This was the proposition. He'd give me an idea out of the file; I'd develop it into a first-person short story by Bernie Silver, between one and two thousand words in length, for which immediate payment was guaranteed. If he liked the job I did, there would be plenty of others where it came from—an assignment a week, if I could handle that much—and in addition to my initial payment, of course, I could look forward to a generous percentage of whatever subsequent income the material might bring. He chose to be winkingly mysterious about his plans for marketing the stories, though he did manage to hint that the *Reader's Digest* might be interested, and he was frank to admit he didn't yet have a publisher lined up for the ultimate book they would comprise, but he said he could give me a couple of names that would knock my eye out. Had I ever heard, for example, of Manny Weidman?

"Or maybe," he said, breaking into his all-out smile, "maybe you know him better as Wade Manley." And this was the shining name of a movie star, a man about as famous in the thirties and forties as Kirk Douglas or Burt Lancaster today. Wade Manley had been a grammar-school friend of Bernie's right here in the

Bronx. Through mutual friends they had managed to remain sentimentally close ever since, and one of the things that kept their friendship green was Wade Manley's oft-repeated desire to play the role of rough, lovable Bernie Silver, New York Hackie, in any film or television series based on his colorful life. "Now I'll give you another name," he said, and this time he squinted cannily at me while pronouncing it, as if my recognizing it or not would be an index of my general educational level. "Dr. Alexander Corvo."

And luckily I was able not to look too blank. It wasn't a celebrity name, exactly, but it was far from obscure. It was one of those *New York Times* names, the kind of which tens of thousands of people are dimly aware because they've been coming across respectful mentions of them in the *Times* for years. Oh, it might have lacked the impact of "Lionel Trilling" or "Reinhold Niebuhr," but it was along that line; you could probably have put it in the same class with "Huntington Hartford" or "Leslie R. Groves," and a good cut or two above "Newbold Morris."

"The whaddyacallit man, you mean?" I said. "The childhood-tensions man?"

Bernie gave me a solemn nod, forgiving this vulgarity, and spoke the name again with its proper identification. "I mean Dr. Alexander Corvo, the eminent child psychologist."

Early in his rise to eminence, you see, Dr. Corvo had been a teacher at the very same grammar school in the Bronx, and two of the most unruly, dearly loved little rascals in his charge there had been Bernie Silver and Manny What's-his-name, the movie star. He still retained an incurable soft spot for both youngsters, and nothing would please him more today than to lend whatever influence he might have in the publishing world to furthering their project. All the three of them needed now, it seemed, was to find that final element, that elusive catalyst, the perfect writer for the job.

"Bob," said Bernie, "I'm telling you the truth. I've had one writer after another working on this, and none of them's been right. Sometimes I don't trust my own judgment; I take their stuff to Dr. Corvo and he shakes his head. He says, 'Bernie, try again.'

"Look, Bob." He came earnestly forward in his chair. "This isn't any fly-by-night idea here; I'm not stringing anybody along. This thing is building. Manny, Dr. Corvo and myself—we're *building* this thing. Oh, don't worry, Bob, I *know*—what, do I look that stupid?—I know they're not building the way *I'm* building. And why should they? A big movie star? A distinguished scholar and author? You think they haven't got plenty of things of their own to build? A lot more important things than this? Naturally. But Bob, I'm telling you the truth: they're interested. I can show you letters, I can tell you times they've sat around this apartment with their wives, or Manny has anyway, and we've talked about it hours on end. They're interested, nobody has to worry about that. So do you see what I'm telling you, Bob? I'm telling you the truth. This thing is building." And he began a slow, two-handed building gesture, starting from the carpet, setting invisible blocks into place until they'd made a structure of money and fame for him, money and freedom for both of us, that rose to the level of our eyes.

I said it certainly did sound fine, but that if he didn't mind I'd like to know a little more about the immediate payment for the individual stories.

"And now I'll give you the answer to that one," he said. He went to the credenza again—part of it seemed to be a kind of desk—and after sorting out some papers he came up with a personal check. "I won't just tell you," he said. "I'll show you. Fair enough? This was my last writer. Take it and read it."

It was a canceled check, and it said that Bernard Silver had paid, to the order of some name, the sum of twenty-five dollars and no cents. "Read it!" he insisted, as if the check were a prose work of uncommon merit in its own right, and he watched me while I turned it over to read the man's endorsement, which had been signed under some semilegible words of Bernie's own about this being advance payment in full, and the bank's rubber stamp. "Look all right to you?" he inquired. "So that's the arrangement. All clear now?"

I guessed it was as clear as it would ever be, so I gave him back the check and said that if he'd show me one of the file cards now, or whatever, we might as well get going.

"Way-*hait* a minute, now! Hold your *horses* a minute here." His smile was enormous. "You're a pretty fast guy, you know that, Bob? I mean I like you, but don't you think I'd have to be a little bit of a dope to go around making out checks to everybody walked in here saying they're a writer? I know you're a news-paperman. Fine. Do I know you're a writer yet? Why don't you let me see what you got there in your lap?"

It was a manila envelope containing carbon copies of the only two halfway presentable short stories I had ever managed to produce in my life.

"Well," I said. "Sure. Here. Of course these are a very different kind of thing than what *you're*—"

"Never mind, never mind; naturally they're different," he said, opening the envelope. "You just relax a minute, and let me take a look."

"What I mean is, they're both very kind of—well, literary, I guess you'd say. I don't quite see how they'll give you any real idea of my—"

"Relax, I said."

Rimless glasses were withdrawn from the pocket of his sport shirt and placed laboriously into position as he settled back, frowning, to read. It took him a long time to get through the first page of the first story, and I watched him, wondering if this might turn out to be the very lowest point in my literary career. A *cab* driver, for Christ's sake. At last the first page turned, and the second page followed so closely after it that I could tell he was skipping. Then the third and the fourth—it was a twelve- or fourteen-page story—while I gripped my empty, warming ginger ale glass as if in readiness to haul off and throw it at his head.

A very slight, hesitant, then more and more judicial nodding set in as he made his way toward the end. He finished it, looked puzzled, went back to read over the last page again; then he laid it aside and picked up the second story—not to read it, but only to check it for length. He had clearly had enough reading for one night. Off came the glasses and on came the smile.

"Well, very nice," he said. "I won't take time to read this other one now, but this first one's very nice. 'Course, naturally, as you said, this is a very different kind of material you got here, so it's a little hard for me to—*you* know—" and he dismissed the rest of this difficult sentence with a wave of the hand. "I'll tell you what, though, Bob. Instead of just reading here, let me ask you a couple of questions about writing. For example." He closed his eyes and delicately touched their lids with his fingers, thinking, or more likely pretending to think, in order to give added weight to his next words. "For example, let me ask you this. Supposing somebody writes you a letter and says, 'Bob, I didn't have time to write you a short letter today, so I had to write you a long one instead.' Would you know what they meant by that?"

Don't worry, I played this part of the evening pretty cool. I wasn't going to let twenty-five bucks get away from me without some kind of struggle; and my answer, whatever sober-sided nonsense it was, could have left no doubt in his mind that this particular writing candidate knew something of the difficulty and the value of compression in prose. He seemed gratified by it, anyway.

"Good. Now let's try a different angle. I mentioned about 'building' a while back; well, look. Do you see where writing a story is building something too? Like building a house?" And he was so pleased with his own creation of this image that he didn't even wait to take in the careful, congratulatory nod I awarded him for it. "I mean a house has got to have a roof, but you're going to be in trouble if you build your roof first, right? Before you build your roof you got to build your walls. Before you build your walls you got to lay your foundation—and I mean all the way down the line. Before you lay your foundation you got to bulldoze and dig yourself the right kind of hole in the ground. Am I right?"

I couldn't have agreed with him more, but he was still ignoring my rapt, toadying gaze. He rubbed the flange of his nose with one wide knuckle; then he turned on me triumphantly again.

"So all right, supposing you build yourself a house like that. Then what? What's the first question you got to ask yourself about it when it's done?"

But I could tell he didn't care if I muffed this one or not. *He* knew what the question was, and he could hardly wait to tell me.

"Where are the windows?" he demanded, spreading his hands. "That's the question. Where does the light come in? Because do you see what I mean about the light coming in, Bob? I mean the—the *philosophy* of your story; the *truth* of it; the—"

"The illumination of it, sort of," I said, and he quit groping for his third noun with a profound and happy snap of the fingers.

"That's it. That's it, Bob. You got it."

It was a deal, and we had another ginger ale to clinch it as he thumbed through the idea file for my trial assignment. The "experience" he chose was the time Bernie Silver had saved a neurotic couple's marriage, right there in the cab, simply by sizing them up in his rearview mirror as they quarreled and putting in a few well chosen words of his own. Or at least, that was the general drift of it. All it actually said on the card was something like:

> High class man & wife (Park Ave.) start fighting in cab, very upset, lady starts yelling divorce. I watch them in rear view and put my 2 cents worth in & soon we are all laughing. Story about marriage, etc.

But Bernie expressed full confidence in my ability to work the thing out.

In the alcove, as he went through the elaborate business of getting my trench coat out of the closet and helping me on with it, I had time for a better look at the World War I photographs— a long company lineup, a number of framed yellow snapshots showing laughing men with their arms around each other, and one central picture of a lone bugler on a parade ground, with dusty barracks and a flag high in the distance. It could have been on the cover of an old American Legion magazine, with a caption like "Duty"—the perfect soldier, slim and straight at attention, and Gold Star Mothers would have wept over the way his fine young profile was pressed in manly reverence against the mouth of his simple, eloquent horn.

"I see you like my boy there," Bernie said fondly. "I bet you'd never guess who that boy is today."

Wade Manley? Dr. Alexander Corvo? Lionel Trilling? But I suppose I really did know, even before I glanced around at his blushing, beaming presence, that the boy was Bernie himself. And whether it sounds silly or not, I'll have to tell you that I felt a small but honest-to-God admiration for him. "Well, I'll be damned, Bernie. You look—you look pretty great there."

"Lot skinnier in those days, anyway," he said, slapping his silken paunch as he walked me to the door, and I remember looking down into his big, dumb, flabby face and trying to find the bugler's features somewhere inside it.

On my way home, rocking on the subway and faintly belching and tasting ginger ale, I grew increasingly aware that a writer could do a hell of a lot worse than to pull down twenty-five dollars for a couple of thousand words. It was very nearly half what I earned in forty miserable hours among the domestic corporate bonds and the sinking fund debentures; and if Bernie liked this first one, if I could go on doing one a week for him, it would be practically the same as getting a 50 percent raise. Seventy-nine a week! With that kind of dough coming in, as well as the forty-six Joan brought home from her secretarial job, it would be no time at all before we had enough for Paris (and maybe we wouldn't meet any Gertrude Steins or Ezra Pounds there, maybe I wouldn't produce any *Sun Also Rises*, but the earliest possible expatriation was nothing less than essential to my Hemingway plans). Besides, it might even be fun—or at least it might be fun to tell people about: I would be the hackie's hack, the builder's builder.

In any case I ran all the way down West Twelfth Street that night, and if I didn't burst in on her, laughing and shouting and clowning around, it was only because I forced myself to stand leaning against the mailboxes downstairs until I'd caught my breath and arranged my face into the urbane, amused expression I planned to use for telling her about it.

"Well, but who do you suppose is putting up all the money?" she asked. "It can't be out of his own pocket, can it? A cab driver couldn't afford to pay out twenty-five a week for any length of time, could he?"

It was one aspect of the thing that hadn't occurred to me—and it was just like her to come up with so dead-logical a question—but I did my best to override her with my own kind of cynical romanticism. "Who knows? Who the hell cares? Maybe Wade Manley's putting up the money. Maybe Dr. Whaddya-callit's putting it up. The point is, it's there."

"Well," she said, "good, then. How long do you think it'll take you to do the story?"

"Oh, hell, no time at all. I'll knock it off in a couple hours over the weekend."

But I didn't. I spent all Saturday afternoon and evening on one false start after another; I kept getting hung up in the dialogue of the quarreling couple, and in technical uncertainties about how much Bernie could really see of them in his rearview mirror, and in doubts about what any cab driver could possibly say at such a time without the man's telling him to shut up and keep his eyes on the road.

By Sunday afternoon I was walking around breaking pencils in half and throwing them into the wastebasket and saying the hell with it; the hell with everything; apparently I couldn't even be a goddamn ghostwriter for a goddamn ignorant slob of a driver of a goddamn taxicab.

"You're *trying* too hard," Joan said. "Oh, I knew this would happen. You're being so insufferably *literary* about it, Bob; it's ridiculous. All you have to do is think of every corny, tear-jerking thing you've ever read or heard. Think of Irving Berlin."

And I told her I'd give her Irving Berlin right in the mouth in about a minute, if she didn't lay off me and mind her own god-damn business.

But late that night, as Irving Berlin himself might say, something kind of wonderful happened. I took that little bastard of a story and I built the hell out of it. First I bulldozed and dug and laid myself a real good foundation; then I got the lumber out and bang, bang, bang—up went the walls and on went the roof and up went the cute little chimney top. Oh, I put plenty of windows in it too—big, square ones—and when the light came pouring in it left no earthly shadow of a doubt that Bernie Silver was the wisest, gentlest, bravest and most lovable man who ever said "folks."

"It's perfect," Joan told me at breakfast, after she'd read the thing. "Oh, it's just perfect, Bob. I'm sure that's just exactly what he wants."

And it was. I'll never forget the way Bernie sat with his ginger ale in one hand and my trembling manuscript in the other, reading as I'd still be willing to bet he'd never read before, exploring all the snug and tidy wonders of the little home I'd built for him. I watched him discovering each of those windows, one after another, and saw his face made holy with their light. When he was finished he got up—we both got up—and he shook my hand.

"Beautiful," he said. "Bob, I had a feeling you'd do a good one, but I'll tell you the truth. I didn't know you'd do as good a one as this. Now you want your check, and I'll tell you something. You're not getting any check. For this you get cash."

Out came his trusty black cab driver's wallet. He thumbed through its contents, picked out a five-dollar bill and laid it in my hand. He evidently wanted to make a ceremony out of presenting me with one bill after another, so I stood smiling down at it and waiting for the next one; and I was still standing there with my hand out when I looked up and saw him putting the wallet away.

Five bucks! And even now I wish I could say that I shouted this, or at least that I said it with some suggestion of the outrage that gripped my bowels—it might have saved an awful amount of trouble later—but the truth is that it came out as a very small, meek question: "Five bucks?"

"Right!" He was rocking happily back on his heels in the carpet.

"Well, but Bernie, I mean what's the deal? I mean, you showed me that check, and I—"

As his smile dwindled, his face looked as shocked and hurt as if I'd spat into it. "Oh, Bob," he said. "Bob, what is this? Look, let's not play any games here. I know I showed you that check; I'll show you that check again." And the folds of his sport shirt quivered in righteous indignation as he rummaged in the credenza and brought it out.

It was the same check, all right. It still read twenty-five dollars and no cents; but Bernie's cramped scribbling on the other side, above the other man's signature and all mixed up with the bank's rubber stamp, was now legible as hell. What it said, of course, was: "In full advance payment, five write-ups."

So I hadn't really been robbed—conned a little, maybe, that's all—and therefore my main problem now, the sick, ginger-ale-flavored feeling that I was certain Ernest Hemingway could never in his life have known, was my own sense of being a fool.

"Am I right or wrong, Bob?" he was asking. "Am I right or wrong?" And then he sat me down again and did his smiling best to set me straight. How could I possibly have thought he meant twenty-five a time? Did I have any idea what kind of money a hackie took home? Oh, some of your owner-drivers, maybe it was a different story; but your average hackie? Your fleet hackie? Forty, forty-five, maybe sometimes fifty a week if they were lucky. Even for a man like himself, with no kids and a wife working full time at the telephone company, it was no picnic. I could ask any hackie if I didn't believe him; it was no picnic. "And I mean you don't think anybody *else* is picking up the tab for these write-ups, do you? Do you?" He looked at me incredulously, almost ready to laugh, as if the very idea of my thinking such a thing would remove all reasonable doubt about my having been born yesterday.

"Bob, I'm sorry there was any misunderstanding here," he said, walking me to the door, "but I'm glad we're straight on it now. Because I mean it, that's a beautiful piece you wrote, and I've got a feeling it's going to go places. Tell you what, Bob, I'll be in touch with you later this week, okay?"

And I remember despising myself because I didn't have the guts to tell him not to bother, any more than I could shake off the heavy, fatherly hand that rode on my neck as we walked. In the alcove, out in front of the young bugler again, I had a sudden, disturbing notion that I could foretell an exchange of dialogue that was about to take place. I would say, "Bernie, were you really a bugler in the army, or was that just for the picture?"

And with no trace of embarrassment, without the faintest flickering change in his guileless smile, he would say, "Just for the picture."

Worse still: I knew that the campaign-hatted head of the bugler himself would turn then, that the fine tense profile in the photograph would slowly loosen and turn away from the mouthpiece of a horn through which its dumb, no-talent lips could never have blown a fart, and that it would wink at me. So I didn't risk it. I just said, "See you, Bernie," and got the hell out of there and went home.

Joan's reaction to the news was surprisingly gentle. I don't mean she was "kind" to me about it, which would have damn near killed me in the shape I was in that night; it was more that she was kind to Bernie.

Poor, lost, brave little man, dreaming his huge and unlikely dream—that kind of thing. And could I imagine what it must have cost him over the years? How many of these miserably hard-earned five-dollar payments he must have dropped down the bottomless maw of second- and third- and tenth-rate amateur writers' needs? How lucky for him, then, through whatever dissemblings with his canceled check, to have made contact with a first-rate professional at last. And how touching, and how "sweet," that he had recognized the difference by saying, "For this you get cash."

"Well, but for Christ's sake," I told her, grateful that it could for once be me instead of her who thought in terms of the deadly practicalities. "For Christ's sake, you know *why* he gave me cash, don't you? Because he's going to sell that story to the *Reader's* goddamn *Digest* next week for a hundred and fifty thousand dollars, and because if I had a photostated check to prove I wrote it he'd be in trouble, that's why."

"Would you like to bet?" she inquired, looking at me with her lovely, truly unforgettable mixture of pity and pride. "Would you like to bet that if he does sell it, to the *Reader's Digest* or anywhere else, he'll insist on giving you half?"

"Bob Prentice?" said a happy voice on the telephone, three nights later. "Bernie Silver. Bob, I've just come from Dr. Alexander Corvo's home, and listen. I'm not going to tell you *what* he told me, but I'll tell you this. Dr. Alexander Corvo thinks you're pretty good."

Whatever reply I made to this—"Does he really?" or "You mean he really likes it?"—it was something bashful and telling enough to bring Joan instantly to my side, all smiles. I remember the way she plucked at my shirtsleeve as if to say, There—what did I tell you? And I had to brush her away and wag my hand to keep her quiet during the rest of the talk.

"He wants to show it to a couple of his connections in the publishing field," Bernie was saying, "and he wants me to get another copy made up to send out to Manny on the Coast. So listen, Bob, while we're waiting to see what happens on this one, I want to give you some more assignments. Or wait—listen." And his voice became enriched with the dawning of a new idea. "Listen. Maybe you'd be more comfortable working on your own. Would you rather do that? Would you rather just skip the card file, and use your own imagination?"

Late one rainy night, deep in the Upper West Side, two thugs got into Bernie Silver's cab. To the casual eye they might have looked like ordinary customers, but Bernie had them spotted right away because "Take it from me, a man doesn't hack the streets of Manhattan for twenty-two years without a little specialized education rubbing off."

One was a hardened-criminal type, of course, and the other was little more than a frightened boy, or rather "just a punk."

"I didn't like the way they were talking," Bernie told his readers through me, "and I didn't like the address they gave me— the lowest dive in town—and most of all I didn't like the fact that they were riding in my automobile."

So do you know what he did? Oh, don't worry, he didn't stop the cab and step around and pull them out of the backseat and kick them one after the other in the groin—none of that *My-Flag-Is-Down* nonsense. For one thing, he could tell from their talk that they weren't making a getaway; not tonight, at least. All they'd done tonight was case the joint (a small liquor store near the corner where he'd picked them up); the job was set for tomorrow night at eleven. Anyway, when they got to the lowest dive in town the hardened criminal gave the punk some money and said, "Here, kid; you keep the cab, go on home and get some sleep. I'll see you tomorrow." And that was when Bernie knew what he had to do.

"That punk lived way out in Queens, which gave us plenty of time for conversation, so I asked him who he liked for the National League pennant." And from there on, with deep folk wisdom and consummate skill, Bernie kept up such a steady flow of talk about healthy, clean-living milk-and-sunshine topics that he'd begun to draw the boy out of his hard delinquent shell even before they hit the Queensboro Bridge. They barreled along Queens Boulevard chattering like a pair of Police Athletic League enthusiasts, and by the time the ride was over, Bernie's fare was practically in tears.

"I saw him swallow a couple of times when he paid me off" was the way I had Bernie put it, "and I had a feeling something had changed in that kid. I had a hope of it, anyway, or maybe just a wish. But I knew I'd done all I could for him." Back in town, Bernie called the police and suggested they put a couple of men around the liquor store the following night.

Sure enough, a job was attempted on that liquor store, only to be foiled by two tough, lovable cops. And sure enough, there was only one thug for them to carry off to the pokey—the hardened-criminal one. "I don't know where the kid was that night," Bernie concluded, "but I like to think he was home in bed with a glass of milk, reading the sports page."

There was the roof and there was the chimney top of it; there were all the windows with the light coming in; there was another approving chuckle from Dr. Alexander Corvo and another sub-mission to the *Reader's Digest*; there was another whisper of a chance for a Simon and Schuster contract and a three-million-dollar production starring Wade Manley; and there was another five in the mail for me.

A small, fragile old gentleman started crying in the cab one day, up around Fifty-ninth and Third, and when Bernie said, "Any-thing I can help with, sir?" there followed two and a half pages of the most heart-tearing hard-luck story I could imagine. He was a widower; his only daughter had long since married and moved away to Flint, Michigan; his life had been an agony of loneliness for twenty-two years, but he'd always been brave enough about it until now because he'd had a job he loved—

tending the geraniums in a big commercial greenhouse. And now this morning the management had told him he would have to go: too old for that kind of work.

"And only then," according to Bernie Silver, "did I make the connection between all this and the address he'd given me—a corner near the Manhattan side of the Brooklyn Bridge."

Bernie couldn't be sure, of course, that his fare planned to hobble right on out to the middle of the bridge and ease his old bones over the railing; but he couldn't take any chances, either. "I figured it was time for me to do some talking" (and he was right about that: another heavy half-page of that tiresome old man's lament and the story would have ruptured the hell out of its foundation). What came next was a brisk page and a half of dialogue in which Bernie discreetly inquired why the old man didn't go and live with his daughter in Michigan, or at least write her a letter so that maybe she'd invite him; but oh, no, he only keened that he couldn't possibly be a burden on his daughter and her family.

" 'Burden?' I said, acting like I didn't know what he meant. 'Burden? How could a nice old gentleman like you be a burden on anybody?' "

" 'But what else would I be? What can I offer them?' "

"Luckily we were stopped at a red light when he asked me that, so I turned around and looked him straight in the eye. 'Mister,' I said, 'don't you think that family'd like having somebody around the place that knows a thing or two about growing geraniums?' "

Well, by the time they got to the bridge the old man had decided to have Bernie let him off at a nearby Automat instead, because he said he felt like having a cup of tea, and so much for the walls of the damn thing. This was the roof: six months later, Bernie received a small, heavy package with a Flint, Michigan, postmark, addressed to his taxi fleet garage. And do you know what was in that package? Of course you do. A potted geranium. And here's your chimney top: there was also a little note, written in what I'm afraid I really did describe as a fine old spidery hand, and it read, simply, "Thank you."

*

Personally, I thought this one was loathsome, and Joan wasn't sure about it either; but we mailed it off anyway and Bernie loved it. And so, he told me over the phone, did his wife Rose.

"Which reminds me, Bob, the other reason I called; Rose wants me to find out what evening you and your wife could come up for a little get-together here. Nothing fancy, just the four of us, have a little drink and a chat. You think you might enjoy that?"

"Well, that's very nice of you, Bernie, and of course we'd enjoy it very much. It's just that offhand I don't quite know when we could arrange to—hold on a second." And I covered the mouthpiece and had an urgent conference about it with Joan in the hope that she'd supply me with a graceful excuse.

But she wanted to go, and she had just the right evening in mind, so all four of us were hooked.

"Oh, good," she said when I'd hung up. "I'm glad we're going. They sound sweet."

"Now, *look*." And I aimed my index finger straight at her face. "We're not going at all if you plan to sit around up there making them both aware of how 'sweet' they are. I'm not spending any evenings as gracious Lady Bountiful's consort among the lower classes, and that's final. If you want to turn this thing into some goddamn Bennington girls' garden party for the servants, you can forget about it right now. You hear me?"

Then she asked me if I wanted to know something, and without waiting to find out whether I did or not, she told me. She told me I was just about the biggest snob and biggest bully and biggest all-around loud-mouthed jerk she'd ever come across in her life.

One thing led to another after that; by the time we were on the subway for our enjoyable get-together with the Silvers we were only barely on speaking terms, and I can't tell you how grateful I was to find that the Silvers, while staying on ginger ale themselves, had broken out a bottle of rye for their guests.

Bernie's wife turned out to be a quick, spike-heeled, girdled and bobby-pinned woman whose telephone operator's voice was chillingly expert at the social graces ("How do you do? So nice to meet you; do come in; please sit down; Bernie, help her, she can't get her coat off'"); and God knows who started it, or why, but the evening began uncomfortably with a discussion of politics. Joan and I were torn between Truman, Wallace, and not voting at all that year; the Silvers were Dewey people. And what made it all the worse, for our tender liberal sensibilities, was that Rose sought common ground by telling us one bleak tale after another, each with a more elaborate shudder, about the inexorable, menacing encroachment of colored and Puerto Rican elements in this part of the Bronx.

But things got jollier after a while. For one thing they were both delighted with Joan—and I'll have to admit I never met anyone who wasn't—and for another the talk soon turned to the marvelous fact of their knowing Wade Manley, which gave rise to a series of proud reminiscences. "Bernie never takes nothing off him, though, don't worry," Rose assured us. "Bernie, tell them what you did that time he was here and you told him to sit down and shut up. He did! He did! He kind of gave him a push in the chest—this *movie* star!—and he said, 'Ah, siddown and sheddep, Manny. *We* know who you are!' Tell them, Bernie."

And Bernie, convulsed with pleasure, got up to reenact the scene. "Oh, we were just kind of kidding around, you understand," he said, "but anyway, that's what I did. I gave him a shove like this, and I said, 'Ah, siddown and sheddep, Manny. *We* know who you are!' "

"He did! That's the God's truth! Pushed him right down in that chair over there! Wade Manley!"

A little later, when Bernie and I had paired off for a man-to-man talk over the freshening of drinks, and Rose and Joan were cozily settled in the love seat, Rose directed a roguish glance at me. "I wouldn't want to give this husband of yours a swelled head, Joanie, but do you know what Dr. Corvo told Bernie? Shall I tell her, Bernie?"

"Sure, tell her! Tell her!" And Bernie waved the bottle of ginger ale in one hand and the bottle of rye in the other, to show how openly all secrets could be bared tonight.

"Well," she said. "Dr. Corvo said your husband is the finest writer Bernie's ever had."

Later still, when Bernie and I were in the love seat and the ladies were at the credenza, I began to see that Rose was a builder too. Maybe she hadn't built that credenza with her own hands, but she'd clearly done more than her share of building whatever heartfelt convictions were needed to sustain the hundreds on hundreds of dollars its purchase must be costing them on the installment plan. A piece of furniture like that was an investment in the future; and now, as she stood fussing over it and wiping off little parts of it while she talked to Joan, I could have sworn I saw her arranging a future party in her mind. Joan and I would be among those present, that much was certain ("This is Mr. Robert Prentice, my husband's assistant, and Mrs. Prentice"), and the rest of the guest list was almost a foregone conclusion too: Wade Manley and his wife, of course, along with a careful selection of their Hollywood friends; Walter Winchell would be there, and Earl Wilson and Toots Shor and all that crowd; but far more important, for any person of refinement, would be the presence of Dr. and Mrs. Alexander Corvo and some of the people who comprised their set. People like the Lionel Trillings and the Reinhold Niebuhrs, the Huntington Hartfords and the Leslie R. Groveses—and if anybody on the order of Mr. and Mrs. Newbold Morris wanted to come, you could be damn sure they'd have to do some pretty fancy jockeying for an invitation.

It was, as Joan admitted later, stifling hot in the Silvers' apartment that night; and I cite this as a presentable excuse for the fact that what I did next—and it took me a hell of a lot less time to do it in 1948 than it does now, believe me—was to get roaring drunk. Soon I was not only the most vociferous but the only talker in the room; I was explaining that, by Jesus God, we'd all four of us be millionaires yet.

And wouldn't we have a ball? Oh, we'd be slapping Lionel Trilling around and pushing him down into every chair in this room and telling him to shut up—"And you too, Reinhold Niebuhr, you pompous, sanctimonious old fool! Where's *your* money? Why don't you put your money where your mouth is?"

Bernie was chuckling and looking sleepy, and Joan was looking humiliated for me, and Rose was smiling in cool but infinite understanding of how tiresome husbands could sometimes be.

Then we were all out in the alcove trying on at least half a dozen coats apiece, and I was looking at the bugler's photograph again wondering if I dared to ask my burning question about it. But this time I wasn't sure which I feared more: that Bernie might say, "Just for the picture," or that he might say, "Sure I was!" and go rummaging in the closet or in some part of the credenza until he'd come up with the tarnished old bugle itself, and we'd all have to go back and sit down again while Bernie put his heels together, drew himself erect, and sounded the pure, sad melody of taps for us all.

That was in October. I'm a little vague on how many "By Bernie Silver" stones I turned out during the rest of the fall. I do remember a comic-relief one about a fat tourist who got stuck at the waist when he tried to climb up through the skyview window of the cab for better sightseeing, and a very solemn one in which Bernie delivered a lecture on racial tolerance (which struck a sour note with me, considering the way he'd chimed in with Rose's views on the brown hordes advancing over the Bronx); but mostly what I remember about him during that period is that Joan and I could never seem to mention him without getting into some kind of an argument.

When she said we really ought to return his and Rose's invitation, for example, I told her not to be silly. I said I was sure they wouldn't expect it, and when she said "Why?" I gave her a crisp, impatient briefing on the hopelessness of trying to ignore class barriers, of pretending that the Silvers could ever really become our friends, or that they'd ever really want to.

Another time, toward the end of a curiously dull evening when we'd gone to our favorite premarital restaurant and failed for an hour to find anything to talk about, she tried to get the conversation going by leaning romantically toward me across the table and holding up her wineglass. "Here's to Bernie's selling your last one to the *Reader's Digest*."

"Yeah," I said. "Sure. Big deal."

"Oh, don't be so gruff. You know perfectly well it could happen any day. We might make a lot of money and go to Europe and everything."

"Are you kidding?" It suddenly annoyed me that any intelligent, well-educated girl in the twentieth century could be so gullible; and that such a girl should actually be my wife, that I would be expected to go on playing along with this kind of simpleminded innocence for years and years to come, seemed, for the moment, an intolerable situation. "Why don't you grow up a little? You don't really think there's ever been a chance of his selling that junk, do you?" And I looked at her in a way that must have been very much like Bernie's own way of looking at me, the night he asked if I'd really thought he meant twenty-five a time. "Do you?"

"Yes, I do," she said, putting her glass down. "Or at least, I did. I thought you did too. If you don't, it seems sort of cynical and dishonest to go on working for him, doesn't it?" And she wouldn't talk to me all the way home.

The real trouble, I guess, was that we were both preoccupied with two far more serious matters by this time. One was our recent discovery that Joan was pregnant, and the other was that my position at the United Press had begun to sink as steadily as any sinking fund debenture.

My time on the financial desk had become a slow ordeal of waiting for my superiors to discover more and more of how little I knew about what I was doing; and now however pathetically willing I might be to learn all the things I was supposed to know, it had become much too ludicrously late to ask. I was hunching lower and lower over my clattering typewriter there all day and sweating out the ax—the kind, sad dropping of the assistant financial editor's hand on my shoulder ("Can I speak to you inside a minute, Bob?")—and each day that it didn't happen was a kind of shabby victory.

Early in December I was walking home from the subway after one of those days, dragging myself down West Twelfth Street like a seventy-year-old, when I discovered that a taxicab had been moving beside me at a snail's pace for a block and a half. It was one of the green-and-white kind, and behind its windshield flashed an enormous smile.

"Bob! What's the matter, there, Bob? You lost in thought or something? This where you live?"

When he parked the cab at the curb and got out, it was the first time I'd even seen him in his working clothes: a twill cap, a buttoned sweater and one of those columnar change-making gadgets strapped to his waist; and when we shook hands it was the first time I'd seen his fingertips stained a shiny gray from handling other people's coins and dollar bills all day. Close up, smiling or not, he looked as worn out as I felt.

"Come on in, Bernie." He seemed surprised by the crumbling doorway and dirty stairs of the house, and also by the white-washed, poster-decorated austerity of our big single room, whose rent was probably less than half of what he and Rose were paying uptown, and I remember taking a dim Bohemian's pride in letting him notice these things; I guess I had some snobbish notion that it wouldn't do Bernie Silver any harm to learn that people could be smart and poor at the same time.

We couldn't offer him any ginger ale and he said a glass of plain water would be fine, so it wasn't much of a social occasion. It troubled me afterwards to remember how constrained he was with Joan—I don't think he looked her full in the face once during the whole visit—and I wondered if this was because of our failure to return that invitation. Why is it that wives are nearly always blamed for what must at least as often as not be their husbands' fault in matters like that? But maybe it was just that he was more conscious of his cab driver's costume in her presence than in mine. Or maybe he had never imagined that such a pretty and cultivated girl could live in such stark surroundings, and was embarrassed for her.

"I'll tell you what I dropped by about, Bob. I'm trying a new angle." And as he talked I began to suspect, more from his eyes than his words, that something had gone very wrong with the long-range building program. Maybe a publishing friend of Dr. Corvo's had laid it on the line at last about the poor possibilities of our material; maybe Dr. Corvo himself had grown snappish; maybe there had been some crushing final communication from Wade Manley, or, more crushingly, from Wade Manley's agency representative. Or it might have been simply that Bernie was tired after his day's work in a way that no glass of plain water would help; in any case he was trying a new angle.

Had I ever heard of Vincent J. Poletti? But he gave me this name as if he knew perfectly well it wouldn't knock my eye out, and he followed it right up with the information that Vincent J. Poletti was a Democratic State Assemblyman from Bernie's own district in the Bronx.

"Now, this man," he said, "is a man that goes out of his way to help people. Believe me, Bob, he's not just one of your cheap vote-getters. He's a real public servant. What's more, he's a comer in the Party. He's going to be our next Congressman. So here's the idea, Bob. We get a photograph of me—I have this friend of mine'll do it for nothing—we get it taken from the backseat of the cab, with me at the wheel kind of turning around and smiling like this, get it?" He turned his body away from his smiling head to show me how it would look. "And we print this picture on the cover of a booklet. The title of the booklet"— and here he sketched a suggestion of block lettering in the air— "the title of the booklet is 'Take It from Bernie.' Okay? Now. Inside the booklet we have a story—just exactly like the others you wrote except this time it's a little different. This time I'm telling a story about why Vincent J. Poletti is the man we need for Congress. I don't mean just a bunch of political talk, either, Bob. I mean a real little story."

"Bernie, I don't see how this is going to work. You can't have a 'story' about why anybody is the man we need for Congress."

"Who says you can't?"

"And anyway I thought you and Rose were Republicans."

"On the national level, yes. On the local level, no."

"Well, but hell, Bernie, we just had an election. There won't be another election for two years."

But he only tapped his head and made a faraway gesture to show that in politics it paid a man to think ahead.

Joan was over in the kitchen area of the room, cleaning up the breakfast dishes and getting the dinner started, and I looked to her for help, but her back was turned.

"It just doesn't sound right, Bernie. I don't know anything about politics."

"So? Know, schmow. What's to know? Do you know anything about driving a cab?"

No; and I sure as hell didn't know anything about Wall Street, either—Wall Street, Schmall Street!—but that was another depressing little story. "I don't know, Bernie; things are very unsettled right now. I don't think I'd better take on any more assignments for the time being. I mean for one thing I may be about to—" But I couldn't bring myself to tell him about my UP problem, so I said, "For one thing Joan's having a baby now, and everything's sort of—"

"Wow! Well, isn't that something!" He was on his feet and shaking my hand. "Isn't—that—something! Congratulations, Bob, I think this is—I think this is really wonderful. Congratulations, there, Joanie!" And it seemed a little excessive to me at the time, but maybe that's the way such news will always strike a middle-aged, childless man.

"Oh, listen, Bob," he said when we settled down again. "This Poletti thing'll be duck soup for you; and I'll tell you what. Seeing as this is just a one-shot and there won't be any royalties, we'll make it ten instead of five. Is that a deal?"

"Well, but wait a second, Bernie. I'm going to need some more information. I mean what exactly does this guy do for people?"

And it soon became clear that Bernie knew very little more about Vincent J. Poletti than I did. He was a real public servant, that was all; he went out of his way to help people. "Oh, Bob, listen. What's the difference? Where's your imagination? You never needed any help before. Listen. What you just told me gives me one idea right off the bat. I'm driving along; these two kids hall me out in front of the maternity hospital, this young veteran and his wife. They got this little-biddy baby, three days old, and they're happy as larks. Only here's the trouble. This boy's got no job or anything. They only just moved here, they don't know anybody, maybe they're Puerto Ricans or something, they got a week's rent on their room and that's it. Then they're broke. So I'm taking them home, they live right in my neighborhood, and we're chatting away, and I say, 'Listen, kids. I think I'll take you to see a friend of mine.'"

"Assemblyman Vincent J. Poletti."

"Naturally. Only I don't tell them his name yet. I just say 'this friend of mine.' So we get there and I go in and tell Poletti about it and he comes out and talks to the kids and gives them money or something. See? You got a good share of your story right there."

"Hey, yeah, and wait a minute, Bernie." I got up and began dramatically pacing the floor, the way people in Hollywood story conferences are supposed to do. "Wait a minute. After he gives them money, he gets into your cab and you take off with him down the Grand Concourse, and those two Puerto Rican kids are standing there on the sidewalk kind of looking at each other, and the girl says, 'Who *was* that man?' And the boy looks very serious and he says, 'Honey, don't you know? Didn't you notice he was wearing a mask?' And she says, 'Oh no, it couldn't be the—' And he says, 'Yes, yes, it was. Honey, that was the Lone Assemblyman.' And then listen! You know what happens next? Listen! Way off down the block they hear this voice, and you know what the voice is calling?" I sank to the floor on one trembling knee to deliver the punch line. "It's calling 'Hi-yo, Bernie *Sil*ver—away!'"

And it may not look very funny written down, but it almost killed me. I must have laughed for at least a minute, until I went into a coughing fit and Joan had to come and pound me on the back; only very gradually, coming out of it, did I realize that Bernie was not amused, He had chuckled in bewildered politeness during my seizure, but now he was looking down at his hands and there were embarrassing blotches of pink in his sober cheeks. I had hurt his feelings. I remember resenting it that his feelings could be hurt so easily, and resenting it that Joan had gone back to the kitchen instead of staying to help me out of this awkward situation, and then beginning to feel very guilty and sorry, as the silence continued, until I finally decided that the only decent way of making it up to him was to accept the assignment. And sure enough, he brightened instantly when I told him I'd give it a try.

"I mean you don't necessarily have to use that about the Puerto Rican kids," he assured me. "That's just one idea. Or maybe you could start it off that way and then go on to other things, the more the better. You work it out any way you like."

At the door, shaking hands again (and it seemed that we'd been shaking hands all afternoon), I said, "So that's ten for this one, right, Bernie?"

"Right, Bob."

"Do you really think you should have told him you'd do it?" Joan asked me the minute he'd gone.

"Why not?"

"Well, because it *is* going to be practically impossible, isn't it?"

"Look, will you do me a favor? Will you please get off my back?"

She put her hands on her hips. "I just don't understand you, Bob. Why *did* you say you'd do it?"

"Why the hell do you think? Because we're going to need the ten bucks, that's why."

In the end I built—oh, built, schmilt. I put page one and then page two and then page three into the old machine and I *wrote* the son of a bitch. It did start off with the Puerto Rican kids, but for some reason I couldn't get more than a couple of pages out of them; then I had to find other ways for Vincent J. Poletti to demonstrate his giant goodness.

What does a public servant do when he really wants to go out of his way to help people? Gives them money, that's what he does; and pretty soon I had Poletti forking over more than he could count. It got so that anybody in the Bronx who was even faintly up against it had only to climb into Bernie Silver's cab and say, "The Poletti place," and their troubles were over. And the worst part of it was my own grim conviction that it was the best I could do.

Joan never saw the thing, because she was asleep when I finally managed to get it into an envelope and into the mail. And there was no word from Bernie—or about him, between the two of us—for nearly a week. Then, at the same hour as his last visit, the frayed-out end of the day, our doorbell rang. I knew there was going to be trouble as soon as I opened the door and found him smiling there, with spatters of rain on his sweater, and I knew I wasn't going to stand for any nonsense.

"Bob," he said, sitting down, "I hate to say it, but I'm disappointed in you this time." He pulled my folded manuscript out of his sweater. "This thing is—Bob, this is nothing."

"It's six and a half pages. That's not nothing, Bernie."

"Bob, please don't give me six and a half pages. I know it's six and a half pages, but it's nothing. You made this man into a fool, Bob. You got him giving his dough away all the time."

"You told me he gave dough, Bernie."

"To the Puerto Rican kids I said yes, sure, maybe he could give a little, fine. And now you come along and you got him going around spending here like some kind of—some kind of drunken sailor or something."

I thought I might be going to cry, but my voice came out very low and controlled. "Bernie, I did ask you what else he could do. I did tell you I didn't know what the hell else he could do. If you wanted him to do something else, you should've made that clear."

"But *Bob*," he said, standing up for emphasis, and his next words have often come back to me as the final, despairing, everlasting cry of the Philistine. "Bob, *you're* the one with the imagination!"

I stood up too, so that I could look down at him. *I* knew I was the one with the imagination. I also knew I was twenty-two years old and as tired as an old man, that I was about to lose my job, that I had a baby on the way and wasn't even getting along very well with my wife; and now every cab driver, every two-bit politician's pimp and phony bugler in the city of New York was walking into my house and trying to steal my money.

"Ten bucks, Bernie."

He made a helpless gesture, smiling. Then he looked over into the kitchen area, where Joan was, and although I meant to keep my eyes on him, I must have looked there too, because I remember what she was doing. She was twisting a dish towel in her hands and looking down at it.

"Listen, Bob," he said. "I shouldn't of said it was nothing. You're right! Who could take a thing six and a half pages long and say it's nothing? Probably a lot of good stuff in this thing, Bob. You want your ten bucks; all right, fine, you'll get your ten bucks. All I'm asking is this. First take this thing back and change it a little, that's all. Then we can—"

"Ten bucks, Bernie. Now."

His smile had lost its life, but it stayed right there on his face while he took the bill out of his wallet and handed it over, and while I went through a miserable little show of examining it to make goddamn sure it was a ten.

"Okay, Bob," he said. "We're all square, then. Right?"

"Right."

Then he was gone, and Joan went swiftly to the door and opened it and called, "Goodnight, Bernie!"

I thought I heard his footsteps pause on the stairs, but I didn't hear any answering "Goodnight" from him, so I guessed that all he'd done was to turn around and wave to her, or blow her a kiss. Then from the window I saw him move out across the sidewalk and get into his taxicab and drive away. All this time I was folding and refolding his money, and I don't believe I've ever held anything in my hand that I wanted less.

The room was very quiet with only the two of us moving around in it, while the kitchen area steamed and crackled with the savory smells of a dinner that I don't think either of us felt like eating. "Well," I said. "That's that."

"Was it really necessary," she inquired, "to be so dreadfully unpleasant to him?"

And this, at the time, seemed clearly to be the least loyal possible thing she could have said, the unkindest cut of all. "Un-*pleasant* to him! Un*pleasant* to him! Would you mind telling me just what the hell I'm supposed to do? Am I supposed to sit around being 'pleasant' while some cheap, lying little parasitic leech of a *cab* driver comes in here and bleeds me *white*? Is that what you want? Huh? Is *that* what you want?"

Then she did what she often used to do at moments like that, what I sometimes think I'd give anything in life never to have seen her do: she turned away from me and closed her eyes and covered her ears with both hands.

Less than a week later the assistant financial editor's hand did fall on my shoulder at last, right in the middle of a paragraph about domestic corporate bonds in moderately active trading.

It was still well before Christmas, and I got a job to tide us over as a demonstrator of mechanical toys in a Fifth Avenue dimestore.

And I think it must have been during that dimestore period—possibly while winding up a little tin-and-cotton kitten that went "Mew!" and rolled over, "Mew!" and rolled over, "Mew!" and rolled over—it was along in there sometime, anyway, that I gave up whatever was left of the idea of building my life on the pattern of Ernest Hemingway's. Some construction projects are just plain out of the question.

After New Year's I got some other idiot job; then in April, with all the abruptness and surprise of spring, I was hired for eighty dollars a week as a writer in an industrial public-relations office, where the question of whether or not I knew what I was doing never mattered very much because hardly any of the other employees knew what they were doing either.

It was a remarkably easy job, and it allowed me to save a remarkable amount of energy each day for my own work, which all at once began to go well. With Hemingway safely abandoned, I had moved on to an F. Scott Fitzgerald phase; then, the best of all, I had begun to find what seemed to give every indication of being my own style. The winter was over, and things seemed to be growing easier between Joan and me too, and in the early summer our first daughter was born.

She caused a one- or two-month interruption in my writing schedule, but before long I was back at work and convinced that I was going from strength to strength: I had begun to bulldoze and dig and lay the foundation for a big, ambitious, tragic novel. I never did finish the book—it was the first in a series of more unfinished novels than I like to think about now—but in those early stages it was fascinating work, and the fact that it went slowly seemed only to add to its promise of eventual magnificence. I was spending more and more time each night behind my writing screen, emerging only to pace the floor with a headful of serene and majestic daydreams. And it was late in the year, all the way around to fall again, one evening when Joan had gone out to the movies, leaving me as baby-sitter, when I came out from behind the screen to pick up a ringing phone and heard: "Bob Prentice? Bernie Silver."

I won't pretend that I'd forgotten who he was, but it's not too much to say that for a second or two I did have trouble realizing

d it's just now occurred to me, is that very often in trying to
t on the right wording for some touchy personal letter, I've
ought of: "I didn't have time to write you a short letter today,
I had to write you a long one instead."

Whether I meant it or not when I wished him luck with his
omic strip, I think I started meaning it an hour later. I mean it
now, wholeheartedly, and the funny part is that he might still be
able to build it into something, connections or not. Sillier things
than that have built empires in America. At any rate I hope he
hasn't lost his interest in the project, in one form or another;
but more than anything I hope to God—and I'm not swearing
this time—I hope to whatever God there may be that he hasn't
lost Rose.

Reading all this over, I can see that it hasn't been built very
well. Its beams and joists, its very walls are somehow out of kilter;
its foundation feels weak; possibly I failed to dig the right kind
of hole in the ground in the first place. But there's no point in
worrying about such things now, because it's time to put the roof
on it—to bring you up to date on what happened to the rest of
us builders.

Everybody knows what happened to Wade Manley. He died
unexpectedly a few years later, in bed; and the fact that it was the
bed of a young woman not his wife was considered racy enough
to keep the tabloids busy for weeks. You can still see reruns of
his old movies on television, and whenever I see one I'm surprised all over again to find that he was a good actor—much too
good, I expect, ever to have gotten caught in any cornball role
as a cab driver with a heart as big as all outdoors.

As for Dr. Corvo, there was a time when everybody knew
what happened to him too. It happened in the very early fifties,
whichever year it was that the television companies built and
launched their most massive advertising campaigns. One of the
most massive of all was built around a signed statement by Dr.
Alexander Corvo, eminent child psychologist, to the effect that
any boy or girl in our time whose home lacked a television set
would quite possibly grow up emotionally deprived. Every other
child psychologist, every articulate liberal, and very nearly every
parent in the United States came down on Alexander Corvo like

that I'd ever really worked for him—that I could ever really have
been involved, at first hand, in the pathetic delusions of a taxicab
driver. It gave me pause, which is to say that it caused me to
wince and then to sheepishly grin at the phone, to duck my head
and smooth my hair with my free hand in a bashful demonstration of *noblesse oblige*—this accompanied by a silent, humble vow
that whatever Bernie Silver might want from me now, I would
go out of my way to avoid any chance of hurting his feelings.
I remember wishing Joan were home, so that she could witness
my kindness.

But the first thing he wanted to know about was the baby. Was
it a boy or a girl? Wonderful! And who did she look like? Well,
of course, naturally, they never did look like anybody much at
that age. And how did it feel to be a father? Huh? Feel pretty
good? Good! Then he took on what struck me as a strangely
formal, cap-holding tone, like that of a long-discharged servant
inquiring after the lady of the house. "And how's Mrs. Prentice?"

She had been "Joan" and "Joanie" and "Sweetheart" to him
in his own home, and I somehow couldn't believe he'd forgotten
her name; I could only guess that he hadn't heard her call out to
him on the stairs that night after all—that maybe, remembering
only the way she'd stood there with her dish towel, he had even
blamed her as the instigator of my own intransigence over the
damned ten bucks. But all I could do now was to tell him she
was fine. "And how've you people been, Bernie?"

"Well," he said, "*I've* been all right," and here his voice fell
to the shocked sobriety of hospital-room conferences. "But I
almost lost Rose, a couple of months back."

Oh, it was okay now, he assured me, she was much better and
home from the hospital and feeling well; but when he started
talking about "tests" and "radiology" I had the awful sense of
doom that comes when the unmentionable name of cancer hangs
in the air.

"Well, Bernie," I said, "I'm terribly sorry she's been ill, and
please be sure to give her our—"

Give her our what? Regards? Best wishes? Either one, it
suddenly seemed to me, would carry the unforgivable taint of
condescension. "Give her our love," I said, and immediately

chewed my lip in fear that this might sound the most condescending of all.

"I will! I will! I'll certainly do that for you, Bob," he said, and so I was glad I'd put it that way. "And now, what I called you about is this." And he chuckled. "Oh, don't worry, no politics. Here's the thing. I've got this really terrifically talented boy working for me now, Bob. This boy's an artist."

And great God, what a sickly, intricate thing a writer's heart is! Because do you know what I felt when he said that? I felt a twinge of jealousy. "Artist," was he? I'd show them who the hell the artist was around *this* little writing establishment.

But right away Bernie started talking about "strips" and "layouts," so I was able to retire my competitive zeal in favor of the old, reliable ironic detachment. What a relief!

"Oh, an *artist*, you mean. A *comic*-strip artist."

"Right. Bob, you ought to see the way this boy can draw. You know what he does? He makes me look like me, but he makes me look a little bit like Wade Manley too. Do you get the picture?"

"It sounds fine, Bernie." And now that the old detachment was working again, I could see that I'd have to be on my guard. Maybe he wouldn't be needing any more stories—by now he probably had a whole credenzaful of manuscripts for the artist to work from—but he'd still be needing a writer to do the "continuity," or whatever it's called, and the words for the artist's speech balloons, and I would now have to tell him, as gently and gracefully as possible, that it wasn't going to be me.

"Bob," he said, "this thing is really building. Dr. Corvo took one look at these strips and he said to me, 'Bernie, forget the magazine business, forget the book business. You've found the solution.'"

"Well. It certainly does sound good, Bernie."

"And Bob, here's why I called. I know they keep you pretty busy down there at the UP, but I was wondering if you might have time to do a little—"

"I'm not working for the UP anymore, Bernie." And I told him about the publicity job.

"Well," he said. "That sounds like you're really coming up in the world there, Bob. Congratulations."

"Thanks. Anyway, Bernie, the point is I really have time to do any writing for you just now. I me like to, it isn't that; it's just that the baby does ta time here, and then I've got my own work going— novel now, you see—and I really don't think I'd b anything else."

"Oh. Well, okay, then, Bob; don't worry about it. you see, is that it really would've been a break for us if made use of your—*you* know, your writing talent in t

"I'm sorry too, Bernie, and I certainly do wish with it."

You may well have guessed by now what didn't occu I swear, until at least an hour after I'd said goodbye to h this time Bernie hadn't wanted me as a writer at all. He'd t I was still at the UP, and might therefore be a valuable close to the heart of the syndicated comic-strip business.

I can remember exactly what I was doing when this k ledge came over me. I was changing the baby's diaper, loo down into her round, beautiful eyes as if I expected her to gratulate me, or thank me, for having once more manage avoid the terrible possibility of touching her skin with the po of the safety pin—I was doing that, when I thought of the way voice had paused in saying, "We could of made use of your—

During that pause he must have abandoned whatever elaborat building plans might still have lain in saying "your connections there at the UP" (and he didn't know I'd been fired; for all he knew I might still have as many solid connections in the news paper business as Dr. Corvo had in the child psychology field or Wade Manley had in the movies), and had chosen to finish it off with "your writing talent" instead. And so I knew that for all my finicking concern over the sparing of Bernie's feelings in that telephone conversation, it was Bernie, in the end, who had gone out of his way to spare mine.

I can't honestly say that I've thought very much about him over the years. It might be a nice touch to tell you that I never get into a taxicab without taking a close look at the driver's neck and profile, but it wouldn't be true. One thing that is true, though, a plague of locusts, and when they were done with him there wasn't an awful lot of eminence left. Since then, I'd say offhand that the *New York Times* would give you half a dozen Alexander Corvos for a single Newbold Morris any day of the week.

That takes the story right on up to Joan and me, and now I'll have to give you the chimney top. I'll have to tell you that what she and I were building collapsed too, a couple of years ago. Oh, we're still friendly—no legal battles over alimony, or custody, or anything like that—but there you are.

And where are the windows? Where does the light come in?

Bernie, old friend, forgive me, but I haven't got the answer to that one. I'm not even sure if there *are* any windows in this particular house. Maybe the light is just going to have to come in as best it can, through whatever chinks and cracks have been left in the builder's faulty craftsmanship, and if that's the case you can be sure that nobody feels worse about it than I do. God knows, Bernie; God knows there certainly ought to be a window around here somewhere, for all of us.

This book is set in BEMBO which was cut
by the punch-cutter Francesco Griffo
for the Venetian printer-publisher
Aldus Manutius in early 1495
and first used in a pamphlet
by a young scholar
named Pietro
Bembo.